RUNNING THROUGH CORRIDORS

ROB AND TOBY'S MARATHON WATCH OF DOCTOR WHO

Volume 1: THE 60s

ROBERT SHEARMAN & TOBY HADOKE

mad
norwegian
press

Des Moines, Iowa

Also available from Mad Norwegian Press...

Running Through Corridors Vol. 2: The 70s (forthcoming)
Running Through Corridors Vol. 3 (forthcoming)

Wanting to Believe: A Critical Guide to The X-Files,
Millennium and The Lone Gunmen by Robert Shearman

Chicks Dig Time Lords: A Celebration of Doctor Who
by the Women Who Love It

Whedonistas: A Celebration of the Worlds of Joss Whedon
by the Women Who Love Them

Chicks Dig Comics (forthcoming)

Resurrection Code (all-new AngeLINK prequel) by Lyda Morehouse

Redeemed: The Unauthorized Guide to Angel (forthcoming, ebook only)

Dusted: The Unauthorized Guide to Buffy the Vampire Slayer

AHistory: An Unauthorized History of the Doctor Who Universe
by Lance Parkin [2nd Edition now available]

THE ABOUT TIME SERIES
by Lawrence Miles and Tat Wood
About Time 1: The Unauthorized Guide to Doctor Who (Seasons 1 to 3)
About Time 2: The Unauthorized Guide to Doctor Who (Seasons 4 to 6)
About Time 3: The Unauthorized Guide to Doctor Who
(Seasons 7 to 11) [2nd Edition now available]
About Time 4: The Unauthorized Guide to Doctor Who (Seasons 12 to 17)
About Time 5: The Unauthorized Guide to Doctor Who (Seasons 18 to 21)
About Time 6: The Unauthorized Guide to Doctor Who
(Seasons 22 to 26, the TV Movie)
About Time 7 (forthcoming)

TIME, UNINCORPORATED: THE DOCTOR WHO FANZINE ARCHIVES
Volume 1: Lance Parkin
Volume 2: Writings on the Classic Series
Volume 3: Writings on the New Series

Published by Mad Norwegian Press (www.madnorwegian.com). Cover & interior
design: Christa Dickson. Editor: Lars Pearson. Cute little "running men" action: Katy
Shuttleworth. **Please join us on Facebook!**

ISBN: 9781935234067. Printed in Illinois. First Edition: November 2010. Second
Print: September 2011.

TABLE OF CONTENTS

FOREWORD BY PETER PURVES

I was extremely flattered to be asked to write this foreword for *Running Through Corridors* – and came to realise that had such a request been made of me about seven years earlier, I would have been totally ill-equipped to accommodate it. Toby and Rob have spent this book discovering *Doctor Who* anew after having seen it many times, but it's fair to say that throughout my life, the time I devoted to making the show has far surpassed the time I've spent watching it. You see, when I appeared in *Doctor Who* in the mid-1960s, no domestic recording of programmes was possible, except through the old reel-to-reel audio machines of the time. Consequently, I hardly ever saw any of the 44 episodes in which I played Steven – the show was transmitted early evening on Saturday, when I would be out making personal appearances and the like. My stories were never repeated, so if I missed an episode, then that was that.

When the commercial video era came about, it turned out that the BBC had – in its great wisdom – wiped many of the two-inch videotapes of the show, and so only a few of my stories were available for release. I was sent videos of *The Ark* and *The Gunfighters*, but I only had fleeting and poor memories of the latter, and so I never bothered to view it. (More on that story in a moment.) I did watch *The Ark* – which again, I didn't see on first transmission – but to be entirely honest, I was dreadfully disappointed with it. The story itself was excellent and imaginative, but the execution – particularly the design of the Monoids – was very poor, almost laughable, I felt.

My first proper re-exposure to my time on *Doctor Who*, as it happened, occurred through the audio rather than the video medium. Luckily for me (and for many *Doctor Who* fans), there were people who liked the show so much, they made off-air audio recordings of the 60s stories. These were eventually tracked down, and it's very pleasing that a full archive of *Doctor Who* now exists in audio form. And so, when audio producer Mark Ayres asked me to record the narration links on every serial in which I appeared, it was very exciting. In

many cases, this would be was the first time I had revisited the show since 1966!

Starting in 1999, we recorded these rather excellent (is that immodest of me to say?) narrated soundtracks. In some cases, I had the occasional recall of the scripts involved, but to a large extent, I came to it all afresh. And the great joy was that I loved these stories! I liked the scripts, I enjoyed the plots, and I threw myself into the narration with genuine pleasure. I was surprised by the extent that the recordings remained (if you will forgive the pun) undoctored, but Mark assured me that the *Doctor Who* aficionados would not be pleased if the pauses, occasional *Billyfluffs* and other extraneous noises were cut out. Everything had to remain in its exact original form. If you haven't experienced these audios, then I can highly recommend you have a listen. (My favourite *Billyfluff* of all time, by the way, occurs in *The Myth Makers* when Bill Hartnell says, "I am not a dog – a god!")

I returned to the world of televised *Doctor Who* some time later, in 2003, when *The Time Meddler* was broadcast in its entirety. I can't say my opinion changed much upon this viewing – I had liked this story at the time, and still liked it upon seeing the final product. Steven's character was at its strongest (just as Dennis Spooner had envisaged), Peter Butterworth was a joy to watch (and had been a joy to work with), and Dougie Camfield was a super director. The Viking/Saxon fights were admittedly pretty awful – embarrassing really, and patently performed in a set the size of an old sixpence – but there was some good acting, particularly from Alethea Charlton.

Then in 2004, my "journey" of re-experiencing *Doctor Who* continued when I was asked to watch *The Gunfighters* as part of a live commentary at a convention in Chicago. I hope everyone reading this will forgive that I expected to hate watching this story, mainly because I just hadn't enjoyed making it. How can that be, you might ask, given that every boy of my era wanted to play a cowboy, and this story was my best chance to do so? Well, the director, Rex Tucker, seemed to rather ignore me – actually, not only me, but Jackie

Lane and Bill Hartnell too. I now suspect it was because Rex, who had been overlooked as the show's original producer, felt that directing a *Doctor Who* serial was a little below what his talent deserved. He did, at least, cast the story extraordinarily well – the Clanton gang looked genuine enough, and Hollywood cowboy actor John Alderson was present as Wyatt Earp, so the authenticity was remarkable. The sets were amazingly good, and the mix between Ealing film sequences and the studio matched very well indeed. But, perhaps owing to the fact that Rex hadn't cast the three regulars, he largely left us to our own devices, and spent much more time focused on the other actors. I also remember being acutely embarrassed at having to sing "The Ballad of the Last Chance Saloon" – I shouldn't have been, because I had always been a singer, but somehow I really found no pleasure in it.

But do you know – as I did that commentary in Chicago, I found myself thoroughly enjoying what I could now see was a subtly funny story. Mind you, there was nothing subtle about my comedy – there were several huge double takes, a couple of trips over my own spurs, I was bumped in the back by the saloon doors – but I think it worked. Having spent some decades thinking ill of this story, I have certainly warmed to it. (*The Ark*, however, hasn't improved for me on a second viewing, nor a third.)

Having now re-experienced all of my episodes on either audio or video, I continue to find it such a shame that the audience of the time liked the historical and pseudo-historical stories less than the hard SF ones, because they were amongst my favourites. The mix of SF and history in *The Time Meddler* was a delight, and *The Myth Makers* and *The Massacre* were powerful stories – the latter being, I think, my best performance and the best script of them all. What the historical stories lacked in SF content, they made up by being script-led rather than character-led. I'm told that the historical stories did not long survive my departure from *Doctor Who*, but continue to think that the historicals we made (is this also immodest of me to say?) were of the highest calibre.

Throughout *Running Through Corridors*, Toby and Rob have noted the many ways in which *Doctor Who* has kept reinventing itself. My era was certainly one of change – not just for the series, but for television in general. In the early 60s, the theatre was the thing, and actors generally were quite disparaging about "television actors". I suspect that, deep down, much of this disdain owed to there only being three TV channels – something that didn't change in the UK until 1982 – so the opportunities to appear on TV were in short supply, and the attitudes towards TV may have contained an element of sour grapes about them. But by the middle of the decade, actors with a good theatrical pedigree were beginning to appear on television more and more – and nowhere more than in *Doctor Who*. To watch and listen to my time on the series, I feel very fortunate to have worked with big names such as Max Adrian, Barrie Ingham, Andre Morell, Leonard Sachs, Michael Gough, Laurence Payne, Peter Butterworth, Stephanie Bidmead and Eric Thompson.

Enough of my reminiscences – the authors of this three-volume study have far more to offer than the ramblings of an elderly actor. I don't know Rob, but have worked on a number of occasions with Toby, whose knowledge of *Doctor Who* is far greater than mine. The two of them have here produced a book worthy of a degree in *Doctor Who*-ology! It's always a pleasure to read, and has such tremendous insight into the series. Whether you're enjoying *Doctor Who* for the tenth time or the very first, *Running Through Corridors* is a must-have for viewers the world over.

Peter Purves
Steven Taylor,
Doctor Who companion, 1965-1966
Suffolk, England, 2010

January 1st

ROB: Last night I had a brilliant idea! The last brilliant idea of 2008. So brilliant is this idea, that by morning, I can still remember it – unlike all the other brilliant ideas the sparkling wine gave me.

I wake my wife and tell her all about it. This, in itself, is *not* a brilliant idea. Indeed, I soon realise that it's the first really *stupid* idea of 2009. I'm lucky to escape with my life.

I tell Janie I want to embark on a quest. Something mad and impulsive, something insane. Something that'll be a voyage of discovery. And I want her to be there right by my side. For some reason she thinks that I'm proposing a round-the-world cruise, and she even manages to look quite interested. Then I explain to her – no, I think I'm going to watch every single Doctor Who episode in order. Her enthusiasm wilts somewhat.

"Why?" she asks. "Because it's there!" I say, with pride. "Are you sure?" she asks. "I *am* sure," I say, "I'm really, really sure." I invite her to watch the entire run with me. It'll be fun, I tell her. And quite an experience! To see a series develop through 45 years right from the start. She tells me she won't. Thanks. Ever so much. But no. "Last chance," I say, "are you sure?" "Oh yes," she says. "I'm really, really, *really* sure." And just so I'm left in no doubt of her sureness, she informs me to what degree she'd rather have her eyes gouged out with rusty nails.

She might be right. It is something of an intrepid journey. Not for the faint-hearted. But it's not something I want to do on my own. I need someone brave by my side. Like a sherpah. Or one of those furry dogs with brandy kegs around their necks, St Bernard's, those are the fellers. Only one person springs to mind.

I text Toby Hadoke. His reply seems a bit abrupt. I check the time, and see it's not quite seven in the morning. I wonder if I woke him too early.

TOBY: I work nights, I'm a stand-up comedian. My head rarely hits the pillow before 2 am. My friends know this, and know not to call a)

before midday and b) when Doctor Who is on. As it happens, I wasn't working last night, but that's *because it was New Year's Eve*, when even people less curmudgeonly than myself are entitled to be grumpy if texted at half-six the next day.

It's Rob Shearman, though, and he's easy to forgive – so even as my outbox pings, I feel a bit guilty for the torrent of abuse I have just unleashed in response. I got to know Rob last year when he came to see my one-man show, Moths Ate My Doctor Who Scarf, and ever since have exchanged texts (usually at a more civilised hour) and met him for lunch every now and again. Rob has an idea: to watch every Doctor Who story, in order, and accentuate the positive. To rediscover why we love the show at a time when its popularity is at such a height, it's all too easy to take it for granted. I waver slightly, because I simply don't anticipate for a minute that we'll be able to keep it up.

I also have other niggles. I've never really wanted to be a part of organised fandom; Doctor Who has always been something I'd enjoyed on my own. The year just gone, however, found me dipping my toes into the world of moderating DVD commentaries and agreeing to appear at conventions. Christmas was a bit sullied when one of our greatest playwrights, Harold Pinter, died on 24th December – and yet, this event reopened the tiresome Internet debate as to whether or not he played Ralpachan in The Abominable Snowmen. (He really didn't, you know.)

2008 was also the year, however, that I discovered the joy of spending time with other fans. Yes, I'd had chums who loved the show: my good friend Mark had 40 or so videos when I was his roommate, but he wasn't such an encyclopaedic fan that he'd have been able to play "Name That Obscure Non-Speaking Background Artist" with me, or have been moved to laughter by jokes about signal howlround or jabolite. But last year, as I toured my show and schlepped from one strange town to another, I enjoyed some wonderful times amongst people I'd never met before, but who proved to be fluent in my language. It turns out that every corner of this fair isle has someone with an opinion about, say, The Androids of Tara, the Cartmel Masterplan and quite what The Eye of Harmony was doing in Paul McGann's TARDIS. Such people would wait behind after my performance, and we'd have excitably geeky chats over a drink or two.

And yet, I've never been to The Tavern – the fabled monthly get-together of Doctor Who pros and fans alike – and have never really hung about at conventions. But I *do* relish the times I spend with Rob. (We once sat in a pub in Liverpool and went through the Pertwee era in order, assessing its merits – I'd *never* done that with anyone before!) We make the effort to get together whenever we're in the same vicinity, and I even rang him up in-between spots at The Comedy Store after the transmission of Journey's End. I kept rushing off stage, dialling his number and shouting "and another thing ...!", to the polite confusion of some of the nation's most respected funsters.

So I think, yes, that might be a fun thing to do. One day. I text Rob again. And I go back to bed.

R: Toby's second text – the one in which he doesn't swear so much – is heartwarming and affirmative. But it's also a bit stupid. He seems to miss the point, that this is something we need to start *today*. Because it's the first of January *now*. He doesn't reply to my new text. So I'm forced to phone him up and tell him to *read* his text. No, I tell him, I don't want to chat on the phone – it's early, I don't want to wake the household. I'm not entirely inconsiderate.

This is the Gap Year – Doctor Who has been back in regular production since 2005, but for the first time since then, we have no complete series to look forward to at Easter. A few special episodes will appear during the year to prepare us for David Tennant's departure, and to introduce... well, who? So 2009 is the perfect year to do this undertaking, when filling our each and every day with Doctor Who will seem quite reasonable. And not the obsessive act of thirtysomething mentalists.

I love Doctor Who. So much so, I even wrote an episode of it once! Oh yes. So I think it's important this quest is a celebratory quest. Toby and I will watch two episodes a day, every day, without fail – and write to each

other saying why we *like* them. What there is to admire. Because Doctor Who's brilliant, isn't it? Always. Even when it's being very rubbish too. We'll watch it to find the bit of magic everyone keeps missing from The Power of Kroll episode three, or Arc of Infinity episode two. We'll cherish how amazing it can be when it's on form, and find what there is to adore in it when it isn't.

We come to praise Doctor Who, not to bury it.

Each and every day. Come on, Toby, I say. Do you have a lot on this year? He writes back and says he hasn't.

T: Actually, I write back and tell him I'm getting married this year. Rob doesn't seem to pick up on this.

But, yes, I've always known Doctor Who is brilliant. I've always known that despite its faults, it's a unique and thrilling programme every week. But I've oddly never worked out *why* – and why I've never never got around to reading Far From the Madding Crowd, and yet have watched, say, The Mutants more than a dozen times.

I remain slightly tentative, though. Rob is a nice person; he's a cheery optimist. And I know from long conversations with him in the pub that he can find intellectual justification in any old piece of tat. (In other words, he can be very irritating.) Whereas my artistic endeavours tend to revolve around bitterness, disappointment and thwarted ambition. But all right. Yes, then. I'm game. We love this show, now let's find out what and why we love...

R: Good. Well, let's get started.
T: What, now?
R: Better had. We've got a long way to go.

An Unearthly Child (episode one)

R: There is so much to goggle at here – aside from the obvious weight on its shoulders by dint of being the Very First Episode, it's also an extraordinary piece of television. It's inventive and clever and full of imagination and, because the series hasn't yet even got the semblance of a house style, Anthony Coburn's script and Waris Hussein's direction do things that will, quite simply, never be used on Doctor Who again. But let's start with the Doctor himself, because he deserves the attention.

At the time of writing, the most recent new episode transmitted was the 2008 Christmas adventure, The Next Doctor. I watched it on the sofa next to Janie, and she tells me she actually felt me quiver with excitement the moment we got a clip sequence of all the previous Doctors. (She rolled her eyes at my reaction, I must admit. But I'm a fanboy. Typically, in the midst of an exciting story set in Victorian London with huge King Kong-size Cybermen, what really sets my heart racing is a three-second excerpt from The Time Meddler.) And there he was, with all the others: William Hartnell! The oldest Doctor, and the one most taken for granted.

Aside from thinking how bemused Hartnell himself would have been, 45 years on, to be part of an adventure told at a pace he wouldn't have followed, in a style he wouldn't have recognised, I also was reminded just how little credit we give him and what he achieved. Fan lore will paint him as an unlikeable old git, played by an irascible actor who could barely remember his lines. And it's simply not true. Hartnell is incredibly good in An Unearthly Child. Whilst the other regulars – William Russell (as Ian), Jacqueline Hill (as Barbara) and Carole Ann Ford (as Susan) – are all sensibly making the effort to give some consistency to their characters within the 25 minutes provided, to give some sort of platform from which they can develop later, Hartnell is brilliantly jumping all over the place. He'll be distant and superior one moment, amused and eccentric the next – the camera will focus upon him listening with intent suspicion to Ian and Barbara, and then he'll wander off and be distracted by a dirty painting frame. He can give breezy speeches about the fourth dimension, but his most chilling moment is a simple "No," turning away from camera, as he dispassionately rejects Susan's pleas to give the teachers freedom. I especially love the bit where his concern for a broken clock almost has him turning to Ian as a confidant, giving us a wonderful glimpse of the amiable Doctor we'll come to know – before he realises he doesn't like this intruder yet, and freezes on him.

And then there's the very real oddness of the way this episode is told, still striking after all this time. A policeman pokes around outside a junkyard, but doesn't go in. But the gates open magically for us – it's as if in its very first scene, Doctor Who is breaking the fourth wall, making us complicit. There are flashbacks – we very rarely get those – but when we do, the audience become the schoolteachers who seem to be hectoring Susan, offering her no sympathy from the mocking laughter of the other children. Waris Hussein actually steers the camera straight at Susan, so that it seems to be stalking her, making her squirm. The best example is the real distress she shows being made to do a maths problem in only three dimensions – and the awed, almost fearful wonder as she identifies the fifth dimension as "space".

An Unearthly Child deliberately sets itself up as a puzzle, right from the very first moments of the title sequence. (What on Earth is it, all that white noise and strobing patterns? We find out before the episode is over, and it's one of the very few times in the series' history that the conceit of travel through time and space is given the breathtaking wonder it deserves.) The genius of this episode is that it makes you believe this series can break all rules; it's only defined by not having any rules at all, next week it could be anything. It's bonkers, and it's brilliant, and in less than half an hour it's taken this rather jaded and complacent fan and made him excited all over again. Not a bad piece of work.

T: Let's go, then... I slide the DVD into the machine and press Play All, and my expectant relaxation is scuppered approximately two seconds later, as a sound effect in the title sequence reveals that I've accidentally chosen the unbroadcast Doctor Who pilot, not the actual first episode. My fiancée, Katherine, is slightly stunned that something so trivial could tell me which episode I'm watching, and I realise that she doesn't quite understand the depths of my depravity. A quick skip later, a lowering of the lights and a legend, as they say, begins...

Those titles and that music establish the show's unearthly nature a good 30 seconds before the actual episode title unassumingly burns itself onto the screen. The most modern synth technology and computer wizardry cannot compete with the impact of these fledgling audio and visual techniques as they are bent, bled and morphed into ethereal alien sounds and shapes. You cannot date this episode from the title sequence, or from the use of a defiantly unfuturistic (and thus, undateable) font to form what initially appears to be the legend "Doctor Oho".

Then we get to the episode, and it's very creepy, the camera itself acting as if it's an extra character. The creak you hear as it pans into the junkyard only adds to the atmosphere, especially as Norman Kay's evocative, spine-tingling incidentals seem designed to have been played on the very bric-a-brac that litters the junkyard – and, indeed, forms the instrumentation in the Doctor's ship.

But it's the people on screen that I most wonder about. There's Reg Cranfield, playing the aforementioned wandering policeman, and therefore literally the first man to appear in the show. (Quite what Fred Rawlings, originally cast in the role, did wrong in the pilot is anyone's guess.) I was often tempted to write to Cranfield, to quiz him on his legendary status, but never did. I wonder if he'd bounced his grandchildren on his knee, regaling them with the information that he was the first human being ever seen in Doctor Who... or whether he went to his grave unaware that no matter how small, his contribution to a television legend was a landmark. I imagine him having a bath that morning, washing in carbolic soap and putting on a crisp, starched shirt before heading off to partake in the genesis of something of huge cultural significance. And how great is that gaggle of students in Coal Hill School? Like the one who rhubarbs with such gusto, eliciting an archly raised eyebrow from a stunning girl whose icy facial expression hints at a feisty, sexy self-assurance that I've always found inappropriately beguiling. She's probably someone's grandmother now. Or dead.

Yes, the regulars are brilliant – but for now, as far as they know, this is just another job. As they loped off to the BBC bar afterwards, they were probably just relieved that (unlike the pilot episode) those infernal doors hadn't clattered, and that Ford didn't fluff her "nineteen to two" line again (something I rather miss, as I thought it was a genuine addition to her

unearthliness rather than an all too prosaic cock-up). There's a lovely moment in the broadcast episode where Hartnell's scarf falls off and he pats himself around the body before realising what's happened and picking it up – all the while playing the scene with the intensity it calls for. It adds quirkiness to his character, and a moment which nowadays would have been stopped whilst the cast dissolved into self-satisfied giggles is allowed to continue, rooting you in reality just as everything is about to go doolally.

But the thing that strikes me most about this episode? It's *alien*. Hartnell's alien, Ford's alien, as is the music and the eerie camera sweeping. It has a spookiness I don't generally associate with Doctor Who. Perhaps it's because I'm aware of the weight these 25 minutes bear on the subsequent 40-odd years, and to newcomers, the whole episode may look as creaky as that camera I earlier lauded.

When Leslie Bates makes his debut as the silhouette seen outside the TARDIS in the cliffhanger and the theme music oozes in, K turns to me and says, "That was quick... I can't believe how fast paced that was. [Jacqueline Hill] is brilliant – she gave a really modern and layered performance. I wasn't expecting that." And nor was I. Hill gave what I assumed would appear to a layperson's eyes and ears as a slightly mannered, over-enunciated performance in an old TV show – but there she is, reaching out from November 1963 and impressing someone on 1st January, 2009. I wasn't expecting that.

But then again, I suspect that "I wasn't expecting that" is precisely what viewers said on 23rd November, 1963... whatever they'd just seen in this very first Doctor Who episode of all, they *can't* have been expecting it!

The Cave of Skulls
(An Unearthly Child episode two)

R: Fandom would have it that the long discussions between cavemen about the secret of fire, and the particular perks that being a firemaker might give an up-and-coming Stone Age leader, are rather less exciting than the imaginative leaps shown in the very first episode. But what's smashing is that director Waris Hussein seems to acknowledge this from the very start.

The first group scene entails the camera panning around all the caveman as they watch with awe and fervour as Derek Newark (playing Za) attempts to ignite a stick by rubbing it with his hands – until finally, we're shown a child extra who, displaying some obvious irritation and boredom, turns away from Za as the camera passes by. It *could* be accidental – but the child seems too foregrounded for that, and it seems to me instead rather a witty comment upon the action of the scene. We've moved from a spaceship travelling through the time vortex to the almost-comical contrast of a hairy man grunting with enthusiasm as he caresses a bit of wood.

It's in the contrast that the episode works, though. Barbara is pleasingly all too eager to accept the insanity of the Doctor Who premise, even before the TARDIS doors are open. It's rather a lovely character note that the woman who teaches history is more open to the technological impossibility of what's before her very eyes than the man of science. But as Ian steps out into the Stone Age, actually knocked giddy by the shock of it all, he still finds himself denying what he sees before him and tries his hardest to rationalise it all away. It's very human, and very real – and not so very different a reaction from the grubby cavemen squatting at the other end of the studio to the bogglingly new invention of fire.

There's also a lovely bit of comedy in the way that Za keeps insisting upon, as leader's privilege, his rights to take Hur as his significant other. Hur is presumably the best looker in the Tribe of Gum – she's certainly the only one of fertile age who has any dialogue. But given – and I mean no disrespect to actress Alethea Charlton – Hur's blacked-out teeth and grubby face, the constant offer of her as top prize in this leadership struggle looks more and more like something of a poisoned chalice.

Anyway, there we are. First day of the year, and two episodes under my belt. Only another seven hundred plus to go. I wonder how Toby got on?

T: It's my birthday tomorrow, and although K is packed off to wrap my birthday presents, my hope that I'll get a Dalek cigarette lighter is dashed as I'm reminded I'm supposed to be giving up smoking. So to take my mind off the fags, I watch Doctor Who: The Difficult Second Album...

I've worked on shows where everyone thinks they're doing a piece of crap, and the finished product is awash with lazy acting and little invention. Well, Derek Newark may have justifiably wondered why the hell he was being made to shout at a stick, but there's nothing in his performance that suggests this is the case. Nobody involved seems to think they're above all of this, or that they're appearing in a disposable piece of ephemera. In fact, I remember that Newark's Guardian obituary in 1998 received a follow-up article from the great Harold Pinter... that one of our country's greatest dramatists noted and mourned the passing of this jobbing (albeit excellent) actor made me feel proud that Newark had made a palpable contribution to the genesis of my favourite programme.

And then we get the first "Doctor who?" gag, when the Doctor is a bit befuddled at Ian calling him "Doctor Foreman". Hartnell wonderfully fits Sydney Newman's brief by being the tetchy outsider – here he's all imperious and haughty, looking splendid in that hat and brilliantly patronising Ian. Then there's his lyrical talk about being able to touch the alien sand, just as evocative as the previous episode's poetic lament about what it would be like to be wanderers in the fourth dimension. Under scrutiny, this episode isn't merely a historical – Kal's world is as alien to us as any mocked-up Mars or Venus, and it's far more visceral and shocking than any planet inhabited by a silver clad, bewigged alien with a silly name. Doctor Who starts out as a *strange* (in the proper sense of the word) programme, and this very strangeness keeps us rapt.

Oh, and brilliant, the Doctor bloody smokes... this is taking my mind off kicking the habit how, exactly?

I'll send my thoughts to Rob, but he's probably hibernating. Either that, or texting some poor bugger in Australia.

January 2nd

The Forest of Fear
(An Unearthly Child episode three)

R: One of the most interesting early discussions we had at BBC Wales, in those talks on the revived series of Doctor Who, was about death. What could we get away with? Could it be shown on screen? Could it even, frankly, be implied off screen? The standards for what was deemed acceptable for family viewing were very different in 2004 than they were in 1963. This was why Russell T Davies' pilot script, which all of us freelancers were using as a template, was so shy about the Auton killings – all the stage directions clearly indicated that everyone who got blasted down by a shop mannequin did so comfortably off camera.

The Forest of Fear is the episode which sets the tone for all the death and carnage that follows Doctor Who ever onwards – because, let's face it, for a show which is at least partly designed to appeal to pre-teens, it's extraordinarily bloodthirsty. (And it's an interesting side note that although The Sarah Jane Adventures is clearly billed as a Doctor Who spinoff, it's far more wary about the whole matter, and sometimes almost seems to bend a storyline just to avoid anything fatal befalling even the monster of the week.) So with all of that in mind, this episode is a big tease – it keeps on inviting the audience to second-guess it, to work out whether the series has the balls to kill anyone off. Old Mother takes a knife into the Cave of Skulls, and we imagine she intends to murder the TARDIS crew... but instead, she just wants to cut their bonds and set them free. Then Barbara falls over a dead body in the forest – but it's okay, it's just a wild animal. Then Za gets attacked by some savage beast and ends up covered in blood – but again, it's okay, the blood isn't his, and the caveman will pull through with just a bit of water sprinkled on him. The Doctor looks bemused throughout the whole sequence, where all his fellow companions stop racing for freedom and instead start dishing out medical advice – it's as if he too is asking what sort of adventure serial this really is. Are their lives genuinely ever going to be at stake, or is this the sort of kids' pro-gramme which will offer a *hint* of jeopardy, but in fact be directing its young audience towards safe moral homilies – such as "Stop and help a wounded caveman chasing you with an axe, and he too will become your friend"?

And then, after 20-odd minutes of Anthony Coburn playing around with the *idea* of death, he gives us a corpse. Even here it's a tease – Kal pretends to the Tribe of Gum (and therefore to the audience watching) that Old Mother is sitting upright alive and well. And then she topples backward, eyes staring open, dead as a doornail, and at last we understand that this is a programme where life and death really *are* at stake. These adventures in the TARDIS can kill.

Someone should tell the Doctor and his friends pronto, because they may not realise they're genuinely under threat. Much has been made of the sequence where the Doctor picks up a rock, presumably to bash Za's brains in so the travellers can dispense with helping him and continue their flight through the forest – it's as if the Doctor, at least, has some inkling of what a very dark and dangerous programme they're all embarking on. But although it's Ian who stays the Doctor's hand, only a few minutes before, *he* was the one who wanted to take advantage of Za being attacked by something with a loud roar and have everyone make their escape to the TARDIS. What I love about these sequences is that there's really no simple morality on display here: Barbara does the humane thing in wanting to tend Za's wounds, but isn't she just risking the lives of her fellows by doing so? Isn't that act of charity the exact thing that forces the Doctor to contemplate murder? We're clearly invited to side with Ian as the Voice of Reason – but because Ian's stance itself is ambiguous (allow a wounded man to die, maybe, but don't actually have the honesty to kill him yourself), the episode rather brilliantly stops short of trite moralising.

Happy birthday, by the way, Toby. Did you get a Dalek cigarette lighter? Do they even exist? Bloody hell, they'll be selling Judoon flickknives next.

T: I didn't get a Dalek lighter, alas. Actually, I'm not even sure they're allowed to make them any more. The one I had in mind was a big, chunky table lighter that was displayed in a

Manchester shop of ephemera and gadgets years ago. I got a fob watch though, suggesting that K wants me to wipe my memory and become somebody else.

Anyway, she joined me again for The Forest of Fear. I was slightly worried that all the good-will generated from that venerable opening instalment would soon evaporate at the sight of some mucky character actors arguing with each other about fire, but as it turned out...

The first thing that strikes me about these first two episodes (gloriously restored on DVD) is the sharp contrast between the black and the white – I remember most of this era as being resolutely greyscale. Here (and I don't know whether it's the quality of the print or a conscious lighting design) the blacks provide a spooky, inky darkness, with the light flashing brightly in the gloomy recesses of the Cave of Skulls. Waris Hussein also specialises in close-ups, wisely telling the story by concentrating on the characters – he looms up on Derek Newark as his face twitches, intimating that his caveman character is assessing a complex situation, with realisation slowly dawning. Or look at how Hussein holds on Hartnell as Za lies injured, the Doctor's eyes darting about as he formulates the dastardly plan you mentioned.

For all that fandom has questioned the Doctor's morality in this episode, he's a great character – one who begins the episode by telling his companions that he's "desperately sorry" for getting them into this predicament. (K liked that vulnerability, delivered as the travellers are trussed up in the corner of a cave looking a bit useless.) But before long, there's the oft-quoted moment where he tries to take Za's life. We tend to create Doctor Who in our own image, and so I've often just tried to pretend this moment didn't happen, that it was an aberration on the part of a production team who weren't quite sure what the show was about. Now, thanks to the new series, I can assess it differently – perhaps it's the Doctor's proximity to humans that makes him a better person. He needs Ian to be a moral arbiter, and fortunately Ian himself isn't a dull do-gooder – his anger at the Doctor's actions makes for a great, sparky dynamic at the centre of the show. Indeed, the shifting allegiances and lack of cosiness makes this far more interesting than the story's simple premise might suggest.

It's often great to act in Doctor Who – to relish the fruity dialogue of a powerful alien warlord, or to play an overblown, pompous grotesque. But getting trussed up in flea-ridden animal skins and grunting? By all rights, that *should* be embarrassing, so let's give the cast credit for pulling it off. Hur's keening as Za lies injured is brilliant – it's recognisable as grief and fear, but it's not expressed in modern terms, and so comes off almost animalistic. Alethea Charlton isn't playing a sophisticated character, but she's made a very sophisticated acting choice. Then when Barbara offers to take Hur to water, to help, she accepts but brushes her off physically. These creatures operate with a completely different moral code – and their unpredictability is what creates the tension in this story. This is a far more complex piece than I'd hitherto believed, the only downside being the hysteria with which poor old Carole Ann Ford and Jacqueline Hill are expected to react to everything.

But as much as everyone fixates on the Doctor's attempt to brain Za, a moment from the outcome to that scene strikes me as being the essence of Doctor Who. Recognizing that the travellers have shown mercy, Za tells Hur: "Listen to them, they do not kill." If ever there's a mantra for the show, that's it.

The Firemaker
(An Unearthly Child episode four)

R: There's a bit in the previous episode where Za and Hur suspect Old Mother intends to kill the TARDIS crew, and suggest that if they prevent her from doing so, the Doctor and his companions might feel so indebted that they'll give them fire in return. It's a sort of Sesame Street logic that you get in a lot of children's television – happy moralising that says that if you're *nice* to people, you'll get a reward. And all this business about the cavemen's believing that Ian's name is "Friend" seems part of that – you automatically know where you are with it, it's a bit twee, and very pat, but offers clear values of decency and fair play that all the children watching should aspire to. (Even if you do wonder why the cavemen, all of whom speak fairly sophisticated English, know the word "enemy" but are so baffled by its antonym.)

So the happy ending is set up that the Doctor will drive away Kal, show Za how to make fire, and then be set free with waves and cheers and promises (no doubt) that the Tribe of Gum will be much more genial to newcomers in future, and maybe even elect leaders with some sort of democratic system. You can see the expectation on Ian's face – rather patronisingly, he teaches Za how to rub two sticks together, as if he *knows* this is the way that the story should work.

But it doesn't. It's another tease on behalf of Anthony Coburn, and rather a brilliant one. Once Za's life has been saved, and his authority has been secured, he's an even greater threat to the travellers than he was before. Ian is left to berate himself that by giving into Za's demands, he's effectively demonstrated that he's weak and vulnerable. A few weeks before The Daleks shows us the evils of pacifism, here Doctor Who is criticising appeasement. It's worth remembering that this programme was being made in the wake of the Second World War – if the Daleks we'll see waving a plunger next week are clearly Nazis, then there's something about Chamberlain's failure to secure peace at Munich with Hitler about the TARDIS crew's dealings with the Tribe of Gum. The conclusion offered here is a bit of a shock, because Doctor Who very soon becomes a programme which (to all intents and purposes) is very liberal minded. Za *ought* to have killed Kal, his rival for leadership, from the moment he saw him rather than offer shelter to the only survivor from a different tribe – because outsiders *are* dangerous, and will challenge you. And the Doctor *ought* to have brained Za with a rock when he had the chance, because you can't teach savages such concepts as friendship or loyalty.

It's wonderful just how *dirty* the regulars are at the end of the story, as they stand in the sudden brightness of the TARDIS control room, smeared with grime. It's an element of realism we won't see very often. But it's also very appropriate – we're still learning what the parameters of Doctor Who can be, and in its morals it's a much dirtier programme than we might have supposed.

T: Talk to actors and they'll bemoan the state of the industry, the lack of rehearsals, the limitations on spontaneity. And watching these episodes, you'll see another now-lost performing art that probably took half a term to conquer at drama school: the Stop-What-You're-Doing-For-Several-Moments-So-The-Episode-Title-And-Writer's-Credit-Can-Be-Superimposed-Over-You Masterclass. Howard Lang (playing Hur's father Horg) has to do it this time by looking inscrutable, and last week Eileen Way's Old Mother had to pause, knife in hand, while Anthony Coburn's name got its five seconds of allotted screen time.

Talking of whom: goodbye, Mr Coburn. He was there at the beginning and a key instrument in the show's genesis, and yet both he and another important contributor, production designer Peter Brachaki, don't make it beyond the first story. But Coburn's dialogue has some wonderful qualities – as well as all the quotable stuff from the regulars (the Doctor's "Fear makes companions of all of us"), the material Coburn gives the cavemen wonderfully crafts their earthy inarticulation – "Za does not say he did this or did that," the animal "took away your axe in its head", etc. These aren't just grunting savages – Coburn suggests character and thought processes whilst not allowing them to express such things in modern parlance.

The staging helps too: the fight between Kal and Za is really nasty. Jeremy Young (Kal) bites Newark at one point, and Kal's death rattle is piercingly offbeat and bloodcurdling; likewise, the ungainly way his twisted body is dragged off is unpleasantly, bluntly realistic. Then when Hur (whose name, by the way, makes you wonder if Horg would have called his son "Hym") pops in, and Alethea Charlton brilliantly plays the scene with her back to the regulars, rubbernecking Kal's crumpled cadaver with animalistic fascination. I'd always had her down as a rather prim, mumsy actress who got shoehorned into playing dowdy roles, but she's been great in this.

As the credits roll, K unconsciously echoes my previous thoughts about the alienness of this civilisation – she tells me she was "gripped" even without the diversions of funky aliens. Fight arranger Derek Ware's name pops up in the credits, and as it turns out, he's a mutual acquaintance – he taught K how to fight (and did a bloody good job, if some of our past arguments are anything to go by).

I still don't think that having the TARDIS crew encounter cavemen the first time out of the gate was necessarily a *wise* choice, but I do feel sympathy for an adventure that's always been overshadowed by the seminal episodes that surround it. However primitive the setting, this is an estimable piece of work.

January 3rd

R: It's all very odd, this. Last night I was invited to a dinner party. And who do you imagine was seated opposite me? Waris Hussein! Only the bloody director of An Unearthly Child. Our host put us together, rather endearingly, because we'd both worked on Doctor Who, so thought we might have some connection. (Yeah, but it was 40 years apart!) Oddly enough, though, we *did* have a connection – we both realised we had the same enormous pride in Doctor Who. Hearing Waris speak with such enthusiasm about the scene in which Za dropped a rock on Kal's head (he told me he'd had an argument with Verity Lambert about it, as his cabbage-crushing sound effect was much more gruesome), I realised that it was never going to leave me alone either, that it was always going to be a fundamental part of my life. Janie asked me later whether that bothered me, but do you know? – I actually found it heartwarming.

What was amusing was that Waris kept on asking me if I knew who the eleventh Doctor was going to be – as if I had some insider knowledge! (And as often happens nowadays, the 13-year-old fanboy in me flipped somewhat, knowing that the director of Marco Polo was pressing me for Who spoilers.) I got home, though, to find out that later today the new casting is going to be announced on BBC1. It's almost too exciting to go back to the Hartnell episodes. But these ones are pretty momentous, aren't they...?

T: There must have been something in the water yesterday – you met Waris Hussein (I'm very jealous), and there's a new Doctor on the horizon. As I type this, the announcement is two and a half hours away and I'm furiously batting off text messages from people who

think the fact that I've done a mildly successful one-man show about Doctor Who means I've got a hotline to the production office. Irritatingly, they're the same people who spent the whole of December shuffling up to me, sagely tapping the side of their nose, and informing me (with no little self assurance) that they had it on good authority that David Morrissey was the new Doctor. I genuinely have no clue who it will be, and am very excited indeed. So shall we kill a bit of time watching some Hartnell?

R: Do you know, I think we should.

The Dead Planet
(The Daleks episode one)

R: To state the bleeding obvious: this is the first episode of Doctor Who set on an alien world. It's a funny thing, though, but whilst the series has often celebrated the sheer wonder of going backwards in time – companions from the black-and-white era to the present day beaming with enthusiasm to find that they're either in an Aztec tomb or in Dickensian Cardiff – it's much more mealy-mouthed about space travel. The Hartnell years almost seem to be deliberately avoiding the opportunity to show a contemporary character marvelling at the prospect of setting foot on a distant world – after Ian and Barbara depart, we'll be given a whole stream of replacements from the future, to whom planet hopping is no more remarkable a concept than catching a bus. (Russell T Davies' new series, with its emphasis upon wonder, surprisingly shies away from it as well – so much so that Rose Tyler, the first character to represent the audience's point of view, first steps off Earth in an untransmitted adventure, so we never get to see her reaction to that locale.)

It's worth asking why that's the case. It can't just be that the programme makers are more *comfortable* showing off historical costumes and pageantry, so can do so with greater confidence. (Besides which, Skaro here doesn't look *that* much more alien than the rocky wastes where Ian and Barbara first encountered the cavemen.) Instead, it's that the settings of the past are much more familiar, and our schoolteacher characters are able to offer information and points of view which make them seem useful. Ian and Barbara are unwilling travellers – given the opportunity to walk around a petrified jungle and encounter strange horned creatures made out of metal, all they really want to do is complain about the journey diversion. It's a dangerous game for the series to play, to turn its first alien world not into a place of magic and beauty, but instead somewhere no-one much wants to be. We'll see in the 1980s, when Tegan Jovanka in Season Nineteen regularly reacts to mind-popping spectacle with sarcastic cynicism, how this approach can be a bit wearying. But it works so very well here, precisely because Barbara's despair, and Ian's over-cheery attempts to make the best of things, are so very realistic. We're five weeks into this show, and yet none of our lead characters have yet given themselves over to the stereotypes demanded by adventure series, where the excitement of the chase and death-defying thrills are actively being sought. Here, we have a couple of ordinary people from sixties England being given a sight that no-one else on their world has ever seen – and they show more genuine enthusiasm at the bacon 'n' egg sweet they get from the TARDIS food machine.

What the episode does, though (and most usefully), is put the Doctor centre-stage. For the last few weeks, the TARDIS crew have shared a common aim: run away from wherever their Ship takes them. (It'll be a recurring plot point of most of these early adventures, and it's telling that even when Terry Nation sits down to write Destiny of the Daleks some 14 years later, he includes in the first episode something which *prevents* the crew from just getting back inside the TARDIS and taking off, as if that'd still be their first impulse in that phase of the programme.) The sight of the Dalek city in the distance is the first thing in Doctor Who that is meant to inspire awe – but in spite of that, only the Doctor has the slightest interest in exploring the thing. It's as if the Doctor alone understands the sort of TV series he's appearing in – it'll be a great deal *safer* every week if no-one bothers to get involved in an adventure, but it'll be a duller show for the audience to watch. Much has been made of how Hartnell's Doctor is a darker, more selfish character for the scene in which he sabotages

the Ship just so he can have his own way, but I think that viewpoint misses the tone completely: it's actually very *funny*, Hartnell playing his concern for the TARDIS breakdown with very mock sincerity, and giving us a delightful little chuckle as we fade to the scene change.

And the upshot of all of these attempts to *avoid* the alien city is that it makes it all the more threatening. It's nothing more than slanting corridors and whirring doors, but Barbara's panic as she loses herself amongst them is tremendously well played by Jacqueline Hill, and very credible: you really believe that within minutes of venturing into the unknown, she's fallen apart. Which builds up all the better to that stunning cliffhanger – again, what we *see* isn't any more impressive than the cheap sets, but by now we so share our characters' dislocation from the ordinary, the sight of a wobbly sink plunger represents something truly terrifying.

It's also an episode in which William Hartnell fluffs a lot of his lines, as he becomes increasingly wont to do. But I find it curiously moving that his biggest stumble is in the scene where he asks Barbara to talk to his granddaughter – it's a confession that he needs someone else's help, and his first real attempt to talk to Barbara on an equal level. The awkwardness of Hartnell at that moment, intentional or not, is very real and very touching.

T: Well, this episode is very evocative for me. I remember a visit to Longleat where I gawped at the book The Early Years in the shop. It oozed class: it had big black and white photos and design drawings, and – most importantly – it was about "old" Doctor Who. I'd yet to see any of the episodes shown before I was born, but anything broadcast prior to about 1976 (except, of course, The Gunfighters) was officially regarded as Good Doctor Who. So imagine my delight when I was searching our old house for things to do one day when everyone was out (or Mum was busy in the garden), and I happened upon a copy of the aforementioned book hidden in a cupboard in a plastic bag, obviously set aside for a Christmas gift. I'd guiltily go back to that cupboard in the ensuing months, reasoning that if I looked at the pictures but didn't read the text, I was somehow not cheating. And so the images of these stories – The Cusick Stories – became extremely familiar. When I finally watched the episodes, there were very few things on screen I hadn't seen in massive close-up or drawn from every angle.

So I hope it's with no disrespect to Mr Nation when I say that it's not really the dialogue that strikes me with this episode; it's what we see, and most evocatively, the sounds we hear that fuse to make the titular dead planet such an evocative place. The visuals of this story hit you first – asked to create a jungle, a ledge with a view to a sprawling city below and the corridors of that city itself (and to fit them all into a cramped BBC studio), designer Ray Cusick doesn't flinch. He's aided by a curious visual effect (one which I previously thought was just a symptom of bootlegging, but which the VidFIREd-DVD reveals as a deliberate production decision): an overexposed lens used for those early moments in the jungle gives everything a curious, blasted quality.

And yet, I feel as if sound-designer Brian Hodgson is the unsung star of this episode – the haunting, unrelenting caterwauls of the jungle, the scraping of the TARDIS door and even the sound of the TARDIS scanner all aid the storytelling in abstract ways. Meanwhile, Tristram Cary's discordant, subtly menacing music is creepy and alien. Then – and just as important – there are the contrasting moments where they decide *not* to use sound: the camera that follows Barbara, the city-doors that close silently around her... moments like these are the most effective in an episode that, fittingly, ends with a treated, echoed scream climaxing in darkness.

The Survivors
(The Daleks episode two)

R: This marks the Daleks' first appearance, so it's clearly a very momentous episode (even if part of its charm is that there's no way anyone making it can know that yet). But watching it back, there were two little reactions that really stood out for me, amidst the bombast and significance.

One of them is the way that William Russell, playing Ian, reacts with such relief and delight when he begins to get feeling back in his legs.

He's paralysed by a Dalek gun at the top of the episode, and spends the majority of the next 20 minutes, in macho hero way, insisting he can walk (and then collapsing onto the floor) and beating at his thighs in anger. By the time he recovers, it's too late to help him – Susan has already been sent out into the mutant-filled forest, and Barbara and the Doctor are nearly dead from radiation exposure. Still, there's that moment of pride when he discovers he's on his feet again, able to move one leg in front of the other. He takes a few steps with growing confidence – and then doubles over, clutching his stomach as the full force of his own radiation sickness hits him. If it's not one thing, then it's another! It'd be almost comical, were the reaction not so very human, and it only helps to reinforce the desperation of the situation.

The other is the laugh that Susan gives when Ian and Barbara solemnly ponder whether there are any little men hiding inside the Dalek machines. It's a real gurgle of a laugh, too, just responding to the bizarreness of it all – and although I'm sure it was scripted, it almost feels like Carole Ann Ford is corpsing. Ford has had a tough job since An Unearthly Child, simultaneously playing an ordinary teenage girl who at times screams so much, she falls over the set, and also someone alien and futuristic and unknowable. That single laugh is the most natural she's been since her introduction, and it's terrific – partly because the Daleks, for all the brilliance of their design, the elegance of their movements and that wonderful staccato voice, *are* ultimately ridiculous-looking pepperpots. And it takes that laughter, that suggestion that *someone* in the story also thinks they look funny, that somehow makes them more credible. They're the first Doctor Who monsters, gawp at 'em, have a chuckle – and now you've done that, look at what they're doing and what they represent.

And the Daleks aren't necessarily the villains of the piece yet either. Their treatment of the TARDIS crew is unfriendly and opportunistic, but at least they can be reasoned with, unlike the cavemen of the Tribe of Gum. At this stage, they're hardly more callous than the supposedly "good" characters we'll meet later in the season, like Marco Polo or Arbitan, who also blackmail or imprison our heroes for their own ends. It's clever that the cliffhanger still suggests that although her fellows are dying in a Dalek cell, it's *Susan* who may be the one in greater peril, having to journey through a forest that may be home to worse monsters still. The stronger of these Hartnell episodes are the ones that focus upon a moral dilemma, just as The Forest of Fear asked us to ponder whether or not the ends justify the means in allowing a caveman to die. That Ian is here obliged to ask a terrified Susan to risk her life for the greater good is only a taste of what Nation has in store for us later in the story, but it's very effective.

T: It's easy, considering everything that follows, to forget the scene before the Daleks first appear. It's great – the lighting is much darker, with the white glare from the instruments dancing on the sweat on the actors' faces. The camerawork here isn't as fluid and well-framed as it was the first four episodes (that Waris Hussein went on to great success is increasingly unsurprising), but the few close-ups we get here (especially on Hartnell's craggy and expressive face) are among memorable and powerful moments.

And given the proportions they'll achieve later on, don't these Daleks seem tiny? They're really little, but I think it works. The pull back that reveals them in their very first shot is wonderful, as is the fact that the travellers are made to get on their knees so the Daleks can be framed towering over them. Quite why the Daleks are seen watching what looks like rejected Doctor Who title sequences on their round telly is anyone's guess, but I like the way one scene ends with them starting to talk at the same time. It's a peculiar choice, but it oddly makes it seem more realistic to end halfway through their babble, as opposed to when the salient dialogue has run out.

This all *looks* and *sounds* amazing, but none of the lines are vying for my attention in the way they did in the first adventure. Thus far, this story has been 50 minutes of set-up, and so I'm fascinated to see what Susan encounters on her way back to the city, and to finally meet a few more humanoid characters...

Back in the here and now, though, I'll know who the new Doctor is in about an hour!

R: And since we watched those Dalek episodes, the BBC have announced our eleventh Doctor is Matt Smith.

I remember the days when the casting of a new Doctor was something you'd get as one of the late "fun" items on BBC News. Now, the News carries a story about how a special programme following it will reveal the new Doctor, which seems just a mite cart before the horse to me. It's astonishing to see, as someone still a bit poleaxed by just how massive a success Doctor Who now is, how cannily the BBC have handled David Tennant's departure. To begin with, his resignation is announced midway through an award ceremony hosted by a rival channel, in one fell swoop guaranteeing that whatever else the evening was *supposed* to be about, all the papers the next day will only cover the scoop from Doctor Who. (I don't know, but if I were up as, say, best actress appearing in a soap opera, I'd be a bit miffed by that.) They then broadcast a Christmas special which deliberately plays upon the idea that a new actor is being cast for the role (they even titled it, of all things, The Next Doctor!), thus sending bookies into a frenzy. And then, as soon as the hoopla of *that* has died down, they announce an entire half-hour programme given over to the casting reveal, on BBC1, only a little before prime time. It's stunning, really.

So, of course, the announcement that the new Doctor is one Matt Smith is something of an anticlimax.

Good.

It's funny, really. With all that build-up, the only way that the new Doctor *wouldn't* have seemed like an anticlimax is if he'd been someone so incredibly famous, everyone had already heard of him. (And I mean, *everyone*. Anyone short of Tom Cruise wouldn't have been appropriate to the fanfare.) That it's an actor the majority of the audience would never have heard of is comically delicious. And, I think, entirely fitting to Doctor Who too. Since when *should* a new Doctor be someone we already know? Of the ten previous incarnations, three of the actors, four at a pinch, would have been immediately recognisable – and none of them necessarily famous enough that their names were on the lips of your everyday man on the street.

The temptation must have been there to do

it differently this time, now that Doctor Who really isn't just seen as a funny little family show with a cult following, and has become a genuinely global concern. Now, that it's a programme which has sold two of its Christmas specials principally upon its guest stars, and which earned its biggest ratings by featuring Kylie Minogue on a Radio Times cover. They could have reached out for the Robert Carlyles of the world, the Alan Rickmans, the names we fans have seen bandied about for well over a decade every time a tabloid story ponders a feature film. Or, failing that, they could have gone down the popular celebrity route and cast a soap star wanting a new vehicle, or a TV presenter choosing Doctor Who as a means for further exposure rather than appearing in the Big Brother house or learning how to do the cha-cha in front of Bruce Forsyth.

Quite rightly, I think, the role of the Doctor has gone to an actor who'll come with no baggage whatsoever. Who can make whatever he wants of the part, without any audience expectations of whatever he's done before. Matt Smith has got everything to play for. David Tennant has cast such a huge shadow over Doctor Who, and I think any actor trying to follow him will find such resistance from the public that it needs to be someone, as a result, who has *nothing to lose*. Put Robert Carlyle in the part, and all he can do is not quite measure up to his predecessor and watch as his reputation suffers. What's in it for him? Give it to someone who instead has *everything* to prove, who can use the part as a stepping stone in his career whatever happens, someone indeed who has the right to fail – and let him off his leash.

I have no particular opinion of Matt Smith yet, and that's precisely because I've never seen anything he's done before, and I think that's wonderful and exciting. At a time when Doctor Who could have been easily forgiven for playing it safe, for trying to follow the brilliant success of David Tennant with a name, they have gone instead for an unknown they feel is right for the job. Good for them. Good for Matt Smith. And good for us, too.

T: I'd previously seen Matt Smith in the first episode of Party Animals, and on that occasion looked him up on IMDb because I'd been

impressed with his performance. I didn't keep up with the series, though, and promptly forgot his name. That actually causes me some disquiet – I can remember the name of every actor that's ever been in Doctor Who, but my brain failed to retain even the most basic two-syllable nomenclature.

Nonetheless, and despite the BBC's best efforts, Smith's name had leaked on some forums as a possibility. So when I heard that the new Doctor would be "the youngest ever" and that "he's only 26," I guessed that it was him. I then cracked open my birthday bottle of Talisker to welcome in the new guy, and was delighted to finally see him as a slightly offbeat interviewee with delightfully expressive fingers. I'd anticipated that, for the first time, the Doctor would be younger than me – but Smith is *nine years* younger! It was enough to make me apply for my old age pension, dye my hair, and forget the names I've read on IMDb. After raising a glass to him, though, I logged onto the Internet to gauge fan reaction to his casting... and immediately wished I hadn't. We're striving to be positive in this book, so let me just sweep that bit of unpleasantness under the rug.

It's entertaining, though, to see some commentators criticize Smith *because* he's an "unknown", even though by "unknown", what they really mean is "someone held in high regard within the industry with a string of leading stage and screen credits, but who has, for all these achievements, never been featured on TV Quick's list of Best-Dressed Men". He'll do splendidly in the role.

January 4th

The Escape
(The Daleks episode three)

R: Ah. Hmm. Oh dear. I said to you that we should look for the positive in all these episodes we watched, and I knew that eventually I'd come across one that I didn't much like. I just didn't anticipate it happening quite so soon.

The problem, really, is with the bloody Thals, isn't it? Terry Nation perhaps tries too hard to characterise them too quickly, giving them all different personalities – here's the cynical one (Ganatus), here's the one who pontificates a lot (Temmosus), here's the annoying one who's a bit dim and a bit humourless and who can't act very well (Dyoni) – and the overall effect smacks of too much effort. The problem is that they're not very interesting; Nation's attempts to give them moments of banter are woeful, because the rest of the dialogue they have to utter is so terribly stilted. It isn't helped, by the way, that Susan keeps on talking of the Thals with all the dreamy, drippy enthusiasm of a schoolgirl with a crush on the latest boy band. It's nauseating.

Positive. Must try for the positive.

But – and here comes the positive, can you feel it? – maybe that's all for the best. Because the very vague emptiness of the Thals only throws the Daleks into sharp relief. They emerge now as the bad guys, of course, but they're all the better for it – they're sly and scheming and cunning. You don't like the Thals. Who'd want to like the Thals? Temmosus talks of how their Thal ancestors were warriors, and now they're *farmers*. Offer any child the choice between rooting for a farmer, or for your actual reconstructed warrior – preferably in a metal casing and with a grating voice and a gun that makes the screen go negative – and who do you think they'll pick?

As characters, the Thals are failures. And by being failures – by keeping the goodies blandly simple and positively tedious – every time they're on the screen, you're left hankering for another scene featuring the Daleks instead. I guarantee that if you were ambivalent about the Daleks at the end of last week's episode, you'll have been converted to their side after sitting through a discussion from Alan Wheatley (as Temmosus) about the causal effect of random events. The boring sod.

I'm not saying that the *reason* children went crazy for the Daleks – and the reason why the production team were taken by surprise and forced to commission a new story featuring the Daleks for the following Christmas, why Doctor Who suddenly was given its first hit and why its longevity was assured – was all because Virginia Wetherell's performance as a lisping Thal girl makes you want to exterminate everyone in sight. But it can be a contributory factor, can't it? Doctor Who has done

something unexpected – it's produced a villain that can be more popular and loveable than its hero. That little grey area of morality that the show has been exploring has, in a trice, become all the more ambiguous – and the programme is all the richer for it.

T: Crikey, Shearman, I thought I might have to encourage you later on, maybe through the likes of The Space Museum episode four or Underworld episode two... but you're flagging after only *seven* episodes?!! Where is your backbone? If it were down to the likes of you, Dalekmania would have lasted a fortnight, maximum. We've got 40-odd years to get through, man, get a hold on yourself!

Let's start with the episode title: "The Escape". Terry Nation hasn't quite got the same flair for naming scripts as Anthony Coburn, has he? In fact, watching this has really put into perspective just how strong Coburn's four-part script was. The only dialogue that sticks out here is the memorably quaint – "Yes, I was rather clumsy" says Alydon, as if he's just spilled the Pimms on the cucumber sandwiches. Much of the remainder of the Thal-speak is, as you say, pretty rotten – it's mannered 60s fare, much as could be found in any dated series from long ago.

And yet, this is where Doctor Who becomes different from anything on TV – where those making the show learn what the series' strengths are. I'm really enjoying watching these 60s Daleks freed from the shackles of received wisdom about how they should behave – this bunch is quite shifty; just notice the way they're sneaky with Susan, are bewildered by her very name and react harshly to her innocent laugh. Such attributes would seem clichéd coming from a humanoid with a spangly hat, but they're creepily alien when delivered by these gliding, menacing machines. I even love the way we blur from an eavesdropping camera into the earwigging Daleks in their control room.

Back in the cell, the regulars apply a bit of nous to the situation and orchestrate a fight, providing the first look inside a Dalek. Or, rather, the first *implied* look inside one – we're actually shown nothing, and it's left to William Russell (and a bit of frantic scratching inside the Dalek shell) to sell us on the nightmare of the creature that inhabits the Dalek casing. Fortunately, he's more than up to the task. And the cliffhanger – in which a Dalek mutant extends a clawed hand from under the cloak that's covering it – is odd and wonderful; it's a stolen moment that has little to do with plot or the actual danger facing our heroes. And yet, had I not experienced this episode before, I'd be waiting with baited breath to see what horror might emerge from the cloak, and what unspeakable beastliness it would bestow upon our heroes.

And it's not *all* bad with the Thals, is it? Philip Bond capers around gamely as Ganatus, clearly embracing a more modern acting style than his cohorts, and lounging insouciantly on a rock. He's great even though he's given so little to do, and of the cast is clearly The One To Watch. (And, interestingly, he's got his two-year-old daughter – who in future will play Mrs Wormwood on The Sarah Jane Adventures – to kiss goodnight after he gets home from recording this episode.) Also, one of the delights of Doctor Who is observing how designers and directors choose to depict something from "space" – and so here, the Thals have holes cut in their trousers. Okay, there are no beneficial or practical benefits to this that I can see, but it's pleasingly "space", that.

I will grant you that the Thals have a lisping problem, though. Alethea Charlton as a cavewoman was one thing, but the three way lisp-off here between (pardon me) Temmothuth, Alydon and Dyoni gets almost comical. (Temmosus: "Yesth, but we've changed over the centuries... the onth famouth warrior rath of Thals...") For all we know, some viewers watched that exchange and came away thinking that the good guys were actually called the "Sarls", but that none of them can actually pronounce the name of their own species.

The Ambush
(The Daleks episode four)

R: This is a much stronger episode – and not only because it's knee-deep in Thal corpses. It shows the first really sustained piece of *action* in Doctor Who yet, as the TARDIS crew escape from magnetised floors and lift shafts and the like. It's genuinely tense, and the entire sequence in which Ian is left trapped in a

Dalek casing, unable to move, makes the claustrophobia of the first few episodes of the story seem positively breezy in comparison.

At first, I'll be honest, I was a bit bemused by the sequence in which the crew defend themselves from the Daleks by throwing a bit of modern art down upon them in the ascending elevator. Since when would Daleks bother with something as imaginative and emotional as *art*? And then it occurred to me that, in spite of all my attempts to free myself from prejudice, I was looking at these Daleks from the jaded perspective of someone who's got used to all their clichés. (And no doubt, written a fair few of them into the series himself.) At this stage, Terry Nation's canvas is still empty – why *shouldn't* these new enemies of his have a culture, and a complexity indeed, that future stories make incongruous? This is the Skaro that we see in the Dalek annuals, or the pocketbook, at the height of sixties Dalekmania. Where Terry Nation and David Whitaker (rather charmingly) pretend that they're translating chronicles of real aliens from interplanetary cubes they find in the garden, where Daleks have a fear of the letter Q and occupy a continent called Darren. If the Daleks seem slightly off-beam in this first adventure – rather given to wordy explanations, content to talk of "extermination" but never ranting the word "exterminate", then that's all to the good. And they're as surprising to watch here, after 45 years of getting overused to the things, as they would have been to the first-time viewer.

I love the staging of the ambush itself, as the Daleks offer the Thals some provisions so they can lure them into the open and blast them. I love Tristram Cary's scraping music, ever-growing in threat as the Daleks emerge from their hiding places to gun down Temmosus; I love the blocking of his dead body, draped over the meagre offerings of fruit... I even love the suggestion that the Daleks were trying to tempt the Thals further by giving them what looks like some rolls of toilet paper. I'm pretty sure that's what it is, toilet paper, the corpse of the Thal leader stretched out before it as if, in death, still reaching for one final wipe. One wonders which Dalek scientist worked on the toilet-roll invention – quite possibly, it was the same one who practised modern art.

And the cliffhanger is wonderful, especially

as the previous story had suggested that this adventure might last for four weeks too. There's the promise that the danger is over – the Thals have their own battles to face, but the regulars are free to escape in the TARDIS. Having spent a substantial part of the episode trying to get out of the Dalek city, the realisation that they've left their all-important bit of TARDIS machinery behind, and must now go back to the city to retrieve it, seems wonderfully cruel. It's one of the joys of early Doctor Who, sadly lost when the show abandons using individual episode titles, that you could offer the audience the hint of an ending, only to deny them it. I think viewers are very canny about such elemental things as structure – they twig very quickly when Doctor Who's format adopts the traditional four-parter time and time again, meaning that the end of episode one will be a monster reveal, the end of episode three will bring universal calamity and episode four will resolve it all tidily. By comparison, the original Dalek story lasts seven episodes, but the 1964 viewer would have no idea that this episode marks the halfway mark of the adventure. The despair shown as the camera pans across the regulars' faces is so much more affecting when we don't know, any more than they can, just how much longer they'll be trapped in this nightmare. And it gives the illusion that the story is more epic as a result.

T: This is a tense affair – Cary's music is gratingly foreboding as the Daleks glide seamlessly and in synchronicity to await their chance to slaughter the Thals. There's a lovely shot from behind a Dalek as Temmosus enters, cunningly emphasising that the thing is hiding there, listening and seemingly pressed against the wall. You know it spells danger for the Thal leader, who has frankly banged on too much about peaceful coexistence to survive what comes next.

I initially thought Alan Wheatley's rather misty eyed, poised delivery as Temmosus talks about his hopes for peace between the Daleks and Thals was deliberate – a technical necessity so he could stare profoundly into the distance and not notice the four Daleks nestled, oh, *about three inches away* from him. But then he blows it completely by looking around at the end of his speech, and then having to pretend he hasn't seen them before Ian shouts a warning for benefit of anyone who doesn't have eyes. To be fair, though, this is a difficult sequence to pull off, and it's generally achieved very well.

Indeed, the programme-makers successfully orchestrate a fair bit of technical stuff in this episode, don't they? We see the Daleks on film for the first time, in that great, tense sequence as they use a cutting torch to burn through a door. And there's the way the lift shoots up and down with people in it – I still have no idea how they did that effect, but it looks great. The city corridors are similarly wonderful – there are Dalek-shaped and sized doors, which cramp our heroes magnificently in what would otherwise be a saunter down a hallway.

Oh, and if you thought the Dalek sculpture was strange, I'll take your modern-art and raise you a Pac-Man, which clearly adorns the walls of the ambush chamber. Thanks also for pointing out Virginia Wetherell... I'd not really noticed her much, as her character doesn't *do* an awful lot, but now I can't take my eyes off her. She's so bad – utterly bored and not really trying – it's captivating.

January 5th

The Expedition
(The Daleks episode five)

R: "My dear child, this is no time for morals!" Forget threatening to kill a caveman with a rock, there's no more shocking example of how alien Hartnell's Doctor is than here. I love the first few minutes of the episode; I love its anger and its honest attempt to put on screen a genuine moral quandary. For the sake of the action, we know full well that the Thals are going to have to attack the Daleks, simply because that's the standard template for so very many Doctor Who stories. Before too long, the cliché of the TARDIS crew siding with the rebels to overthrow a totalitarian regime will become so second nature, the ambiguity of whether these outsiders have the *right* to topple a government just because they *can* won't even be acknowledged. (And by the time of, say, The Happiness Patrol, it'll be such an endemic part of the programme, the Doctor will go to planets specifically to see whether he can topple regimes in a single night!)

The disgust that Ian shows for the selfishness of Barbara and the Doctor – that they're quite prepared to goad the Thals into revolution simply so they can recover the fluid link from the Dalek city – makes me think, say, of how easily we'll come to accept the way that the Doctor will upend entire societies on Zanak or the third moon of Delta Magna just so he can wave a segment of the Key to Time and then merrily set on his way. Much has been said about how this Dalek story reflects the Nazis and the Second World War – but it's only watching it now that I can be impressed by the dubious realpolitik of the TARDIS crew starting a war to free a bunch of oppressed people they have no kin with (even the Doctor says that the Thals' problems are no concern of theirs), simply so they can gain something for themselves. It's not so unlike overthrowing Saddam Hussein because you want cheaper oil. The sequence where Ian supposedly shows the sham of pacifism, by provoking Alydon into hitting him, is perhaps a bit pat – but it works precisely because before he does so, Ian makes it perfectly clear to his friends that it *is* pat. For the story to work, the Thals have to be prepared to fight; for the story to be an action-adventure, the Thals have to put aside their entire culture and moral convictions. (And the next time we see them, they'll be those strange gun-toting soldiers we meet in Planet of the Daleks – who, if anything, are even blander as characters than the ones we have here.) Once the argument has played out, that's it; the Thals are committed to the Doctor's little war, and we'll never face that moral dilemma again – but at least it *was* a moral dilemma, even if only for a few minutes, and in one of my favourite-ever sequences of Doctor Who.

You've got to admire Christopher Barry too. He's the more dynamic of the two directors assigned to this story, and while he's here given a rather talky episode here, he almost busts a gut trying to make it as visually interesting as possible. Sometimes he almost tries *too* hard – Ian and Barbara's argument about their responsibility to the Thals almost loses its focus because Susan has unaccountably climbed a tree just behind them, meaning that Carole Ann Ford's feet sway into shot above their heads. But there's a delightful moment where the camera pans up from a reflective Alydon in mid-conversation to settle on Barbara behind him, unseen, watching him. Or there's that really strange bit where we see from a Dalek's point of view, not through its eyestalk, but from the hole behind its sink plunger!

T: Christopher Barry really is going for it in this episode, isn't he? I love the Dalek going "Ahh, arg!" – remember: just because something is a staccato creature of hate, it doesn't mean it can't enunciate when it feels pain.

Overall, there's altogether much more going on in this episode, and a feeling of *urgency*. The dialogue sparkles for the first time in this adventure – the verbal sparring between the regulars is very well done, and you find yourself changing sides as the argument about the morality of pushing the Thals to war progresses. William Russell is very good at suggesting that he knows he's doing the right thing, but he's not very happy about it; he gives a much more complex performance than he's sometimes given credit for. And I had to chuckle when Ian grabbed Dyoni, suggesting he could take her to the Daleks so they can experiment on her. He's right – they could inject some life into her, for starters.

But the production team, I think, deserves credit for being mad enough to try this episode *at all*. A modern crew would baulk at having to mount a trek through a swamp with marsh mutations, never mind the additional jungle and metal-city sets thrown in for good measure. And if you told them they'd have to do it indoors and in the space of a week, they'd probably tell you to sod off. So what's achieved in The Expedition seems so miraculous (there's even something malevolent about the eyes on the inflato-octopus that rises from the swamp), I can readily forgive the odd misstep, such as the way the "menacing swamp creature" that Ian kills is quite obviously a stock-footage caterpillar.

This is a very odd way to write a quest story, though – characters are bumped off throughout, but they never have much depth to them. In particular, Elyon is only given anything to do immediately before he's killed. Part of the fun of adventures like this is working out who is going to live or die, but for that to work, you have to have some investment in the characters, no matter how perfunctory. What's funny is that I read the novelisation to this story in my youth, and really liked the strong, brave Kristas with whom Ian forms something of a bond – only to find out that in the TV version, he's a rather tall actor who says about two lines and does his best to look grim when the situation requires it. If you're paying an actor, you may as well give him *something* to do – even if it's just to produce a picture of his sweetheart back home and talk of the unborn son he'll get to see "once this bally war business is at an end".

Towards the end of the episode, there were two things I hadn't ever noticed before. One is the way that Ganatus goes to sleep on Barbara's leg (the tiger), and the other a bit more shocking – it's the way Elyon's scream turns into gurgle, with the noise suggesting he's being dragged under water and is choking. It's grim, but an effective way of ending the episode and raising the stakes.

The Ordeal
(The Daleks episode six)

R: The little romance that develops between Barbara and Ganatus comes out of nowhere – but it's really well played by Jacqueline Hill, and it goes some way to humanising Philip Bond too. I know you've liked his performance, Toby, but I feel he's been a bit inclined to play his lines as if he's declaiming blank verse – and he clearly now seizes the chance to find a lighter side to his Thal in leathers. There's not very much detail given to any of this in the script, but the way that Hill and Bond play against some of their more doom-laden lines helps enormously, finding affectionate banter that probably wasn't intended. It's lovely. And it gives a bit more depth to the relationship between Ian and Barbara too; in the sequence where Barbara jumps over the chasm to be caught by Ian, they're both a bit embarrassed by the physical contact, William Russell clearly trying to be as formal as possible. Smashing stuff.

Ah yes, the chasm sequence. It goes on forever, as we watch each of the characters one by one take a running jump into the darkness. It

ought to be very boring, but it works so well precisely because it *is* so painstaking – and there's one frightened Thal waiting his inevitable turn with dread. There's a similar sequence in Voyage of the Damned, where the starship Titanic survivors are required to make a demonstration of bravery across a yawning abyss – and there you have the CGI effects, the sense of depth and killer robots to boot. But what the 2007 story doesn't have is *time* – and the "ordeal" mentioned in the episode title is so much more awful because as an audience, we're allowed to contemplate how terrified we too would be in that situation. Antodus is really only characterised in the broadest of strokes as "the cowardly Thal", and Marcus Hammond doesn't find much in the part other than to panic at two different volumes – but that shot where Hammond numbly lets the thrown rope fall slack against him, not even bothering to pick it up, is a terrific picture of rigid terror.

And I love the scene in which the Daleks phone up one of their engineers to ask about the progress on the neutron bomb, and how disgruntled they are when told it'll take 23 days to finish. They couldn't be more disappointed if they were told they'd also have to pay extra for a call-out charge.

T: Bless Antodus, he's very stroppy. He's got that puffy lower jaw and permanently down-turned mouth while Terry Nation is busy carving "Sacrifice yourself bravely to achieve redemption" on his forehead. Everyone else seems *very* polite on this escapade, though – Ian compliments Kristas on his chasm-jump in such a way, it's as if he's tacitly apologising for the Thal being much more interesting in the book than he's allowed to be on screen.

Meanwhile, Richard Martin – directing episodes three, six and seven of this story – gives us an ambitious mirrored shot to suggest the camera looking down on Ganatus, and later shoots everyone from as far back as possible, showing the party negotiating the tunnel in a manner that predates a similar effect from Graeme Harper in The Caves of Androzani. He also illustrates the subtext of the Daleks by having them do a Nazi salute with their suckers (so, it wasn't just in The Dalek Invasion of Earth, as I'd always thought!). Then, alas, the

Daleks somewhat spoil the moment by buggering up their supposedly synchronised chanting. Still, it was a nice thought.

"We won't use one of the customs of your planet," says Ganatus, in a wonderfully naive attempt to display the difference between aliens and humans. You'll need to do better than that if you want to crack this sci-fi lark, Mr Nation. Still, I love it for its twee sixties innocence, and I'll forgive Philip Bond almost anything as he's working his socks off again. There's a lovely moment later where he's thrown a torch and gives a brilliant look back to the chucker, acknowledging that they'd done a good throw and suggesting his admiration. It's a tiny moment, but one that keeps things real and interesting.

January 6th

The Rescue
(The Daleks episode seven)

R: In a rush to reach its conclusion, the story strains and buckles under its desire to be epic. After an episode and a half of dodging rockfalls and jumping chasms, Ian and his party reach the Dalek city in time to bump into Alydon's mob in a corridor – which rather emphasises the fact that had they simply gone together and walked in the front door, they'd have saved themselves a lot of bother. And there's an element of farce to the final battle itself – everyone's gamefully putting a bit of welly into it, but there isn't the space to make Nation's climax pay off. As with a lot of Doctor Who stories, the greater the attempt to make the threat, and the grander the scale on which the adventure is framed, the more perfunctory the resolution.

So it's in the smaller, more intimate moments that the episode hits its mark, such as Alydon's bemused acceptance of the Doctor's handshake, or the way that Dyoni bends down in wonder at the space that the dematerialised TARDIS had previously occupied. And the final goodbyes between Barbara and Ganatus are especially effective – all the more so when you consider that with all the blood and thunder and corridor chasing, there hasn't been time this week for them even to share a bit of

dialogue together. Their entire relationship is therefore built upon one scene in episode six, but I still love the way that Ganatus nobly (*too* nobly, actually) kisses Barbara's hand like the Shakespeare tragedian that Philip Bond has largely played him as. Then Barbara, so impulsively, gives Ganatus a kiss on the cheek.

It's also the first time that the Dalek voices begin to sound properly imitable, taking on the panic that we've come to expect as the Thals invade their city. They sound much more like petulant or frightened children here, just perfect for kids in the playground to have fun with. The sequence where the Dalek begs help from the Doctor as it loses power almost forms the template for how they're going to talk ever afterwards; they become less concerned with conversations involving long words, and are more interested in barking hysterical orders. You've got to admire, too, the way that in its last moment before death, the Dalek flips its eyestalk up at a right angle. It almost feels like its final action is to give Hartnell the finger.

T: Well, at least the cowardly Antodus dies bravely – cutting his support line so his teammates won't also plunge to their deaths. We can be safe in the knowledge though, that his bloodline of baffling grumpiness and petulance will continue, as history teaches us he has impregnated the mother of every single character subsequently played in the series by Prentis Hancock.

The countdown to the Daleks unleashing nuclear waste into the atmosphere is a staple in drama of this kind, but this one reminds me of when I'm counting sternly at the kids to try to stop them from doing something naughty, but with no actual intention of meting out a punishment. The tick-tock towards doomsday proceeds so laboriously, our heroes are given just enough time to sneak in and be victorious, and you can almost hear the Daleks going "When we get to zero, you're definitely in trouble, three, I'm warning you, two and a half, seriously, you'll be for the high jump when I get to zero, two and a quarter, please just do as you're told or, oh alright, but next time I'll definitely release a nuclear holocaust and not let you watch Lazytown for a week!"

I keep getting diverted, though, by the status of my hero, Kristas. First off, he doesn't appear to be blond anymore! Go on, take a look... perhaps he cast his wig off in protest about his lack of lines, and that's why Jonathan Crane's credits on IMDb stretch this far and no further. But then I see that Kristas has survived being shot by the Daleks! He's emerged (at least, in my own little happy place) as a Thal superhero! Casting off his wig has given him special powers!

And so the Doctor's first battle with his most iconic enemies comes to an end. It's been spooky and experimental, and yet what I love most about this story (especially when you consider that the show as it currently stands can occasionally be *too* knowingly iconic) is that this was all chucked together by people who had no idea what it was they'd started. To those involved, it was just a day at work, a confluence of ideas – and yet it was so successful that it's directly responsible for Doctor Who surviving to see the vast number of Who-related events that are going on all over the world on this very day.

The Edge of Destruction (episode one)

R: This is utterly bonkers, isn't it? You'd never get away with screening an episode as bizarre as this on television nowadays. I'm pretty amazed they got away with screening it *then*.

Faced with a need to make two episodes on the cheap – and with no new sets and no additional actors – the production team made this quickie inside the TARDIS. With that in mind, David Whitaker – Doctor Who's first script editor and the writer of this story – could have gone down several different routes. He might have written a story which served as some sort of intriguing mystery – and at times you feel that's the approach he's opting for, but the clues are too thinly drawn, and don't point to any solution. (Besides, at the episode's end, a whole halfway through the story, you don't get a sense of anything really being at stake.) So instead, he could have gone for the character study, the cost-cutting option seen on many a Star Trek near the end of a series, sacrificing action and adventure for dialogue and depth. But even *that* isn't happening, as the TARDIS regulars are quite purposefully drawn from scratch, and are at times quite unrecognisable

from any previous episodes. Actually, it's even odder than that – they're even acting in completely different *styles*. William Russell affects a sort of zombie air for most of the proceedings, giving an eerie sing-song quality to a lot of his early dialogue; Carole Ann Ford goes flat-out playing Susan either as swaying drunk or scary psychopath. William Hartnell seems very puzzled by the whole thing, and so falls into his default "brash" persona. Thank God for Jacqueline Hill, who in spite of the odds actually mines something emotional and true out of all the weirdness, becoming wonderfully angry at the Doctor's ingratitude and suitably distressed by his suspicion.

It'd take a braver man than me to suggest that The Edge of Destruction actually works. (You up for that, Toby?) And yet... this is an episode so utterly ill-conceived, so entirely off the rails, that it actually impresses with its sheer chutzpah. You can tell that none of the cast have the slightest idea how to read what's going on – and yet, rather than muttering the lines and looking embarrassed, they're all really *going* for their contrasting interpretations. If the following scene contradicts what they've just done, they don't worry about it, they just commit wholeheartedly to the new approach instead. (Watch Carole Ann Ford in particular, who moves from hysteric to sinister scissor-wielding nutter to troubled peacemaker within minutes – and does so with such utter gung-ho conviction, it almost joins the dots.) Had the episode been played in a uniform style, with the cast fully clear about the direction their characters should be going, this would all be rather tepid stuff. But because it's so deliriously flying by the seat of its pants, it at times feels genuinely chilling. When even the *actors* don't appear to know what to expect next, neither can we the audience, and the effect is disorientating. The camera keeps on surprising us, with actors taking up different positions off screen – the most obvious example is when Ian happens upon a Susan who's brandishing a pair of scissors, but I honestly shuddered when Ian, having been set up as lolling unconscious in a chair, is revealed as standing up, impassively staring at Barbara in the background.

Because this episode breaks all the rules, because we can never for a second work out what the threat is, almost *everything* has the potential to be creepy. It could be the smile on the Doctor's face as he hands out drinks to all his companions, it could be the somewhat too self-conscious shrug that Ian gives when Barbara asks him why the Doctor is staring at them. There's a wonderfully disturbing idea at the heart of this episode – that something has entered the Ship, and is hiding in *one of the crew*. If you can forget the depressingly prosaic explanation that's instead offered next week, and if you can pretend that you're watching The Edge of Destruction as viewers did in 1964, then this is unnerving stuff.

You also have to cherish a series that can be as insane as this. Having just played out a monster serial with fights and explosions, it offers *this* – this strange, ugly, unwieldy thing. At a time when Doctor Who acts as if it's one ongoing serial, the contrast between what the show has been promising its audience and what it's now giving them is extraordinary. No, The Edge of Destruction doesn't really work. But it's probably the single maddest thing it's ever attempted in its 45 years of history, and it does it only 12 weeks in.

T: I watched this episode while unwinding after my first gig back, so I'm typing these thoughts after having taken a couple of relaxing drams... which I'm hoping in some way goes to explain what I've been witnessing. This is bonkers! As you say, the cast are acting each scene in a completely different manner; it's as if they're contestants on Whose Line Is It Anyway, and the audience is shouting for them to perform "melodrama!", then "kitchen sink drama!", and then – to William Russell – "drunk vicar!" Even the regulars' dress sense seems mercurial – Barbara seems to be wearing Thal trousers (an odd present to give someone), and Susan has been reduced to floating around in a maternity dress. And now she's got a flannel on her head! I'm half expecting her to stick two pencils up her nose and plead insanity.

Among the genuinely weird vignettes, there are some chilling moments – the way that Jacqueline Hill's voice cracks in a brilliant evocation of full-on fright, and the eerie manner in which Susan suggests that if an intruder has penetrated the TARDIS, it might be hiding "in

one of us". Carole Ann Ford in particular seems very much in her element with this story – she's able to channel the spirit of An Unearthly Child, which suits her visage and the disarmingly offbeat look she can muster in her eyes. It's especially disturbing when she becomes so demented that she produces a huge pair of scissors, has an orgasm and starts stabbing her bendy space chair (or wibbly space bed, take your pick). And is it wrong of me that, amongst all this madness, I find Susan quite sexy while she's lolling about on the wonky space divan clutching those scissors? (I *did* mention that I've had two winter warmer whiskeys, right?)

You're right, though, to highlight Jacqueline Hill, who delivers a smashing retort to the Doctor's paranoia and accusations that she and Ian have sabotaged the Ship. Not for nothing has this fantastic confrontation – where Barbara, bristling with principled and righteous anger, really sticks it to the old man – been cited by some commentators as a turning point in the Doctor's character, and therefore in the entire series. The only downside to this smashing performance is that Hill is made to top it off by over-reacting to a melting clock, and then a wristwatch. I do feel sorry for her and Ford: they get all the rubbish stuff to do despite the occasional gems they're thrown. People wouldn't as fondly remember the Doctor musing "Have you ever thought what it's like to be wanderers in the fourth dimension?" in the first episode if he'd followed it up by immediately screaming at a bit of shrubbery and tripping over a hillock.

Then things get *even stranger* when the English countryside appears on the scanner, and I react with twenty-first century aloofness at the basic technology being employed by the production. "It's obviously just a photograph," I think smugly to myself. "It's just a photograph," the Doctor says on screen. *What?* This is becoming metatextual in my head now. I pour the remainder of the whisky down the sink.

And so everyone goes to bed and the Doctor is doing something crafty at the controls, the camera jauntily highlighting his nifty hand acting (he's got very expressive digits – see, I told you this Smith bloke has what it takes). Someone then grabs the Doctor by the throat, and as the credits roll, I can't help but think, "What the *hell* was that all about?" – but I say that as a positive rather than a negative. One of the many things I love about about Doctor Who is how there's an episode to suit me no matter what mood I'm in: action-adventure, SF epic, knockabout comedy, morality play... the series can be (and has been) all of these. And sometimes, just *sometimes*, I might want to watch a bunch of people being chucked in at the deep end and asked to pull off what's possibly the oddest 25 minutes ever committed to television – and when I do, I'll watch this.

January 7th

The Brink of Disaster
(The Edge of Destruction
episode two)

R: On the one hand, this is much better because you feel at least that the actors have read the end of the script before coming to the set this week, and so have a reasonable idea of what to work towards. But it's also much worse, because what they're working to is so determinedly anticlimactic. "We must all work together," says the Doctor, and that's a reasonable moral – but it's also the same one the band of travellers employed escaping from savage cavemen, or in defeating alien mutants, so it doesn't have appreciably more dramatic value now that they're pitting their wits against a stuck button. It's been argued that this is the story where the regulars throw off their suspicions towards each other and through the mystery become *friends* – and you can see the value of doing a story like that – but in fact, the earlier two adventures have done their jobs too well and already achieved it.

The one thing that really works, though, is in watching how William Russell, Jacqueline Hill and Carole Ann Ford all snap back into their previous personae at the story's end, but that William Hartnell resolutely *doesn't*. He takes the Doctor on an extraordinary journey in this instalment, having seemed rather bewildered by the last. He seizes upon the Doctor's capriciousness and cruelty early on – he positively looms over Ian threateningly as he sneers at him to get up off the floor. And this

is in marked contrast to his new defining of the Doctor as a cuddly grandfather by the story's end, where he awkwardly tells Barbara how valuable and clever she is, or tells Susan that he fears he's going round the bend. This is by way of an *extraordinary* monologue given while the Doctor is darkened against the central console, in which he describes the birth of a solar system – it's melodramatic, it's over the top, and it ends with the Doctor giggling at the cosmic implications of it all like a lunatic, but it *works* because it feels incredibly alien. It's not an easy scene to watch, and I have friends who deride it as Hartnell at his hammiest, but that sequence seems like the bridge between the brusque Doctor of the early stories and the loveable old eccentric he'll now become. Hartnell also fluffs a lot this week – most amusingly, at the episode title itself. ("We're on the brink of... of destruction!" he says, forcing William Russell, rather charmingly, to repeat the mistake back at him.) But you can forgive that, I think, for the intelligent way that he steers himself into this new characterisation – and especially for that gorgeous moment where he admits to Ian that he's lied to the women about how much time they all have left to live, then asks whether the schoolteacher can stand and face oblivion with him.

T: The weirdness of this story seems to be bleeding into the real world – my TARDIS money box has, with no external stimulus or prompting, just starting randomly making stuttering sounds! I'm not kidding. This would only have been more perfect and strange had it coincided with Susan's line that "*Everything can't be wrong!*"

Meanwhile, the approach to doomsday is very effective – the lighting gets very atmospheric, helped no end by the recurring explosions that rock the Ship. It builds a fantastic, oppressive momentum that climaxes as the camera creeps up on Hartnell as he delivers his big moment. I sympathise with your mates who mock him (especially the slightly mad hand clasp he does at the end), but he looks *so* magnificent, and the scene is lit with such brilliance, I think it's churlish to criticise. The Doctor is awed by the magnificence of the birth of a solar system, so of course he's going to get a bit hysterical.

But what's important about this two-parter is that the regulars all pull together – Susan does some helpful counting, and the Doctor confides the truth about the oncoming oblivion to Ian, but most importantly Barbara becomes the brains of the outfit and pieces a solution together from the clues they've witnessed. (Just how the hell she does this, though, I've no idea – when all is said and done, does the evidence actually add up the way Barbara *thinks* it adds up? Clearly, she's a dab hand at cryptic crosswords, and we're not meant to question her methodology.) Later on, Jacqueline Hill is great when the Doctor tries to apologise for his behaviour, with Hartnell suggesting that a lot of the Doctor's jolly bluster is to cover up his embarrassment at pesky interpersonal interaction. It lays the groundwork for so much characterisation to come.

The fact that the production team did this story at all is amazing, and it beautifully complements the previous two adventures in terms of variety: so far, each story has been markedly different to the one before it. My knowledge of sixties TV is limited, but I like to think that the people making this programme went for broke and decided they could do anything, and did it wholeheartedly. For all I know, there's a Z-Cars episode that's told from the point of view of one of the cars, but I very much doubt it. This isn't a story I'll watch again in a hurry, but the fact that it exists is proof that Doctor Who is the flexible, crazy, unformulaic show we all love it for being.

The Roof of the World
(Marco Polo episode one)

R: Our first missing episode! And it's hard, when you listen to the soundtrack of Marco Polo, and look at the telesnaps, and pore over the gorgeous colour photographs, not to feel cheated – that of all the stories to be wiped, this is Doctor Who's first casualty. After two episodes stuck inside the TARDIS jumping at shadows, this adventure sounds sumptuous – and you want to see the pictures *move*. And there's an irony of sorts, I think, in that following a story that purported to be *about* the TARDIS, we have here a story in which the TARDIS is the pivot around which the plot turns. The Edge of Destruction featured a

TARDIS that was revealed as sentient, that was trying to communicate with its travellers, but it's this episode that makes it seem *especially* magical and mysterious. It's a flying caravan, a piece of Buddhist wonder and the key to Marco Polo's freedom.

And after the fairly simplistic portrait of goodies and baddies on the planet Skaro, it's refreshing to have an episode in which the threats that the TARDIS crew confront are somewhat more ambiguous. The warlord Tegana is clearly shown to be the story's villain – but he is an enemy purely because of cultural difference, not because he is intrinsically evil. And Derren Nesbitt plays the role so subtly – just listen to him. Swarthy Mongol with an earring he may be, but there's nothing in his voice which marks him out as a caricature, nothing which suggests that Tegana doesn't see himself as a heroic patriot. The scene where he encounters the Doctor and friends, and gives orders for them to be killed as evil spirits, is all the more startling because Nesbitt makes the argument sound eminently reasonable. In his discussion later with Marco Polo, you almost find yourself warming to Tegana's point of view, until you catch yourself realising that he's coolly advocating the murder of our heroes. In any other story, too, Marco Polo would be presented simply as an obstacle to be thwarted, but Mark Eden makes him so affable and courteous that, again, you can appreciate his reasons for stealing the TARDIS. And it's extremely clever the way that writer John Lucarotti uses the poignant scene in which Susan talks about her not having a home, to make us sympathise more with Marco Polo's position. He has not seen his home for 18 years, and fears he will be killed at court upon Kublai Khan's death.

And William Hartnell continues to be a joy. Irascible at one moment when he realises the TARDIS is broken, charming with Ping-Cho whilst eating her soup... and, best of all, overcome with delighted hysteria when he realises he's lost his only means of travel through time and space, and has no idea what to do next.

T: The TARDIS might be a space/time vessel, but it's no sanctuary – if something simple goes wrong with the Ship, even the snowy environment in which our heroes land becomes as palpable a threat as any robot or cyborg. If they don't do something quick, they're going to die of hypothermia, and not even the "magical" TARDIS interior can save them.

What's funny is that although we know *now* that this story is a historical, it's at first played as if it's science fiction. Something as simple as a footprint is used to generate menace, and Barbara thinks that a beast or creature – which is finally revealed as a fur-dressed Marco Polo – is stalking them. The longer pace of sixties TV allows the mood and suspense to build up in a manner that wouldn't be countenanced today. Similarly, I love the narrative device of Marco reciting his diary entries – it's a very nice flourish that's not seen in any other Doctor Who story, and the uniqueness of this makes me realize just how much modern shows can be bloody hidebound by format or concept. 24's raison d'etre relies upon a "real-time" gimmick that necessitates the unlikely conceit of something dramatic happening on the cusp of every hour, and a protagonist who appears to have had a bladderectomy and owns a mobile phone with a limitless battery. Doctor Who, however, will dispense with such gimmickry in one episode, then try something new next week. It's the only prime-time British TV show that dares do such a thing.

Strangely enough, by the end of the episode, the biggest threat to the crew – the person who forcibly takes the TARDIS, their most prized possession, and announces his plan to trade it away to end his exile – is actually a very affable and reasonable man. This puts the audience in a strange position: after spending just 20 minutes in Marco's company, you *want* him to get home, but also know that if he gets his wish, our heroes are scuppered. This is subtle, clever and brilliant character work. We love Marco's intellect and reasoning, but at the same time must acknowledge that from the Doctor's perspective, Marco is also something of a savage.

January 8th

The Singing Sands
(Marco Polo episode two)

R: I think it's really rather terrific that the most alien thing we've yet encountered in Doctor Who hasn't been found on some remote planet, but on Earth; the singing sands are genuinely eerie. And it's a reminder that at this point in the series, much of the true wonder comes from history rather than just science fantasy. When Susan looks up at the sky and bemoans the fact they're not exploring distant galaxies, it sounds almost odd and irrelevant, quite rightly so – and within minutes, she's marvelling at the beauty of the Gobi desert.

And it's this push-pull effect of Lucarotti's writing – that he invites us to stand back and be a slack-jawed tourist one moment, then realise how much danger we're in the next – that gives this instalment its edge. It's an episode about nothing more grand than sand and water – swords are drawn, but only in jest, and a king is killed, but only on a chessboard. And yet, there's such an earnestness to the real-world threat of thirst that the closing minutes, in which Ian persuades Marco to gamble all on a sprint to a distant oasis, are brilliantly tense. What's so remarkable about the confidence of this story is that, only two episodes in, it feels so tonally different from what we've seen before, so much more magisterial somehow. Doctor Who has become a road movie of sorts, and, set as this story is to run for seven episodes, you can somehow sense that this adventure could be the basis for the *entire* series. Had Sydney Newman come up with the idea of a group of contemporary people travelling not through time and space in a police box, but journeying to Cathay alongside Marco Polo, then I think the premise would have sustained itself for quite a while.

William Hartnell has only one line this episode, but you hardly notice his absence because Mark Eden (playing Marco) and William Russell effortlessly take on the lead roles. (I love the explanation for the Doctor being missing from the action – he's usually unconscious or captured in stories to come, but here it's because he's sulking, which is delightful!) Carole Ann Ford is very good this week too. In this story alone does a writer think back to that strange girl in the classroom who didn't quite add up – the one who knew the future and was a scientific genius, but still danced to John Smith and the Common Men on her transistor radio. The portrait of Susan as a mixed-up kid who can fantasise about the metal seas on Venus, but so desires an identity that she's fallen in love with sixties England, has been rather left by the wayside; she's been reduced somewhat to a girl who'll scream for her grandfather. But it's really very endearing here that she'll dig that crazy desert in her sixties slang. It all sounds unreal and self-conscious, of course, just as Ace did with her toecurlingly unlikely eighties yoof speak 25 years later – the difference here being that it's *meant* to be.

T: The marvellous soundscape created for the titular sandstorm is reminiscent of the Radiophonic Workshop's unnerving crepitations in Quatermass and the Pit (the only programme to have *ever* rivalled Doctor Who in my affections). It's uncanny the way the elements themselves become the threat, and the consequent moaning, roaring, screeching aural assault suggests something alien and dangerous just as much as anything we encountered on Skaro. Ian's line that "it sounds like all the devils in hell are laughing" is wonderful, and underlines my previous assertion that John Lucarotti is cleverly making the past not so much another country as another planet. Fandom has always considered Lucarotti as a writer of evocative historicals, but he's far more sophisticated with the brief than is generally accepted.

No, there's not an awful lot of incident in this episode, but it still works because Lucarotti is cunningly engaging in an exercise in mood. The manoeuvring of the chess game between Ian and Marco, the lurking shadows in the threatening night-time, the horses acting uneasy – all of this builds up the sense of menace and impending doom magnificently. I'll take this over any badly orchestrated fight scene or a randomly generated piece of jeopardy involving a pesky space door, because the writing is so skilful and the characters are so real.

Derren Nesbitt continues to purr his way through his role as Tegana – he lays his nastiness out in the open but stops short of being *too* blatant, almost as if he's willing everyone involved to accuse him of being a baddie. It's most beguiling and, strangely, rather civilised. Tegana is a sneaky, manipulative presence who smiles, and murders while he smiles.

I don't think we'd ever get a story like this now. It's not a criticism of New Who at all – it's just that this adventure belongs to its period. But then, I'm not sure I'd *want* them to do it now either – Marco Polo exists (or rather, frustratingly doesn't on video) as a period piece and a very fine example of its genre. And, indeed, of sixties television.

Five Hundred Eyes
(Marco Polo episode three)

R: I agree with you, Toby, that one of the joys of watching this series in order is how there's such a strange *variety* of styles on offer. Doctor Who still hasn't worked out what it wants to be yet. There's a glimpse here of a road not taken, I think – the series as educational children's programme. We get a science lesson about condensation, and a story about the Hashashins which almost feels like the sort of insert you'd get in a magazine programme like Blue Peter. What's great is how *well* these little bits of instruction are dropped in. The demonstration of how water is produced by temperature change is very clever, and the fact that Marco doesn't respond with the cooing interest of a schoolchild – but instead the fury of a man who thinks that the travellers have tricked him – is spot on. And Ping-Cho's mime dance is extraordinary, not because Zienia Merton has the grace of a ballerina (if she does, the telesnaps aren't telling), but because all the action *stops* so the characters can sit about and watch a performance of a history lesson. The Doctor wants to get to the TARDIS with his new key, Barbara wants to tell Ian about her suspicions of Tegana – but then everyone seems to turn to camera and say, "Now we'll take a short break whilst we have this word from our sponsor, the Education Board." It's absolutely splendid, full of charm and only adds to the richness of the setting. It's as if we're reading a history book, and are being sent to the back of the volume to read a particularly interesting footnote.

And so it should come as no surprise that the plotting is influenced by children's literature too. I rather love the idea of Barbara going off to the very caves where all the villains have chosen to meet and chat about their nefarious plots. It's all so wonderfully Enid Blyton, you can just see the Famous Five getting mixed up in a similar scrape. But that's where Doctor Who and its strange shifting tone leaps up and bites you – just as you recognise the genre, you cut to a sequence where Barbara is tied up on a cave floor, the painted faces of dead bandits staring down at her, as Mongols giggle about her and mime they're going to slit her throat. That never happened to the kids on Kirrin Island.

T: This is, I think, as close to Sydney Newman's view of Doctor Who as we're ever likely to get – and Lucarotti here fulfils the brief perfectly, carefully placing the "educational" elements into his script with elegance and panache. One is expected to pay attention to things like plot when reviewing television, but if an episode has *no* plot and yet still manages to entertain, move and excite the viewer, then it's done its job. The history lessons here aren't the patronising asides like the safety lessons at the end of Inspector Gadget, but they augment the story and the characters in an interesting way. Marco needs to have the process of condensation explained to him – and so yes, we get a bit of science, but it also informs us about his character and impacts upon his relationship with the regulars. Ping-Cho's delightful interlude is a triumph – even if I can't *see* it, experience tells me that the loss of this dance is much more regrettable than that of what may well have been some slightly limp fight scenes elsewhere in this story.

You can get away with not a lot happening if the stuff that doesn't happen, er, doesn't happen in an *interesting* way. In that regard, all the elements that make up this jewel of a story come together superbly. I know a number of fans write off the historicals as boring, but I could listen to these performances and savour this dialogue a lot more than any number of routines given by some poor sod with a silly haircut talking about the Bandicoots of Venus or somesuch. There is an intelligence going on here, one that has the confidence to weave the story with subtlety and sophistication, and gently lure us along for the ride (or, rather, meander). I will happily spend further time in the company of these characters on their quest.

January 9th

The Wall of Lies
(Marco Polo episode four)

R: Marco Polo's a real butterfly of a story – it never quite settles down to be one thing long enough, then it's off again, whether this means a change of location or tone (or both, really). In that way, I think that it symbolises all that is great about the potential of Doctor Who. Take this rather brilliant episode as an example, and note the way that within 25 minutes, the tenor of the story shifts from something which is basically amiable (it is to Polo rather than to the Doctor that Ian calls when he finds something interesting in the cave wall) to one tense enough that Ian and the Doctor plan on taking Polo hostage, in a desperation that recalls their struggle against the cavemen. Last week, this was all an entertaining travelogue; here, all the danger is restored.

What's fascinating, as we react to the Doctor's plans to attack Polo, is how much we are still invited to sympathise with Polo rather than with the regulars. The device of having Polo narrate the journey is very inspired – this is *his* adventure, we are seeing the story through *his* eyes, and it makes the TARDIS crew far more alienating as a result. To survive, everybody plays for Polo's good opinion of them, and everybody lies to him. Ian may call Polo his friend, but he's just as prepared to deceive him as Tegana is. I wince as the Doctor and Ian are caught out in their treachery, and it isn't because their attempt to escape has been foiled, but because they've been shown to have lost the moral high ground we expect of our heroes. And therefore there's a strange cynical edge to this episode, especially in contrast to last week's, which had the trust and familiarity of all the characters sitting around together watching a dance. Tegana manipulates Polo against the regulars, the Doctor immediately distrusts Ping-Cho... and there's a truly terrific cliffhanger, in which Ian creeps up to attack a guard only to find that someone has got there first and already attacked him. There's a corpse on the ground and Ian's not the killer – and yet, he still seems strangely culpable, because you know he just *might* have become one. Here we are, just four stories in, and the series is *still* refusing to tie the regulars down into easy stereotypes; it's still playing around with how the audience should be responding to them.

What a truly extraordinary story this is. I just love it.

T: The morality here is complex and murky, and I find it fascinating. The regulars come across as interlopers in the guest cast's story, flies in their respective ointments. The Doctor laughs at Tegana's superstitions (played dead straight by Nesbitt), and this makes us squirm uncomfortably at the old man. Such is the Doctor's patronising scorn, it legitimises Tegana's hatred of the travellers, and makes it absolutely plausible that Marco would trust the warlord rather than the Doctor and his friends. Especially when, later in the episode, the Doctor *again* hoots at Marco for being a savage, putting us even further into the curious position of having more sympathy for Marco than our leading man does.

I have to highlight the gripping scene where Barbara's captors play dice to decide which of them will get to kill her, and Jacqueline Hill pitches Barbara's horror at this with just the right level of fear and disgust. The barbarity of this era – as alien as it might seem at times – is all the more frightening because the perpetrators of the evil deeds are humans, like us.

Rider from Shang-Tu
(Marco Polo episode five)

R: Wang-Lo – the pompous landlord – is a bit of a breakthrough, isn't he? He's obsequious and fat and oily, like one of those people who show up on your doorstep trying to get you to change your gas supplier. And yet he's also the first comic character in Doctor Who, the only one so far who's there purely for light relief, to make us laugh. It's a further indication of just how Marco Polo is expanding the series, and using its epic length generously, trying to nudge Doctor Who into all new areas.

The shifty looking criminal Kuiju is rather amusing too – both Wang-Lo and Kuiju are wonderful contrasts to the complexity of Tegana and Polo and our heroes, because they're so guilelessly and shamelessly interested only in money, and have caricatured themselves in the process. Oh, and Kuiju has a monkey and an eyepatch. There's only one thing that's funnier than a monkey, and that's a monkey owned by someone with a facial disfigurement.

But what really stands out in this episode, perhaps *because* of the comparatively broad comedy, is the very dignity of everyone else. I think the scene where Ian honestly tells Marco Polo that they intended to escape, and Polo as calmly tells him that he'll need to redouble his vigilance as a result, is just smashing – it's two enemies discussing the matter without rancour or apology in the face of a greater threat from bandits. And even better is that beautiful sequence in which Susan refuses to compromise Ping-Cho by asking her to break her word to Polo and tell her where the TARDIS keys are hidden – even though she knows that her entire freedom is at stake. This is all such a marked contrast to the amorality of the early stories, where the ends justify the means, where you'll lead the Thals into battle just to save your own skins. I think it's all part of an ongoing debate the series is making, and these differing approaches to responsibility towards individuals is what gives Doctor Who its unity – and for all its shifting styles, makes this feel like one long continuing story.

It's why the cliffhanger is so effective. This is the third story in which the audience has been led to believe that the regulars have reached the sanctuary of the TARDIS, only to be thwarted in the closing seconds. Doctor Who plays an awkward game sometimes with the credibility of its companions, where for the plot to work your typical girl assistant needs to go out and foolishly get herself captured. But for all the Doctor's bluster about Susan, it's entirely *right* that she jeopardises their escape by going to say goodbye to Ping-Cho. Because Ping-Cho has put her own honour at risk to steal Susan the keys, and all she wanted in return was a farewell. The Doctor of The Forest of Fear would have broken that promise, the Ian Chesterton of The Expedition would have put his own safety first. But there's a different moral centre to this episode, and there are some things that are just more important than the TARDIS crew getting their way and flying off to their next adventure.

T: "Classy" is the word for this. After a very talky instalment last week, this is all-action from the kick off, with the underbeat of drums rattling us along. Marco gets a great line when giving a weapon to the Doctor, stating that if he's half as aggressive with it as he is with his tongue, then they can't lose. The science lessons continue to be seamless and integral, whilst demonstrating the smartness of our regulars – in this case, Ian's application of his scientific knowledge from the future (the burning of the bamboo) exploits the bandits' superstitious beliefs. When the Khan's courier – Ling-Tau – arrives, we get a fascinating litany of information about how he manages to ride so quickly (he keeps changing horses every three miles, but this means he travels 300 miles in more than 24 hours with no sleep). It's meticulously researched and fascinatingly presented, without feeling like an unnecessary longueur.

There's so much formality about, in fact. Tegana is now happy to be blatant (but not in a sneering, cod, villainous way) in his dislike for our heroes, and Marco and Ian openly discuss their differences and what tactics they might employ in dealing with each other. Then there's the fine moment where Marco does a "good" thing by saying that they're no longer officially prisoners of the Khan – but that they're still *his* prisoners. "Thanks for nothing," mutters Hartnell, brilliantly. It's a bit like telling the Guantanamo Bay inmates that they're no longer prisoners of the state but are still prisoners of war, and that they're not going anywhere. The powerful often use semantics to make their actions seem honourable.

January 10th

Mighty Kublai Khan
(Marco Polo episode six)

R: This episode is dominated by two excellent scenes. The first is between Ian and Polo, and it's so cleverly written. After everything I wrote about the moral code at work in the last episode, Ian here loses his opportunity to convince Marco that they should get the TARDIS back – all because he tries to protect Ping-Cho by taking blame for the theft of the TARDIS

keys in Marco's possession. Because Ian has lied, even with the best of motives, it only means that he is *capable* of lying in the first place – and so Marco cannot make the leap of faith required to accept that the TARDIS can travel through time. There's never any question that Ian shouldn't have leaped to Ping-Cho's defence, but Lucarotti is subtly demonstrating that there's a sacrifice to be made for doing the right thing. It's another version of the argument played out in The Expedition, in which Ian battles with his conscience to lead the Thals into a war in which some will die for the greater good.

Suddenly, that chess game that was played in The Singing Sands takes on a whole new meaning; every time Ian acts altruistically, he risks losing a pawn. By chasing after Ping-Cho when she runs back to Cheng-Ting, he only gives Tegana the chance to drive a further wedge between him and Polo. For all the fact that this adventure appears to be an educational story for children, it firmly resists any attempts to teach easy differences between right and wrong in a way that's wholly admirable; just look at the stuff we get on CBBC nowadays, which strongly sets out moral messages in which naughty acts are punished and selfless ones are rewarded. In Lucarotti's tale "for kids", instead, we're shown things are never quite as simple as that. And that's so much more valuable a lesson – here I am, age 38, and *I'm* trying to debate whether Ian should have told Marco that white lie or not.

The other great scene is the introduction of Kublai Khan. The first Dalek adventure showed us that the more epic you make the story, the greater the risk of it falling flat when the climax can't be as grand as you want it to be. For six weeks' viewing (and several months' adventuring!), all the travellers in Marco Polo have done is set out to meet the great Khan. The danger, surely, is that the reveal of this warlord Mongol could only be disappointing – and Lucarotti brilliantly faces that head on, and trounces it, by playing it as comedy, by showing the Khan as a frail old man who finds a common bond with the Doctor by bemoaning the agonies of old age. It's the dramatic power of finding out the Wizard of Oz is just a little man pulling strings, or Deep Thought announcing the answer to everything is 42, or revealing after all the press hoopla that the eleventh Doctor is Matt Smith. And yet, what's terrific is that the tension doesn't lessen – the scene might smack a little of The Mikado, but it's impressed upon us that this apparently doddery arthritic has the supreme power of life and death. And that carries so much more awe than had he been simply another Tegana with better robes.

Incidentally, Toby, you're an actor – what do you make of all the different accents? For a while I was thrown that there was no consistency to them at all. Some were putting on cod Chinese, some speaking in BBC English. I've rather grown to like it, though, I think it lends rich variety to the setting. Does it make that classically trained noggin of yours seethe?

T: Actually, I don't mind the accents; complaints about such things are, frankly, the first weapon employed by lazy critics. Quite often, I've seen actors getting stick for using an accent that is actually their *native* one, which just goes to show how little weight such objections can have. In the case of this story, once you've accepted a Czechoslovakian Kublai Khan, such things cease to matter.

I'm likewise struck by our meeting with the Mighty Kublai Khan. Hartnell's overt comedy refusal to kowtow to him seems initially like a misstep, but it's worth it for the reveal of the aching, moaning warlord. The Doctor needs to rail against his condition (even if it does make him seem a little daft, seeing as he's facing a man with the power of life and death over everyone present), so that the two old codgers can bond over gout! The Doctor and Khan hobbling out, groaning far longer than you expect, their exit protracted with comedy grunts, is nuts but great fun!

By this point in the story, the loss of the TARDIS – which is stolen while en route to the Khan – cannot be taken too lightly. When the Ship, say, falls into the chasm in The Impossible Planet, we know it'll somehow come back because we're on an alien planet surrounded by strange, SF goings-on. But the sheer length of this tale, combined with the travellers having no technology at their disposal in this time period, and this being a point in the series' history where seemingly *anything* can happen,

makes searching for the missing Ship become like looking for a needle in a haystack.

Special mention should be made that there's yet-another riveting cliffhanger: Ian, who *finally* gets proof after six episodes that Tegana is a ne'er do well, is denied a triumphant denouement when the Mongol – expert swordsman that he is – calmly beckons Ian towards him.

Assassin At Peking (Marco Polo episode seven)

R: And, after nearly three hours of screen time, the story ends – and not through any logical plot development, not because any characters' plans have come to fruition – but because of random chance, and the whims of a tyrannical old man. Now, that's brave. It'd even look a bit clumsy, but Lucarotti knows *precisely* what he's doing; the backgammon scene between the Doctor and the Khan is certainly very funny (Hartnell's polite regret to his opponent that he has now won a year's income from Burma made me laugh out loud), but it also sets up in miniature the way that the outcome of this entire adventure will depend upon the vagaries of fate and luck. Nothing comes to pass the way the characters expect – Ping-Cho's husband dies the night before his wedding, Marco's bid to curry favour with the Khan only achieves the opposite. The only person in the drama who is in charge of his destiny – and, indeed, of everybody else's – is someone introduced only in the previous episode as something very like comic relief. Now, *that's* the power of a monarch. Once again, the Khan is like the Wizard of Oz, with the power to send everybody home – but he's much more capricious than his outward appearance as a genial old man might suggest, and is just as likely to sentence death as to grant freedom.

Once again, we're watching a historical adventure where the big fight at the end is between the two guest stars, and none of the regular cast get a look in. (The format of the programme has yet to properly establish itself.) And we're left in no doubt that although the day is saved because Marco Polo happens to beat Tegana in their bout of swordfighting, it could so easily have been the other way around – one different thrust of a blade would have meant the entire adventure was concluded differently. Again, this could so easily be seen as a fault – after seven weeks of build-up, the ending is shockingly abrupt. There are no time for proper goodbyes, no chance to take a breath as the Doctor and his friends escape quickly in the confusion of Tegana's suicide. But I think that's the entire point – even up to the last drop of the story, Lucarotti *never* allows the characters to relax, never lets us think that the situation is now safe and cosy. In their very first adventure, the TARDIS crew escape by the skin of their teeth from a bunch of cavemen. In this story, they've been exposed to art, and history, and a culture bursting with riches – and it makes no difference; when the chips are down, they still have to seize the chance to scamper away. In the (very dull, frankly) Target novelisation, Lucarotti tries to correct the plotting of this last episode. Tegana is defeated as a result of the Doctor's guile, and we get that conventional ending in which everyone departs as friends, with the Khan even gratefully offering the Doctor a position in his court as personal secretary! It's smoother, yes, and it's more what we expect from Doctor Who – but it also entirely changes what the story is *about*. At this stage, the Doctor and his friends haven't the power to influence events. They've barely the power to keep their lives. And it's fascinating.

I did love this story. It's been such a joy these last few days, looking forward to the next episode. I honestly don't want it to end... what do you say, can we just forget the next story, and move on to The Aztecs? Because I know we're being upbeat and only looking for the good in these episodes... but isn't The Keys of Marinus a bit pants?

T: John Lucarotti has already proven to be smart, elegant and poetic, but the scenes with the Khan allow the writer to flex his not-unimpressive comedy muscles. To that end, Clare Davenport is perfect casting for the Empress, lumbering in and bossing Kublai about so much, he wishes he was more like Genghis. It's a sweet and very funny cameo, with Kublai genuinely scared of the wrath of Mrs Khan.

But this frivolity just helps to disguise the numerous reversals of fortune throughout this final episode. Just as it looks like the Doctor's

skill at backgammon will win the TARDIS back, Lucarotti throws a final spanner into the works by having the Doctor *lose* – he emerges from his game against the Khan with only a bit of paper currency (the start of the show's mischievous stance regarding the pointlessness of money) and starts giggling like a lunatic. Again. Then, when it seems as though Ping-Cho's story will end unhappily, it turns out that her aged finance drank "a potion of quicksilver and sulphur to prolong life... and expired", which means her marriage contract is terminated and she's now free.

Other characters have darker endings: there's a bit of black comedy when the kowtow insistent Vizier is killed before what sounds like a hell of a fight, and while Tegana's suicide lets him to die with a certain dignity, it is, concurrently, a very brutal moment. Even the death of Kuiju – who is killed by the Khan's men while trying to escape – shows the different moral compass of this time period. It's shocking because he was, as you said, something of a comedy turn. (Incidentally, the actor playing Kuiju – poor old Tutte Lemkow – seems cursed in that none of the episodes he appeared in survived the BBC's purge. Despite Lemkow being in three stories – Marco Polo, episode four of The Crusade and three episodes of The Myth Makers – we can't *see* any of his performances. Judging by their, ahem, eccentricity, this is something of a shame.)

Marco, at least, weighs in on the story's resolution by besting Tegana in a duel, and then by allowing the travellers to reclaim the TARDIS and escape – and yet there's no time here for reflection, goodbyes, or even a post-adventure bon mot followed by a group giggle. With the travellers back on the run, we're left with Polo rounding off back home – whilst handily explaining why none of these exploits will make it into his journals. Phew!

My goodness, this was a beautiful adventure. I'm sad to see these people go, and I'm even sadder that I'm tidying away telesnaps of Marco Polo while dusting off the shiny disc of The Keys of Marinus, rather than the other way round. Still, if the stories to come even match in quality the adventure we've just experienced, we're in for several treats.

January 11th

The Sea of Death
(The Keys of Marinus episode one)

R: Do you know, I think the most interesting thing about this episode is what *isn't* there. The story opens without a reprise, without any real link to the previous story – save for the fact, I suppose, that Ian is still wearing that fetching Oriental garb. The past 20 weeks have run into each other consecutively, giving the sense this programme is one long serial with one common goal – which is to get these interfering schoolteachers safely back to sixties England, thank you. But now, that element has been dropped. There's a break in the show's overriding imperative for the first time, and this must have been deliberately done. But if so, why?

I think it comes out of a new understanding of what Doctor Who is all about. For a start, against the odds, it's now a hit show, with viewing figures regularly reaching over nine million. It's not on borrowed time any more, and it doesn't need, therefore, to be looking towards a conclusion. As a result, it has to start taking the attitude that these travellers are enjoying their adventures, that all of this time-and-space lark is as exhilarating for them as it is for the audience.

With all of that in mind, it's interesting that The Sea of Death seems to echo The Dead Planet – although since they're both first episodes by Terry Nation, and since he'll become renowned for using the same structure again and again, I wouldn't count on it being all that calculated of a decision. The TARDIS arrives somewhere strange, the crew wonder over the peculiar landscape (here it's a poison sea; in The Daleks it was a petrified jungle). They see a mysterious city in the distance, go to explore it, get separated in the process for a bit. But whereas no-one save the Doctor was too keen on exploring last time, here everyone's behaving like jolly tourists. On Skaro, it took the Doctor sabotaging the Ship to get his companions to venture into the mysterious city they've seen; on Marinus, the Doctor need only suggest that they look around as an afternoon excursion, and Ian nods cheerfully. Even when Susan goes missing, Ian and Barbara are relaxed enough to coo over the architectural use of building blocks, with all the fervour that suggests they've just read about it in a local guide book.

All of this had to happen. This is what Doctor Who needs to be – a collection of adventures in which the regular characters *want* to participate. This about-face admittedly feels rather glib after the previous 20 episodes that we've watched (and especially when contrasted against our heroes' desperate efforts to leave in Marco Polo), but this is going to be the template for now on, and that's not in itself a terrible thing.

The shame of The Sea of Death, though, is that it doesn't really offer much for this new holiday-making TARDIS crew to be impressed about, in spite of their most affable efforts. A petrified forest on Skaro *looked* sinister, but the sea of death on Marinus... is somewhere off-camera. I'd love to pretend there's something very clever about the Voord – creatures who at first glance merely seem like men dressed in rubber suits, but who then turn out to *genuinely* be men dressed in rubber suits – but I think I'd be reaching a bit. They're not very interesting because they never say a word, and they're not very threatening because all they seem to do is stumble into all of Arbitan's traps. And though the Doctor pays some lip-service to being blackmailed into a quest to retrieve the missing keys to the Conscience of Marinus, the rest of the TARDIS crew are in holiday spirits, and so don't mind too much. They have the resigned look on their faces of tourists who've been told their flight home has been delayed for a couple of hours. Oh well, nothing for it. Back to browse round the Duty Free shop for a few more episodes then.

There's one delightful line that I must draw attention to. It could well be one of Billy's fluffs, but it's actually so absurd, it has a wit to it that suggests it really *must* have been scripted, surely? Asked whether the sea is frozen, the Doctor replies, "No, impossible at this temperature. Besides, the sea is too warm." Which has the same sort of skewed logic as a Douglas Adams joke. Almost.

T: Memo to Arbitan: if you want to keep the Voord (or "Voords", as they're credited) out, you might want to stop making walls that give way when you lean on them, thus granting access to your abode. Oh, and that forcefield of yours might come in handy as a Voord barrier: surround your dwelling with it, and no one will be able to get in and stab you. Oops, too late.

I know I'm being cheeky here, but it's because my pleasure in watching The Sea of Death is mainly due to my having discovered a different way to enjoy Doctor Who. For years, when I collected videos of Doctor Who stories, I was often disappointed that the actual images didn't live up to the pictures my wild imagination had conjured upon reading the Target books. Also, I watched the vids in a climate in which Doctor Who was a joke, an unloved relic, and so I resented these old tales if they didn't satisfy modern standards. I watched them with half an eye on what the cherished "casual viewer" would make of them, and got angry if I didn't think they'd appeal to my cocksure teenage mates. But why the hell *should* they? It took me a long time to realise that I could enjoy Doctor Who when it wasn't necessarily at its best and not get hung up about it. With time, I could still admire the show's scope, ambition and imagination while having fun with its imperfections and short-comings.

Such a mindset has served me well at times, because with the best of goodwill and charity regarding imperfections and shortcomings, this episode is bloody full of them! The technical faults (crew-members can be glimpsed behind revolving walls at least twice) aren't as intrusive as one might think, because I had to have these slip-ups pointed out to me, and even then had to remain eagle-eyed to spot them. However, the bit you mention about Ian and Barbara commenting on the walls demonstrates the huge gulf between the quality of writing in the script for Marco Polo and this one. John Lucarotti's asides grew organically from his story, whereas in The Sea of Death, knowledge is shoehorned into a bit of perfunctory chit-chat. It sounds tacked on, and the actors involved can't muster much interest in it. Even George Coulouris – in his one-episode cameo as Arbitan – seems quite befuddled and as unsure of his lines as William Hartnell.

And rewatching this story has only reminded me that the core of this adventure entails

the Doctor and his friends being sent on a mission to rearm a machine that, er, takes away free will. After the sophisticated morality chess game of Marco Polo, we're suddenly in the realm of such trite definitions as "evil" – from which the Conscience of Marinus can apparently free people. Even the machine's name is a bit presumptive, as if nobody on Marinus has a "conscience", and requires science to provide one for them. Somehow, I had self-edited the whole raison d'etre of the story from my subconscious, but it now seems very un-Doctor Who to me, and stands out more starkly because the rest of the script is just Doctor Who by numbers.

I know we're supposed to stay positive in this undertaking, so I apologize if I've skewed too negative here. Despite my misgivings, I do find it hard to call The Sea of Death a disaster, and can find bits to enjoy. I like the little TARDIS that appears on the beach (surely the first such model ever made – I wonder what happened to it?), and Norman Kay's music is evocative and seems to trot along. Coulouris was quite a name to get in his day, so we should give the production team some casting kudos. But I do find that my chief comfort in rewatching this story, warts and all, is that it gives me a feeling of familiarity and warmth. It falls short in the details, but at least Doctor Who is still taking us to places that no other series can go.

The Velvet Web
(The Keys of Marinus episode two)

R: The best way this episode could have been improved is if it hadn't survived the BBC's purge. No, honestly... this would be *so* good if we were unable to *see* the thing! Think about it – if we only had an audio soundtrack and a few gloomy telesnaps at our disposal, our imaginations would have filled in the gaps, and led us to believe that the utopia of Morphoton had the same opulence of set we were given just a couple of weeks ago in Marco Polo.

What we get instead, unfortunately, is a really good premise that's compromised by cheap design and awkward direction. This won't be the last Doctor Who adventure to have suffered from that – but because The

Velvet Web is all *about* contrast of perspective, in that we're invited to see beauty and decadence through the Doctor's eyes and grime and filth through Barbara's, it's especially galling that there isn't the budget to achieve the former or the imagination to achieve the latter. We're meant to be shocked when we see that Morphoton as previously viewed through Barbara's eyes has been reduced to just a shabby BBC set, but instead we're presented with just a different sort of shab.

It's such a pity, because in concept there's so much to admire here. At a time when scenes are recorded sequentially and in long takes, it's brilliantly jarring that Altos wears relatively plain clothes when the camera favours Barbara, but he's dressed more elaborately when it favours the rest of the regulars. It's the sort of thing you wouldn't even blink at were it made on modern television, where we passively accept that any TV show has been compiled from numerous takes, but to an audience trained to see television drama as a form of theatre, this is really striking. From one angle Susan can be holding a pretty dress, from another a bunch of rags. And it leads to the best joke of the story, where the Doctor thinks he's admiring an advanced laboratory but is actually extolling the marvels of a dirty mug.

What's clever, too, is that Nation plays with our perception of time as well. At first it seems very peculiar that Barbara has, in the few seconds available to her since leaving her companions on Arbitan's island, been welcomed into, and become so familiar with, the Morphoton society. But that's as nothing in a story where our heroes settle down to sleep *twice*, even as the storytelling elsewhere seems to suggest that Barbara's section of the story is told at an entirely different pace. It might all be a mistake – but it also enhances this idea that what we're looking at can't be taken for granted, and gives a nightmarish feel that reaches its peak once Ian's memories have been wiped and he no longer knows Barbara. Nothing that we look at can be taken on face value, because the story so schizophrenically refuses to settle down and show a consistent perspective to the audience; time seems to speed up, then slows. It's eerie.

Or, at least, it *should* be. John Gorrie has been handed a tricksy, somewhat surreal

script, and directs it as if it's a kitchen sink drama. The sets don't help, and Barbara is required to hide behind a particularly shallow pillar and not be seen *several times*. Even at the climax, when she's required to smash the globes that house the brains of Morpho, the attacks she rains down just bounce off. As I say, this isn't the last Doctor Who story that'll be affected by fluffs and goofs and unsympathetic direction... but it is the *first*, and that matters.

T: Time really is skewed: Barbara has managed to be measured and accoutred in a dress, plus learn all about Morphoton, in the 20-second gap between her and the others arriving there. After Lucarotti's meticulousness, I'm finding Nation to be so brazenly sloppy, it's almost heroic.

But, I have to take you to task, and say that there's actually is plenty of opulence in the ersatz reality (I got quite peckish when they brought all the food in). I also really enjoyed the Morpho brains. Yes, talking brains in jars – that's the kind of thing this show does so well. I regret not being able to see them from the front a bit more, but they're terrific, as are their creepy, superior tones as provided by Heron Carvic. Oh, and check out the bored-looking extra with the messy hair in Morpho HQ. Bless her, her entire role seems to entail standing there fidgeting so the brains can enunciate their plans to someone while Altos is chasing after Barbara.

Also, did you notice William's Russell's acting in the early scenes? I very much enjoyed it – Ian is polite but detached, not entirely ready to embrace a utopian society until he knows "what the price" of it is. It's a practical, intelligent reaction to this situation, and he plays it well. On the other hand, the brains' mind-musher must also make everyone perceive Altos' weird, goggly acting to be normal politeness, otherwise the game would be up immediately.

Following Barbara's early departure last episode, though, the Doctor's party *still* hasn't picked up on the importance of leaving for their next destination at the same time. It's as they've had an off-screen chat along the lines of: "Let's all leave together, so that one of us doesn't walk straight into danger."

"Ah, but then how would we contrive a cliffhanger?"

"Good point. Bugger off Susan, we'll give you 20 seconds to get into some sort of scrape. Ta-ta!"

January 12th

The Screaming Jungle (The Keys of Marinus episode three)

R: Things to love about The Screaming Jungle:

Last week, Robin Phillips got to play Altos as the villain of the episode. But Altos now has his true identity back, so he's accompanying the TARDIS crew on their quest – and he's bouncing around a bit like a puppy eager for approval. There's a lovely bit where he's delighted they have found the next key, only to be slapped down by Ian, who is more concerned about the missing Barbara. The flash of hurt on Altos' face is rather endearing.

What else? Oh, I love the bit where Susan tells Barbara she hates saying goodbye to her grandfather. There's foreshadowing for you! If this Susan character ever leaves the series, they should get that Terry Nation chap to script that awkward farewell. Indeed, Carole Ann Ford is very good this week, in spite of the fact that she's largely required to shout a lot and blub. She brings such intensity to her assertion that the sound inside her head was evil, it actually gives the episode some much-needed atmosphere for a while.

Otherwise, though, this is a bit of a squandered opportunity, isn't it? Once again, at the heart of this there's a decent idea; the notion that the jungle is overrunning them not because it's evil, but because the course of time and nature has been accelerated, is rather creepy. The moment of this revelation, in fact, gives a momentary shiver of claustrophobia. But this time, it's Terry Nation's script rather than the direction which stifles the concept. All the interesting little quirks of the episode are pushed into the background in favour of the key-hunting quest – which in itself has no real urgency, and seems to require precious little ingenuity. (In his dying breath, Arbitan's friend Darrius tries to help Ian and Barbara by giving them a sequence of letters and numbers; later, at the very last instant, they realize this is a chemical formula and locate the key by finding the correct jar-label. Wouldn't it have required much less effort for Darrius to have said, "The key's in the jar"? But then, he also tells them that he set booby traps knowing that any associate of Arbitan would have been safely forewarned about them – which, of course, Arbitan clearly didn't bother to do. Maybe Arbitan actually *wants* the travellers dead? Maybe Darrius does too? Or maybe I'm trying for some of the character complexity and plot twists that we saw on the journey to Cathay. Yes, that seems more likely.)

The best thing about The Screaming Jungle, though – and the real reason to cherish it in spite of its faults – is that it puts the focus almost entirely upon William Russell and Jacqueline Hill. They're centre stage at last, and although they deserve better material than this, they've earned a real rapport that was only hinted at the last time they had any sustained scenes together, in An Unearthly Child. They here give an urgency to a scene in which they need to whirl around a greenhouse whilst stage hands wave plant fronds at them, whilst still demonstrating not only an affection for the other but a shared humour. And all of this attention on Ian and Barbara is because William Hartnell is absent from this episode. (He's a shrewd man, he knows when to take a holiday.)

T: Most of this episode centres around the Terry Nation Ludicrous Random Jeopardy Generator. It's all here: falling prison bars, moving statues, spikes descending from the ceiling and Barbara fortuitously shouting out to warn Ian about the Noisiest, Slowest-Ever Moving, Axe-Wielding Statue of Doom. And it *almost* gains a pre-Edge of Darkness grandeur with nature turning against the blight of humanity... except, of course, that it's all a bunch of nonsense.

Still, while it's easy to write this off as daft, by-the-numbers B-movie peril, stories such as this one grabbed the children watching, and made them *keep* watching Doctor Who as it progressed and got more sophisticated. But they needed that grabbing in the first place, and there's enough going on here to keep them coming back for more. It's easy for me to forget that when I first encountered these Hartnell stories (courtesy of the Target novelisations), the incident-packed sci-fi tales sparked my fevered imagination much more than the worthy-but-nowhere-near-as-heady historicals. All right, so my adult eyes and ears are far more receptive *now* to the subtle subtext and characterisation that the more intelligent scripts provide, but the kids of the 60s were kept behind the sofa more by killer plants than bearded Mongols.

Incidentally, have you noticed how the episode titles here are unlike the normal Hartnell style, in which name of the episode and writer are both superimposed over the recap? Here, they strangely foreshadow the style we're all familiar with, whereby they appear over the final moments of the title sequence. I must keep watch to see if it happens again (as it has done for the last two instalments) – this sort of thing interests me, which is why I've never been considered cool.

The Snows of Terror (The Keys of Marinus episode four)

R: William Hartnell doesn't appear in this episode either. Which leaves us with a bit of an oddity! Here we have, to all intents and purposes, a self-contained adventure – five people on a quest looking for a key, fighting a villainous trapper and a few soldiers. There's no reference to the TARDIS, there are no monsters, and only a couple of minutes from the end is there a single use of the word "Doctor". It's about as atypical a story as Doctor Who will ever have, lacking all the trappings and fixtures that one can associate with the series. And it's a measure, still, of how the programme is finding its voice – and how much bolder it's prepared to be with the format when it doesn't realise what the limitations are yet.

The tone of it is also very peculiar. There's a strange brutality to the episode that sets it apart from the rest of what we've seen on Doctor Who, let alone from the other instalments of The Keys of Marinus. Vasor the trapper is the ugliest villain we've yet encountered – he has no creed, no beliefs, not even the courage to lift a weapon against Ian, preferring

instead to fill Ian's bag full of raw meat so wild wolves will kill him. And – there's no way of drawing a veil over this – Vasor clearly wants to rape Barbara. His lust for her is brilliantly conveyed from the moment that he strokes her chilled hands to help restore her circulation; it's subtle enough that it'd pass over children's heads, and adults will deny the import of what they're seeing until it erupts into violence. It's cleverly done, and bold, and seems somewhat inappropriate because it's slap-bang in the middle of a rather childish boy's-own adventure. What's wonderful is that the contempt Ian shows for Vasor afterwards is greater than any disgust we've seen displayed towards anything else yet in the show – the Daleks included. It's as if real-world cruelty and selfishness and evil have crept into the teatime family series inadvertently, and it leaves a bad smell under all the characters' noses.

Peter Davison once recalled in an interview that his earliest memory of being frightened by Doctor Who concerned the ice soldiers in this episode. There's something a little Monty Python and the Holy Grail about them in their visors and chainmail, especially when they do a double-take on the crevasse when Ian destroys the rope bridge. But when they're introduced – frozen, impassive and apparently dead – there's something genuinely eerie about them. It's partly, I think, because again they're so inappropriate; there's been no attempt to dress up the fact that these are stock costumes, and to stumble across medieval Crusaders in the middle of an ice mountain on an alien planet is startling in spite of itself.

T: Terry Nation here takes advantage of William Hartnell's absence by writing a mini-adventure that would have been hindered by his presence. The Doctor wouldn't have been much of a match for Vasor, or very handy at making an ice bridge, so even if he *had* been about the place, he'd probably just be incapacitated and left out of the way. Fortunately, William Russell has plenty of steely grit; Ian here is a grimly heroic lead, although his slightly swaggering dismissal of the doomed, panicking Vasor – who doesn't stand a chance against the oncoming ice soldiers – is unpleasant, and miles away from the ambiguous morality we're given from better writers. Even so, Russell just acts what he's given, and we can't blame him for that.

Otherwise, the acting is a bit of a mixed bag. Carole Ann Ford is very nice on the ice bridge – she's brave, determined, and wholly convincing (possibly because she fell off it during the camera rehearsal). Francis de Wolff, though, is pure ham as Vasor – he charges round his cottage after Barbara looking like that Chaplin villain Eric Campbell, all bewhiskered and wild-eyed, arms raised and fingers arched into claws. I suppose he's just doing what the guest actors before now have done. They've generally responded to the individual scripts they've been given because there is, as yet, no template or house style for how to act in Doctor Who. So the cavemen were all grunts, the Thals were rather postured and worthy, and the journeymen to Cathay were subtle and layered. Sadly for de Wolff, his response to the one-note villain presented to him in this week's episode isn't very dignified.

What chiefly comes across to me in watching this episode, though, is how we've gone from a terrifying jungle to terrifying snow. The series continues its running meme that the environment itself is as powerful an enemy as any – indeed, Vasor uses it as an effective method of trying to murder Ian rather than having to indulge in any fisticuffs himself. I really fear for Altos, though: there's so little separating his crown jewels from the inclement weather, and I suspect his chances of furthering his line have been frozen off.

January 13th

Sentence of Death
(The Keys of Marinus episode five)

R: The first thing that really struck me was the telephone that Tarron – a police interrogator in the civilized city of Millennius – uses to call security. It's just so *ordinary,* with its curly wire and its plain handset; my family used to have one like that when I was a kid. And I snorted with disdain for a moment that the designer couldn't even be bothered to try and make it look a bit more space-age – but then it dawned on me that this is the closest we've got, and are going to get to a long time to come, to an adventure which looks in any way as if it's set on contemporary Earth. The show's format is so dependent on Ian and Barbara being lost in time and space, unable to get home, that the one thing Doctor Who really *can't* do at this stage is something which looks and feels like a standard drama. And so, this is it! Rather cleverly, this episode makes the clichés of the courtroom play and the modern-day thriller look somehow weird and jarring – we've got so used to our heroes wandering petrified forests or confronting history, it looks somewhat bizarre to see them taking part in a story which, if you squint enough, could just about be set in sixties Britain or America. (By the end of the episode, it's as if the designers have woken up, and people are now talking into telephones that resemble hair tongs. But it doesn't matter – that link to the everyday has been made.)

And so, I begin to find myself, at last, rather falling in love with The Keys of Marinus. Because although it's daft and cheap, and the individual episodes themselves feel a bit thin, there really is an attempt here to change the style every week – so that wherever those travel bracelets may take us, it's genuinely unexpected. We've now gone from the mind games of The Velvet Web to the horror of The Screaming Jungle to that strange and ugly thing that was last week's Snows of Terror. I'm not saying they're especially *good* takes on the different genres, but they are at least distinctive, and with every episode Terry Nation seems deliberately to be pushing the series into entirely new areas. So here, we've got a detective story in what seems a roughly modern-day setting (and yes, again, it's not a very *good* detective story), wherein the culprit makes that cardinal error time and again of jumping up and giving away his guilt. Nonetheless, it's still good fun to see Doctor Who being quite so different. The idea of a society in which you're guilty until proven innocent is the series' first stab at anything truly satirical, as broadly sketched as it may be. However paperthin the courtroom proceedings are, the death of the duplicitous guard Aydan is very well handled. There's a sudden flash from a gun, there's a corpse on the floor, and then a silence falls upon the cast, as if they too have been surprised by the change in tone, what with this lightweight action yarn suddenly evoking the televised murder of Lee Harvey Oswald.

And hurrah: William Hartnell is back! Beautifully, he's here put into a role in which he can shine – there's no better Doctor you'd want to act as your lawyer, and Hartnell clearly has great fun being autocratic during the court scenes. (The best joke being, of course, that for all the Doctor's efforts, he only convinces the judges all the more of Ian's guilt!) He's wonderful in the scene where he gets to play detective too, fairly shoving Barbara to the floor in his enthusiasm to act out the crime. For the first time in the series, there's suddenly no question that the Doctor is the lead character – we've missed him, and the story makes great play of building up his return.

Prior to this, The Keys of Marinus has hardly been the best-acted of productions – but here, either through luck or the cast being able to better identify with a setting that seems less fantastical, we finally get some proper and solid performances. Donald Pickering and Fiona Walker are great as the conspiratorial baddies, and flesh out what are little more than sketches. And I also love Michael Allaby as Larn – the character is a bureaucrat who is part of a society that's condemning Ian to death, but Allaby plays the role with a straightforward affability that seems very credible.

T: This episode gives us yet another type of adventure-within-an-adventure. It's fairly simplistic (though top marks for Tarron saying that everyone admitted to the vault undergoes a "probity check" – hopefully a few kids will have asked Mummy what that meant), but nonetheless, there is much to savour. Hartnell is in his element in the court; he has an air of authority as he puffs himself up and faces everyone down. I'd never noticed the nifty space pen Altos gets for the little cutaway in the library – it indicates some attention has been given to detail, even for the most peripheral of scenes. Matters then turn pretty grim when Barbara, having brilliantly faced down Aydan's threats, listens behind the door and hears a slap as Aydan hits his wife! Attempted rape last week, wife-beating this week – there's plenty that was done in this era that you'd be hard pressed to find on teatime TV today, and it's effectively jarring to a modern viewer.

I do feel a bit sorry, though, for Henley Thomas, who is here playing Tarron. He doesn't appear to have done much before or since his appearance in this story, and yet he was considered important enough to get guest-star billing in the Radio Times. Oh, how proud he must have been, showing this to his Mum, thinking this was the beginning of something good for him, and then... nothing. He had a couple of other telly bits, and then obscurity. Donald Pickering and Fiona Walker, at least, went on to much more successful fare – especially the former, whose cool underplaying here is an early entry in a career filled with such glacial, watchable performances. And if we're playing "Where Are they Now?", I should point out that Michael Allaby has become a leading writer on climate change. Perhaps he got into the zone by watching The Screaming Jungle a couple of weeks ago, was gripped by the idea of nature destroying man and thought "half a mo', there's something in that!"

Oh, and what with the production team having spent money on three Voords in The Sea of Death when just one would have been enough (as only one Voord is visible at any given time), we here get two actors credited as "First Judge" and "Second Judge" despite the fact that they aren't allowed to deliver a line, and are forced to rhubarb with Raf de la Torre (the "Senior Judge"). At one moment, Torre's judge-posse laboriously nod far longer than any human being has ever nodded before or since, as if to make up for their being robbed of dialogue. In particular, quite why the judge on the left bobs his head up and down like the Duracell Bunny when a simple "yes" would have sufficed is anyone's guess.

The Keys of Marinus (episode six)

R: Yartek – the leader of the Voord – isn't a very intelligent villain. He attempts to deceive Ian by wearing Arbitan's hood over his head and keeping his distance – but he hasn't even taken off his wetsuit helmet, suggesting even to the most gullible of people that Arbitan's head has grown corners since they last spoke. It was established in episode one, after all, that the Voord wear their costumes as protection against the acid sea; it's not their actual skin. Or maybe Yartek isn't wearing a helmet at all

– maybe he isn't even humanoid – and he has the misfortune to be an alien who happens to *look* like he's in a wetsuit, and lead a group of people who always happen to wear wetsuits. It's enough to make anyone a little power-crazy and unbalanced.

This isn't the only time that Doctor Who will create a monster, and then casually forget the details of that monster on its return – a warrior found encased in ice will, in future serials, refer to its own race as Ice Warriors; the third eye that a Silurian uses to open doors becomes something which flashes during speech; and the Daleks, after their first serial, no longer need to drive around on metal like bumper cars. Those sort of changes are inevitable – from story to story, monsters can only carry the characteristics that the viewers at home remember, no matter how inaccurate. But in the case of the Voord, it's possibly the only time that the production team throws away what the monsters are all about mid-*story*. And it's telling, because it's been so long since we've seen last them, and we've watched so many mini-adventures in the interim, that it does actually feel that the Voord are a returning villain from the past.

One could argue that any story which is about the collection of vital keys, which only ends with them being destroyed before they can be put to any practical benefit, is going to come across as a massive anticlimax. Peculiarly enough, in its truncated six-episode form, The Keys of Marinus predicts the disappointment many will feel 15 years later at the end of The Key to Time season, which has much the same let-down after *26 weeks* of adventuring. But rather than making the quest here feel like a waste of time, the destruction of the Conscience feels like a positive conclusion to the serial. Although this story has hardly had the greatest depth to offer, its support of free will in all its forms is very winning. It's especially appropriate too, coming as it does at the end of a story which, however clumsy some of the little adventures it has given us, has tried its level-best to celebrate so much variety of locations and characters. The idea that the inhabitants of Morphoton or Millennius should be controlled by Arbitan's machine seems as daft as suggesting that the Thals or the Mongols should be as well.

Two especially nice moments here: I love the way, after losing the trial to the point that Ian gets a death sentence, we see the Doctor sitting quiet, staring into space. We've seen him bluster before, or face crises with pride or anger or even a fit of giggling, but we've never seen him so still and composed. It's very powerful, as is the dignified way he accepts the commiserations of the prosecutor. And in a lighter vein, the little romance between Altos and Sabetha may feel as contrived and unmoving as any romance between two sheets of cardboard – but as they depart, it's interesting to see the interplay between Ian and Barbara as they stand in the TARDIS doorway. Ian puts his hand on Barbara's shoulder, grins, beckons her into the Ship – and she smiles in return. That's the real romance of the series, right there, subtly developing under our noses with barely a word of dialogue to mention it – and Russell and Hill are playing it beautifully.

A final reason to take note of The Keys of Marinus: the novelisation. It's not that it's an especially good book, because it isn't – but it is written, of all people, by Philip Hinchcliffe. And the idea that the man responsible for turning Doctor Who into something so horrific – a man that was the bane of Mary Whitehouse and BBC censorship – had to watch The Screaming Jungle over and over again does something funny to my head.

T: Whilst Terry Nation cannily wrote episodes requiring more physical action during Hartnell's absence, he's rightly put him centre stage here – and he's rewarded by an actor in commanding form. The Doctor makes up for buggering up Ian's defence last week by cunningly unmasking the murderer, and reveals he actually knew where the missing key was the whole time. Oh, he's a clever manipulator, this one. Who knows what he might have been up to in the weeks before Ian and Barbara stumbled into the TARDIS: burying an ancient Time Lord power source, perhaps? In light of this, it's plausible!

Otherwise, though, we're now back in slap-dash territory. Barbara asks Tarron if the "psychosymetric" test is back on the murder weapon, and he says it isn't. No matter, she replies, it will say that Kala (Fiona Walker's character) killed her husband. Hang on –

you're telling me that Ian's trial has finished, and the clock is ticking down to his execution *before* the forensic reports are back on a related murder? It's rough justice on Millennius methinks. Have these people no Conscience? (Oh, wait a minute...)

Then our heroes return to Arbitan's island, and I'm reminded that I rather like the design of the Voords – despite, as you say, confusion as to what exactly they are. Personally, I see no reason why they can't actually look like rubber outercasing, meaning they're monsters, not men. Or perhaps they *are* men who happen to look like rubber monsters. Or perhaps they're wearing rubber suits, but underneath they're *still* just as rubbery, only slightly thinner. Oh God, I don't know. If the script is confused, you can't blame me for so being.

And so, finally, after six long weeks of adventuring to retrieve the keys so the Conscience can re-exert control over the populace of Marinus, the Doctor takes the position that, "I don't believe man was made to be controlled by machines." *What?* So, what was the bloody point of the quest, then? It seems rather a glib payoff, doesn't it? Yes, the assertion that free will is important is laudable, but it hasn't really grown organically from what we've seen in the last five episodes. It's bunged on at the end, like a naff joke at Spock's expense at the end of a Star Trek episode.

To look over the entire story, I don't think much of The Keys of Marinus was good, necessarily, but I did wind up enjoying it. None of the storylines outstayed their welcome, and each episode had plenty of incident to keep us occupied. There were some neat ideas at work, and a heck of a lot of labour for that inventive designer Ray Cusick. Was this adventure childish in parts? Yes. Was much of it far fetched? Yes. And we're wrong to expect that from a family programme about a time-travelling police box for what reason, precisely?

January 14th

The Temple of Evil
(The Aztecs episode one)

R: Up to now, the TARDIS crew have essentially been spectators of the times they've vis-

ited, unwilling to do more than observe, and only breaking out of that because they've been forced to win back their freedom. The Keys of Marinus followed that basic idea, but really only paid lip service to it – our heroes never seemed *that* threatened by the loss of the TARDIS, and the forcefield put around it was treated so glibly, the story never even felt the need to take it down again. Instead, the Doctor and his pals blew up the Conscience and defeated the Voord – and, like it or not, put themselves at the very centre of change upon the planet.

The Temple of Evil is a reaction to that. It's all very well for the Doctor to take an active involvement in the affairs of fictitious planets – but what about in these history stories he keeps popping into every other adventure or so? Barbara's decision to take advantage of her new guise as the goddess Yetaxa and save the Aztecs from themselves is only arrogant and wrong because she's doing it in the wrong type of Doctor Who adventure – the Doctor happily encouraged Ian to rewrite the culture of the Thals, so Barbara trying to get rid of human sacrifice here in Mexico seems only a logical extension of that. The resultant argument between her and the Doctor is fascinating, firstly because by doing so, John Lucarotti has immediately dived into the essential inconsistency of the show's premise (and one that is still being teased at in 2008, like a nagging itch – why is it acceptable for Donna save the Ood, but not the victims of Vesuvius?). And what's terrific about the debate is that the Doctor *loses* – because his only real argument can be that Doctor Who Stories Don't Work That Way, and all the moral rightness lies with Barbara. The climax to the episode, in which the sacrifice is prepared, is just terrific – the expression on Ian's face speaks volumes, that of a liberal twentieth century man unsure just how far he can go along with this, knowing full well he's promised the Doctor not to interfere, but for all that becoming an accessory to a man's death.

The brilliance of it is, of course, that Lucarotti refuses to patronise the Aztecs. Barbara technically saves a man's life by calling a halt to the sacrifice, but all that the intended victim shows in response is shame and embarrassment. The last look he throws her, just before he jumps to his death, is the petulant defiance of an angry child who is sulking because his mother's taken away his favourite toy. Up to that point, we might have sided with Barbara entirely, thought the Aztecs would *want* to be rescued from their savagery – but this character who gets only one line, and whom we might have assumed was only an extra, throws Barbara's mercy right back at her.

The opening scene is very also clever – Barbara emerges from the TARDIS, clearly delighted to find herself at her hobbyhorse period of history, and proudly proclaims herself to Susan an expert on this era. Susan's face is a picture; she's rather less enchanted by what she sees about her, focusing on the horror rather than the beauty Barbara enthuses about. And while Susan claims that she knows little of the period, she knows it well enough that she can reference the Spanish, date Cortes' arrival exactly to the year and give an account of the horrors of human sacrifice, which isn't bad going. By contrast, the best that Barbara can do is pick up a bracelet. The suggestion Lucarotti makes from the outset is that Barbara *may* not be the voice of experience after all. It's probably not deliberate, but the way that the other members of the TARDIS later discover her – all dolled up and lounging in luxury – is essentially a repeat of the opening of The Velvet Web. And just look how Barbara's assessment of Morphoton society was back to front as well. The Velvet Web was all about skewed perception, how the beauty presented to us might just be rags. And now we have the whole of the Aztec culture to wonder at in the same way – truly, what is barbaric here, and what is not?

T: Yes… it's often stated that the main job of the companions is to stand about and ask questions, but that's not the case here, as both Susan and Barbara impart necessary contextualisation in an informative and interesting way. We then learn about the cleverness of Aztec engineering at the same time that it becomes a vital plot point – these people have built complex structures, and one of these impressive architectural feats instantly becomes the barrier between the travellers and the TARDIS.

What strikes me the most about The Temple of Evil, though, is how it's all very theatrical –

and I don't at all mean that as a slight. One of the reasons I like Doctor Who is because I get characters and dialogue I'd never see in any number of programmes about vaguely grumpy detectives, or tough times in grotty housing estates. I've read critiques that dismiss the dialogue in stories such as this one as "cod-Shakespearean", but I have to strongly disagree – Lucarotti's lines are rich and elegant, and it's a perfectly reasonable conceit to convey a sense of place and time through hyper-real, "grander" language. It would jar if Tlotoxl – the High Priest of Sacrifice – and his contemporaries talked with twentieth century colloquialisms, and we'd gain nothing by losing such fine language as Cameca's comment, "Better to go hungry than to starve for beauty." As part of this approach, John Ringham's cruel, lizardlike performance as Tlotoxl is perfectly apt – he's a truly memorable villain. Just watch the way Tlotoxl makes his first entrance by shambling into the corner of the picture; it's a subtle and effective trick.

But despite the lofty position afforded to the travellers, the Doctor expertly enunciates the undercurrent of danger: it's all very well that Barbara is regarded as a god, but if these people discover she's not one, it won't be pretty. It's interesting, then, that Ian acts with such confidence when he's chucked into the soldiers' barracks – he's understandably wary regarding his rival for command, Ixta, but never displays a fear of him. A middle-class science teacher from our time might seem rather out of place in such a setting ("I will fight you Ixta, but first we need to assess your social, emotional and interpersonal development and ensure we give you enough positive integrational encouragement so as not to curb your self-esteem levels"), but Ian comes from a generation who grew up as the most devastating war the world had ever seen was being fought. He just gets on with the business at hand, hoping that words will suffice, but seemingly ready to use action if it comes down to it.

As an aside, Rob, let me say that so far, we've largely agreed on the plusses and minuses of the episodes we've seen. I can't wait till we vehemently disagree. I can see it now… "I tell you again, Hadoke, if you don't accept that the High Priest Lolem in The Underwater Menace is the greatest villain of the series so far, I will never give you Bruno Langley's phone number," followed by, "Damn you, Shearman, for vomiting on the legacy of the Morok Commander!"

The Warriors of Death
(The Aztecs episode two)

R: Oh, you can tell that John Lucarotti wrote this, can't you? Everybody's manipulating everybody else – Ixta is using the Doctor to win a fight, the Doctor is using Cameca to find a way of opening the tomb, and Tlotoxl and Barbara are using absolutely *everybody* for political reasons. It's plotted so tightly, and has all the various little bits of subterfuge converge splendidly in the episode's closing moments: Ian is poisoned as a result of the Doctor trying to buy information about the tomb, and Tlotoxl at last dares Barbara to make a public demonstration of her divinity. This has the perfect structure of a theatre play, with all the disparate subplots affecting the other in the most calamitous way just before the curtain falls for the halfway mark.

It's told with greater pace and efficiency than Marco Polo, and maybe a little of the charm is sacrificed as a result. But the scenes between the Doctor and Cameca in the gardens are delightful – however calculating the Doctor's reasons may be for flirting with the old girl, there's more than a sense he's genuinely smitten with her. Hartnell clearly enjoys playing this new Doctor as someone who can be sentimental and fond. The awkwardness he displays upon realising that there are always a group of extras staring at him from behind as he begins his courtship of Cameca is a subtle piece of comedy, and especially lovely.

T: The biggest similarity I can see between this and Lucarotti's previous story, Marco Polo, is the way that everyone puts their cards on the table, but *just* stops short of showing them. Tlotoxl is cagey and patient – he'll make his move in his own good time – while Barbara tries to use her composure and unflappability as a weapon against him. So the cliffhanger boils down to Barbara playing her "I'm a god, do as I say" ace, and Tlotoxl responding with his "If you're a god, prove it" joker. This Aztec priest is such an adaptable, shifty character;

he's far more palpable a threat than any clod-hopping rubbermen who fall through walls and fail to disguise their triangular heads.

But I also enjoy the interplay between the Doctor and Barbara – William Hartnell and Jacqueline Hill work really well together, don't they? Their reconciliation was one of the highlights of The Brink of Disaster, and their confrontation here – as the Doctor tells Barbara how her ignoring his advice has made everything worse – is just as impressive. He chides her, yes, but only in the sense that he's commanding and pragmatic, not that he's unkind or unfair. Her response – to cry – is, for once, a genuinely understandable outburst. She's not upset because he's being a git; it's because he's right and her plan didn't work – and she's now feeling pressured and vulnerable. And then the Doctor melts, and becomes understanding and tender. It's such a lovely dynamic, coming as it does in a flawlessly written and acted scene.

Visually, director John Crockett's style seems similar to that of Waris Hussein, which suggests that Crockett's missing episode of Marco Polo probably didn't jar particularly with those that surrounded it. He favours the close-up (a great move when you have such expressive, interesting actors as Keith Pyott – who plays Autloc, the reasonable and agreeable High Priest of Knowledge – and John Ringham) and framing background figures in-between foreground ones. It's visually stimulating and helps isolate some characters whilst cementing the strength of others. The way that Barbara is set back, framed by the open curtains of the high priests' heads, says as much about her position in this drama as any dialogue.

Everything about this is lovely, even the soundtrack. Richard Rodney Bennett's twittering flutes meld seamlessly into the pretty birdsong in the garden. I don't want to change this historical, not one line.

January 15th

The Bride of Sacrifice
(The Aztecs episode three)

R: "I serve the truth," the Doctor says smugly – and that's precisely what the TARDIS crew *don't* do this episode. The development of the benevolent priest Autloc, whose world beliefs are being shattered by Barbara, is especially moving. As he begs her not to deceive him, you are made uncomfortably aware that this most sensitive of the Aztecs is suffering the most thanks to the time travellers' interference. The guilt on Jacqueline Hill's face is perfect and just. Ian later says that Autloc is the one reasonable Aztec, but by "reasonable" he only means conveniently stupid; the faith that means so much to Autloc is being destroyed, owing to someone preying upon his gullibility and gentleness.

The irony of the story, of course, is that although the Machiavellian Tlotoxl is cast as the villain, his suspicions are perfectly valid, and none of his schemings are anything more than attempts to protect his society. The cornerstone of his universe is being threatened by an impostor – what *else* should he be doing? And just as Barbara shows guilt when she's forced to lie to Autloc, there's an angry relief to her outburst when she finally confides to Tlotoxl, her mortal enemy, the truth that yes, she's mortal, yes, she's a liar – and no, there's not a bloody thing he can do about it. Barbara is the one who is callous here; Tlotoxl's delight that he technically has the proof he's sought is at once balanced by the agony of realising he's underestimated Barbara and been outmanoeuvred by her. And the burgeoning romance between Cameca and the Doctor, no matter how charmingly played by Margot van der Burgh and Hartnell, is just as morally suspect. We can accept that the Doctor proposes to her accidentally – and the double-take Hartnell gives to camera is priceless – but before long, he's amiably playing the happy gardener to his new fiancée.

In this atmosphere, it's hardly a surprise when Susan's riposte to the Perfect Victim is so very brutal – let him die if he wants to, it's nothing to do with her. Which sums up the amoral stance of the TARDIS crew perfectly. They either don't care enough (like the Doctor) or they care far too much (like Barbara) – either way, they are warping the fragile world around them, and people are suffering. The scene where Ian and Barbara argue over whether Tlotoxl or Autloc most accurately represent the Aztecs is very telling – both of them, from different stances, want to stereo-type the entire race. Susan makes no distinction between them either; when Autloc tries to reassure her after she's been threatened with punishment, her retort that she finds the Aztecs hateful and barbaric is directed wholly at *him* – and Keith Pyott steps back as if he's been physically slapped. Lucarotti is so clever at this sort of thing; his last story asked us to consider at times that Marco Polo was a hero having to struggle against these unruly strangers who threatened him, and in this episode, that ambiguous treatment of the regular cast is developed even further.

I love the scene, too, where Ixta decides that now that he's proven he can defeat Ian in battle – meaning that Ian is sure to die in future – he can now be considered a friend. It's just another example of the cultural divide played out in the story, and is a wonderful little taste of black comedy.

T: I have a slightly different take on Barbara's confession to Tlotoxl that she's not a goddess. Yes, she's telling him there's nothing he can do about her deception, but it's telling that she confesses her falseness when she's outmanoeuvred his plan to poison her. He hasn't got her in a corner and dragged a confession from her – she says it because she needs to say it to *someone*, even someone who could use the knowledge against her. She's a woman pretending to be a god, a thing of perfection. And it's too much, she can't keep up the pretence. It's a complex moment of human frailty sold fantastically by Hill. The fact that Ringham's such a worthy opponent helps – mark how he clings to the rock, his head darting from side to side like a gecko.

The camera work continues to be brilliant here. It's hard enough to ensure that everyone is in the right position at the right time when you do a stage play, so it's all too easy to underestimate the skill involved in framing a decent picture while making sixties TV, in which there was only one chance to get it right. So whilst there's the odd jarring pan or skewed moment, the fact that the director was prepared to push for interesting pictures is worthy of great praise. There's a fantastic shot of Barbara and Tlotoxl in focus, set back from Ixta's raised arm (as he prepares to kill Ian), that exhibits a good eye coupled with a desire to visually illustrate the story-dynamics.

And let me say that I adore the conversation between two of the gentlest characters we'll ever see in Doctor Who: Cameca and Autloc radiate respect for each other, and their chat doesn't explicitly give away what she's intending (that the Doctor make her some cocoa, and thereby propose to her). It's only on that great close-up of Hartnell almost choking (so good, I feel the hot cocoa in his mouth) that their discussion makes complete sense. Lucarotti trusts his audience, and I hope I'm returning the respect he's given me by hanging on his every expertly crafted word. I especially love the Doctor's observation about cocoa being a currency you can drink, and Tlotoxl's slimy statement that "for once, the High Priest of Knowledge will be in ignorance." There's nothing cod about this; in dialogue terms, it's caviar.

The Day of Darkness
(The Aztecs episode four)

R: Let's just consider a moment. This is the final episode of The Aztecs, but the audience at the time wouldn't necessarily have known that. Events certainly *seem* to be drawing to a conclusion; access to the TARDIS at last seems possible, so it's only a matter of getting all the regulars into the temple at the same time so they can make good their escape. But we've been here before. An Unearthly Child episode three, The Daleks episode four, Marco Polo episode five... all of them suggested to the viewer that the adventure might be coming to a hasty end, but something always prevented their flight, and the TARDIS crew were forced to see out the final act of the story. The Daleks still need to be defeated, Tegana still needed to be given his comeuppance.

By the time of The Aztecs, any careful viewer will have spotted this pattern – and also that the series seems to have worked out just how long these adventures last. Discounting The Edge of Destruction (which was bonkers anyway), the typical structure of a story is that it's told in six or seven episodes. As the Doctor and his friends begin to believe that they'll soon be away from Mexico, as the last few minutes of episode four play out, the Careful

Viewer knows differently. They can't leave yet. Tlotoxl is not only unpunished, he's in the ascendant. The "goodies" in this story, Cameca and Autloc, are the only characters who have suffered – the former's heart has been broken, and the latter has miserably gone into exile to die in the wilderness. If the Doctor takes off now, the rules that Doctor Who has established about the nature of these adventures will have been broken – he'll have escaped, but he'll also have *lost*. So as our heroes rush towards the TARDIS, we still wait for a last-minute reversal of their fortune – a fluid link to be missing, a Tegana to emerge from the shadows and grab hold of Susan.

And yet, off the Doctor goes. Imagine the closing scenes in light of what the series has already led us to expect – think about that last image of Tlotoxl, his power at his most supreme, in delighted fervour as he begins to carve out his victim's heart. I suggest it's as big a dramatic shock as the end of Mindwarp, over 20 years later, where because the sixth Doctor has suddenly been removed from the story, it can only be left to play out to tragedy. Even Genesis of the Daleks, the series' most famous example of a story in which the Doctor is seen to fail, ends upon a note of optimism – that the battle may have been lost so the war can be won. The best the Doctor can manage here, though, is to say that Barbara's influence has led to the salvation of one man, and that's enough – and it's quite clear that Jacqueline Hill is as unconvinced by the success of Autloc's redemption as we the audience must be.

I particularly like the way that, after Ian knocks out a guard whom Cameca first tried to buy off with the seal to Autloc's property, she has enough honour to place the seal in the unconscious man's hand. I also like the way Lucarotti doesn't shy away from showing that Ixta subsequently kills the guard as a consequence of Ian's impatience. There is also a beautiful scene in the tomb where Barbara leaves Yetaxa's bracelet behind, but the Doctor can't find it in him to abandon the brooch Cameca gave to him.

T: They lose.

They achieve nothing. Thanks to the Doctor, Cameca is crestfallen. Because of Barbara,

Autloc casts off his title and possessions, and the obsequious Tonila becomes the next High Priest of Knowledge. And owing to Susan's choices, the Perfect Victim doesn't get any nookie. Only Ian's story has him triumphant, as he hurls Ixta's stunt double off a building (in a scene made a tad more confusing on the spanking DVD print, where it's more obvious that Ian's double is David Anderson, who also plays the Aztec captain). It's a glorious fight, because the filmed sequences allow the painted backdrops to convincingly suggest the scale and height of the building more effectively than the studio work did. And bringing things full circle with the resolve Ian showed in episode one, it's shocking that he actually *waits* for his mortal showdown with Ixta. As the Doctor's party gets busy opening the tomb, Ian stands his ground – knowing, or rather accepting, that a reckoning with Ixta is inevitable. To my lily-livered generation, it's quite shocking.

Hartnell plays the Doctor's guilt over Cameca very well – he doesn't let himself off lightly. Despite all the giggles and dottiness, this weighs heavily on him, and his non-vocal acting speaks volumes. He's helped, of course, by the graceful Margot van der Burgh – I just love how Cameca's parting shot to the Doctor, "Think of me...", is said twice. The first sounds a little like a (justified) dig, but she can't bring herself to leave it like that, so the second utterance has no malice and much dignity. I find it absolutely bloody heart-rending.

So, the Doctor says that while Barbara failed to change Aztec civilization, at least she saved one man, does he? If anyone other than John Lucarotti were writing this, I'd have probably taken it on face value. But *saved*? The Doctor's opinion seems to be that Autloc has lost everything, including his firmly held core beliefs, but at least he won't hang around watching people getting stabbed any more. It niggles, and Jacqueline Hill is right to play it as if Barbara isn't convinced. Part of me likes to think that if the travellers hadn't come, Autloc would eventually have steered the Aztec civilisation on a less barbaric path, and they'd have abolished sacrifice thanks to his wise council. The Aztecs would have thus become a robust society with which Cortes wouldn't have wanted to tangle. For all we know, Barbara *did* change history, but only in the sense that the

Aztecs were wiped out because of her interference.

January 16th

Strangers in Space
(The Sensorites episode one)

R: The Doctor gets to fly a spaceship! He shouts about stabilisers and thrusts and things! I find that oddly very exciting. Considering that grabbing hold of some space-age throttle and trying to prevent something crashing into a planet becomes a staple requirement for future Doctors – it's such a cliché, you think it's probably written into their audition – it still seems peculiar to see this most old-fashioned of them all doing things which are so delightfully techno.

This is a very peculiar episode. It starts off being almost determinedly reassuring. Everyone stands around the TARDIS listing all their previous adventures in order, as if they've been memorising some early version of the Jean-Marc Lofficier Programme Guide, and underlining the fact that they're all by now seasoned travellers who enjoy each other's company and the perils they face. There's an easy affection between them all; Hartnell is tactile with Russell, while Hill and Ford relax and joke together. It's so charming, it's tempting to forget that as they step out of the TARDIS and confront the Mystery of the Moving Spaceship, united as four friends, they've never seemed quite so *efficient* before. Barbara is able to check the pulse on what she thinks is a dead body without flinching, and Susan is curious rather than distraught. They've never been in so much control. They analyse the situation, and conclude that they can do nothing to help the poor dead people they've found, and make to return to the TARDIS. Then they realise the people aren't dead after all, revive them, listen to their story – and conclude they *still* can't help them, and decide to leave anyway. It's amiable and relaxed and utterly out of tune, coming as it does from a programme that's usually pitched just beneath mild hysteria.

And then, there's a shift. The spaceship is under attack. There's a suggestion that strange aliens are manipulating everyone, that they're playing a game of nerves on their human captives. And that the *other* human on board – the one stalking the corridors outside the flight deck – has been driven to violent psychopathy by the experience. The Doctor speculates it's an exercise in fear – and that, suddenly, is what the whole episode becomes. Barbara and Susan trying to hide from a shuffling sick man given to bouts of sobbing is the eeriest thing we've yet seen in Doctor Who. Stephen Dartnell is terrific as the deranged crewman John; he's sinister and touching at the same time. His promise to defend the women against the Sensorites of whom he's obviously terrified – and, especially, the way Barbara allows him that dignity – is lovely. And the cliffhanger, as the cast wait patiently for the aliens to show their faces, is extremely tense. There's absolute silence for over 30 seconds, and nothing to see but the anticipation and dread on everyone's faces. What began as something rather light and affable has become genuinely frightening – Norman Kay's music and Mervyn Pinfield's direction make this so suspenseful, the episode sticks out as by far the scariest Doctor Who has yet produced.

This is also our first glimpse of Earth's future – I love the way that Big Ben is used as the most identifiable and reassuring landmark we have, and everything goes all science-fictiony when the episode casually mentions that it's been destroyed. (Russell T Davies did exactly the same thing the first time he got the chance – admittedly, in a more spectacular style.) It's rather endearing the way that these astronauts from the twenty-eighth century accept the arrival of time travellers from the twentieth with so much ease. And, because I'm an anal-retentive fan, I also enjoyed the way that Susan and Barbara are so surprised by the way spaceship doors open, even though it's *exactly* the same method as was used in the Dalek city, down even to the same sound effect. Pay attention, girls!

T: Well, this is odd! I'm certain that if we took a poll of Doctor Who fans, and averaged out their viewing habits of the past ten years, The Sensorites would be a contender for the least-rewatched story of them all. But I have to say:

on the evidence of this first episode, it's difficult to see why.

The recap scene in the TARDIS is, admittedly, somewhat awkward – Barbara's dismissal of her experiences with the Aztecs is so casual (first she says, "I've got over that now," and then she again mentions the Aztecs with a bit of a smile on her face), you'd think the Doctor had hit the Continuity Reset Button while he was fiddling with the console. But otherwise, there's something genuinely creepy about this episode. By use of sound, camera wobbles and especially Stephen Dartnell's performance as John, this is all very atmospheric. Even though the dreaded "they" are eventually revealed at the cliffhanger to be a balding Father Christmas peeking through a spaceship window, I'm still looking forward to next time.

Mervyn Pinfield's direction seems a bit old-fashioned – while the other Doctor Who directors were young mavericks anxious to do something ambitious or groundbreaking, Pinfield's approach seems to belong to a previous decade. Ian checks a crewman's pulse and stoically announces that the man is "dead" – and then, as if that weren't dramatic enough, there's a big thump of music to remind us that this is quite a bad thing! Some of Pinfield's flourishes work well, though: the bit where the Doctor's party walks straight out of the console room and into the spaceship is often regarded as a gaffe (because we don't see the outer TARDIS doors open, and they seem to automatically close once the travellers exit), but I think it's a very clever way of selling the fact that all that space inside the TARDIS can fit into anywhere.

My favourite bit in this episode: the unhinged John telling Barbara, "You look like my sister," which is really sweetly delivered by Dartnell.

The Unwilling Warriors
(The Sensorites episode two)

R: There's an attempt to ratchet up the tension still further in this episode, most notably in a long sequence where Ian and Barbara search the spaceship for invading monsters. But there's only so far the story can go once you reveal that the Sensorites are really rather timid beasts, clearly as frightened by the humans as they are of them, and have a propensity to clutch their heads in pain if William Hartnell so much as raises his voice. (He didn't raise it *that* much either, chaps – this is the new, cuddlier Doctor he's playing. You should have seen him during The Edge of Destruction, your heads would have throbbed!) I rather like the idea that we're encountering at last an alien race that, whilst dangerous and suspicious, are clearly not evil and are open to negotiation – it's a step onwards for the show. But the episode then wastes too much time on playing off an atmosphere of horror that's no longer there. The title itself is a bit of a giveaway: "The Unwilling Warriors". Whatever next? The Well-Meaning Invaders? The Assassin Who'd Really Rather Not Shoot and Would Prefer to Talk About It?

I rather like the design of the Sensorites. They're cheap, certainly, and the disc-shaped feet are probably a bad idea – the actors don't seem to realise when they're standing on each other. But the faces are lovely, and – again, rarely for a Who monster – individually distinctive. Besides, the thinner of the two Sensorites bears an uncanny similarity to a maths teacher I had when I was 14.

Stephen Dartnell continues to give a great performance as John; I love the way that he tries to resist the aliens' mind-control, turning to camera and pleading as if the audience at home are the ones tormenting him.

T: I'm watching this on a grotty old VHS tape (not the commercial BBC one, but a multi-generational copy). So I'm denied the crystal-clear images of The Aztecs, where I could pick up every nuance in an actor's face, and here I'm seeing fuzzy, blobby shades of grey, populated by aliens who appear to be talking through a sock. But, I rather like it. As a kid, I was always fascinated by the 60s stories because they were on before I was born; they were ancient, fusty, awe-inspiring pieces of history. The cold light of day (and the VidFIRE restoration process) can make these episodes appear less antique, but I actually like the metaphorical cobwebs. It also makes me look forward to the eventual release of The Sensorites on DVD, as within the doubtless sharpened pictures and crystal-clear sound, I will discover this story all over again.

This time around, though, the lack of clarity in the picture makes those little Sensorite eyes look really interesting and alien. In fact, even though they're just men in body stockings with plates on their feet, I think the design of the Sensorites is unfairly maligned. I find them convincing, and the simple trick of the actors husking their voices up a bit sells me on their alien qualities. I also like the spaceship set, and even though much of this episode consists of people just walking very slowly, the languid camerawork and Kay's music (though basically a retread of The Keys of Marinus) make it all seem very spooky. The scene with Ian and Barbara creeping towards their confrontation with the Sensorites, in fact, has no dialogue for ages (yes, it's true: this episode is the Doctor Who equivalent of Buffy the Vampire Slayer's Hush), and keeps you on the edge of your seat.

William Hartnell again proves that he's so much better at the haughty or resigned one-liner than at giggling, as the Doctor – when Captain Maitland explains John's condition by saying his hair tuned completely white – delivers a bluff "There's nothing wrong with that" as a riposte. It's worth noting too, that even though the Doctor Who Annuals of this era refer to the Doctor as an Earthman, Ian explicitly tells him that, "On Earth, we have a saying..." It's interesting that whilst taken as read, the Doctor's being an alien isn't an issue.

Stephen Dartnell is still the best thing on offer here, though (facially and physically, he bears a striking resemblance to David Tennant – have you noticed that?), though Carole Ann Ford gives him a run for his money when she's allowed to channel her inner unearthly child, and delivers a moody and effective cliffhanger where Susan says she must go with the Sensorites to their homeworld or all of her friends will die.

January 17th

Hidden Danger
(The Sensorites episode three)

R: Do you know, I really love it when we stumble upon things that simply wouldn't work the way television is made today, but can still have surprised and wrongfooted the contemporary audience. Take the cliffhanger, for example. The Doctor, Ian and Susan are having a meal with the Sensorite leader, and William Russell coughs during one of his lines. He clears his throat, throws in a "sorry", and we think nothing of it – we've been watching Hartnell stumble his way through the script many a time, and we're used to the fact that the BBC can't afford many retakes, so seeing an actor get a fly in his throat is nothing. Then the camera gives its attention to Hartnell when he gives a speech, and we can hear Russell once again give a little cough. Then he keels over unconscious. The coughing *was* scripted. The man's dying! Now, there's no way that could work in the new series, or even for much of the seventies onwards. If a character starts coughing, and it's left for broadcast, it *must* be significant. A director can't hide surprise moments like that from the audience any more; the slickness of television nowadays would rob it of any ambiguity.

The highlight of the episode, though, comes early on. Susan's little rebellion against her grandfather is beautifully played by Carole Ann Ford, who clearly seizes the chance to give the character a little more welly. The lines she has to say – insisting that she's no longer a child, and has opinions of her own – could almost have been written by the actress herself. It's a nice development from the stance she took in The Aztecs against her arranged marriage, stating boldly that she has the right to her own choice. How right it feels, then, that she reacts so strongly against the Doctor when he suggests here that she has no right to exercise her judgment around him either.

There's a laudable attempt to give all these Sensorites individual characters – and it's the first time in the series this has happened, as all alien races before this acted as one. The actors do their best, but they're rather defeated by the masks and the longwinded bits of dialogue that feel more like speeches than conversation (and have wonderful bits of exposition, with the Sensorites telling each other things about their own anatomy!). That said, you get the feeling that the performers are trying to get more humanity into the parts despite the lines being a mouthful; there's a lovely bit where the Second Elder takes the firing key from the Administrator and gives him the deathly warn-

ing, "Take care lest my doubts are become realities" – and then, as he's leaving, he turns in the doorway and gives the Administrator an admonishing look as if to a naughty schoolboy, which makes everything light and natural again.

At least the effort is there, and I like the idea of a society that has good reason to fear and dislike the humans. The Administrator himself isn't evil; he's merely arguing a point of view that is opposed to the First Elder's policy of appeasement. He's no Tegana, and no Tlotoxl (there's none of that depth), but in theory the character should have a dignity to him. That's all rather threatened by the fact that John's mania seems to have given him the ability to be moral arbiter of everyone he meets, and to categorise them as "good" and "bad". It's touching when, on the spaceship, he calls his fiancée "good" – which makes Carol turn away in distress, realising that that childish simplicity is all the complexity he can give her. It's less effective on the planet when John identifies the First Elder in the same way, partly because there's good reason to believe the Elder won't *have* any greater character complexity for John to miss, and also because John does it straight to camera as an aside. It does feel a bit like he's trying to help out any audience members who may have lost their way.

T: And two episodes in, we finally meet the serial's main guest star. Ladies and gentlemen, it's Peter Glaze! At the time, I suspect that this was a casting coup equivalent to getting the Chuckle Brothers to play Nazis in the new series. I just can imagine, though, Glaze being pleased to hear his agent say that he's going to be playing the lead villain – and then being rather nonplussed to discover he's credited under the illustrious name of "Third"! Especially as he's always referred to as the City Administrator in the script. It seems a rather sloppy way of going about things; Arthur Newall's character is called "Engineer", but is credited as "Fourth". This will get even more confusing later in, when the First and Second Sensorites disappear, and so top Sensorite billing goes, oddly, to the Third! Was it too much of a stretch of the writer's imagination to give these characters names?

In the same vein, the caste system of the

Sensorites feels like a vague attempt to give them a discernibly different culture, but it's all a bit lazy. The Sensorite warriors fight... what, exactly? Each other? They must do, as the Sensorites are a peaceful race who have no contact with anyone else. The Fourth Sensorite asks the Third if humans' hearts are "in the centre, like ours", which is a bit like me saying to you, "Fish breathe with gills, not with lungs – you know, like we humans have in our chests."

Am I straying from this book's brief and being overly critical, you might ask? No, because The Sensorites is showing me that Doctor Who could have been written like this every week! We're being given unsophisticated, two-dimensional aliens who don't have individual names, and live in a simplistically sketched societal hierarchy. Clues to each mystery are set out in such proximity to one another, it seems intended to make the children watching at home think they've been very clever when they work them out. Not that there's anything wrong with this approach per se – it's just that when one considers the programme's timeslot and central premise, we probably wouldn't be writing about it 40-odd years later had the production team not opted for more sophistication from subsequent scripts.

Oh, and I promise not to use a Doctor Who book to make too many cheap political gags. Otherwise, I'd point out that the actor playing the creepy, xenophobic, self-interested, dishonest Fourth Sensorite quit acting after this and became a Tory Councillor for Enfield.

A Race Against Death
(The Sensorites episode four)

R: To be fair, it's not so much a "race" against death as a gentle trot. There's a very funny montage sequence of the Doctor testing various samples of water for poison – alongside the First Elder painstakingly writing "negative" against each one and shaking his head sadly at Susan – only at last for a positive result to come up, and the Doctor to confirm what he'd already worked out five minutes beforehand. Meanwhile, William Russell plays someone dying from contamination the way a man plays having a head cold and phoning up his boss to get off work for the day – he makes his voice a bit weak and raspy.

There's a much-mocked scene in which Carol suggests to the Administrator that were he to change his clothing, his physical similarity to all the other Sensorites means that no-one could recognise him. "I'd never thought of that!" says our evil egg in the Sensorite regime, as if he's a seventeenth century man just hearing Newton's take on gravity. But, really, why *should* he have thought of it? If you're part of a culture where everyone is identical, and your badges of your office identify you, it takes a radical mind to make the leap to question that and see it from an outsider's perspective. You can see this being a really witty idea – say, if a sudden genius grunt in the ranks of the cloned Sontaran realises that he could be commander if he only put on a different helmet. It only falls down here because the Sensorites manifestly *aren't* identical – Peter Glaze in particular looks nothing like any of the others. And since they're all facially dissimilar, the little differences between the Sensorites would be all the more obvious. All of this smacks a little bit like an Englishman who believes that all the Chinese look the same, and actually *expects* that the Chinese can't tell each other apart either.

T: Yes, in the days when I'd read about The Sensorites but not actually seen it, I was thrilled to read that different masks had been designed to give each Sensorite a unique character. It's cheaper to lift every visage from the same mould, which explains why Doctor Who monsters tend to all look exactly the same, even though this isn't altogether believable. So it's typical of this daft series that I adore, that the only two species who are cited in the scripts as being identical – the Sensorites and the Sontarans – resolutely aren't!

And while the Doctor's laborious gathering of evidence wouldn't have detained Sherlock Holmes for even a minute, I like the cross-cutting and fading from the stricken Ian, to the Doctor, to the test tubes. When director Graeme Harper does this in 20 years' time, we'll be lauding him. There are a couple of fluffs, though – the First Elder says, "Give my Doctor the compliments," whilst the Doctor talks of "the First Elder... err, Scientist." But to be fair, Peter R Newman (or the Fourth Writer, as he shall be known from now on) hasn't exactly made it easy for everyone.

And did you notice, with regards the way the Doctor is more and more becoming the series' central character, that the First Elder refers to him as the "commander" of the TARDIS crew? Perhaps he's just reciprocating a bit of courtesy – the Doctor here is far more respectful of court ritual and authority than he was whilst hooting like a maniac in front of Kublai Khan.

Finally, let me point out that when John says "evil", we get another socking great musical sting, just as we did with Ian's declaration of "dead" in episode one. Subtlety has taken a holiday, alongside the absent and much-missed Jacqueline Hill.

January 18th

Kidnap
(The Sensorites episode five)

R: Well, the "kidnap" of the title takes place – ooh, I'd say, five whole seconds before the end of this week's instalment. Things are coming to a pretty pass when the selling point of the episode is only at the cliffhanger. It's strange, watching this, how all that wonderful tension evoked in Strangers in Space has now ebbed away. There's the odd attempt at it – I love how Hartnell has mastered the act of "silent acting whilst the credits play over your face", getting suspicion and fear into a single and slightly affected hand movement to the chest. (Peter Purves once said in an interview that Hartnell's film experience taught him to keep his hands in shot during close-ups because they're so expressive – it's mannered and unnatural, but it really does work well.) And Norman Kay is working overtime with his musical stings, trying to make the action here more melodramatic than it really is.

But to be honest, Kidnap is rather on the dry side; when Ian tells Susan that he wishes they were all in the TARDIS and away from the Sense-Sphere, he says it just a little *too* feelingly. And it's peculiar that the cast are so much looking forward to Jacqueline Hill being back from her holiday next week, they men-

tion it on no less than four separate occasions – you can always tell there's a problem with the pacing of a story when it keeps on stopping so all the characters can anticipate the thrills they can expect *next* week.

It's a funny affair, this episode. The best scenes are the ones where the Administrator and the Second Elder argue about a policy of appeasement towards the humans. It's interesting in part because Peter Glaze's fervent attack on the pacifism of his brothers is really just the flipside of Ian's discussion with the Thals – only this time, the TARDIS crew are on the receiving end of the aggression. Although Glaze is clearly portrayed as the story's villain, without a shred of ambiguity to it, it's easy to sympathise with his stance – especially when Susan openly laughs at the way the Sensorites run, or John and Carol treat them as if they're tardy waiters. There's still a clever twist or two up this story's sleeve (thank God), but watching it now is a faintly uncomfortable experience, as the amiable racism of the humans (and the way Doctor *continues* to shout at the Sensorites, even though he knows it causes them pain) isn't challenged by the episode at all, and the distrust the Sensorites show in response is labelled purely as evil. It's all a bit too simplistic – we've seen during this first season how Doctor Who keeps on trying to find a tone to play off, and at this point it's clearly Children's Television. But not in the way that John Lucarotti interpreted it, with subtle instruction and shades of depth. No, here the Administrator is rumbled as a baddie primarily because he was a bit abrupt with Ian and Susan once he'd been put in a position of power. Because that's right, kids – evil people give themselves away because they're *rude*.

Pah. I'm grumbling too much. I'm supposed to be pointing out what's good and worth celebrating. Peter Glaze, then. They've stuck him behind a mask, they've given him the broadest of characters to play – but the funny little feller from Crackerjack is really going for it, blowing the cobwebs off the staid Sensorite society. He's worth the admission price alone – the regular cast are going through the motions a bit, but Glaze mines the most out of every scene he's in, a single tilt of the head suggesting pride at his elevation, or haughty disdain to the humans he so despises.

T: We get one of the biggest and most obvious fluffs in the entire series: "I heard them over... er... t-talking." And yet, William Hartnell isn't to blame. Stand forth (or Fourth), Arthur Newall, your place in history is assured!

Some of the Sensorites' attributes continue to raise questions – we're told that loud noise hurts them, but when Third shouts at the Second Elder, the latter is caused pain while the perpetrator of said noise feels nothing. So, it seems that a Sensorite could charge about shouting and banging, giving everyone around him tinnitus, but would be perfectly fine and oblivious to it himself. (Actually, I know a busker like that in Manchester City Centre.)

Good on the Third Sensorite, though, for releasing the Fourth to help instead of doing that ridiculous and boring strategy employed by villains on 24: killing their useful ally for incompetence. Oh, and note how the cliffhanger – in which Carol is kidnapped – is the first instance of a non-regular in peril being used to entice us back next week.

A Desperate Venture
(The Sensorites episode six)

R: John Bailey does a wonderful turn as the Earth commander, who's been hiding in the aqueducts poisoning water for years, and yet still believes he's fighting an honourable war. His soldiers wear long beards and carry pointed sticks, but he still has the hearty bonhomie of a colonel who believes in the well-ordered discipline of the drill. It's a lovely performance because it's very funny – here is a man who genuinely cannot see to what a ragged state his xenophobia has brought him – but it's dangerous too, teetering on the edge of paranoia. He rails against the Doctor and Ian with threats of courts martial, and is only reassured when he's promised all the attention of a welcome committee. Subtlest of all, though, is the way that Bailey clearly feels *disappointed* that the war is over – his underlings emerge into the sunlight with such relief on their faces, they almost don't mind that they're captured by the Sensorites, but this is a soldier who, in supposed victory, has lost all his life's purpose. He's only on screen for a few minutes, and yet he plays the part with such energy, and with such thought, that it livens up the entire epi-sode and reminds you how long we've had to do without performances of this calibre. Hartnell and Russell clearly perk up too as a response.

There are some lovely moments here – Carole Ann Ford is very affecting when she talks to the First Elder about her home planet, and by the end of the episode, she clearly feels homesick and wishes that she could have a permanent base. (Not much longer to wait now, love. You'll see, contracts are up for renewal soon.) And I love the way that as Ian and the Doctor venture into the lair of the Earth soldiers, Hartnell rolls up his map and passes it to him wordlessly as a weapon. Russell's bemused facial expression is priceless – but he brandishes it ahead of him nonetheless.

So, that was The Sensorites then. It's a little hard to see what it was trying to do, really. It tries to be a tale about the evils of racial hatred, with the Sensorite Administrator and the Earth Commander both so caught up in their fears of the unlike, they are determined to exterminate the other. In that sense, this is really quite a moral little tale, and a clear development of the first Dalek story; it's a more complex and more realistic take upon war, where extremists on both sides are responsible for the sufferings of those caught in the middle. But for all that it has two and a half hours to play with, Peter R Newman's script barely finds time to bring out any of that depth – it prefers instead to give attention to the relationship between John and Carol, who by the story's end behave like pseudo-companions, and who by patronising the Sensorite culture are only a subtler form of the racism we see from those humans trying to poison the aliens.

I think The Sensorites' intention is honourable, but it's naively written. The Administrator doesn't even get an exit scene – he's been the most interesting character for the past four episodes, and he deserves *some* conclusion, whether it be a comeuppance or a redemption, but he's packed off into exile off screen as an afterthought. It's just another symptom of the way that the story pays lip service to respecting the Sensorites – to treating them as a civilised culture – but at the end of the day doesn't really feel they're worthy of our attention. We wave Maitland and his crew off back to Earth

– those are the characters we're meant to identify with, not these funny little aliens with the big feet.

T: Yay, Barbara is back! And without Maitland... perhaps she couldn't tell if he was comatose again or not (I found it hard at times, I have to say). Unfortunately, her arrival, for some reason, makes everyone talk in exposition.

It's worth bearing in mind that, for all my chiding of this tale for its childishness, the seeds were sown for the plot twist involving Bailey's group of aqueduct-skulking humans over a month ago! Nowadays, you'd never be allowed to expect an audience to remember that far back without copious use of flashbacks or Previously Ons. But it's interesting that all this death and disaster was caused by a petty little war, perpetrated by the equivalent of those Japanese soldiers you read about, hanging about the jungle, refusing to believe that they've surrendered.

And you're right – Bailey is truly stunning, aided by the sympathetic reactions that Hartnell and Russell feed him. Yes, this man is the enemy, and yes, he's committed a number of murders, but in some measure they actually feel sorry for the guy. And so do we, thanks to Bailey's fragile dignity. It's an established scientific fact that we don't make actors like him anymore.

For all the criticisms one can level against The Sensorites – and for all the logic-holes I've mentioned – I enjoyed watching this story, and feel that it's a bit of a neglected piece. It's also, if I'm remembering correctly, the only Doctor Who story where the principle director and the writer had died – or, at very least, were missing and presumed so – before the series had become a huge phenomenon. I wonder how they felt about what they'd done for a few weeks in a tiny studio.

January 19th

A Land of Fear
(The Reign of Terror episode one)

R: All the regular cast look so much more happy now that they know they're in another historical adventure, don't they? I must say, I feel the same. I think I'll be relieved when these Doctor Who people phase out all those odd monster and planet serials, and just stick to sending the TARDIS back in time. They'll be doing that soon, won't they, Toby?

The opening TARDIS scene is a joy, as William Russell and Jacqueline Hill flatter William Hartnell's ego to the point where the Doctor seems to positively purr with the attention. It's lovely – and quite a reversal of the sudden coldness the Doctor displayed at the end of the last episode, when he abruptly decided to put Ian off the Ship at its next stop. It felt like a rather crass way to shoehorn a cliffhanger in and generate some unnecessary tension, but here – especially as the Doctor thinks he's taken Ian and Barbara back home, and so isn't portrayed as just giving them the boot on some alien locale – it seems all rather like a charming bit of banter. There's something very touching about the way that the TARDIS crew all react to the possibility that their travels have come to an end, that they really have reached contemporary Earth... Susan hugs her teachers in a whirlwind, and then rushes from the room; the Doctor, most touchingly of all, tries to deny he's feeling anything at all, and becomes gruff and terse. And Ian and Barbara *try* so hard to be mature adults, and reason that they have to stop travelling some time – and then clearly feel such relief when they're able to persuade the Doctor out of the doors and into another adventure. I also love the way that as soon as the teachers discover a chest of eighteenth century clothes, they begin to dress up in appropriate garb. By now they know the drill, and can even have fun with it.

There's such a beautifully light tone to the episode... and it's deceptive, of course, because it's set to contrast with the horrors of the French Revolution. Stanley Myers' music, too, all ironic refrains from The Marseillaise, adds to the idea that this is going to be something of a romp – and, as Susan indicates, this is the Doctor's favourite period of history, so he'll just *love* it here. Then we meet a couple of characters with guns, but it's all right – within minutes they show themselves to be friendly. The standard structure of a Doctor Who story allows us to believe that the fugitives Rouvray and D'Argenson will be like Altos and Sabetha or Carol and Maitland – that they'll be the supporting cast for this story, and share the adventure with our regulars. So it's a genuine shock that they're killed so brutally, especially since Rouvray's brave stand in front of the peasants suggests he's going to be a heroic figure like Marco Polo, but he's cut down anyway. D'Argenson's death is even nastier, as he's perfunctorily shot off screen; he's treated like a coward who deserves nothing more than an afterthought.

Suddenly, the revolutionaries seem much more threatening, and it's telling that when Ian is told to shut up, he does. Ian, Barbara and Susan are imprisoned and led away by a mob while the Doctor is trapped inside a burning building – the fire so intense, it seems, that it's even allowed to burn away during the closing credits. And all those jaunty little pieces of music from Myers don't sound quite so funny any more – there's something strained about them, almost mocking.

T: Yes, Rob, the teachers do flatter Hartnell delightfully... but what really wins him round, I think, is Ian's offer of buying him a pint. And then we're told that the French Revolution is the Doctor's favourite period of Earth history! What a time to choose – I take it he loves watching scores of upper-class toffs getting their heads lopped off.

Nonetheless, this is a great start to an adventure which seems anything but safe. There is the odd comedic beat, but it usually comes from such unpleasant characters, and we're left in no doubt that there's a genuine air of menace and danger for everyone, everywhere. The Doctor's party really has arrived in a land of fear.

Dramatically, D'Argenson and Rouvray are the perfect characters to illustrate the backstory to the events that are about to unfold, and give us an insight into the societal makeup of this adventure's setting. The former is terrified as his whole family has been slaughtered, whilst the latter is a polite, honourable man with an air of class about him. We're told what they represent through character as much as exposition, which marks the return of a welcome complexity to the scripts. And then we see the soldiers that arrive to capture/execute the runaways – they're spectacularly uncouth, a rabble who are in it for the killing more than anything else. They're genuinely unsettling, and seem more *alien* than even the Sensorites.

Laidlaw Dalling makes a huge impact as Rouvray, although he's aided by Ken Lawrence (playing the soldiers' lieutenant), who tries to reaffirm his authority in the face of Rouvray's commanding confrontation. Rouvray only mucks it up when he gets a bit too hoity-toity for his own good (note to self: it's probably best not to call people pointing guns at you "peasants"), which helps us to understand both sides of the divide in this conflict. D'Argenson's death taking place off screen is a conscious decision that forces our imaginations to run riot: Heaven knows what that horrible mob did to him before administering that final bullet. It's blood curdling.

And do you know... I just remembered that I'd meant to keep a tally of how many times the TARDIS lands silently (as it does here), but didn't. (Curse this book, it's taking me away from valuable list-making duties!) I have an interest in such things because although we now take various aspects of the TARDIS as constants (the materialisation sound, the Ship's interior, etc), certain details haven't yet been decided upon, even as we enter the last story of the first season.

Guests of Madame Guillotine (The Reign of Terror episode two)

R: I absolutely love this episode. But there are some very odd things about it.

To kick off – it appears to be told in two entirely different time periods! We start the episode with Ian, Barbara and Susan arriving in Paris. Then they're sentenced before a judge. Then they're taken to the prison. Barbara attempts to reassure Susan that her grandfather will have escaped the burning house... and we then cut to the Doctor, who's only now recovering consciousness, with smoke still visible behind him! How long has he been out? Even assuming that the captives were taken to Paris by carriage – and the episode before suggests that isn't the case, that they were marched there in all discomfort – and even assuming they were sentenced and imprisoned at a breakneck speed, a couple of days must have passed at the very least. But the scenes with the Doctor *can't* be taking place in-between the scenes featuring his friends – the series has always told its stories in chronological order before (save for some clearly signposted flashbacks in the first episode), but now it's not even pretending to be sequential. Just in case you thought we should be turning a blind eye to it, the episode then makes it perfectly clear that the Doctor's journey to the city is a long and arduous one – as if to emphasise still further that his companions' journey there must have also taken a lot of time.

I don't for a moment think it's a mistake; it's a very deliberate way that the writer, Dennis Spooner (soon to be the series' script editor), is telling the story. And it suggests that he's not interested, like John Lucarotti was, in marking the passage of time in a logical and accurate way. On the contrary, he's going to go for the structure which best tells the story, and we accept it – even though it's pretty obvious we're leapfrogging backwards and forwards in time every instant that the episode cuts between the two plotlines. But what it does, very cleverly I think, is give a vague unease that you don't quite know as a viewer how you should be interpreting what's going on. Which is made even more obvious by the second odd thing:

... which is that, by the end of the second episode, we *still* haven't worked out who the important guest characters are yet. Very oddly, not a single person introduced in A Land of Fear makes it into this one, except for the little boy who rescued the Doctor from the burning building. (He gets a lovely scene too; Hartnell's rapport with the little tyke is terrific, and the salute they share absolutely gorgeous.) You watch this episode therefore waiting to identify who's going to be significant, who's going to be this adventure's Za, this adventure's Marco or Tlotoxl... and time and time again, you get completely wrongfooted. When a prisoner is thrown into Ian's cell, you think he might be the one – and then he promptly dies the moment he starts saying something interesting. The Doctor encounters a road-works overseer on his journey, and you think maybe *he* might be significant – but within a few minutes, he's been brained by a spade, and he's out of the story. By the episode's end, the most

screen time has been given to the jailer – and he hasn't even been given a name!

The cleverness of this is that it makes our heroes' plight seem all the more real; they can't even bond with anyone, and you really feel at the episode's end that Barbara and Susan really might be lost in the anonymity of history. In The Aztecs, they were under threat because they were divine and all-powerful – here, they're just caught up in someone else's story, and no-one even cares enough to ask them who they are. And it helps the spy story element of the adventure too; the government official Lemaitre only makes his first appearance some 40 minutes into the adventure, and the story has been structured in such a way that we're given very little reassurance we'll ever see him again, let alone that he might be the master-spy James Stirling that Ian has been told to watch out for. After all we never saw Rouvray or D'Argenson again, did we? In a story that has often been remembered as the first "comedy historical", it's notable how unsettling all this is.

And it means that whereas very little really *happens* this week – Barbara and Susan realise their attempts to escape from their cell are futile, Ian is stuck in *another* cell altogether, and the Doctor can't even get to the centre of the action without being waylaid by a bit of padding – that lack of forward momentum is very effective. It genuinely suggests that for once, our heroes are in a hopeless situation. Oh, and we get our first bit of location work! That's the Doctor, that is, walking down country lanes and across fields! ... okay, it's not *actually* William Hartnell. But Brian Proudfoot does a good job of imitating his walk, even if it does stray a bit too close to being jaunty.

T: Dennis Spooner's voice is still prevalent in the show today. The series may not have survived were it not for the Daleks, but I don't think it'd be as beloved without its wit, satire and fun – all of which Spooner here brings into play. Hartnell clearly enjoys these aspects too, spitting his hands before knocking out the boorish works-overseer (who, brilliantly, calls the Doctor "skinny"!). And when asked if he thinks he's clever, Hartnell gets the wonderfully Doctorish line, "Without any undue modesty, yes!"

Despite all the levity, however, much of this is grim stuff. The image of a guillotine – which at first looks like a photograph, then unfreezes as the blade sails down – evokes the opening titles of the Classic Serial's A Tale of Two Cities, and this cruel icon hangs forebodingly over the whole episode. The prison cells are dingy and dirty, and Lemaitre seems quite a threat as he pins Ian against the wall. Our heroic science teacher is having none of it, though, facing Lemaitre down and putting much ice into his addressing the man as "Citizen". Yes, it's true: Ian Chesterton is a latter-day Jack Bauer. With the passage of time, it's easy to mock Ian's middle-class earnestness and manners, but we've seen him a) fight Ixta to the death, b) leave Vasor to his fate, and c) here hold his nerve against the powerful man who has his life in his hands. Ian is as hard as nails were allowed to be at teatime in the 1960s.

Also appearing opposite Ian is Jeffry Wickham (playing the dying prisoner Webster), who is a charming man and a good actor. It's amazing how someone could appear so early in his own career and the show's history, and yet, whilst continuing to be gainfully employed for the next 45 years, somehow conspire never to appear in Doctor Who again. And did you notice, Rob, how Ian's cell is glossier and more impressive than Barbara and Susan's, by dint of it being recorded on film? Of course it's symptomatic of William Russell being the last of the regulars to take a holiday, and only appearing here in pre-recorded sequences.

The jailer keeping everyone locked-up, though, is a curious fellow... although Wang-Lo in Marco Polo put paid to the myth that the jailer is the show's first attempt at an out-and-out comic character, it's interesting to note how Jack Cunningham plays the part in a broad Northern Accent. We don't question for a second that this is a kind of shorthand to suggest he's a different kind of Frenchman to others we've seen – and yet, when the same trick is played with aliens, we don't buy it so easily. Which is funny in its own way, because this is a long-held technique (think about the number of Chekhov productions you've seen where actors adopt regional accents to signify what class of Russian they're playing). We'd have howled with laughter had the Fourth

Sensorite used a Geordie accent to show that he's a bit rougher than his posher fellows. It seems we can accept a Frenchman from, say, Bolton, but not a Voord from Hull.

And the jailer wants to give Barbara a seeing to as well – if this behaviour keeps up, she's going to get a complex. Perhaps if some of these guys unleashed their lust for her in front of Ian, he might start to notice her a bit more! But later on, it's rather reassuring how Barbara gets all practical and treats her escape attempt in the efficient and homely manner with which you might imagine she'd make jam.

Oh, isn't Hartnell really lovely in his scene with little Jean-Pierre? It's not just the salute he gives the boy, it's the way he turns back and gives a really grandfatherly, affectionate wave. One can imagine Hartnell being like that with any young fans he might have met – he'd have melted their hearts.

This story is good – it trots along really engagingly, and it has character. The blending of styles is such that you effectively get the sense that Doctor Who itself is undergoing some sort of revolution.

January 20th

A Change of Identity (The Reign of Terror episode three)

R: The resistance pop up out of nowhere into the story, and start swearing they won't rest until Barbara and Susan are safe! Barbara starts flirting with a rather dandy looking Frenchman! Ian manages to break out of the Conciergerie prison! The entire tone of the adventure changes in one fell swoop, and we're rather delightfully within the realm of romantic melodrama. It's the first time that a historical period has been used not to explore the society or the setting itself, but instead to feed off an entire familiar genre – in this case, inspired by The Scarlet Pimpernel by way of (as you mentioned) A Tale of Two Cities. The grimy realism of the last episode has vanished almost altogether – although you still get glimpses of something darker under the surface, most notably as the doomed Barbara and Susan are mocked by the watching peasant women. And if there's some sacrifice to be made – most obviously with the character of Susan, as the source material Spooner is feeding off makes her abnormally wet and spineless – it also ensures the story becomes decidedly more *fun*.

There are some lovely little bits of comedy here. Hartnell's in his element, of course, at his best whenever he's bullying some poor tailor or jailer into submission. But he knows too when he's been trumped – however good Billy is at bluster, his deadpan reaction to Lemaitre's insistent invitation that the incognito Doctor should accompany him to see Robespierre is perfect. I also love the joke that the Doctor goes to all the trouble of putting on a disguise to effect a rescue of his friends from prison – only to find, of course, this adventure series being what it is, that the girls and Ian have already escaped... separately!

Then there's the bemused expression on the rebel Jean Renan's face, as it dawns on him that although *he* thinks he's taking part in some derring-do melodrama, Barbara and the dishy rebel Leon Colbert are switching genre right under his nose, and going for something much less boy's own stuff. And I also like the lovely cross fade from Colbert elegantly seducing Barbara over a glass of wine, to the jailer guzzling at his bottle.

T: John Barrard gets much mileage out of playing the weasely shopkeeper from whom the Doctor acquires his "regional officer" uniform, although I question the likelihood that the tailor would be selling sashes that denote such a high rank. Surely, such things would be issued when you were appointed to your lofty post? It's not like I can nip into a shop and get some clothes that will grant me entrance to Number 11 Downing Street.

It's all right though, because it gives us another chance to see Hartnell manipulate a conniving prole, and he's clearly having great fun with Spooner's script. And there's a lovely moment where he quite openly admits to having no money and Barrard instinctively snatches his coat back! The feathered hat that the Doctor eventually acquires is wonderful – it's so ludicrous, I love it. And Hartnell plays against it in a self-assured and cocky manner that's priceless; he's clearly in his element, bluffing his way haughtily and running rings around the stupid jailer. Cunningham plays

the part as an obsequious fool – as someone who is convinced of his own brilliance and dispenses his addled wisdom in such a way that you could imagine Johnny Vegas playing the role today. The Doctor, of course, uses his intellect and understanding to exploit the shortcomings of this arrogant ninny so effectively, we've no reason to doubt that the Doctor will prevail... until Lemaitre appears, and then we get worried.

I can't help but notice the odd lapse in logic: Jules says that everyone involved in his resistance cell should use Christian names only, but then refers to his two dead mates as D'Argenson and Rouvray. No matter – everyone in the serious part of the story is doing their turn with appropriate gravitas. I'm delighted when a favourite of mine, Edward Brayshaw, strides in as Leon Colbert. He has such presence, being handsome, dashing and full of virility – sad, then, that he's now chiefly remembered as the bloke who played Harold Meaker on *Rentaghost*.

And I have an odd confession to make... I've seen every existing Doctor Who episode countless times, and I have a number of recons. But because the majority of this story's episodes exist, and I know what happens in the tale, I've never quite got around to acquiring the soundtracks to the missing episodes four and five. Until now. So yes, the next two instalments will be particularly interesting for me, as they're the only two episodes in the entire history of Doctor Who that I've *never* experienced. And I call myself a fan!

The Tyrant of France
(The Reign of Terror episode four)

R: This clearly sees the Doctor's meeting with Robespierre at its centrepiece – and that's a pity for two reasons. First, because it happens at the top of the episode, the remaining 20 minutes of Barbara fussing around a feverish Susan are the definition of anticlimax in comparison. And second... because, well, it's really not very good. Dennis Spooner is at his very best when he's creating colourful characters of his own: the jailer, the shopkeeper, the road works overseer, all without names, but all little cameo gems. You can see *why* he had to introduce Robespierre sooner or later; it's a mark of these early historical adventures that the TARDIS crew had to interact with schoolboy history, and at this stage it'd seem criminally wasteful if the Doctor didn't face off with someone extremely famous sooner or later.

But it's very awkward. You can sense that Spooner would love to have the Doctor rip into Robespierre, attack the regime of terror he'd created. But he can't – because just as The Aztecs demonstrated that you can't interfere with history, so this demonstrates that a writer can't interfere with historical icons. There's a respect that is shown to Robespierre here – not by the Doctor per se, but by the production team, who can't challenge a factual monster here in the way they could a Tegana or a Tlotoxl. The conversation between the Doctor and Robespierre is toothless and undramatic, and it's such a contrast to the vigour we've seen in Spooner's writing in the previous episodes that it pulls us up short.

I believe, though, that what Dennis Spooner is doing in The Reign of Terror is creating the *real* template for the structure of what Doctor Who will become. He's the first writer really to get that balance between action adventure and comedy and – let's face it – excessive padding that'll become a staple of the show. He pitches lower than a Lucarotti, but the framework that Marco Polo and The Aztecs offered wasn't really sustainable – the Doctor and his friends were reduced to sightseers in spite of their best endeavours to interfere. The Lucarotti historical *depends* upon famous real-life characters to give the setting the thorough educational grounding that he's aiming for. The inclusion of Robespierre here is a valuable lesson for the Doctor Who producers – it demonstrates exactly *why* you don't want these people from the past popping up and getting in the way of the action. There'll be a few more attempts, of course, to get this right – with The Crusade being a notable example – but from this point on they'll be sidelined, the story will be more important than the historical figures who inspired it. You may pop back into the past from time to time, but if you go to visit Leonardo da Vinci, he'll be unavailable, and if you bump into King John, he'll turn out to be an android. If you want Renaissance Italy or Victorian London, you'll use the archetypes, not real people. After The Gunfighters, we'll

never again see a real-life historical figure on Doctor Who for 19 years, not until George Stephenson pops up rather awkwardly in The Mark of the Rani. And although this might seem like something's been lost, I think actually the reverse is true: the Doctor is too overpowering a character to pay homage to someone more famous than he is. The reason the encounter between the Doctor and Robespierre is such so dissatisfying is because, by the end of Season One, this has clearly become Hartnell's show, and the viewer should be paying him more attention than someone they've read about at school. (It's only with Russell T Davies that that all changes, and the celebrity historical comes back with a vengeance! But more of that later. Much, much later.)

So although I don't think this is a very good episode on its own terms, I think it's invaluable for what it represents. Modern Doctor Who sprouts from this. And even more from next week's episode...

T: Well, you can tell we're in France, because everyone's drinking. Susan has a brandy, and Colbert's knocking back the wine...

I agree with you about the Robespierre meeting – it doesn't really advance the plot apart from giving Lemaitre another reason to keep the Doctor hanging around. In fact, the only really interesting thing that I can see about this episode is Ronald Pickup appearing as the duplicitous physician who treats Susan. How many actors cropped up in minor parts early in Doctor Who before disappearing completely, their CV tailing off as other less-precarious ways of earning a living took away the lure of greasepaint and stardust? Loads, I should imagine (here I'm thinking in particular of Jonathan Crane, whose sole acting credit on IMDb is playing Kristas in The Daleks). But Pickup has never stopped working, and one has to wonder if he hates Doctor Who because, despite all of his leading roles on TV and in classics at all of our finest theatrical institutions, he probably gets more mail about a week's work he did four decades ago (and which doesn't even exist on video, or even as telesnaps!) than he does about the rest of his accomplished career together.

And speaking of people with prolific careers... it's about this point that I think your previous comments on Stanley Myers' music were a tad generous. You're very good, Rob, at being able to turn something a bit naff into a metatextual piece of genius – but to a layman like me, it sounds like Myers has been briefed to score a kids' show set during The French Revolution, and produced a childish, rompy piece of fluff that suggests he's not really taking it that seriously. It might be telling he was never asked back to the series – and typically, went on to have perhaps the most illustrious career of any Doctor Who composer ever! This is the same Stanley Myers, after all, who consistently found work until his death in 1993, wrote the theme to The Deer Hunter and scored such works as Moonlighting (the Jeremy Irons film, that is, not the Bruce Willis/Cybill Shepherd dramady).

One last point: it's sometimes cited as a scripting cock-up that the dying Webster mentioned "Le Chien Gris" – a pub that Jules and Jean frequent – when he should have said the drinking establishment "The Sinking Ship" instead. So far, though, this makes sense: Webster wanted Ian to go to Le Chien Gris and hopefully find the spy James Stirling, and then go to The Sinking Ship, where... well, that can wait until episode six. It's just worth noting that for now, that part of the script is watertight, and it only, er, springs a leak when we're forced to presume that Webster mentioned The Sinking Ship off camera.

January 21st

A Bargain of Necessity
(The Reign of Terror episode five)

R: There's a really important scene in this episode, and if it only existed in the archives, I think it'd have much more attention. But it's not, so it doesn't. It's the argument between Barbara and Ian about the death of Colbert. There's not been an awful lot of anger in this story, and all the death and treachery has been played mainly on the level of melodrama or black comedy. But Jacqueline Hill has a wonderful way with fury, and she tears into Ian, reminding him that while Colbert betrayed them, he was a patriot to his side. In this way,

she insists that Ian look at history from a different perspective.

But it's Ian's reaction that is so telling – the travellers, he insists, are *involved* now; they're no longer cool onlookers to history, they're actually part of it. And it's the pivotal point at which Doctor Who changes. Ian tells Barbara he could just as easily have fired the gun that killed Colbert – they can no longer afford to be as dispassionate as they have, in retrospect, been for most of this season; their first instinct can no longer be just to run back to the TARDIS the moment there's trouble, and hang the consequences. They have responsibilities to the people who befriend them, who take risks for them, and who can't *ever* have Barbara's perspective that they're all figures in history and can be part of an academic debate. It blows a wind through the story, and demonstrates exactly what Spooner sees the future of Doctor Who as being – a series that is a lot more immediate than it has been before. Once upon a time, Barbara was judging history and even trying to alter history to the side she preferred; hearing her talk about the *good* that the revolutionaries have done – and their modern-day legacy – within the very house of the resistance group that saved their lives from those very same revolutionaries is tactless at best. It's also clearly shows how looking at history from the outside-in even sounds faintly ridiculous. All the historical theorising in the world counts as nothing beside real emotional ties.

And what's great is that although Ian's argument carries (sort of – it's certainly the stance that the series from this point on adopts), Spooner has strengthened Barbara's argument with the way he has written Colbert. The interrogation scene between him and Ian is fascinating – Colbert all but *pleads* with Ian for information, refusing to see himself as a villain, using the word "traitor" only in inverted commas, clearly believing he's the hero in this story. Obviously, our sympathies are meant to remain with the resistance – Renan's rather colourless speech in which he's making a stand against anarchy makes that very clear – but it's still refreshing to have that ambiguity here.

T: You've rightly highlighted the most important scene. History tells us that the French Resistance members are the good guys, but – as Ian points out – when time-travel places you thick of it, it's difficult to be quite so objective. Jules and company are only the "goodies" because our heroes were mistaken for the same kind of people they automatically try to rescue. The Doctor himself has toppled the decadent and powerful often enough (though, to be fair, never with something as cruel as the guillotine). But it's easy for us to see people from the past as naive because they've not discovered electricity or Kellogg's Pop Tarts, and yet here it's a character from a supposedly more sophisticated time (Barbara, one of the audience identification figures) who comes across as green by trying to intellectualise their situation.

Ian has indeed learned from Marco Polo, and his candour does him credit. We should pity poor Colbert, though – he's the first Frenchman to learn that time travel exists, and he's gunned down about five minutes later. And note how Ian tells Barbara he'd have killed Colbert himself, and that he got what he deserved. I keep telling you, he's Jack Bauer! Next, he'll be torturing people in the name of democracy.

No, this isn't as successful as Lucarotti's work – it's a template that is far more sustainable. If not for this paradigm shift, Doctor Who might have ended up as the equivalent of a show about football, but in which we only spend time with the people watching the match.

Prisoners of the Conciergerie
(The Reign of Terror episode six)

R: This is a peculiar episode, and no mistake. It heads off in a completely different direction, into the area of unfolding history. Which means that one of the big showpieces of the episode involves watching one historical figure we've never seen before engaged in political discussion with *another* historical figure we've never seen before. It reduces our heroes to spectators again, and more pointedly than they've ever been before – with Ian and Barbara watching the Napoleon meeting through a spyhole, there's not even the pre-

tence they're still part of the action. Rather delightfully, though, the Doctor seems to take issue with all of this – he wanders off whenever Lemaitre is talking exposition, and has to be summoned back with a scowl.

The best moments, again, are those involving Hartnell – his final scene with Jack Cunningham's jailer is beautifully played, with the Doctor so wrapping him around his finger, it makes the little drunk's head spin. With all these reversals of who's in power – how one person can represent the state one day and be a traitor the next – it's hardly surprising that the jailer can't keep up with whether he's meant to lock Hartnell up or be locked up *by* him. I did the French Revolution as a special subject for A-level, studying it in day-to-day detail, and I couldn't understand most of what was going on with an index at the back!

It also occurs to me that while William Russell is a very good actor, Ian Chesterton really isn't. He wasn't a good drunk in Marco Polo, and he doesn't make a very good country bumpkin here. You should ease off on the amateur dramatics, mate – you're going to get yourself killed if you carry on like that.

And that's it! The very first season of Doctor Who over. What a milestone! I'm very proud of myself. I just went downstairs and told Janie. She just stared at me, and asked me if I'd really spent the best part of an *entire month* on just *one single year* of the series. Weren't there forty-bloody-five of the things? How long was this going to take? And I didn't quite know what to say, really. So she and the cat exchanged looks, both sighed, and together trotted into the kitchen for a cup of coffee.

T: We're back to that football match analogy again, because, as you say, the regulars are simply watching the action rather than participating in it. Which is doubly odd since, if they know their history of this era, why do they *need* to dress up as yokels to identify who is involved in this historic meeting that will lead to Napoleon's rise to power? Couldn't they just have saved some hassle by telling Jules and Stirling that they had it on good authority that Napoleon was being groomed for office? Sod Ian's poor acting, though – Jacqueline Hill has a rare off-day by being the only person in this story to put on a cod French accent. If this was a David Tennant story, you can bet that Barbara would have been told, "No, no... don't do that...", but nobody here seems to have instructed her to stop sounding silly. I love, though, the way that Napoleon comes to the pub incognito... but dressed as Napoleon! He's almost begging for Barbara to offer him a drink so he can say "not tonight, Josephine..."

We open this episode, though, with the regulars standing around, for what seems like an age, as the title caption appears. Those involved cope with this in different ways: the regulars are used to this and stand firm, but James Cairncross (as Lemaitre) elects to nod sagely, whilst poor old Donald Morley (as Jules) looks uneasy and then cracks, looking straight at the camera as if asking for permission to start acting again! Shortly thereafter, the Doctor gets very impatient, coming across as a stand-offish observer. History can jolly well take its course, but he just wants to retrieve Susan – who has, as it happens, recovered from her fever and illness very quickly. (They needn't have given Ronald Pickup his TV debut as the physician after all, it seems; the travellers could probably have romped home two episodes earlier.) And as Robespierre here becomes a victim of the mob rule he perpetrated, we get to see that comic everyman, the jailer, switch sides once again as it suits him – for all his stupidity, he has a survival instinct which outweighs any moral conviction. Oh, This common body/ Like to a vagabond flag upon the stream/ Goes to and back, lackeying the varying tide/ To rot itself with motion.

This story – and the entire season – comes to a close, though, with the Doctor and Ian's echoing voices over a starscape, as if the travellers have just rounded off something momentous, and are off to find their destiny amongst the stars. Whereas the new series' sense of self-awareness could become arch at times, here it's surprisingly pleasant. The Doctor, Ian, Barbara and Susan have been about their travels together for a year (and we've chomped through them all in less than a month), and it's been quite an achievement. Doctor Who has taken its first steps towards becoming something that's truly remarkable – it's already a strong series, with a lot of the hallmarks that make it stand out even today, and the series' flexibility will make it capable of almost infi-

nite form in future (even if nobody involved in making the programme yet realises just *how* diverse a format they're dealing with – at present, doing the show without William Hartnell was surely unthinkable).

Roll on Season Two – see you in four weeks! (Well, all right... tomorrow.)

January 22nd

Planet of Giants (episode one)

R: Imagine it – Doctor Who has been off the air for ages! (Or a month and a half, anyway. They had it easy in those days.) And the audience knows the formula by now – there are the historical adventures, and there are spacey ones. The episode title reveals that the story is set on a "planet of giants", and from that point on, you know to expect the latter – with lots of monsters, and maybe some dashings of bad science. The twist is brilliantly handled; the Doctor and his crew do what they always do, they set off to explore this alien world separately – Ian even rolls his eyes in exasperation to see that they're all conforming to the cliché. And then, after finding strange creatures of unearthly size, they stumble upon enormous lettering telling them "Made in Norwich". (That's what's especially funny about it – Norwich is such a decidedly anticlimactic place in which to find that *anything* is made.) The reveal that they've made it back to modern-day Earth – but are now wandering around a garden at the size of an inch – is one of the best jokes that Doctor Who has yet played. There's something very appropriate about the fact that after so many bizarre adventures on planets with petrified trees and acid seas, our heroes now find themselves exploring *crazy paving*.

And Hartnell is so impressive in that opening scene. He plays his first few lines in as deliberately neutral a tone as possible, so that he can best contrast it with his angry outburst when he believes the TARDIS is in danger, and then his winsomely charming self when he apologies to Barbara straight afterwards. It's very skilfully done; he now understands all the contradictions of the Doctor's character, and effortlessly plays them off each other to maximum effect. He's never been as much in control.

It's childish of me, I know, but I also love this episode for the way that Frank Crawshaw plays the hapless Farrow. Bless Crawshaw's heart, he whistles the letter "s" every time he uses it, and yet he's stuck with having to discuss "insecticide DN6" and to say things like "This isn't science, this is business." It somehow makes this poor old fool, who seems to be almost *inviting* some unscrupulous businessman to shoot him dead, all the more real and sympathetic. He's not just a bureaucrat from the ministry, he's a bureaucrat who has a speech impediment.

T: Now that we've become accustomed to the regulars and guest-cast facing all manner of outlandish forms of jeopardy, Forester pulling his snout little gun on Farrow seems quite odd. A slick-haired, besuited moneyman drawing a pistol feels like it'd be more at home in Dragnet than on Doctor Who at this point in its history. (And how fortunate for Forester's fiendish plans that he brought a gun to his meeting with a man from the ministry – foresight is essential in business matters.)

Ian has undergone something of a transformation – after the clueless outburst "What do you mean 'close the [TARDIS] doors'?" (the ways one can interpret that statement are very few, Chesterton), he suddenly gets all groovy when the TARDIS lands, telling his mates to "sing out" if anything happens, and describing a cadaver as "stiff as a poker". He's pretty hip this teacher – I can imagine him shaking his booty at the school disco to show that he's down wid da kids. The other regulars are on form though: Hartnell is quite amusingly detached in response to Susan's hysteria about Ian being in the matchbox, and is curiously dismissive when he says, "someone picked [the matchbox] up, I suppose..." And when the Doctor snaps at Barbara as she helps him down from his peek at the house, Jacqueline Hill gives a very believable and naturalistically exasperated response.

But of course, the most remarkable thing about this episode is the design work. As the camera pans up the garden path and see the house, the viewer assumes it must be a very good model – until Farrow is seen sitting in front of the full building later on. It's quite brilliantly rendered, and doesn't look like it's studio-bound at all.

Dangerous Journey (Planet of Giants episode two)

R: When I first saw this as a cynical teenage fan, I found the idea of Barbara's refusal to tell anyone she'd been infected by insecticide rather silly, and very contrived. I now think I was only half-right; yes, it is a bit contrived, but it seems to me a wonderfully *human* reaction of embarrassment and denial, and the ever-wonderful Jacqueline Hill (my God, why isn't she praised more often; she's fantastic!) sells it perfectly. It's a great scene anyway; Ian is so distracted by giant litmus paper that he absently hands Barbara a handkerchief to wipe stickiness from her hands, whilst telling her in the same breath that the grains of wheat he's left her with are covered in deadly poison! The way he so dispassionately shrugs off her cheery attempts to get him to contemplate other possibilities for why the wheat is glistening, and the way he reacts with bemusement when Barbara hopes to find in the briefcase something that will better explain the DN6 she now knows is threatening her life, sounds almost callous.

And what about the giant housefly?! It's one of the most effective Doctor Who monsters *ever*. It's disgusting; it *quivers*. It's little wonder that Barbara is so transfixed by it. This entire story really ought to look rubbish, the demands on the design team beyond any reasonable expectation for what we've come to expect on their budget. If this story were missing from the archives, we'd all assume it looked embarrassing. But when it exists for all to see, the design is *so* good, but so deliberately functional, we utterly take it for granted. Those sequences with the Doctor and Susan resting against the plug in the sink, or Ian trying to open the latch on a briefcase, are frankly extraordinary. Raymond Cusick has done an amazing job in designing this story – forget his work on the Daleks (and anyway, they're all dead now, aren't they, who'll remember them?).

This is, in so many ways, the most atypical of Doctor Who stories – the only one in which the regulars never interact with any of the supporting cast, for starters. But it's also the introduction of a theme that serves as a series staple: the way that the mundane can be turned into something deadly. The camera follows the briefcase from the perspective of the "giants", but we're invited to imagine what's happening to Ian and Barbara inside; the final image focuses upon the water running out of a sink, in what on the surface must be the most banal cliffhanger ever transmitted. Doctor Who is at its best when it wants the audience to look for threats in the most innocent of places – it's from this that we lead to shop-window dummies coming to life, and the mythical Yeti sitting on a loo in Tooting Bec.

T: You do have to pity Ray Cusick – he had to achieve all these technically complex designs, and was probably rather galled when he discovered that pretty much the only pre-filming allowed was for a cat! "Yes, Ray, we know you have to realise a fully functioning giant fly, but you'll have to do that as live because little Tiddles refuses to attend rehearsals." I still have no clue, actually, how that fly was done. It's *that* good, and so unshowy that it's been unfairly neglected over the years; it has to be one of the best special effects in the programme's history. And it's not just the *scale* that makes the sets look impressive, it's the textures given to each object to ensure close-up accuracy, to the degree that they look impressive even in a cleaned-up print on a large, modern TV with good definition. Design-wise, this is a gigantic achievement.

The environmental catastrophe threatened by DN6, interestingly enough, has become a timeless concern: champions of the Pertwee era should herald this as a worthy forebear of that period of the programme, and Forester is a selfish moneyman who'd be right at home as the central protagonist in a Russell T Davies script. On the other hand, Smithers – the scientist who created DN6 – believes that this insecticide will boost food production and help starving people all over the world, so he aids and abets the criminal Forester to achieve what he thinks are noble ends.

And I can't help but think that Alan Tilvern, playing Forester, is the sort of actor who could well have cropped up in Doctor Who more often – he has a suave villainy which suggests

he could've stepped in had Phillip Madoc ever been unavailable. (Appropriately then, it was while filling in for someone else that Tilvern got his best notices – he took over from a stage-frighted Ian Holm at the last minute in the West End run of The Iceman Cometh.) And "Forester" is such a good, ironic name – an appropriately verdant moniker that serves as a sweet juxtaposition, considering how little the man cares for the environment. Perhaps his fellow businessmen are named "Woods", "Spring" and (cough) "Bush".

January 23rd

Crisis
(Planet of Giants episode three)

R: There's no clearer indication of the way the series has changed in the space of a year than this. In Season One, our heroes would have scuttled back to the safety of the TARDIS the first moment they could. And if that was ever a justifiable course of action, it surely would be in this story: Barbara is dying from an incredibly powerful insecticide and can only survive if returned to her own size, and the rest of the crew have no way, given their shrunken state, of communicating with the normal world. (They've mentioned this fact a lot over the last two episodes, but here seem to have forgotten about it, so they even try to make a phone call to the police.) The thing is, even though they're powerless to bring a murderer to justice, or to stop the licence for a bug-killing poison, they still insist upon behaving as selflessly as possible, unable to leave in the Ship until they're as certain as can be that they've saved the world.

And of course, they do no such thing. The Doctor delightedly tells his friends that before they left the laboratory, a policeman had come to arrest Forester and Smithers (how would he have been able to see that?), and supposes that's a result of their intervention. In fact, Forester has been brought to justice by a nosey switchboard operator, and the fact that he rather stupidly thought he could imitate Farrow on the telephone just by wrapping the Universal Voice Changer (i.e., a handkerchief) around the receiver. He should have remembered that Farrow whistled his "s"s, that might have helped. The last season entailed a whole run of stories in which the Doctor didn't particularly *want* to help anybody – and yet somehow managed to change entire lives in the process. And in this episode, the Doctor and friends decide they *will* help, but do nothing of any consequence whatsoever, and yet at the story's end somehow think they've had an impact. Intentional or not – and I sadly suspect it isn't – I think there's a delightful irony to this. From this point on, with the TARDIS crew actively taking a heroic stance and battling evil where they can, the Doctor will become an ever-more dominant force. Look, next week he's even going to be given an arch-enemy. But here, for the very last time, he's a deluded old man who thinks he's more important than he really is.

T: What beguiles me most about this episode is the fact that, of course, it's two episodes hacked together into just one. This must have been a monumental decision – no episode made since has been deemed unsuitable for broadcast. The show has always gone on, even if a silly pantomime lizard with wet paint has reared its lolloping head. But here, Verity Lambert judged that this story was so deathly dull that action had to be taken for the ultimate good of the show. The remounts of the pilot and The Dead Planet were a case of trying to get it right on the second try (the latter on purely technical grounds), but this is a bit different – it took great skill to take fifty minutes of material, cut them *in half* and still have the coherent instalment we're shown here. And who knows? Even though the longueurs were probably removed for good reason, it means that some never-before-seen William Hartnell Doctor Who could, for all anyone knows, be languishing unnoticed in a film can somewhere.

I've enjoyed this story more than I thought I would, because if you're watching the show in broadcast order, there's plenty that seems new here. In particular, two frequently seen names make their way into the credits for the first time: the fantastic Douglas Camfield gets to sit in the director's chair, though Dudley Simpson's debut doesn't so much involve music as it does random jaunty noises. But I also note the

appearance of Fred Ferris, playing the husband of the telephone operator. He was a stand-up comedian, but an actor too – a useful riposte for anyone who bemoaned the casting in future of Ken Dodd, Peter Kay and Lee Evans (and, indeed, Ian Boldsworth, Thomas Nelstrop and Bernard Padden – but most fans don't moan about *them* because they're unaware that they're comics).

I do wish that the script for Planet of Giants had been as memorable as the set-design, but if the programme-makers could only have one and not the other, they got it the right way around. The selling point here is that everything is *large*, and the production team admirably rises to the task of making it seem very real. But it's also worth noting that Planet of Giants was pitched as the very first Doctor Who story of all, and that by the time it's finally shown as part of Season Two, there's already a feeling that the programme has moved beyond such gimmickry, and deserves (not to mention desires) a little more on which to hang a story. Which will be good for us, good for those making the show, and good for Doctor Who itself.

World's End (The Dalek Invasion of Earth episode one)

R: It's very jarring to see the regular cast actually walking around *on location*. We've got so used by now to seeing what the house style of Doctor Who can be, in all its studio-bound glory, that to see it played outside makes it suddenly look so much more epic, somehow. What I love about this episode is that, for the very first time, there's a self-conscious anticipation about the series – it *knows* that this is a big story. And the audience at home know too; the Daleks are back, the adventure has been well publicised – for the first time, the viewers know more about what's waiting around the corner than the characters do. It's a subtle difference in the way the episode is told, and a very stylish one. There's an atmosphere to this that is grimmer and thicker than anything we've yet seen on Doctor Who, and it really feels like a different programme – the children's series has grown up. The lack of a reprise subtly suggests that this is a different thing altogether, and that a clean break has been made. And rather than opening with Hartnell pondering over a broken scanner in the TARDIS, instead we're presented with a grotesque image of a man screaming out like an animal and all too eagerly committing suicide, leaving only a sign in the background telling us that it's forbidden to dump bodies in the river. It's astonishing they got away with it; Doctor Who has been experimenting with shifts in style ever since it started, but never quite as abruptly as this. It's brave and exhilarating and more than a little unnerving.

It stands a comparison with the other opening episodes we've seen from Terry Nation so far. Once more, it's an exercise in the slow burn – the characters explore their surroundings for 25 minutes, and marvel at what they find. But this time, instead of remarkable bits of fantasy to goggle at, they find a London so dead that Ian wants to run away without further investigation. It's the drab and ordinary turned into something sick and poisonous. Every time a Nation story opens, the cast find a dead body – in The Dead Planet, it was of a fossilised animal; in The Sea of Death, it was little more than an empty wetsuit. Here, it's a strange parody of a man hidden amongst the rubbish with a knife protruding from his back. Any regular viewer watching this will have recognised the structure of what was going on – and also that it was being presented in a starker, realer way than ever before.

And then, just as the episode can test that viewer's patience no longer, at last a Dalek appears. It hasn't even emerged from the water before the end credits roll. Almost tauntingly, the screen reads: "*Next* Episode: The Daleks."

T: It really does start well, with that horrible, grisly self-inflicted death. But then – as if to prove that director Richard Martin is only at his best when using film – we cut to a TARDIS scene where the framing is cack-handedly sloppy, and the camerawork poor. On some occasions, the character we're supposed to be looking at (say, the Doctor) disappears from shot altogether. It's an ugly piece of work, although it does at least emphasise how good the outside images are. At the episode's climax, the iconic image of the Dalek rising from the Thames isn't helped by the jarring cut from

studio to film – it looks curiously detached from events occurring in what's supposedly the same scene and location, and the action doesn't flow at all seamlessly. That said, it's the climax to a grim, moody episode; plague is mentioned, floating bodies are seen, London has been desolated. You can see why Terry Nation liked an apocalypse; it really helps to drench everything in a morbid atmosphere.

William Russell keeps getting the job of telling the audience how serious the situation is, and he does it well. He has a different kind of authority to Hartnell, but an equally important one. "Intelligent", the Doctor tells Ian approvingly – the old man's starting to respect the schoolteachers. And just as he despaired that they all split up in the previous story, Ian now berates the absent girls for their tendency to wander off (and into danger). He's aware of what the clichés are.

I also really like the bit where Ian falls though the door-leading-to-nowhere – stunt-arranger Peter Diamond often gets overlooked because people interested in such things tend to focus on the work Havoc did on 70s Who, but Diamond was a damn good stuntman who later choreographed one of the best sword-fights in cinema ever (for The Princess Bride) and worked on a number of motion pictures, Star Wars included.

Oh, and a special mention should go to Susan spraining her ankle – something cited as a cliché of Doctor Who, but which doesn't actually happen very often. I wonder if Carole Ann Ford was revelling in the knowledge that she's been made to trip over clumsily for the very last time, not realising that she'll have to do it again, 19 years down the road, in The Five Doctors. (If only the Doctor had installed a Wii in the TARDIS, so she could have sorted out her co-ordination!)

Had I seen the first broadcast of this as a kid, I'd have been really looking forward to the return of the Daleks – and been pissed off when the credits rolled and promised them *next* week. I'm sure I would have cursed the Radio Times and its cover-spoilers (that revealed the creature that appears in the cliff-hanger) – thank goodness that sort of thing doesn't happen any more.

January 24th

The Daleks
(The Dalek Invasion
of Earth episode two)

R: We've never had a story on this scale before – and in a way, we never will again. As we get ever further into Doctor Who (and, tellingly, ever further away from the Second World War and a genuine fear of Nazi occupation), alien invasions are the sort of everyday thing that the Doctor *prevents* from happening. On the odd occasion when there's a tale that tries something similar – to show an Earth already subjugated by alien aggressors – it'll be as in Day of the Daleks, something that can be handily rewritten from history owing to some helpful time paradox. But there's nothing so reassuring in this story – Doctor Who is here doing an adventure in which (technically) contemporary Earth is destroyed. (I know that this adventure is set in the twenty-second century, but that's just a storytelling necessity – in every part of the design, in every part of the plotting, there's no attempt to suggest that what all this represents is anything more than the world that the TV viewers intimately know being wiped out. Terry Nation likes this sort of modern doomsday thing – if he'd written Survivors as a Doctor Who adventure, he'd have had to knock it into a so-called "twenty-second century" too.)

The ambition of this instalment is tremendous, which makes its awkward moments and clumsy beats forgiveable. Nation is not the most elegant of writers, but it's actually that very bluntness of his which makes this episode so strong. No, there's nothing especially subtle about the scenes of Dalek propaganda over the radio, or the way they're leading prisoners into work camps – but there's a satirical *anger* to it all that would make subtlety look lily-livered. "Daleks offer you life," indeed. The epic nature of what Nation is attempting here all but dwarfs the regular cast. Never before have the TARDIS crew been so companion clichéd – Susan twists her ankle, Barbara busies herself with the cooking, Ian's only on hand to ask questions and look confused. But with the scale of Doctor Who changed, it's apt that only the Doctor is now big enough a character that he remains imposing and unaffected; it's the Doctor who gets to give the big speech about the futility of the Daleks' victory, it's the Doctor who gets to shine as a genius. The brilliance of this episode is that it finally accomplishes what the last few stories have been edging towards – it turns the Doctor into the star. This is the moment he gets defined.

And can I just say how much I love the Robomen too? They might look like a bunch of extras with metal helmets, but, actually, that's the point. No snug fitting black PVC costumes as is in the Aaru film, just a group of captured prisoners automated in whatever rags they happened to be wearing at the time. The body horror that's suggested by this – that they're really the walking dead, with all identity and hope removed – anticipates the Cybermen two years early.

T: You have to wonder if Terry Nation ever set foot in a BBC studio, because he's demanding a *hell* of a lot from the production team. (For instance, I've just realised that the brilliant warehouse set in World's End was a one-week wonder, never to make an appearance in the five remaining episodes.) So it's perhaps understandable that some of the action here is pretty messy, and the slightly bewildering way that the cliffhanger is shot suggests either that the camera has magically moved through a wall, or that the Dalek Robo-machine – which the baddies start to lower onto the Doctor – is situated on a bench in the lobby of their spaceship.

(Okay, I have to admit it... I'm *trying* to cut Richard Martin some slack here, given the requirements for this production, but I worry that I'm only half-succeeding. To his credit, there's a curious illustrative scene that takes place outside the Dalek saucer, in which a pretty blonde girl waits to get karate chopped by a Roboman – it's an offbeat choice, directorially, but it works. But then we get the rather stupid way the Supreme Dalek *clears his throat* before making an announcement, which just makes me want to give Martin a hard slap.)

But, most importantly for this episode, Nation has worked out what kids want – it's as if he wrote this story from a checklist of things that would seem cool or intriguing to an 11 year old, then found a way to bung them in.

Examples so far include a man with a Germanic name in a wheelchair, zombies with whips and a bloke chucking himself into a river. At times, though, this proves interesting for the adults as well – as you say, the concept of the Robomen is indeed horrific, and David Campbell's claim that they smash their heads against walls or jump off buildings when they malfunction is deeply unpleasant stuff.

All right, so this looks a bit slapdash in places, but there is lots going on, and so I'm eager to see the next episode...

Day of Reckoning (The Dalek Invasion of Earth episode three)

R: In the first season, the attack upon the Dalek city by the Thals was more than a little perfunctory, but they won through anyway; the moral seemed to be that so long as you confronted your demons, you could beat them. Here we have a restaging of that attack, this time on the spacecraft standing on the heliport: it's much more dramatic, and it's *much* better directed. The human resistance put lots of welly into it – but it's a complete and utter disaster for them. There's never been a better demonstration of just how powerful the Daleks are, nor how brutal or callous. There's that poor extra who gets blasted into negative just as he thinks he's reached the safety of a trap-door; there's Baker, who only has to say goodbye to the Doctor and wish him luck before unluckily running into a Dalek patrol and being exterminated without even a farewell speech. But my favourite of all is the death that we hear off-camera – that of a panicked man pleading for his life and being killed regardless, the horror of it all being played out on Susan and David's faces as they hide, unable to help.

What a very brutal episode this is – there's the realisation that the Roboman that Ian confronts is none other than the same chap who shared a cell (and lots of exposition) with him only the week before. Then, more horrifyingly, there's the very dispassionate way that after the Roboman is electrocuted, Ian tips his corpse down a service duct without sparing him sympathy. Or the cruelty of the scene in which the wheelchair-bound Dortmun tests his bombs

against the Daleks himself, not wanting to accept that his own failure got most of his followers killed already, not wanting to give into his disability. It should be a powerful image of hope and victory, the brave man rising to his feet and stumbling towards the invaders – and his death is for nothing, because the bombs don't work. I love the way that the shot is framed, the wheelchair rolling away from him once it's abandoned. If there's ever a scene that proves the lie to the simple optimism that was offered by the Dalek defeat on Skaro, it's this one.

The sequences in which the Daleks parade around London, riding over Westminster Bridge, hobnobbing under Nelson's Column, are justly famous. It's not that they look especially impressive, really – indeed, they seem a bit like tourists out to see the sights, and they look dwarved by the lions in Trafalgar Square. But it's the very *wrongness* of the image that makes it work, these strange looking pepper-pots from last year's children's TV serial holding their own against the city backdrop. Remembering that this episode is long before the Daleks became icons in their own right, what we've got here is surreal and silly, and just a bit unnerving.

I also love the anger David Campbell shows when Susan suggests they escape together in the TARDIS. It's quite clear now that there's a moral purpose to these adventures we're watching – a duty in righting wrongs, not just selfish survival and hopping off to the next planet when things turn ugly.

And to lower the tone a moment, is it wrong of me to find Dortmun's helper Jenny so fetching when she's wearing that little balaclava of hers? That's Richard Briers' wife, you know.

T: At this point in the series, we're so used to seeing Doctor Who done "as live" that the actors getting from one set to another is often witnessed in laborious detail. So here, it's curious how one minute we have the rebel Tyler telling Baker to help the Doctor and then – bang – he's opening a cell door and freeing prisoners, with no scene to bridge the gap. Mind you, the Dalek ship is clearly a very efficient place – since the rebels infiltrated it, the baddies have found the time to repaint the Supreme Dalek and robotise Craddock.

But the film sequences are again impressive, and the music helps them trot along nicely. Inside the museum, though, those annoying "Vetoed" signs (which the resistance members use to communicate with each other, sort of) again draw attention to themselves. I believe this started out a gag on Martin's part (tellingly, they aren't mentioned in Terrance Dicks' novelisation of this story) because he'd wanted to do something and been, er, vetoed – but unless you're aware of this, the "joke" simply becomes an intrusion. It's a shame, as other little touches like the Dalek graffiti are rather fun – putting an insignia on an invaded country's monuments is the sort of thing petty dictators do.

You're right, though: Baker is (or rather, *was*) a nice chap, isn't he? There are so many little touches of humanity here – David gives Baker a hip flask, Baker tells the Doctor he hopes he finds his friends, etc. – that you can't help but warm to the character despite his limited screen time. And then my stomach lurched when he surrendered and the Daleks shot him anyway! Dialogue and characterization haven't always been Nation's strong suits, but – as with the Thal being dragged under the water at the end of The Daleks episode five – he's often very good at writing horrifying vignettes.

Unlike some people, by the way, I don't mind the bit where the Dalek talks to a dummy and mistakes it for a real person – it's a quite alien thing to do, I suppose, in a way that the Dalek leader clearing his throat really wasn't.

January 25th

The End of Tomorrow
(The Dalek Invasion
of Earth episode four)

R: I know the actor who's inside the Slyther! That's dear old Nick Evans, who does charity work with Janie. Once in a while, he tells me proudly of his days spent inside a Dalek casing. He never shows off about being inside a Slyther, though. But, do you know, watching it now, I think the Slyther is actually rather good! It's clearly just a bag with a bit of a claw poking out of it, but it's so misshapen, so expression-

less, that I actually find it rather disgusting. Maybe it's the effect of watching all the episodes in order, but I'm actually adjusting to expectations of the time. Or maybe I'm just getting soft in the head. What do you think?

One other thing that really oughtn't to work is the absence of William Hartnell. He's ill this week, having injured himself in a fall on set, so a hasty bit of rewriting means we only see the back of Edmund Warwick's head doubling for the Doctor after he's inexplicably fainted. But actually it does a lot of good to the story. David Campbell is given a lot of the Doctor's lines, and a certain genius in disabling ticking bombs – and suddenly, there's a chance of rapport between him and Susan, and a more credible reason why she might be attracted to an also-ran character and want to settle down with him. It's a curious episode because besides not featuring the Doctor, it doesn't feature a lot of Daleks either – I'm quite sure that if there was an episode that the production team would have chosen Hartnell to be injured during, it wouldn't have been this one.

But again, mainly by accident, it works because it shifts the emphasis upon human villains instead. Up to now, the only human characters we've met are either resistance members or the poor souls who had been forcibly converted into mind-controlled slaves. Now, Terry Nation gives us the chance to see the uglier consequences of totalitarian occupation and plague disaster: the human race doesn't necessarily just bond together as one, but also produces scavengers and black marketeers. Once again, it's a depth you don't usually get with Doctor Who alien-invasion stories; yes, you get the odd misguided traitor here and there, but not those who are amorally taking advantage of the situation. After an episode in which we've seen the human race portrayed as something which is heroic and proud, where men seem to queue up to display their willingness to die for the greater good, the likes of the black marketer Ashton leave an unpleasant taste in the mouth. And that there *are* Ashtons about only makes the memory of Dortmun's sacrifice all the more powerful.

T: It's worth going over again – the leading actor is unexpectedly absent, so as everyone prepares for the next episode, they have to rewrite and re-jig the whole bloody thing! And so they do, because there's so little time between recording and broadcast, and they've no choice. Modern producers would sob into their lattes and have an extra line of coke before finding out who to blame for the episode not being completed, but these young turks just got on with it. By the way, I've met Nick Evans too – he's a lovely chap. Do you think the other blokes inside the Daleks were jealous of him getting to play the Slyther as well?

But oh, if only Richard Martin had been able to do *everything* on film – I love the shots of the Robomen atop the wagons, whipping and cajoling suitably grimy (and plentiful!) extras. And look, they've had to pay Alan Judd for an extra week, just to get that shot of Jenny emerging from the museum with Dortmun's corpse in the frame. It's a great shot, but the money might have been better spent on using something other than a still picture of a paper plate to represent the Dalek saucer. Or some footage of an alligator that doesn't look about three inches long (although the shot of Tyler framed in the hatchway, firing his gun at the little creature, is so good it almost sells the sequence).

The Waking Ally
(The Dalek Invasion
of Earth episode five)

R: What's this "waking ally" mentioned in the title, then? Did I miss this?

The women in the wood who give Barbara and Jenny up to the Daleks change the tone of the story completely; they look like something out of a Grimm fairy tale. In the *one* concession we ever get to the twenty-second century, we get the older of the two nostalgically remembering the moving walkways and the astronaut fair – which makes it all seem unreal, as she and her partner look as if they'd be better suited to joining the Tribe of Gum than the space-age future that Nation has dreamed up. The younger woman is almost positively feral! I think it's so clever, this, that the moment we get an allusion to the utopian ideal of 200 years hence, it's from the mouths of those who have been brought so low that they've become Dalek collaborators – and can easily justify

their actions, rummaging through a grocery bag for sugar like kids opening a Christmas present, and reasoning that the women they've betrayed would have been captured anyway.

No, it's not a good week for Barbara or Jenny – they're caught like Hansel and Gretel and bundled off to the mines. It's not a good week for Ian's friend Larry Madison either. Amidst all the epic plotting, and the attention given to the *national* implications of an invasion, there's been this little background storyline of a man searching for his missing brother. In some ways, it foreshadows Abby's search for her son in Nation's later Survivors series – but it's not overplayed here, it only surfaces in the way that Larry can't resist referring to what his brother Phil says and believes; it's clear that Larry idolises him. There's a certain grim inevitability that nothing good will have come to Phil – but Larry's discovery that he's become a Roboman, his desperate pleas to make Phil remember his wife Angela, and the determined way in which he chooses to die alongside him are the most touching moments yet in a story which has rather forgotten gentler feelings of love and affection.

T: Larry's self-sacrifice actually brought a tear to my eye. It's so sad, and the mutual death is horribly touching – kudos to Peter Badger, who I understand added Robo-Phil's final utterance of "Larry" in rehearsal. This allows the two brothers to be together, fleetingly, one final time, in their dying moments. It's a typically grim Nation subplot, but he's smashing at this kind of Boys' Own stuff.

But yes… the "waking" what? The "ally" who? Perhaps this refers to the Doctor being on his feet again, but he woke up last week (albeit out of shot). And anyway, he wasn't supposed to be *out* of action then, and I've not heard of the title being altered at the last minute due to Hartnell's injury. And even if that were the case, is there *nothing* else of note about which they could have named this episode? How about "Slyther Me Timbers" or "Fratricide of Doom" or (sorry) "Prisoners of Cod Science". Whatever the reason, I bet it's the only time in the history of the English Language that the words "waking" and "ally" have ever resided next to each other.

And I really must try to perfect the "flirting

over dead fish" technique that David uses on Susan sometime – it's terribly effective and results in (for Doctor Who, at least) quite a passionate kiss. And the Doctor's being a wily cove about this: "Something's cooking," he says gleefully, twinkling at the young lovers.

January 26th

Flashpoint
(The Dalek Invasion
of Earth episode six)

R: I suppose, if you wanted to be critical, you could argue that wrapping up the entire invasion of Earth in 15 minutes flat is just too easy. And of course it is – but I think that rather misses the point. The *plot* of The Dalek Invasion of Earth is nonsense. For Heaven's sake, it relies upon the idea that the Daleks want to mine the magnetic core of the planet, replace it with an engine and fly it around the galaxy like a bus. But Nation was always more interested in the symbols that the story offered as opposed to its hokey science – and so it is here. The problem with almost *every* Doctor Who story (classic series and new) is that however epic the crisis offered, the conclusion will inevitably feel a bit glib – and this story is about as truly epic as Doctor Who will ever be.

But the symbols of the victory *do* matter, even if the plotting of said victory is rather muddled. After five weeks of Doctor Who being at its most sour, the triumph here as slaves and Robomen alike turn upon the Daleks is very powerful. There's even a bit of comedy to those symbols, in that lovely scene where Barbara bluffs to the Daleks about several imminent uprisings against them by drawing upon her history teaching – and reminds us in the process of mankind's ever present desire to fight for freedom through the ages. Yes, it's ridiculous, the sounding of Big Ben as soon as the invasion has been foiled. But it's extremely moving too, and Hartnell knows how to play the sentimentality of it perfectly – a hand on Tyler's shoulder, a smile of hope and a soft repeat of "Just the beginning". Wonderful.

And all that is as nothing to the departure of Susan. She's not been the best written of char-

acters, shame to say, and her potential was clearly squandered. But right up to the end, Carole Ann Ford has tried her damnedest to find that ground between teenage cry baby and strange alien girl, and her final scenes are amongst her very best – she finds at last a cause that gives her identity and a man who loves her, and yet she's unable to leave her grandfather, unable to *grow up*. William Hartnell sometimes looks a bit flustered when he's dealing with plot-mechanics, but give him a scene which invites him to focus on truthful emotion, and he's heartbreaking. He's never been better than in the sequence where he puts all his attention upon a hole in Susan's shoe, awkwardly pretending even to himself that he'll repair it – that he can continue travelling with the granddaughter he loves so much. It's not so much the speech that's later repeated at the start of The Five Doctors that made me cry – oh yes, I'm embarrassed to admit it, but I cried all right. It was more the way that having delivered that speech, he rushes the TARDIS dematerialisation with a couple of farewells, quickly, before he can change his mind.

Did you cry, Toby? Oh go on. I hope it wasn't just me. I'd feel like a right prawn.

T: Tears welled, but they didn't cascade – but then, I'm a tough nut to crack. But before we got to that last scene, there was some fun to be had along the way...

As you say, final episodes are very difficult when the scale is so large, but I think they get away with it here. Well, almost. You have to wonder, retroactively, why Dortmun put so much effort into perfecting a Dalek-killing bomb when it turns out that simply whacking the Daleks with rocks will be more effective. And there's a *lot* happening in that final explosion that finishes off the Dalek mining operation, isn't there? The stock footage goes all over the place – I can just about buy the lava flow, as the Doctor mentions a volcanic eruption, but is the explosion really so powerful that land falls into the sea and then deserted buildings tumble down?

But, who cares – this episode is about Susan's departure. I'll happily put up with a perfunctory plot resolution because these last ten minutes are the best. Hartnell is just superb, holding his granddaughter close because he knows that when he goes back into the Ship, he'll never be able to do so again. Carole Ann Ford is good too (although unfortunately, she's forced to clutch onto a drainpipe at one point), and it remains a shame that she was rarely allowed to be as alien as she was in the pilot. She's lovely in her parting scene, though, especially when the TARDIS disappears and she puts her hands out to feel where it once stood. It's a worthy send off, and Hartnell's oft-quoted final speech is played magnificently.

I have to say, Terry Nation has come out of this much better than I expected; the successes in this story are largely down to him and the actors involved, but I'm not sure how I'll cope if they get Richard Martin to do another six-parter. Especially if it involves, say, very little film work and lots of complex and technically demanding studio scenes – that'd give me butterflies.

The Powerful Enemy
(The Rescue episode one)

R: I was expecting the Doctor to be especially abrasive in this episode, reacting to Susan's departure by snapping at Ian and Barbara and sulking. But, rather charmingly, he instead wants to fuss over these two companions that he never wanted in the first place, joking with them and showing concern for them and treating them much as if he's their doting aunt. It gives the impression that he desperately wants to cling to the friends he has left, and it's the most endearing portrait of the Doctor yet – and a very touching one too, as we can see just how much he's suffering from the expression on Hartnell's face when he accidentally asks Susan to open the doors. Barbara's careful response – that he could perhaps teach her how to do it instead – and his gentle willingness to do so, is pitch perfect. We've seen the Doctor hide his feelings before beneath bluster and complaints, but never so vulnerably as here.

Not an awful lot else really *happens* in this story, but for once that tranquillity is rather the point, and feels reassuring after the epic crises of the last adventure. The Doctor would far rather take a peaceful nap than explore the caves they've landed in, and Ian and Barbara

too react to their new surroundings with the cheerful vague interest of a pair of backpackers. The story's one real attempt to up the ante is when Ian says that he finds the enigmatic alien Koquillion more intimidating than a Dalek – what, really, mate, you'd rather take on a metal Nazi than some chap wearing a spiky headdress? – but it only adds to the charm of this instalment that you can't really believe him. David Whitaker always seems to write these peculiar two-part filler stories that serve to take into account the state of the TARDIS crew and rethink it. In The Edge of Destruction, he depicted them at their most paranoid and embittered, but through the muddle and confusion of their adventure with a stuck button, they emerged as a recognisable team. Here, he starts from the reverse position, with the TARDIS as comforting an environment as it's ever been, soon to be shaken by Vicki's arrival.

The peculiarity of the episode is that for all you might think it's there to introduce Maureen O'Brien as Vicki, it doesn't really give her that much to do. But O'Brien mines every emotion she can out of a script which pretty much confines her to the kitchen – she shows elation, she's frightened, she stands up to Koquillion, and, best of all, she's proud enough to reject the look of sympathy she spies on Barbara's face.

T: Re-watching the show in order is making me reassess some of my attitudes – for example, I've always lauded David Whitaker and pooh-poohed Terry Nation. That might have to do with my in-built resistance to following received wisdom – Nation is probably classic Doctor Who's most famous writer (well, all right... after Douglas Adams), so obviously I wanted to celebrate the more obscure writers to demonstrate that I don't follow the herd – because, er, I'm a pretentious twit instead. But so far into this marathon watch, Nation has delivered in spades whilst Whitaker has trotted out the most bonkers 50 minutes in the series thus far.

Whitaker redeems himself here though, first in providing a nice intro episode for O'Brien – she gets a big emotional scene, and, unlike her predecessor in the last story, doesn't feel the need to clutch onto a pipe or anything. But do you know, Whitaker shines most in his handling of the regulars, providing a script that demonstrates the great dynamic between the characters and actors alike. Hartnell is very funny here – when Jacqueline Hill informs him that "the trembling" (i.e. the TARDIS engines) has stopped, he excitedly tells her, "Oh, my dear, I'm so glad you're feeling better..." And he's brilliantly dismissive when Ian shines the torch in his face to ask about the culprit of the growling Sand Beast-noise – "Well, it's not *me*, is it?", he snaps, hilariously. And I love the way the Doctor refers to sleep as being in "The Arms of Morpheus"; I do the same in Moths Ate My Doctor Who Scarf. It's a phrase that was obviously dormant in my subconscious, as I hadn't knowingly pilfered it from the programme.

As you can probably tell, this project of ours is making me appreciate William Hartnell in ways that I never have until now. Yes, he makes some blunders (there's a terrible one here, where he stumbles through his explanation that the TARDIS can travel through solid matter, so they needn't worry about being trapped underground), but he's brilliant at complicated material that requires his character to display one emotion while he's actually feeling another on the inside. And Hartnell has got a face that's so good in close-up – you get all the nuances of his character if the director is smart enough to exploit this (which is often the case here, including a terrific shot of Hartnell being seen through a magnifying glass).

Other bits of this episode amuse me... when Ian and Barbara get into the spookily lit cave, they muse about what Susan is up to "now" in post-Dalek invasion Earth – milking cows, they suspect. But, as "now" is several centuries in her future, "being dead" is actually a more probable postulation. It's a bit more depressing, I know, but that's time travel for you. Also, isn't it interesting that Koquillion uses yards as a measurement? He clearly rejects the metric system, and probably resents rules imposed by the EU (Exo-Space Union). And speaking as someone who watches the perilously dwindling population of Battlestar Galactica, I'd like to suggest that Dido's 100 inhabitants aren't enough to ensure propagation of the species – at least, not without an awful lot of incest.

On a final note, I'm thrilled that credited the fictional Sydney Wilson as Koquillion. The production team clearly thought people would be reading the credits and in need of hood-winking. You hear that, modern TV chiefs? People read the credits. So stop shrinking the bloody things and zipping them through at 200 miles an hour. Just because *you* can't read, it doesn't mean that the audience can't either.

January 27th

Desperate Measures
(The Rescue episode two)

R: I really love the titles to this story – The Powerful Enemy! (Who?) Desperate Measures! (Where?) They're just so wonderfully melodramatic and misleading. There are occasional moments in this episode when it thinks about rousing itself and having a bit of action – but rather like an elderly dog by a radiator, it thinks better of it, puts its head back under its paws and goes back to sleep. This might be considered a problem if you felt the story *ought* to be rousing itself – but it clearly doesn't see this as its raison d'etre, and I don't think we should either. It's interesting how, as Doctor Who fans, we get into the habit of looking at all these stories individually and judging them as separate entities – whereas that was clearly not the way the series was viewed at the time. The point of The Rescue is that it's a couple of weeks' respite before the major adventuring begins all over again. It's broadcast straight after Christmas, when everyone's feeling fat and lazy and too full of turkey to move – this is the Doctor Who equivalent, an amiable enough little diversion that wants to be tackling all its New Year resolutions but hasn't got the energy to get off the couch yet.

So we have a main story that is so secondary, the Doctor tells Ian and Barbara about its resolution as if it's an anecdote: "That Bennett, he turned out to be Koquillion, you know!" No, the purpose of The Rescue is to get Maureen O'Brien on board as a regular, and so its climax is therefore not some strange maniac falling to his death with a scream, but a little girl shyly accepting an invitation around the universe with a smile. The best moments in the episode are from William Hartnell; the way he bonds so easily with the upset child, and immediately establishes a rapport with her; the dignity with which he confronts the murderer Bennett in the hall of judgment and with such bored disdain tells him to get out of his ridiculous costume; and, best of all, the delightful scene in which he hears his friends talk about him over the intercom, and realises what an impression he's made on Vicki, and how much he's come to mean to Ian and Barbara. It'd be wrong to describe this latter scene as a defining moment for Hartnell's Doctor, because it's far too passive for that – but it's sweet and uplifting, and nothing else demonstrates just how precisely he's been redrafted now as a dotty grandfather. (You can see precisely why when Peter Cushing takes on the role in the Aaru movies he plays it the way he does – it's an imitation of the benign old man with a twinkle in his eye that we see here.)

T: Indulge me for a moment would, you? I'm watching this off a scratchy VHS recorded off UK Gold, as we're just a month too early for the release of this story on DVD – which I'm on, as a commentary moderator! So these episodes (and the next four) are among those that I've seen more recently than most, because I had to scrutinise them for my moderation duties.

Picture the scene: on 9th April last year, I was set to make my West End debut. By coincidence, the commentary for The Rescue was scheduled for the same day, so I set off at 6 am to get to TV Centre in time to sit alongside Christopher Barry, William Russell and Raymond Cusick. We watched this story, and I endeavoured to elicit their 40-year-old memories of it. I don't say this to brag – instead, I try to imagine phoning my 14-year-old self as he illicitly pored over the pages of The Early Years, to tell him that one day he'd be watching this story in the presence of those mythical names who'd created the episodes he was reading about. He'd have been beside himself with joy! It's occasionally worth reminding ourselves of such elation, and to not let being too close to the show (as we both are, professionally) dissipate that magic.

And even though I've seen this story recently, there are so many little things about it that keep me from being bored: there's the distaste-ful way with which Jacqueline Hill handles the flare gun, the Sand Beast's evocatively lamenting cries as it dies, and the angled set (because the spaceship is lying there broken) allowing for brilliantly abstract shapes in the framing of the shots. And isn't the way the Doctor smashes his way into Bennett's room a bit of a cheek? (If someone tells me I can't come in, I tend not to break their door down – for all the Doctor knows, Bennett's indulging in an intimate moment with Space Razzle.) The actual appearance of the Dido residents, though, provokes a mixed reaction – while I do think a potential sitcom about the last two survivors of this race was a squandered opportunity, I even more strongly wonder how the 100 people of Dido kept their species going until now (certainly, the two rather fey chaps seen here won't cut the mustard in that regard).

Hartnell is once again so good in this – even at this early stage of her tenure, it's clear that O'Brien already adores him. The Doctor is so sweet with Vicki (sending Barbara and Ian away so that he can have a quiet word with her), and she gleefully takes his hand as she leads him to Bennett. There's such good rapport between them – indeed, between everyone. I really enjoy being with these people.

I have a confession to make, however: I was a bit in awe of everything that was happening during the commentary of this story, and so I neglected to ask William Russell precisely what he meant by calling Koquillion "Cocky-Licken". It's one of the eternal mysteries of Doctor Who, unanswered, and it's all my fault. Sorry.

The Slave Traders
(The Romans episode one)

R: Oh, this is just enormous *fun* – full of great verbal gags and witty bits of direction, and the cast all relaxed and making the most out of a script which gives them all plenty to feed off. But what makes it so enjoyable is that for once, it's a fun shared by the characters as well. Everyone's in Roman times, and they're getting to do what any normal person would do if suddenly thrown back into an era so familiar from popular culture – they send it up, they walk around in their togas quoting Julius Caesar, they giggle over the exotic foods they can buy at market. They even laugh at the quaint backward society they're visiting because the villa hasn't got a fridge. In short, they're actually properly behaving like *tourists* and it's wonderful to see, because in all their hopping about through space and time, there's been plenty of jeopardy to run away from but precious little pleasure to embrace.

There was a taste of this, very briefly, in Dennis Spooner's first script, where the first thing Ian and Barbara do when they find eighteenth century clothing is get dressed up in it – oh, Ian may *claim* it's a way of staying inconspicuous, but you can tell it's because he likes the frocks. Here, uniquely, the cast have had a chance to lounge about an empty villa for a whole month. We've never seen them so relaxed and at peace – and, tellingly, we've never seen the cast this contented either. William Hartnell in particular just goes from strength to strength – he almost acts with a completely different *voice* when he's chuckling over his larks' tongues at dinner, as if he's a drawling fop from an elegant Noel Coward play, and the conspiratorial acknowledgement of the "liar" pun he gives to Vicki is delightful. Hartnell's Doctor is never as entertaining as when he's caught on the hop, a blustering character forced into situation he can't extricate himself from, and his gift for hangdog expression and double take ensure that he'll be at his best for this comic adventure.

But what Dennis Spooner does so well is contrast the frivolity with something just a bit grimmer hiding beneath the surface – the slave traders of the title are callous thugs, and the brilliant scene in which they invade the villa shows a collision of the two styles; Ian and Barbara have grown so soft and complacent, you can see they almost expect Sevcheria and Didius to play along with the comic style they've established. Barbara even mistakenly breaks a pot over Ian's head to prove it – and it's not until they're chained up that they seem to accept they're in dire straits after all. Jacqueline Hill so cleverly plays the contrast between a wisecracking Barbara who almost winks to the camera with her "Oh boy" as Ian goes off on a spot of Mark Antony, to a woman who is so scared and defeated by the crisis ahead of them that her voice becomes quiet and inflectionless.

Oh, and Ian and Barbara are an item now, surely? The scene where they loll about drinking wine on each other is about as post-coital as you can get on a family show in 1965. I can only presume that they're relieved to romp about in proper beds at last – the ones on board the TARDIS would have broken their spines.

T: This is clearly what you'd do if you travelled in time – find somewhere nice to hang about and soak up the culture, weather and environment (while hopefully avoiding being sold into slavery along the way). And Spooner cleverly avoids the plausibility drawbacks of the need for a continuous adventure element by jumping from last week's cliffhanger to a month later. This also helps to establish Vicki as a permanent and trusted member of the team without stretching our credulity.

It's all a hoot isn't it? And, yes, everyone's playing it absolutely bang on. Jacqueline Hill has always been great as the moral arbiter, and here she shows that when given the rare opportunity to play comedy, she's damned good at that too. And look, Nick Evans clearly demonstrated enough skill whilst Slythering that he's been given a human role as Didius. Okay, so he's never seen in Doctor Who again after this, but at least we know what he looks like (something I can't say about, say, Murphy Grumbar, who spends a decade being stuck inside Dalek metal and various alien costumes). Derek Sydney is great while playing Evans' partner-in-crime, and shoots him a nice disdainful look when Didius ineptly tries to question the stallholder. Oh, and it should be noted that Edward Kelsey's appearance as a slave-buyer here, by dint of his future casting in The Power of the Daleks, makes him the first guest-star to appear alongside two lead actors in Doctor Who. That Kelsey is also Joe Grundy in The Archers and Colonel K in Dangermouse makes me smile.

And yes, Ian and Barbara have clearly had sex. I didn't ask about that on the commentary either. Sorry again.

January 28th

All Roads Lead to Rome
(The Romans episode two)

R: This time last year, Doctor Who was broadcasting a story in which the Doctor willingly led his companions into danger just for the sheer thrill of exploring the Dalek city. And here we are now, and he's beating off assassins, having a fine time as he does so, and he *still* can't resist travelling on to Nero's palace even though he's aware that he's borrowed the identity of a marked man. Vicki can hardly believe her ears, but the Doctor packs off her to bed with a chuckle. Technically, it's the same scenario as Skaro – in that the Doctor is pursuing excitement against all sense – but the tone has changed completely. At the beginning of the series, only the Doctor seemed to understand he was in an adventure serial, and now everyone else has caught up with him. It's odd to think how rapidly the style of the series has moved on; for all of the variety of stories and backdrops in Season One, the same grim determination to survive and escape back to the safety of the TARDIS was there. Now, we can juggle apocalyptic tales of totalitarian oppression with comedies like this – and they still have more in common with each other than the stories in the first season, because there's an acceptance that there's no point in having a time/space machine if you don't make the most of the adventure into which it propels you.

Where this episode really differs from what we've seen before is the extraordinary pace! Dennis Spooner skilfully juggles three separate storylines, and gives each of them a flavour all of their own – but also ensures that enough happens in them all that you're never confused or bored. This week, we have Ian getting shipwrecked, Barbara being sold at a slave auction and the Doctor fighting a murderer – all this in 25 minutes, *and* with the sort of ease that allows room for lots of lovely character comedy, such as the Doctor getting to meet Emperor Nero and play off his vanity. It's astonishing just how much Spooner is able to cram in – and all with the single aim of getting all of his characters into the same building by the episode's end without any of them spotting the other. He does it by such sleight of hand too; if Ian had merely been sold as a gladiator to play before Nero, or Barbara had been merely bought into the imperial household, it'd have felt like a grinding coincidence. But even the episode title suggests that no matter what hoops these characters jump through, it's destined they're all going to end up in the same place – Barbara is bought because she's caught making a show of kindness to a fellow prisoner (played by the wonderfully named Dorothy Rose-Gribble), and even the elements conspire to bring Ian back to shore. There's no escape from the pull of the adventure – all roads lead to Rome.

T: Ah, Dorothy Rose-Gribble. She's up there on my favourite name list, alongside Basil Tang (who was the office foreman in Marco Polo, and gets my vote as the worst actor thus far in the series) and Laidlaw Dalling (who was Rouvray in The Reign of Terror). I nearly met her, but she didn't attend the commentary session because she wouldn't correspond with the DVD producer by email or phone – only handwritten letter, which added a pesky time factor and prevented her from being in that warm studio on that April day, when I had to go four long hours without a cigarette. I'm reminded of this by Tavius' gravelly tones (clearly the result of an anachronistic 40-a-day habit). But it's not all laughs and good times for Ms Gribble in this story, especially when she's singled out by Sevcheria to become lion fodder.

This episode also marks the first appearance of the slave Delos (played by the adept Peter Diamond), but his bond with Ian establishes itself immediately. There's so much man-love between them, I half expect a lost scene to be unearthed one day in which they discuss the relative merits of peaches. And they get to share scenes with Gertan Klauber, who's fresh from his appearance in Carry On Cleo (in which he played Marcus, *not* the Galley Master, whatever Doctor Who: A Celebration might claim).

Conspiracy
(The Romans episode three)

R: There's a story told about I Claudius, which is that when Jack Pulman adapted it for the television, he got so self-conscious about writing for these big famous historical figures that it was only when he interpreted them as a dysfunctional family that he was able to relax and produce the black comedy classic it became. I think much the same thing happened with Dennis Spooner; last year's Reign of Terror only stumbled when he felt obliged to stick these real-life men from school textbooks onto the screen, and although I'm not claiming that his own Roman adventure has *quite* the scope or depth as I Claudius, he's certainly a lot more liberated here. The Caesar family are funny because they're in such a position of power that their whims and irritations have global consequences; Nero doesn't stop to think or care that his designs on Barbara will put her in mortal danger from his jealous wife, any more than the Doctor considers that performing *well* at the emperor's banquet is just as likely to get him executed as performing badly. Derek Francis' Nero is a joy – he's very funny and likeable, and his asides to camera make the audience feel as if he's on their side – but he's also delightfully dangerous. He spends the episode being pestered by an irritating slave, Tigilinus, who keeps standing too close or tripping him up – and, ultimately, he poisons the man just to satisfy a bit of curiosity. And we're clearly *still* intended to find it funny, making this the first comedy death we've had on the series. Similarly, Locusta can take a professional's pride in her poison craft, and is so amoral that she sees no responsibility for the fact that people die as a result – if anything, she's indulgently amused by the Caesars who will always keep killing each other for tradition's sake. But Barbara survives a botched attempt to poison her, and so Locusta is dragged off to be eaten by lions.

Life is cheap in Rome, and so whilst all the farce is genuinely very skilful (the fact that the TARDIS crew keep missing each other in corridors is beautifully well done), and the tone is wholly charming, you're always aware that this is a comedy about dispassionate killers and self-indulgent psychopaths. The Doctor can be lying around in a sauna with Nero one moment, then incur his displeasure the next – with potentially fatal consequences. And the strange thing is that this black streak to the humour only makes it funnier. Nero is perfectly realised as a man so used to everyone giving into his every demand, he doesn't even realise he's being an unreasoning tyrant – it must be a bit how Tom Baker felt on set during the late seventies. The best and coldest joke in the episode isn't even one that's intended to raise a smile; Delos assures Ian that he'll fight him to the death, but because Ian's his friend, he'll make the killing quick. That's the society our friends have chosen to have a holiday in. And like I Claudius, it's written as comedy because if you depicted it as tragedy, you wouldn't believe it.

T: You know how I wrote yesterday that there was a danger in getting so close to a programme, you're not childishly thrilled about it anymore? Well, today I was rehearsing a show with Sanjeev Bhaskar, Marcus Brigstocke, Phill Jupitus and Hattie Hayridge (illustrious names, and the first time I'd met any of them), and was patting myself on the back for resisting the urge to be totally awestruck, and for treating them like fellow professionals. But when I turned around during a break, *who* do I see framed in the doorway of the Drill Hall corridor? Only the new Doctor Who, Matt Smith! This was it, my Livingstone and Stanley moment... what words would I say, as fate presented me with this once-in-a-lifetime opportunity?

None, as it happens, because my mouth stopped working, and after a brief moment of eye contact and a weak smile from me, he was whisked off. I went outside to text my friends and Adjoa Andoh walked past, as if to rub in the fact that today was some kind of Doctor Who/Toby Hadoke confluence that I'd entirely failed to capitalise on. Although I've gone over any number of witty things I could have/ should have said, part of me is rather pleased that a vestige of an excitable kid still resides somewhere beneath this creaky, cynical frame.

Anyway, back in ancient Rome, I too enjoyed the way Nero dispatched Tigilinus – dear Brian Proudfoot, an erstwhile William Hartnell body-double, is wonderful as he capers about after Nero and perfectly times his comedy expiration. Sad to say, he will be reduced to playing "walk-on Aridian" in The Chase in just a few weeks, and then history will lose track of him entirely. Still, it's wonderful that Doctor Who can serve as a historical record of the talents of so many extraordinary actors who would otherwise be entirely forgotten about.

But Tigilinus' death is just part of a challenging endeavour to do farce (which is hard enough on a theatre stage) "as live", with three cameras in a pokey studio. That takes some chutzpah, and makes this feel unlike anything we've seen in Doctor Who thus far. The Nero scenes in particular are a delight – Derek Francis pitches his performance just right, being delightfully funny but with an undercurrent of menace. When Nero corners Barbara for a drink, she downs a big goblet of wine (either with the intention of keeping the Emperor distracted, getting pissed, or both) – and it's interesting that it was terrifying when Vasor had similar designs on Barbara, but here she treats the Emperor's attentions as a slightly intolerable chore. That's why Doctor Who works so well: it adapts to the tone of every adventure, and yet is still recognisably the same show.

And next week's episode is entitled Inferno? I take it that Ian will be saved as a herd of Primords storm the Coliseum.

January 29th

Inferno (The Romans episode four)

R: At first the Doctor is utterly floored by Vicki's assertion that he had a hand in the Great Fire of Rome – the notion that he might have shaped history, however accidentally, simply doesn't fit in with his worldview. And it's only because there's a new companion aboard the TARDIS who doesn't understand the rules yet (at the story's end, in spite of spending a month in his company, Vicki still hasn't twigged that the Doctor can't steer the Ship) that she's able to open his eyes to the possibility. The series can be different from this point on, and the regulars can intervene more in the action, because Vicki can't see why they shouldn't.

And that's very apt, because Maureen O'Brien genuinely is a breath of fresh air for the series – she's got a great gift for comedy, downplaying the lines beautifully (the bit where she matter-of-factly told the Doctor in last week's episode that she's poisoned Nero was perfect), and hasn't even come close to hysteria so far. For all the crises we've seen unfold, Vicki stubbornly insists on keeping the story light and playing the tourist – as she heads back to the TARDIS, she's able to marvel at watching the Great Fire, and she delights in telling Ian and Barbara all about her adventures in such breathless detail that they're unable to get a word in edgeways. It's all part of Dennis Spooner's plan to make the series a bit more *fun*, to make the idea of travelling on these adventures something any child watching would jump at. And it shapes the tone of the series for the next 15 years or so... right up to the eighties, when companions start finding the idea of popping around time and space in the TARDIS once again something of a chore.

There are some dark moments to this episode – the best surely being the way Nero stabs the soldier holding Barbara because he didn't fight hard enough. But part of the joy of the story is that it's so determinedly superficial. For all that Barbara and Ian have been through, within *seconds* of arriving back at the villa, they're making jokes about "the fridge" once more, and cavorting about as if they've never been sold into slavery. How do you feel about this, Toby? Is it a bad thing? I feel it's very clever – the more sophisticated audience can see the more serious themes in the story; the way that William Hartnell's delighted giggling at the idea he might have started the Fire merges into Derek Francis' madman laughter speaks volumes about the contrast between the protective bubble that surrounds these happy adventurers and the real-life world they leave behind them. But this way, the series can continue. You can explore all aspects of Roman society that you wish, no matter how brutal, safe in the knowledge that you won't traumatise the regulars in the process, leaving them fresh for their next adventure. It's the beginning of Doctor Who as an anthology series rather than a continuous storyline – and I think it's that change which guarantees its survival.

T: It's absolutely fine that Ian and Barbara recover from their ordeals so quickly; the onset of post-traumatic stress wouldn't have been in keeping with the world of this story. And by "world", I don't mean physical location, I mean the dramatic world created here, where death is funny, assassins are blundering dolts and the razing of a city is the punchline. Each Doctor Who story has its own world (well, *ideally* it does), with the creative team setting the tone and thus the rules to be followed. Fortunately, the series' lead actors are versatile enough to effectively deliver whatever style they're asked. Just note the deadpan way Hartnell reacts to Nero's outlandish threats to put him on an island and raise the alligator-infested waters – he's going for the laugh, not attempting to give a psychologically plausible reaction to the idea (which he's perfectly capable of doing as well).

And whilst much of this is very funny, the casual murders and terrifying plight of those in the arena jails isn't sugarcoated. It's interesting, for instance, that nobody went back for Dorothy-Rose – so one must assume she's lion lunch. Even Sevcheria (who has somehow gone from being an independent slave-trader in episode one to here working as Nero's lackey) is rather harshly dispatched by a burning torch to the face.

But if we're talking about killing, there's one element of this story that retroactively sticks out: we're here told that the real Maximus Petullian was going to assassinate Nero, but do you *remember* the character as seen from episode one? He could barely walk! Unless he's continually acting decrepit to pass himself as a doddering old man (in which case, he should've fared better against the slave who killed him), he looks like the sort of person who could hardly harm a stalk of broccoli, let alone murder an emperor. In an era where nobody had recourse to repeated viewings, the programme-makers clearly expected the audience to remember the pot gag and fridge joke made three weeks ago, and yet not to recall the geriatric infirmity of a would-be assassin. Glorious!

Overall, this story had been such a ball, and proves you can get away with virtually any humour if the world you've created supports it. I don't admire The Romans as much as some of the straighter historicals, but it's not asking for admiration, it's mostly asking for chuckles – and it delivers those in spades.

Oh, and Ian and Babs have clearly had sex again.

The Web Planet (episode one)

R: The planet Vortis feels unlike anything we've yet seen in Doctor Who. It isn't just the Vaseline on the lens to give the atmosphere an "alien" feel – although I like that, and think it sets up a really nice contrast between the scenes on the planet's surface and the ordinariness of the TARDIS interior. It isn't just the sense there's a *scale* to this place – I love the moons in the background, and the crags, and just how odd all the shapes are. It isn't even the peculiar sounds of those giant ants, which are so invasive they even give the cast a headache. No, it's actually a deceptively small thing – that to roam about on the planet safely, Ian and the Doctor are obliged to change their costumes, and put on Atmospheric Density Jackets. However exotic some of the trappings of Skaro or Marinus, the fact you could walk around on either in ordinary clothing did rather suggest it was a BBC set. Here at last, there's attention being given to the notion we're somewhere very distant and very alien, and it brings back a sense of wonder and danger to the series. In any other story, the TARDIS disappearing at the end might be seen as an inconvenience, another of those plot devices used to keep everyone from just popping off into the next adventure. Here, it strands the Doctor in an environment which seems unknowable, and that's far more frightening.

I love too the way that Bill Strutton's script emphasises the difference between Barbara's culture and Vicki's – the way that Future Girl looks at Sixties Teacher as something really rather primitive, and how Barbara's attempts to fob Vicki off with aspirin are rather the equivalent of our being presented with leeches. It's funny, but it also gives Vicki just that bit of extra character she needs. Before too long the series' format will mean that she's required to have just the same reaction to things as anyone else, and then Ian and Barbara will disappear altogether and we'll lose any real sense of a contemporary viewpoint upon the series. So it's important that we get these distinctions between the regulars when we can. Maureen O'Brien, like Carole Ann Ford before her, seizes upon moments that can accentuate her "otherness" – the way she laughs in reaction to Barbara's concern about what's happening to her arm, and the look of hurt surprise upon her face when Barbara persists in taking the crisis seriously.

And, look! A quadruple cliffhanger! Ian caught in a snare, Barbara walking towards a pool of acid, Vicki in an out-of-control TARDIS, and the Doctor looking utterly bereft to find the Ship has vanished. It's beautifully done.

T: I have a confession to make. This is the only Doctor Who story I have ever recorded over. The Kevin Costner film The Untouchables was playing, and I'd really enjoyed it when I saw it at my friend Jon's house – and, er, I figured I'd probably rewatch it more than this. I felt dirty doing it, and never again erased even a moment of Who from my collection. Even now, I still have hundreds of videos I'm not quite sure what to do with (I haven't the time or technical nous to efficiently move everything over to DVD).

It's a surprise then, that I find this opening instalment to be very impressive. The lens distortion provokes odd shafts of light and abstract glistening that is very effective, the soundscape is horribly invasive (especially when Barbara is being dragged from the Ship) and there are some neat tricks (the echoing voices, Ian's pen whizzing out of his hand). I also take solace in the fact that Barbara chides the Doctor for being messy... a genius doesn't have time to tidy up! (That's what I'm trying to convince K, anyway.)

And the Vicki/Barbara culture-clash scene you mention is nice, yes, but it curiously seems a diametrically opposed vision of the future to the one I expect. Instead of learning medicine at ten, I fear that the way things are going, the kids of the future will be getting GCSEs in Thomas the Tank Engine and degrees in Walking in a Straight Line and Talking at the Same Time, just to fulfill government pass rate targets. (Sorry to digress, but I saw an apostrophe on a plural on the whiteboard at my son's school this morning – these have been medi-

cally proven to turn radical young bon vivants into grumpy old farts.)

January 30th

The Zarbi
(The Web Planet episode two)

R: This episode we get the chance to see the monsters in greater detail, and I have to say – the Zarbi look fab. Really. I think it's telling that these are the first alien beings since the Daleks to break away from using the human form, and it makes them the most honestly alien and unknowable lifeform we've encountered since then. There's something very unreasonable about a giant insect: you can't chat to them, you can't confide in them, and their motives seem emotionless and calculated as they round up all the travellers and prod at them with their legs. The trick is that they don't *talk*, and that's so much more threatening. And it leads to a wonderful cliffhanger when they've finally shepherded the Doctor under a strange alien tube, and at last the civilisation is given a voice. It's an unexpected voice at that, strong and feminine – "Why do you come now?", it asks. It's hostile and it's demanding, and it wrongfoots the viewer entirely.

If the Zarbi are the new Daleks, then I suppose the Menoptra are the new Thals. There's just a bit *too* much effort going on to make the Menoptra more interesting than the Thals, when simply sticking them in butterfly costumes and making them consider whether to kill Barbara or not would have sufficed. Roslyn de Winter is the best actor amongst them, but she's also credited in the end titles with "Insect Movement", which suggests she's responsible for the strange hand wavings and head tiltings – and, no doubt, the rather fey and over-deliberate manner of speaking. But even if all of this is just a tad too distracting, and you're so busy marvelling at all the attention given to making these new creatures different that you forget to listen to their dialogue, they still feel intriguingly exotic.

Opening episodes which establish wholly alien worlds usually blow it in the second instalment when mysteries need to be solved and characters to be introduced. The opening episode of The Web Planet doesn't do this, and that's to be admired; it's sold largely by the efforts of the regulars. Hartnell contrasts his rather giggly performance last week with something much more sombre now he feels the situation is desperate, and Hill, who was invited to faint at the sight of a giant insect a few stories ago, struggles to be brave in front of them here. My favourite scene of all, though, shows the calm practicality of William Russell, as he persuades the Doctor to take off his jacket and get used to the planet's atmosphere. It has a brave stoicism to it that suggests he's stripping away his life support, and needing to determine whether or not the shock will kill him.

T: If we're considering the effectiveness of the creatures on Vortis, then I should note that in the novelisation, the Menoptra are better portrayed as individual characters. But they don't really manage that here, with the actors involved are lumbered with those crazy staccato speech patterns, and hand movements that suggest they're applying nipple clamps. It's decent of them to have a go at it, yes, and this is probably a more realistic way of conveying that they're alien than if they'd moved and spoken like humans (as they do on so many alien worlds), but it doesn't exactly help sell us on the drama.

What *does* work in terms of dramatic intent is that genuinely horrifying moment when the Zarbi force Hrostar to his knees and nibble his wings off. It's made worse because we can't *see* exactly what's happening, but the close-up of Barbara's face tells you it isn't anything nice. The only shame here is that this is prefigured by Hrhoonda's wings dropping off when he's shot, causing everyone to trip over them.

By the way, is this the first time that something other than the regulars has been in the TARDIS? Even though the Zarbi's attempt to enter is thwarted, seeing that giant ant framed by the roundels feels like a genuinely threatening moment, because no-one has hitherto crossed that threshold, defiled that sanctuary. Also, it's telling that this is the second time in a row that the Doctor has a pre-knowledge of the planet on which he's landed – it'll be interesting to see how soon this becomes the norm,

and he transitions from being a daffy amateur traveller to the omniscient wiseacre we now recognize him as.

And for benefit of fans of The Untouchables (again, the prized movie that compelled me, back in the day, to tape over The Web Planet), let me just say: The Menoptra aren't that well armed. You shouldn't bring a stick to a grub fight. And if they send one of yours to The Crater of Needles, you need to send one of theirs to The Centre of Terror. That's the Vortis way.

Escape to Danger
(The Web Planet episode three)

R: All the scenes where the Doctor talks to the Animus are *fantastic*. For a start, Catherine Fleming's voice-performance really is spot on – this is a peculiar story of actors doing insect movements, flying about, and even running into the camera underneath giant ant costumes, and what makes the central villain so fascinating is that to contrast all this overelaborate design, Fleming downplays the role. She's cold and inhuman and – above all else – *invisible*, and when so much else in the story tries to distract your attention with its curious visuals, with voice alone she makes these scenes have a focus which feel so much more dangerous. And Hartnell is terrific too. He plays the Doctor at first with a polite distance, trying to size up the entity he's communicating with. And then, over the course of the episode – as he deceives her and cajoles her and tries to bargain with her – he establishes too with his very *deliberate* and (rarely for this Doctor) minimalist acting that he's a shrewd diplomat. We haven't seen the Doctor be this cool and this manipulative and this controlled since... well, ever, actually. At his most likeable, Hartnell's Doctor is a creature of giggles and tics and fluffs – it's only in scenes like these we can see that this is all as much of an act as Tom Baker's clowning, or David Tennant's boyish exuberance. When the chips are down, there's a steely intelligence to this Doctor that he often masks for his companions.

And speaking of future Doctors... I rather love the sequence where the Doctor tries to comfort Vicki by offering her a sweet. Okay, he's not picked up any jelly babies yet – it's just a slab of chocolate – but out comes the bag of sweets from his pocket, and he's that loveable old grandfather figure again.

T: Hmm... I take back what I said last week about the Menoptra's mannerisms interfering with the drama; as I spend more time in their company, I've stopped being distracted by them (much like, I suppose, the way you're no longer distracted by aeroplane noise if you live near Heathrow for a while). Also, let me give some credit to the Zarbi operators – they have to spend the whole episode not standing up straight, being weighed down by a pretty hefty costume, so I find it forgivable when one crashes into the camera (especially in the days when editing out such a mishap wasn't really feasible; these days, such a goof would never have been left in the story). Whoever's inside the Zarbi that Ian tussles with deserves a medal, as he remains upright under quite a hefty onslaught from Russell.

The cliffhanger leaps out at me as being terribly odd, though – *I* know what happens, but I'm not sure it's clear to a virgin audience. Vrestin says the ground is giving way and Ian moves to help... all right, but then sand falls *on top* of him, and it doesn't help matters that we then move to outside the cave and see a lot of confused-looking Zarbi. I would hazard a guess that the script read "Ian and Vrestin fall through the floor – cue titles," not "Ian and Vrestin fall through the floor, then we see some Zarbi milling about for a bit, then cue titles at a random juncture, thus robbing the cliffhanger of a climactic moment," and can't help but think (sorry about this) that it's a haphazard addition on Richard Martin's part.

But if I'm trying to stay positive here, I should mention that I'm finding enjoyment in lots of little places. With all the aliens on show it's easy to ignore some of the lyricism in Strutton's writing – the strange crying that de Winter does works really well and shows that some of her insect inventions have real plausibility. And whatever the datedness of the costumes, Vrestin looks damned impressive when she unexpectedly takes off and starts flying. Also, I *love* the title "Escape to Danger": those three words became ubiquitous when used for Target novel chapter names, so I feel comfy and nostalgic every time I see them hit the

screen. It's like wrapping myself in a large, geeky blanket.

January 31st

The Crater of Needles (The Web Planet episode four)

R: Look who's just come flying in! It's Martin Jarvis! Martin's been my producer at BBC Radio for nearly ten years now, and is one of my best friends. When you and I are in Los Angeles for the Gallifrey convention in a couple of weeks, Toby, I'll go and stay with Martin for a bit once the show is over. We sometimes talk about Vengeance on Varos. Once in a while we'll dip our toes into Invasion of the Dinosaurs. But we never – repeat *never* – discuss The Web Planet. Hmm. I wonder why.

I suppose it could be that no-one really looks all that good in a big butterfly costume. I have to be honest – there are a few stories out there I was rather dreading watching again, and The Web Planet was one of them. I've really been enjoying it, though, and that's probably because as I watch the series in order, I'm seeing it in the right context, and can appreciate just how the series is building. But The Crater of Needles is pretty much what I remember from the last time I gave it a go, some 15 years ago: lots and *lots* of characters I can't tell apart all chatting away to each other in furry costumes. What stands out to me now is just how many of them are rebelling against the attempts to make their speech artificial, and give it a bit more distinctive oomph. Martin's really very good as the haughty and regal Captain Hilio; Jocelyn Birdsall clearly has decided she can't possibly echo Roslyn de Winter's mannered Vrestin, and makes her own Menoptra much more naturalistic. It's a relief, because when you *do* get performers like Ian Thompson as Hetra – who is really getting his teeth into the alien rhythms – you better appreciate their efforts as a contrast to those about him.

The Crater of Needles is a tough episode, because it's really the first of these Vortis episodes where a lot of strange aliens with subtly different characterisations and motives repeatedly outnumber the regular cast. But there's a real chutzpah to a lot of it, and sequences like the one at the episode's climax – where there's a pitched battle between Zarbi and the Menoptra invasion force – have a certain grandeur to them. It may be a folie de grandeur, but the flying of the butterflies – with those camera pans as you see Menoptra battling ants and dying elegantly after being shot by woodlice – is like nothing else. And it works a lot better than it has really any right to.

Oh, and I love the way the Optera manacle their captives by having them dip their hands into some strange liquid gunk that hardens. It's those little touches of originality that make Vortis *interestingly* alien, rather than merely a bunch of actors jumping about in boiler suits. (Poor old Optera. Martin shouldn't complain – at least his costume was better.)

I feel guilty seeing Martin there on screen. I'm supposed to be writing a radio commission for him this very moment, and instead I'm watching Doctor Who and the Antmen. But if I try, I just pretend that isn't my commissioning boss on screen at all. Actually, I don't need to try *that* hard.

T: My nervousness about watching The Web Planet hasn't yet gone away, and I've been sitting here waiting for it to get awful... but do you know, it hasn't – it really hasn't. Okay, I continue to think that Richard Martin is a clumsy director; there are moments where it's really not clear what the hell is going on, or where it's only possible to discern what the action is because I've read the book. And astonishingly, the cliffhanger here is possibly *more* inept than the one before it! The clear intention was that the climax was meant to entail Babs and everyone with her trapped against a rock as the venom-grub charged up its nose-gun. It sounds so simple, and yet we don't actually cut to the titles until they have started to run away and thus... escaped the danger. It's not exactly a successful cliffhanger if you see the heroes elude the threat, is it? For all of Martin's high-falutin' and often impressive ideas, his basic storytelling is appalling.

But visually, there's more than enough to keep me interested. The Menoptra and Zarbi both look good enough in long shot, and for all I've just complained about him, Richard Martin tries to keep his camera back to over-

come the limitations imposed by the cramped studio conditions. I also like how there are two sorts of Menoptra here – the ones recorded on film and ones in the studio have differing masks. (My favourites, though, didn't actually make it to screen... photos exist of a third type of Menoptra with furry cowls.)

And the more this story continues, the more Vortis' ecosystem seems textured; the idea of the vegetation being broken down by the acid and channelled into the Carcinome, which explains why the planet is becoming barren, is a smart and well-described idea. The tunnelling Optera are a nice addition (and not part of Strutton's original scripts, apparently) and even if their appearance and gait is somewhat laughable, in concept they're a credible and interesting extra layer to this world. It jars a little when Vrestin compares the Opera to slugs – she's describing them in Earth terms, which is a bit like the Judoon announcing themselves as space rhinos. Vrestin is pretty cool when she displays her wings in full spread, though.

One more thing... there's a great moment where it's postulated that the Doctor might be helping the Zarbi; Barbara says she's certain he would never do such a thing, but Jacqueline Hill puts enough doubt into her voice to suggest that Barbara might be lying to herself. It's a clever choice that re-injects some of the crew's earlier, more ambiguous dynamic.

Invasion
(The Web Planet episode five)

R: Back in 1982, to commemorate the return of the Cybermen to our screens, the BBC produced a special documentary about Doctor Who's monsters on a magazine review programme called Did You See? And those clips they used on it for a long time were the only taster I had of the show's black and white era. I couldn't keep the documentary on video – they were so expensive in those days, and I was only 12 – but I copied it all onto audiotape. And I listened to it so often when I was a kid, over and over again, trying to imagine what these strange stories from the past could possibly be like. There's a scene from this episode that I suddenly found I could recite, word for word – and the joke was, of course, that for so many years I had no understanding whatsoever of this rather dry scene in which a bunch of Menoptra discuss their invasion plans. Oh, the stories I imagined around that little scene during my childhood! "They too will be massacred. The Menoptra will be no more!" Gave me nostalgic shivers that did. Lovely.

The deeper you get into The Web Planet, the narrower the tightrope it walks between wonderful ambition and toecurling clumsiness. To be fair to it, it's only here in episode five that it finally falls off. But look past the scenes of all the Optera bouncing up and down, or the long dialogue bits where Menoptra argue about Isoptopes and electron passwords, and there's still much to admire. I love the way writer Bill Strutton has tried to give the story a language of its own – from the way that no-one can say Ian or Barbara's names correctly, to Hetra's description of digging as trying to make something talk with light. Yes, it's all a bit mannered, even a bit pretentious – but it suddenly contrasts with the dispassion shown when poor little Nemini saves everyone's lives by using her body to block a flow of acid, and the way that only Ian is moved by the sacrifice. The *effort* that has gone into making this an alien culture is almost bonkers in its detail – and yet, every once in a while, there'll be a scene where the emotional reaction shown by characters is so skewed, and you realise they really are *alien*.

T: I'm increasingly starting to think that I didn't enjoy this story previously due to the muddied, grotty print I had – now that The Web Planet has been all spruced up on DVD, it's so much easier to follow, and there are so many interesting visual touches that the longueurs aren't quite so painful. Even things that had annoyed me before – such as Ian Thompson's very odd performance as Hetra – now work much better. His face is constantly twitching, struggling to form the words, which makes his guttural drawl a much more understandable acting choice. He seems to be giving the impression that his character is just learning how to speak and to enunciate – in other words, his speech is evolving in the same way that his species soon will. That may sound a bit strange, but it's no less believable than aliens speaking RP, so good on him for having

a bash at something different. His references to smashing teeth of stone and the hole being a mouth which speaks more light are brilliant – it's an inventive approach to creating an alien viewpoint that we can translate and understand.

The set for the Temple of Light is very impressive, especially with those mummified Menoptra cadavers spookily hanging about the place. Likewise, it's no mistake that the centre of the Animus – the "Carcinome" – has a cancerous moniker, meaning that the Isoptope is a kind of portable chemotherapy machine. This disease analogy helps the audience to understand the sci-fi concept of the Animus and its baleful effect on the planet.

And while you praised some of the guest-cast last week, notably your mate Martin Jarvis (you wait till The Time Warrior episode three and I'll start the name dropping – oh yes indeed, I was once in a play with the non-speaking mate of the sentry in that brilliant scene where the Doctor is disguised as a friar), I here note that Jolyon Booth (playing Prapillus) gets lots of lyrical language to chew on and does it brilliantly. In contrast to all the visual oddities, there's a poetic beauty in his descriptive vocabulary that's most pleasing. But it's perhaps no surprise that Booth handles such words so well – a friend of mine from university went to a posh public school (Winchester, I think) and Booth was one of his teachers.

I must stop to mention the very bizarre moment where a tendril appears to fart at the Doctor, and he ripostes "And the same to you!" But on the plus side – hurrah, we're back to having successful cliffhangers! The Doctor and Vicki are here shown shrouded by web, in what's a startling, chilling image.

February 1st

The Centre
(The Web Planet episode six)

R: The Animus is defeated quite early in the episode, which leaves lots of time at the story's end for Vrestin to teach the Optera how to enjoy the bright lights, and to give flying a go. It's all done with much conviction by Roslyn de Winter – and then it dawns on you that this is probably *exactly* how she's been treating the cast these past six weeks! "Be brave, be brave!" It's so easy to picture her, leading masterclasses on hand waving in the mornings, and speech inflection in the afternoons.

"Be brave!" It's not a bad way to approach The Web Planet, all told. There's much here to admire, but let's face it – it is (deliberately) the most alienating of all Doctor Who stories *ever*. (There are one or two of the Virgin New Adventures novels which come close, but even the ones which deal with the psi-powers arc aren't as much of a culture shock as this.) And it's also (not deliberately) one of the most dated. The latter is hardly the story's fault. Indeed, if anything, it's something to be cautiously admired.

Certainly, Doctor Who never even attempted to be quite this extreme ever again; there will never be another story without humanoid characters within it. That makes sense – at its best, the series is always *about* humanity, even if only in a form that is symbolic. But in a funny way, by attempting something as bold as this – to see whether Doctor Who could possibly survive without any of the familiarities that give it tone and theme – it shows just how limitless its scale can be. Doctor Who never *needs* to do anything like this again; now it's been done the once, we can imagine, should we want to, that the strange adventures the Doctor often alludes (but which we don't actually witness) may all be like this. Consider the off-handed mentions of the planet Quinnis where they nearly lost the TARDIS, the planet Esto where everyone communicated by thought – or even, in the new series, the planet Woman Wept, where the waves are like rock. The Web Planet conjured up all these imaginings, and serves as the bedrock for the breadth of its ambition.

Now let's get away from those talking butterflies and get back to Earth. Pronto. What's this? Next Episode: "The Lion"? I hope it's not a talking lion.

T: Much of what goes on here at the end, I'm sorry to say, and with the best of goodwill, probably earns this story its brickbats. The Menoptra actors have previously done well enough with the odd speech patterns and the

"Insect Movement" by Roslyn De Winter, but the way they clamber around the set screaming "Zaar-biiiiii-eeeeeee-eeeeeeeee" probably didn't make it onto any of their showreels. I suspect that Ian Thompson's copy of this episode had a suspicious looking edit just before Hetra decides to have a go at flying, and the final confrontation with the Animus is a mess – Barbara's gun doesn't work, then Ian appears, then Barbara perseveres with holding the weapon whilst everyone else falls over.. and then suddenly the Animus dies, with the camera apparently picking out random bits of action. It's all very confused.

But, look! There are still plenty of good moments – Hrostar and Hilio clearly don't like each other and have a little ritual hissing as they face off, and Prapillus has a sweet "dotty old man" moment where he bustles about the Doctor's astral map and then tells everyone to hurry, unaware that they've already buggered off. (He also calls the "Sayo Plateau" the "Isop Plateau", but you can't really blame him for getting confused.) And as we finally see (or rather, can *actually* see, in this sparking new DVD print) the water breaking out onto the surface of Vortis, the leisurely pace at the end is quite welcome after what has been a bustling two and a half hours.

Whatever my reservations about The Web Planet – and whatever fandom's low opinion of it – I think much of this works in context. Sure, much of it *doesn't* work, but let's remember that this is the show's second year, and they're not resting on their laurels. This adventure was a work of madness, but there was definitely some method in it.

The Lion
(The Crusade episode one)

R: In its own way, this is as dated as The Web Planet. You start off being distracted by all the alarming facial hair – but it's the blacked-up actors you remember. But, as we've seen in Marco Polo, the Saracens are treated with respect – because although their skin colour marks them out as foreign and exotic, their accents don't; Bernard Kay, as Saladin, acts with the same rich Shakespearean delivery as Julian Glover's King Richard the Lionheart. Certainly, this is going to be an issue that

Doctor Who contends with for some time to come – and we're still 12 years away from the wince-inducing portrait of the Chinese in The Talons of Weng-Chiang – but however awkward it looks from today's perspective to see Caucasian actors wearing dark make-up, there's nothing in the script or the performances which indicate that this is racist. Indeed, what's remarkable about the episode is the way that it treats its two Famous Historical Characters. Saladin is *terrific* – the way he's introduced, listening unobserved and unsmiling behind the curtain, gives him a real power; and once he emerges, Bernard Kay so effortlessly commands respect and fear without ever raising his voice or even appearing to change his inflection. There's a wisdom and subtlety to the man, and for a moment we allow ourselves almost to *patronise* him, to think that this is the Kindly Arab. But there's one magnificent moment in particular where Barbara, like the audience, is lulled into a false sense of security, as she contemplates how her storytelling will make her like Scheherazade. Saladin reminds her that the threat of death hung over her skills too... It's his amorality that makes Saladin so compelling, and Bernard Kay is the equal of Julian Glover at commanding natural authority.

Indeed, if anything, it's the amorality of Richard too which is so striking. Schoolboy history held that Richard the Lionheart was our hero king – that's certainly what I gleaned from my Ladybird books when I was a kid – and all the Robin Hood legends, of course, paint him as the kindly monarch whose mere showing up at court could put an end to the schemes of the Sheriff of Nottingham. We know from *real* history, though, that Richard was one of the biggest gits ever to have sat on the throne of England (not that he was in England enough to warm the throne in the first place), but that's not the point; it's more that Doctor Who here refuses to paint Richard in the way that anyone watching in 1965 would have expected. We see in his first scene a king who is so capricious that he gets his fellows killed, and in his second a man given to bouts of melodramatic temper, who just can't be reasoned with. (The cliffhanger has a double whammy – it's not just that Barbara's in danger, it's that with Richard's retort that she can rot in

a cell for all he cares, the audience unequivocally are made to realise he's not the great symbol of England they were hoping for, and it's a real shock. It's the equivalent of depicting Marco Polo as a villain, or Robespierre as a hero.) There's a wonderful fluff that Julian Glover makes, and it actually *helps* this bold portrayal when he bemoans the fact that Richard des Preaux (not, more correctly, *William* des Preaux) has been captured. It gives the impression that for all his crocodile tears, this arrogant king can't even remember his friend's name.

T: Douglas Camfield is setting himself up early as the Doctor Who action director – all right, this inevitably looks a bit clumsy to modern eyes, but the ambition in the staging of the early scuffles marks this out as bold work. There are carefully timed and cunningly hidden arrows, Ian gets a fight on film (with Val Mussetti, a racing driver of note when he's not playing a Saracen warrior), and best of all, stuntman Derek Ware gets thunked in the chest by a whacking great sword. It's impressive, even if the rather mimsy underarm sword-throw that butchers Ware would have caused the weapon to just bounce off his chest rather than pierce his armour and ribcage.

But what's so striking about this episode is that it makes as its core the two elements that are central to all good drama: namely, writing strong dialogue, and getting talented actors to speak it. This first makes me wonder what transformation David Whitaker has undergone since he stopped being script editor – the man who formerly wrote The Edge of Destruction and The Rescue here gives us such excellent dialogue and characterisation; episode one alone is a work of ambiguity and poetry. And while Julian Glover happily plays up Richard's weaknesses and petulance to the point that he's as big a threat to the travellers' safety as anything else in this strange land, you're absolutely right, Rob, to highlight Bernard Kay as Saladin. This is an *astonishingly* powerful performance – the best yet seen in the series, even – and a lesson in the art of underplaying. Saladin's face is locked in the aspect of a man wearied by war, who has no time or inclination to dress things up or even strut his power. He completely deadpans when telling des Preaux

89

"I salute your chivalry," leaving you in no doubt that while he means what he says, he's not someone who needs to get all flowery and twee. He's at war, after all.

The only thing detracting from Kay's performance – and as you've already mentioned – is the way he and other actors are "blacked up". In fact, dark make-up isn't the only means by which the producers have juggled with ethnicity here: one of the extras is Oscar James (later one of the original cast on EastEnders), who is of West Indian descent. (Imagine his agent telling him that as a West Indian, he'd be perfect casting in the role of an Arab!) But while I am almost painfully politically correct, I can't say this damaged the story's dramatic intent for me – you'd never get away with this today (and rightfully so), but it's easy to view this theatrical practice as the product of bygone era. Donald Sinden played Othello once, for goodness sake, and – in the very same year that The Crusade was broadcast – so did Laurence Olivier, in full blackface! He was even nominated for an Oscar for it!

In the very first preview version of Moths Ate My Doctor Who Scarf, I did a joke about the whole race issue – mentioning that only in the 60s could you get twelfth century, Arabic Muslims played by actors called "Bernard", "Roger" and (best of all) "Reg". It got a decent response, but I didn't really know what I was trying to say, and it seemed like an easy dig when there's so much else to enjoy in this rich, lyrical tale. What is funny, though, is how this episode has a selfish, thieving opportunist named "Thatcher".

February 2nd

The Knight of Jaffa
(The Crusade episode two)

R: What I love about The Crusade is just how many different stories it juggles with at once, how tonally different they are from each other, and at what a terrific pace they're told. So we open with a really clever scene in which the Doctor manages to manipulate Richard into reinterpreting the capture of des Preaux and Barbara as something to his political advantage; it's delightfully done, and Richard's com-mendation of Ian's courage and the Doctor's wit nicely assigns them their individual roles for the rest of the story. But we then contrast this with pure melodrama, as the scarred El Akir ponders revenge upon Barbara for humiliating him. And we contrast *that* with a scene of rare pomp within Doctor Who, as Ian is knighted by the King with all due solemnity. The Doctor can laugh about it all afterwards, and wish *he'd* been knighted too, but even he daren't mar the tone of the ceremony. Just compare this to the corresponding scene in Tooth and Claw some 40 years later, where the Doctor and Rose are tourist bystanders to the same event even as it's happening to them. And then we contrast that with a wonderful scene of comedy in which the Doctor runs rings around the chamberlain, who has realised our heroes are wearing stolen clothes. We're watching a story about kings and sultans, about merchants and thieves.

In a typical historical adventure we might expect this story to be taking twice as long. El Akir hatches a plot against Barbara – and it's succeeded within ten minutes' screen time. Ian is knighted so he can journey to Saladin – he's there within the same episode. The distinction of the (serious) historicals before this has been the way they've explored the setting with respectful depth; The Crusade offers us almost a snapshot portrait of an epic. We're presented with a whole array of characters who are painted in vivid detail, then disappear out of the story. The first episode seemed to establish the idea that William des Preaux would be an important friend to Barbara – the job done, they're never in the same scene ever again. The merchant Luigi Ferrigo becomes lackey to El Akir, smarms his way around Saladin and is exposed at record speed. Sheyrah establishes herself as loyal ally to Barbara, in a role you'd expect in any ordinary story would make her a confidante like a Ping-Cho or a Cameca... and then she's gone. David Whitaker's script feels like an extraordinary synthesis of the historical he established as story editor in the first season, coupled with the quicker paced action approach adopted by his successor Dennis Spooner. And the result is all rather exhilarating.

T: You're right... David Whitaker is so immersed in this world, he gives depth to characters with limited screen time; they fulfill their plot function with economy, but don't feel at all sketchy or perfunctory. And because Doctor Who can't do pitched battles at present, manners and guile are the weapons used in this engrossing historical drama.

But Whitaker nurtures his supporting cast while playing to each of the regulars' strengths – this is perhaps no surprise, as he was the show's original script editor and understands the characters very well. But he does a great job of using the TARDIS quartet in different dramatic ways, while insuring that their stories are packed with incident and peril. The Doctor is a clever manipulator, and has a little sabbatical in an amusing subplot with Vicki as his witty sidekick (fortunately, Maureen O'Brien has got the comedy stuff licked). Ian is the square-jawed hero, volunteering to go off, flirt with danger and rescue Barbara. And Barbara herself gets the meaty drama – she's thrown in and out of jeopardy so much, she has to be brave and clever in equal measure. She needs all of her wits, in fact, to avoid winding up in El-Akir's harem – all this travel through time and space, and she's once again an object of lust. It's enough to give a person a complex!

Oh, and look – the telesnap of Sir William throttling Luigi is exactly reproduced in the Target novel.

The Wheel of Fortune
(The Crusade episode three)

R: This series is certainly very keen on its forced marriages, isn't it? It seems that whenever the TARDIS pops back into history, somebody is being wed to someone else! For the first time, though, we're being invited to *sympathise* with this marriage and see it for the common good. That's odd in itself – even odder, perhaps, within a context of an adventure serial with aliens and monsters and guns, that we're being told we should prefer the dramatic resolution being something in a church with confetti and cake, as opposed to lots of sword fights and deaths on a battlefield. And it's interesting to see that whereas we were supposed to baulk at Ping-Cho's arranged marriage in Marco Polo from a twentieth century

perspective, here Joanna's arguments are that she doesn't want to be wed to an *infidel* on point of principle. She defends herself on grounds of xenophobia, rather than freedom of choice.

It's a measure of how much weight these scenes have that the Doctor's attack upon the Earl of Leicester seems so unjust. Because the Earl has a rather good point to make – that whilst the politicians can play around with honeyed diplomacy, it'll be the grunts on the battlefield like him who'll have to pick up the pieces when diplomacy fails. John Bay could have played the part like the thug that the Doctor accuses him of being, but he makes good use of Whitaker's Shakespearean spoof dialogue (deliberately aping Henry V here) and giving his case a convincing righteous anger. Just look, later on, when he's required politely to praise Vicki's dress – he'll play the game of courtier, but only to a point.

And if Joanna objects to being married off to a Muslim, so in contrast we does Barbara resist being put inside El Akir's harem. On the face of it, Barbara's storyline is a lot less sophisticated than all these court scenes of intrigue, as she hides away from a melodramatic villain – but it's a really clever parallel to it. And Jacqueline Hill continues to amaze. David Whitaker introduces a new character, Barbara's protector Haroun, and has him detail his life history minutes after we've met him... and it's through Hill's reaction that we find it moving. The bravery she shows as she sacrifices herself for the safety of Haroun's daughter Safiya, but more particularly the very human fear that Hill shows as she comes out of her hiding place *still* hoping against hope to make good her escape, is just wonderful.

What a magnificent episode. And on top of all that, we get a chamberlain who rolls his eyes to Heaven at the thought of modern-day transvestitism. You can't get much better than this.

T: The way that we here leap from gripping storyline to gripping storyline puts lie to the occasional assertion that the historicals are dull. Ian gets a bit of a scrap, and Barbara spends the whole episode essentially engaging in an aborted escape attempt – but her meeting with Haroun, and her sacrifice to save Safiya, keep this potentially perfunctory diversion interesting, moving and exciting.

Even better, the scenes between Richard, the Doctor and Leicester – and then Richard and Joanna – are the best written and acted we've seen in the series thus far. Bernard Kay got my vote for "best performance" in episode one, but here we're given such incredible ensemble pieces. Jean Marsh bristles with righteous anger as Richard's sister, whilst Glover's impotence, and exasperation at his inability to bend Joanna to his will, seize every fibre of his being. And yes, our loyalties are severely tested as we hurtle from one moral grey area to another – the Doctor is great in facing down Leicester, yet the latter is clearly a brave man. Joanna is absolutely entitled to feel like a pawn in a game of politics, but her assertion that all of England reside in the heathen land to fight and kill and butcher sits uncomfortably with her moral outrage. Richard struggles to find a way to avoid confrontation, but is still a wilful bully. And the Shakespearian dialogue is delivered with such aplomb, it's in no way forced or unrealistic. Douglas Camfield could have picked a British thesp to play Leicester, yet he oddly went for an American – fortunately, John Bay plays the part well. And then there's George Little as Haroun, his voice quavering as he prepares us for how cruel and callous El Akir will be when Barbara is captured. Oh, it's hard to imagine a finer cast.

As part of this, neither Richard nor Saladin are depicted as being the goody or the baddy – they're both men burdened with enormous responsibility, and while they're honourable on one hand, they're pragmatic about awful bloodshed on the other. It's a clever study on the responsibilities of power and the human being beneath the crown (or turban). Saladin only appears in one short scene, but he's weary and wily, playing with his brother by alluding to his ambition. Bernard Kay's face only registers the barest flicker of emotion, but those tiny little nuances speak volumes about this shrewd, utterly believable character.

And even though El Akir is hardly in this episode, we've heard so much about his sadism (the way that people keep telling of his cruelty and butchery is far more effective than depicting it on screen) that the cliffhanger – as El Akir tells Barbara, "The only pleasure left for you is death. And death is very far away..." – is genuinely horrifying. I'll take that approach over the likes of "Kill them, kill them now!" or "Crikey, it's a monster!" any day. Whilst it's again frustrating that half of the best story of this season is missing from the archives, we should be grateful that the wheel of fortune (and, I suppose, the BBC Film Library) somehow kept this episode safe from the purge.

February 3rd

The Warlords
(The Crusade episode four)

R: So – what happens to Fatima? This episode is missing from the archives, and the telesnaps of it are frustratingly vague. Fatima is the Judas of the harem, the woman who sells out Barbara to El Akir for the price of a shiny ruby. The last we see of her, after El Akir has been successfully foiled, is when all the other members of the harem surround her without saying a word... and Fatima starts to scream. (I don't imagine viewers in 1965 saw *anything* of what happened to her, but the suggestion is very unpleasant.)

This is the story's final episode, and it all ends happily, with our heroes laughing at puns in the TARDIS. But it's the *suggestion* of a darkness under the surface that makes this episode interesting. Maimuna – Haroun's other daughter – is moved to hear from Barbara that her father wants to rescue her. She says that she'd have expected he would be unable to forgive her – because, although it's not spelled out, she's clearly no longer a virgin and has been defiled by El Akir. And, of course, historically Maimuna would be right; Haroun could never have taken her back. This being an episode of children's television, of course, Haroun's views are much more enlightened. But Whitaker darkly suggests what the real-world consequences of her capture would be. In a similar way, Julian Glover speaks in interviews about how the script could never have made reference to the incestuous relationship between Richard and his sister Joanna, but how he and Jean Marsh alluded to it anyway in their performances – and there's certainly something cooking between them in episode two. All of this makes The Crusade a curious beast – it acknowledges in a very subtle way the adult themes, then with a wink heads off in another direction. An illustration of this is how, in the novelisation of this story, Richard never forgives the Doctor for the supposed treachery of his telling Joanna about the marriage plans – whereas here in the broadcast version, he pops in for a final scene to reassure the kids at home that he knows the Doctor wasn't to blame.

That's what is so remarkable about The Crusade – the way that it plays off a darker storyline whilst accepting it needs to give a happy ending. In its own clever way, this is as unrealistic a historical adventure as The Romans. Where Spooner's story buried its crueller excesses beneath black comedy, Whitaker does so with pageantry. It's why we get glimpses of these characters, no more – by episode four, the story has moved away from Richard and Saladin altogether (indeed, Bernard Kay doesn't even feature in this episode, and Jean Marsh vanishes as well), and we're concerned with the revenge story of Haroun (introduced only last week), and the menace of the Earl of Leicester (ditto), whilst building up one-episode wonders such as Maimuna or Ibrahim. It means that everyone is simplified, but by being so allow *hints* of the reality that Whitaker bounces off. We accept Haroun's decency towards his daughter, because we barely know them as characters, so accept without question what they represent.

Why is Doctor Who doing this? Well, because it's already finding itself at something of a crossroads. The writers can easily control the tone of the sci-fi adventures and turn them into morality plays with whatever level of sophistication they like; they can have happy endings in which the villains are bested and the heroes triumph unequivocally. The historical stories are already to be found in schoolbooks, and have an ambiguity to them that contrasts rather wildly. To fit in with the tone of the series Dennis Spooner is aiming for, there has to be a "take" on history – just as Russell T Davies offers in the twenty-first century. And it's telling, I think, that for the rest of Spooner's tenure on the series as script editor, we'll never get another "pure" historical, and he'll allow the sci-fi stories to collide with them completely.

T: And herein lies the problem: as you say, the Richard/Saladin story fizzles out – because historically speaking, what role *could* the travellers have played in it without stretching our credulity? The political gamesmanship between them has been a brilliantly written and acted non sequitur, but now the individual storylines that seemed as if they were there just to generate random thrills (Ian's journey, Barbara's capture) become the focus of the story. For any viewer not familiar with what the history books say about these events, there's no resolution at all to the Joanna/Saphadin proposal, and the Doctor's not even that explicit about what becomes of Richard, apart from mentioning that he won't make it to Jerusalem.

But I'm fine with this – the plotting may not be rigorous, but I'll excuse it because of the brilliance of the script in other areas. I find it harder to forgive a loosely structured script if the writer is just being lazy, but if it's the result of their having other priorities, then more power to his/her elbow. And there *is* a resolution here (just not with the most prominent historical figures), as Haroun gets to indulge in a spot of (very swiftly dealt) poetic justice when he dispatches El Akir.

Woven into all the drama of this climactic episode are some great laughs – the bandit Ibrahim is bananas (and Tutte Lemkow is having a whale of a time in the role), even though he's a most unlikely ally for Ian. (Let's face it, we're having fun here with a character who has probably tortured and killed people for tuppence.) And it's entertaining how the telesnaps show the sequence with the ants' nest as being shot through the carcass of a cow – it suggests that, even this early in his career, this was directed with Douglas Camfield's trademark visual flare.

Even though it's hard to make a proper judgment unless a story exists in full in the archives, everything that *does* exist of The Crusade is so marvellous, I would venture to say that this is one of the best Doctor Who stories of all time. However, I'm afraid to tell you, Rob, that Fatima is toast. History is a cruel place to hang about in, but one of the many things that's great about the series at this stage is that it's not afraid to confront us with that unpleasant fact.

The Space Museum (episode one)

R: A space museum is rather a good idea. If I ever write an episode of Doctor Who, I think I'll nick it!... oh, hang on. I did.

The last time Mervyn Pinfield directed a story it was Planet of Giants, in which the regulars didn't interact with the rest of the cast. This time the same thing happens, in spite of Vicki's most hysterical sneezing trying to force them into the narrative. As associate producer, Pinfield was always most interested in the odder, "sideways" stories that the series could tell – so it's highly appropriate he was allocated to this, as it's as determinedly odd as it can get. Doctor Who has done odd before, of course – The Edge of Destruction is still a chilling memory – and the reason why this is so much better is because the regular cast are a solid rock against all the deliberate inconsistencies. Indeed, it's perhaps telling that within seconds of the episode starting, they are magically popped back into their default costumes. With all the mysteries on offer, the story needs to present the leads as identifiable and dependable (which is why Hartnell pops back into the familiar grumpy version of his Doctor characterisation, and O'Brien plays up the clumsy girl).

And what's brilliant is that the more the mysteries pile up, the more the TARDIS crew are forced to try to work out what's going on – and by doing so, invite the audience to do so as well. At the very start the Doctor, rather wonderfully, takes the first oddity purely on face value – rather delightedly, he tells his friends that now they're all in their familiar garb, it'll save them all the effort of having to get changed. Pretty soon, though, everyone is coming up with theories which get ever more elaborate. From supposing they've landed on a dead world (they haven't), to wondering whether everyone's voices are on a higher frequency (they aren't), they eventually come to the simple conclusion they *simply aren't there.*

As writer, Glyn Jones builds up the clues so skilfully – once our heroes alight upon an answer, it's as if he cruelly rewards them with the evidence of their own dead bodies. What's so clever is that he makes the audience so intent on what the puzzles can mean, he makes us take our eyes off any possible threat

– he even gives us a harmless Dalek to reinforce the point – and then shocks us with one of the most striking images the show has yet given us. And the final five minutes – as the crew are genuinely helpless for the first time, unable to connect with a story they haven't yet taken part in but in which they finish up as corpses – has a wonderful clarity to it. At last the footprints appear, the bodies vanish, and the Doctor acknowledges they're ready to start the story... with none of the complacency with which we're by now used to, and with all the dread which comes of knowing that this adventure is destined to be his last. It's the best cliffhanger the series has yet shown.

T: This is a decent episode, but it's not quite as bonkers or surreal as its reputation. Much like The Dead Planet, it's a good, old-fashioned 25 minutes of being presented with a set of clues, and having to work out what type of story we're dealing with. These days, it's the sort of preamble that would be dispensed with before the opening credits roll, but here the creepy way it takes longer to play out, layering mystery upon mystery, is very intriguing. I believe Mervyn Pinfield was assigned to direct this because of the various bits of trickery required (his role as executive producer, I think, had been primarily the result of his nous with all things experimental), and there certainly is a lot of technical virtuosity on display.

While I don't know how many "sideways" stories the series could have done before they overstayed their welcome, I don't resent this one at all – it uses the fact that we're in a sci-fi universe to explore all sorts of possibilities we couldn't get in a normal setting. The travellers are here faced with an *entirely* fictitious problem (as far as I know, there's no such thing as a "time track", but perhaps the likes of Stephen Hawking know better), so we're thrust into very imaginative realms, and can't second guess how our heroes will survive.

Two other things about this story stand out for me... I was delighted to hear some stock music that I've only previously heard in the Quatermass serials; they have an especially spooky effect on me, as I associate those sounds with the dark, foreboding horror of Nigel Kneale's wonderful work. And while I'd never really liked Maureen O'Brien's performance prior to starting this exercise of ours, I'm starting to find her invaluable. No matter how peripheral she is to any given scene, she just keeps on acting – and yet she doesn't overdo it at all. Her commitment to keeping her character doing interesting things is to be applauded.

Eventually, we arrive at that great final sequence where the travellers – having seen the doom that awaits them – "arrive" in the museum, accompanied by some stirringly melodramatic music. Hartnell's apprehensive face fills the screen – and is it wrong of me to notice his very expressive teeth? Those two fangs bestriding his truncated upper middles really add to his beguiling, characterful visage.

February 4th

The Dimensions of Time
(The Space Museum episode two)

R: Okay, this is inevitably something of a disappointment. We go from one of the strangest episodes in the canon to... well, 20-odd minutes of our regular cast walking up and down sterile corridors. But there's still much to find interesting.

To kick off with: the Moroks are rubbish. Really, rubbish. But that is the whole point. We're encountering an aggressive race of alien conquerors past their prime. Once, they conquered galaxies. Now, they sit around and moan about the hours they work, like bored bureaucrats – and, in their boredom, perk up with childish enthusiasm when a handful of aliens wander around their museum in need of being captured. The dialogue therefore must either be perfectly awful or is secretly rather clever – Lobos, a governor so dull that no-one can respect him, spends his first scene talking exposition so long-winded and obvious, it surely *must* be a joke. (Glyn Jones clearly thought it was – in his Target novelisation, he repeatedly depicts Lobos' underlings as staring at the ceiling in embarrassment whenever he opens his mouth.) We've seen the outcome of alien invasion explored to great dramatic effect in The Dalek Invasion of Earth; now we see the flipside of totalitarianism, the tedious pointlessness of it, the museums erected in honour

of victories won long ago that no-one any longer cares about. In a way, I feel, it's the more realistic depiction. And if you can be judged by the quality of your enemies... well, it's telling that the only species on the planet more inept than the Moroks are the Xerons. You can tell they're inept because even the Moroks can't be bothered to subjugate them properly. The Xerons dress around in black polo neck sweaters and trainers, like first-year students in the university coffee bar, and seem to have elected as leader a boy purely based upon his ability to put his hands on his hips in any given number of situations. Their big plan this episode to free their planet is to capture the Doctor. This they do, only promptly to lose him again. The Moroks have nothing to fear from this bunch.

The Space Museum has a very bad reputation, and it's based upon the idea that after a brilliant opening instalment, the successive runaround episodes are cheap and formulaic. Cheap they certainly are, there's no denying that. But the "formulaic" part is surely deliberate. Here we are, exactly halfway through the Hartnell era, and we're presented with something which parodies the structure of one. It's a comedy. The only problem is, no-one making the story really seems to understand that. You can hardly blame them – there's nothing within the first episode, which was so atypical, to suggest that what would follow would be a send-up of the series' conventions. Only William Hartnell really rises to the occasion; the Doctor has a great time this episode, hiding inside a Dalek and giggling all the while, and making light work of the Morok mind-probe during his interrogation.

T: I like your reinvention of this as a comedy (and the novelisation, which is very funny in places, does indeed back you up on that). How else can you explain a story where the travellers are scuppered not by gun-wielding psychopaths or horrible monsters, but by getting lost in a building and spending a whole episode trying to find the exit? (After a first instalment that's "way out", the second sees the TARDIS crew unable to find one.) Why else would the show invoke the myth of the minotaur, and then re-enact it using, of all things, a cardigan? Even when events get spooky, and Hartnell is bathed in evocative lighting while he's trapped in the interrogation chair, it's not long before we're back into comedic territories – it's difficult to make out, but I sincerely hope that Hartnell himself is the bloke in a bodys-tocking (or whatever it is) who appears on Governor Lobos' monitor. That would have made for a terrifying moment for the PA on this episode: "Here are your call times, Mr Hartnell. We'll need you half an hour earlier tomorrow for the photo session with you in a Victorian swimsuit."

There's also a bit of seriousness here, though, in the way that Richard Shaw – who plays the governor (and of whom I'll talk more about later) – goes to the effort of putting on a South African accent. Let's take this as sign (rightly or wrongly) that he's delivering a little bit of sub-text, which makes his muted performance seem more like a deliberate choice rather than lazy acting. As for the Xerons – hmm, well, anyone who thinks that Doctor Who only got camp when JN-T climbed aboard should have a butchers at this lot! I note they're wearing converse trainers too (so, David Tennant got his wardrobe choice from these lovely lads did he?).

But the ongoing dilemma makes me want to ask: why, exactly, would the Moroks *want* the TARDIS crew as exhibits? It's not as if they look manifestly different to everyone else on the planet, so as items preserved in glass cases, they'd hardly be worth a gawp. If the Moroks had been purple octopi, I could understand them being fascinated by humans, but I can't really envisage a typical Morok family being all that interested in the Doctor's party. "Look dear, they don't have spiky hair and have only one set of eyebrows – how fascinating!"

Despite all the nice things I can say, though, there's no avoiding the fact that this is clearly a downturn in quality from last week. Perhaps this should stand as a warning to future production teams: never put the words "Dimensions" and "Time" together in an episode title ever again. Whew! Glad that's sorted.

The Search
(The Space Museum
episode three)

R: Ever since Doctor Who began, the writers have been pondering the ramifications of put-

ting time travel at the very core of the series. At what point do the lead characters need to stand back and be observers, and when are they allowed to muck right in and be dynamic? So far, all the shifting arguments about that have taken place in historical adventures – The Aztecs clearly stated that any attempt to inter-fere with destiny is doomed to fail, The Romans suggested that the TARDIS crew are maybe *responsible* for making the history they're trying to preserve. The Crusade had the most muddled position of all: the Doctor sadly tells Vicki in the final episode of Richard the Lionheart's failures in future, and that events cannot be altered, and yet has spent the pre-ceding episode and a half advocating a war-ending marriage that he knows full well didn't take place.

But the sci-fi adventures are fair game, aren't they? It's as if the worlds of Skaro and the Sense-Sphere don't actually *have* a history the Doctor need worry about preserving – or so we thought. What's fascinating about The Search is the way that the TARDIS crew are made so very aware that their own future deaths have become history on Xeros – and that whatever they try to do, whether they resist the guards or hide in the shadows, whether they let events take their course or try to overthrow the gov-ernment, might very well be the very steps that get them embalmed in glass cases. It's really rather an existential argument – the freedom we take for granted to make decisions is all an illusion.

Fortunately, the TARDIS crew are a fairly pro-active bunch, and decide to resist the inevitable anyway. Ian gets to fight a lot – rather impressively, since he's so outnumbered – and even makes an unwilling friend in the form of a cowardly Morok. (He's really very amusing, this Morok – I've no idea who plays him, but I bet Toby does.) And Vicki starts a revolution. You almost get the sense she starts a revolution solely because she's so sick of the inertia – and because the Xerons are so woe-fully colourless beside her that she wants to change their entire society just to make them wake up and take notice. She gains access to the armoury so wonderfully easily, it seems that even the computer has been waiting all this time for someone to have the gumption to override it.

T: Of course I know who your favourite Morok is! It's Peter Diamond – latterly Delos in The Romans, and stuntman extraordinaire. In the novelisation his character gets a name ("Pluton"), and has a much more impressive story arc. Diamond, who died in 2004, can also be found in documentary footage on the Star Wars DVDs – where, amongst other things, he's the Tusken Raider who looms over Luke.

As we continue with this story, I'm more and more aware of Pinfield's directing style. He's got something of a trademark for spooky lighting – there's the recap (Hartnell is hauled to his feet as Lobos orders the Doctor be taken to the "preparation room"), but also the unnerving scene when Barbara nervously hides in a storeroom with two mannequins. One does wonder if Pinfield was as good working with actors, however, as the cast overall seem pretty limp. That said...

I can't help but fixate on Richard Shaw, who plays the governor – he was so very good as Sladden in Quatermass and the Pit, and delivered one of the best performances I've ever seen. It was *way* ahead of its time in terms of naturalism and conveying sci-fi moments without appearing daft or hammy. He's neither of those things here either, but he does play Lobos a little low key considering he's the main villain. To be fair, there might be a reason for that – Shaw wrote to me once, saying that he sustained a severe blow to the eye during the making of this story, but had to carry on. That's why I can be so forgiving when he's Lobos: the man was concussed! The most *colourful* performance in this story, though, is Ivor Salter as the Morok Commander. He's bellicose, but an unfortunate side-effect of his testy bluster is that he clearly hasn't had time to learn his lines properly, and you breathe a sigh of relief when he gets to the end of a sentence with its meaning still vaguely intact.

Finally, Rob, how much do you think Vicki will be venerated in the history books of this planet? If not for her help, the Xerons would still be standing around being wet and sincere. They even seem lame when they tell Vicki, "You can see we're nothing like [the Moroks]". No, you're not, sweetheart – they're not the ones wearing plimsolls or drinking space coffee from space cups, and unable to muster enough intelligence to overcome a security machine that can be defeated by silence. (Had Ascaris led the rebellion on Xeros, they'd have won within minutes. Still, Maureen O'Brien takes great delight in outfoxing a blithering machine that seems less complicated than Windows XP.)

Oh, all right... I must have just one more jab (but a *loving* jab, I promise you!) at this episode, because it contains one of my absolute favourite stupid moments in the show's history! A guard confronts Ian and company at gunpoint, then allows them to plot amongst themselves for what seems like five minutes, and then says, "Enough talking!"... as if, somehow, his being out of shot allows the viewer to forget that he's present whilst our heroes discuss how they're going to deal with him.

February 5th

The Final Phase
(The Space Museum episode four)

R: At the end of the day, it seems that whatever the TARDIS crew did in the museum, they *were* just working towards getting captured and made into exhibits. But, rather wonderfully, ever since they arrived on Xeros, they'd been changing events more subtly – by speaking to people and making a difference to them, they've set into motion a chain of events that allows them to be rescued. It's what Doctor Who is about, fundamentally – that these journeys through space and time *do* have an influence. And it's a very new-series idea, that the day is saved not directly by the Doctor, but by those who have had their lives touched by him. But this is the first time that the classic series comes right out and says it, and it's as if this is the answer that the production team have been working towards for the last two years now, the reason why Doctor Who matters.

The Space Museum might be a bit unloved, a bit naff – but I think that it makes a statement like that is very important. And it can do so purely because it's within a rare context where we're invited to consider the consequences of what would have happened had the Doctor and friends *not* gone down a certain corridor, or *not* encouraged the odd Xeron or two. "Our lives are important; at least, to us," said Hartnell at the very close of the first season, in a scene which could give no conclusion to a discussion about whether or not the Doctor makes any real difference to anyone. Now it's stated, unequivocally, that he does. It's optimistic and it's vital.

I did a DVD documentary for this story a little while ago called "Defending the Museum". I was rather surprised when I got behind the camera to realise that no-one else was prepared to be taking part in such an exercise – *that's* how bad this story's reputation is! And, yes, I exaggerated how much I liked it for comic effect, and I can't pretend it's all that successful a production... but I *do* think there's much here to admire. Not least for the line, "Have any arms fallen into Xeron hands?" A line like that is *so* bad, you just know it had to be deliberate.

T: Oh, you weren't the *only* person they asked to defend The Space Museum, Rob – I was just too expensive.

Here at the end of the story, I realise I came to it the wrong way round upon my initial viewing of it. I had first read Glyn Jones' wonderful novelisation, and so all I could see when I actually watched the story was what I thought was missing from it. And there *are* some frustrating glimpses of what could have been – it seems odd to see poor old Sita being gunned down whilst Dako is only coshed on the head, but the book clarifies that the Morok who bashes Dako (Peter Diamond's character – "Pluton", if you prefer) changes sides. He also spares Gyar (a dishy Xeron who doesn't even appear in this TV version) out of mercy and heroism. Little touches like that are completely absent here, alas, and the next time we see Diamond's character, he's zapped to death while beating a hasty retreat.

And did you notice that whereas The Crusade entailed each regular being given a plot strand that played to their strengths, here it's almost the opposite? The Doctor spends most of the story frozen or locked up, Ian wanders around with a babbling Morok and Barbara is stuck in a gas-filled room. Only Vicki really has an impact on events – fortunately, it's just enough to save the travellers from being freeze-dried. Speaking of which, it's

worth noting that Lobos implied the freezing process might have a permanent effect on the Doctor's brain – and, to judge by the Doctor's giggles and muddled delivery here, it might be worth keeping an eye on him in future. Perhaps Lobos was right, which would help us to rationalise any future piece of Hartnell flubble!

The Executioners
(The Chase episode one)

R: Ha! This one has a tone so unlike anything we've seen on Doctor Who before, and it seems determined to bemuse the audience from the very beginning. We kick off with a reprise from last week, where a Dalek takes orders to arrange for our heroes' extermination. Nice and dramatic, you might think... and then we cut straight to Dudley Simpson playing some inappropriate lounge music. For the next 20 minutes, everyone has a jolly good time watching TV, doing a spot of dancing to The Beatles, catching up with sunbathing and some light reading – in fact, the basic equivalent of your average 60s family on holiday at the beach. And you might be forgiven for thinking that the most terrible consequence likely to happen all episode is that Vicki has ruined Barbara's sewing project. And then, rising out of the sand, comes a Dalek grunting like a pig.

And suddenly, it all makes some sort of weird sense.

Probably the most identifiable image in Doctor Who so far has been the cliffhanger to The Dalek Invasion of Earth episode one, where a Dalek is seen rising majestically from the Thames. What we're given here is a parody of that same sequence; it's too much of a coincidence otherwise. And all that we've been watching is to be seen in that spirit; we've never seen the TARDIS crew as complacent as this before. At first it seems ridiculous that they're all getting so excited about the Time and Space Visualiser, a television that allows them to see any event in history – wow! – but hang on, chaps, look about you. You can *go* there in a moment! But this is a portrait of our regulars being lazy – it's far easier to watch Marco Polo passively on a TV than go and meet him yourself, just as it's far easier to read about space monsters than it is to confront them.

And so it goes on. The TARDIS lands on a strange new planet, and Ian is given a magnet – a device so remarkable that he literally ignores this alien world he's standing on so he can marvel at the gadget instead. No-one can be bothered any more. When Ian and Barbara first arrived in the TARDIS, it was a source of fear and wonder and unimaginable adventure; now, it's a place where they can laze about on a Sunday in their dressing gowns. The magic is over. They've taken it for granted. It's time they went home.

There are lots of little touches to admire here. They obviously haven't room for the TARDIS console this week, so there's a terrific shot of the Doctor reaching out to the viewer to operate the knobs and levers. And I love the fact that the Doctor's the sort of man who can sunbathe without even taking his jacket off. And the Shakespeare sketch is actually quite funny – I can sympathise with any writer who keeps on being stopped and given ideas for stories. (If I were in a pretentious frame of mind, I'd point out how the three sequences we see on the Time and Space Visualiser sort of echo the way that Doctor Who treats its history stories. The first is a bit didactic and po-faced, and the historical figure is treated with enormous respect. The second sends it up a bit. And by the third, no-one can be bothered with historicals any more, and would much rather try to be up to date and funky. But I hate pretension. So I shall say nothing of the sort.)

T: Right, cards on the table – I have a confession to make. The Chase is, as I write this, one of my least favourite Doctor Who stories of all time. It's in my personal bottom five, definitely; I'd rate it a zero out of ten. So, you'll have to forgive me if this gets difficult, but I thought I'd better be honest with you (and anyone reading this) up front. Okay, see you in 25 minutes...

Hello, I'm back now. What's interesting is that for an episode that's menacingly entitled The Executioners, this was actually written with comedy at the forefront. The regulars' insouciance is very much a dramatic irony, as we know the Daleks are on their way to wipe them out. Unfortunately, as part of this, the regulars are all out of form – William Hartnell is written as much more of a consistently dod-dery old buffer (which allows him a couple of nice gags, but also some way OTT "comedy"), William Russell seems disinterested, Jacqueline Hill is unusually shrill and Maureen O'Brien is just drunk. ("I am redundant round here," Vicki says – careful love, future producer John Wiles might be listening.)

Really, that's my problem here. The Executioners isn't bad per se, but almost everything about this – the script, the acting, the direction – well, it just feels a tad slapdash. Ian (a schoolteacher!) says "Barbara and I" instead of "Barbara and me". Richard Martin's predilection for getting the Daleks to repeat everything all the time leads to an unintentionally funny moment where Hill dramatically says, "Doctor, he said TARDIS!" (Yes, he did, Barbara – about 25 bleeding times.) Also, as the three Daleks expertly glide into their time ship (twice over, for benefit of boosting their numbers), one of them noticeably uncouples his mid-section. I'm very sorry to say this, but I've never seen the series this *complacent*, to such a degree that when Abraham Lincoln talks of a "Nation... so dedicated", it's pretty clear that he's not talking about Terry. (Top marks for Robert Marsden's cameo as Lincoln, though – he was something of a Lincoln specialist, so getting him was a bit like securing Simon Callow as Dickens. I said "a bit", okay?)

And, all right, the Dalek emerging from the desert and coughing is an oh-so-clever subversion of the iconic cliffhanger from the year before. And yes, there's no realistic reason why a Dalek *wouldn't* clear its throat if it had been submerged in sand. But the coughing does somewhat undercut the dramatic intent of the cliffhanger: the much-garlanded cliffhanger to The Caves of Androzani episode three, one supposes, wouldn't be so revered had the Doctor shat himself just before impact – even though you could hardly blame him for doing so.

I'm trying to stay upbeat here, Rob – I'm really trying. If I were being honest, this isn't as bad as I'd feared. It's okay. It's fun and frothy and odd. I'm just not sure it's any of these things in the way it was *intended* to be.

February 6th

The Death of Time
(The Chase episode two)

R: This is altogether a rather more thoughtful affair. Terry Nation continues his analogies about the way society responds to totalitarian aggressors – the Aridians are rather a spineless bunch, who adopt a policy of appeasement, and resign themselves to handing over our heroes to the Daleks in return for their own lives. It's an alternate take on the pacifist creed of the Thals, and an altogether more treacherous one – and Nation makes it very clear that the Daleks have no intention of sparing the Aridians once they have the hostages they want; notice how they blast away at a couple of especially effete examples who are polishing sand from the TARDIS with all the efficacy of someone cleaning a toilet with a toothbrush. What gives them a dignity denied them by the plot is William Hartnell's forgiving acceptance; he's understanding, if not condoning, why these strangely fey aliens would sacrifice him. What's really rather impressive is that within a single episode, we are invited to sympathise with the Aridians, and to see them much like the Menoptra from a few weeks before – indeed, their strange hand movements and vocal inflections have a touch of Roslyn de Winteritis about them. We hear the story of their society, and how they've been threatened by the Mire Beasts. And then, so quickly, we're required to do a volte face and to despise these apparently benevolent creatures for their treachery – to despise them because they haven't even got the honesty to be obvious threats like the Daleks, and would instead kill the Doctor with such timid apologies. Hywel Bennett appears to play one of the Aridians as if he's constantly on the brink of tears. Doctor Who has no time for appeasement, and clearly indicates that it's no better than active collaboration with the enemy.

There's still room for humour, though. Nation is still parodying the conventions of the series; Ian snaps at Vicki and call her a fool for stopping to scream at a monster, and seconds later Vicki does the same thing back at him for gawping at another. There's the first real moment of Dalek comedy, where a subordinate is told off by its impatient commander for being a bit thick. And, rather weirdly, Ian wants to call this same Dalek "Fred", whilst the Doctor insists on waving at it and calling it "Auntie". No-one quite bothers to explain why.

T: In this case, what you call "parodying a convention", I would – with great reluctance – call "crap comedy". There's admittedly no reason to *not* to have a coughing Dalek, or a dim-witted (or at best, "work experience") one, but they're impossible to take seriously. What makes the Daleks such chilling adversaries is their very alienness – take that away, and you remove their core brilliance. It doesn't seem worth it for the sake of some rather limp humour.

Which is such a pity, because while we've previously seen Daleks in their city, and on twenty-second century Earth, and in water, they're now on sand and look very impressive gliding about on it. Also, notice how they exterminate the first Aridian they see (it's Brian Proudfoot! – oh, how the mighty Tigilinus has fallen into an uncredited role!), and *then* identify the species and decide that they're not necessary. The Daleks' strategy here is "kill first, decide what to do with the rest of the population later". It shows that they're nasty to the core, and their amorality and coldness regarding death is so very effective. If I get techy about Dalek humour, it's because it threatens to hamstring so much of this – the scene where the Daleks gun down Proudfoot, for instance, wouldn't have been improved had Richard Martin yielded to the temptation of adding a line like, "Oooh, it gets your gun sore, all this shooting, doesn't it Timmy?" You know, to be funny and all that.

(And so long as I've "broken the seal" and am venturing into criticism of Martin for just a little bit, let me say that he continues to be such a clumsy director, I can't even work out which Aridian gets killed because the Mire Beast attack is shot so ham-fistedly. Also, the bit where the Dalek pitches over the cliff is visually impressive, but seems so disjointed from everything else – largely because it was shot in broad daylight and then inserted into a "night" scene – it looks like a random incident, not part of the narrative. There, I feel better now. Let me switch gears back to being positive...)

The Doctor is magnificent in this episode. His pragmatism in the face of the Aridians' decision to hand him and Barbara over to the Daleks shows great dignity, and is sensitively played by Hartnell. I wouldn't agree with you that the programme is too heavy on appeasement – we're made to feel sorry for the Aridians, and the Doctor doesn't condemn them for their actions, because they're understandable. These people appear to have no weapons or means of defending themselves whatsoever, and they're being compelled to surrender two strangers. What choice do they have?

As part of this discussion, there's a superb moment when Hywel Bennett (as Rynian, one of the Aridians) beats about the bush and rather gently asks if the Doctor and Barbara have eaten, and the Doctor in reply – but without malice – bluntly asks what the decision is regarding their fate. He's stoic and impressive, but it's quite a sweet Aridian moment too, as Rynian shows concern for the captives despite being prepared to, however reluctantly, sell them out. (In fact, I have a theory about Bennett's performance – perhaps all the Aridians are *trying* to cry. If they weep long enough, their planet might stop being arid, and they'd have to re-Christen it Lachrymosious or something.) It's also worth noting that the Doctor doesn't save the Aridians – yes, he manages to get the Daleks off their backs, but they're still stuck with a Mire Beast infestation. It'd be unthinkable today that the Doctor would just shoot off and abandon people in such an oppressed and increasingly dangerous situation.

As with the previous episode, this is okay. It's not great, but it's okay. I'd still caution against using the words "Death" and "Time" in a title ever again though, no matter what the medium. (Fingers crossed...) And one last thing – we never *did* find out what that smelly stuff Ian and Vicki found last episode was. Mire Beast poo?

Flight Through Eternity (The Chase episode three)

R: As Toby and I pack our bags so we can jet off to Gallifrey convention in Los Angeles in a few days' time – sunshine! jacuzzis! theme parks! I can hardly wait! – it's easy to forget how in sixties Britain, travel to the USA was almost ridiculously expensive, and the idea of New York was exotic and alien to the average Doctor Who viewer as the planet Aridius. My parents moved to New York in 1962 and lived there for the best part of a decade, so that when Barbara and Vicki look over the side of the Empire State Building, it could well be my mum and dad they see walking the sidewalks beneath. My parents have always stressed to me just how strange a world this city of skyscrapers seemed to them when they first arrived, and that's the image you get here. To see the TARDIS crew as tourists once more – however briefly! – and in *America*, is really rather exciting. And there's a charm to this very long comic scene where Alabaman idiot Morton Dill meets first Doctor Who and then the Daleks on top of one of the most iconic buildings in the world. It's such a strange mix of American clichés that don't really fit together – Dill's belief that he's watching Hollywood movie stars, even though Hollywood is two and a half thousand miles away, makes some curious sense because movies are the things everybody just *does* in the USA. And because Dill is the focus of the scene, and we're seeing our heroes and their mortal foes entirely through his eyes, his delight at the crazy magic of what Doctor Who represents is really rather infectious. The accent Peter Purves adopts while playing Dill is awful, but that's part of the joke, and his double takes are priceless.

I accept I have personal family reasons for liking this half of the episode. The Mary Celeste segment leaves me a bit cold, though. Perhaps Toby has reasons for liking it? Maybe he has family members who used to travel around on nineteenth century sea clippers. Let's ask him.

T: We're first transported back to the present day atop the Empire State Building, and it's mainly an excuse to get a juicy comic turn from a guest actor. Fortunately, Peter Purves delivers in spades. It's not a *hilarious* outing, because he's not given much to work with, but he acquits himself very well. It's easy to see why they were so keen to bring him back as a series regular, even though he'd already appeared here as a different character. And some thanks are due to my friend Peter Crocker, who pointed out to me that the way the Dalek eyestalk rotates 360 degrees as Dill goes around it is unnervingly alien as well as technically proficient. The later Daleks had a catch that prevented such motion, so I believe that this is a unique moment. And the extras all look suitably American – I especially like the fat man who gives Morton Dill a funny look, and wonder if Arne Gordon, playing the tour guide, ever tried to sue Peter Falk for his later portrayal as Columbo, because the one feels very similar to the other.

And if you're asking about the Mary Celeste sequences... what I find most interesting about them is that once again, Barbara finds herself lusted after as soon as she arrives somewhere, and here seems an object of temptation for a bunch of "lonely" sailors. (No wonder she's getting increasingly uptight.) But the action to follow also has some notable moments (we get the vivid image of a Dalek tumbling into the water, even if this happens because – once again – a Dalek was stupid enough to keep gliding along after it had run out of solid foundations). And it's quite unnerving, in amongst all the comedy charging about from the superstitious and panicking sailors, to see a woman clutching a baby jump into the sea (especially as we later discover that they couldn't have possibly survived...). At least David Blake Kelly, playing the ship captain, adds a bit of class by removing his jacket and diving into the water with dignity and authority. Nice touch, sir.

Otherwise, all I can offer about this story is a little knee-jerk response: Hartnell does his best to underline the fact that the Daleks are closing in on the travellers, but his work is to no avail as the subsequent model shot shows the Dalek time machine – what we affectionately call "the DARDIS" – going in a completely different direction!

February 7th

Journey Into Terror
(The Chase episode four)

R: The haunted house sequence is really rather fun, because it gives all the regular cast a chance to play against type a bit; after all their attempts to be brave and heroic in the face of danger, it's funny to see them give in so easily to every bump or creak or lightning flash. Jacqueline Hill is able to look on Count Dracula with a dread that is so middle-class and polite, it's wonderfully endearing, and Maureen O'Brien is particularly funny with her deadpan reactions to all the nightmare imagery around her. I can't help but think that Terry Nation's original idea to set an episode within the recesses of human thought is a lot more interesting than Verity Lambert's compromise suggestion that this all takes place in a theme park. (Nation's proposal is a lot more logical too; why would a robot version of Frankenstein's Monster turn upon tourists as violently as that?) But it's fun, for once, for the audience to be in on the joke rather than the TARDIS crew.

But the most interesting scene in the episode is the one where the Doctor, Ian and Barbara all mourn the loss of Vicki. There's a despair about it which is very effective, especially after so much time spent running about not really taking anything seriously – and it uncannily predicts a similar conversation in the console room in Time-Flight, where the characters all argue about whether there could be any way of going back to save Adric. Vicki isn't dead, of course – but the implication is that, with a TARDIS that has no way of returning to a previous location and which cannot be controlled, she might just as well be. Certainly, there's no reason to believe they'll ever see her again. Considering that within the next two weeks this crew really *will* be fractured forever, this is a wonderful little piece of foreshadowing.

T: This is a tricky episode to talk about, because, well, I'm not seven years old, and Terry Nation clearly isn't writing this so that future wannabe scholars such as ourselves could dissect it in minute detail. Instead, Journey Into Terror involves Nation wanting to entertain the kids for 25 minutes with as much exciting adventure as he can pack in – and what better way to do that than with the ultimate in horror icons, Dracula and Frankenstein?

To be fair, I've rarely found sci-fi scary – fear for me tends to revolve around the ancient, not the futuristic. And I've enjoyed the way those cheesy old Universal flicks are drenched in spookiness; it's partly that they're in black and white, and partly that I always seem to watch them with the slightly disconcerting knowledge that all the players involved are themselves long dead. So while modern eyes might view this episode as being random, tacky jeopardy, it's excusable because I know if Doctor Who had served up a haunted house to *my* young self, I would have been terrified – and ultimately pleased that a rational explanation was used as to the presence of the horrific.

And it's rare that the audience gets to outsmart the Doctor – he's had nothing, even to this very day as far as we know, to tell him that visited a funfair in 1996; he seems convinced that he actually *did* have an adventure in the human mind. As with the Aridian episode, there's some unfinished business here that's necessitated by the chase scenario – one could dismiss this as sloppy and ill defined, but it actually seems disconcerting.

As does the comedy, but, er, not in the same way.

The Death of Doctor Who (The Chase episode five)

R: The death of Doctor Who? Oh, come on. It's not quite that bad...

I've been meaning to say this for ages, and it may as well be here. Nowadays, we expect our special effects to be impeccable. Doctor Who is a mainstream hit TV series today, and the audience who watch it are just as likely to be the same people who watch EastEnders or Top Gear. They may not even think of Doctor Who as sci-fi – not as *such*. Now, having good quality FX is in some ways a rather limiting factor. For example, back in the sixties you could visit the planet Aridius fairly easily; it was just another studio bound planet, and production team and viewers alike accepted that. Nowadays, you'd be flying to do location filming in Dubai. So Chris Eccleston never had the

opportunity to visit an alien world, because for that first year of the revival, no-one could guarantee that it could be done convincingly enough not to frighten away our new audience. I remember that my Dalek story opened with an effect of an enormous face of the villain breaking in half, and revealing itself to be the ceiling of a hangar admitting a helicopter. It was in so many drafts, but was cut from the shooting script because it wouldn't have looked good enough on the budget allowed. If it had been the 1970s, they'd probably have done it with bad CSO. If it had been in The Chase, God knows how they would have pulled it off – but they'd have done it anyway, you can be sure of that.

This is because where modern TV asks the audience to take things at face value, classic Doctor Who asks it to take things on trust. The people who made The Chase weren't stupid. They didn't really think that Edmund Warwick wearing a wig was a dead ringer for William Hartnell. Look at him! He's a different height! He's got a longer nose! Nor would they have seriously thought we'd believe that, say, the Fungoids weren't actors shuffling about in giant toadstool costumes. But the Daleks tell each other that this robot is an exact duplicate of the Doctor, and later Vicki asserts the same thing. So the programme is inviting the viewers to fill in the gaps – to see Doctor Who not as an accurate depiction of the story, but a fictive representation of it. It's compounded by the fact that Hartnell ends up playing the robot at certain moments of sustained drama, and as a result Warwick has to play the *real* Doctor. Nowadays, you'd make Time Crash, and find a line that explains away jokingly why Peter Davison looks so much older than he did when he played the Doctor some 20 years before. As late as the mid-eighties, though, you could dress up a middle-aged Frazer Hines in a kilt, and within the story pretend he was the same age as when he made The Ice Warriors.

And *that's* what dates The Death of Doctor Who, because it's the single grandest example of the series asking the kids watching at home to suspend their disbelief. We'll laugh or smirk at the Skarasen in the Thames, or the Myrka, although it's part and parcel of the same thing – because they're individual *moments* when we have to pretend the special effects are decent.

But to a production team who'll use locations as varied as the Aztec city or Xeros as painted backdrops, to take an entire story concept that there is no way it can achieve on screen, and then *to do it anyway*, isn't quite the act of folly it might appear. In the same way that any theatre production of Twelfth Night knows full well that they'll never find two actors who can play identical brother and sister, but sticks their Viola and Sebastian in the same clothes, and assumes the audience will have the wit to understand what that's meant to indicate.

Of course, this doesn't excuse incompetence, laziness or both. There's plenty of that in Doctor Who throughout its history. But when an episode like this one clearly doesn't *care* that it can't do the effects, and just gets on and tells its story, it seems rather churlish to blame it for what it never intended to do in the first place.

The Death of Doctor Who is not a *great* episode. But it does have two versions of the Doctor fighting each other with walking sticks. That's the sort of thing I like. You saw Edmund Warwick and William Hartnell? Pish and tush to that.

T: I don't know... having Warwick double as Hartnell is one thing, but to have Warwick's face clearly visible in long shot, and then to make him mouth Hartnell's pre-recorded words, and *then* to cut to a close-up of the real deal is utterly bonkers. Why didn't they just have Hartnell play the Doctor-robot, save for scenes where a body-double was unavoidable? I can try to be kind, I can try to be understanding, but the whole robot-Doctor Who section of this episode just seems terrifyingly inept. The Daleks even tell each other that they'll follow the android... then go in a completely different direction. And you know things aren't quite right when the normally dignified Barbara pretends to machine gun the Daleks!

Fortunately, once Edmund Warwick has received his just desserts (and the Doctor issues a parting joke about him needing a doctor!), the pace actually ramps up quite nicely. There's a wonderfully downbeat "things aren't too good are they?" moment between the Doctor and Ian – Hartnell is pleasingly grim in his outlook, while Russell is very stoic and brave. I'm less sure about what Dudley

Simpson is doing, though – as the Daleks surge forward in force, the music decides to evoke a romp around Monte Carlo. And then Camera 5 strangely appears in the background. (My friend Peter Crocker, entertainingly enough, maintains that this is a Mechonoid probe, planted there to spy on the Gubbage Cones.)

But if nothing else, there's a sense in this episode that as far as our heroes are cornered, the chase itself is over and the confrontation between them and the Daleks is imminent and unavoidable. As part of this, the Doctor does the right thing and, without consulting his companions, bravely (and unsuccessfully) tries to delay the Daleks by posing as the robot-Doctor. It's a superb moment for the character, and a scene in which, without ceremony, the Doctor becomes the hero and Ian's usefulness to the programme comes to an end.

February 8th

The Planet of Decision
(The Chase episode six)

R: This is by far the most satisfying, and the most exciting, of all the episodes in The Chase. The Mechonoids are actually rather a witty idea: a bunch of robots who have been abandoned by the colonists who designed them and have since "gone native", and are now capturing the odd hapless human and putting him on exhibition in a zoo. (It does make you wonder what pleasure the robots can possibly derive by staring at humans, but that's part of the fun.) There's a terrific battle between the Daleks and these new robots, which rather bizarrely manages to look expensive (all that film!) and cheap (those cartoon explosions!) at the same time – and that, actually, sums up The Chase admirably. And Maureen O'Brien very creditably takes the part of a whimpering girl who's scared of heights and makes her fear honest and realistic.

But it's ironic, nevertheless, that this rather epic finale with the Daleks is upstaged entirely by the departure from the series of Ian and Barbara. The last ten minutes or so are just wonderful. That quiet realisation from Jacqueline Hill that, at last, there's a means by which she can get home – it hadn't even occurred to Ian, and it's beautiful that before he decides whether he even *wants* to leave the TARDIS, he checks with Barbara what she would like to do. Once she's committed to the idea of returning to Earth, then so is he – my God, the love he feels for her just shines through. They utterly deserve that photo montage of their messing about with pigeons at Trafalgar Square – if any two characters had a right to celebrate the joy of home comforts and the glories of being *ordinary* once more, it's these two. And Hartnell, typically, is extraordinary in these scenes: he is so *good* at the heartfelt. He can't bear to lose them. When the Dalek ship dematerialises, he daren't even turn around to watch it vanish. He watches them on the Time and Space Visualiser, his face ashen and pained as he realises that, happy as they are, he'll never see them again. "I'll miss them," he says. Right with you, Doctor. I'll miss them too. They were magnificent.

Mind you, Peter Purves looks very promising as Steven, the new companion. He's given a standard bit of long exposition, and makes it seem a result of two years' worth of isolation. The way that he can barely contain his delight at seeing fellow humans once more – and yet backs away from them as the disbelief keeps kicking in – is really well observed. The toy panda will have to go, though. If Steven keeps throwing really good escape plans into chaos every time he forgets his panda, the Doctor will come to a very sticky end.

T: Morton Dill is back! Or, not really... while playing Steven, Purves is pretty unrecognisable as the well-meaning Alabaman who laughed at the Daleks in New York City. The incoming companion has a splendid moment where he asks the travellers to repeat his name, and bites his lip as it is said back to him. He's *deeply* affected by hearing another human being address him, and he has such a natural delivery in his reactions to the crew. First he shakes Ian's hand, then the Doctor's, and then apologetically yet vigorously does Ian's hand *again* – it's very human, very clever and very subtle. I do have to question Steven's choice of risking life and limb for a teddy bear, but hey – a guy gets lonely in prison.

But it's Ian and Barbara that we're meant to concentrate on now. Setting aside the fact that the Doctor becomes so happy to see Ian that he says he could kiss him (move over, John Barrowman!), we really will miss these two. The realisation that they could return home is performed beautifully – they're desperate to get back, but they'll be sad if they do. It's also spot on that the Doctor reacts to their announced departure by being spiteful and ranting, and that Ian loses his cool and yearns for the comfort of having a pint in his native time! And of course, just as it looks like their argument will end in tears, it's down to Barbara to smooth things over with the old man. Her admission that her life will never again be this exciting is just lovely, and Hill plays the lines with a composed but heart-rending modicum of wistful regret. It's interesting that we don't see Ian and Barbara actually say goodbye to their friends – the Doctor testily takes the two of them into the DARDIS, and then exits alone. Perhaps witnessing the actual moment where they part would be too much to bear.

The photo montage that shows Ian and Barbara back in London, 1965, might seem very unusual to a modern viewer, but – as directed by Douglas Camfield, as part of pre-production on the next story – it's a great send off with them happily charging about and scattering pigeons. They're deliriously happy, and I can only hope that after Ian gets his pint in the pub, there's a bit of hand-holding and some fumbled offers of coffee back at his place. While Jacqueline Hill has always been (rightly) lauded for her acting, I do feel that William Russell is something of an unsung hero of these early years of Doctor Who. He generally takes on the brunt of the action and arbitration, and he's always delivered and done so with authority. I salute them both.

And do you know, while I've been less than kind to Richard Martin's work, he wraps up his Doctor Who tenure in the best way possible. The pitched Dalek-Mechonoid battle is terrific – there's a good use of camera cranes, gun close-ups and animated explosions. I'd be fearful about Martin doing more stories, but I do appreciate that he here goes out in style.

Did I really say this adventure was in the bottom five stories of all time? Does it really score nought out of ten? Nope, not with episodes like this up its sleeve.

The Watcher
(The Time Meddler episode one)

R: You remember how yesterday I was banging on about TV conventions expecting the audience to suspend their disbelief? It still happens today, of course – everyone accepts that the incidental music isn't really there. So it's gobsmacking when, at the end of the episode, William Hartnell all but appears to wander off set to find a gramophone playing Now That's What I Call Monastic Chanting. The series has spent so long asking its viewers to accept that its regular trips back into history have a certain truth to it. And yet here we are, back at the most famous date in English history – oh, and look! There's Alethea Charlton again, with many of the same dirt stains on her face now that she's playing a Saxon peasant as when she was playing a cavewoman. It all looks very proper, and as the Doctor says, we'll soon give that arrogant new companion a dressing down and prove that we *can* time travel after all. But it suddenly looks as if Steven's scepticism is warranted – a Saxon is found with a wristwatch, and the BBC Radiophonic Workshop have just been discovered hiding behind a curtain. Perhaps Steven was right after all. Perhaps that hat thing with horns on really was just a space helmet for a cow.

T: I'd like to ask: why *couldn't* it be a space helmet for a cow? Given all the space pigs/space rhinos/space wasps in the new series, this just about seems conceivable. And didn't Gareth Roberts once write a story with some gun-toting space bovines for a DWM comic strip? I know he did! It was called The Lunar Strangers, and the space-cows had little protuberances in their environmental helmets to accommodate their horns. Why, this is sounding more plausible all the time...

Anyway, back in 1066, this whole episode is quite a meandering tease, and a definite first for the series in that we're made to question the veracity of the *when* it's occurring in a way that we haven't really done before. There's not much by way of danger, though – the Doctor has a dainty little chat with a rather too lovely and prim lady Saxon villager, and the villain of the piece spends most of his time eavesdropping. The script does have many comedic

Dennis Spoonerisms, but it's less full on than The Romans, and so finds itself stuck in an odd no man's land between that story's excesses and the lofty worthiness of Lucarotti and Whitaker's efforts.

But even if we're meant to be uncertain about the time period, and exactly what sort of genre we've found ourselves in (it *looks* and *feels* like a pure historical – but why, then, does the Monk have a wristwatch?), the people involved in making it are showing no such vagueness as to what they're doing. Director Douglas Camfield isn't settling for "this'll do", or "that'll be fun" – he's clearly striving for everything to look *good*. He uses angled shooting (the shot of the TARDIS from above, for instance) to sell the lie that we're outside rather than in a studio, and he's aided by Barry Newbery's astonishing design work (that moving sky is exceptionally convincing). On the acting side, Hartnell is very low key and magnanimous in the first scene, and the new TARDIS dynamic gets off to a flying start. The Doctor is crotchety with the bullish Steven, whilst Vicki is bouncy but not afraid to chide. It's curious, though, that the Doctor seems delighted that they're in 1066. (What is it about this man? He seems to revel in visiting periods of history renowned for their mass slaughter!)

On a somewhat minor note, this is the first time the "D" in "TARDIS" is said to refer to the word "dimensions" plural, not "dimension". It's a mistake that won't get rectified till 1996, and it's also interesting to discover that in Steven's future of astronauts, space rockets and dubious toy panda use, they still have police boxes.

And I'm sorry, but someone has to say it. Peter Butterworth is very underused – he barely gets a line. It turns out that, in this episode at least, he was just The Watcher all the time.

February 9th

The Meddling Monk
(The Time Meddler episode two)

R: We cut from a scene of the Doctor's captor laughing at our hero to his singing to himself while he's preparing a nice fry-up breakfast for him. Like the sudden appearance of the gramophone, this wrongfoots the audience – villains in Doctor Who are often funny, but they never *know* they are. Peter Butterworth's Monk was an eerie figure in the first episode – he barely said a line, hid in shadows and was generally weird and enigmatic. Now, with Hartnell off on holiday for a week, he gets to take charge. The Monk's attempts to take snuff in a howling wind are amusing, his ingratitude to the Saxon women who bring him food is nicely deadpanned. And for all the fact that the Monk is clearly meant to be a comic character, there's still something rather unnerving about him. Indeed, it's *because* he's comic – we can't get a handle on him. The best scene is the one where Steven fools the Monk into revealing that he's seen the Doctor, using that hoary old plan of making the villain reveal things that they couldn't possibly know. (All copyright Terry Nation, by way of The Keys of Marinus in several instances.) But Vicki suspects that the Monk's apparent stupidity is just a ruse to lead them into a trap. Here's a character who wants you to underestimate him, with his comic bumbling, double takes and funny faces only masking a great intelligence. Who does that remind you of? And you suddenly remember just how big a part Dennis Spooner later played in shaping the character of the second Doctor. Here he is, a prototype Patrick Troughton, all in monk's clothing.

Peter Purves continues to impress, mostly because he doesn't in any way try to elicit the audience's sympathies. The viewers at home will still be missing Ian and Barbara – I know I am – and rather resenting this new upstart. Steven works well precisely because he doesn't care. He's like Edmund in The Lion, the Witch and the Wardrobe – the child who refuses at first to play along with the fantasy of Narnia. The way that he beats up a peasant out hunting makes us feel uncomfortable, and he's hotheaded to the Saxons who fear he might be a Viking. But Purves very skilfully allows him to thaw bit by bit – the way that he grudgingly thanks Edith for the food that she gives them, after all of his rudeness, is wonderful.

T: As you say, Purves is superb, especially the way he uses steel and modern parlance – "I'm not mad about you either!" – in response to Eldred-the-clichéd-mistrustful-villager's braying. Vicki then chimes in too, and what's *really* interesting about this scene is how much – a mere two weeks after Ian and Barbara left the series – the new TARDIS team is gelling together. With Hartnell on holiday (*again?* He had one only two months ago!), Purves and O'Brien carry the story adeptly. There's such nuance in the way Steven thanks Edith twice for her kindness, and gives a stately "God be with you..." as he goes, giving the impression that he's genuinely embarrassed about his patronising behaviour towards the good-natured villagers. And I love the bit where Vicki suggests that the Monk is double bluffing them, putting the layers of second guessing into the story, and suggesting that the next episode's promise of "A Battle of Wits" won't be too wide of the mark.

But for all the compassion and comedic elements on display in this episode – for all the cosy business with cod Vikings and a funny monk – there's no escaping the conclusion that the Vikings rape Edith off-screen. This is pretty unpleasant stuff, and actually quite difficult for modern viewers to get their heads around (almost undoubtedly, nothing like this would appear in the new series). Any children watching this might well gloss over the event – either not comprehending what's happened, or knowing (as I did, when I was eight) that the Vikings traditionally did rape, murder and pillage without understanding what that really meant. At 35, having gained adult knowledge of what rape is, I find this all the more disconcerting. Michael Miller, playing Edith's husband Wulnoth, expertly sells us on what's happened to his wife without saying anything explicit, but then... well, the scene isn't helped by the appearance of the bewhiskered and bulging-eyed peasant Eldred, who reminds me too much of Michael Palin's shriller characters in the Monty Python films.

Nonetheless, this sub-plot raises the stakes, and makes clear that the Vikings aren't *quite* as silly as they appear at times. (It's easy to make fun of Ulf and Sven because they're a bit weedier, but Geoffrey Cheshire looks excellent as the Viking captain – his massive frame is bedecked in an impressive costume, and his strong, pock-marked features are augmented by his hefty beard. And Gunnar the Giant –

killed in a throw-down with the Saxons – is a great sight too.) I'm just glad that things are kept from getting too mature and depressing by Dennis Spooner writing in such frivolity as the Monk making breakfast (there's something rather jolly about seeing an eleventh century monk pottering about frying eggs), and the joyful way that the Doctor chucks water over the Monk's head.

A Battle of Wits
(The Time Meddler episode three)

R: The first thing that leaped out to me was the high quality of Douglas Camfield's direction. The second season of Doctor Who has entailed some pretty ropey and don't-give-a-toss direction to its stories; it'd be against the spirit of this diary to name names, but if Toby gave me a Chinese burn, I think the words "Richard Martin" might pop out.

What we have here is so striking in contrast. Take the scene where the two Vikings in the woods argue about whether they should take refuge from the Saxons or not. We don't care about the Vikings, frankly – Sven and Ulf are hardly the most rounded of characters, nor the best acted either, and this little part of the storyline isn't half as interesting as a time travelling monk. But Camfield provides real energy to a rather dull discussion, giving it danger and edge, and eventually frames it so that both Vikings are in extreme close-up, so that one of them looks complicit at last to the other's cowardly plan. It's brilliantly done, because it's the work of a director who tries to maximise the drama or the comedy at every turn. For comparison's sake, there's that bit where the Monk needs to leave the monastery to see who's knocking at the door, and get surprised by Hartnell from behind. These sorts of things are very theatrical, and always a bit eggy if they're not blocked properly, but here it's surprisingly tense and pays off as a good joke, with a stern-looking Doctor pretending that the stick he's holding against the Monk's back is a rifle. A few weeks ago, there was a sequence in which Vicki had to somehow sneak into the Dalek time ship, avoiding detection while the Daleks were distracted by Count Dracula and Frankenstein's Monster. All it needed was good blocking, and it would have worked – but

because it looked as if it was being filmed without rehearsal, it's a confusing and illogical mess. What Camfield brings to a production is *smoothness*. The Time Meddler is not the fastest paced of stories, but you can relax with it completely, because it all feels deliberate and crafted.

All this gives space for Hartnell and Butterworth to spar off each other delightfully. This isn't the battle of wits that the title would suggest, but instead a lot of amusing banter – and yet, the rapport between both actors fairly crackles. There's lots of nice throwaway jokes from both: the way that Butterworth gets into monk character, relaxing his "naughty" face into something much more cherubic, even before calling out to Wulnoth in another room altogether; the way that Hartnell so delightfully thanks the Viking he's just knocked unconscious for coming into the room, because he thought he'd be waiting for the chance to attack him for ages. And out of this tale which is as light and amiable as can be, there's a chance for a real shock – that Steven and Vicki discover the Monk has his very own TARDIS is another moment in which the series just flips over, and you wonder what the rules can be any longer. Only a few weeks ago, in The Chase, the Doctor was talking about how he built his TARDIS – now it's suggested that it's one of an assembly line.

T: For an episode entitled A Battle of Wits, one might more correctly say that it's *full* of wit. There's a brilliant moment where Vicki postulates that the Doctor's cell must contain a secret passage – as if, of course, the presence of such a thing were an everyday occurrence. Steven is immediately scornful about the idea, but Vicki knows better because she's already bought into the clichés of an adventure serial and he just hasn't yet. The end result is Doctor Who at its most metatextual – we're being dared to buy into the mores of a daft and bonkers adventure, then to get over ourselves and just join in the nonsense. It's so easy to criticise sci-fi adventures for being ridiculous and unbelievable, but there are times when Doctor Who embraces the ridiculousness with glee, pointing out that if you're inclined to be churlish, you'll be missing out on a whole heap of fun.

And fun is what's largely on display here:

Hartnell is remarkably funny with the way he prods the Monk with a stick and assumes the demeanour of a 1930s gangster. (You almost expect to him drawl, "No funny business or the Monk gets it.") The way that the Doctor and the Monk independently brain the stupid Vikings is a hoot – one might almost call it a battle with twits. And despite the mass-murder implications, the idea of the Monk using a bazooka to wipe out the Viking fleet is hilarious – the word is in itself funny, and even more so when the weapon in question has been placed on an eleventh century clifftop by a cherubic nuisance with a comedy checklist.

Back in the village, Edith is up and about remarkably quickly after her violation last episode – evidently, mediaeval crones such as her are made of stern stuff. Wulnoth even deems her fit enough to be a nursemaid for the wounded Eldred. Yes, Edith may be traumatised, but it seems that whatever her problems (oh, do I *dare* say it?...), Eldred *must* live. But what's most interesting about the village scenes is the way that the Doctor talks about the Battle of Hastings before muttering to himself, "At least, that's what the history books said happened...", as if history all of a sudden isn't this unalterable certainty. It's funny how everyone fixates on the game-changing revelation that the Doctor's TARDIS isn't unique, when this Dennis Spooner chap has also managed – in terms of what the travellers can and can't do in relation to their adventures – to change the whole ethos of the show monumentally. And all for the sake of facilitating a story that's in so many ways a charming romp.

And amidst all this low-key silliness, Spooner slips into the biggest gear-change imaginable: there's another TARDIS! It's like the Doctor revealing that he's Rassilon in the middle of Delta and the Bannermen.

February 10th

R: It's my birthday! And, just like you, Toby, I didn't get a Dalek cigarette lighter. In my case, though, that was just as well, since I don't smoke. (I never have. At school I was never one of the cool kids behind the bike sheds – I was with all the other nerds who hid near the portaloos, discussing how much we liked Adric.)

No, my best present this year is getting to the end of the second season of Doctor Who. That's rather good timing, isn't it? It seems that Verity Lambert arranged it deliberately. And tomorrow, I'm up early in the morning, and getting to Heathrow Airport for a flight to Los Angeles and the Gallifrey convention... you *are* bringing your laptop, aren't you, with a DVD drive? And I'll be bringing Season Three (at least, what exists of it). What fun! Whilst everybody else will be in the bar drinking beer, we can hide in our hotel rooms listening to Hartnell soundtracks. Lovely.

Checkmate
(The Time Meddler episode four)

So amiable is this story's conclusion, and so perfunctory the plotting (and all the more so in the version that survives today, in which the Viking deaths have been neatly censored from the prints), that you can happily enjoy this rather light adventure and barely notice that a large part of the series' credo has just crumbled away. All the way through the second season, script editor Dennis Spooner has been nagging away at the show format he inherited from David Whitaker. Whitaker perceived the series as something by which the Doctor and his crew became unwilling adventurers, running away from crises and only intervening in situations in order to better facilitate their escape later. Spooner clearly saw this as dramatically rather sterile and also – more importantly – less *fun*. And here, we have the Monk say as much to the Doctor – that it's more fun his way. The Monk represents the way that Doctor Who *could* have been, something of a romp in which he travels about all of space and time having adventures merely for the sake of it. And although Hartnell clearly rejects the idea and foils the Monk's scheme, it must be said, he doesn't foil the scheme *very well*. Indeed, the Doctor's basic solution to dealing with a time meddler wishing to interfere in the backwaters of Earth's history... is to leave him stranded in the backwaters of Earth's history, where he may well turn his hand to a bit of meddling. It's almost as if Spooner sides with the Monk, because he refuses to give the Doctor a particularly good argument against *why* the Monk shouldn't change past events –

and it's telling that when the Doctor comments at story's end on how history can now run its natural course, Vicki chimes in with him, as if he's a boring old windbag who keeps on trotting out the same old killjoy phrases.

The Doctor may have won this battle, but he's actually lost the war. It's hard now to hear of the Monk trying to influence Leonardo da Vinci without thinking of how the Doctor does the very same thing himself in City of Death. From this point on, and aside from a few hiccups where the idea of preserving history is paid some sort of lip-service, Doctor Who becomes a series where more or less everything is up for grabs. That's Dennis Spooner's legacy. And that lovely final image, where the TARDIS crew's faces play against a star background, seems to suggest that the whole universe is now theirs for the taking.

T: Happy birthday, Rob! I'm sorry I didn't call, but I was packing and panicking for Gallifrey. I can't wait – we're soon going to cross the Atlantic, and what's the first thing we're going to do? Yep, that's right – watch (or, rather, hear) Galaxy Four!

I wrote last episode about how Dennis Spooner has altered more of the series' foundations than he's usually given credit for; he's reversed course on Whitaker's assertion that the travellers *can't* change history (all together now: "not one line!"), and yet when Spooner's name comes up, it's usually in relation to his use of comedy. This isn't without good reason, and it's here in abundance. The Monk putting money in a bank and then using time-travel to claim a fortune in compound interest is funny and smart. And the idea that he used a gravity lift to aid the ancient Britons in building Stonehenge is a pleasingly cheeky deflation of any pretensions to earnestness the show might have.

But all of these historical/temporal shenanigans are just part and parcel of the way that Spooner has completely opened up the potential of the programme, and deployed the idea that time-travellers can *change* things rather than just observe them passively. In many ways, The Time Meddler is the culmination, Rob, of what you were talking about in The Reign of Terror: actual historical figures are sidelined (certainly, we don't meet any in

1066), and there will be a greater expectation of the regulars getting involved. The Monk here wants to change history just because "it's more fun his way," but what's notable is that after this story, there's no escaping the idea that you *can* change history – you can get your hands *dirty* in it, even – whatever the Doctor's previous protests about it.

While this paradigm-shift will give Doctor Who a new and extended lease on life, it will also, in effect, sound what will be the slow death-knell of the pure historical. No longer will the machinations of a particular time period be interesting in themselves; future production teams will go out of their way to bung outer-space elements into pseudo-historicals just to spice things up. Spooner himself made this approach work, and it's certainly a decent way of keeping a series going for decades.

As for The Time Meddler itself... well, I found so much of it to be terribly endearing, but I do think I preferred the previous historicals. The design and direction here are excellent, yes, and Butterworth and the regulars are fab. But there's just not enough colour (so to speak) for my taste, the supporting characters are all pretty dreary and much of the fun stuff was mentioned, not shown. And yet, no matter how unassuming this story is, no matter how much I have the suspicion that it underperforms a bit, I can't deny the seismic effect it will have on the series to come.

Dr. Who and the Daleks

R: And yet, in a funny way, *this* is what changed everything.

Between Season Two and Season Three, Doctor Who was suddenly on the big screen, and in colour! Just weeks after we've said goodbye to Ian and Barbara, and the original TARDIS crew we loved so dearly, here they all are again... but not in a way we've ever seen before. Ian is now an accident prone boyfriend, "Susie" (as the Susan character is called) is a rather humourless little wunderkind who reads enormous physics text books, Barbara is... well, it's rather hard to say what Barbara is, actually, because the script doesn't do anything with her, and actress Jennie Linden looks a trifle bored by the whole thing.

And Doctor Who is... Peter Cushing. And *that's* what's so revolutionary about this. Cushing is a brilliant actor, and it's something of a shame that he doesn't seize the part and make it his own – it's not his fault, but you can see that he's trying a mid-tenure Hartnell performance of loveable old granddad, with some of the same quirks and added winking. (It's particularly odd seeing the sort of Hartnell Doctor who appears in The Time Meddler and having him transposed into one of his earlier adventures, where we expect him to be much spikier and dangerous. It's a great illustration of just how much the Doctor has changed over the last two years.) But the fact that someone else is playing Doctor Who is enough. In the third season, as Hartnell's relationship ever sours with new production teams, they'll have been shown a successful crowd-pleasing truth: that you can replace the man in the lead role, and the audience will accept it.

What's so striking is just how much more childish the feature film is compared to the TV serial it was adapted from. As director, Gordon Flemyng downplays moments of tension, and so needs something else to fill the void – and he opts for strange humorous set pieces, such as Ian's frustrated attempts to get through a motion-detector door. The sets may be larger and more colourful, but the world of Skaro seems much smaller this time round. And, understandably, the film producers want to simplify everything. You can accept that Doctor Who is an eccentric inventor, but what has repercussions is how they also simplify the Daleks. The faltering attempts to characterise them individually in The Chase may not have been wholly successful, but it was at least well-intentioned – the Daleks shouldn't necessarily come across as comic-book villains with no depth to them at all. That's what we get here, and it's so impressive – the voices are harsher than on the TV show, the costumes are sturdier and filmed from more flattering angles – that from this point on, that basic stereotype will become the template for how they're depicted. The scene in which a Dalek leads a room full of his fellows in a triumphant chant is quite brilliant. But it also sheds any ambiguity from the creature.

The best bits of the movie are those which deviate from the original series. The sequence where the Doctor leads the Thals to turn mirrors upon the Dalek sensors looks stunning – and the way that the Daleks react, by pulling apart the entire mountain rockface like James Bond supervillains, is audacious and exciting. And that final battle in the control room seems at last to be climactic – and gives Ian a chance to be a hero, as he makes the Daleks destroy their own countdown by firing at him. That's very neat and clever. But it also keeps sticking to old bits of the original for no particular reason. In the TV version, the only dramatic justification for cowardly Antodus falling down the chasm was so that he could come good and sacrifice himself – to keep the moment in the motion picture, but save his life anyway, is unintentionally hilarious. And I didn't ever think I'd say this, but... seeing the movie Thals makes me appreciate how much I preferred the ones from the telly. This movie bunch *act* better. But they're a bunch of sarcastic unlikeable thugs, really – it's astonishing how, after the Doctor teaches them the evils of pacifism, just how sarcastic and sulky they become.

Ultimately, that's the best reason to love Dr Who and the Daleks. I'm glad it exists, if only to show me how much I prefer the subtlety and charm of the original.

T: I remember when the BBC once showed this movie on a Saturday afternoon – but I only realised too late that I'd missed it, and was inconsolable. In the days before videos, DVDs and iPlayer, Doctor Who wasn't available much, and so I had a massive tantrum upon missing a rare opportunity to immerse myself in even an ersatz version of the programme – knowing that there was little chance of it being repeated for least a couple of years. I vividly remember the pain I experienced to this very day, even though when I *did* finally get to watch Dr Who and the Daleks... well, let's just say that I wasn't massively impressed.

The introductory scene demonstrates how the producers have misunderstood the essential ingredients of Doctor Who: instead of this dealing with mysterious goings-on at a school, or even a car accident in Barnes Common, what we get is Roy Castle (whom I loved in Record Breakers, but who is so deeply irritating here, he's immensely punchable) sitting on a box of chocolates and doing comedy double takes. The movie's production team also seem to believe that the central character's name is "Doctor Who" (although to be fair, the TV show itself will make that mistake), and as for the Thals... sorry, but what nightclub have they just come from? The Thals on TV were lisping posturers with holes in their trousers, but in the movie, they're skipping, false eyelash-wearing mimsies with waxed chests. In so many ways, this all looks like a distorted image of the TV serial upon which it's based – it's told with more economy, but in doing so they seem to have ejected *all* the layers and edginess. The movie version seems very squarely aimed at kids, and unlike the parent show doesn't make an attempt to give adults in the audience much to get their heads around.

There are some positives, though. The movie's larger sets are very impressive and allow for much more streamlined action sequences, and the lighting in the jungle is terrific. Some of the special effects are impressive – there's a great moment in a lift where a Dalek shoots upwards and the floor fizzes and blows out, forcing our heroes to leap back. The score in general is quite groovy and catchy, and fits the tone of the whole film. And I too like Peter Cushing – he's not remotely dark or cranky like Hartnell, but it's a good performance, full of neat little touches.

I'm sorry, Rob – as I watch this, I'm unable to say much that you haven't expressed already. But if this review is a bit like a watered down, slightly less effective echo of yours – well, under the circumstances, I can't help but feel that it's somewhat appropriate.

February 11th

R: And here we are in the States! What an extraordinary thing this is. I've just been in your hotel room, Toby, sharing a couple of episodes of Galaxy Four. There's nothing much to look at, just a strange soundtrack of lots of Chumbley noises, really. And here I am, typing my diary entry to you by email, even though I can clearly see you sitting on a rather nice-looking sofa not a hundred yards away drinking an even nicer-looking glass of wine.

The flight over was long but comfortable. On the entertainment system, they had a Doctor Who episode to watch – The Doctor's

Daughter, dated 2008. But I didn't watch it, because annoyingly enough, they *weren't* showing Four Hundred Dawns, dated 1965. (It'd have been great if they had been, though, wouldn't it? Missing episodes have been found in Mormon churches and behind BBC filing cabinets, so it would have been so amusing to find another on a British Airways Airbus.)

Four Hundred Dawns
(Galaxy Four episode one)

We've been spoiled. So much of the first two seasons of Hartnell's tenure survives intact in the archives, we're only now hitting the waste-lands. There are no telesnaps of Galaxy Four, only a few pictures. There's a strange six-minute excerpt, and a complete soundtrack. These require concentration to get through, because, to be completely honest, this episode of Doctor Who does not boast the most quotable dialogue, the most riveting set pieces – or, for that matter, an awful lot of drama period.

What it *does* have is Brian Hodgson's sound effects. The man was a genius. There's something so full of character about the Chumblies – the robotic servants of the unseen Rills – from all the different whirrs and beeps and strange background purrs; there are ambient albums you can get on iTunes which sound like this. And shorn of the visuals, you really do appreciate just how ahead of its time the BBC Radiophonic workshop really was – what you hear in the show is so distinctively *different*. There's not an awful lot going on on this new planet, and the Doctor's comparisons to Xeros frankly make it sound rather cheap and nasty. But Hodgson has still managed to make it alien and exotic.

I love the way that William Hartnell's Doctor can only take the politest of interests in this new adventure – hearing the Drahvins (the alien females in conflict with the Rills) speak of their war, he seems to tut with the concern due if he'd hear them tell how they'd stubbed a toe. He's done all this before – if you want to impress the Doctor in his third season, you've got to try harder than that. He gets most excited about his (frankly rather hasty) theory that because it's quiet and he can't see anybody, the whole planet must be lifeless. Maureen O'Brien has a jolly time cutting Steven's hair and naming cute robots. And once Peter Purves realises that his chat-up lines aren't working on the Drahvins, he spends the rest of the episode being rather snotty with them.

T: You had The Doctor's Daughter on the plane? You lucky bastard – I had High School Musical 3, and a cup of tea that was of a colour no tea has ever been before. Sorry that K was comatose in the hotel room when you stopped by – she decided to utilise a traditional method, handed down through generations of shamen, to combat flight stress: six diazepam and a bottle of vodka.

Anyway, this is William Emms' sole contribution to the series, and his voice is at odds with much of what we've heard before. And yet, there's some offbeat and archaic phraseology that gives the story a curious verbal landscape – I love the substitution of "dawns" for "days", and little touches like "metal mesh". And it's rather thrilling that after ten minutes of listening to the soundtrack, we suddenly get a bit of movement, courtesy of that hefty video clip recovered back in the 1990s. It gives some indication that Derek Martinus is as effective with the camera as Douglas Camfield; his framing of the characters shows he's taken care with the visual makeup of the picture. And I really like what we see of Stephanie Bidmead as Maaga, the Drahvin leader – beneath her clipped formality and posturing, there's a weariness that suggests she's tired of both war and hanging around with staccato clones.

I don't know what to make of the title, though. "Four hundred dawns"? Where, exactly? We're told that the Drahvins left their homeworld 400 dawns ago, but the action of this episode revolves around an anticipated planetary explosion in 14 dawns; at the climax, that's shortened down to a scant two dawns. So, why refer to "four hundred" in the title at all? It's like calling Underworld episode one Departure From Minyos. And we're not actually in Galaxy Four either – it's where the Drahvins are from. So to review: we're in a story named after where it isn't set, and the opening episode has a title depicting a time span that isn't relevant. It's most peculiar.

And it's also hard to deduce just how much Emms expected the audience to be fooled by the old "beauty is in the eye of the beholder"

switcheroo concerning the beautiful Drahvins and the "evil" Rills, or if he thought they'd know the score from the very start. After all, Steven has already deduced that the Rills' offer to help the Drahvins escape the dying planet might be genuine, and Vicki senses that Maaga would enjoy killing them. Even the Doctor mistrusts the Drahvins from their very first encounter, which suggests that any story-twist where the Drahvins are concerned might not have quite the same impact as the one in The Sixth Sense.

Even so, I *do* think the premise of two spaceships marooned on a doomed planet is a novel one, whatever the script's bizarre desire to spoon-feed us. And isn't it interesting that if the new series wants to do a race against time, the Doctor and company only have 42 minutes to prevent total disaster? Here, the shocking cliffhanger is they've only got *a day*!

Trap of Steel
(Galaxy Four episode two)

R: There's a lovely moment where the Doctor searches inside his pockets for... a screwdriver. Not a sonic screwdriver. Not yet. But we'll get there.

It seems to sum up this episode rather well. Galaxy Four feels like an interim story between two different styles. It's not the adventure series we were promised by Dennis Spooner's time as story editor, nor is it the more experimental drama we'll be getting when his successor Donald Tosh gets to work with incoming producer John Wiles. This is the fag end of Verity Lambert's time on the show, and it feels like as everyone swaps their work overalls they've taken their eye off the conveyor belt. William Emms' story feels as if it's been written by someone who has a vague idea of what Doctor Who is like – and, because it's a script which has a lot of the tropes (weird robots, people getting captured, ugly monsters) but absolutely none of the heart, it's absolutely *not* like anything we've ever seen before. There's not much going on in Galaxy Four. But as with the screwdriver, the elements are in place – and we'll get there.

There's still stuff to enjoy. Hartnell and O'Brien sparkle together nicely, and make the most of a script which has some witty lines.

(The bit where Vicki works out how to best a Chumbley is really very funny: "I noted, observed, collated, concluded, and then I threw a rock.") And Peter Purves' attempts to introduce a Drahvin drone to the concept of equality are really rather delightful.

T: I'm sorry to be so fixated on the episode titles, but they're getting increasingly enigmatic. *Is* there a "trap of steel" in this episode, or is William Emms just mucking about with us? I suppose the Drahvin's broken spaceship could be one, in a way, sort of, but otherwise I just don't know what it means.

Like you, Rob, I can mine some good points from this. The episode starts out with some strong dramatic dialogue – the Doctor's comment that "Tomorrow is the last day this planet will ever see" sets up the tempo very effectively at the start, and for a time the audience feels as if the heat is on. There's a good, foreboding moment where Vicki notes the size of the Chumbley corridor, and then looks at the Rill corridor and gets a bit freaked out – this sets us up nicely for the cliffhanger, which has Vicki screaming at her first sight of the Rills, and cuts into an otherwise cutesy scene. The regulars are on good form, and the Chumblies wibble sweetly enough.

But really, what strikes me most about this episode is that for all it promises a fight for survival on a dying planet, not a lot actually happens, does it? The Doctor and Steven get stuck in the TARDIS for a bit, then they walk from the TARDIS to the Drahvins. Then the Doctor and Vicki walk over to the Rills. Steven argues with a Drahvin, then Maaga. The Doctor and Vicki continue walking, and we learn that the Rills are ugly. The End.

I wouldn't so much mind the slower pace if the story seemed to be going somewhere interesting, but I'm not feeling very confident about this. In fact, the scene with Steven and the Drahvin – although an effective demonstration of *his* intelligence – if anything just demonstrates that the clones Maaga commands are thick as two short planks. It's hard to feel intrigued by what's coming next when the baddies we've seen so far amount to a gun-wielding harridan and her posse of the dimmest aliens in the galaxy. I know, I know... we're

supposed to stay positive here, but I need *something* to work with!

February 12th

Air Lock
(Galaxy Four episode three)

R: It's okay, I'm beginning to find my way into Galaxy Four now. I had a bit of a shaky start, partly because it wasn't the story I *imagined* it to be. I'd always had this idea it was a simple moral tale about how the ugly Rills were (shock!) nice, and the beautiful Drahvins were (no, what?) evil. But it's clear right from the beginning of episode one that Maaga is about as affable as a driving instructor, and I was floored. I find I rather like the Drahvins now. There's a certain world weariness to Stephanie Bidmead which is very appealing – and I love the way she pulls out from that to describe with such enthusiasm how the Rills and the TARDIS regulars will die horribly on an exploding planet. Because her Drahvin soldiers are just drones, it comes across a bit like she's telling a gruesome fairy tale to infants – only to give up, and get bored with her audience, because they haven't the imagination to appreciate horrific deaths they can't see for themselves. It's all rather wonderful. There's a downside to being the most evil person in the army, and that's when your subordinates haven't got a clue just how nasty you're actually being.

The Rills, in contrast, are a bit humourless and dry. But it's very funny that they use the Chumblies to be the voiceboxes for the alien voices – Robert Cartland is so solemn and sonorous, it's a bit like imagining the Quarks suddenly voiced by James Earl Jones.

T: Hooray, as the episode title promises, there's an airlock in this episode! Okay, it's probably not the most dramatic or riveting of story-elements, but it is as advertised!

I too appreciate Stephanie Bidmead – it's so novel to have a commander whose frustration with her underlings is understandable because they've been *created* as grunts, as opposed to their just happening to be rather ineffective and hapless. Drahvin high command has evidently issued an edict requiring that a creature with brains, emotions and imagination serve as the leader of each task force, whilst the other members are expendable labour. It makes sense up to a point, and results in a terrific scene where Maaga berates her troops for lacking the imagination to picture and savour the destruction of her enemies. All of this makes the Drahvins more interesting than episode one suggested.

But really, my attention keeps being drawn to the Rills – who for a time were widely regarded by fandom as the only Doctor Who monsters for whom no visual representation existed. (Remember that in those days, we'd never *heard* of Celation, an alien from The Daleks' Master Plan who was for a while only represented by nothing, and then only a tiny, rare photo, and finally was revealed when episode two of that story was found.) Now there's... what? One, maybe two surviving photos of the Rill that the Doctor and company meet? The lack of moving pictures means that we'll never know how effective the Rills were on screen – something that I fear is the case with a lot of this story. We know from elsewhere that Derek Martinus is a director who can keep things flowing and looking good, so it's incredibly frustrating that much of what we glean from this is guesswork. It's a neat idea, for instance, that the creatures are dependent upon ammonia and thus obscured by gas – I would like to think that this was rendered in an interesting way, but there's no way to find out.

It's not a shot in the dark to say, however, that this episode is fundamentally about contact – or rather a discourse – between the Doctor and the Rill, who to look at them are two very different creatures. When the Doctor asks where a Chumbley is off to, the Rill – in Robert Cartland's dignified tones – gently admonishes him by pointing out that it's off to repair the damage he has caused. Hartnell then gets very flustered and embarrassed, and it's a lovely bit of interaction between them. What's more telling, though, is when the Doctor gives the Rills' embarrassment about their appearance very short shrift: "We're not children," he sagely points out. We could, if we wished, mock this story because this core message – judging by appearances is just immature – is

overly simple, but it's one that society is still struggling to learn, even 40 years after this was made.

The Exploding Planet (Galaxy Four episode four)

R: What's to like about The Exploding Planet? That's honestly a tough one. It's as if William Emms gave up writing after episode three, and decided to wait out the 25 minutes until the story was over – it's pretty much what the characters do. The Doctor spends the time siphoning energy from the TARDIS into the Rill ship, whilst constantly getting time updates from his companions, and reassuring them they're under no particular pressure to do this any more speedily. And he's right: watching this is a bit like pretending that someone fixing your car is high drama. The Drahvins know that unless they attack the Rill spaceship in a desperate attempt to get off the planet, they'll die – and yet, somehow, they don't quite get around to doing anything more urgent than bashing a single Chumbley on the bonce with a bit of metal piping.

I was at a convention in the mid-80s, where William Emms sat on the stage with the likes of JN-T and Eric Saward, and spoke of how the current production team, sitting only inches away from him, wouldn't read the scripts he submitted to them. And he grumpily concluded that was because "modern" TV was all about sparkly special effects, and not about intelligent drama. (I was 14, but even I could tell at that age this wasn't the best way to endear yourself to people you were trying to get work from.) After relistening to Galaxy Four, I'm still waiting for Emms' intelligent drama. Actually, I'd even put up with a few lowbrow brain-dead special effects.

Peter Purves complained of this story that he'd simply been given lines written for Jacqueline Hill, and that Steven didn't come across as a character at all. I'd disagree, actually; he gets the one interesting scene in the episode, in which – cynical space pilot that he is – Steven refuses to believe that the Rills are quite as selfless and altruistic as they claim, and demands to know their real agenda. It's like a breath of fresh air through all the moral homilies. And it's only a shame that he's wrong, because it might have made the episode a little more dramatic.

And I do quite like the end. In these days of modern Who, when one story every season has to find a way of writing out the Doctor, they haven't yet hit upon this idea: simply having our heroes point at the scanner, pick out a planet, and wonder what's going on there. As it is, the brief lead-in to the next story entails Barry Jackson being rather brilliant, remembering that he should kill – and saying so in such a reasoned and affable manner that it sounds rather chilling. It's a lot more interesting than what happened on the exploding planet, at any rate.

I'm sorry, Toby. I really tried hard to find something good to say. I was defeated. It's up to you to rescue this baby. I'm now off to the hotel bar downstairs to talk with fans about some *good* Doctor Who. You salvage this Galaxy Four review – do it well, and there's a nice shiny glass of wine in it for you.

T: I saw William Emms at a convention too – although not the one you mentioned – on a very grumpy panel about the Hartnell years that bemoaned the current state of the series. Along with countless others who – like myself – hadn't actually seen any of these 60s "classics", I applauded heartily. We'd never watched the work in question, and so perhaps weren't in the best place to judge, but by Heaven – we knew *for certain* that Doctor Who wasn't as good as it used to be!

Fortunately, times have changed – not only are *we* now working professionals and convention guests (I find this somewhat impossible to believe, and am a bit daunted by it all), but also, the new series is in such rude health that fandom is very proud of it and isn't quite as strident and defensive about bygone eras of Doctor Who as it once was. I very much doubt that we'll see panels in which people previously associated with the show will take shots at the current production team. (Well, maybe a little, but not very much.)

As for the final instalment of Galaxy Four... hmm, as you say, it's less a "race against time" and more a "saunter against time". It begins with a certain amount of incident, though – a bomb gets chucked through a window, Steven is freed and our heroes escape from the

Drahvins with lots of breathlessness and urgency. It's only afterwards that things start slowing down, but I don't seem to mind this as much as you – there's lots of build-up to the planet disintegrating, and events keep upping the dramatic ante. It's a bit like the constant eruptions in the TARDIS in The Edge of Destruction. And the Drahvins work better than you might think – there's an interesting scene in their spaceship as Maaga falls back on shallow military catchphrases to calm the nerves of her soldiers.

All in all, this is a reasonable stab at doing something different. I like the Rills' dignified nature, and feel sorry for the poor old Chumbley who sacrifices himself to get the travellers back to the TARDIS. To put it another way, Doctor Who is such a strange series that I'm here made to admire a noble warthog and get emotionally attached to a twittering dustbin.

And now, as I didn't whine, I think I've earned some, er, wine. Time to hit the bar and take you up on your offer... if, of course, I can prise you away from your adoring fans.

February 13th

Mission to the Unknown

R: Aha! Now that's more like it. We all think of this, of course, as being the only classic Doctor Who story that has neither the Doctor nor any of his companions in it. But structurally, it's a lot weirder than that. You could call this the first of a 12-part adventure... which then unexpectedly has a couple of comedy stories (The Myth Makers and The Feast of Steven) in the middle of it. But this gives us a sense of the genuinely epic; it's a story that *can't* be told in one go, and needs a couple of breathers put in. And if we were talking about how you could play around with audience expectations in Season One by simply never letting them know how long a story was going to last, then they'll be confounded absolutely by this. Everyone watching would be sitting there waiting for the sound of the TARDIS to cut through the weird alien shrieks of the jungle – and waiting in vain. And because the regulars never show up, *everyone* here dies. You get the feeling not only that the Doctor is a genuine saviour, and that his presence alone can make things better, but that the world is a far more brutal place without him. So, who do we look to in his stead? Space security agent Marc Cory, that's who – he's clearly smart and resourceful, but he's also an emotionless killer who'll get his mission accomplished at the cost of his own life and anybody else's.

As in Turn Left so many years later, the absence of the Doctor – the fact that the most the regular cast can do at this stage is to point at Kembel on the scanner screen – defines how powerful he is. Without him, the Daleks run riot and seem like a credible political force. The Nazi allusions are at last complete; Cory's associate Gordon Lowery (and by implication, humanity in general) can't see the harm in the Daleks occupying lots of other planets, so long as they're far away from home. And the Varga plants are horrific too; the very idea that they turn people into savage plant-creatures – meaning that even after you're dead, you lose your humanity completely and become a walking vegetable – is a terribly repulsive one. It's the perfect synthesis of the Robomen and the Fungoids, and a good deal more unpleasant than either. So the "heroes" in this story face destruction of their very identities, as an alliance forms behind them to destroy the entire galaxy...

... seems to me like it's time for the TARDIS to touch down in ancient Troy.

T: For all that Mission to the Unknown might seem like a "filler" story, it's a gutsy melodrama. The stock music ups the tempo, and Edward de Souza, playing Marc Cory, gives a biting and unsentimental depiction of a pragmatic professional. (It's a bit over the top, though, when Cory says that he's "Licensed To Kill" – come on!) And the Varga plants *are* a chilling concept, evoking those horrid wasps that later inspired the Wirrn in that they consume your body and use that succour to propagate themselves. It's such a frightening proposition, it overcomes the way the Vargas themselves look like a massive candyfloss.

But you'll have to forgive me if I indulge in a bit of high geekery, because Mission to the Unknown features that marvellous array of alien delegates – a group made all the more

tantalising because despite all the documentation we have on the 60s stories, it remains one of the Great Doctor Who Mysteries as to which delegate has which name. It's a question that has vexed all sorts of Doctor Who historians over the years, and re-experiencing this story now, the anal-retentive side of me has to speculate on this a bit, as I'm still not convinced by the most popular hypotheses about the delegates' identities...

We know from the paperwork that the uncredited performers are Ronald Rich as Trantis, Sam Mansary as Sentreal and Len Russell, Pat Gorman and Johnny Clayton (he was Reg Cox, the guy who dies in the first episode of EastEnders, you know!) as the Planetarians. Now, it's generally accepted that Trantis is the small spiky delegate who looks like the character with the same name in The Daleks' Master Plan, but... we've already seen Ronald Rich on screen when he was Gunnar the Giant in The Time Meddler, and he's massive, whereas Mr Spiky is clearly the tiniest delegate of the bunch. I'd therefore venture a guess that Rich must be the tall white spacesuit man or the big black Christmas tree. (Perhaps Douglas Camfield rejected the latter costume for Trantis because it looked like an overgrown chess piece, and used one of the other design ideas instead; only Malpha is formally identified at this point, so it's not like Camfield was tinkering with established continuity.) Also, given that Len Russell was a diminutive Optera a few weeks back, I'd suggest that *he* is Mr Tiny Spikeface. And surely, Sentreal is the space-helmet chap, as Sam Mansary is the only black actor in the cast.

I realize that not every fan cares as much about this as I do, but I do love that there are a few issues about Doctor Who that we'll never have a definitive answer for, no matter how much Who scholars debate them. (Even if this episode were recovered and we could finally *see* it, it's doubtful that we'd be much more clear on which delegate is which.) Piecing things together and postulating is so much more fun and engaging than just being handed answers on a plate (it's what makes history and archaeology so fascinating), and it just reinforces my belief that Doctor Who is so complex and has so many forms, it's so very, very hard to get bored with it.

Temple of Secrets
(The Myth Makers episode one)

R: Donald Cotton's script for Temple of Secrets is *very* clever. It starts off sounding earnest and melodramatic enough, aping the ancient classics – and then, the characters begin to drop their battle cries and posturing, and reveal themselves as ordinary bored people with the same irritations about love and life as the rest of us. Achilles may know the right lingo when he's waving a sword about, but he's really just a man desperate to prove he's worth taking seriously. No-one does, though, with Odysseus clearly believing the only way Achilles could have defeated Hector in battle would be had he worn him out by running away for long enough. And the scenes between brothers Menelaus and Agamemnon are especially rewarding – they behave not as great kings from Greek literature, but as brothers getting on each other's nerves; the way that Menelaus keeps on whining about the ten-year war, and how he's glad to be shot of Helen in the first place, brings a modern outlook upon ancient history that pre-empts Blackadder by over 15 years. And William Hartnell, of course, always relaxes when he gets to play with comic lines – we can't *see* his reaction to Achilles worshipping him in the guise of an old beggar, or to Agamemnon inviting him to eat a ham bone, but we can still hear that his timing is spot on.

If there's a problem, it's only that all of Cotton's wit doesn't yet give the rest of regulars an awful lot to do – after the pedestrian plotting of Galaxy Four, and their absence from Mission to the Unknown altogether, it does feel rather a long time since Steven and Vicki got a moment in the spotlight. Vicki doesn't even get to leave the TARDIS at all, still nursing a bad ankle she picked up two weeks ago! (Ailments lingering on between stories is something of a theme this year, with sword wounds and toothaches still to come.) But it's hardly a crime that a writer has come onto the scene who is so clearly delighted with his background characterisation – we haven't seen anything as rich as this since The Crusade.

And I love the gag about Odysseus interpreting Cyclops' mute gestures to him in such accurate detail. I only hope that the rest of the cast reacted to it in suitable deadpan.

T: It's wonderful how Doctor Who keeps reinventing itself so often. Last week, we had a rather grim space adventure, with everyone behaving with requisite gravitas. Now, the crew witness a fight and the Doctor is whimsically blasé about it, noting that the jousters are doing more talking than fighting (which is to say: the Doctor's as in on the joke as we are). And it's particularly interesting that in some ways, this is a reversal of what happened in The Aztecs – in that story, Barbara being mistaken for a god was handled very dramatically, and you were never in doubt that her mere presence was a matter of life and death for those around her. But here, Donald Cotton's tongue is firmly in his cheek as plays on the Doctor's vanity, with the old chap rather chuffed when he's assumed to possess divinity. The suggestion that he's Zeus is justified, hilariously, by Achilles mentioning that the father of Mount Olympus once disguised himself as an old beggar – which to look at the Hartnell Doctor is a priceless thing to say. The secret of great comedy interaction is to have at least one good straight man, and so credit must be given to Cavan Kendall for not lampooning Achilles, but instead playing him as the sincere soldier he thinks he is, despite overwhelming evidence to the contrary.

Much of this story's charm, though, lies in the fact that Cotton doesn't seem to favour either side in this conflict. It looks initially as if he's more accommodating to the Greeks, in that Hector is cocky, patronising and a hammy posturer whilst Achilles seems to be quite brave. But then Achilles' famous victory over Hector is depicted as the result of cowardly opportunism, and it's clear – as you've mentioned, Rob – that Achilles' allies see his heroic bluster as the braggadocio of a self-promoting halfwit. Such a stunning manipulation of dramatic mores would be completely lost on any kids in the audience (who, in all likelihood, would be happy enough with lots of fighting and shouting), but this turnabout is there to allow the adults their own take on the story. You mentioned Blackadder, and I'll raise you The Simpsons.

All of which means that Temple of Secrets couldn't be further from Wolfgang Peterson's Troy if it tried – and that it's about ten times more entertaining. Peterson's version was awash with humourless musclebound hunks being drearily honourable, but this episode entails the likes of a bellicose Ivor Salter (as Odysseus) guffawing his way through proceedings with a drunken swagger and a fantastically dirty laugh. Doctor Who is all about creating worlds, and I feel as though ancient Troy in Donald Cotton's hands has been made by taking fragments from classical literature and applying a contemporary eye for characterisation, thereby creating a comedic tour de force. The guest cast very much seems on the same page as this – as Hector, Alan Hayward gives what I presume is a deliberately OTT performance that mocks the conventions of the historical epic (which is a pretty sophisticated acting choice for someone who's on screen just long enough to get slaughtered). And back in Agamemnon's tent, Jack Melford's put-upon Menelaus is delightful, and Francis De Woolf (as Agamemnon) is far more subtle and deadpan than the mad growling he doled out as the would-be rapist Vasor in The Keys of Marinus.

And yet, for all that this episode might *seem* like a comedy – for all the opening sword fight, for instance, is accompanied by parping music to let us know straightaway that this is a bit of a romp – the setting itself provides a bit of necessary jeopardy. Call this a "comedy" if you like, but there's also a gory on-screen death (that we can't see because the video is lost, sadly) and threats of tongue removal – so it's not *all* frivolity on the fields of Troy, is it? It's best to keep this in mind as we consider the next three episodes.

This is bloody fantastic, and quite unlike anything the show has yet served us. The production team weren't wrong when their press release heralded these scripts as the most sophisticated yet seen in the series – I had a ball "watching" this episode.

February 14th

Small Prophet, Quick Return (The Myth Makers episode two)

R: Isn't Barrie Ingham fantastic? I found him rather anaemic in Dr Who and the Daleks as Alydon, but here he gives a performance that's

laugh out loud funny, doing his turn as Paris by way of Bertie Wooster. His (whispered) calls to Achilles so he can do the proper thing and take revenge for Hector, his eagerness for praise when he brings to the Trojan camp both the TARDIS and then Steven, and his boyish attempts to chat up Vicki are all utterly delightful.

It's a very funny episode altogether – but the tone is only deceptively light. There is a flippancy towards death which is quite striking; Priam treats the power he has over Vicki's life so affably, as does Odysseus with his over Steven, and both regulars give a similar response: "That's very comforting!" This new, jaded look the TARDIS crew take to their life-threatening adventures is something we shan't see again until Tom Baker. What makes it quite chilling is that the soldiers in both armies share this jaded reaction; it's been a ten-year war, and matters of life and death have become trivial. Paris is surprised when Steven suggests he be taken prisoner rather than killed after he loses a duel: "But that isn't done!" Odysseus' macabre speculation that the Trojans may or may not take prisoners of war depending what mood they're in is extremely funny, but also says a lot about the way both sides regard the other as being essentially without values or humanity.

Max Adrian is lovely as Priam, playing him at once as a doddery old father who despairs of his children, and also as a king who is perfectly at peace with his ability to command death. And Frances White is great fun as the doomsaying Cassandra, pitching it just enough over the top that the bored reactions of the Trojans who listen to her are hilarious.

This historical is one of the most intriguing experiments of the third season. For the first time, the TARDIS lands in a historical era where it is impossible to distinguish legend from fact, making the Doctor's knowledge of the time unreliable at best. Ordered to find a way to end the siege of Troy, he dismisses the Trojan horse as a fanciful invention of Homer's. It's a far cry from The Time Meddler, where William Hartnell is able to reel off in detail the events leading up to the Battle of Hastings. And it's an experiment which will be used to more dramatic effect later in the season, where both the characters' and the audience's unfamiliarity with the events of The Massacre only contributes to the suspense.

T: The title of this episode is a great gag. It's so great, in fact, that I mention it in Moths Ate My Doctor Who Scarf – which, by a curious coincidence, I'm performing at the convention tonight. I've found that this joke provides a nice bit of funny info for my audiences, which ordinarily aren't composed of hardcore Doctor Who fans. But tonight it'll be different, and I'm interested to see what happens if I tell about 600 fans something they already know. Will they laugh anyway?

Turning our attention back to ancient Troy, we continue to get a comedy of manners that's juxtaposed with the trappings of a completely different genre. It's almost entirely dependent upon the dialogue, and the actors all rise to the challenge with aplomb. You've mentioned Barrie Ingham, who strikes me as Hugh Laurie in Blackadder – he's the jolly public schoolboy you can laugh at and still love. But I also enjoy Frances White as Cassandra – her colourful foreboding is a dramatic device, but the story's knowing treatment of her inherent ridiculousness serves a comedic need as well (just look at Priam's assessment that Cassandra's doom-mongering, for all its lofty dramatics, is really just a means of her hedging her bets).

But as with the previous episode, there's some jeopardy in spite of all the hi-jinks. The cliffhanger entails some Trojan guards advancing on Vicki and Steven, whom they believe are spies for the Greeks. As the "next episode" header promises "Death of a Spy", surely one of them is due for the chop? Unless, of course, the writer does something very clever – and on the evidence of what we've seen thus far, I have no doubt that he will.

Death of a Spy
(The Myth Makers episode three)

R: In future years, we're going to get a lot of this – the Exiting Companion Suddenly Falling In Love motif. If you thought Susan taking a shine to David Campbell was a bit out of the blue, that's nothing to this – which is based on Vicki going goo-goo eyed at Troilus within a few minutes of airtime! (And you can tell it's important, because in her neighbouring cell,

even Steven has noticed she's got a boyfriend – relationship stuff must be written in big lettering if another regular acknowledges it; even Barbara's dalliances were never deemed worthy enough of actual comment.)

This ought to be rubbish, of course – but it really truly isn't, because Donald Cotton is playing a clever game with his audience. For a start, anyone watching when Priam renamed Vicki "Cressida" last week should have felt their inner alarm go off – and once more, as Toby would say, there's an expectation that the viewing public will have heard of Troilus and Cressida and know what that represents. It's impossible to imagine that taken on trust nowadays. But although Cotton seems to be setting up a relationship, because he's subverting the audience's understanding of who all these classical characters are – Odysseus as a boor, Achilles as a loser – it's just as likely that when Troilus pitches up in the story, he'll be as attractive as a Drashig.

So we get this lovely scene of flirtation between Troilus and our new Cressida. And it teases the audience, that we *know* how this love story is supposed to work out, but we also realise that nothing that we think we know about these legends is working out as we'd expect. To underline the point, we've got the Doctor rubbishing the Trojan horse gambit, and then resorting to it when he needs to break the siege and can't come up with anything better. As a result, we don't need to be moved or touched by the romance taking place here – we're asked instead to consider whether or not it'll be resolved as an intellectual puzzle. It's as abrupt as Leela, say, running off to have Time Tots with Andred – but it's far from being as stupid. It's brilliant sleight of hand plotting. We accept what's happening because it's playing off the myth – but we're not obliged to see Vicki's exit next week as inevitable, and by the time it happens, it's not a bit of awkward plotting but the resolution to a literary joke.

Still, with romance in the air for Vicki, it's ideal to be listening to this on Valentine's Day. (Hmph. I miss Janie. You've got your K with you here at the convention, but I'm lacking my J.) Not that the literary jokes involved are all that sophisticated, of course – this is probably the only time in the series' history that we're catapulted into a cliffhanger by the threat of a groan-inducing pun, as Paris says, "I'm afraid you're a bit late to say *whoa* to the horse, I've just given instructions to have it brought into the city."

T: It *is* Valentine's Day – the very day that I've been booked to do my show. A cynic might say that my performance was slated for tonight because most Doctor Who fans won't have an awful lot else to do – but that would be cruel (not to mention very unfair). Anyway, you may not have your beloved here, but I'm a bit nervous, and so can't pay mine much attention as the hours tick away towards the gig.

I first have to comment on the resolution to the "Death of a Spy" business, as it here turns out that Odysseus' agent – a mute man named Cyclops – is killed by one of Paris' soldiers. As far as I recall, Donald Cotton elaborated on the backstory of this in his terribly witty chapter in The Doctor Who File, in which he said that some wet-behind-the-ears BBC type imposed the title on him. As a result, he had to contrive the Cyclops' demise, and thus lose out on calling the episode Is There a Doctor In the Horse? (Though episode one's lost title, Zeus Ex Machina, is the one I regret the most.) The mute's execution does seem arbitrary – but then again, the seemingly random violence reminds us that despite all the merry banter, our heroes are caught up in events where life is cheap.

Amidst the ongoing frivolity (including the way Priam says that the dungeons are nice, and that he hangs about in them when it all gets too stressful), it's intriguing how Cotton redefines the Doctor. He's here depicted as a dotty improviser at odds with a witty and wise opponent – Odysseus, who actually knows what a paper aeroplane is and consistently outsmarts our hero. This would come across as a betrayal of the Doctor's character in less skilful hands, but here it just *works*. And what a rude line Odysseus gets, when he tells the Doctor that he's feeling as "nervous as a Bacchante at her first orgy". Glorious!

There continues to be so much about this story that we can't evaluate (what was the lighting like inside the horse, how many soldiers were in there, etc?) because the video no longer exists, which is galling. However, if The Myth Makers can keep me *this* nourished with

only a soundtrack, scant photographic representation and the merest scraps of moving pictures, it's a lasting testament to its superb writing and acting.

February 15th

Horse of Destruction (The Myth Makers episode four)

R: This comedy reveals its teeth – and my God, the teeth are sharp. Dennis Spooner's Romans story had a certain grimness beneath its merry surface, but that's nothing to what Cotton does here. The humour is more exaggerated, and the corresponding violence more shocking. We're so used to seeing Paris and Priam as likeable bumblers, that the calm manner in which Odysseus tells his men to kill them – denying them last words, or even last pratfalls – is completely jarring. And that is, of course, Cotton's point. He treats war as such a big joke for three episodes, and then in the final one wipes the smiles off our faces. It's not subtle, and it's not pretty, but there's an anger to this and it's quite startling.

But perhaps it's all a bit too much? Removing the comic moments from a comedy doesn't turn it suddenly into serious drama. It leaves behind instead a vacuum, which, arguably, is what much of this episode is – a big, gaping void in which a number of characters we thought we knew get killed rather violently in a burning city. Achilles and Troilus, neither of them the big heroes of legend, fight to the death – accompanied by incidental music so jolly, it seems even the composer can't really believe that the story's going to go through with it.

Taken as a story in isolation, The Myth Makers ends in messy confusion. But this is where, seeing these episodes as part of an ongoing narrative, the story works so brilliantly. What appeared at first to be a jolly run around The Iliad becomes an adventure that shatters the TARDIS crew. Vicki is left with Troilus and a determinedly uncertain future, her last scene not being the romantic happy ending we might have expected, but a desperate attempt to convince a lover who suspects she's sold his civilisation out to the enemy to be strong and survive. Steven had an amusing little sword fight with a Trojan in episode two – now he's dying from a skirmish that was much more serious. And in a particularly wonderful exchange, the Doctor tells Katarina, one of Cassandra's handmaidens, in quiet seriousness never to refer to him as a god – even though in the opening instalment, his pretence at being mistaken for Zeus amused him greatly. It's as if all the gags that the regulars indulged in have come back and bitten them. And then you realise quite *why* the apparently bonkers decision was taken to insert this four-part Trojan comedy into The Daleks' Master Plan narrative. It's not a detour from the action on Kembel – it's a wryly comic examination of the themes of war which are about to unfold in the series over the next three months. "You think this is funny?", the story says to us, "All this war, all this fighting? It's not funny. Look at what it's done to the TARDIS crew, just *look* at them. And this is nothing. We haven't even started yet. Next Week: The Nightmare Begins."

T: Well, the nightmare for *me* started last night when I went on stage about an hour after I was scheduled, and the sound guys got the very first cue wrong. At least they were consistent – they screwed up all the other ones as well. I was touched, by the way, at how furious you were on my behalf. Everyone seemed to enjoy it though, and I've been flattered and moved by some of the kind things people said. Nervousness compelled me to smoke all the cigarettes in America before I went on, though!

Anyway, back to an example of Doctor Who and comedy that was put together long before I was even capable of thought... by now, we've seen this amazing show change in form or tone from story to story (or even episode to episode), so – because we've been watching Doctor Who in order – the sudden dramatic shift here in episode four isn't quite as unnerving as it might have been, because the idea of a "story" hasn't become the norm. There's a change of gear, yes, but there's a similar shift between the sci-fi ludicrousness of The Web Planet episode six and the grandiose Shakespearean antics of The Crusade episode one. If you're a Doctor Who viewer, you've become acclimatised to such sudden changes in tone.

What *does* seem out of left field is the way that the new companion, Katarina, is bizarrely introduced so late in the day – we've already spent three episodes in the environs of Troy, and she hasn't even made a cameo appearance before now. This, of course, brings up the debate about whether Katarina should even be considered a companion: Adrienne Hill never gets proper billing in the Radio Times, and she filmed her death scene (four episodes hence) before recording this episode, so she knew her days were numbered even on her first day at TV Centre. More to the point, this is such a perfunctory introduction to the character that one wonders why the production team decided to get rid of Vicki rather than kill her off in the Dalek epic we're just about to experience. If you're going to horrifically kill someone in the depths of space as part of a 12-episode saga, the death of someone who's already been around for a year or so would have been far more affecting.

That said, Vicki's exit is lovely – there's that wonderful scene she has with Troilus at the end, which just proves that Cotton can deliver drama and emotion as well as comedy; he's much more than just a glib tongue. Note too, how we're back into The Chase territory in that we don't get to witness Vicki and the Doctor's farewell scene – they disappear into the TARDIS, and then it's just Vicki who emerges. Squandering the opportunity to play with those big emotions wouldn't be countenanced today, but I actually think it works better – it makes me try to think how those characters would have parted, and the scenarios I can conjure up in my mind are more touching than might have been realised on screen.

Where the supporting characters are concerned, director Christopher Barry once lamented to me that today's kids don't have a proper grounding in classical education – meaning that while Odysseus *seems* to win the day, a lot of children watching this would have known that he's in for a few grotty times ahead, and that his *real* troubles only start after his face-off with the Doctor. Whether or not it's true that modern-day children don't know their *Iliad*, it's a neat trick on the part of Cotton and Ivor Salter that we're made to view Odysseus as such a distasteful, boorish pig, and yet root for him anyway because he's very funny.

I have to say, Rob, that thus far into our journey, The Myth Makers is my favourite story. Someone find the video of these episodes, please – this adventure desperately needs to be seen and eulogised, rather than to languish half-forgotten as it does at the moment.

The Nightmare Begins (The Daleks' Master Plan episode one)

R: It's a little hard to believe that this is from the same series as The Chase, isn't it? As soon as we recognise that there are Space Security agents stumbling around the jungle, we know that we're right back in that Dalek story that was postponed a few weeks ago. And just like Kert Gantry, licking his lips and edging forward with his gun raised, we're waiting for the pepperpots to appear and put us out of our misery. That's a brilliant sequence, by the way – one of the few from the episode that exists in full. Gantry knows he's going to die, and is terrified of the prospect of it, but can't bear the suspense of it all the more. There's no question of the Dalek he encounters being *funny* – and this single tense scene does more to re-establish the Daleks as indomitable monsters than any other we've yet seen on the show. It's the difference in directors – whereas Richard Martin would point the camera every which way, Douglas Camfield here so carefully frames the Dalek from below to make it look merciless.

And there's another remarkable scene – one which really ought to be rather rubbish. It's a long sequence where two bored technicians chat about fast cars and their favourite telly programmes, whilst watching a smooth politician being interviewed by the forty-first century equivalent of the BBC. It's all exposition, of course – but it's skilfully done, it's so natural, and it illustrates the complacency of a society that has such a corrupt leader as its figurehead. Roald openly mocks Mavic Chen, the Guardian of the Solar System, whilst Lizan admires his style – but neither of them engage with Chen seriously, both treat him as a TV celebrity rather than their spokesman, and they're exactly the sort of people therefore who won't even notice as he sells them out to the Daleks. Both of them are the types for whom Facebook was invented. They're very minor bit parts, but their appearances lend the impression there's a whole real world outside this strange Terry Nation-planet of screaming jungles and killer plants.

T: Initially, this episode looks like it's going to be a retread of Mission to the Unknown – first in the unsentimental and manly patter shared between the two Space Security agents, Bret Vyon and Kert Gantry, and then in the surviving clip that (as you've noted) gives us Gantry's trembling face in close-up as he sinks to his knees and a Dalek looms over him. But while the tone here is certainly more serious than The Chase, it's not *all* a dry comic strip: Chen has a great line about getting away from interviewers, and William Hartnell has already established a sweet and unpatronising rapport with Adrienne Hill. It's just a shame that he fluffs his line about using brain instead of brawn, which rather undermines his point!

With so many of the visuals for this episode gone, I find myself fixating on the wonderfully horrid soundscape – the screeching of the jungle is fingernails-on-blackboard uncomfortable. Brian Hodgson's contribution to the effectiveness of these early serials is not to be underestimated – his work is consistently superb, innovative and atmospheric. And I very much appreciate the forward thinking in that Vyon's distress signal contains a futuristic metamorphosis of the phonetic alphabet, so that Charlie becomes Charlo and Echo becomes Egan. (We should probably credit this revamped terminology to Douglas Camfield, as he suggested that the character-names should be futurised. And he certainly had a point – the very next scene would seem somewhat quainter had it been, as was the original plan, an exchange between characters called Ronald and Liza!)

But overall, it's very frustrating that we've entered a telesnap-free zone, and so much of what's here is difficult to picture. The scant clips that remain, at least, tell me that Mavic Chen's spaceship, the Spar, is rendered as a great model, but I so eagerly want to *see* the rest of it! John Wiles was a very good producer, but he clearly didn't anticipate any long-term interest in the show, even from the people who made it (who were the principle purchasers of telesnaps). Fortunately, three episodes of The Daleks' Master Plan have managed to wend their way back to the archives over the years – and one of those is up next! Hooray!

February 16th

Day of Armageddon
(The Daleks' Master Plan
episode two)

R: You're right, Toby – we're back to moving pictures again! And it gives me a certain pang, right here in my heart, because this episode is *so* full of little moments to enjoy that it makes me wonder what else we've been missing by having to resort to the soundtrack. There's the weird futuristic manner in which Mavic Chen holds his pen, and his squiggly back and forth handwriting. The way all those alien delegates clap their appreciation for Dalek conquest, but all in subtly different ways. That wonderful shot of the Dalek studying all the seated aliens one by one, all strange teeth and spots, and for a moment we're put exactly into the same position as the Dalek – reacting with curiosity and some disdain to all the weirdoes gathered in the conference hall. And although you can get some measure of just how good Kevin Stoney (playing Chen) is from hearing his lines alone, we'd miss the amused contempt on his face as he contemplates Zephon, Master of the Five Galaxies but Fashion Icon of None. Douglas Camfield's direction is, frankly, brilliant – he mines each and every scene for interesting camera angles and close-ups. The conversations between Chen and Zephon, which on paper alone are hardly crackling with wit or depth, feel energised and somewhat dangerous. Chen drops his amiable façade when insisting that he needs air, and suddenly there's a real tension to all of this.

And this is the only existing episode to feature Adrienne Hill as Katarina. For years, this sometime-companion (well, according to all the lists we compiled in the 1980s, and I'm

enough of a fanboy to stick to them) was constantly represented by the same BBC publicity photograph – it's all they have of her to use as the Doctor inexplicably remembers all of his companions (bar Leela) as his mind is sucked out in Resurrection of the Daleks. And yet, with Day of Armageddon having been re-discovered in 2004, we've at last got a chance to *see* Hill in action. It's a very stylised performance, and there's something of the idiot savant to Katarina – she looks a little as if she's having to retreat into her own private world because there's simply no way she can cope with what she sees around her. A lot of actors would choose to portray such a character in a permanent state of distress – but Hill, rather bravely (and very oddly) instead smiles a lot and nods her head, as if this is all something very weird she's dreaming about after eating too much Trojan cheese. It's hard to imagine how such a performance could have sustained itself if Katarina had survived into Proper Companion Territory, but as it is I find it rather winning.

T: I vividly recall the excitement that was generated when Day of Armageddon was found in 2004. A missing episode had returned to us! And, owing to its limited overseas distribution, from one of the most *unlikely* stories to turn up somewhere! And it's also thrilling that we're able to properly see so many of the delegates – some of them are a wonderful surprise! Trantis has some nifty pointed teeth, and Zephon delightfully looks as though he's made of seaweed. It's a shame, though, that between Mission to the Unknown and this episode, the programme-makers have set aside the delegate who looks like an evil Christmas tree.

Being able to *see* this episode makes such a difference... Kevin Stoney is all nuance in his performance as Chen; I just love it when he steals behind some scenery that resembles prison bars, and gives an amused look of mock hopelessness. Douglas Camfield's camerawork is excellent, as is the set-design, which allows Zephon's entrance to be very grand. He's so nicely silhouetted in that doorway, and I adore the way he doesn't fold his arms! (The Doctor makes the mistake of folding his arms while impersonating Zephon, though, which is one of *many* clues that he's a substitute, but which the other delegates strangely fail to pick up on.)

The only thing dampening my giddiness is a pet peeve of mine – it's only episode two, and the Daleks are already vowing to exterminate Chen once he's served his purpose. It's lazy writing to suggest that the villains will dispose of one another, thus saving the Doctor a moral quandary about how to deal with them. Besides, we don't *want* the Daleks to exterminate Chen – he's far more interesting than they are! Oh, and it seems that Hartnell is now choosing *exactly* the wrong lines to fluff. His supposed witty rejoinder to Bret Vyon's "Sir, will you *shut up!*", is so mucked up, it doesn't make the Doctor's resultant superiority seem justified.

Finally, how have we made it this far without discussing the oddness of watching Nicholas Courtney play Bret Vyon, now that we're so familiar with his later role as the Brigadier? I particularly note with interest the way Courtney delivers the line "Who cares about history?" not as the crabby retort the writer intended, but as a mused philosophical point. It's as if, even this early in his relationship with the programme, Courtney is so thoroughly decent that he's doing everything in his power to refrain from snapping at the Doctor.

Devil's Planet
(The Daleks' Master Plan
episode three)

R: I love the way the Daleks threaten our heroes with "space extinction"! That sounds like the most wonderfully exciting way to die. That's how I want to go.

This is all a bit like The Chase, isn't it? Except it's being played straight. There's a far greater sense of desperation to the Doctor's theft of the Taranium core than we've seen before – it feels like a last-ditch attempt to stop the Daleks' plans, rather than the cheerful self-confidence that has characterised all Hartnell's encounters with them since the first story. When the Doctor realises the Daleks are in pursuit, all the optimism and life go out of Hartnell's voice in a moment of rare fear. Although he doesn't sound at all convincing talking about gravitational points and what-

not, he turns in a lovely performance as he shows increasing tenderness towards Katarina. There's an especially touching moment when she tells the Doctor she feels safe so long as she's with him. Considering how little dialogue the two of them have together, the charming way Hartnell has of building a relationship with Hill is very impressive – and works towards making her death next week all the more affecting. And I love the way he cheerily chides her for asking questions "like the other two" – we know he's referring to Bret and Steven, but I like to think he's thinking of her two predecessor Doctor Who girls, Susan and Vicki. Ask too many questions and John Wiles will sack you. Oops, too late.

The Daleks, too, have a sense of authority restored to them. They wait patiently as Chen and Zephon squabble over which of them is responsible for the loss of the Taranium – and then calmly exterminate Zephon, the loser of the debate. It's calculating and callous, with more than a touch of black comedy to it.

T: Isn't it curious how in the future, it seems that every spaceship will have a cassette player fitted? Not that today's SF shows or books have their forecasting down perfectly. I wonder what new piece of whizzo technology will emerge in the next 40 years, immediately dating any piece of SF that currently uses shiny discs as memory devices.

Hartnell is once again displaying a rare gift for the lines he's fluffing – this episode, it's the line with the words "to be precise" that he doesn't deliver precisely!!! He *does*, however, successfully utter the line, "That's why we're stuck on this pimple of a planet whilst you footle with a fusebox!" Why fans haven't quoted this for generations escapes me – its awfulness makes it utterly brilliant!

But I'm trying to find some levity in an episode that is otherwise pretty grim – the desperates of Desperus (which is to say, the convicts exiled there) do seem a grotty bunch, and it's clear that these bedraggled beardies will stop at nothing to escape. It's odd though, with so many thugs on display, that Nation elects to use the weediest of them – Kirksen – as the one who sneaks aboard the Spar for the brilliantly screamed cliffhanger. Mind you, the only reason Kirksen takes Katarina hostage is because the Doctor forgot to shut a door. He's becoming a menace, this man.

February 17th

The Traitors
(The Daleks' Master Plan episode four)

R: William Hartnell exposes Bret Vyon's associate Daxtar as a traitor, and by the most simplistic means possible – it's because, once again, the silly villain has revealed information he could never have known unless he was on the wrong side. We've had this little bit of plotting going on as far back as The Keys of Marinus – and it's fun for the kids, because they can point out before the TV characters do that a mistake has been made. And then the episode turns down this bit of childlike problem-solving on its head – Daxtar is shot down in cold blood, and Hartnell is left reeling and furious at Bret Vyon's callousness. It's no greater demonstration that this story isn't quite playing by the same rules we come to expect from Doctor Who; Katarina's death is shocking and sudden and leaves you utterly floored, and then, later in the same episode, Bret Vyon is killed too. And if anything, Vyon's death is even *more* surprising – at least Katarina was given some sort of eulogy by the Doctor, whilst Vyon suffers the indignity of no more than his executioner going through his pockets, and then not even pausing to give him a backward look.

We know that Hartnell was unhappy with the new direction John Wiles was taking the show in, and felt that it was getting excessively brutal. This episode has to be the crowning example of that. Even the Daleks dispassionately kill their own kind when they fail to catch the Doctor on the planet Desperus – failure will not be tolerated. It's a far cry from the comedy "thick" Dalek of The Chase who stuttered a lot; you rather suspect he'd have been exterminated without benefit of a court-martial by these chaps. It's not just the dispassionate attitude towards death that the episode exhibits; there are real power struggles taking place here.

The warning that the Daleks give Trantis – that they will eliminate their allies if they fail

them – mirrors Chen's own warnings to his henchman Karlton. Now that we see Chen away from the Dalek influence, we can at last appreciate him as a powerful character in his own right, and Kevin Stoney excels. There is a gritty cynicism to each character, and nowhere before have the Doctor's childlike ideals of goodness and pacifism seemed more out of place. The Daleks are depicted as active, ruthless strategists; they're neither simply bogeymen to resist nor clowns to laugh at. And the simple sequence with Daxtar elegantly demonstrates that no-one can be trusted on Earth at all – and that the entire mission of the last two episodes to warn the authorities there has been naive. It's very clever – what was settling down into becoming a repeat of The Chase has had the carpet pulled from under its feet.

I love it all, of course, because I'm 39 years old. But was Hartnell right? Up to this point, the show has never really been about the corruption of mankind, but about its innate morality. Never before has Doctor Who's basic worldview been so casually shattered.

It's clever, too, how the script hides from the viewer the fact that the ruthless killer working for Chen is a woman. Chen and Karlton only ever refer to Sara Kingdom by her surname – they clearly see no importance in her gender whatsoever, merely in her efficiency. After the awkward sexism of Galaxy Four, in which military women were clearly something to be ogled at, it's refreshing to see Sara treated immediately with far more dignity.

T: Ah, this is a rare example of a reblocked cliffhanger – Kirksen's appearance aboard the Spar had to be a surprise last week, and come out of nowhere. But this week, we open on him, it seems, and he engages in the stalemate that results in (depending on how you define terms) the first death of one of the Doctor's companions. Given that the Daleks are the major protagonists in this adventure, it's odd that such a milestone is achieved by a relatively banal villain whose grand, evil scheme is to force our heroes to literally change the direction they're going. It comes across as a bit of a wasted opportunity, but it's brilliantly sold. Purves really gets his teeth into the stand-off, and the thumping silence after Katarina's self-sacrifice – as she ends the impasse by blowing both her captor and herself out of an airlock – is extremely effective.

As Daxtar, Roger Avon imbues his defiance of the Doctor's cross-examination with a hefty note of hysteria in his voice. Tension is heightened, and events get even more dangerous when Bret coldly shoots him down. Hartnell has time to berate Bret with some wonderfully righteous indignation, and then Bret himself is slain. One half of the team we've been watching – Katarina and Bret – are both dispatched in the same episode, and the Doctor and Steven are on the run. Whether this adventure is working for you or not, the stakes just got very, very high.

Counter Plot
(The Daleks' Master Plan
episode five)

R: What a very bizarre story this is – tonally, this episode is nothing like the one before it! It's almost as if the writing staff were making the whole thing up as they went along, and took Hartnell's criticisms of its brutality to heart. (I don't know whether that's true, but it wouldn't surprise me.) So this week, the only characters to get exterminated are... a couple of white mice.

I've no problem with that, actually – it's something of a relief to get a bit of comedy into a story that's been so relentlessly grim and pessimistic. There's almost the sense of the plot catching its breath here – after all, we've got (my God) another eight episodes to go, so the best way to pad it out still further, just as the Doctor and Chen are in striking distance of the other, is to have our heroes broken down into atoms and sent spinning halfway across the universe.

And this gives everyone a chance to work out how the relationships should be played out from this moment on. Sara Kingdom, as played by Jean Marsh, needs to be reinterpreted as the new girl companion instead of being viewed as an inhuman killer – and if dramatically the scene in which she comes to see the Doctor and Steven as allies is a bit rushed, Hartnell and Purves go a long way to helping her with the transition. Hartnell is full of sad sympathy, Purves shows angered impatience – and then Marsh drops the bombshell

that by following her soldier's orders, she's just killed her brother. As melodramatic as that revelation obviously is, the scene just *clicks* into place beautifully.

And isn't Maurice Browning outstanding as Karlton? He's sly, he's ambitious, he's rather camp – and he's wonderfully bald into the bargain. The scene where he silently realises that his master Mavic Chen is insane is brilliantly understated – and Stoney too is terrific here, almost embarrassed to catch himself on the slide to megalomaniacal lunacy. And I'm very fond too of the scientist Rhymnal, as played by John Herrington – as the universe is threatened, and fascists stomp over his planet, he has the innocence to obsess over his experimental pet mice.

T: As with Day of Armageddon, it's nice to have moving pictures again. It almost makes up for the fact that I'm no longer with Katherine in sun-drenched California, luxuriating amongst the nicest bunch of people I could ever hope to meet, and instead am jet-lagged in Manchester, on my own, in the rain.

The survival of this episode on video reveals some interesting quirks on the part of the baddies – for a start, Karlton goes about his business with a limp, and I think it's a real one. I've seen Maurice Browning in something else – an episode of The Avengers, I think – and he hobbled in that as well. Actually, Browning's delivery, expressions and movements are such that he reminds me a little of Servalan... yes, that it! He's a bald, male Jacqueline Pearce, so good for him! And Kevin Stoney continues to be terrific as Chen – his ability to express himself while wielding a pencil remains second to none, and the bit where he proclaims his suppressed appetite for power is even better. In lesser hands, this sort of bombast would be awful, but Stoney is spot on, pitching it perfectly.

And the video also lets us know that the set design, considering how much the story jumps from location to location, is rather impressive – once again, we get an effective establishing shot (on film) of an expensive-looking jungle with bubbling water pools and smoke. Things don't look nearly as shoddy as they did on other multi-location sagas like, say, The Keys of Marinus, and this jungle has a very different character to the one on Kembel.

I should also mention how sad I feel that the Daleks exterminated the mice – poor little things, they're the first mice ever to be successfully disseminated through space and reconstituted on an alien planet, and all they get for their trouble is zapped. Conversely, isn't it funny that we only see Sara and Steven bouncing through space, even though the Doctor is transported with them? Maybe that's why Hartnell really fell out with John Wiles – he was livid at his producer for trying to force him to jump about on a trampoline!

February 18th

Coronas of the Sun
(The Daleks' Master Plan
episode six)

R: It's a lovely (albeit irrelevant) episode title. But "coronas" aside, this is all a bit drab. The Doctor and friends capture an enemy spacecraft – again. There's a lot of anxiety as the spaceship readies for take-off – again. The Daleks drag them off course by overriding their navigation – again. The lovely yarn that Terry Nation and Dennis Spooner wrote this story as a series of "get-out-of-that's" is all well and good, but it's a bit unfair on the audience when we see the same trump cards being played over and over.

There's a nice attempt of character reversal with Steven, though – having been a futuristic space pilot when compared to Vicki and Katarina, he's here reduced to primitive caveman status alongside the Doctor and Sara. It almost justifies the act of bravado by which Steven illuminates the fake Taranium core and puts himself in a handy Dalek-proof forcefield for the rest of the episode. But it's all fairly desperate plotting, to be honest – the entire instalment marks time until the Doctor can confront the Daleks, fool them with a forgery he's just knocked up in ten minutes, and recover the TARDIS.

There is, inevitably, the odd good moment. I love the shift of power when the Black Dalek at first interrogates Chen for his failure in recovering the Core – "You make your incompetence sound like an achievement" is a great line – and is then reduced to justifying itself

and its race hysterically. And the subtle way in which Sara shows her disgust for her treacherous leader is quiet and powerful. But there's a real sense in the repetition here that the story has run out of steam, and that the strengths of character manipulation and machiavellian intrigues suggested in episode four have been lost for good. It's the first time that this strange epic adventure, which keeps darting about from planet to planet and from tone to tone, stumbles – and that's a pity.

Never mind. It's Christmas next week!

T: I hate to sound like a broken record, but Kevin Stoney remains the best thing on offer here (and I say this without the benefit of visuals for this episode – he's even *better* when we can actually see what he's doing). He's such an inventive and surprising actor, I can only guess at his reaction to Sara calling him a traitor – a sustained music cue suggests he gets a lengthy close-up at this point, but it's hard to say. *None* of the lines Stoney delivers are done predictably – even when he says something as perfunctory as, "It appears everything is going according to plan," it's done with purred amusement, almost as if he's daring things *not* to go to plan, and that he'd actually enjoy the fallout if things went wrong. Then the Dalek Supreme tries to get a word in edgeways, and Chen keeps interrupting, resulting in the Supreme screechingly justifying itself and losing its composure and confidence. Chen is such an arch manipulator – you might think that this scene was included to send the Daleks up, but it doesn't. It's there to underline Chen's brilliance. If he can control this lot with his silver tongue, he's a powerful enemy indeed.

Otherwise, this is a very strange episode. We've now gone from Earth, which has loads of supporting characters and increasingly complex machinations, to the swampy planet Mira, where only one of the guest actors isn't playing a Dalek. And where there is a lot of blather. It's almost as if the Daleks' cunning plan is to take the TARDIS crew away from the interesting places in an attempt to (excuse the phrasing) bore the Taranium out of them. Perhaps this is why Steven behaves very out of character, resulting in a piece of technobabble so horribly contrived, if anything of its ilk appeared in the new series, the Internet would probably commit suicide rather than contain the fan-reaction.

And so we're halfway through one of the longest (if not *the* longest, depending on how you view The Trial of a Time Lord) Doctor Who stories ever made. It's started to tread water a bit, and it doesn't help that Hartnell delivers the cliffhanger line – that the air outside the TARDIS is poisonous – with all the gravitas of a weatherman. Still, with the Doctor's party having regained the Ship, it seems that we can somewhat clear the decks and move into the next phase of the story.

Plus, as you say – next up is a Doctor Who episode broadcast on Christmas Day! They never had those when I was a lad.

The Feast of Steven
(The Daleks' Master Plan
episode seven)

R: It is some measure of Doctor Who's popularity at this stage that it was given its own Christmas special. Quite how much you enjoy it depends on how much you appreciate the series poking fun at itself – back when I became a fan, in the very earnest early eighties, the episode was mentioned in hushed tones of horror. Audio recordings had the infamous last line – in which Hartnell raises a glass to the viewers at home, demolishing the fourth wall – cut out. And in subtler ways, earlier in the story, he acknowledges the BBC's habit of casting actors who've already appeared in the show when he recognises Reg Pritchard – here appearing as Man in Mackintosh – as a bit player in The Crusade. The delightful thing about The Feast of Steven is that although you can see the whole thing as a rather clever breaking down of the show's limitations, it's clearly all being done in fun, and the audience is required to do nothing more than bask in the comedy.

Which is fine – much of it is actually quite funny. The laconic policemen are great, and the increasingly surreal conversation about rebels stealing a man's greenhouse is positively Pinteresque. Having Steven disguise himself as a policeman (complete with comical Mersey accent) to rescue the Doctor is a witty comment on the clichés of the show, as well as a nice piece of farce. The second half of the epi-sode, set in a Hollywood film studio, is rather messier, and trying a bit too hard perhaps; it's all a big chase, consciously or unconsciously parodying the main Master Plan plot, as everyone runs after the TARDIS crew and gets horribly confused. Complete with silent film captions and tinkling piano background, this is perhaps the single oddest piece of comedy ever seen in the series – but its inventiveness is really quite surprising. Hartnell loves comedy, of course – and the exchanges between him and a depressed clown who realises that every gag he wants to perform has already been copyrighted by Chaplin is a real highlight of comic timing.

The only real downer of the episode is the killjoy moment when it bothers to remind us of the Daleks and all that Taranium core business. Not because it's a bad thing in itself to remind the audience of the ongoing story – but because it all sounds just as silly as the rest of the proceedings! The seasonal runaround also plays a clever trick on the audience – we more easily accept Sara as a fully fledged member of the TARDIS crew, and we'll be all the more shocked by her death in a few weeks' time. It's typical of Doctor Who that even when it promises innocent fun, a darker consequence is around the corner.

It's of interest that the production team resisted the idea of sending up the Daleks alongside the TARDIS crew. Only six months ago, Nation was fully prepared to use them as comic relief – now, in a fully fledged humorous romp, he's unwilling to sacrifice them for cheap laughs. It's a telling shift in tone.

T: I dunno, Rob... one of my chief rules with comedy is that the louder something is, the less funny it generally tends to end up. So it's ironic that the whole section dealing with the silent film studio is bloody loud – Sheila Dunn screams and wails, Royston Tickner bawls and everyone in the background shouts. Obviously, we can't actually see what they're going on about, but the physical comedy here would need to be bloody hilarious for this to work, considering the lines themselves aren't up to much. It's really difficult to discern what's going on at times, but it's hard to imagine that this is the laugh-a-minute that the script is aiming for. It just sounds messy, with everybody thinking that the way to make it funny is to belt it out.

It's not all a waste, though. It's nice to have Norman Mitchell showing up – he's one of those "I know the face but..." actors without whom Britain wouldn't have won the war, and he makes for a very sweet and kindly copper in his dealings with Sara. Mitchell could have interpreted the lines he's given as requiring overbearing comedy exasperation, but the much softer tone that he uses makes him all the more likeable. He even tells the departing Sara to "have a swinging time" – as if he's trying to be down with the kids!

And it warms my heart that Robert Jewell – here appearing as a clown – finally appears in the flesh; he's only been "seen" inside Daleks and Zarbi before now, and he'll spend the rest of the 60s stories he works on as Daleks or the Macra. (Camfield made a habit of promoting extras and people inside monsters so they could have a shot at the limelight – in future he'll cast John Levene, who starts out his Who tenure operating a Yeti, as Benton – and good on him for doing so.) Jewell also took some off-screen stills, so he's the reason why we still have the odd image from this, the most elusive and visually unrepresented of Doctor Who episodes. I saw these pictures when missing episode rumours were the meat and drink of fanzines, and they were published with a frenzy along the lines of, "...and The Feast of Steven was never sold abroad, but these pictures were found in Australia, so it could actually exist after all, and if *this* episode could exist, then statistically *all* the other episodes could too!", etc, etc. All of which is terribly amusing, considering the photos were actually taken in England on its only broadcast there, by a man who subsequently moved back to Australia, so they provide absolutely no indication about the potentiality of anything else turning up anywhere, anywhen. But why let the facts get in the way of some returning episode speculation?

This episode has been such a curious and odd interlude, I'd be fascinated to actually see it – not because I really think it'd be very good, but because there are certain things you just have to witness for yourself (such as the delivery of the line, "This is a madhouse – it's all full of Arabs"), if only to convince yourself that

they actually happened. The visuals would also help us to evaluate the in-joke with Reg Pritchard – do you honestly suppose that anyone watching this would have comprehended that he played Ben Daheer in The Crusade about eight months back? But whether or not the gag worked at the time, at least it gives we fanboys something to appreciate 40 years later.

February 19th

Volcano
(The Daleks' Master Plan
episode eight)

R: This is absolutely bonkers – the maddest, most atonal episode of Doctor Who there's yet been. It makes The Feast of Steven look quite restrained in contrast. We start off with a wonderful bit of Dalek callousness, as Trantis finds himself helping with the Time Destructor experiment in a manner he may not have been bargained for. The dispassion with which both Chen and Celation contemplate their ally's fate, and then the eagerness as they wait to see how horribly he'll die, has a sick cruelty to it. The cruellest bit, of course, being at the very end – after Trantis survives the Destructor, the Daleks coolly blast him down without even allowing him a word.

And it's contrasted with... what, exactly? A scene in which the TARDIS arrives during a cricket match, the whole sequence played through the reactions of two BBC commentators whose only concern is checking to see whether a test match has been similarly interrupted before, and how it'll affect England's chances. It's a piece of whimsy so Douglas Adams in tone, it's hardly surprising that Adams himself wrote the *exact* same scene in Life, the Universe and Everything nearly 20 years later. It's very funny and perfectly performed, but it's so at odds with what we've just seen that it leaves you flummoxed.

And so the episode goes on. We go from scenes of the Daleks threatening the alien delegates, and assuring everyone of their future annihilation, to sequences of delightful comedy. The best joke of all is that, just as the Daleks are planning to pursue the TARDIS, the Doctor finds another old enemy is out for revenge. Against all the odds, that jolly Peter Butterworth is back as the Monk! Imagine the shock for contemporary audiences – you're expecting the threat of a Dalek, and instead out of a rock steps this bumbling comic figure. The dialogue between Hartnell and Butterworth is delightful as always, and the echoed laughter they both share as the Monk tells the Doctor he's getting his revenge is very funny and, somehow, rather insane at the same time. And then we're off to the London New Year celebrations, conducted for real only hours before. The bells of Big Ben cut back and forth between the countdown of the Dalek timeship as it prepares to hunt the Doctor down and destroy him.

This episode is so *very* strange and all over the place, it almost looks as if it's been thrown together as it went along. Instead, I think it's trying to tell the story on two different levels at the same time, and is glorying in how jarring it seems. It makes the Doctor look complacent, wasting time on jokes when he should be worried about his survival. And it makes the Daleks look as cold and as humourless and as threatening as they've ever been. Volcano is either dreadful, or quite quite brilliant. What do you think, Toby?

T: With The Daleks' Master Plan, it's becoming more and more evident that the writers have little to no idea how they're going to resolve the plot strands of the promising opening instalments, and so are trying to distract us with some very arbitrary murders or some romping comic experimentation. Yes, it's true: this entire adventure is a microcosm of The X-Files.

The cricket scene, at least, is utterly adorable. As an aficionado of Test Match Special, I can verify they get the tone of this just right. It's a funny idea that seems to be a hangover from last week, and the characters are lovely – Trevor is all jolly and eccentric, and Scott is a slightly dull and bemused Aussie prone to repeating what's just been said. Doctor Who does this sort of comedy scene so well.

But, setting aside the pleasant surprise of the Meddling Monk showing up, it's all downhill from there. Having already killed Zephon, the Daleks now pick Trantis to be part of a lethal experiment – then slaughter him anyway when the test fails. "I wonder why they chose him," hisses Celation blithely, as if using one of your allies as an experimental guinea pig is somehow normal behaviour (if it were, surely no one would ally themselves with you). The way that the delegates are so easily dispensed with is making them seem increasingly redundant... by story's end, it's a miracle that the Daleks haven't killed them all. I'm also wondering what this means for the planet(s) Trantis represents? After all, if Gordon Brown went off to ally himself with France in a war against China and Nicolas Sarkozy suddenly killed him, you might expect there to be some repercussions.

All of my attempts at wry commentary, though, are being sabotaged because so much of this episode is little more than techno-nonsense. Let me try to summarise events: the Meddling Monk locks the Doctor's TARDIS with a thing. The Doctor does a thing with his ring and the sun, which causes a thing to happen, and undoes the Monk's thing. That's about as much sense as can be derived from about ten minutes of screen time – these people may as well have been talking in Swahili. We don't even find out what happened until everyone is back in the TARDIS – and when we finally do get an explanation, it's a nonsensical one. Even Steven seems to realise this, forcing the Doctor to say, defensively, "I don't want to discuss it anymore!", which is the grumpy and less amusing equivalent of "I'll tell you later." We then round things off with a sequence that takes place on New Year's Day (to coincide with when this story was broadcast), but it's little more than an excuse for some stock footage of fireworks and an odd reference to Mafeking.

Meanwhile, the contrived cliffhanger entails the Daleks suddenly chanting about how their time machine will bring them victory, even after it's been around for half an episode. It's an ersatz moment of significance/jeopardy and just underlines how bunged together this whole episode feels. The Feast of Steven got away with some of its shortcomings because it was a bit silly, but this week doesn't, because it's a bit stupid. And there's a big difference between the two.

Golden Death
(The Daleks' Master Plan
episode nine)

R: Look, Walter Randall's turned up again – this time playing an Egyptian! It's like the BBC keep him in a cupboard and dust him off for historical adventures.

There's a nice, basic idea at work here – that a rather low-key comedy menace like the Monk can accidentally become the agent of a much greater threat. The best scenes of the episode are Peter Butterworth's – whether he's playing for laughs (like putting on sunglasses to face the Egyptian sunshine), offering a Dalek monastic greeting or being forced to play the unwitting ally of Chen and the Daleks, you can tell he'd be much more comfortable giving up all idea of revenge and chumming up with the Doctor. Butterworth and Hartnell play off well together in their one scene, with the Doctor laughing in genuine amusement as he advances on his irritating adversary with his walking stick.

But for the rest of the episode... oh, I don't know. It is all very dull, really. The Doctor spends the majority of the instalment fixing the TARDIS lock, and Steven and Sara get captured and escape from a bunch of Egyptians. The locals are the most shabbily characterised historical figures in the Hartnell era; even the crew of the Mary Celeste were given a bit more life than this poor lot.

It does feel such a pity that The Daleks' Master Plan is now on such a treadmill. With the scope afforded by 12 episodes, there really ought to have been room for something more epic than this. But the story has abandoned any attempt at that, and instead seems more content to tell self-contained little stories. It's ironic that there just doesn't seem *time* to develop anything. All the most interesting characters, like Karlton, were forgotten a month ago – and by now, Mavic Chen only gives sporadic hints at being a credible politician rather than a camp cardboard cut-out. The writers seem prepared to try any trick to keep the story plodding on – the cliffhanger here tries to suggest a mummy horror movie – and in the process fail to realise that the story will sustain itself far better if it reined itself in and concentrated on what it has already estab-

lished. As you watch the Doctor's exploits in ancient Egypt, you're left with the nagging sense that some time next week, he'll take off in the TARDIS and land somewhere else altogether; there's no build-up, no hint of resolution, no development. The Daleks' Master Plan can go anywhere, do anything – it's a microcosm of the series itself in a way – but it resists doing anything interesting with any of its new settings, or any new characters it introduces. The 12-episode length by now feels completely arbitrary; this story will end when its slot comes to an end, and for no other reason. We must be grateful, I suppose, that Huw Wheldon's mother didn't want it to be any longer.

Pah. Sorry. It seems that it's my turn to be grumpy. But I was *really* enjoying this story.

T: No need to apologise; something very strange has happened here. The Daleks' Master Plan started out brilliantly – Earth in the far future was awash with traitors and dangerous undercurrents, and the most trusted man in the Solar System was selling humanity out to the Daleks, who had also assembled an eclectic and exciting looking war force of disparate alien races. Only a few fearless Earth Agents and the TARDIS crew were aware of the conspiracy to hold the universe to ransom with a Time Destructor; bravery and cunning were the only weapons they had to expose the traitors and thwart the Dalek alliance. It was all very comic strip, sure, but in a good way. But now, we've left all of that behind, and Dennis Spooner – here trying to take the baton from Terry Nation, and finish the last half of the story, somehow – decided give us what no-one has ever asked for before or since: that's right, another few episodes of The Chase. There's no Celation, Malpha, Sentreal, Beaus or the much-missed Karlton... instead, it's some rather dull Egyptians and another contrived cliffhanger.

So it's in the individual moments of this story where we have to find some greatness. Peter Butterworth continues to be brilliant as the Monk, and look how William Hartnell (who seems to have a frog in his throat for the first five minutes) perks up the minute they bump into each other; he seems so chuffed to be facing off against this fun adversary. Kevin Stoney – who has yet to put a foot wrong – also rises to the occasion, and his face-off with the Monk is beautifully done. It amounts to a charming manipulator trying to outmanoeuvre a cheeky chancer, in a jolly scene with an underlying menace. You can tell that the Monk amuses Chen, but also that he'll happily kill him if he doesn't deliver. The two of them get the best scene in the episode, although it's also quite amusing later on, when the Doctor mucks about with the Monk's chameleon circuit.

And hooray! Sara gets to do some karate. What a shame that we can't see it!

February 20th

Escape Switch
(The Daleks' Master Plan episode ten)

R: I'm in a better mood today, and I very much enjoyed this. It's not that it's substantially better plotted than the last episode, actually; there's a battle scene between Egyptians and Daleks again, and lots of weasel to-ing and fro-ing with the Monk. But this instalment exists in the archives, and *watching* it made me remember just how good Douglas Camfield's direction is. He never wastes a scene, wanting to make each and every one as visually interesting as he can. The Daleks look threatening here – so much so that you wince as Mavic Chen gets above himself and slaps one about the eyestalk with impatience. And I was very unfair to Kevin Stoney too. On audio, the silkiness of his voice can sound at times a little one note – but watching him, you realise how much of this is an act. So much of his performance is in asides, showing his frustration with the Monk, or his horror at the Daleks – they may be his allies, but he fears them as much as he uses them. He seems to understand that it's only by being the arrogant politician who *demands* their respect that he can keep them on his side.

And I just want to point out: there's a brilliant scene here, where Chen shows surprise that the Daleks so readily gave into the Doctor's terms, and agree that only one of their number should go to the hostage-exchange. By way of justification, Chen is told, "One Dalek is capa-

ble of exterminating all!" – and it's that single line which, all those years ago, was the inspiration for the Big Finish audio play I wrote, and which was adapted for the new series as Dalek. So there you go.

T: Like you, I'm feeling a bit bad that I was so harsh on the last few episodes. Much of the problem continues to be the loss of the video – whatever the handy pictures, soundtrack, reconstructions and odd clip are at our disposal, there's so much that you can only appreciate by *watching* the damned thing. And with Escape Switch existing in the archives... well, it's making me question some of my previous assertions. Perhaps Galaxy Four episode two had loads of clever little visual and acting touches that lifted it out of the realms of the mundane, or perhaps The Myth Makers episode four was as shabbily staged as The Keys of Marinus, making my assessments of both episodes ill-informed and irrelevant. The simple truth is that with so many of the missing 60s episodes, we're resorting to guesswork.

There are some odd moments in this (particularly the big fight with the Egyptians, which doesn't really go anywhere and seems a waste of resources), but as you say, Douglas Camfield for the most part distracts you from the shortcomings. There's a very well focussed three-person conversation in which Steven and Sara blather to each other whilst the Monk talks to them (and us), and – better still – there's a fantastic shot of the sun metamorphosing into a gleam of light on a Dalek's head; it's all very inventive and shockingly smoothly done. The last three episodes in particular need to be recovered so we can reevaluate them – Camfield is so good, and makes it all look so easy, who knows how much they might improve if we could watch them?

Otherwise, and while I'd admit that some of this amounts to faffing about in ancient Egypt for no particular reason, the cast continues to be superb. Kevin Stoney gives a consistently elegant performance; not for nothing was he named Villain of the Year by the Daily Mail – or was it the Express? (It doesn't make a difference; they're both pretty nasty papers.) His relationship with the Daleks is so intriguing – as you say, there's that great moment when he arrogantly pushes away a Dalek eyestalk when it muscles in against him, as if it's an intimidating hard-nut in a pub altercation. And there's some pleasant frivolity from the Monk, with Peter Butterworth treading that fine line that lets him be comical without undermining the threatening nature of the Daleks. I love how the Monk innocently asks at one point, "You mean my performance was that good?" Yes it was, Mr Butterworth, yes it was.

But it's William Hartnell who benefits most from this episode existing on video – the Doctor is sidelined for vast chunks of Escape Switch, then surfaces to deal with the baddies. As good as Peter Purves and Jean Marsh are when the Doctor isn't around, he's so commanding and wise during the confrontation with Chen and the Daleks, I realised just how much I'd missed him. Plus, he does look great in that straw hat.

The Abandoned Planet (The Daleks' Master Plan episode eleven)

R: And after all the rushing around of the past few months... it stops. And it's brilliant. Ever since the Doctor first touched down on Kembel all those many many episodes ago, there hasn't been an instalment when he's not been taking off in a spaceship or being transmitted across the galaxy – even the comedy instalments haven't provided the viewer with a chance to catch their breath. It's made the story play on a more universal scale than ever before, that's true – but it's also made watching it somewhat exhausting. And lately, the programme itself has been looking a mite exhausted into the bargain.

But now... the promise of a climax! And slow-burn tension, as Sara and Steven explore the abandoned Dalek base on Kembel. It's a reminder of what Doctor Who has always been good at, because as fun and frenetic as The Daleks' Master Plan has been, its real atmosphere comes from something a bit less driven than the Doctor having a *mission*. As the two companions edge ever deeper into the Dalek city, at any second expecting to be challenged, at every footfall expecting to run for their lives – we're forcibly reminded of where all this started, with Barbara getting lost and panicked on Skaro, and the wonderful tension that pro-

duced. Now, on the eve of universal conquest, the story brilliantly goes *inwards* and becomes claustrophobic. It's the most eerie the programme has been since The Sensorites, and it feels great to have this back.

T: I wrote last time about how much I'd missed William Hartnell when the Doctor was gone for a long stretch, but here – and even though he's out for *most* of the episode – his absence is less profoundly felt because Steven and Sara are made to deal with an eerie calm before the storm. Even in the Daleks' chats with Chen (or chats *about* him), there are some shifty, tension building silences. Something is afoot here, and it plays to the Daleks' strengths – they're always scariest when they emanate guile and subterfuge, and their creepiness in this story makes some necessary villainous exposition more interesting. Meanwhile, Chen is certainly losing it – but the escalation of his arrogance as power slips through his fingers works, both for the character and the drama.

Please indulge me, though, if I bang on some more about which delegate is which, because – as anyone keeping score at home will know – we have another identity conundrum here. I previously stated that in Mission to the Unknown, Sentreal must be the black man with the space helmet. However, while Sentreal isn't credited for this episode, it seems safe to assume that space-helmet man is present because he was in Day of Armageddon (albeit probably played by a different actor in both Mission and here, as all the non-speaking delegates are). Now, Gerry Videl was black, but he's listed on the paperwork as Beaus. So we have yet another identity swapping delegate – probably the result of Douglas Camfield choosing his favourite costumes from Mission and discarding the others. After all, nobody in Mission is referred to by name apart from Malpha, just as none of the "extra" delegates are named specifically here.

Or should I just drop this, and mention that Malpha now sounds like Alf Roberts from Coronation Street? Either way, this episode is good stuff, well done.

February 21st

The Destruction of Time
(The Daleks' Master Plan
episode twelve)

R: The effect of this episode, even just with the audio soundtrack, is like being punched in the stomach. God knows what it would be like if we had Douglas Camfield's direction to watch as well. You know, it reminds me a bit of the sort of feeling that Russell T Davies aims for in his season finales: the sensation that everything is vast and epic, but that that's all smoke and mirrors, and what he's *really* interested in is something much more intimate – a collection of powerful moments. And that's what we have here. After five hours or so of drama, set on half a dozen different worlds, and boasting a *huge* supporting cast – we're left, really, with just four characters and a bunch of Daleks on three sets. It's a shock that the fate of the universe is as small as this – or as devastating.

And even here, the story refuses to offer us the climaxes we might be expecting. For all that he's been the lead villain for the last three months of screen time, Mavic Chen has never squared off against the Doctor. To him, the Doctor has always been a nuisance, some strange thief who's nicked his Taranium core – he's never understood what the Doctor's purpose could be, which leads to his frankly wonderful assertion here that all the time traveller could want is to be a bigger chum of the Daleks than he is. In his growing lunacy, Chen is reduced to a child in a playground, jealous that this newcomer might take away his friends. Kevin Stoney's death scene is terrific; he parades fearlessly around the Dalek control room, refusing to believe that they will kill him, refusing to believe even that he *can* die. You know that the Dalek Supreme will take him out and shoot him sooner or later – and that the most painful thing for Chen will not be death but his humiliation. It's not a question of whether they're going to shoot him, just *when* they're going to get fed up of his preening antics and squash him – and the whole sequence is a masterpiece of tension.

Ultimately, this is all wonderfully simple. The Doctor defeats the Daleks by turning their

universe-destroying gizmo upon them, and Sara unwittingly gets caught in the exchange. The sound effect accompanying the Time Destructor seems amusing and chirrupy at first, and gets progressively crueller as the episode goes along and it wreaks such damage. There's a poetic justice to this, coupled with the Doctor's pained realisation that the greater the victory over his mortal enemies, the greater too the sacrifice that will be asked of him. (Again, very new series, that – Russell can disguise the almost arbitrary way in which he wipes out the Daleks each season finale by ensuring that the Doctor loses a companion in the process.) The Doctor is left giggling at the sight of the Dalek embryos, and is brought up short by Steven's list of all those characters who died over the course of this adventure – it's the starkest ending we've yet had in Doctor Who. It's perhaps the series' first attempt at doing a story which feels in some ways *definitive* – and you feel after this that it needs to take a break, just to let the audience catch its breath back, something. And yet the screen would have read, "Next Episode: War of God." I'm telling you, Toby, I'm exhausted of war, I'm exhausted of the whole thing.

T: Events have finally caught up with Mavic Chen, and he's finally lost any vague tenancy agreement he had at Reality Towers – but thanks to Kevin Stoney, it's a well-handled descent into madness that never stretches our credulity. It also gives us the added plus of the whispering Daleks that plot to double-cross him – I love it when the Daleks are cunning, and it's great to be in on their secret while Chen is strutting about oblivious. You've already mentioned the increasing tension, Rob, but *here*, most of it comes from the fact that the Daleks just... stop talking to Chen, and regard him as a defeated irrelevance. There's something genuinely creepy and unsettling about those silences, and the Daleks once again seem like alien machines. When they finally drag Chen away to kill him, the Dalek Supreme doesn't even bother to gloat – it just doesn't want any vital equipment to be damaged when they dispose of this pest.

But the converse is also true – with the Daleks having become so formidable and daunting, it's fantastic that when they find the

Doctor with the Time Destructor, they back off! To see them so scared and wary just confirms the device's potential for devastation. It's no longer a simple plot device – it's now a harbinger of death. Although the Doctor is once again absent for loads of the episode, he's rightly allowed to handle the brave face-off with his arch nemeses, and sends his friends packing while he remains behind to do the right thing. It's something of a pity that Sara doesn't achieve more when she turns back to help him (like, say, killing the Dalek Supreme, rescuing a cat or retrieving a stuffed panda) – as matters stand, she loses her life while trying to help but not actually doing so to a large degree. That her death is meaningless and avoidable is surely part of the point and makes it all the more horrifying, but one could argue that Doctor Who is supposed to have more soul than that. (Then again, the next time we see a companion die, he'll similarly fail in his final self-appointed mission – and fandom-at-large tends to regard that story as a classic.)

The more I think about it, the more those final few minutes seem hellish. Sara's death is protracted and terrifying, Hartnell unleashes a most unearthly and harried screech when berating Steven for leaving the TARDIS, and the Doctor's ensuing frailty demonstrates that he's really been through the mill. It's a grim denouement with Hartnell and Purves leaving the stage like shell-shocked victims, the names of the dead hanging in the air over the wasteland of the once verdant Kembel.

With a bit more forward planning and structuring, The Daleks' Master Plan could indeed have been the epic masterpiece those involved clearly thought it was. But it meanders in the middle and seems very muddled at points (you get the impression that the episode titles were chosen before the scripts were actually written, and nobody bothered to go back and amend them to something more suitable). And yet, I *do* like the adult tone it took – for all that I understand, Rob, your weariness of it – and it gave us such praiseworthy items as a karate-chopping female security agent, Dalek embryos and one of the best-ever Doctor Who villains. You can see why some fans speak of this story in such hushed tones of reverence, and why it's such a shame that only a quarter of it is in the archives.

War of God
(The Massacre episode one)

R: Steven is dropped right into the deep end here, at a point in history that's simply not iconic enough to reverberate through the history books. Earlier historical adventures had the benefit of knowing that the viewing public would be fairly well grounded in the settings – but here, at last, the production team deliberately choose an event that leaves even our heroes wrongfooted. Quite simply, we don't know who we're supposed to treat as the goodies and who as the baddies – there's no Marco Polo here, striding purposefully out of the school books, and nor is there a Tlotoxl, all deformed and hunchbacked. We suppose that the Huguenots *might* be the characters we're supposed to side with – they do buy Steven a drink, after all – but that Gaston chap seems far more concerned with intimidating the frightened girl chased by the soldiers than in reassuring her. There's nothing for us to grasp on to. Not even a spot of incidental music, which might give us a clue what we're supposed to be thinking or feeling. And after all the melodramatic hi-jinks of the previous few months, it feels incredibly refreshing.

It seems like a development, too, of our last "pure" historical. The Myth Makers traded upon the Doctor's uncertainty of what was history and what was myth, so he couldn't be sure what the course of true events should be. In writing The Massacre, John Lucarotti is simply too good a dramatist to be dull, but there's a deliberate obscurity to things here – and although there's no indication of any threat to the TARDIS crew for the entire episode (which may well be a first), there's a brooding sense of sombre menace. Whereas once Lucarotti's joy seemed to be in dropping our heroes into a historical period and then milking all the dramatic opportunities from it, here he leaves us truly lost. It's brave – the biggest revelation is when the word "Vassy" is dropped in conversation, but the script leaves Steven in the dark whilst all the other characters react to it with such awe. The past really *is* a foreign country here, and we don't know how to read the signposts yet.

The best bit for me, though, is that gorgeous scene where the Doctor reassures a little-known scientist that, in spite of the accusations of heresy he must endure, his work is brilliant and of great importance for the world. We'll get a few such moments through the years – Binro told by Unstoffe that he was right in The Ribos Operation, Dickens being told in The Unquiet Dead that his work will endure – but this is one of the best. Erik Chitty (playing Charles Preslin, the scientist in question) is so clearly delighted to find someone out there who will believe in him rather than condemn him that it's extremely touching – and gives a bit of much-needed warmth to this otherwise rather frosty episode.

T: This is a very literate script – words such as "dogma" and "badinage" appear in the first pub scene – and the interweaving characters all make some narrative sense. Yes, we've been dropped into a period where we don't know much about the political landscape, but we're fed droplets of information that designate, at the very least, who stands for and against whom. All of the characters are very well drawn – Nicholas Muss is an arbitrating, sensitive, decent man, whilst Simon Duval is an arrogant, snivelling conniver. Eric Thompson imbues Nicholas' companion Gaston with a smooth mischievousness which is endearing, then undercuts that with a dismissive disdainful superiority. It's clever, complex characterisation for a character who's not even that vital, delivered strongly by a good actor.

At this stage of the game – and especially given the shocking cliffhanger in which it's revealed (or so it seems) that the Abbot of Amboise is the Doctor – it's a bit hard to predict where all of this is going. But the tone of this intelligently crafted and serious-minded episode is very brooding, and it deftly portrays Steven as a hapless witness to these events. We might not yet know what type of adventure we're watching, but we do know that the Paris where the Doctor and Steven have found themselves isn't very safe.

February 22nd

The Sea Beggar
(The Massacre episode two)

R: This episode ends with a terribly clever cliffhanger, I think. Steven learns that there's a plot to assassinate "the Sea Beggar", but his limited knowledge of history means he has no idea who that might be. Every time he tries to find out, he's foiled – he either gets shouted down by those high enough on the social ladder to know, or he's met with bemusement by those lowly enough to listen. And it's only in the closing seconds that identify the Sea Beggar as Admiral de Coligny. It's a measure of where The Massacre is aiming for, that the climax is to give us a further piece of historical information that's so far eluded us.

For the first time, Peter Purves is put firmly in the spotlight, and it's hard to imagine any other companion working as well in this story as Steven does here. Ian would be far too resourceful, somehow – as soon as Gaston drew his sword, Ian would probably have beaten him off in some trick he learned during National Service, whilst Steven's recourse (rather charmingly) is to run away. Steven has been depicted – during The Daleks' Master Plan in particular – as a man who just gets increasingly impatient with those around him; he's always ready to cut through the Doctor's concerns and tell him to get on with the action. So it's wonderful that he's here dropped off in as sensitive a situation as a period of religious hatred. The way that he manages to alienate his former allies so completely is quite remarkable – and yet somehow extremely human, and very well-meaning. The Massacre is a rather intellectual script, and it's Steven Taylor who thaws it, who in his honest struggles to understand what is going on makes the confusion of the society so much more approachable. He asks at one point why on earth the Catholics would want to hurt the Huguenots, and the baffled response – because they're Huguenots – is at once insultingly simple and terrifying. Steven has never been as sympathetic as he is here, pleading with Gaston to listen to his news, and anxiously persuading Nicholas Muss that he isn't a spy.

T: These days, the accepted title of this story – The Massacre – hints that matters in sixteenth century Paris probably aren't going to end terribly well. But for anyone watching this at the time (and even allowing for the first episode being titled War of God), there's only the *threat* of violence all around. People are quick to draw swords, an old woman suspects Preslin was murdered and there's an assassin in the wings. Death seems to be lurking off screen, creeping ever closer. As a result, The Sea Beggar seems as paranoid as any modern-day conspiracy story, but is endowed with elegant dialogue, and has great actors such as Andre Morell (as Tavannes) and Leonard Sachs (as de Coligny) to give real weight, dignity and authority to these historical figures.

You've already mentioned how Steven owns this episode, but the *way* that this happens – with Hartnell only present on film, and barely figuring into the action – is interesting. For the only time in the entire history of Doctor Who, these middle episodes lack a credit for the titular character (Hartnell was even credited as Doctor Who in Mission to the Unknown, even though he didn't get a minute of screen time!). Even with "Doctor-lite" episodes such as Love & Monsters and Turn Left, it's almost impossible to imagine this happening today (but might make for a fun little twist if they did).

Oh, and did you notice how the opening scene has Gaston criticising Prince Henri of Navarre because he "refuses to take precautions". Ha! Perhaps our Huguenot prince is more Catholic than we thought...

Yay! This is a brilliant, intelligent story with much dramatic weight, and it's got a fun bit of credits trivia too. I'm in Heaven (though let's not get into that whole religion business right now – it's clearly a can of worms).

Priest of Death
(The Massacre episode three)

R: Every review I've ever read of The Massacre makes great mention of William Hartnell's performance as the Abbot of Amboise – how it's utterly different from his interpretation of the Doctor, and how it's completely free of all the tics and mannerisms and fluffs. Am I missing something here? For a start, it's a surprisingly *small* part – he appears in a couple of scenes,

then gets murdered (shockingly swiftly) by Tavannes, the Marshall of France. And it feels pretty Doctor-ish to me; Hartnell sounds a bit posher perhaps, but there's nothing of the radically different performances you get, say, from Peter Purves playing Morton Dill in The Chase or Jean Marsh playing Joanna in The Crusade. Surely, the whole point of the episode is that even after Steven has seen the Abbot, he *still* believes this must be the Doctor pretending to be someone else? The story hinges upon the ambiguity of Hartnell's performance, not upon a reinvention of it. I think he does it very well, don't get me wrong. But in my usual fanboy way, The Massacre was sold to me as a story about a doppelganger Doctor – when it's actually the smallest of subplots in something else altogether.

And it's also tonally rather jarring. We've got this strange story about religious intolerance and medieval politics and assassination attempts – and stuck in the middle of it, there's a bit with Hartnell playing someone else. It feels somewhat inappropriate – in the same way it might have seemed out of place, after five episodes of journeying to Cathay, to find that Jacqueline Hill was a dead ringer for Kublai Khan's missus. There's a reason to all of this, and it's not a terribly pleasant one. Script editor Donald Tosh has said in interviews that the sidelining of Hartnell here was the start of a process by which they could persuade the viewers he really wasn't *that* essential a part of the series any more, and so the production team could safely sack him. In The Celestial Toymaker they'll reduce Hartnell to a mute disembodied hand; in The Savages, they'll give his part to Frederick Jaeger. Most of the Doctors approach the end of their tenure with something like a climax – apart from Tom Baker, only Hartnell is given a slow death, and this is where it starts.

So if the episode's not about William Hartnell impressing us with his acting versatility, what is it? The political discussion is taken out for the bars and alleyways and put into council chambers. Barry Justice's Charles IX is perfect, a man trying to be a good king without the strength or intelligence to maintain his authority. But good performances aside (Andre Morell and Leonard Sachs in particular), I can't help feel that all this intelligent dialogue is taking place within a vacuum. There is a vague sense of doom – the cliffhanger, where Steven is chased by a vengeful mob from Hartnell's corpse, is strikingly grotesque! – but little of this massacre coming to fruition. The story's concerns are a little too lofty, perhaps – what it needs is some honest-to-God plain emotion. The streets of Paris are to be covered in blood the very next day, so at this stage, I really don't care much about alliances with the Dutch in a war against Spain.

T: A real-life concern of mine is the power of the mob – specifically, the way the media and politicians can whip society into a rage, to hate or condemn this or that social group, nationality or celebrity. Common humanity is so easily forgotten when such a frenzy is unleashed, and so the final scene here – in which screaming hordes chase Steven down the street, baying for his blood on the scantest of evidence – is all too plausible and terrifying. I'd love to say that we've progressed as a society since then, but there are times when I wonder...

Fortunately, not everyone we meet here acts like a savage – the Huguenots, despite all they face and fear, never lose their humanity and retain a dignity common to many of Lucarotti's more sympathetic characters. On the other hand, Tavannes deals with life and death as political tools, dispensing them with little compunction. (Compare this to the supposed Protestant "zealot" Gaston – who, when confronting Steven in the previous episode, found he couldn't kill a man who wouldn't defend himself.) One of the most intriguing things about this story is the way a sense of honour might get you killed – with the two factions demonising each other and increasingly headed towards bloodshed, to what degree can someone in the middle of this retain their sense of decency and still survive? It's a depressing subject (and not one Doctor Who ventures into very often), but can nobility withstand an assault of sheer ruthlessness? There are no easy answers here, which makes The Massacre such a brave and captivating story.

But from a production point of view, what we're again given – as I've cited before as the core of great drama – are great actors performing great scripts. Everyone in the cast is up to

scratch here – and of especial note is Barry Justice, in one of the best one-episode Who cameos as Charles IX. Justice rationalises the seeming discrepancies about Charles into a constant characterisation – he's a regal King who wants to do the right thing, but is easily bored and prone to fits of pique. Essentially, Charles has developed a sense of decency in spite of his upbringing, but he just isn't strong enough to stand up to his mother or the political climate. Joan Young, playing Charles' mother – Catherine de Medici – is similarly wonderful; she's a beguilingly quiet presence whilst others are in attendance, and only opens up to manipulate, scold, chide and threaten Charles when she has him to herself.

It's telling, though, that these moments aren't cut off from the main story like the scenes with Barass and Napoleon were in The Reign of Terror – Steven's actions greatly impact upon the lives of those at court, and vice versa. This is a story about inexorable disaster, and the ordinary man's powerlessness against of the whims of the dominant and the cruelty of fate. Ultimately, history is the enemy here.

February 23rd

Bell of Doom
(The Massacre episode four)

R: Hartnell's soliloquy in the TARDIS – as he reflects upon his loneliness now that all his companions have abandoned him, and considers (ever so briefly, and with such regret) the possibility of his returning home – is heartbreaking. It may be the very best performance Hartnell ever gives in the series. And although we only have the audio soundtrack to rely upon, that long gap between his two "I can't"s – as he realises that there's to be no end to his wanderings – is enough to choke me up. It comes out of a truly startling scene in which Steven rounds upon the Doctor for his callousness in abandoning Anne Chaplet to die in the massacre, and the way that Hartnell so glumly recites the appalling statistics of the carnage that took place in France draws us up short too – here's a story which relied upon the way that we've so comfortably pushed the atrocities of the distant past into obscurity. We don't know about this civil conflict between sixteenth century Frenchmen, because – in truth – it's not part of our history, and so we don't much care. Woodcut drawings of the time depicting the slaughters in 1572 are graphic and shocking, and it's only to be hoped that the ones used in the episode were too. Seeing Nicholas Muss or Gaston or the Admiral de Coligny run through with a sword on a small BBC set wouldn't have been enough – the genuinely epic scale of the killings could only be conveyed, ironically enough, by distancing us even further from the action, and just showing us the art it inspired.

It could perhaps be argued that the speed with which the Doctor returns to the TARDIS once he realises what the date is – thus avoiding the risk of his changing history – is at this stage of the series a little out of character. Even at his most extreme moments in Season One, the Doctor wasn't quite as concerned with protocol as this. And it's telling to have a Doctor Who story in which the evil isn't rationalised by moralising, or even confronted. Joan Young and Andre Morell are horribly credible as they discuss the ensuing massacre with such dispassion – that kind of evil just wouldn't be dramatically viable opposite a science-fiction hero's posturing. It's a brilliant scene, but it does beg the question – if this were a subject too grim for the Doctor to engage with, surely it was too grim for Doctor Who to engage with too? You wouldn't set a Doctor Who story at Auschwitz; was there really much point in setting one during the Huguenot killings either?

Don't get me wrong. This is an extraordinary story... in every sense of the word, as there's very little that's ordinary about this. The brooding solemnity of the opening few minutes of this episode alone, as Steven searches for the "dead" Doctor's clothes just to find the TARDIS key, have a cynical and despairing tone quite unlike anything the series will ever offer again. But, where do we go from here? Steven bawls the real Doctor out; the Doctor crumbles. And then... it's as if a magic reset button has been pushed. Dodo arrives! She's unarguably the dimmest companion of them all, whose only response to the impossibility of the TARDIS interior is to ask the Doctor if he's a policeman. Who gets whisked away through

time and space because the Doctor claims she looks a bit like Susan (well... sort of), and who's quite happy never to see anyone from her life again because she's an orphan and hates her aunt. The two of them are acting more like sociopaths than actual people you might meet. It's a scene of such incredible shallowness, in such marked contrast to what we've just experienced, that it can surely only be deliberate. It's as if Donald Tosh has tried his best to explore the potential of Doctor Who, both here and with The Daleks' Master Plan, and to have shown the real implications of space and time travel: that you can achieve nothing worthwhile, and that there's death, always death. And having brought the audience to that bleak conclusion, he acknowledges that the show is going to continue without him now – this is the last episode he'll be contributing to – so here you go, he says, here's your jolly little adventure serial in all its banality.

The third season of Doctor Who is a very odd one, isn't it? No-one seems very happy any more.

T: I take your point about Doctor Who being a bit dour under the John Wiles-Donald Tosh regime, but if so, it's because they're trying to explore the potential of the show beyond the cosy romps we've fallen into. Just compare the characters here with the clichéd, sanitised Vikings we met in The Time Meddler – in real life, the Vikings were pretty brutal, what with all the raping and pillaging, but Sven and Ulf come across as slightly dim ballet dancers. The Massacre, by contrast, has believable historical figures who work so effectively, that we're rightfully made to sit up and feel guilty for our ignorance concerning this monumental atrocity. And isn't one of the points of visiting history to draw parallels with our own times and learn some lessons? If The Massacre existed in the archives, it should be required watching today – it's a credible attempt to do a play about intolerance and fundamentalism, and how religion (which is supposed to be a moral code for guidance and spiritual goodness) can, in the wrong hands, become a weapon of cruel political expediency.

To put it another way, Rob... deep down I'm a bit of a grumpy person, and I'm a pessimist.

So I like it when Doctor Who occasionally confirms that there's a lot of nasty darkness in the world, and that sometimes even the best of intentions fail to overcome that. You wouldn't want Doctor Who to be like that all the time, of course, but in taking such an approach, this show can help to educate us on why man is still cruel to man, why unfair things happen to good people, and that why – despite all the terrible, unjust and unpleasant things that happen – we must hang onto our humanity at all costs. We do it because there's a future, and because the Doctor encourages us to work towards it; as he continues and strives onward, so must we. Otherwise, what's the point? It's possible to draw a positive lesson from this, but it's a positivity based on reality.

If I have a complaint about this, it's the way that Steven – having severed his relationship with the Doctor – abruptly changes his mind because he sees two policemen walking towards the TARDIS. Yes, we can celebrate that beautiful speech that Hartnell gives, but it's made possible because Steven is here, despite everything we've seen about the character to the contrary, unbelievably fickle. And you're not wrong to point out how the new companion is introduced in an extremely offhanded fashion. We've been moving away from stories such as The Rescue – which was tailor-made to introduce a new companion – for some time now, but Dodo's arrival seems fast even compared to the way that Katarina came on board. And of course, if the Doctor will so readily accept someone as a new companion, it begs the question of why he didn't just take Anne Chaplet along with him and Steven for her own safety. (And by the way, why does so much of the literature written about this story discuss Jackie Lane's Cockney accent? She's clearly doing Mancunian – indeed, she'd done seasons at The Library Theatre, just up the road from me here in Manchester. Though her accent may well have changed subsequently at the behest of the BBC, there's not a Cockney inflection in sight – or rather, sound.)

But, the final scene is just a sour note on an otherwise bulletproof adventure; as with The Myth Makers, this is one of the best Doctor Who stories. Allowing that John Wiles and Donald Tosh had The Daleks' Master Plan foisted upon them (and that Tosh here parts ways with the show, and is replaced as script editor by Gerry Davis), we never really got to see the full extent of what they wanted to achieve with the series – and I, for one, think that's a terrible loss.

The Steel Sky
(The Ark episode one)

R: There's an elephant! I like elephants. Director Michael Imison plays a clever trick on the viewer here. We know that Doctor Who can't really pull off animal action – be it the cat in Planet of Giants, or the lions in The Romans, we accept that they're stock footage. And when we first get our glimpse of Monica the elephant, we're led to assume the same thing; we cut from the sight of her walking through a jungle to a close-up shot of Jackie Lane's face. And it's only *then* that the TARDIS crew walk over and *touch* it, demonstrating they really did squeeze one onto the BBC studio floor. It surprises us in a way that simply plonking the actors next to the elephant could never do; it asks us to accept the limits of Doctor Who's resources, and then confounds us.

There's lots to enjoy in The Ark. It's all terribly high concept; just a couple of seasons ago, we were invited to marvel in The Sensorites at the fact we were on a spaceship at all, and now it's been reimagined as an entire world that's so big, you need futuristic buggies to get around in it. The steel sky of the title rather sums up the scale of it all. And there are so many ideas we're hit with – to suggest that all the adventures we've so far enjoyed have taken place within the first segment of time, and that we've now popped into the 57th! (It's a good comedy number, 57. It suggests something big and imprecise, in precisely the way The Daleks' Master Plan taking place in 4000 AD didn't. And it's the number of varieties of Heinz Baked Beans into the bargain.)

We're immediately invited to consider the rigorous capital punishment that exists on this ship, and whether being executed outright might be a more humane fate than being miniaturised and stuck on a microscopic slide for 700 years. As a result, we can't be certain whether or not to trust these remnants of the human race. Certainly, Eric Elliott (as the commander) smiles a lot – with a wideness so disconcerting at times, I feel he's about to take a bite out of Hartnell's throat – but there's something so humourless and so stylised about our descendants (all dressed in the same uniform, all making frantic sign language at the Monoids) that they're not very likeable.

So thank heavens for Jackie Lane. I never thought I'd say that; I've never liked Dodo before now. But in context of how grim the series has been recently, and in stark contrast to all these frowning humans around her taking everything so seriously, at least she's having *fun*. She laughs and jokes and has all the zest of someone just starting out on her travels through time and space without having yet stumbled over a single corpse or watched the destruction of a single civilisation. We need something of her childish innocence in the show again... oh, and she brings the common cold to a society that's long lost her immunity towards it. Oops. Looks likes those corpses might start piling up after all.

T: You're a bit more kind to Dodo than I am, Rob... yes, she's enthusiastic, but Jackie Lane is only as good at acting "enthusiasm" as she is any other emotion – i.e. not very. It doesn't help matters, of course, that she's given such an alarmingly dim character to work with. Dodo accepts with thigh-slapping glee that a Police-Box-That's-Bigger-on-the-Inside-Than-it-is-on-the-Outside can travel to Whipsnade, but not anywhere else in space and time. And did you notice the curious moment in the cave, where Steven grabs her close and holds his hand over her mouth and nose for what seems like an age? After what's come before, you have to flirt with the idea that he's actually (and understandably) suffocating her. I do like her costume though – it's very cute.

But this is an ideas episode, which is why I can forgive Dodo being thick, the consistently limp guest cast (Inigo Jackson is hilariously bad as Zentos, the deputy commander) and the tasselled costumes, which remind me of the similar draping between the front and back of a shop. As writer, Paul Erickson brings a new voice to the proceedings; he increases the show's scale and template by having the audacity to confront us with the very thing that the Doctor usually has to prevent in his adven-

tures: the complete and total destruction of Earth. The introduction of the Monoids is cleverly handled, and the concept of these two races travelling together is sold without contrivance. And then there's Dodo's cold – it's an irritating bit of comic business that turns out to be the very thing on which the plot centres. It's a cerebral notion, one that provides us with a different sort of jeopardy than we've seen before.

And it's an interesting introduction to the Guardians too, with the trial of one of their own resulting in – as punishment – his miniaturisation. Paul Erickson's excellent novelisation of this story gives added pathos to this little subplot, and wouldn't it have been great if this had been a speaking character, and the story had dovetailed with his revival on Refusis in episode four? It's a very strange means of punishing someone, though – at least the condemned man will live to see Refusis, whereas the Guardians seen here are doomed to die centuries before they arrive. Why don't they work in 20-year shifts, reviving a new bunch and putting the current lot in the drawer? Then more people can play a part in the journey, and everyone involved gets a chance to settle on Refusis. Come to think of it, why have they decided to settle on Refusis, when Zentos gives the impression that he thinks that the indigenous population of that planet are untrustworthy ne'er do wells?

If I'm nit-picking, it's because I so very much love the scale, ambition and originality of this story. Much of this is down to director Michael Imison's stunning visuals – he uses crane-mounted cameras to emphasise the scale of Barry Newbery's extremely inventive sets. Do you know, until they started to move, I genuinely didn't notice the large number of Monoids who rise from the jungle floor to face the travellers? It's very impressive, especially as I've seen this before and knew they were there!

February 24th

The Plague (The Ark episode two)

R: There's a clever bit of misdirection going on here. You think this is all a story about the future of humanity catching the cold, and you begin to think of the Monoids as just a bit of alien window dressing. And then there's that cliffhanger. And the words appear on the screen telling you the title of the next episode – and you *still* can't yet see what the fuss is about, and what Dodo is reacting to – the camera begins to pan upwards... and we see that the giant statue in the Ark has a Monoid head, and realise with a real shock that we've taken our eye off the ball. The story was about the Monoids all the time, and we took them for granted.

This makes you look back through the episode for clues... the way the humans casually profess the aliens to be their friends, but nevertheless treat them as court secretaries and as labourers; the way that the trial only *really* becomes serious once a human has died, regardless of how many Monoids perished beforehand. The only person who's actually remotely nice to a Monoid is the Doctor, who tells the one waiting on him as a nurse that he couldn't do without him; at the time it seems odd, like a harmless bit of Doctor eccentricity, because no-one else appears to acknowledge them as *people* whatsoever. Even the funeral procession – which is quite beautifully staged, with the Monoids bearing a plague victim down to the main hall to be ejected into space – has Dodo innocently commenting that they sound like a bunch of savages.

So what's brilliant about this episode is that it hides its main theme – the way that these complacent humans treat their subordinates – in full view. As Steven says, nothing's really changed – Man still responds to mob rule, he'll still strike out in paranoia at the unknown. And what's a little casual racism between friends either?

Which is not to say that the crisis of this episode – the cold epidemic – isn't an interesting idea in its own right. At last, the Doctor is forced to consider the responsibility of his travels, in a way that it is normally only considered in historicals. The scene where Steven ponders just how much damage the TARDIS crew have potentially caused to other civilisations, by unwittingly spreading diseases throughout time and space, has the Doctor tell him that it doesn't bear thinking about – but that's just it, it *has* to. Straight after The Massacre and Steven's tirade against the Doctor

in the TARDIS, we have new darker implications to face about the consequences of these funny little adventures we go on every Saturday night on BBC1. That John Wiles, do you think he was much fun at parties?

T: I'm really enjoying this, because it refuses to conform to how Doctor Who is supposed to be, and is resolute in giving us a different kind of story. Okay, there's a trial and a gathering together of stuff in test tubes – which we have seen, respectively, in The Keys of Marinus and The Sensorites. But here, they actually function in terms of the wider plot and character. And it's brilliantly directed – Michael Imison even takes the time to restage last week's cliffhanger, so that an assembled crowd actually *reacts* to Zentos' announcement that they might all die (as opposed to last week, when one of the extras greeted the news by wiping her hair away from her face and noticing something on her shoe). And the director's eye continues to help convey the sense of scale – there are the different monitor-shots of Monoids collapsing across the Ark, and there's a lovely effects shot as the dead Monoid's body is ejected into space. There's also a great visual of a Monoid feeding Monica.

But the script has some excellent moments too, particularly Steven's speech about however advanced mankind might seem, its fear of the unknown is still great. I hate optimistic futures where no-one is acquisitive and each man knows his place; call me a cynic if you must, but human nature isn't like that. Even in this supposedly advanced and idyllic society, "every fibre" of Zentos' being is unjustifiably prejudiced. And Hartnell gets a lovely moment too, when Dodo starts crying and he doesn't quite know how to react – he looks around uselessly, unable to deal with this display of emotion. (I'm less sure, though, when Dodo uses the word dodgy and he tells her that things are about to get "doggier" (sic) – is that what they get up to in the Monoid buggies?)

At the end of this skilful and smart episode, we get that fantastic shot of the Earth being destroyed *and* the Doctor skilfully counselling Zentos that he must "travel with understanding as well as hope", *and* that absolutely superb cliffhanger. All of this, and Michael bloody

Sheard makes his first Doctor Who appearance! Three cheers for all of that!

The Return
(The Ark episode three)

R: ... and sometimes you're left just thinking, "Everything I *thought* was good about a previous episode, all the cleverness I found there – was I just imagining it all, or what?"

With a reminder to myself that I'm meant to be finding the things to enjoy in these episodes... I think Eileen Helsby, playing Venussa, one of the subjugated humans, gives one of those lovely sincere performances that always tend to get overlooked. She shows the right sort of hope against her friend's defeatism when she hears about the legendary Doctor returning, and the right sort of disgust when talking to a collaborator. They're not complex scenes, these, but she pitches them perfectly. And you can tell that the director is working as hard as he can to keep this episode as inventive as the previous two. Those camera shots from above are interesting to look at, and rather cleverly suggest the importance of the statue to the story as well. But sometimes, the cleverness runs away with itself. It's great fun to have sequences showing that you can produce a heap of potatoes by dropping a tablet into a bit of water, but it does rather suggest that the slaves working in the security kitchen (I love that phrase, security kitchen) aren't having to exert themselves too much. And although there's a good reason why the house on Refusis looks a bit like the front room of where my parents used to live – with nice tables and vases everywhere – it's neither jarring enough for any of the characters to comment upon it, and far *too* jarring to fit in with the design elsewhere.

And otherwise... oh, hell with it, let's be honest. This is a bit rubbish, isn't it? The scene in which the evil Monoid gives away his plans to Dodo, and then tries to backtrack when like a finger-wagging schoolteacher she calls him on it, is tooth-hurtingly twee – it's drama pitched at the infant level. It's even worse than the sequence in which that same Monoid tries to anger the Refusians by smashing a vase and throwing their flowers on the floor – and that's saying something. The Monoids had a strange presence to them before, when they were hidden in the background and patronised by the cast; now that they sound like Roy Skelton and waddle about with big guns, they just look ludicrous. The worst of it all is that any themes about the way Man treats its slave races is not only squandered by turning them into two-dimensional villains, but even seems to *justify* that very treatment. We're not in Planet of the Ood territory here; the Monoids didn't revolt because they were oppressed. On the contrary, the lead Monoid (wonderfully named One) says that the reason they took charge was because the humans ultimately were a bit too *nice* to them. The message being, I suppose, if you want to keep your fuzzy wuzzies in check, don't give them an inch.

Bah.

T: Well, I'm not sure... One says that the Guardians helped the Monoids to develop their voice boxes and heat prods, but not that this was the reason for the revolt. Sort of. Either way, discovering the consequences of the Doctor's actions by revisiting the same place some centuries in the future is a great, interesting concept that we haven't seen before. The idea that the formerly lethal cold mutated and sapped Man's will is a clever one, and puts the onus of setting things right on the travellers' shoulders. And the Monoids' gesticulation makes absolute sense, as they used sign language before they developed their Zippy synthesisers, so it's logical that they'd continue to be demonstrative. I'll take what's seen here over bringing in Roslyn de Winter to do, for instance, some "Monoid Movement" any day.

The Refusian Barratt Home that you rightly mention is a curious blip in what's otherwise an exemplary design; the space-launcher chair that flips when the door opens and turns into steps, and the mountain-backdropped Refusian jungle are most impressive. (When this story is restored for its DVD release, it's going to *look* fabulous.) And who cares about the logic of it – I love the space-potato pills. It's another throwaway effect that looks impressive without making a song and dance about itself.

I do get the nagging sense, though, that after the thoughtful and elegant ideas at work in his previous two episodes, Paul Erickson has given up trying to be clever. His attempts at futuristic dialogue are unintentionally hilarious – Dassuk asks how the Doctor's party has returned after all these centuries with "How in space could you do it?" And Venussa does that impossible thing you often find in a Terry Nation script – she's already conversant in the language, idioms and culture of people she's only just met, when she describes one of the subject Guardians to Steven as, "What you'd call a collaborator."

The biggest mystery here, though, is why Two's manservant Yendom seems to die with his arms sticking up in the air, as if he's a dead cat.

February 25th

The Bomb (The Ark episode four)

R: Even though the story is working its way towards a climax, there's a lot more time this week for little moments of subtlety. Take for example, the look that's passed between Venussa and Dassuk when she elects to stay behind on the Ark with Steven to search for the bomb; it's as if she's dumped him for Peter Purves, and he goes off to Refusis spurned. At the end of the story, as they contemplate future generations, Eileen Helsby and Brian Wright manage to make it look as if they're referring to their *own* children – they've patched things up, and going to make a go of it. It's an example of two actors getting together and finding *something* to do, some little character arc they can play out to make the job more interesting, even if there's no script evidence for it whatsoever. And it's really rather wonderful.

Or there's the little subplot concerning Maharis, the quisling human. He's genuinely distraught to find out that the Monoids have betrayed him in his slavery, and the resigned disgust that Steven shows him when he refuses to help search for the bomb lends him a depth that the dialogue itself only hints at. So his eventual death, crying out with delight when he sees his masters, only to be gunned down automatically, has a certain pathos to it.

It's little things like this that make The Ark work, in spite of itself. The actual scene-to-scene plotting is pretty wretched, all told – but the cast and director are putting in enough

effort to make sure the incidentals count. Even though he's trapped inside a limiting costume, Edmund Coulter tries his level best to make Monoid One a distinctive villain, patronising when talking to his slaves, and madder and madder with his arm movements the closer he gets to taking over the world.

And it must be said – after all my ranting yesterday, there *is* some attempt to suggest that the Monoids shouldn't be merely demonised as evil villains, and that their corruption was in part the fault of the original humans who marginalised them from their society. Indeed, the whole Monoid civil war goes a long way – in theory – to establishing them as a bit more complex than The Return suggested. (I say "in theory", because it's still a bit hard to think of them as individual characters when the main bone of the revolution is Four picking a fight with One, much to Three's disgust. Pity poor Seventy-Seven, lying there dead on the surface of Refusis, the victim of another Monoid's war. And with 76 Monoids more important than him still unaccounted for.) But the intention is there, and I accept that.

So – this is the last story produced by John Wiles. I know it's a little against the spirit of this book to say so... but I'm rather relieved. The joy of Verity Lambert's Who was its diversity, not only in location but in tone. Wiles made sure that the TARDIS travelled the length and breadth of the universe, but the tone has been much the same throughout – and that tone is chilly. The Myth Makers is a wonderful comedy that, nonetheless, ends in chaos and despair. The Daleks' Master Plan is a romp, the closest Doctor Who has ever come to a comic book, but which ends in death and ruin. And frankly, The Massacre isn't full of the jollies either. It's all very *clever*, and I honestly admire his intent to push the boundaries of the series and see it as a more thoughtful concern than a children's tea-time serial. But not only has he lost the fun of the thing, he's also misplaced its wonder and vision. I've found Doctor Who a little hard going recently, and I want to enjoy myself again, please.

T: I've already discussed how I wish John Wiles and Donald Tosh had overseen more stories, and can only continue to applaud Wiles for broadening the kind of stories the series should be attempting... even if I do, Rob, grudgingly accept your point about the lack of humour.

Looking at the last instalment of The Ark itself, I can only encourage anyone reading this to check out Erickson's novelisation of this story – in this, he succeeds (as Glyn Jones did with his book version of The Space Museum) in fleshing out his original storyline, and making things chock-full of nuanced touches and character moments. (Although I do seem to recall mention of Steven "ejaculating" – i.e. "snapping"/"sharply expressing" – himself once too often. Now that I think of it, Dodo "ejaculates" once too.) The Monoid rebellion in the book is far more plausible, and there's a big showdown by a waterfall – as opposed to the load of paunchy, waddling actors zapping each other and falling over that we get on screen. It's a shame, actually, that although the latter two episodes of The Ark are marginally better acted than the first couple, so much potential complexity has been squandered.

Still, visually this continues to be engrossing – Imison not only has great flair, he's a bit cheeky too. We see many a shot of finished Monoid food or drained Monoid glasses, but of course we don't *see* them actually eating, do we? It's as if he's daring us to ask where their mouths are. Many of Imison's shots are impressively long and wide – there's a fantastic forced perspective shot of the launcher taking off with a Monoid in the background – meaning there's nothing small or cramped about this story. It's the same on the Ark itself – we have a close-up of Venussa's nodding head, and then she walks out of frame, leaving the statue in the background.

If The Ark hasn't been overwhelmingly successful, its ultimate message of multiculturalism comes across strongly enough. And even if this story doesn't amount to the sum of its parts, it's more original, well made and beguiling than many of the better-remembered and better-lauded adventures of this era.

Which brings us, neatly, to The Celestial Toymaker ...

The Celestial Toyroom (The Celestial Toymaker episode one)

R: Do you know, there was a time when it seemed everyone actually *liked* The Celestial Toymaker? Not now, of course, when fan consensus seems to regard it as something rather evil smelling – but back in the eighties when I was growing up, it was seen as odd and brave and different. In fact, it's a measure of its reputation at the time that John Nathan-Turner tried to bring the character back as a foil for Colin Baker. (It's tempting to see Michael Grade as a twenty-first century fan, quickly cancelling the entire season at the very thought.) I remember that a boy from school had got an audio recording of this story, and gave me a copy. I listened to it a lot when I was growing up, and pretty soon had memorised all the dialogue. (There isn't much.) The tape played slightly fast, actually, which made it all sound even more bonkers: William Hartnell and Michael Gough (playing the Toymaker) squeaked, and Carmen Silvera (playing a clown, Clara) spoke at a pitch that only dogs could hear. And I loved it.

And against the weight of fashion, I do still – especially as a contrast to the episodes we've been watching over the past fortnight, which have been so earnest and grim. Instead, this is just sinister – and what makes it all the more macabre somehow is that it doesn't emphasise that sinister streak too forcefully. Twenty-odd years later in The Greatest Show in the Galaxy, we would see the programme deal with killer robotic clowns in a circus of death. But this first proper dip into the surreal works because, for the most part, it truly suggests that the games that Steven and Dodo play to win their freedom really may just be an entertainment for them, and that the clowns who cheat are being loveable rascals rather than psychotic murderers. Brilliant as Greatest Show is, it very quickly decides that it is a story about good and evil, and becomes a much more conventional story with surreal trappings; The Celestial Toymaker walks a much more disconcerting tightrope. It plays upon the trivial and the childish, the Toymaker trapping his victims not for material gain but because he's bored. And the more that the threat becomes unspoken, the more genuinely disturbing this becomes. The scenes in which the Toymaker makes the Doctor invisible at a whim are fine – but it's the mocking fact that he then leaves the Doctor one hand to play his game which hints at how much power he has. The Doctor's urgent cries that Steven and Dodo must not look at images of themselves is never properly explained, and is so much more potent for that.

I would criticise Jackie Lane, whose performance of a companion with the mental age of ten is still in full force, except for the fact that she fits neatly into a world of child's playthings. The story wouldn't work at all if the companions treated the situation with the full gravitas it deserves, because the principle pleasure of watching Steven is not that he's playing for his life, but that his self-respect is equally at stake. The deadly Blind Man's Buff game is smashing: accompanied by music which is just a little too jaunty, and performances from the clowns which are just a little too annoying, it is actually unsettling. A lot of this atmosphere is the responsibility of Peter Purves; the scene in which Steven adamantly insists that the clowns play on until death reveals a hard edge which suddenly makes the episode more serious.

Anyway. It's different. What do you think, Toby? I know we're not going to agree on this one...

T: I've already confided in you that I was dreading having to rewatch this story because I think it's nonsense, but I'm determined to give it the benefit of the doubt here. As you know, normally if a story flouts the usual Doctor Who rules and conventions, I'll be the first to champion it, even if my reasons for doing so don't hold much water. But even then, this adventure has never quite done it for me, possibly because it's a Donald Tosh-John Wiles story put on the screen by Gerry Davies and Innes Lloyd. It's a bit like having a Coen Brothers film reimagined by Jerry Bruckheimer and Roland Emmerich.

All of that said, it's quite unsettling just how little preamble there is. In an era where it can take the entire opening instalment for the regulars to find out exactly what the story is and who's going to be in it, it's to be applauded

how swiftly the Toymaker (so to speak) puts his cards on the table. The opening is spooky and unsettling, and the episode cleverly exploits that old childhood bugbear of the nightmarish clowns. Setting the story in a moody world of games and illusion is a new one for Doctor Who (we're more than two years away from The Mind Robber), and there's a sense of the series boldly venturing into new frontiers. It even seems a novel threat that the Doctor's very tangibility has been removed, even though – as you say – it means that poor old Hartnell has been shuffled off to the side again. (Perhaps it's a punishment for his mucking up the story title again when he refers to the "Celestral Toymaker".)

As far as the episode's main plot goes... hmm, well, Peter Purves does his best to be grumpily affronted that he's having to engage in such childish flim-flam, but as Clara and Joey's terrifying machinations include such horrors as squirting you in the face with water and popping a balloon behind your back, we're not exactly left on the edge of our seats. The Blind Man's Bluff game is pure nonsense, with the level of villainy exhibited by the clowns being that, er, they're cheats. And when they're rumbled, the game simply has to be played again. This is hardly the stuff of high drama, is it? It really needed to be a ghoulish abstraction of child's nursery, not just an over-sized recreation of one. It only flirts with the nightmarish when Joey is coldly forced to play the game properly – Dodo's "he's not funny anymore" is the best line in the whole episode.

Then everything gets wrapped up with a very limp cliff-hanger in which some dolls come to life because Dodo asks them to, although I will admit that flashing the words of the riddle on screen gives the pleasing suggestion that the adventure has been lifted from the pages of a book.

So, this isn't nearly as bad as I had feared, Rob... there are some interesting moments, and a definite atmosphere in places. Dudley Simpson's rattling wooden percussion is a cannily conceived musical conceit, and I very much like the way the Toymaker refers to the Doctor as an undefeated enemy of old, because it gives our hero an air of epic grandeur. And isn't it doubly a shame that this episode hasn't shown up somewhere, as it features clips from similarly missing instalments of The Daleks' Master Plan and The Massacre? I've reassessed my preconceptions before, Mr Shearman, so who knows? Let's see if I continue to warm to this story...

February 26th

The Hall of Dolls
(The Celestial Toymaker
episode two)

R: I think more than any other episode we've yet heard, this one all depends on what it actually *looked* like. There's an interesting vein running through the dialogue about whether the Heart family are real people or not. Certainly, they act like comic caricatures – the Queen is by turns Lady Bracknell and Queen Victoria, and poor foolish King Henry is any hand-me-down old duffer. But that all may be just what happens to you if you get trapped in this realm forever and become toys – you lose your identity a bit, you go insane. Amongst all the bizarre jokes, the only thing that pulls them up short is the notion that they're not actually human beings – and you get the sense that this strange game of deadly chairs is their last gamble to hang onto the scrap of humanity they have left. This is what Steven and Dodo will end up like.

And that's all fine and good, but therefore the threat of the chairs has to be real. All the dialogue and sound effects suggest that the dolls look like real people too – the same height, the same weight. And that means that whatever devices the chairs use to despatch their victims, it should always be made clear that these could be used against a human body – just like those disturbing ads we had in the seventies, with crash test dummies going through windscreens of cars. The first chair that we see turn on its victim shakes it to death. When we return to the scene a bit later, it's still shaking – and it's clear that by now *the doll's head has come off*. That's a disturbing image. And we get an episode where Steven and Dodo, as real people, are playing against people who are only *half* real (and whom, by implication, they wish to die instead of them), using dolls which just *look* like people. That's

creepy stuff. All done to heightened comic dialogue, and the sort of japery where the King amusingly tries to persuade both his son and his fool to take one of the Russian roulette bullets for him.

It *really* depends on how it looks, though. If the dolls' destruction is violent and grotesque, then this is wonderful. One gets cut in half with a knife, for God's sake! But if the production holds back and plays it too safe, then this would be entirely pointless. As pointless, one might argue, as listening to the soundtrack and *imagining* it as eerie as I want. But hey. Them's the breaks.

William Hartnell literally phones in his performance this week, doesn't he? His one voiceover part is clearly delivered with absolutely no understanding of what the context of the lines could be. "It's chair number," he says, as if that were a complete line in itself, not a revelation that gets interrupted.

T: I'm trying to be charitable to this episode, but too many things are niggling at me. First off, I'm finding it very odd that the programme-makers went to the expense of hiring an actor as talented as Michael Gough, only to consign him to being stuck in a room, playing a tedious game with a recording of the leading man's voice. Second, and as I mentioned last week, the Toymaker's minions cheat. So, what's the bloody point of playing the games at all, then? If the Toymaker doesn't take doesn't take joy in the game-mechanics – if he doesn't delight in the fun of playing the games – why go through all the rigmarole? He could spare us an episode of British Bulldog With Spikes or Hunt the Exploding Thimble and just turn the Doctor, Steven and Dodo into his playthings and have done with it. You can only really justify such an odd and potentially silly set-up if it takes you into the realms of dark surrealism, but this doesn't, instead offering us overblown whimsy at best.

And isn't this getting a trifle repetitive? We get almost exactly the same cliffhanger as last week, and Dodo's enthusiasm here simply exposes her weakness as a character, completely failing to sell the idea that any of this is in any way threatening. Tellingly, Steven has to keep saying the same things to Dodo over and over again to remind us that this is supposed to be scary. Also, the way that even the Doctor's voice is taken away makes me a bit angry on Hartnell's behalf – he may as well trip over on his way back to work, thus adding injury to the litany of insults he's being dealt.

(Right, things are getting a bit negative, and I need to adjust my perspective here. Go to your happy place, Toby... go to your happy place...)

On the plus side, I do like the way the Hearts mention their desire for liberty, and that the King and Queen sit on the final, deadly chair together – both moments give a touching hint of their latent humanity. It's rather fun that each chair kills in a different way, and the music remains suitably childish and plinky-plonky (that's a technical term). I also like the groovy robot with a TV screen on its chest – it's like a cross between a Dinky toy and a Tellytubby.

See, Rob? I've just reproved the rule that Doctor Who is such a fantastic show, you can milk a few compliments even out of a story you normally can't abide. Unlike the Toymaker's underlings, I'm at least *trying* to play by the rules we set out for this book...

The Dancing Floor
(The Celestial Toymaker
episode three)

R: Crazed Toymaker apologist as I am, I have to admit this episode tests my patience a bit too. I'm enjoying seeing Campbell Singer and Carmen Silvera pop up each week in a different guise – the Toymaker's realm is a bit like an impoverished theatre repertory company – and they both banter very well as Sergeant Rugg and Mrs Wiggs the cook. But who cares? – their current guises have none of the immediacy of clowns or playing cards, and are utterly unrecognisable figures. And the games that Steven and Dodo play against them this week are paltry fare, neither "hunt the key" nor "avoid the annoying ballerinas" having any of the macabre edge seen in the previous two weeks. There's pleasure to be derived from watching Dodo try to seduce a tin soldier, I suppose, and there are actually some good witty lines to be had between Rugg and Wiggs – but there are so *many* lines between them that this does get a bit wearisome.

Things do pick up, though, with the arrival of Billy Bunter. (Sorry, "Cyril" – no copyright problems there, then.) It's not that the image of a fat jolly schoolboy is so very odd, it's more that they've got a middle-aged man playing him. The best bit of the episode is Steven's reaction to Cyril telling him that he's one of his heroes, and that when he grows up he wants to be just like him: "You seem pretty grown up already!" There is some relief to be had when the next episode is announced as being the *final* test.

T: The dramatic high point of this episode is when a character who doesn't really exist threatens a pie. That should tell you all you need to know.

With the best of will, the majority of this episode is very stupid, and one can only hope – given that this episode is missing from the archives – that the impassive ballerinas looked spooky and jerky, and that the dance was macabre rather than lamely unconvincing. That Dudley Simpson seems to have popped a few happy pills before scoring this doesn't exactly fill me with hope, I'm afraid to say. And do you know, I was joking earlier when I said they'd be playing Hunt the Thimble – I'd forgotten that that's precisely what they do. Oh yes, and Sergeant Rugg proves he's up there with the vase-tossing Monoid Two in the palpable threat stakes – smashing, as he does, a number of plates. (I can't wait to till the epic end-of-season finale where some dastardly fiend threatens a whole cabinet of Wedgwood.) So much of what Rugg and Mrs Wiggs do is pointless banter; I know they're supposed to be *deliberately* annoying, so as to distract Steven and Dodo – but they're still annoying! I'm sure I could come up with a character whose speech sounded like nails on a blackboard, but I don't think the audience would be terribly grateful.

I should be nice, though... none of this is to criticize Campbell Singer and Carmen Silvera, whose versatility and commitment throughout these three episodes has been admirable. They've given very distinct and utterly different performances in each of their roles. I'm assuming they were hired to play George and Margaret in the original, Donald Tosh-edited version of the script, and I'd love for that version to be uncovered. Whilst the George and Margaret idea might not have hit home with the kids or stood the test of time, I know in my bones that Tosh would have ensured that proceedings were beguiling, strange and offbeat.

And while the ballerinas may have been scary – much like the clowns are in The Greatest Show in the Galaxy – I really, really love the doll's house set. That's what Doctor Who is all about – making our childhood staples into nightmarish, distorted (and in this case, oversized) mirror images. And as ever, Peter Purves admirably carries the proceedings while Hartnell is away; Steven keeps us rooted in reality and is surprisingly harsh and single-minded – he's prepared to accept the fate of his opponents if it gets him closer to his goal.

The programme-makers really do seem to be flirting with a trademark violation when Cyril says that he's known to his friends as Billy. No wonder Frank Richards, the creator of Billy Bunter, was annoyed. What next, putting Bertie Bassett on screen with an alias? That would never happen! Oh, and look... Tutte Lemkow's name is in the credits. If that's not going to get your episode marked for destruction, nothing will.

February 27th

The Final Test
(The Celestial Toymaker
episode four)

R: Hmm. Oh, bugger it, I'm finally coming round to your point of view, Toby. This really isn't very good. Graham Williams once said, after watching this one surviving episode to research his abortive Nightmare Fair script for Colin Baker, that he was amazed the audience in the 60s put up with watching a game of hopscotch for half an hour. It's not that the hopscotch in itself is the problem, I think – and look, they've made the floor electrified, so at least unlike last week's games, there is an iota of jeopardy! – but the way everyone reacts to it. Dodo says at one point that she thinks she's going to enjoy this game – as if she hasn't yet twigged that if she loses, she's going to be turned into a Barbie accessory – and Steven is sulky and bored. Those would be fine reac-

tions if this were episode one, but it's episode *bloody four*, and although we're reaching some crisis point, no-one seems to feel any urgency whatsoever. There are the elements of a good episode here, I think, in spite of the fact that, yes, it really is watching three people play hopscotch for half an hour. Peter Stephens is rather brilliant as Cyril, and it's his sudden swings from jolly schoolboy to something much more scheming and spiteful and then back again that gives the proceedings an edge; his performance, frankly, also suggests the way the tone of this whole thing might have been played. But if there were only the sense that Steven and Dodo realised what was now at stake, and played the game in as deadly earnest as their Bunterish opponent, this might be rather exciting. As it is... it just isn't.

And so the story rather dribbles to a halt. And though there's the hint that there might be a twist to all this – that even having won the games that the Doctor has lost the war – it's resolved in such a contrived manner (the Doctor just happening to give a perfect imitation of Michael Gough's voice) that you wish the hint hadn't been made in the first place. It's a niggling problem that's effected a lot of Doctor Who lately: the raising of an Interesting and Difficult Dilemma, which is minutes later solved so haphazardly as to make it redundant. This isn't as bad as that whole sequence in Volcano where the Monk destroys the TARDIS lock just so the Doctor can magically restore it two minutes later – but it comes close.

At the end, you only get glimpses of the macabre story in my head that I cherished as a kid, the best example being the charred doll of Cyril after he's been electrocuted. It's really rather gruesome. I'll hang onto that image, and pretend the rest of the episode was that nasty.

T: Peter Stephens *is* magnificent isn't he? In previous instalments, when we were robbed of his facial and physical presence, he came across like Christopher Biggins – but here, the audience can see how he switches with consummate ease from the smug, smiling faux schoolboy into the terrifying grotesque we know he is underneath. He does all the "Yaa-boo" sucks stuff excellently, but is also creepy and threatening. The production as a whole could have done with a bit more of this duality.

Good though Silvera and Singer were, there was never a psychotic undertone to their japery as there is with Stephens; oddly enough, he's the only thing that hints at what this story is renowned for being – a nightmarish, dark spin on the nursery.

Michael Gough is also a great actor, but as the Toymaker, he doesn't get to do much except order big bits of Toblerone to move about. Still, he does look great in that splendid costume, and he exudes a polite, feline menace – but it has to be said, he's not the most memorable villain, and there have been more impressive performances thus far in the series from lesser-known actors. I'll grant you that he has some nice moments – I like the way his hand stiffens in anticipation as Hartnell goes to make his last move, and the way he vanishes from the robot's telly tummy to appear behind Steven is very effective – but at the end of the day, he's the villainous equivalent of someone who challenges you to a game of cards you've never played before, and keeps bringing up new rules that coincidentally play to his favour and against yours.

I'd probably be over the line of this book's parameters to comment upon the way that Dodo is written as possibly the stupidest person in the history of time (she is, though – when she falls for Cyril's "hurt foot" trick, despite his having demonstrated a number of times that his key characteristic is duplicity, she loses all dignity). But it might be fair of me to mention that for all of this story's good intentions, its main fault is that everything is just a bit *too* literal. In trying to invoke the sort of episodic jeopardy of other Doctor Who stories, Gerry Davis has removed everything that was unusual and therefore remarkable about it; thanks to the constant rewrites, it seems to have lost its raison d'etre. I'm not saying Tosh's version would necessarily have worked, and I'm aware that I'm talking as an adult (if the Davis version was suitably entertaining for the kids in the audience, good for him), but I suspect that it would at lest have been interesting. And I'm not sure this is.

I actually feel a bit bad that with The Chase, I was able to admit that rewatching it made me reconsider my lowly expectations of it – but The Celestial Toymaker really hasn't, and even the surviving episode four doesn't desperately convince me that this story is badly in need of re-evaluation. But, we can only *try* to look for what's positive in each story we encounter on this journey – and you can't win them all, can you?

A Holiday For the Doctor (The Gunfighters episode one)

R: Fan reputation is a funny thing. You remember that convention panel we were on a couple of weeks ago in LA, Toby? We were discussing the future of the series, and what we might expect under the aegis of Steven Moffat. And a woman in the audience piped up, as if she were delivering holy writ, that there were two monsters she didn't want to see make a return appearance in Doctor Who. The Zarbi were one, and the Gunfighters were the other. Leaving aside the rather odd idea that BBC Wales *might* be planning Revenge of the Clantons or The Bat Masterson Stratagem, it reinforced again this peculiar idea of The Gunfighters as the show's nadir. That was based on the fact that it had the lowest ratings ever (not even remotely true), looked cheap and nasty (nope) and had jokes in (aah... guilty as charged there, your honour).

Of course it has jokes in. It's a Donald Cotton script! You can tell that much from the appalling pun in the title, and I wouldn't have it any other way. It's not the comedy classic that The Myth Makers tried to be, but something far more restrained and gentle. In a way, I rather prefer that. The Myth Makers could afford to be bizarre and self-parodic, its characters speaking in anachronisms, because it was set at a time of myth and legend that was only on mild speaking terms with established history. The Gunfighters is set less than a hundred years before its first broadcast, and had Cotton's comedy been as freewheeling, it'd have looked as silly as The Feast of Steven. So instead of verbal tricksiness and broad satire, what Cotton gives us instead is character comedy. And it's lovely – to see Steven and Dodo excited at the story's setting, and get carried away playing cowboys, restores that element of fun that's been missing from the show for months.

And better yet... look, everyone, William Hartnell's back! I don't know who that strange intruder in the TARDIS was while John Wiles was on the watch, but the actor playing this Doctor has brilliant comic timing and subtlety, and there's a sense of joy to Hartnell's performance again. Notice his exasperation as his friends forget about his toothache as they play about, his fear as he realises he's going to have a tooth extracted without anaesthetic by a first-time dentist, and his delightful naivety as he misinterprets Seth Harper's summons to be shot as the greetings of a new friend wanting to buy him a drink. It's a relief to see this Doctor again, the one I want to share adventures with in time and space. The one who has the skill of a deadpan comedian – the moment where he mutters after his operation that he's grateful he didn't need his tonsils out is probably the single funniest we've had all season.

T: There's an interesting sociology experiment in which a teacher is told at the beginning of the year that six pupils are the best, and six others are trouble. A year later, the top six and bottom six in the class match what she had been told – and yet, the kids had initially been picked entirely at random. And this is what has happened with The Gunfighters... back in the days when so much of Doctor Who wasn't commercially available, Doctor Who – A Celebration (1983) famously informed us that The Gunfighters wasn't just a bad Doctor Who story, it was *the* bad Doctor Who story, and it's suffered from an inherited negative perception ever since. I vividly recall, in fact, overhearing a young fan ask another (they must have been 11 or 12, the little whipper-snappers – this is when I was a wise old sage of, ooh, 15), "What's the worst Doctor Who story... apart from, of course, The Gunfighters, which everyone knows is rubbish." I very much doubt that they had *seen* it, of course, and yet these young rascals felt certain that this adventure was horrid – even though, I would argue, it's got far fewer shortcomings in the departments of writing, direction and acting than so much of what surrounds it.

As you say, Rob, this is nothing like as bold as Cotton's script for The Myth Makers... nor should it be. It's a witty pastiche that asks us to have fun with the conventions of a popular form. The comedy works very well – Hartnell is great (and slightly more restrained than nor-

mal; his grasp of the deadpan is much better than all that dotty giggling), I particulary like his exhortation to his "fellow thespians" and the way he keeps referring to Wyatt Earp as "Mr Werp". Speaking of whom, John Alderson is splendid in the role – he's comfortable in the genre (he acted in the States a lot, and indeed died there), and has the authority to pull it off. There's an openness and a lightness of touch about him, which means he can handle the funnies too. When the slightly embarrassed Steven is forced to apologize, "No, you see, I'm not really a gunman...", Alderson's polite response – "You did kinda make that look obvious, didn't you, boy?" – is charmingly amusing.

And if we're highlighting the key actors on display this, Peter Purves is game, isn't he? If ever there's a lack of consistency in his character, he adapts his performance to fit whatever style the week's script demands from him. So today, he's come over all Morton Dill, with a blizzard of comedy double takes and nervous bravado. The zealous comic gusto Steven displays here is completely different to the angry pragmatism he used to make events in The Celestial Toyroom have the appearance of being even vaguely threatening. In this era where the lead character is being more and more sidelined, Purves is an unsung hero.

For good measure, this first episode also gives us a dentist's shop advertised by a massive molar hanging outside, and a great scene between the Doctors Who and Holliday, where the latter offers a bash on the bonce as an anaesthetic before removing the Doctor's tooth, and whose response to our Doctor's haughty "I never touch alcohol" is to say "Well I do..." and knock back a mouthful before operating. It's wonderful stuff! I hate to say it, Rob, but perhaps the reason this story isn't very beloved is that they don't understand that it's not taking itself entirely seriously? Is it wrong of me to point out that some quarters of fandom aren't famed for their sense of humour? I've even seen the Doctor's response to Holliday's "Good bye and good luck" – "The same to you and many of them!" – listed as a mistake, as a goof, when it's clearly a deliberate choice. With every scene, Donald Cotton is trying to strip away all the dour seriousness and gritty moodiness of this genre and muck about with it. If some people don't get how much of this is meant to be a joke... well, don't shoot the writer.

February 28th

Don't Shoot the Pianist
(The Gunfighters episode two)

R: The thing is, though, you can see why fandom didn't embrace The Gunfighters. They weren't (just) being curmudgeonly, or failing to have a sense of humour. The plotting is slow, to say the very least. And it's a story that hinges entirely on the Clanton brothers wanting to kill Doc Holliday, and mistaking him for the Doctor. That's it. There are no other frills to this. It's structured very oddly, so that every time you think the story is getting somewhere, the Ballad of the Last Chance Saloon pops up to make you feel distanced from it. (It's not that it's a bad tune, or that Lynda Baron can't sing – but we've heard it in so many contexts already by the end of episode two, performed by Peter Purves and Sheena Marshe as well, that it does begin to grate.) And although the acting from all the supporting cast is pretty strong – especially Anthony Jacobs as a charming Holliday – the accents are *abysmal*. Across the board. And from line to line. You might feel that within the comedy they're intentionally bad, but they're not – there's nothing intrinsically funny in being pulled out of the action every time someone opens their mouth.

So although I'm really enjoying The Gunfighters, I can understand completely why a fandom who was picking its way through the black and white stories, and looking for monsters while doing so, might prefer The Dalek Invasion of Earth. It's all a matter of context. More than ever, watching these stories in order, day after day, I can appreciate The Gunfighters for its charm and its sense of fun – it really does feel like a breath of fresh air, and to be given permission to *laugh* at something is a joy. And William Hartnell continues to shine. I just love the Doctor here – watch his childlike delight in being able to show "Mr Werp" that he can swivel a pistol, and his bemused irritation that everybody keeps giving him guns. It's a performance that recalls the

dotty old grandfather from Season Two, but played with less fumbling about, less tics, and more down-to-earth accurate comic timing. This isn't the greatest story of the Hartnell era, or the greatest comedy of its time either – but it may just be a collection of Hartnell's finest moments. And if for nothing else, that makes it something to cherish.

T: I'm a bit reluctant to lay into accents – it's usually something done by lazy critics, and often erroneously. (A number of my mates mocked the American accents in some of the new series episodes until I pointed out that the actors in question were actually using their own native brogue.) But on this occasion... well, your highlighting of the vocal shortcomings is fair enough. John Alderson's Wyatt Earp is spot on, but the baddies are all over the place, save for Shane Rimmer's Seth Harper. So it adds insult to injury when Harper is the first person to get killed! What? Why didn't they cast Rimmer (a Canadian) as Ike Clanton? The man they've cast instead, William Hurndell, is giving one of the oddest performances I've ever seen – it's not just the accent; physically and verbally, he's a real mush. At times he reminds me of the Scarecrow in The Wizard of Oz! And it's to this charisma-free plank that they've given the job of rallying the lynch mob.

Otherwise, William Hartnell continues to give a kind of performance that really suits him; he's blithely pulling this off with all the skill of an old sweat who knows what the gags are and how to throw them out. Peter Purves likewise hurls himself into this and emerges pretty unscathed, although there are occasions where he flirts with reminding us of Roy Castle in that Dalek movie! And it's a bit odd that Purves is singing live, whilst Sheena Marshe (as Kate, Doc Holliday's girlfriend) is so badly dubbed, you think for a moment she might have been replaced by a Dalek-made robot double. But I love that everyone seems to be having fun with this – it's a great moment when the actors playing the baddies opt to deliver the line "Alive, that is!" in unison, even if they spectacularly fail to pull it off. And isn't Anthony Jacobs terrific as Doc Holliday? I adore the way he tips his hat to Harper's corpse, then smacks Dodo's bum!

It sometimes happens in entertainment that

when the tone is comic, everyone decides that that's enough and they don't really bother in any other department... but that's not the case here. For all we might enjoy the comedy aspects of The Gunfighters, it's wonderfully designed – the sets are absolutely fantastic, the costumes work both in terms of authenticity and what they say about the character of the people wearing them, and they've even got a horse in the studio! And there's an underlying current of tension to all of this – the darkened scene in Holliday's salon is moodily lit, benefiting from the sly quips and mutual respect issuing from the veteran gunslingers. There's also a shocking moment in the pub where Bat Masterson shoves the Doctor with some force. It's quite unusual to see the leading man (played by an actor we know is frail) chucked about quite so unceremoniously.

For my money, this Corral is a lot more than OK.

Johnny Ringo
(The Gunfighters episode three)

R: It's the first time since Kublai Khan popped up on our screens that a character (apart from the Doctor) has been deemed worthy of taking the title of an episode. And the first time since then too that by making a late appearance in a story, a real-life historical figure has changed the entire tone of the drama. As Johnny Ringo, Laurence Payne blows like a cold wind through the plodding comedy of The Gunfighters. Death suddenly seems more serious, the stakes more tense. We go from one scene where it's inferred that Doc Holliday has gunned someone down just to steal his breakfast, to Payne's fantastic introduction, in which he amiably terrorises poor barman Charlie and then shoots him dead before turning in for the night. Payne is excellent; he crafts Ringo as the first character in this story who isn't hiding behind a silly accent or comic shtick, and by playing it so completely straight, he allows the rest of the comedy to seem much funnier in retrospect. Certainly, the scene where Dodo orders Doc Holliday at gunpoint to take her back to Tombstone has a different feel to it in the context of Charlie's death – but it's probably the high point of the episode, and Jackie Lane's finest moment on the series, as she so reluc-

tantly turns protagonist and then visibly crumbles with relief once her demands are met, asking her victim for a glass of water.
T: Anyone doubting the intentions behind this story need only to listen to the fantastic (but irritatingly catchy) ballad, which goes bonkers this week! "So pick him up gentle/And carry him slow/He's gone kinda mental/Under Earp's heavy blow." You say that he's gone kinda mental, Lynda? Well, if he has, he's not alone!

The comedy is again superb, and the actors are clearly relishing the opportunity it presents. The Doctor's suggestion that Holliday is a friend of his ("He gave me a gun, extracted my tooth, what more do you want?") and Steven's sotto voce repudiation of it are very funny, and Hartnell is also great in the prison scene – the moment where he innocently shows Earp Ringo's Wanted poster is blissful, especially when Earp rolls his eyes and chucks the picture away.

That some of the acting is rubbish (the Clantons are, at least, consistently awful) is less of a hindrance here than it would be in other stories – this is *supposed* to be a send up, after all. I don't think these actors deliberately chose to play it that way, but that almost adds to the charm – there's a really odd moment, after Phin has been arrested, where Ike Clanton suddenly gets very camp and minces off, which is very bizarre but also a bit wonderful.

But I absolutely agree that the episode belongs to Laurence Payne, who is all subtle menace and impressively cool in his black leather trousers. It's great how his method of chatting up Kate entails threatening her with a pistol ("Marry me or I'll shoot you" – try it lads, it works!), and his scene with Charlie is fantastically amoral and effortlessly menacing. And with my having fallen off the non-smoking wagon and only just climbed back on it, I also note with annoyance how cool he looks puffing on his cheroot.

After New Earth was broadcast in 2006, Payne wrote to one of the national papers (The Times, I think) praising the imagination of the new series. I therefore find it doubly sad – especially when I've just watched his performance here, in which he's strong, powerful, robust and untouchable – to hear that he died just a few days ago. In real life, regrettably, we can only travel through time in one direction.

March 1st

The O.K. Corral
(The Gunfighters episode four)

R: It's the last time that Doctor Who uses individual episode titles (that is, until that Slitheen story in 2005 upsets the apple cart, provoking wails of concern about whether it should be called Aliens of London or World War Three), and by doing so spoils the fun for fans arguing about how they should actually refer to all these adventures. Personally, I don't see why the fun should stop. I'm still going to think of, say, The Sontaran Experiment as The Destructors (as made canon by the BBC Sound Effects Album!), or Delta and the Bannermen as Flight of the Chimeron, or Dalek as The One Where I Panicked Over Deadlines For Seven Months.

The episode opens with the Doctor and the Earps taking off their hats in respect of the dead – and it's a marked change in tone from the merry comedy of the past three instalments. As if to acknowledge this, there's a lovely moment where Hartnell rests his hand upon the table – only to realise grimly that he's touching a corpse. Just as he did in The Myth Makers, Donald Cotton here lets the laughs die outright, and we're presented with a massacre. What began as a running joke – with the Doctor protesting against being given guns – becomes an earnest appeal for peace and reason, as he tries to dissuade both Wyatt Earp and Pa Clanton from a course of action that can only result in bloodshed. The odd thing about this new, more sober approach is that it doesn't really leave any room for our series regulars at the climax, and for the first time since The Reign of Terror, the show is somewhat gazumped by proper history. Dodo gets to be a hostage for Johnny Ringo for a minute, but otherwise it's remarkable how unimportant the TARDIS crew are to the resolution of this adventure – especially considering that Cotton clearly wasn't concerned with the accuracy of the history. He tries to rectify this in his novelisation by allowing the Doctor to shoot Billy Clanton accidentally – but by doing so, of course, he keeps the comedy coming even through the death-filled finale. I rather prefer

the TV version, even if it means our heroes are sidelined. Rex Tucker stages the gunfight impeccably, and for a few minutes the BBC really *are* doing a Western, and there are no holds barred – for once, there's a climax to a story which genuinely feels grand and effective. Truth to say, that's only because there's no sign of the Doctor anywhere – it only works because you can let yourself believe for a while you're not watching Doctor Who at all.

T: The grand finale of this story entails us leaving the studio (and the medium of videotape) behind for an impressively staged gunfight, all done on film, with sweeping crane movements, high angles and loads of gunfire. The Earps look cool walking calmly up the street, and even the ballad suggests things ain't so much fun any more. What was a comedy for so long ends with brutal stuff: Doc Holliday coldly shoots Billy again and *again*, and Ike's doomed ascent up the stairs is pretty horrifying. He finds himself out of bullets and with nowhere to turn, as the "good guys" calmly and calculatedly take aim and take turns shooting him down. The only thing missing from this slaughter is Johnny Ringo's parting shot from the wonderfully witty novelisation – in which, having been shot, Ringo quips that his gall has just been divided into three parts.

There's more substance to this episode than the final shootout, though – Hartnell has a commanding face off with the excellent Reed de Rouen (who as Pa Clanton gets to wear a fab costume), and Sheena Marshe acquits herself well in the same scene; she's full of faux coquettishness before delivering a killer revelation. John Alderson's grief at Warren's death is dead straight, and his hoarse voice is laced with proper emotion. But it's Doc Holliday himself who provides most of the colour for this episode – his hand-on-hip, self-aware entrance is as much fun as his cackling when he's asked about "his way" of dealing with Johnny Ringo and the Clantons.

But ultimately the whole gunfight (the whole episode even) gives lie to Doctor Who – A Celebration's hypothesis about this story. In labelling this the worst Doctor Who adventure of all time, that book accused the script of being pure Talbot Rothwell (it ain't – there *is* silly wordplay sure, but it's actually much more sophisticated than a Carry On film), of having acting that's bad vaudeville (there's a plethora of worse performances in The Ark and The Keys Of Marinus, to name but two) and direction that's more West Ham than West Coast (a nice bit of wordplay there, but with no basis in truth). The piece then says this story was "not good – it was bad and ugly" – again, that's well punned, but it's also the sort of thing it accuses the script of doing. And then, of course, it's blatantly wrong to say that this was the lowest-rated story ever (the worst of these episodes, at 5.7 million, still outperform the best of the very next story in line, at 5.6 million).

I worry here, Rob, that nothing we can say, and no amount of proof we can offer, will alter the embedded, general feeling that The Gunfighters is somehow worse than most of the black and white era – it really, really isn't. Still, I should stop defending it – otherwise, some reviewer might get annoyed with my stroppiness and decide that the book they're holding is the worst Doctor Who project ever. Even worse, they may that write that down, and then everyone might believe it for the next 25 years at least.

The Savages episode one

R: Raymond Jones' incidental music is fascinating, at one moment sounding like it's aping the classical, with soaring violins giving a strange dignity to the proceedings – then suddenly becoming off key and dissonant and harsh. It sums up the mood of this episode very well, which at first feels like a real throwback to what we've seen before; even Dodo's assertion that the TARDIS has brought them to the Iron Age echoes the setting of the very first adventure. And there remains a peculiar off key sense to the drama, filled as it is with tons of exposition offered very freely and amiably by quite the most welcoming people the Doctor has ever met on his travels (the council-leader Jano in particular, having charted the Doctor's adventures, comes across a little like a leading member of the Doctor Who Appreciation Society), and yet sporadically spotted with dispassionate demonstrations of pleading savages undergoing medical operations. You long for the Doctor and company to

get involved in the action, and I stifled a cheer when Dodo (of all people) becomes suspicious and inquisitive and goes off to look for a bit of drama rather than a guided tour. It's at once the most didactic episode we've yet seen – it's extraordinary just how much of this comes across as prose narrative – and whilst that doesn't make for the most dramatic of episodes, its very oddness, like Jones' music, does give a sense of unease. It's Doctor Who, yes. But it's not quite as we're used to it.

I'm not necessarily saying that's a good thing, or even a deliberate thing, but it is at least interesting. None of our regular characters seem to be quite right. Hartnell seems a mite confused by a Doctor who's written as someone blander than he's used to. Dodo picks a fight with Steven early on because she thinks he's the Doctor's lapdog who'll never do anything for himself – which is so far removed from the way Steven has been written in every single other story since he was introduced. And, against the odds, Dodo has a backbone.

Now, of course, there's a new producer on board in the form of Innes Lloyd, and Ian Stuart Black is here introduced as a new writer – and neither of them yet seem fully conversant with the style of the series. (It's only a few weeks before this team have a computer talking openly about how it requires some bloke or other called "Dr Who", of all things.) It's as if all either of them have ever seen of the programme was some movie in the cinema, in which the lead was some slightly two-dimensional old duffer who had an interrogative as a surname. But, peculiarly enough, all this dissonance, this feeling that the programme just *isn't quite right*, only makes this episode feel all the more fresh and skewed. This strange talky thing ought to be tedious, but it's like a bridge between the old and established (Hartnell hanging on by his fingernails) and the completely new (everybody knowing who the Doctor is, and lots of action set in a quarry).

T: Hmm... one of the disadvantages of "going second" in this guide book, Rob, is that there's the rare occasion when you brilliantly say everything that needs to be said, leaving me with nothing to follow with! I don't have much to add here beyond the fact that you're right... this *is* an odd episode, but I think the oddness works in its favour. Despite the slow pace and innocent naivety on display here, a couple of ingredients make it curiously palatable. As you've already mentioned, the most striking element is the music – the use of strings is inspired; they can be at turns spooky and poignant, and (when the tempo is upped) add drama to the chase scenes. This is quite possibly the most effective and versatile score we've yet heard in the series – it's unsettling and beautiful, all at the same time.

And the *other* key component that lends a sense of strangeness is the location filming. We no longer have the video of this story – so in truth I'm doing some guesswork here – but the telesnaps, for instance, suggest a great use of high angles in the Exorse/Nanina chase. It's a cliché to say that Doctor Who does all its location filming in quarries, but *here* the quarry (again, as far as I can tell) is used very convincingly, and makes it look like the Doctor and his friends have indeed arrived at a stunning, sun-drenched alien vista.

So far, this story is unfolding at a leisurely pace, but I'm diverted enough. You're right to say that it's not quite like Doctor Who as we've come to know it, though, and hopefully the next episodes will help us determine why.

March 2nd

The Savages episode two

R: If I thought Hartnell was at a bit at sea last week, here he finds a whole heap of righteous anger, and seizes it for all he's worth. His fury against Captain Edal, and his assertion that all human life is precious, feels now like a mission statement for the series – and the caveman trappings of the story only serve to emphasise just how far we've come with his character since those early days of selfishness and amorality. It's really rather a political script, this; it may seem none too subtle to modern eyes, with its tale of how the ruling elite come to subjugate and exploit the poor and less educated, but it's so refreshing to see it tackled head on. It's not a million miles away, of course, from the tale of the Guardians suppressing the Monoids we saw a few weeks ago – but this time the gloves are off, and the pro-

gramme isn't hiding behind the metaphor of mute monsters wearing ping pong balls in their mouths; these are *real* people being tortured. And if the Daleks couldn't get on with the Thals, or the Drahvins with the Rills, they could always point at the aliens they hated and mention they were unlike themselves – when Jano and Edal do the same, and the only thing we can see different is that these animals they're tyrannising have scraggy beards and don't wear smart uniforms, then the effect is highly ironic. It makes these Elders, who claim to be so wise and sophisticated, look instead deeply stupid – for all of their technology, they can't see they're victimising their own kind.

And another cliché is introduced here, before it actually *becomes* a cliché – the amoral scientists so cheerfully flapping about their laboratories (the bubbling vats sound terrific!) that they've utterly shut themselves off from the implications of their work. The closest we've come to this before is in The Space Museum, where the Doctor got frozen for an episode – but that was nothing to the long cliffhanger here. The scientist Senta is so positively cheered by his wonderful success draining the Doctor's life force that the episode ends upon a note of excited triumph – one that's all the more sick for its affability. Senta isn't crowing over his success like a villain, because he doesn't *see* himself as a villain – he's a well-spoken hard working scientist who's just satisfied with a job well done. That's what makes him so much more horrifying; an ordinary man who's simply no conception that what he's doing is evil.

T: I'm trying to get an angle on this story – whereas I previously thought the quarry-filming was effectively used to convey an alien locale, we now seem to have moved into a slightly un-Doctor Whoey, cheesy yet dully sincere attempt to portray "the future". To look at the pictures of Hartnell in his space costume, and the overall appearance of Jano and the Elders, I'm reminded of some of the futuristic episodes of Out of the Unknown, and it just doesn't feel quite right.

Hartnell is once again in full command, though – he rattles off his lines without stumbling, and bristles with authority and indignation when standing up to Captain Edal. He's doing what the Doctor does best – advocating for the weak and defenceless – and the oft-quoted "protracted murder" scene is the defining one of this serial. It's a joy to see Hartnell and Frederick Jaeger (as Jano) reward the solid writing with performances to match. In fact, it's a good episode all around for the regulars – Dodo is remarkably feisty when she wanders into the laboratory, and her stroppy side is brought out with brio by Jackie Lane. It's telling though, that Steven gets the line "not even Dodo would be that stupid..."! Even the series itself seems to be admitting that she'd probably be out in the first round of Companion Academy.

I'm not quite sure why the guys in the lab mistake Dodo for a savage though. Didn't her lack of animal skins suggest otherwise?

The Savages episode three

R: When Frederick Jaeger finally emerges from the experiment, clutches his lapels and says "hmm" a lot, you get the feeling that at last the punchline has been delivered to a joke that's had two and a half episodes' set up. It's a lovely, clever idea to give another character the Doctor's life force, and to see the first Doctor performed by another actor... but it doesn't actually work. Jaeger never sounds comfortable doing the imitation, and the best he can make out of it is a high-pitched caricature.

And thank God for that, because I think we've just dodged a bullet. We know that the production team are now actively considering ways that the series can survive Hartnell's departure. Now, imagine if Jaeger had been a mite more impressive in the role. It might have convinced Innes Lloyd that, really, *anyone* could have a bash at the Doctor just by putting in all the same tics and mannerisms that the audience are already used to. And it would have meant that, in only a few months' time, they might have approached the new incarnation much more conservatively. The show survives the transition to Troughton precisely because it *doesn't* play safe – it doesn't do a Cushing from the movies, or a Jaeger from The Savages, and instead looks for the contrasts rather than the similarities between the two Doctors. Jaeger's failure here may mean that The Savages suffers, but Doctor Who as a

whole benefits hugely. Senta's tinkering in the laboratory really wasn't the only experiment going on this week.

In The Space Museum (again), Hartnell sat out an episode, and the cliffhanger was simply Ian reacting with shock to an as-yet unseen Doctor. What makes the drama here work so much better is that this isn't just an excuse to give Hartnell a holiday. He's here in person, but dumb and weak – just one episode after he gave his fabulous tirade against the evils of the Elders, we've never seen him so feeble. What's effective is that we really see the consequences of Senta's life-draining device, and there's nothing in the episode more shocking than hearing Hartnell manage no more at the episode's end than groans and heavy breathing. And, once again, the production team's experiment has failed – they've not even given him a single line this week, but still the most impressive thing about this episode is William Hartnell.

T: Well, Rob, that's a wonderfully thought out and argued hypothesis, but – as your friend – I have to say that it looks like you're attempting to fulfill on your word count by spouting a load of old nonsense. You *seriously* think that this was a trial run on the production team's part, to see if they could replace the leading man with a ringer? I'd argue, then, that you're giving them a bit too much credit – it's hard to swear that they're even *watching* the show, let alone that they're thinking about what's happening all that closely.

Thanks though, for giving me something to argue with – it helps me to fill a paragraph about one of the most unremarkable episodes the programme has ever given us. Who knows, the visuals of this story may have been incredible, but I doubt it; Christopher Barry is a good and efficient director, but he doesn't worry about pretty pictures. And without the benefit of moving images, I can only clutch at straws for commentary – from the telesnaps, it seems that Ewen Solon (playing the primitive Chal) has great make-up, and the set for the planet exterior looks pretty well realised. And I'm now getting seriously vexed on William Hartnell's behalf – he's not out on holiday here, he's made to hang around all week so he can lie down and be a bit doddery at the end. He's been treated pretty shoddily for about the past six months (except by Donald Cotton, actually).

But hang on a minute... it's just hit me. This is an adventure where a rather dull and pious future society is revealed to be not-so idyllic, and where our series regulars must teach them the error of their ways by bringing our morality to their world, thus leaving it an equally dull (but more just) place. Meanwhile, a guest star gets to flex different acting muscles, and consequently has a bit of fun. Yes, that's it! I know why this story seemed so odd in Doctor Who terms! It's because I'm watching bloody Star Trek!

March 3rd

R: Oh, come *on*. You don't think that's what the production team are doing here – that it's a deliberate (and frankly very unpleasant) process in which they're trying any means possible to get the programme working without Hartnell? You say yourself he's been badly treated; it feels that every other story we've been watching recently tries either to give him as little air time as possible, or makes him literally invisible! So, yeah, I really *do* believe that had Frederick Jaeger done some lovely comic stint, clutching his lapels and saying "hmm" a lot, that in a week's time we'd be analysing in our diaries some replacement actor getting up from the floor of the TARDIS doing nothing more than a Hartnell impersonation. Except we wouldn't be analysing it at all, because Doctor Who would have ground to a halt long ago, and so we probably wouldn't be doing these diaries in the first place.

It makes me very grumpy (though not, I think, as grumpy as you). I know that at the moment, Russell T Davies is working hard to ensure that David Tennant gets the biggest and most triumphant exit a Doctor could wish for. But the 1966 production team are doing the opposite to Hartnell, so that when he finally shuffles off to the unemployment office, the viewers at home may not even notice. It's shameful.

But I'm glad to see the spirit of Hartnell still exists, even if it's only in Toby Hadoke getting peevish when things are going wrong around him, and lashing out at his companion. Admit it, I'm not the source of your irritation at all. It's

The bloody Savages! Don't worry. It's coming to an end now.

The Savages episode four

What I love about this ending is how unequivocally triumphant it is. As with so much of The Savages, all the standing about at the end and thanking the Doctor is something we're going to get used to terribly quickly. (And it's amusing to consider that just as it starts becoming familiar, Ian Stuart Black subverts it again in time for The Macra Terror!) But it's very rarely happened before. Under Verity Lambert, the regulars either wanted to nip back to the TARDIS and escape, having done nothing more decisive to the status quo than having survived it, or at least stood apart from the other characters in the story sufficiently that a hearty handshake from them at the end would have seemed a bit inappropriate. When you *do* get something of that nature – say, in The Daleks or The Keys of Marinus – it's more a parting from people with whom the Doctor has *shared* an adventure, not saved them himself per se. And under John Wiles, of course, the story conclusions became more about the Doctor looking depressed and working out how great the body count was.

So the build up to a climax here feels actually very redemptive. In the joyous scene where the laboratory is smashed up, the Doctor talks about the satisfaction of destroying something which is evil. And he's absolutely right – although the story very deliberately tried to sideline William Hartnell, it was a celebration nonetheless of the *Doctor*, the way his conscience infected Jano, and the way his humanist ideals have given a society a new way to live. In light of that, and how in context the optimism of the ending and the forefronting of the TARDIS crew seems so fresh, it feels absolutely right that this should be the moment that Steven departs to take on new challenges. Yes, it's abrupt – but it's beautifully abrupt; for the very first time, Steven is part of an adventure where at the story's end all the characters have a respect and a need for him. The Doctor says he's very proud of him – and, sentimental old git that I am, I feel rather proud of him too. Peter Purves has worked so very hard on the character, taking all the things that made him at first somewhat unlikeable and turning those bouts of impatience and stubbornness into things which have made Steven wholly credible. He's never given a bad performance.

T: I hope you'll cut me a bit of slack, Rob... it's now Day Three Without Cigarettes. I think I'm allowed to be grumpy.

Listening to Peter Purves' final episode makes me remember a time long ago when I got the Radio Times 20th Anniversary Special, and saw a picture of him in the chapter about companions. "That's Peter Purves from Blue Peter," I thought, "was he a companion on Doctor Who?" At the time, the Target novels were my only source of Who knowledge, so I'd never heard of Steven Taylor at all, let alone had any idea who played him. So I've always thought of Purves as a "Blue Peter Presenter who in His Acting Days was on Doctor Who"; it was an interesting trivia factoid, a curio, but nothing to boast about.

In execution, however, Purves has been so much more – at various stages, he's been an action hero, a comedy stooge and a moral centre. He's been adaptable to the point that no role has been beyond him, whilst remaining solid at the ailing Hartnell's side. So it's wonderful that he here gets a decent send off, as he becomes the man best suited to mediate between the Elders and the Savages.

If I'm overly fixated on Steven, it's probably because if this *wasn't* his final story, I'd be struggling to say anything about it at all. (Except of course, for the fact that – as if to counterbalance the John Wiles era – everybody lives!) This could well be the most innocuous Doctor Who story of all time – which is an accolade of sorts, I suppose. I'm hard pressed to call this "interesting"; "curious" is perhaps a better descriptor for it. But that's perfectly fine – Doctor Who should be willing to do such material, there shouldn't be a formula to it. Even if this hasn't been the most exciting of stories, it has its charms and it's been *about* something. Best of all, Steven's departure is given necessary weight, and both Hartnell and Lane act their socks off in response. We will miss him, but we trust him to rise to this new challenge.

Did you notice, though, how we pretty much leave Steven as we found him, stuck on an alien planet? Only this time, he hasn't got a stuffed panda to keep him company. Never mind, Clare Jenkins is certainly more than adequate recompense.

The War Machines episode one

R: Something that's always puzzled me: the rogue computer is called Wotan, so why does everyone pronounce it as if it begins with a "V"? The "W" stands for "world", and yet no-one goes around referring to how the war machines are going to enslace the vorld's population for the next four episodes. For a while you think that maybe it's Professor Brett's own affectation, but everybody else does it as well – perhaps he's got some strange speech impediment, and Sir Charles and Major Green are merely imitating him rather cruelly to take the piss. It's rather odd. I suppose it's an attempt by the production team to give all this a Cold War sense – which is fine, 60s movies are full of East German scientists making armageddon devices. But then why not just go the whole hog, and have the Professor called Himmler rather than Brett?

And, of course, that's where the oddness just starts. If I said that The Savages had an air to it that no-one involved had ever watched the programme, then that goes double here with knobs on. To see the Doctor in a contemporary setting for the first time is weird enough – what makes it all the weirder is that no-one producing the show seems to realise it's never happened before, and treats it as if, like The Avengers, this is what Doctor Who has *always* been doing. (And before too long, of course, they'll be absolutely right! But what's bizarre is that we go from a situation in which contemporary adventures were unthinkable to one where they're the norm immediately, with no blurring in between.) Professor Brett knows who the Doctor is, and Sir Charles accepts his presence immediately. Verity Lambert once complained that the Jon Pertwee Doctor was too much part of the establishment, but that's nothing to a William Hartnell who has a personal secretary, waltzes into scientific establishments and press conferences as if they're routine day job stuff, and whose fab gear gets compared to disc jockeys in trendy London nightclubs. Frankly, at the end of the episode, when Wotan expresses his interest in a certain chap called "Doctor Who" paying him a visit, that they even get his name wrong is hardly a shock at all.

But the episode works well. At times it all feels staggeringly naïve, at others it feels fresh and real – and, bizarrely, it's the collision of that which makes it so much fun to watch. There's something wonderfully charming about seeing the Doctor be amazed at a huge computer – just because it can work out a square root of a small number at a speed considerably slower than a pocket calculator. And though the Inferno nightclub is a rather peculiar mix of groovy cats dancing and kids drinking soft drinks, the scenes there are utterly unlike anything we've seen in the show before. Anneke Wills as fun-lovin' sailor-cheerin' good time girl Polly makes Dodo look staid and old-fashioned within a single episode. And it's peculiar to note that although the BBC put the kibosh on Jackie Lane speaking in a Cockney accent when she was introduced, it's only a few months later grumpy sailor Ben Jackson can get away with it. (Someone should keep an eye on him. He beats up a fellow patron, and makes a lunge for the barmaid a huge leer on his face. I reckon his Coca-Cola has been spiked.)

All this, and John Cater (as Professor Krimpton) in a frankly *tremendous* scene fighting against his possession and insisting upon the superiority of human life over machines.

T: *Jackie Lane never did a bloody Cockney accent, it was Mancunian!* Will this torment never bloody cease? If you mention Harold Pinter when we get to The Abominable Snowmen I'll have you shot...

Other than that, though, you've hit the nail on the head. Innes Lloyd has clearly never seen the programme before... first he had a grotesque children's nightmare rewritten into a load of unthreatening parlour games, then he gave us an episode of Star Trek (albeit three months before the first Trek episode aired), and now we have a twentieth century larks in which the Doctor (sorry, "Doctor Who") gains access to everywhere with ease. If the latter isn't very convincing with what we've seen before, though, I do like it – having the Doctor trusted from the outset gets rid of lots of tedi-

ous to-ing and fro-ing whilst he proves himself and wins everyone's trust.

In terms of style, this episode is a self-consciously hip depiction of 60s life (just look at how the nightclub-owner tells the Doctor "I dig your fab gear"!). Polly is a breath of fresh air – she's funny, upbeat and stunning. And Hartnell looks wonderfully incongruous in this contemporary setting, especially when he walks the London streets in that hat (it's obviously his twentieth century hat, as we haven't seen it since An Unearthly Child). His performance in the opening scene is shockingly all over the place, though – you almost have to wonder if he's rattled because he's just seen Innes Lloyd at the other end of the studio, linking arms with Patrick Troughton and taking him up to his office for coffee and a little chat.

Is this story that made Doctor Who the programme we've come to know and love, though? Wasn't it inevitable that the series would eventually come to Earth so the viewers had some sort of investment in, or identification with, the proceedings? The Savages was a curiously detached experience, and I found it difficult to care about what was going on. The War Machines by contrast isn't perfect, but it starts to shape Doctor Who into a series that is about confronting our fears, or creating fear out of the everyday. It's a cracked mirror, one that gives us skewed reflections for comedic, satirical, frightening or entertaining effect.

Intentionally or otherwise, Innes Lloyd has happened upon that something we now take for granted: the modern setting. As a result, Doctor Who will never be the same again. The Doctor's visits to the present won't happen with a lot of frequency just yet (even in this story, the Doctor will become saddled with two *more* modern-day companions whom he can't take home because he can't pilot the TARDIS properly), but before too much longer, his returns to twentieth century Earth will become a default setting; they'll be a matter of course, of habit. The Doc returning to Earth is like me with cigarettes... I don't know *why* I do it, but if I don't do it on a regular basis, I'll get all testy.

Like you, though, I've no idea why they pronounce Wotan as "Votan". But I love the fact that he gets his own credit!

March 4th

The War Machines episode two

R: The murder of the tramp is incredibly brutal. Right up to the moment he dies, he's playing the part as a comic cameo, doing jokey coughs and pretending he's just come out of the 'ospital. The look of horror on his face, when he realises these workmen are in earnest and are actually going to kill him, is like a realisation that he's strayed into the wrong TV show; this isn't Steptoe and Son after all. And it's the very inhumanity of the death that's so memorable. Mob lynching has been a recurring trope in the third season – it was used for comic effect in The Gunfighters, and rather more chillingly in The Massacre. But right after the broadcast of The Savages, in which the elite victimise the underclasses, the destruction of the homeless man by all the people with jobs looks very deliberate. The tramp even *looks* like he's wandered off the set of The Savages, all scraggly beard and rags.

And it's that inhumanity which makes The War Machines work so well. Yes, you can laugh at its fumbled attempts to be "with it", or its hugely dated understanding of computers. And the War Machines themselves, let's face it, are as impractical and ungainly a bunch of killing machines as Wotan could devise. But it's scenes such as the one where Major Green decides to test the efficacy of a War Machine's gun by trying it out on the first hapless technician he points at – and, even more powerfully, the way that the victim just stands there without fear and gets shot – that give the story such power. And no-one is safe; just by picking up a phone you can become enslaved to Wotan's will and lose your identity. This is the very first story to exploit a contemporary setting to the full, and it hasn't taken long before the programme has insidiously turned innocent everyday objects into instruments of fear.

Michael Ferguson directs all the warehouse scenes wonderfully; there's a cold beauty to the way these workmen, their individuality sucked out of them, work like machines to produce more machines. (And this comes only a couple of stories from the debut of the Cybermen – you can see Kit Pedler's influence on the story premise seen here.) Weighed against this is the Doctor – Hartnell is superb at displaying, in contrast, real warmth and tenderness. The gentle way in which he relieves Dodo's hypnotism, in what turns out to be her last scene, is gorgeous.

And, yes, Jackie Lane's gone! Just like that! It's staggeringly abrupt. Ironically, Dodo leaves the series on something of a high, as she's far more interesting as someone possessed than she ever was when left to her own devices. Lane plays these scenes really cleverly; if there's one thing that has typified Dodo, it's that she behaves like an infant, and you can see Lane playing her character as evil merely by... not doing that, and acting her age. Dodo becomes an adult for her last gasp of screen time, and we don't like her very much. Her innocence has gone, and so is her point. Bye.

T: It's probably fair to say that The War Machines tends to be one of the more popular stories from Season Three – certainly, it has the advantage of actually existing in the archives (not that this has helped The Ark or The Gunfighters as much). And yet, for my money, this isn't in the same league as the much-less-feted The Myth Makers, The Massacre or even (yes, a controversial choice, this) The Gunfighters – not because The War Machines is *bad*, but because, apart from the direction, it's a pretty pedestrian affair. You can make some accommodation because this is something of a template for future stories, so it's a bit excusable that so many subsequent adventures did this sort of thing much better... but, er, the truth still remains that the subsequent adventures *did* do this sort of thing so much better. Script-wise (and wherever Innes Lloyd was when he wasn't watching Doctor Who, Ian Stuart Black was clearly with him), nothing much happens here, except for an aborted attempt to kidnap the Doctor and the very lengthy construction of a hugely impractical tank-monster. And poor old John Harvey, as Professor Brett, isn't just forced to do zombie acting – he's a zombie who spouts exposition at two other zombies.

Some of the elements you've already hinged on, Rob, are amongst those I'd have a go at. Look, there's a comedy tramp played by a bloody awful actor! Oh, and the newspapers already have a picture of him on file, and so can get the story in their first editions with such speed and efficiency, despite the murder happening in the early morning hours. And yes, it's a bit creepy when the workman willingly stands before the machine as it tests its gun – but he's also obliged to fall over dead when it seems to miss him completely!

Still, there's plenty of good in this – the production values are on the whole excellent, and there are some impressive film sequences, with the director choreographing everyone's movements with an eye towards interesting visuals. Ben Jackson is proving to be a sprightly addition to the series – he's polite, thoughtful, resourceful, respectful of the Doctor and played with chirpy charm by Michael Craze. And speaking only for myself, I'm very entertained by the way John Harvey provides No. 1 in what's to become an occasional series called Hadoke's Hilariously Rubbish Sci-Fi Bits. When Brett gets the line, "He must be destroyed...", his voice (for some inexplicable reason) goes up several octaves on the final word, thus speaking in a fashion people only do in science-fiction series. I find it hugely amusing that Stephen Fry does a similar thing in the futuristic segment of Blackadder's Christmas Carol, when he orders "Send them to the sprouting *chamber*!"

But by God, Rob, you're right – it was an unforgiving business, being a Doctor Who companion in the 60s. Seventeen minutes in, we get our last shot of poor, plucky Jackie Lane. Saddled with a dopey character, she was never less than enthusiastic – and while she maybe wasn't up to much as an actress, I do feel a bit sorry for the way she gets to spend her valedictory moments. Whatever your feelings towards Dodo, she deserved better than to end her time with us snoozing on a chair.

The War Machines episode three

R: There's a protracted action sequence which lasts *over five minutes* where the army take on a War Machine in a warehouse. It's the sort of stuff which will seem a bit passé during the UNIT years, but we've never seen anything like it on Doctor Who before. Michael Ferguson does wonders considering two things especially – that all the soldiers' guns lock so that

they can't actually fire, and that all the War Machine can do against them is fire a fire extinguisher and knock over crates. It ought to be ridiculous. Instead, it feels like Doctor Who from a new era, with a concentration upon the visual rather than the verbal. And it builds up to an extraordinarily effective cliffhanger, in which only the Doctor stands indomitable against the advance of the killer machine. Beautiful stuff.

And, as if to remind us we're still in 1966, there's also a painfully long scene in which Sir Charles has an *entire* phone conversation with not only the minister but the minister's secretary; it's completely from his point of view, and he says not only what the audience already know, but what he's already told the Doctor he's going to say. So it's a strange, unending painful repeat of exposition that was unnecessary the first time. I bring it up not to mock it, but to point out the strange collision in this episode between the old and the new – between the pitched battle on film that Ferguson milks for all he's worth, and the strange, clunky studio-bound drama that thinks it's still a piece of theatre. Isn't that one of the things that's so extraordinary about Hartnell's Who, that you can see the trappings of traditional TV even as it's doing its best to shake them off?

T: If I previously thought that The War Machines was a ho-hum affair, I now have to confess that if Innes Lloyd's intention was to give the series an injection of vitality, it seems to be working. The newcomers shine here – debut director Ferguson finds ways to keep all the bits of business in the warehouse (tossing and lining up guns, filling crates with ammo, etc.) interesting, and there's a great moment where Major Green whacks a worker unconscious and the War Machine tidies him up. But Anneke Wills and Michael Craze are continuing to impress too – there's a lovely connection between them when the brainwashed Polly lets Ben go, and the look she gives him suggests a lingering humanity beneath the robotic conformity. Ben himself is all fired up, full of impetuosity and urgency, and striking the right dramatic note. And while we will eventually take the military for granted on Doctor Who, in this context their presence seems exciting, modern and grown-up.

And while you've rightfully given credit to Michael Ferguson for the battle sequences, we should also give a little nod to the Doctor Who Restoration Team – they've seamlessly woven many recovered clips into the action, and have used clever zooms and other techniques to create footage where the pictures are missing. In fact, the sharpness and clarity with which these old prints are presented on DVD is sometimes extraordinary, and the quality of the film footage of the war machine in the alleyway is breathtaking too.

Finally, I should mention that this is a great episode for playing Spot the Extra (baldy Hugh Cecil and the estimable Pat Gorman both feature heavily) – which makes for a useful diversion, because if you give the script any attention whatsoever, it's clear that much of it is nonsense. The triumvirate of baddies shout the plot out in a most uninteresting fashion, and even the enthralled Polly gets in on the act, inexplicably telling Ben everything she knows, even though she acknowledges he hasn't been programmed. (Even stranger, she admits that there's no guard because nobody would want to escape – which Ben obviously does.) Still, should Wotan ever want to conquer a planet where the main industry and technology is crate based, he's onto a winner.

March 5th

The War Machines episode four

R: It's trying very, very hard – and it mostly succeeds. There's not an awful lot of story, really – one War Machine just sort of fizzles out, another gets reprogrammed and blows up Wotan – but it's the stuff *around* the plot, all the frills and fripperies, which are what make this episode interesting. The use of real TV newsreaders popping up to alert the viewers that there's a menace on the streets of London is actually rather startling. The story has very consciously avoided using real landmarks of the city, almost exactly the opposite of the way The Dalek Invasion of Earth gloated over its famous monuments; the most iconic thing seen here has been a man gunned down in a

recognisable phone box. There's a reason for that, of course – in the Dalek story the aliens had already won, so there wasn't a need for a huge number of extras slowing down the filming and incurring cost. But in spite of radio messages instructing the population to stay indoors, it'd be unreasonable to suppose that a sequence in which a War Machine came gliding over Trafalgar Square would work without a *lot* more budget.

So how does the series get around this? It shows the scale, rather brilliantly, through use of the media. It's telling that one of the very first things we see in the episode is the famous face of broadcaster Kenneth Kendall. It's not the best place in the *story* for the cameo, because the crisis hasn't started yet, and indeed Kendall's message is largely one of reassurance. But it's the best place for the episode as a whole; from this point on, you imagine the events are being played out on every TV and in every newspaper, that this is a situation really affecting the entire world stage. By halfway through the episode, you can resort to an actor on the phone pretending to be an American journalist, and a few voiceovers as people listen to the radio – it doesn't matter, because the job is done, and we've been given enough to *imagine* a scale the BBC simply can't afford.

Michael Craze is really throwing himself into the role of Doctor Who companion, even though the character has no idea that's what he's already become. He's brave and loyal and charmingly self-sacrificial. His willingness to take the risk of capturing a War Machine off the Doctor's shoulders is terrific – mostly because he tactlessly offends the Doctor in the process by saying he's too old to perform such a stunt. And it's touching the way he obsesses about Polly's safety all the time – not because he fancies her or nuffing (of course not), but because that's the bird that saved his life. He'll be great fun in the TARDIS, I think. On the face of it, Anneke Wills hasn't had much to do except get hypnotised – but again, it's the way she acts like a companion, the way she *fights* against her mind control (even though no-one else has that ability), which mark her out as something special. And it's quite clear that Innes Lloyd has no compunction about dropping Jackie Lane. There's not a single companion departure yet which hasn't tried to pluck at the heart strings – not even Adrienne Hill's, and she was only there for five episodes! But here, the Doctor is clearly hurt by Dodo not even bothering to say goodbye to his face, he remarks upon her ingratitude... and that's it, we never hear her even mentioned again. (Well, not until the fifth Doctor has his brain sucked out by the Daleks and she pops up in a little clip. So, he hadn't forgotten her after all! Bless.)

T: The visuals of this story continue to be stunning. I love the zapping of the very British phone box, and a couple of shots featuring the war machine are superb – one that's speeded up shows it moving along at a fair lick, and there's an even better one when it's reflected in a puddle beneath the spinning wheel of a recently abandoned bicycle. And if the presence of the military wasn't enough to conjure up memories of Quatermass and the Pit, the pub scene – complete with the public watching the sci-fi events unfold on television – really does. The use of the media that you've rightly highlighted is an old Nigel Kneale trick; it grounds the unbelievable in a recognisable context, and lends it scale. And not only does Kenneth Kendall add verisimilitude to the proceedings, he's joined by broadcaster Dwight Whylie – who I believe is the first black person to have a speaking part on the show.

There are a few things about this episode that I don't entirely understand – why, for instance, do the highly trained and paid military personnel defer an extremely dangerous job (albeit one that hardly requires specialist skill) to an old man and a young sailor? The real-life answer is, obviously, because the soldiers are just extras, and the Doctor and his incoming companion need more screen time, but within the fiction itself, it's harder to justify. Also, it seems odd that the War Machine enters the trap rather than just extinguishing the soldiers (and Ben) who are each seen a mere foot or so away from it. As killing machines go, Wotan's troops leave something to be desired.

Can I stop for a moment, though, and mention that something I've seen listed time and again as a goof isn't one? It's claimed that Michael Craze hauls the Doctor's cloak over the War Machine, but then knocks the end of

its gun off and has to cover his tracks by bending down, picking it up and replacing it. Nope! That's done very deliberately (after all, the camera would hardly go out of its way to highlight an error) – the clatter is the TARDIS key falling out of the Doctor's cloak, whereupon Ben has to pick it up so he and Polly can later gain access to the Ship! It's amazing how these myths get accepted so effortlessly!

And so, Dodo does indeed get barged away off screen. Welcome aboard, Ben and Polly! I just hope that for your sakes, the producer doesn't get tired of you...

Daleks Invasion Earth: 2150 AD

R: Let's be honest. On any reasonable level, this is a lot better than the TV version which inspired it. It obviously looks better for a start – the special effects, the explosions, the action sequences, they're all top notch. Gordon Flemyng is directing this as an exciting feature film, and Richard Martin is nowhere in sight. The acting is far superior across the board. Ray Brooks turns David (appearing here without the surname he had in the TV story) into a moody freedom fighter who's clearly survived so far because he's bold and brutal; Andrew Keir actually gives resistance-man Wyler the sort of character journey clearly earmarked for Jenny in the original version, so he becomes a man who is humanised by his adventures with Susie; Philip Madoc is extraordinary in only a few minutes' screen time, making his black marketeer someone very credible and very dangerous by downplaying every line he's given. And the plot is better too – it's lean and tight, it actually makes more sense, and in spite of the fact that it's less than half the running time of the original, it still finds a way of elongating the story's climax so that it feels more epic. (This results in lots of smashing scenes where Daleks are pulled magnetically through walls or down mine shafts. Great stuff.) There's an attention to detail here that's missing from The Dalek Invasion of Earth, and makes the ruined London seem much more believable: all those peeling advertisements for Sugar Puffs suggest a society which is dead, but which no-one has bothered to clean away yet.

And Bernard Cribbins is funny and heroic

and likeable in a way that, bless his heart, Roy Castle simply couldn't be in the first movie. He's a bit of a bungler is Constable Tom Campbell, it's true – but the comedy sequences he's involved in portray him as an ordinary man struggling out of his depth, not as a klutz there as light relief for the little 'uns. The food-machine scene is a development of the bit in Dr Who and the Daleks where Castle couldn't make sense of the electronic doors – both show the male hero get into scrapes with future technology. The difference with Cribbins' take on it is that it's only funny accidentally – it's Tom's desperate attempts to imitate the Robomen, and in doing so save his life, which provide the laughs. The stakes are higher, so the comedy is less forced.

But I'm going to be unreasonable anyway. I can't help it – I do rather prefer the original, clumsy and dated as it is. The Robomen on TV look crap compared to these ones, who marching along in perfect time in PVC, and blast away with their explosive ray guns – but it's that very crapness which reminds us that these are just uncared-for corpses being used as an easy work force. It's cheaper and rougher and dirtier in Hartnell's Who, and that's mostly because they couldn't afford anything better – but it also meant that the ruined Earth was an expression of real despair, not just a background for an exciting action adventure.

And I cared more for the characters in the original. I can't help it – I miss Barbara and Ian and Susan, and seeing these paler counterparts (Louise?... even Peter Cushing seems to forget about his niece, and hardly bothers to express concern for her during the whole movie!) only reminds us that there isn't time in a movie like this to give them any background. It's typified by a scene in which Tom is relieved to see his fellow captive from the Dalek spaceship, and calls out to him as "Craddock" – but there hasn't been more than a few lines between the pair nearly an hour earlier into the film, and certainly they never exchanged names on screen. When you see the end credits, with characters like "Man with carrier bag" popping up amidst all the unidentifiable surnames, you really need a few "Man left to be robotised on spaceship" or "Man who makes a break for it and gets shot"s to give you any idea who they are.

I'm being churlish. It's a good, spectacular movie – and it utterly fills its remit, to give us a taste of a big-screen Dalek adventure on a scale and with a budget we'd never have seen on television. It's hardly surprising there's a bit of a trade-off with character depth. It's charming the way the original TV adventure made so much of seeing Daleks on location parading around famous landmarks – the movie doesn't even *try* to do a sequence at Trafalgar Square, because its visuals are already in a different league to anything Verity Lambert could impress us with. (It's interesting perhaps that the only big visual image it replicates, that of the Dalek rising out of the Thames, counts for nothing in the movie – the big reveal on the TV screen is such small fry, it's as if Gordon Flemyng doesn't even realise it's meant to be so iconic.) It's ultimately a matter of personal taste that I find myself hankering after the black and white original, Slyther and all – but I can't deny that the Aaru movie is genuinely very good.

It's such a shame that this wasn't a hit. I'd have loved to have seen what they'd have done with The Chase. (I'd bet they'd have cast Ronnie Corbett this time, maybe as Abraham Lincoln.)

T: Rewatching this movie is very nostalgic for me – I saw it many times on TV, usually after realising I'd just missed a broadcast of the first Peter Cushing film. Then a friend of mine opened a video shop and got hold of this, long before the TV series started being released commercially, I think (or certainly, before they were affordable). This movie is now so cosily familiar, I can even anticipate some of the music cues. And I'm not a late clamberer onto the Cribbins bandwagon either – he'd always been a favourite in our household, long before he won our hearts as Wilfred Mott. He pitches his comedy and his drama just right in this, and proves why he's a national treasure. In fact, I might watch his Fawlty Towers episode later – he's bloody marvellous in that too. Thinking of Cribbins' performances just makes my heart warm, and puts a gentle smile on my face.

My limited ability to watch Doctor Who growing up caused some re-evaluation of this film, though – I distinctly remember when a friend of mine saw The Dalek Invasion of

Earth at Longleat, and was so excited to tell me that the "proper" Robomen didn't have black uniforms, but were just ordinary people with robotic headgear. It deferred some retrospective class onto something that actually predated the assumed images we already had in our minds (both from this movie and the Target novelisation of the TV story, which misleadingly had what looked like a Blake's 7 Federation trooper on its cover). What never paled for me, however, was the way the Cushing film mounted effects shots, exteriors and action sequences so much more successfully than the TV version could ever hope to do – there's a tracking shot in the Dalek base in Bedford that's giddily impressive, the fights and stunts are very well done, and the Dalek spaceship is incredible (especially the way its two sections spin in different directions). The Dalek rising from the Thames does so at one hell of a lick, and is undermined only by the fact that the score begins to sound, at this point, uncannily like the theme to Police Squad!

By no means is this movie perfect – the intelligence test is hardly The Krypton Factor, and Tom runs through the spaceship looking for "the girl" (Louise), despite the fact that he's no reason to know that she's there in the first place. And whilst I adore the music, the opening title sequence is a huge contrast to the eerie, experimental TV-series blobbyness as it amounts to, in all its glory, some coloured water swirling down a plughole!

But I do love almost everything about this film – it's exciting, well staged, funny and economical, and it reminds me of winter afternoons in front of a warm log fire. I could simply list the brilliant moments that stick in my head – the rebel getting tugged back as a Roboman whip wraps itself around his face, the low-angled shot of the imposing Dalek frighteningly looking down at Tom Campbell as he escapes from the mine, and even the crap Roboman with the wonky mask, who sits next to Cribbins in the comedy lunchtime scene.

As you can doubtless tell, I'll probably never be able to view this movie with anything approaching objectivity, as it makes my heart beat faster just to think about it. So I'll just close here by saying that for all the happiness this movie gives me, I've never considered it to

be proper Doctor Who, and still don't. Don't get me wrong, it's an impressive achievement (it's Doctor Who – in the cinema!), but the people making it weren't versed in the history, continuity and essential ingredients that made my favourite programme so special. They actually refer to him as "Doctor Who", for starters. And they'd *never* do that in the TV series, would they?

By the way, I just realised – you're right, Rob! A movie version of The Chase would have been brilliant! Imagine the trailer: "Robin Askwith is Malsan – the Aridian with a confession to make!"

March 6th

The Smugglers episode one

R: The Doctor's got two new companions – and for the first time, the newbies outnumber him. Which means, in wonderfully human fashion, that even though Ben and Polly by degrees have to adjust to the impossibility of the TARDIS and the fact it's taken them from London in 1966, they still are more readily disposed to believe each other's theories about what's going on than listen to the man who actually knows. Some might claim this is a rather unbelievable way for them to behave – but I've been on package holidays to Crete, and if you've ever been on a tour coach where every passenger is more likely to listen to their fellow tourists than the native, then this will seem very familiar. They adapt to things by degrees. The fact they can accept that they've been transported in seconds to the coast at Cornwall, but still refuse to take the Doctor seriously when he suggests they've got back in time, and insist on looking for a train station, is delightfully funny. And Hartnell's Doctor is by turns both frustrated and amused with their antics. Which seems only fair.

It's a new season, and rather cleverly, we're looking at the entire series through fresh eyes. The Doctor is on hand to explain the TARDIS, but no-one's really listening. And so we're plopped down into a story which any seasoned viewer is likely to find fairly familiar fare – but it's energised by the reactions of two new time travellers who react to the whole thing rather like tourists. I especially love the way that Ben and Polly make fun of all the patrons at the inn as if they're just amusing characters in a pageant. And that's what makes the episode so clever. It deceives us with a deliberately slow pace, inviting us too to relax with a pretty low-key adventure – and then in the final ten minutes ignites the action. The Doctor is captured by pirates, and Ben and Polly are arrested for murder. You get the feeling that the story has suddenly sped up without warning, and turned upon the Doctor's all too complacent new pals.

T: The Smugglers is probably one of the least-remembered Doctor Who stories, but I actually think about its first episode quite a lot. As you know, I'm just getting used to that there London, and the Tube especially. I still get that odd feeling where some bizarre impulse tempts me too close to the platform edge – where I dare myself to tiptoe nearer and toy with danger, looking onto the track while simultaneously being terrified of falling off. The connection my mesmerising Tube experience has with this episode? Terence De Marney, who here plays the Churchwarden, died a few short years after making this story when he was accidentally knocked into the path of a Tube train. It's a little morbid, I know, but he's always in the back of my mind as I struggle and tussle through the anonymous throng.

Otherwise, the new TARDIS crew makes for interesting watching (or, rather, listening). Ben and Polly are gloriously game, with her deciding to "like it or lump it" and Ben appreciating the potential virtues of the pub! They're a breath of fresh, funky air, and I adore Polly's costume, even if it makes everyone mistake her for a boy. (Well, if *she* looks like a bloke, I'm not as firmly heterosexual as I'd hitherto thought!)

William Hartnell, sadly, isn't entirely in command of himself – he fluffs a fair bit in this episode, and even gives up halfway though one sentence as De Marney decides to plough on regardless, rather than wait for him to finish. Indeed, at one point, in relation to a question he's just been asked, Hartnell gives all the wrong stresses in the sentence "We don't come from this part of the country." But, there are still traces of what makes him such a special

Doctor, such as his conflicting emotions when he muses that he'd thought he might be alone again, and contrives to sound cheery and wistful at the same time. He also picks up on the Churchwarden's plight, gently pressing him and offering assistance – "You appear to be afraid, Sir, can we help?" That's the Doctor in a nutshell.

For all Hartnell's muck-ups though, De Marney commits the major one, as he gets one of the names wrong in the critical piece of plot info he gives the Doctor. (They could have revised later episodes to accommodate this, but it seems that no-one bothered.) Although the Churchwarden doesn't survive past episode one, his character does offer a good piece of psychology: he constantly refers to his Christianity to remind himself that he's *now* a "good" man, but his reliance on alcohol suggests someone who is haunted, deep down, by his criminal past. He gets drunk to hide his shame and fear, and it's a quite frightening element in an episode that's awash with ripe language and hearty villainy. We shouldn't write off this story as a harmless historical outing; there's a real dark undercurrent to it.

The Smugglers episode two

R: The Doctor is clearly delighted to find out he's caught up in a smuggling adventure – and his enthusiasm is infectious! The way he trades off the gentleman pretensions of Captain Pike, and knows what part to play in ensuring he gets a share of any buried treasure, is absolutely gorgeous. When Hartnell gets the chance to seize on a bit of comedy, there's really no-one better, and it's just great that here in his penultimate story, he's given a final chance to indulge himself. Captain Pike and Cherub make a terrific double act; their mock disgust at Polly and the standards of modern-day youth is absolutely priceless.

Polly and Ben too acquit themselves well, escaping from their guard by making a voodoo doll of him. The best bit is when Ben, quite cruelly, tells the stable-hand Tom that by setting him free, he now too is an agent of Satan and "one of us"... It's all very funny, but it does a first in Doctor Who – and that's to assume that a character is a bit stupid simply because he comes from ye olden days and therefore doesn't know much. It's a somewhat disturbing sign; we've seen so many historical periods in the series now, and they've been treated in such a variety of tones – but never quite this smugly. The closest we've come before now was Barbara's patronising attitude towards the Aztecs, where she felt that by virtue of her modern-day morals, she could better an entire society. And look what happened to her. Up to this point, no matter whether it was played straight or as a comedy, the history settings in the show have been something to which the TARDIS crew had to adapt – they've never before been able to exploit a superiority just by dint of coming from the 1960s.

What do you think of this, Mr Hadoke? There's a whole bit in your Moths stage play where you talk about this very modern-day arrogance towards the past – did this grate on you as much as it did with me?

T: Yes, it did, but only because I read your email prior to watching the episode, and was thus on the lookout for it. I'm not sure I would have made the connections that you did, but yes – the voodoo doll really is a terribly convoluted way of facilitating an escape, when a quick distraction and a whack on the head would have sufficed. The method they use is a bit mocking of poor old Tom, and makes Ben come across as a little cruel.

Everyone involved in this story seems to be enjoying themselves, and because they're entertaining *us* too, it's easy to get carried away with the fun and frolics. So far, The Smugglers is proving to be a "jolly" romp where the villains, behind their smiles, are still palpably dangerous, and the threat of violence lurks beneath all the bonhomie. It would be a stretch to call this highly innovative, and nobody is ever going to hold it up as a shining example of the series, but it does nothing wrong, trots along quite merrily, and is played with plenty of gusto by a colourful cast.

And can I digress to add that one of the cast has become unwittingly responsible for another actor-based myth about Doctor Who? David Blake Kelly, here playing the landlord Jacob Kewper, is in fact the same David Blake Kelly who appeared as the captain of the *Mary Celeste* in The Chase (hence them having exactly the same name!). He is not, however,

David Kelly from Robin's Nest and Waking Ned (hence them having slightly different names). Sadly, this isn't what it says on Wikipedia or IMDb... where someone well versed in Internet matters (but clueless about Doctor Who and actors) has gone to great lengths to suggest that David Kelly temporarily changed his name to that of an already existing actor for four weeks, on only the one occasion in a 50 year career, purely so Doctor Who fans can claim that the bloke who played O'Reilly in The Builders episode of Fawlty Towers did a Doctor Who. By that astounding piece of logic, the Paul Whitsun-Jones who here plays The Squire isn't at all the same Paul Whitsun-Jones who appears in The Mutants, but is actually Paul Jones from Manfred Mann.

I don't know why I get so annoyed at stuff like this – perhaps it's because, like the coveted Avery's treasure, the clues are in the names. The names! Needless to say, I've been on IMDb to change it, and have done my little part to bring truth to the world. (Don't all thank me at once...)

March 7th

The Smugglers episode three

R: And now the Doctor's up to it, escaping from the stupid pirate by predicting the future with a pack of playing cards! There's no odder image than seeing this man of science while away his hours with a spot of tarot reading.

One of the funniest things about the comedy is the way in which this story's writer, Brian Hayles, allows Captain Pike and Cherub to eclipse the small-time villainy of the Squire and his cohorts. You get the impression that the Squire is really rather proud of his smuggling activities; he's probably the sort of man nowadays who'd get a vicarious thrill from speeding his car in built-up areas, or from downloading illegal videos. He *enjoys* being a bit of a rogue, cheerfully showing off where he hides his loot to the first pair of strangers who come sniffing around looking appreciative. When he realises he's been consorting with honest-to-God actual *criminals* – the sort who'd skewer a fellow pirate then wipe the blood off with a lace handkerchief – the smile is wiped from his face. And cleverly, it means that for all their humour, the pirates come across as being genuinely quite threatening in contrast. The Squire is a hypocrite and a bureaucrat, but Captain Pike is psychotic.

This really does feel at moments like it's reinforcing the series' main credo for any new viewers who might be tuning into the start of the season. Ben is all for escaping in the TARDIS the first chance he can, claiming that the events here are nothing to do with them. Does that remind you of anyone from the early days? But now it's the Doctor who insists they stay and see the story out, telling his new friends about the "moral obligation" he feels. We'll get odd flashes of the Doctor wanting to duck out of adventures again – it happens in a couple of weeks' time, actually – but from now on, more or less, the template for Doctor Who is clear. And William Hartnell has never had the opportunity to express it quite so baldly.

T: With all of this story missing from the archives, I find myself drawn to the few surviving clips of it – initially cut out by the Australian censor and left in a box somewhere, then recovered in the mid-90s – and am looking at Jamaica's death scene. We'll probably never know why the censor objected to Pike's "Twill be a merry night" line, as nothing scary seems to be happening at that point. But if nothing else, the bit a couple of seconds later, where Pike wipes Jamaica's blood off his... um... pike is gruesomely effective (especially as Jamaica's eyes coldly stare open in death). It also reminds me of the connection between Pike's name and the old Tony Hawks joke, i.e. "What was Captain Hook's name before he lost his hand?" And the other censor clip from this episode is Kewper's demise, meaning our Australian cousins must have been slightly confused as the credits rolled, having been robbed of the actual cliffhanger! (Funny how censors don't take that sort of thing into account – it wasn't that many years ago that the Buffy the Vampire Slayer story Smashed, in its pre-watershed broadcast, lost the Buffy-Spike sex scene that ends the episode.)

The irony here is that for an episode that lost some scenes for violent content, everyone *talks* about being a gentleman – a rather clever little theme Brian Hayles seems to have slipped

in. The Doctor is versed in certain practices which pass as gentlemanly in the company of rogues, Pike enjoys the status and trappings of gentlemanly behaviour, and the Squire kids himself that he's a cut above the common criminals with whom he consorts; it's all a slyly witty comment on overblown egos and pompous villainy.

And it's a nifty turn of events that the revenue man Blake is allowed to free Ben and Polly thanks to his own guile, as it's refreshing that a guest character from the past doesn't need one of our heroes to educate them (not to mention that it's a nice contrast to the treatment of Tom last week). There's an urgency and authority in John Ringham's performance as Blake, and we're very lucky to have him in a role that seems to consist mostly of dashing about on a horse. (Maybe it was the holiday in Cornwall that convinced him to take the part. We used to holiday in Cornwall when I was a kid and it was lovely; there was winkle picking on the beach, clotted cream and my refusal to swim in the sea because I'd seen Jaws and was terrified.)

Oh, and let's gloss over the fact that the Doctor's tarot readings all turn out to be correct, and that everyone who goes looking for Avery's treasure winds up dead, shall we? Otherwise, you'd think it was a deliberate bit of foreshadowing on the production team's part for what's going to happen in the next story...

The Smugglers episode four

R: Hmm. It's honestly a little hard to know what to make of this one. The scope of the series is changing – it's now becoming increasingly normal to have an episode made up of stunt action sequences and fighting. And there's an awful *lot* of fighting in this episode; according to well-worn interview anecdotes, this involved stuntmen who'd get killed get out of shot, then put on some different clothes and re-enter the fray! Whilst watching the gunfight at the OK Corral, or the army's attack on the War Machines at the warehouse, I considered how lucky we were to be able to *see* these sustained scenes of fisticuffs, because we'd be lost if we were relying upon nothing more than a soundtrack and a set of blurred telesnaps. It's only with this episode that the luck runs out... for all I can tell, amid all the shoutings and death gurgles, Michael Godfrey's Captain Pike sounds as demented as he should be. It's great that a pirate who was so down-played to an assumed level of gentlemanly sophistication should come across as such a nutter when the chips are down.

T: Like you, I can't think of much to say because the video is missing. There seems to be lots fighting and charging about on horses – and of course boats and coasts always look good on screen and are unusual sights in Doctor Who.

The characters, at least, hold my attention irrespective of the action sequences. Cherub is such a gleeful villain that one feels a bit cheated when he gets nobbled early – especially as we get that rather tiresome trait of one villain dispatching another, and thereby doing the hero's work for him. George A Cooper and Michael Godfrey (respectively Cherub and Pike) have both given great performances – they've had fun without sending the show up, and it's been a delight to boo and hiss them.

And Cherub isn't alone in having a face-off with Pike – the Doctor and the Squire get the chance to do so as well. What's interesting about this is that the Doctor, even when bluffing Pike and playing for time, rejects the opportunity to acquire cash and is firm about the sanctity of human life. Strictly speaking, he's only stalling so Blake can come in and defeat the baddie, but the Doctor's presence is vital. Being exposed to the Doctor's generosity of spirit has made the Squire see the error of his ways, and he's the one who prevents Pike from killing the Doctor and emerges a reformed character. (That's very Russell T Davies, that.) This section of the adventure, and last week's "moral obligation" bit, are really most unexpected. They've managed to smuggle something quite fundamental and lasting about the series into one of the least showy and venerated adventures.

At the end, the Doctor buggers off before anyone can say thank you. This is becoming a habit. Speaking of habits, did the baddies *really* have to be smuggling tobacco? It's been 44 years since this story was made, and yet

everyone involved seems intent on reminding me about smoking!

March 8th

The Tenth Planet episode one

R: Well, we *know* this one is special. It's the introduction of the Cybermen, and Hartnell's swan song, so it's hard to rid the story of all its weighty significance and look at it objectively. But I think, even though I'm straining to do so – here I go – that it *still* stands out as something distinctive.

For a start, there's that setting. The snow effects are pretty good, and it looks all so wonderfully bleak; this is the first time the series has given us what is going to be a bit of a hoary old chestnut – the isolated base under siege. You almost couldn't get more isolated, and the way the episode turns the North Pole into a landscape as alien as anything we've ever seen before is very clever. And then there's the time: 1986! It's another first, a dip into a *near* future, which means that everybody can look normal and talk normal and have normal concerns – but that when the gloves are off, the events that take place here can be as far reaching as those on a different world. The series can have its cake and eat it, playing with contemporary characters but without the need to put all the toys back in the box as neatly as it did with The War Machines.

And just listen to all that variety of accents and nationalities, and even – my God – different skin colours! It doesn't matter particularly that the cast are stereotyping the types of foreigners that they're depicting – that we get a horny Italian who sings Verdi, or an American who shouts a lot and calls the Doctor "pop" – because it's a forgiveable shorthand to demonstrate that this story has truly international consequences. It's helped by all the maps in Wigner's office, let alone that there's someone in African dress. It all contributes to an atmosphere of world concern never yet felt in Doctor Who before. And this is compounded by the scenes on Zeus Four, in which the extremely realistic acting from Earl Cameron (playing a Yank) and Alan White (an Aussie) as the space pilots who begin to panic as they lose control of their spacecraft make for some of the tensest scenes seen in the Hartnell era. And all this achieved by two actors, always static, sitting in a couple of armchairs side by side...

The appearance of Mondas, the tenth planet, too is a highlight. A couple of stories ago, we were asked to be in awe of a computer that could calculate square roots – now, for the first time in ages, there is a real sense of intrigue and wonder in the programme. That planet appearing on the screen, that false Earth, is a haunting image. It's the best introduction any alien race has had in the series since the Daleks, and it's a great deal more interesting. As the American sergeant blasts away in panic at the creatures moving towards him through the snow, there truly is a sense of something momentous happening in the programme.

T: Well, this is certainly *different*... Gerry Davis – here co-writing this story with Kit Pedlar – ultimately went off to work in America, and you can see his predilection for American-style TV here. It's all military, macho, space faring stuff. The presence of "Yanks" (including John Brandon, playing a sergeant) in the cast grounds the episode somehow, making it feel more like a prosaic action/adventure than a twee space opera. Having Americans playing Americans over here in Britain tends to make everything more realistic (as the man who wrote Dalek, I'm sure you'd agree)... but then Robert Beatty saunters in as General Cutler, and demonstrates that having Canadians playing Americans does the same trick.

The whole presentation of this is solid, realistic and less fantastical than usual; everyone is dressed relatively normally, so the setting is immediately plausible. The part of me that used to petulantly defend the series against all the slights it suffered in the dark years – particularly with regards its production values – loves this grounded solidity. But another part of me – the one that's rediscovered the magic of this era by doing this exercise – is starting to miss what separated the programme from other TV: its strangeness. Up until recently, Doctor Who was interesting because it was a bit weird; even some of the historicals had a mysterious, frighteningly alien aspect. Not any more, though. For all of the rollicking jeopardy we saw in The Smugglers, the bravura

characters and situations therein were recognisable types. Under Doctor Who's new regime, the past (or in this case, the near future) may be another country, but it comes with a map and interpreter thrown in for free.

That this episode works at all is mostly down to the director, Derek Martinus. The camerawork is slick; he keeps everything moving and doesn't indulge in frivolity. The bustle of the control room is conveyed very effectively, with over-lapping dialogue and convincing bustle. I like little touches like one of the astronauts, Schultz, being referred to as "Blue" (Australian slang for redheads, if I remember the mini-series Anzacs correctly). They use his surname when more formality is required – because not even your friends always address you in the same manner do they Rob, Robert, Mr Shearman? It's little things like this that help us to buy the outlandish; the low-key interactions between the two astronauts, as well as their colloquial dialogue, is bang on the money.

And isn't the music interesting? The infamous piece of stock music named "Space Adventure" is here used for the Cyber-march, but not the part of the piece that will become the norm for the Cybermen. Instead, we get the opening, suspenseful build-up (it's even laid over the reveal of Mondas, but at a slower speed). And in that same scene...

Hurrah! The moment arrives... as the creatures march through the snow, there's that pan-up from their bare hands – which are impervious to the cold – to those odd faces which flirt between the frightening and the ridiculous. It returns that sense of strangeness to a show that recently has been a little more down to Earth than we've come to expect. I *love* the cliffhanger here, and could do with more of this type of eeriness, please!

Why, it's enough to nearly make me forget that one of the soldiers was having a fag (this is getting beyond a joke, now).

The Tenth Planet episode two

R: The Cybermen are great! By later standards, of course, they look very primitive – but that's precisely the point. There's something rather distasteful about the way they proclaim they are the superior race in all their dubious splendour of awkward plastic frames and cloth skull faces. When you see later Cybermen talk about their desire to upgrade the human race, you can perhaps see their point – in their metal robot suits, they *do* look pretty impressive. But this bunch are all the more horrifying because they look like they've been cobbled together by machines with no appreciation of beauty or elegance – such things, of course, are unimportant. To be turned into an Earthshock Cyberman would be pretty cool. To be turned into one from The Tenth Planet would be obscene.

I love their voices too. Nick Briggs told me of the time he played the Mondas Cybermen voices for a Big Finish story, and the way that Peter Davison and Sarah Sutton fell around laughing at the strange sing-song he imitated. But again, it feels like the *parody* of human conversation, all the inflection put into the wrong place; the English language has been turned into something grotesque and alien. And that's all the more emphatic because for all the terrible things they say – for all that they kill and let people die – they're incredibly *polite* about it. "That really was most unfortunate, you should not have done that," says the leader, a little like he learned how to talk from a training film for waiters. The Cybermen have really only seemed properly emotionless *once*, and it's here, in this story, where every threat comes out as something vague and matter-of-fact.

The deaths of Schultz and Williams are so simply conveyed, the monitor screens going blank to signify that Zeus Four has exploded. It's all the more moving for that. Indeed, death is a serious business for this story. The way that the camera lingers just that little bit too long on the soldiers killed by the Cybermen at the top of the episode, their corpses already getting buried beneath the snow; the wonderful smoke effect that comes from a body shot by the Cyberman's gun; best of all, the way that Ben is truly appalled that by taking the Cyberman's weapon from him, he's obliged to shoot him dead – a Cyberman cannot feel fear, so cannot be intimidated. I could say that there's something nicely apt about a Cyberman being blinded by something as frivolous and human as a movie in a projector – but I dare say I'm just taking the metaphor too far.

T: I remember being shocked as a kid when I read the novelisation to this story – it had "The First Exciting Adventure with the Cybermen" on the front cover, and yet it was hard for me to rationalise that statement with the cloth-faced creatures depicted in the illustration. And yet... I think they're *brilliant* for all the reasons you outline above. We're Doctor Who fans, so our default mode is to look for existential body horror where others would mock primitive technology. To put it another way, we don't allow an arrogant modern perspective to colour the impact of these impressive creatures. The Cybermen's voices *could* sound silly, yes, if you were inclined to take it that way, but there's something very apt about its distortion of our speech patterns and the almost benign computerised lilt. It's like being threatened by a Speak & Spell machine.

And what about those open mouths that the Mondasians have?! No wonder they don't bother to synch up the voices – the technology makes the sound variation, so lip movement is redundant. This might initially look a bit laughable, but why *wouldn't* manufactured speech be issued in this way? Besides, it makes them look all the more like dead men walking. The only shame here is that the Cybermen don't know how to pronounce – of all the words at their disposal! – "cybernetic". It's like Monoids being unable to properly say "waddle".

It's also a bit eerie that these Cybermen are so *polite* compared to the ones to follow... certainly, they seem to keep inviting the humans to Mondas in a jolly way that suggests tea, cakes and perhaps a cucumber sandwich. In addition to this anomalous social etiquette, one of the Cybermen has one of the most ridiculous names I've ever heard: "Shav". Granted, all of these Cybermen have pretty rubbish names, but you can at least rationalise the likes of "Krail" because there's something a bit metallic about it, and while "Talon" simultaneously sounds scary and a bit stupid, you know can tell how they got there. But "Shav"? I've no idea what the thinking was behind that one.

As for the humans that inhabit Snowcap Base... well, you know how I wrote last episode that this all seemed a bit American? Here it almost goes too far in that direction, as we get the dreadful cliché of the bullish commander finding out that his son has gone up in the second capsule. This is a very, very silly and spurious addition to the script, I have to say – all we need to discover now is that they haven't spoken for several years, or that the son is engaged to Barclay's daughter. But if General Cutler's motives seem a bit wooden, there are some lovely little touches of realism in his control room – Barclay has a drink, Cutler yells at him, and Dyson asks off camera if he's all right. That sort of thing would only normally happen if Barclay was about to snap under pressure, but here it's just a little moment of truth that helps build up the drama. And Dudley Jones, playing Dyson, also sells what's a very strong line for this programme – I'm quite shocked to hear him say "Oh, for God's sake, Barclay!" The new production team may have rejected the offbeat experimentation sought by the previous regime, but they do know little boys get excited by tough, grown-up language and situations.

March 9th

The Tenth Planet episode three

R: It's the penultimate outing for Hartnell's Doctor – and he doesn't even appear. The actor fell ill during rehearsals, necessitating a quick rewrite. In retrospect, his absence is rather galling; give it a few episodes, and I know I'll be missing this first incarnation like mad, and in his dying fall, I want him to get as much screen time as possible. (It'd be unthinkable to have any other Doctor end his tenure with so slight an appearance – even poor old Colin, knocking his head against the console, gets a better build-up than this.) But even though it's an accident, it does suggest that something very *wrong* is happening to the Doctor, which at least will make his departure less abrupt. And Hartnell's loss is Michael Craze's gain. He takes over a lot of the Doctor's lines, and his character gets an added depth it sorely needs, becoming the focus of the rebellion against General Cutler. (There's a lovely moment when Dudley Jones, playing the scientist Dyson, warns Cutler that "the old man may be right" – clearly he didn't get the rewrites!)

So the Doctor is missing – but, strangely enough, the Cybermen are barely in this either. They get one beautiful sequence where they're massacred in the snow; director Derek Martinus ensures they die so gracefully, you almost feel sorry for them. And that shift of allegiance seems apt this week. The enemy now is, for the moment, not a race that by losing their emotions have ceased to be human, but General Cutler – a man whose emotional concerns for his son have blinded him to reason. It's a terribly clever conceit, and Robert Beatty does a fantastic job making Cutler both a dangerous warmonger and a loving father who can hardly bear to listen to his son's jokes when he first talks to him over the tannoy. As Ben struggles through ventilation shafts trying to prevent an ill-advised attack on the Cybermen, and advising everyone that their best line of defence is to wait, I'm struck by how much a volte-face this is from Doctor Who's usual stance. Time and time again, whether it's Ian persuading the Thals into action against the Daleks, or Vicki leading the Xerons into revolution, or Steven urging the humans to fight the Monoids, Doctor Who has always suggested that active effort is a stronger force than passive acceptance. And quite understandably so – this is an *action* series after all. It's a mark of just how odd The Tenth Planet is that it's pushing so hard in the opposite direction.

T: It's a testament to the quality of the previous episode that I got so carried away with it, I forgot to acknowledge that it was the last full episode with Hartnell's Doctor that we can actually see. I should have given Hartnell a valedictory nod – I'm like that, I salute magpies and everything.

Without Hartnell and the Cybermen though, the cracks really start to appear in this episode. If all the central characters have to do is wait for matters to resolve themselves, then they're probably being invaded by the stupidest creatures in the universe. And if your invasion plan leads to your own destruction and you haven't picked up on that, it obliterates any potential for menace you may have. It's like being invaded by those kamikaze blokes at the end of Life of Brian. Or held hostage by lemmings. That overriding problem aside, there's much to enjoy here. Derek Martinus continues to be game, and just about successfully sells what's happening to us. He's helped immeasurably by a solid cast, the best of whom is the undemonstrative, plausibly professional and likeable David Dodimead (playing Barclay), who keeps things real whilst selling the jeopardy. Plus... hooray for the first major use of ventilation shafts, as Ben attempts to disable the rocket! They're not just adopting clichés, this production team, they're establishing a few of them too, which is no mean feat.

Given the developments in the next episode, I suppose you could say that William Hartnell's illness here was serendipitous... the Doctor's collapse is incorporated into the script relatively simply, and it helps to foreshadow the astonishing transformation that's going to happen in episode four. This isn't some random instance of getting the Doctor out of the way for a bit (such as his suddenly passing out at the start of The Dalek Invasion of Earth episode four, or all the times Troughton will be knocked unconscious); it's part and parcel of one of the greatest make-overs the series will ever get.

The Tenth Planet episode four

R: It's a shame; the Cybermen were much more interesting as something amoral rather than predictably evil. Previously, they actively wanted to help humanity become like them – now they're just thugs who want to blow up a planet. (And although their sing-song voices were weird and eerie when their intentions were so much more ambiguous, they really don't suit the galactic conquerors they are here. The high-pitched Cyberleader Gern exulting from an office in Geneva that he's master of the world is very, *very* funny indeed.) And there's not an awful lot of tension to the episode, as we know that Mondas is going to destroy itself. Having established *how* the story is going to be resolved, the only suspense comes from finding out *when* it's going to happen. And it'd have been a pretty safe bet that it'd happen just a few minutes before the end of the episode. Oh, look. It did!

But of course, we don't care much about such things as plot or monsters by the end of the episode. That must be the strongest,

strangest cliffhanger the series has shown yet – the lights in the TARDIS going mad, the Doctor falling to the ground... and suddenly, Hartnell's gone. What's astonishing is how little attempt there is to make this remotely reassuring. Ben is indeed put out by the Doctor's behaviour, saying that he's lost his sense of humour – and as he shuts himself away in the TARDIS, there's a real sense that he's entirely forgotten his new friends and may well abandon them at the South Pole. Certainly, they're nothing to do with this transformation he's undergoing, and he only lets them witness it as an afterthought. When so much has happened over the last three seasons to shape Hartnell's Doctor into someone grandfatherly and cuddly, it seems wonderfully apt that in his last few minutes' screen time, he's as alien and unknowable and dangerous as he's ever been. And Hartnell is typically brilliant, finding even in his last gasp new ways to play the part – he's driven and insane when released from the Cyberman's spaceship, almost as if he were reeling drunk. Just about every other regeneration sequence (not that we'll call it that yet, of course) has allowed a moment of sentiment, a chance for the audience and the companion to say goodbye to the Doctor. Tragic or triumphant, only here is it sold to us as something *frightening.* Doctor Who is doing something very brave again, all of a sudden. Better hold on tight.

T: Here at the end of the Hartnell era, I'm flooded with mixed emotions. In the first place, I'm in disbelief that the BBC managed to hang onto last week's Doctor- and Cybermen-lite episode, but they misplaced episode four, which is a milestone! The fact that it's gone seems both a criminal shame and, to be fair, symptomatic of just how much television at the time was regarded as virtually unrepeatable and inherently disposable. It's such a marked departure from the world we live in now, where, for instance, the DVD of *Torchwood: Children of Earth* was on sale the week after broadcast.

I'm also struggling a bit to keep up with the technobabble at work here. I'm quite happy with such made-up terminology if it facilitates something exciting, adventurous, satirical, moving or witty, but a whacking great planet travelling through space – that conveniently takes the Cybermen with it when it melts – really doesn't do it for me. (You could have anticipated this reaction, I'm sure, Rob, after I made your ears bleed after the transmission of Journey's End.) All of this seems such a shame because there are some *really* neat concepts in this story – a Tenth Planet is a nice idea, as are the Cybermen. But in implementation, everything seems to fall apart in the final episode. Even the supporting cast seem to undergo personality transplants – Cutler goes from solid, gravelly authority to drooling ham, Gern the Cyberleader just sounds daft and Dyson has turned into an irritating whinger. A bright spot, though, is that the technician Haines doesn't die as he does in the book, poor chap. I always felt sorry for him, as he goes uncredited in the cast list (he's played by Freddie Eldrett, whose partner, Philip Gilbert, played Tim in The Tomorrow People). Dying would be bad enough, but dying and not getting a namecheck seems horribly ignominious.

But most of all, I feel sorrow that William Hartnell – who made such a commitment to Doctor Who, enabled its early success and has given me such great enjoyment over these three seasons – is here pushed out of the series with so little ceremony. I will credit that the final TARDIS scene re-injects some of the oddness I've been missing – the Ship is once again this weird, unsettling environment, in a way it hasn't been for a couple of years! But this doesn't paper over the fact that the Hartnell Doctor doesn't perform a brave or clever act in his final adventure; instead, it's as if he bows out after having a kip. Even at the end, Hartnell manages to infuse the proceedings with some nuance – his statement that, "I must go now" is wonderfully laced with double meaning, and is quite powerful – but he seems to be finding such depth in spite of the script, not because of it.

And astonishingly, no explanation is given regarding what's happening with the regeneration – not even a perfunctory "Look, he's changing!" from Ben or Polly – and the event is so whited out and in such extreme close-up that, had I been watching on first broadcast, I'm not altogether sure I'd have known what the hell was going on. (I probably shouldn't complain about that, though – I've been wanting more mysteriousness in the series, and God knows, this passes the mark.)

For all the nice things I'm sure I'll say about Patrick Troughton, I'm going to miss William Hartnell. Watching his performance from beginning to end has been a real eye opener, and even if I don't buy that his muddled delivery was a deliberate acting choice, it frequently didn't do any harm, and he tended to successfully ad lib himself out of trouble, or to rely on the rock solid support he was given by William Russell and then Peter Purves. He was very good at some forms of comedy, and he had a natural ability to flit between the imperious and the gentle. He certainly gives a *great* performance when you consider the arduous production schedule and limited recourse to retakes in this era. It would be enough to send most modern actors scurrying back to their Pilates classes, but Hartnell was largely up to the task.

And in the end, he generously came back to hand the role over to his successor... and then wound up collapsing on the floor of the TARDIS, and changing for what seems to be the most spurious of reasons. They may as well have saved him the bother, not had him back at all, and just got Troughton to lie on the floor and put on a wig.

March 10th

The Power of the Daleks episode one

R: The first thing that Patrick Troughton does is thoughtlessly step into a dead man's shoes and assume his identity. Whether it's William Hartnell's Doctor, or Martin King's Examiner, it comes to much the same thing; watch out for this man, the story says, he's an impostor. It's remarkable just how little this episode wants to endear you to the new man in the TARDIS. He is at turns desperately irritating, only answering his companions' questions with blasts on a recorder, deliberately unhelpful, always referring to the Doctor in the third person just to give his friends more reason not to trust him, and even strangely sinister – that moment he takes out a dagger, only to identify it as something Saladin once owned, plays directly upon our fears that the man's a threat.

And of course it's wonderful that the episode risks alienating Ben and Polly, and the audience at home into the bargain. The job of this story is to *show* that Troughton is the Doctor, not tell it outright. You wonder why the Doctor is making it so difficult for his friends to accept him, even at moments of great tension. Why, when they discover the Daleks in the capsule, he still wants to keep his silly game going – as if to suggest that he may not be the Doctor after all. And it has to be because he wants his actions, not his words, to be the proof. It's very clever, this; when Ben hits upon the idea that the Doctor has renewed himself, Troughton repeats the line back at him – not in assent, but as if he too is being persuaded by the idea. He wants his audience to do the job of working out this mystery for themselves. He's got other things to do than waste time explaining himself.

T: It's so easy for the two of us to be blasé about this... when we started learning about Doctor Who, things like "regeneration" and "different Doctors" were the norm. Last week we had flashing lights and a silent denouement; there were no valedictory speeches, self-sacrificial set pieces or climactic explanations. *This* week, the show – like the Doctor himself – is wilfully oblique. It's now deemed a bad idea that Colin Baker spent his first story being difficult and unknowable, but the production team at the time could reasonably cite The Power of the Daleks as a precedent. I mean, we're currently experiencing the extreme (and, it has to be said, sensible) measures employed to reassure the audience that the move from David Tennant to new boy Matt Smith will be all right... yet with this episode, the trailer doesn't even bother to mention that there's a new Doctor at all!

It helps to establish the new boy's credentials, though, that he's put through the mill from the start. The "renewal" sounds like a pretty shocking and painful process, and he wails like he's suffering cataclysms, and thus spends the rest of the episode slightly off kilter. The few snatches of 8 mm off-screen footage that we have from episode one (recorded by an anonymous Australian and his cine camera)

are very helpful in this regard – we can see, albeit a bit murkily, how jolted the new Doctor seems by his transformation, and can witness that poignant bit where Hartnell's face stares back at Troughton from a mirror.

Aside from the new lead's tantalising work – and the way he's helped by a believably irritated turn from Michael Craze – the depiction of the colonists contains some pleasing little subtleties. It's clear that Bragen and Quinn (respectively the colony's head of security and deputy governor) aren't pals, with the latter making disparaging remarks about the intellectual shortcomings of the former's guards. It establishes their difficult relationship well, whilst hinting at the power at Bragen's disposal. Meanwhile, Janley's bunch are referred to as – at this stage at least – a pressure group rather than rebels. Everything seems a tad more believable and less generic than the set-up otherwise might have been.

But even if the central character isn't too keen to let us know that it's business as usual, his greatest enemies are. With Tristram Cary's music again employed to great (and – not to be sniffed at – fiscally sound) effect, the emergence of the Daleks draws this episode to a close. It's surely no accident that in his fright, Ben blurts out the final line, and it is but one word...

Doctor.

The Power of the Daleks episode two

R: So, this is the situation. We've got a Doctor who doesn't seem like he's the Doctor. And we've got Daleks who aren't behaving like Daleks. In one fell swoop, the whole series has been turned on its head. And my God, doesn't it feel fresh and exciting?

This is a superb episode, shot through with a comic irony as black as anything ever seen in the programme. The episode depends upon the audience's familiarity with the Daleks in a way that perhaps wouldn't have worked before this story, as you want to cry out to the scientists innocently working around one of the machines to take care. It is a heart-stopping moment when the colony's chief scientist, Lesterson, bends down and looks into the gun stick and says, "Can't imagine what this short stubby arm is for..." And it's telling that the one person who feels disquieted by the Daleks is the one that gets suddenly exterminated – it's as if the Dalek can sense fear. You're only safe from them if you don't realise they're a threat – and that's a great pity for all the kids watching at home, because that puts them next in line of fire. And the Doctor too, of course – at the climax of the episode he's genuinely frightened (and we've barely seen that before) trying to shout down a Dalek, who mockingly grates it is a servant. It's one of the best cliffhangers yet.

And through all this, Troughton is magnificent. Here is a Doctor who can suddenly be distracted from deadly earnest by a bowl of fruit or an accidental tongue twister. Special note must also be made of Robert James as Lesterson, whose eagerness in reanimating the Daleks is so boyish that you feel both sympathetic and revolted at the same time.

I love the way, too, that Ben makes mention of the Daleks as something the Doctor is always going on about. It conjures up this delightful image of him standing around the console room, boring all his companions to death with his anecdotes about The Chase. "They were my only recurring monsters, you know – I thought there was a chance with the Zarbi or the Mechonoids, but it just never happened." But the reason it has an impact here is twofold. Firstly, it suggests a Doctor who is genuinely obsessed by these creatures – and yet to the audience, the Daleks are far more familiar than this Doctor is. It's not that we side with *them*, not exactly, but they may feel oddly safer. And yet, the way that the Dalek clearly recognises the Doctor, even though his human friends cannot, does so much to give Troughton the proper credentials.

T: Remember how the Daleks treated the raving Mavic Chen with silence in The Daleks' Master Plan, and how eerie I found them? Well, the same trick is employed here. Much as I love the Dalek voices, the impression one gets is that the Dalek seen here is observing, conniving and planning its next move. The scene where it observes Lesterson's assistant Resno is spectacularly creepy (aided in no small part by a really menacing soundtrack), and the POV shot of his face in the Dalek's

eyeline sends a shiver down the spine. There's something incredibly unnerving about being *watched*, and all the scenes with the Dalek ooze with menace – with us, the audience, more aware than most of the characters involved in this adventure just how deadly these creatures are. It's like watching kids playing with a hand grenade, but being stuck behind soundproofed glass and unable to issue a warning.

Troughton does absolutely sterling work making the silent Dalek as terrifying a threat to the oblivious colonists as possible – he's still a very shadowy presence, this new Doctor, with Troughton speaking in throaty, hushed tones and still not communicating in anything like a normal fashion. His namedropping is interesting, though – Saladin and Marco Polo are figures that at least some of the audience will know that the Doctor has met, but Ben and Polly don't. Quite why he's playing around with his companions is anyone's idea, but it certainly keeps the viewer intrigued. So long as he doesn't get out a projector and do a planet Quinnis slideshow, this should be fine.

And then there's that terrific line that sums up this new Doctor perfectly: "I want [the Daleks] broken up or melted down – up or down, don't care which." He's a bundle of contradictions – he'll give orders (but in a quirky way) and he'll articulate his fear (but mask it with funny phraseology). I don't know quite how they alighted on this particular characterisation to follow on from Hartnell, but at this stage it's somehow reinforced the "Who?" if not always "the Doctor".

I particularly love the cliffhanger here, as the Dalek seems to eyeball (or, rather, eyestalk) the Doctor just as it did Resno – whom it brutally exterminated. Had I been watching this episode back in 1966, I'd probably have finished it still unsure about what they'd done to the titular character, and wondered if this was still the series I knew and loved. But I'd definitely be back next week, because on its own terms, this is something quite special.

March 11th

The Power of the Daleks
episode three

R: Oh, this is absolutely wonderful. This is the longest story we've had in almost a year – ever since, oh, that last Dalek story. (Odd that.) And it means that with a six-parter there's actually the *space* to explore characters that would be pretty functional otherwise. And they're a funny bunch, this lot on Vulcan – backbiters and politicians, the lot of them. I love the way that Bragen is able to manipulate Governor Hensell, just as Janley does Lesterson. The vanity of them all with their trivial little power games seems so especially banal when they can't see the real threat of the Daleks right under their noses. The irony is that the character who's in greatest opposition to the Doctor is Lesterson – and he's the one man there who's honestly likeable. Listen to his excitement about his new robotic servants – it's always the genuine good of the colony that interests him, not his own personal glory. Robert James plays the part a little like a bumptious child; I love the smarmy way he insists upon a guard being posted outside his laboratory once he's won his argument with the Doctor. That's what's so damning about the way this story treats its humans. Let Bragen and Hensell and Janley and Quinn fight it out and destroy themselves, and there wouldn't even *be* a threat from the Daleks; they'd still be sitting at the bottom of a mercury swamp, no doubt. But with Lesterson – poor well-meaning and socially concerned Lesterson – there's a real danger for evil to emerge.

It's the Daleks and the Doctor who are the stand-outs of the episode, mind you. The humiliation that the Dalek puts itself through answering feeble chemistry questions even I could get right, the way that it pretends to immobilise itself because the Doctor demands it proves it's servile – you can hear the contempt in its voice as it flatters and fawns at Lesterson. It means that the sequence where it resurrects its two Dalek compatriots feels almost like a relief – *now*, you think, it'll show its true colours – and then it has their guns removed. That's what's really chilling, that it's

willing to abase itself still further; its ambitions must be so much more lethal than we supposed. Patrick Troughton is excellent playing a man so obsessed by his hatred that he utterly disregards Ben's concern for Polly. He's something of a clown, it's true, but he's a dangerous clown. Hartnell may have been more cantankerous, but his Doctor was always more concerned with the safety of his companions than his apparently foolish successor.

T: Lesterson also struck me as the most likeable guest character – which is funny, as his actions have caused this entire mess. But this man is far from being an idiot – he's smart enough to ask the Dalek why it disobeyed orders, and he doesn't stumble blindly in the face of logic. It's telling that it's the glimmer of doubt he exhibits towards the Daleks that marks the ending of this smart and nuanced episode.

Indeed, the devil's in the detail in this clever script. It's profoundly ironic that Lesterson mentions that the Daleks have "a *certain* intelligence", since *we* know that they're much smarter than any of the humans present. Along the same lines, it's great that the Dalek stutters when the Doctor tries to outwit it. This isn't a round of cack-handed humanising like you'd find in the Richard Martin stories; instead, it's a battle of wits between two formidable opponents, both of whom have to keep their cards close to their chests. What's fascinating about this is the degree to which you sense that the Dalek is desperately trying to hold its composure in public, rather than rely upon its usual trick of yelling and shooting everyone in sight. Thanks to Peter Hawkins (another unsung hero of the 60s), this Dalek becomes a *character* who exhibits guile and cunning, rather than just being a one-note monster. It's great seeing a Dalek under such pressure, and it helps us delve into its Machiavellian psyche. I especially adore the moment where it fires its empty gun, either as a reflex or in frustration.

And it's also interesting that the Doctor has to turn on the charm to get access to Lesterson's lab – despite his clowning, this new Doctor has plenty of guile. And then he tries to electrocute the Dalek! This story really *was* an influence on your TV script wasn't it, Rob? It clearly wasn't just the war-scarred Christopher Eccleston who would go to those lengths when confronted with his greatest enemy!

The Power of the Daleks episode four

R: Influence on my Dalek episode? Oh, I'm not telling. Yet.

Truth to tell, the rebel storyline isn't really as interesting as the Dalek one. But that's rather the point. We watch these arrogant little humans plot against each other, and all the time there are Daleks *there* – serving drinks, trundling down corridors. The gall of these colonists, to think that they're the ones who are the main plot! The scene where Bragen establishes himself in the Governor's office as a master criminal, only to be surprised by a Dalek ever so politely inquiring whether he's finished with his liquid refreshment, is chilling and very, very funny.

It's all quite clever, and the first time the series has unleashed on us so much subplot just to test our patience. We *know* the Daleks are marking time. We *know* that the rebel storyline is very soon going to be irrelevant. Director Christopher Barry and writer David Whitaker are playing a game of nerves with us. They're giving us padding, and lots of it – just so that sooner or later, the Daleks can start firing a blast a hole clean right through it.

That sequence in the Dalek capsule, where Lesterson sees Skaro's finest reproduce themselves, sounds absolutely extraordinary. On the one hand, it looks like a parody of all that merchandising the audience are well used to from a couple of Christmases ago – see the happy little Daleks pour down the conveyor belt! On the other, it's the only time in the show's history we see Daleks being born, scraped off bits of foam and goo and stuck inside metal containers. It's horrific and utterly alien. No wonder Robert James begins to lose his mind.

T: To talk of the slow pace that you mention isn't to damn this story with faint praise... Ben and the Doctor wander down a corridor, and we realise when they do that there might be an extra Dalek; Lesterson's doubts increase, but Janley manipulates him; Janley herself shows she isn't just a clichéd villain by bravely offering to be the guinea pig when the rebels test the Dalek. There are so many subtle moments of colour here, which are augmented by carefully placed shades of grey, and it's all the more remarkable how the programme-makers flesh out the society of this colony without benefit of the vast canvas afforded to modern television. I particularly like the fact that Hensell is away because he's doing a bit of work outside of the few sets we're obliged to see; it helps to provide a sense of real people doing real jobs with real, mundane obligations.

Meanwhile, it's wonderful how Troughton brilliantly undermines the pathetic trappings of power on display here, especially with his childish glee as he says "I would like a hat like that." Just as he's playfully prodding at authority though, a Dalek enters with a tea tray and the special sounds creepily erect the hairs on the back of our necks. The whole situation is played brilliantly, hinting that everything's just a little bit... wrong. The sense of impending doom is probably more palpable than in *any* other story up to this point.

What I'm getting at is that it's remarkable how this show, which is understandably so unaware of its mythic status at this point, still manages to make its first new leading man's debut so astonishingly special – not by doing anything terribly grandiose, but by establishing a realistic setting, and then having the man-who-claims-to-be-the-Doctor confront a situation with the Daleks that's *unlike* any he's faced with his old adversaries before. It wouldn't have been out of order for us to expect Troughton's debut to have been an inconsequential four-parter with some aliens called Steve and Trevor trying to invade Grimsby. But for all that Hartnell's departure seemed abrupt and low key – and for all that the series of late has been declining to mark its "big moments" (such as having companions depart halfway through a story) – the production team has really put the effort into making Troughton's debut adventure something extraordinary. We're only to episode four, and you can tell that The Power of the Daleks was, and remains, one of the most crucial and successful revamps in Doctor Who's history.

March 12th

The Power of the Daleks
episode five

R: One of the Daleks asks: "Why do human beings kill human beings?" Good question.

Quick digression. The night that my Dalek episode went out on the BBC, I had a few friends over to celebrate – most of them other people who'd been working alongside me on the revival. After the end credits, and a few glasses of champagne had been drunk, I had a phone call. When I answered, a female voice on the end enthusiastically told me how much she'd loved the story, well done, and welcoming me to the Doctor Who family. She was so bubbly it took me a little while to get a word in edgeways and ask who she was. "Oh, sorry!" she laughed. "I should have said! I'm Anneke Wills!" It turned out that she was at a convention, had watched Dalek go out live with some fans – and one of them had my phone number. I was thrilled, obviously – I'd never spoken to Polly before. And I began to tell her that it was all because of the work she'd done with Patrick Troughton. That my episode had been inspired by The Power of the Daleks, that it was the best Dalek story written, and I was just trying to pay homage to all their efforts. It was great. I actually out-enthused Anneke.

What I tried to capture in Dalek – not nearly so well as David Whitaker did, I know – was that sense that however evil a Dalek might be, it has at least its own moral code and personal integrity. In contrast to all those wonderful scenes of efficient Dalek unity on the conveyor belts, you get mankind here at its most base and mendacious. When a Dalek asks Bragen why as a fellow human he would want to kill Hensell, it suggests that we're baser. It's a far cry from the last story, in which the Cybermen were offered as an alternative to all that characterised Man; when at the cliffhanger the Daleks announce they're now ready to wipe out the colonists you feel some sort of relief, because these human beings *deserve* all that's coming to them. The scene where Bragen has Hensell exterminated is quite superb. It's so wonderfully petty; it starts out as a bit of an office argument, with Bragen refusing to stand up when talking to the boss. Ultimately, Bragen only gives up Hensell's chair so that Hensell can be killed in it. It's very tense, and blackly comic – and the Dalek servant ends up looking as the most mature character in the room. I only wish I could have written a scene in my episode that was halfway as profound as this one.

T: Ooh – can I come and watch your next episode at your house? I'll bring champagne! And Anneke's wonderful isn't she? She once stroked my face and called me cute, and (I thought) pretended to be interested in seeing my stage show, requesting a copy. I sent her a DVD, and to my surprise by return of post got a wonderful, enthusiastic and jolly letter back, with some signed piccies for my boys. Moments like that still make me pinch myself!

I have an anecdote about this episode too, but it's slightly more bittersweet. We've been discussing how Robert James is astonishing as Lesterson – and it happens that when he died in 2004, I got commissioned to write his obituary for The Guardian. When it failed to appear, I began to make enquiries, and they kept telling me it was going in – only to rescind after about a month. I subsequently offered it to The Independent (who at that time had more space and a broader remit), and frustratingly was told that they *would* have run it, but that too much time had now passed since his death. The most galling aspect of this was that I'd spoken to James' wife, Mona Bruce, and read her the piece, and it never materialised. She died a short time ago too, and I feel like I let her down (it was a nice article too, but I lost it when my computer committed suicide). I can't help but think about this while re-experiencing this story, because James gives one of the best guest turns we've yet seen in the show; the script demands excellence in so many areas, and he delivers in every one.

For a story that reformats Doctor Who in so many ways, it's the little things – the little choices – that continue to elevate this to greatness. Governor Hensell's popularity among the mine workers on the perimeter is something we're only told about, but lends some texture to a world that we couldn't actually see (even if the video existed) beyond a few rooms.

Later, Quinn's reaction to Hensell's death (in a programme where murder is an everyday event) helps to sell the importance of the governor's killing on both a human and political level. Top marks though, go to Bernard Archard as Bragen – having ordered and witnessed Hensell's death in a cool, villainous manner, he sounds audibly shaken after the event, so much so that he hurriedly shoos the Dalek away. It's a very credible moment, and an unusually psychologically sophisticated acting choice.

And is it wrong of me that I adore that Bragen's got himself a uniform and hat? It's always the meaningless pomp that seems to turn on the power crazed; that the Doctor looks like he's raided a jumble sale and kipped on a bench is the ultimate antidote to such sartorial posturing.

The Power of the Daleks
episode six

R: And, really, this is much better than it *needed* to be. After five episodes of ratcheting up the tension to breaking point, all this episode actually had to do was set the Daleks loose on a rampage and I'd have been satisfied. And it certainly does that, of course. In fact, this does what as a kid I always imagined all Dalek stories did – it has the pepperpots exterminating every human in sight, chasing people up and down corridors, and killing without warning or mercy. After the slow build-up, the carnage is overwhelming, and even in telesnap form you can see that Christopher Barry spends a fair bit of time emphasising the dead bodies. It's all very grim. We have sequences where, to foil the Daleks, the Doctor and Quinn have to lie still amongst all the corpses. And there's an extraordinarily callous scene in which the Doctor seems quite happy that all Bragen's guards get slaughtered just to buy him some time doing something clever with a plug.

And I know that I've been moaning on a bit recently about things getting a bit too brutal in the world of Who – but I do think that this has been so well set up, it's justified. The Doctor has spent five episodes marching about telling people that there would be atrocities. And the story doesn't shirk whatsoever from demonstrating that he was absolutely right. It makes

the Daleks more powerful than ever before – they're cunning and sly, but because they've also been playing *against* their true natures, to see them as they really are depicts their evil more vividly than we've yet seen. And it does its job and makes the Doctor someone we can believe in. He may wear a silly hat, he might do irritating things with a recorder – but he has stayed his ground and warned a community that his voice is the only authority, and if he's ignored they will die. The brilliance of all this is, of course, that his moment of victory plays *against* that – he appears so delighted that he's done something clever that he makes the audience suspect it may all be accidental. No other Doctor would assume power so easily, and then fritter it away once the crisis is over, to the point that the colony suddenly turn on him and complain about the damage he's caused.

As I say, a bloodbath is all it needed to be. But it keeps the power games between the humans going so well – Janley changes allegiances so often in this one episode alone that by the time she's killed, even *she* probably doesn't know which side she's on. The depiction of Bragen as governor of colonists who can't respond to his orders because they've all been killed is very clever. The best bit, though? Lesterson trying to imitate the same sing-song refrain to a Dalek, "I am your servant," quite amiably believing that they are the higher order and that mankind's time has passed. He tells a Dalek it wouldn't want to shoot him, because he gave it life. "Yes," considers a Dalek. "You gave us life." And then, without a word, as nonchalantly as you please, kills him anyway.

T: I've been waiting for this story to let me down, to run out of steam, to cop out or to just get a bit messy – and it hasn't. As ever, I know it's difficult to tell because we can't actually see it, but it *sounds* fantastic. The whole thing has rumbled along menacingly, and – as advertised – now really kicks off with horrible, bloody consequences. The sound of gunfire permeates the action throughout – which works, because automatic weaponry always seems more believable and dangerous than lasers. Towards the end, there's what seems to be a lingering pan over all of the dead bodies, replete with funereal music. Make no mistake, the goodies may win, but the cost has been unpleasantly high. The use of the Dalek POV has been consistently well employed in this story, and is again here, as one of them surveys the carnage, finally resting on Janley's prone corpse.

It helps immensely that we've been able to invest so much in the inhabitants of Vulcan – even minor characters such as Janley's associate Kebble do enough to arouse our interest. Prior to Janley's demise, we're never quite sure whether we should like her or not, but she does seem convincing as someone with wavering morals and loyalties. At the very least, she's not a one-note baddie, and her close personal relationship with the rebel Valmar seems as textured as her mendacious behaviour – even the way she addresses him as "Val" lends a pleasing note of casual realism. Bragen also seems very humanistic as he keeps using the word "governor" in the scenes where he loses control of both the colony and the Daleks; it's as if he pathetically believes that by affirming his title often enough, it will somehow maintain his command of a situation that's now completely beyond him. And Robert James, whom I've praised before, adds a beautifully wistful note to Lesterson's insane assertion that Man has had his day and is "finished now". His appeal to the Daleks with the phrase "I am your servant" is amazingly done, and (despite his actions having caused all of this carnage) makes you cheer for him a little. It's this act of distracting the Daleks – the last thing Lesterson ever does, as they gun him down – that allows the Doctor to succeed in defeating them.

The Troughton Doctor isn't yet the version we've all grown accustomed to, but that's only to be expected at this early stage. Still, it's a bit alarming that when the Doctor is confronted with the question, "You did know what you were doing?", we're by no means certain that the answer is affirmative, especially when he oddly responds with, "What d'I do, what d'I do?" Even allowing for the stories made under John Wiles, there hasn't been an adventure that's climaxed with *quite* so much destruction before, but it somehow seems appropriate to this new phase of the show. The Doctor sorts things out, but he doesn't do it tidily. He's like The Cat in the (Stove Pipe) Hat.

March 13th

The Highlanders episode one

R: It's the last historical adventure until Season Nineteen! (It's so hard, watching these stories, not to be hit by all the facts you learned by rote as a young fan.) Yes, this is the last gasp of a type of story that wasn't much good and nobody enjoyed. (Ha.) Considering just how bloodthirsty these forays back into the past usually are, it seems terribly apt that the TARDIS at last plunges our heroes right into a famous battle. The Ship has been very well-behaved so far, always arriving just a few days before Hastings or the fall of Troy – but now here we are, picking our way through the wounded and the dying. I love the way that the title music is cut off by the roaring of cannons and the groans of soldiers. And by dealing with a historical event from the *wrong* side of the action, we're looking, for once, not at the build-up to something the Doctor needs to escape from, but its aftermath; we're seeing the consequences of war, not the politics behind it. I find that very refreshing. It'd be the equivalent of the TARDIS pitching up and finding all the Huguenots in the street after the massacre – it's another way of looking at the butchery of war altogether. It's very telling that Troughton's first reaction upon seeing a cannonball is to get back into the TARDIS and take off; "You don't want to seem as if you're frightened, do you?" asks Polly. "Why not?" is his surprisingly honest reply.

And it's very funny, Gerry Davis' script – but never funny at the expense of the carnage. Instead, there's a comedy to this blacker than any we've really ever seen in the series before. The mercenary solicitor Grey and his obsequious clerk Perkins make a fantastic double act, but the way they're trading in human lives is genuinely repulsive. Grey's languid appreciation of Culloden as a battle connoisseur contrasts well with how appalled he is to find that his wine has been corked. And the cynicism of the English is so pronounced, it's safer to treat it all as a sick joke: the sergeant's recognition that his lieutenant turns a blind eye to the executions on account of his weak stomach, and the soldiers' eagerness to interpret anything the Doctor says as a reason to hang him. Both Ben and Polly make the faux pas of assuming the English must be the good guys – and just like in The Power of the Daleks last week, where the humans characters were turned into unsympathetic gits only worthy of extermination, so they find that their fellow countrymen are not their friends.

And Polly's great! She spends her time impatiently telling the Laird's daughter, Kirsty, to stop snivelling, and is all full of determination and plans to rescue her friends. You go, girl.

T: We're certainly in grim territory – we open with a slaying, and before long, we're regaled with bleak reports of prisoners being hanged, children being slaughtered and soldiers plundering corpses. There's something tough and gritty about angry rebellious Scotsmen, so that even a potentially daft line like "Sassenach dragoons" sounds pretty fierce. It's a bit of a pity, then, that against all of this drama, it's Ben's carelessness with a pistol that results in our heroes being discovered by the Redcoats; it makes him come across as both cack-handed *and* responsible for Alexander's subsequent death.

Certain bits of dialogue strike me as interesting... not even Troughton can get away with the line, "You'll give us your word you won't molest us?", but I do find the line "Rebels aren't prisoners of war" very telling. I'm always rather cynical about semantics being used to justify atrocities; it's this sort of behaviour that enables governments to get away with detaining people without trial or torturing them in the name of liberty. If you call your enemies "soldiers", you're expected to treat them a bit more honourably than if they're (insert the current acceptable euphemism for baddie, be it "rebel", "terrorist" or "insurgent").

But the most notable line of all? The Doctor declaring, "I would like a hat like this!" He also said that in the last story, didn't he? Is this the sign of an intended but abandoned catchphrase? Hmm, to look at the other ones that have cropped up in recent years – "Fantastic!" "I'm so very, very sorry...", etc. – I suppose it's understandable why the hat-talk didn't last. Still, it would've been nice had they continued the tradition – it's very amusing to think of the nation's schoolchildren running about the

playground, harmlessly declaring "I would like a hat like this!", and putting on whatever headwear they could find.

Oh, and did you notice how the Doctor calls *himself* Doctor Who, albeit in German? In days gone by, I'd have passed this off as a joke, but in the current climate I'm not so sure!

The Highlanders episode two

R: That Troughton's a bit of a bastard, isn't he? He's funny and he dresses up as an old woman, and puts on an outrageous German accent. But there's a darker edge to this Doctor than anything we've seen since the amorality of Hartnell right back in the first stories. When he denounces the highlanders just so he can get an audience with Grey, it may well be the clever ploy Ben says it is – but his sudden turn as traitor is just a little too convincing for comfort. (Even Ben sounds as if he's trying to persuade himself.) It's interesting that he'll only shout out "down with King George" in order to enjoy the echo in the cell, not because he's going to share the affiliations of anyone else in this conflict. And when he says that he's rather enjoying himself, amidst the suffering and the fear of real prisoners fearing death, it sounds just as callous as Hartnell's Doctor contemplating braining a caveman with a rock.

But he really *does* enjoy himself. His turn as the German doctor, persuading Perkins he has a headache by banging the clerk's head on a table, is simply glorious. But what gives such power to this scene, when he tells Solicitor Grey he's only interested in money and his own skin, is that at this stage you really can believe he's a rogue out for himself. We don't know this Doctor yet, and although we're *hoping* this is just subterfuge, we can't be sure. He has his own agenda. And as much as Ben might stick up for him to the suspicious Jamie McCrimmon, it clearly doesn't involve rescuing lots of highlanders from their cell.

Anneke Wills also gets the chance to shine, sparring well with Michael Elwyn's foppish Lt. Algernon ffinch (sic), and showing a real wit and resourcefulness for the first time in the series. Though it's curious that this is achieved, in part, by her being a contrast to Hannah Gordon's Kirsty, who's as wet as a soggy cabbage and will burst into tears at any opportunity. I'm not sure I like this; it seems a development of that rather dubious suggestion in The Smugglers that people in the past were a bit stupid, and this presentation of savvy sixties girl being tougher than her eighteenth century counterpart is rather overstressed. (Especially when you consider that a Highlander woman in rebellion is likely to be a mite more assured than even the hardiest of Chelsea girls.) But I'll bless anything that gives Polly a bit more strength. (Anneke Wills phoned me once! She did!... oh, I've already told you.)

T: In some way, this is another exercise in extremes. The prison is squalid, with unpleasant water lapping at the feet of the prisoners, some of whom are on death's door. Human life is pretty cheap, and the Laird sounds genuinely, painfully ill.

But the *characters* involved in this locale are actually very funny. You're right to mention how the Doctor is a hilarious protagonist as he trusses up Grey and then tortures Perkins – it gives some murky undertones to his character, but I genuinely don't see how he could have carried on being this unpredictable or untrustworthy. (It's bad enough having the villains wanting to kill you, but this Doctor isn't averse to encouraging the good guys to feel the same.) For now, though, everyone around the Doctor is likewise acting naughty... the Sentry sticks around for a tip that Grey makes Perkins pay (much to the clerk's world-weary chagrin), and the Sergeant extorts money out of ffinch whilst maintaining a front of civility. Everyone's a crook, and it's rather delightful. The only bump in the road here is Dallas Cavell's performance as Trask the ship-captain – would I be wrong to suggest that he's not exactly taking this engagement particularly seriously? Oo-ar.

Even if this story isn't the comic masterpiece that The Myth Makers was (it isn't as clever or interested in mucking about with form), it's all good fun, with Gerry Davis displaying aptitude for witty lines – my favourite yet being, "I've never seen a silent lawyer before..."

March 14th

R: Thanks for your email this morning, Toby, that invited me to your wedding. Many congratulations – I'm glad a date has been set. But you'll forgive me if I raise a few concerns.

July 18th. You mean, this year, right? But you are aware that at that stage we'll be somewhere late Pertwee or early Tom? I know you love K, and she's great and everything, I'm quite sure you'll be very happy together. But do you think your priorities are quite in order? If she *really* loved you, don't you think she might be persuaded to delay the wedding? If not until we've finished the book, at least until we're having to watch Sylvester McCoy?

I don't know, mate. You signed up for this task of watching Doctor Who with me perfectly enthusiastically a couple of months ago. We've seen off the Sensorites, we made it through episode three of The bloody Ark. I just hate to see you falter now. Yes, you want to get married, I understand, and marriage is a terrific thing. But I have to ask – what about Doctor Who? (And what about *me*?)

T: I understand where you're coming from, but to be honest, it's taken K 20-odd years to think that nuptials are a good idea, so I'm not holding them off for anything. Frankly, the poor woman is already set to be a Doctor Who widow – she came to Gallifrey, she knows who Robert Holmes is, and she's even agreed for the dinner tables at the reception to be named after the Doctors. I think postponing the big day so that I can concentrate on our magnum opus might be pushing things a little too far!
R: Fair enough. That's up to you. Be selfish. It's your big day, I suppose.

But can you at least guarantee that at some point during the wedding, we can leave the reception and nip off somewhere to watch Genesis of the Daleks episode four?
T: Perhaps we could show the episodes in-between the speeches...

The Highlanders episode three

R: This is a by far more sombre affair altogether. Troughton recognises this by underplaying his performance significantly – which is quite an achievement when he spends much of the episode in a skirt. The scene in which he gently convinces Kirsty to give him the Prince's ring so that they can save her father is perhaps the most persuasive he has yet been as the Doctor. Contrast this with the truly menacing scene where he warns Perkins at gunpoint not to raise the alarm. His Doctor is a wonderful mix of calculation and breezy indifference – he accepts Polly's compliments that he's wonderful – and then, all of a sudden, loses interest in the complications of the plot and wants to have a sleep. If this were an eighties story, there'd be muttering at this point about a regeneration crisis; because such a term hasn't been invented yet, instead the Doctor gives the impression that he's barking mad. Michael Craze does very well too, making the most of the fine set piece in the scene in which Grey attempts to convince the captive highlanders to sell themselves into slavery. Indeed, what is on display here time and time again are scenes in which bravery and camaraderie are pitted against basic inhumanity. Even Grey seems to admire that juxtaposition, in a brilliantly callous scene where he tells Trask that the highlanders are not to be whipped, because it will only make these honourable men resist him the stronger. (But once they're enslaved and working in the plantations, as far as he's concerned they can be beaten to death.)

Most striking of all, perhaps, is when Polly and Kirsty entrap Algernon ffinch. He's the perfect comic foil to the girls, but it is quite clear that he is also a man who thinks nothing of committing bureaucratic murder. In all the comedy there is a real edge of something quite unpleasant to the taste – as Kirsty shows when Polly and herself adopt disguises that quite clearly set them apart as prostitutes.

T: The Doctor reminds me of a small child. He's playful, but can turn sharply and loses interest in events when he decides to have a kip. He's actually rather bewildering, and because of this, his two companions get the best opportunities the series has yet given them – Ben gets to do all the heroic stuff, and Polly is allowed to be independent and feisty. It's telling that the audience needs the moment where the Doctor has to demonstrate that the gun he's holding is unloaded. With most of the Doctor's other incarnations, we'd probably have little doubt

that this was the case, but when the Troughton one wields a pistol (even when dressed as a woman!), it's genuinely disconcerting.

This story continues to be a bit grim, but it's done with an elegant lightness. Grey is a fantastic baddie, and in that great scene with Trask he's cruel, clever and wily, but also has such poise and intelligence that you can't help rather admiring him despite yourself. The ending is a bit of a puzzler, though – there's no dialogue to accompany Ben being thrown off the deck of the Annabelle, so it's difficult to discern exactly how dramatic or exciting it's supposed to be. Normally, if the hero is sent to his doom, he gets something defiant or brave to spout – but Ben is here dispatched without ceremony, with little fuss. But, that seems to be par for the course if you're a Doctor Who companion under Innes Lloyd...

There's just one thing I don't get about this episode. If Trask once served as first mate to the mob-leader Willie Mackay, couldn't Mackay have anticipated that the man might have been trouble, what with him having the speech and mannerisms of a pirate 'n' all? If your first mate says "ahhrr" a lot and storms about calling everyone "swab", you'd probably have good reason not to trust him. After all, you wouldn't hire someone who lives in a lightning scarred castle and has an aversion to garlic to be your babysitter, would you?

The Highlanders episode four

R: This satisfying conclusion makes The Highlanders that rare thing – a consistently good story. The construction is pretty near perfect – the overthrow of Trask aboard The Annabelle is exciting, but also allows room for some surprisingly tender moments, and the Laird's conviction that his hearing Kirsty must be the imagination of a dying man is actually very moving. And still the episode refuses to be predictable – the set piece aboard the boat would act as most story's climax, but, very neatly, the tension of the travellers getting back through the fog and the Redcoats to find the TARDIS is well preserved. (Indeed, the idea that the danger isn't really over until the crew are safely behind TARDIS doors is an early Hartnellism you wouldn't expect to surface again in a comedy historical.) Good to see too that Grey survives the story, albeit within ffinch's custody, and that Perkins' redemption is somewhat grudging. (The Doctor's assertion that the highlanders can trust him as their clerk in France until the winds change direction is wonderful; Gerry Davis refuses to give simple solutions in what by expectations really ought to be a simple runaround.)

It still seems extraordinary that Jamie leaves in the TARDIS at the end of the story. Frazer Hines has acted very well, but the character itself has been thinly drawn. When Ben and Polly express such surprise to see him on shore near the end of the story, I echoed it – I'd all but forgotten he was even *in* this adventure. And of course, from now on, there'll be another regular inside the TARDIS to share all the companions' lines. In a way, it's a great shame that in a story where both Ben and Polly have been allowed to shine, its conclusion condemns them both largely to bit parts from this point on.

T: Like last week's cliffhanger, it's the middle of this episode that's a bit tricky for us to interpret – being, as it is, a big long fight. Even with the soundtrack and the telesnaps to help us, it's very hard to judge if this was well-mounted or an apologetic and scrappily staged shambles. It's worth noting though, that even though the writer has gone to great ends to depict the bloodiness and cruelty of the setting, not one of the major villains is seen to die. In fact, no-one has been killed since Alexander perished in episode one... Trask *might* drown when Jamie chucks him overboard, but it's not explicit. (I couldn't be certain, but I don't think he gets mortally wounded before being pitched into the firth.) And I think it quite right that Perkins gets a let off; he's been an obsequious little creep who, even as he joins the good guys, is explicitly outed as a shifty bounder, but he's been good fun. The bit where he turns on Grey – like a rebellious Ariel spitting at the feet of his Prospero – brings a joyful closure to this entertaining double act.

And three cheers for Algernon ffinch – an idiot and a thoughtless coward who, through interacting with the TARDIS crew, finds the goodness that dwells within him. His subplot has been a delightful addition to this adventure, and I hope that the viewers became very

fond of him. It's a credit to Michael Elwyn's performance, and indeed to that of Anneke Wills, who's gamely manipulated ffinch but has always displayed a sense of humour while doing so.

Then we come to that spurious end scene that you mentioned, where Jamie suddenly joins the TARDIS crew. I have to confess that it's very difficult for me not to use my fore-knowledge of the companions' fates to underscore my opinions of it – I'm trying, as best I can, to contextualise episodes only in light of what has happened in the series thus far, but this is one of the exceptions where that isn't really possible. Michael Craze and Anneke Wills have been fantastic, and pretty much grounded the series when its leading man has been either poorly (Hartnell) or untrustworthy (Troughton). But what of Jamie (whose introduction here spells the beginning of their end)? If he'd stayed aboard the Annabelle, he'd have been safely stowed in France... but because he goes with the Doctor, when he's finally returned to his time at the end of Season Six, it's during the aftermath of a bloody battle, when Redcoats were happily scouring the countryside killing anyone they even vaguely suspected of being a Jacobite. So, for the sake of three years in space and time he won't even remember, Jamie quite probably goes to an early grave at the end of a British soldier's sword. Okay, that's only one possible interpretation, but, rather sadly, it's feasible.

But on a more upbeat note, did you hear it? "I would like a hat like that!" That's it, it's a catchphrase! I can just imagine Troughton blacking up, wearing a wind-jammer captain's costume and striding into Lloyd's office, suggesting that in each story, the Doctor wears a different hat! Why, if they'd followed through with such a plan, just think of all the action-figure variants we could now have...

March 15th

The Underwater Menace
episode one

R: Aha! This one's rather interesting. It's a story which has been written off as a clunker for *decades* – its reputation not helped, I suspect, by the fact that episode three is the only one in the archives, and watched cold seems to be comprised mostly of fish people having a strange watery ballet. But I think this is a story you cannot just watch cold – jumping into the madness halfway through doesn't let your brain click into what the tone should be.

Because this is mad – barking, in fact – and deliberately so. And the key to that is in the wonderful TARDIS scene that opens the episode. Ostensibly, it's all about introducing Jamie to his new home. In practice, though, it's a reminder to the audience that this programme can (and will) do absolutely anything. The camera focuses upon each of the regulars in turn, and we hear their thoughts on where they'd like to end up. ("Prehistoric monsters!" Troughton thinks with glee.) But it's Jamie's reaction that is the most telling, as he wonders what insanity he's wandered into. We're offered present-day adventure, familiar old baddies or something back in time – and the production team ensure that when the TARDIS doors open, we get something completely different to all of them.

So there's a strange high priest who wants to sacrifice our heroes to the gods – but we find out this is set in 1970. There's reference – the first one, I think, in the series – to the Cold War as Zaroff is sought by Eastern and Western governments... and this sudden dose of real-world politics is tempered by the fact that he feeds people to killer sharks. It would have been so easy for writer Geoffrey Orme to have crafted this as either a modern-day James Bond spoof or set it right back in history to better suggest the Dark Ages approach to religion – and it's the fact that he bolts the two together that makes this so frankly weird. It's as if the production team are deliberately playing with the conventions of the series. As soon as they leave the TARDIS, all the crew split up as per usual – which is utterly pointless, because within three minutes they're all imprisoned together as if that hadn't happened. You could say that it's clumsy plotting. But I'd argue that it's part of a process where our expectations are challenged. It's no excuse that Polly suggests at the beginning they're in Cornwall; we've just had an adventure which alluded to its own similarity to The Smugglers, and straight afterwards this next story does the same. And

immediately plonks us into a situation unlike anything we've ever had before. The episode ending, I'll remind you, is of Polly being held down by doctors who want to inject her so she'll end up with fish gills. That's a novelty. Doctor Who has been jumping around from genre to genre for years now, from future to past and back again, until we pretty well know what to look out from either. It's been years since we've had anything like The Edge of Destruction or The Space Museum, which has so consciously wanted to go sideways and challenge us with something new.

T: You make some very good points, but this story isn't that bonkers just yet. In fact – if I were being truly honest about this – the first 15 minutes are actually desperately dull. Yes, the little insight into the thoughts of the TARDIS crew is quite sweet, but the charging about on the rocks seems to take forever – as does, actually, the sacrifice sequence where it's pretty obvious that Zaroff will eventually stop it, as it's only episode one and he's the only person who can.

What strikes me most about this episode, though, is the genre that we're dealing with; when the rather shabby looking Atlanteans come along, it's the closest Doctor Who has ever got to being a shoddy 50s B-Movie. The funny thing is, I actually don't mind watching a shoddy 50s B-Movie, and even a genuine one typically takes a good while to get so-bad-that-you-can-laugh-at-it. This is only episode one, and so odds are high that we're going to be waiting for the plot to take hold, and for things to get truly silly. I guess what I'm trying to say is that the only way is down – but that's probably okay, because the only way this will get any good is, perversely, if it gets worse. The main way this strategy could backfire is if it becomes too difficult to watch this without feeling a little patronising – the Doctor's bluff to Zaroff, for instance, could either be a clever example of our hero's optimistic improvisation, or just a lazy piece of writing. (Sadly, that Zaroff subsequently doesn't kill our heroes only because he likes the Doctor's sense of humour leads me to suspect the latter.)

But the surviving telesnaps reveal something very interesting – the Doctor signs a note as "Dr. W". Watching the series chronologically has made me notice how closely together these hints that his name *is* Doctor Who come. Calling him "Doctor Who" in The War Machines has always been brushed under the carpet, passed off as a mild aberration that was quickly spotted and never repeated. Well, this is the *fourth* such allusion (with, admittedly, different degrees of obliqueness) in eight stories. The fifth, actually, if you count the caption slide at the end of The Gunfighters telling us that the next episode is called "Dr. Who And The Savages."

It's also what he's called in the credits, of course, but nobody seems inclined to count that.

The Underwater Menace
episode two

R: Actually, I'm rethinking what I said about that last episode. I'm not sure that The Underwater Menace is especially challenging. As you suggested, Toby, I think it's really very silly.

But I'm not sure that's necessarily such a great crime. Because what it's done, in its wacky way, is consolidate the second Doctor. During his past two stories, Troughton has come across as something of a wild schizophrenic. He has a catchphrase about wanting people's hats. He keeps on pretending to be other people – sometimes several within the same episode – and it's hard to nail down who he actually is. And so to pit Troughton now against Joseph Furst's Zaroff is a stroke of good fortune. It reins him in. There's no way that Troughton at his most comic can compete with Furst at his most over the top. And so instead he's forced to play the sane one. The scene where the Doctor quietly asks this lunatic scientist why he wants to split the earth open like an egg is a revelation – he's talking carefully to a man who is so unhinged, he'll kill himself and everybody else for nothing more than the achievement of doing so. And the scenes he shares with Tom Watson as the priest Ramo are terrific. Here's a Doctor who will risk his own life just for the chance of persuading others that he is the voice of reason. For the first time, you feel he can pull it off – that there's a calm sincerity to this manic clown, that here there's a figure of real authority.

Yes, very silly, as I say. But it's interesting that the cynicism of The Power of the Daleks, and the depiction of war's currency that made The Highlanders so grim, made Troughton invent the Doctor as a joker by comparison. And that when the tone of the story is made lighter and dafter, that Troughton is the one who allows you to take it just seriously enough you can enjoy it.

T: I'm deeply concerned about Geoffrey Orme – what was he on when he wrote this? Zaroff's motivation for blowing up the world is *because he can*? He's mad obviously, but it's all-purpose TV mad. Medical students watching this may quibble with the suggestion that the best way to diagnose madness is to look at your patient's eyes and try to spot any boggleyness, but where Zaroff is concerned, this isn't a bad idea.

But if anything, the script is even more insane than Zaroff – and clearly written in about 15 minutes. In a repeat of episode one, Ramo asks the Doctor why he should trust him, and what does our cosmic genius say in reply? That he doesn't know – so Ramo trusts him anyway. And neither Ramo nor the serving girl Ara like Zaroff – why, you may ask? Because they're goodies, and goodies don't like the man. In fact, we're evidently supposed to like Ramo simply because the Doctor has decided he's a potential ally, even though they've barely spoken before. All we've really seen of him up till now is him getting cross because a human sacrifice has been cancelled, which is hardly a quality one looks for in a friend.

The telesnaps give us some indication of the design for this episode, and boy, it's a really curious hybrid – everyone from Atlantis wears shells and seaweed (Ara's even got an Oyster bra!), and yet the Overseer has a lumberjack shirt and a hard hat. And only in daft old Doctor Who could you get an actor with the illustrious pedigree of Colin Jeavons (here playing Damon, Zaroff's assistant) and then cast him only in this story and K-9 and Company. And deck him out with massive eyebrows. For that matter, only Doctor Who could get a cast like Jeavons, Tom Watson and Noel Johnson, and have them give such duff performances. It seems that having seen Joseph Furst go in one direction as Zaroff, they've all gone in the other. Whilst he's gone for apocalyptically proportioned OTT, they're all a bit too blandly sincere and (Johnson, particularly) mannered. It's bizarre.

Do you know what, though? The B-Movie strategy that I mentioned is working... I'm man enough to say that The Underwater Menace is so naff, I rather like it. And next up, we get to see the surviving episode in all its glory!

March 16th

The Underwater Menace
episode three

R: I think it's a measure of just how unpredictable The Underwater Menace is, that in the scene where the Doctor's execution is prevented by a voice coming from a large idol, you really can just about believe that the great god Amdo has just popped up to save the day. Tonally, this story is so over the place that literally anything could happen. And this means that such things that would normally be of vital significance to a story – like plot, or logic – are wilfully abandoned in favour of a more freewheeling style. Let's kidnap Zaroff!, the Doctor suggests. Or let's make the fish people revolt! As soon as a character hits upon an idea, it's no more raised than easily achieved. Considering the mine-workers Sean and Jacko spend their time persuading the Fish People to rise up against their oppressors by mocking the size of their manhood, it's utterly bizarre they manage to get their rather disgruntled piscine pals to go on strike. And no sooner have they determined to go on strike, than the community is reduced to its knees! Incredible! Considering Zaroff is the most powerful man in Atlantis, with an armed guard to protect him, it's even more bizarre that two young men in leather, a girl dressed up as a Can Can dancer and a man in drag can capture him within minutes. And having achieved this, that they simply fall foul of his cunning plan to escape – by his clutching his stomach and saying "ow" a lot.

By my reckoning, there are about three points in this episode where you'd traditionally expect the story to end. The scene where Zaroff is imprisoned feels like an end of adventure moment. Later on, when he's hounded by Jamie as he escapes over a rockface, you anticipate him falling Morbius-like to his doom. Or when the Fish People rebel, that King Thous turns against him. And each time the story waves at you cheerily, no no no, I'm carrying on. In some ways, it's truly awful; it feels increasingly like the episode hasn't been so much scripted as thrown together in improvisation. And in others, it's rather exhilarating. The adventure doesn't have a clue where it's going. And so neither can we – it's an insane ride into the unknown. It's like Geoffrey Orme has fitted the Randomiser to his typewriter.

Joseph Furst's performance sums it up. In that final, famous scene, he can scream to the camera that nuffink in ze world can stop him now, and it's outrageous and funny – but it follows immediately after a line in which he dispassionately orders two men to be murdered off camera. It's all over the place, and out of control. Is it any good? Of course not. Is it entertaining? Just about, if you hold on tight, and don't resist where it takes you.

T: I have a confession to make... I've just finished watching this, and I have a big, stupid grin on my face. Did you hear that, fandom? I love it, I love it to pieces!

I'm not exactly unbiased though – this episode has always had a special place in my heart. When I was a teenager and the Doctor Who VHS range was merely a gleam in some savvy marketing guru's eye, I had an exotic day trip to the nearest buzzing metropolis to where I lived. Oh yes, I fondly recall those glamorous city lights that lured me like a moth to the urban flame that was... Wolverhampton. I went to a shop called The Place that had advertised in the pages of Doctor Who Magazine, and whilst I was there, feasting on such rarities as the first edition of Doctor Who Weekly (no transfers), I overheard two guys talking about episodes that you'd expect they couldn't possibly have seen. My older friend (and driver) Derek, much more confident than me, asked about how they'd got access to the existing back catalogue of the BBC archives... and a whole world of bootlegging opened itself up to me. My first order (cost: give the man two VHS tapes, get one back in return) was all of the orphaned Troughton episodes. I figured I'd get more variety that way, and so, of course, the very first old episode I viewed in this manner was – yes, it's true – The Underwater Menace episode three.

It was like blowing the cobwebs off a signed first edition of The Complete Works of Shakespeare. A magic door had been opened, and televisual Narnia was on my screen. Oh look, the music carries on over the action, did it always do that? Is that a cat in the background? (It wasn't, it was studio talkback in the first scene.) And blimey, Joseph Furst is listed second on the credits – oh, I get it, after the Doctor, they're done in order of appearance. I didn't know they did it like that! These were magical, magical times for me, never to be repeated.

But it's not just nostalgia that makes me love this instalment – it's absolutely great, dumb fun, mainly thanks to Joseph Furst. Anyone who thinks this is nothing more than bad acting hasn't got a sense of humour. It's a brilliant spoof performance about 20 years ahead of its time, anticipating knowing, genre-baiting comedies like Airplane! If you want to see him doing "proper" acting, have a butchers at Doctor Korczak and The Children – it's a touching, dramatic tour de force that I guarantee will make you cry. He's splendid in that, and everything he does *here* is deliberate and very, very funny. I also have a video interview with him where he recreates the famous cliffhanger whilst wearing an eyepatch! What's not to love?

For benefit of anyone who says that Doctor Who only got camp and silly in the 1980s, I'll gently point them in the direction of Peter Stephens, who here plays the high priest Lolem. He's hilarious, swanning about in a skirt and wobbling. He even gets to say "Amdo has eaten up her victims" – not "eaten" or "eaten of", but "eaten *up*"! Glorious. And one of my favourite Doctor Who moments, ever, is when he bitchily tells Zaroff that he wants the wrath of Amdo to engulf him, and Furst tells him to get out – in a manner that suggests he's suddenly started acting in a Mel Brooks movie.

I'm not saying that a lot of what makes this good isn't due to the heroic ineptitude in various departments, but seriously – how can you not adore it? Polly forgets to try to save Ramo,

leaving Furst menacingly holding a spear until she audibly kicks herself up the arse. Zaroff's hair gets madder as the episode progresses. His guards wear wetsuits, and some of the fish people need goggles. The music sounds like someone is strangling a cat as it scratches a blackboard with its claws. To top it all off, the loony professor gets hit on the head by a rock, and says "Oof" before running into the darkness bellowing a good, old-fashioned crazy laugh.

Nuffink in ze world can stop me from loving this episode!

The Underwater Menace episode four

R: The telesnaps suggest that this might have looked rather spectacular. (It was certainly pretty expensive!) The Underwater Menace shifts tone yet again, and largely this week becomes a disaster movie. The scale is rather grand, as the Doctor decides the best way to foil Zaroff is not merely by kidnapping him again (go on, it was pretty simple last time), but instead to drown the whole of Atlantis. As ever with this story, the plotting has a make-it-up-as-you-go-along feel, but it does give a sense of urgency to the adventure. It's a race against time, as our heroes battle towards the surface!... and a race against gushing water too, obviously.

But with the visuals wiped, there's a pleasing sense of intimacy to all this. The best bits are those that focus upon the companions' obvious concern for each other. Jamie gently has to reassure Polly when they realise that the chances are the Doctor and Ben have drowned; in a moment so simple, it's heartbreaking, Ben despairingly says just one word, "Polly", as they too consider that their friends may be dead. And if, at the end of the day, this story was too ridiculous and too clumsy for words, episode four does manage to consolidate this rather large TARDIS team. The affection they show towards each other in the final scene, caught in telesnap mid-laugh, Polly wearing the Doctor's hat and Jamie looking around his new home with pride, is absolutely gorgeous. Together they've weathered this very peculiar and very messy story; now, stronger, they can tackle better adventures.

T: Quite a lot happens in this last instalment, doesn't it? Or, more accurately, perhaps I should say that it all seems very hastily bunged together... Richard Dawkins would probably approve that the new and improved Atlanteans decide that the best way forward is to ban religion, but this unfortunately means that the evil, experimenting doctor Damon is suddenly a goodie now. Elsewhere, poor old Lolem gets killed off screen. Elsewhere still, Zaroff doesn't even get a Herculean outburst before expiring; our last sight of the man is his rather lame attempts to stretch his arms far enough through a grille to press a switch. He doesn't even die because he's trapped; he's just mad and/or daft.

But all eyes are on the Troughton Doctor as he must save the entire planet Earth from being blown up. He's not inspiring a great deal of confidence, though – when the Doctor is asked if he knows what he is doing, he replies in the negative, but that there's nothing wrong with trying! It's very sweet, and seems to be Orme's main take on the character: that this Doctor cluelessly dives in and has a bash. It echoes similar instances found in the last three episodes – although I should again mention that I don't think they could have persevered with this characterisation, which would have involved the Doctor saving the universe by accident every week! And I do like that even this anarchy-minded Doctor resolves to go back and try to save Zaroff – it only takes a handy rockfall to stop our hero from doing so, but at least his conscience has been articulated.

All in all, I feel deeply satisfied with this story. I've found it to be rather jolly, and even its flaws have held a certain charm. I suppose you could say that if any script isn't going to hold water, it's more than a little appropriate that it's this one.

March 17th

The Moonbase episode one

R: There's that bit where Hobson, the moonbase-leader, is introducing the Doctor to his co-workers and refers to Nils as their "mad Dane". And it's a fact of life that anyone in an office who's described as the "mad one" is going to be the sort of irritating idiot who'll

photocopy his bum, or send spoof emails to all his colleagues masquerading as a virus alert, or have a mug in the kitchen in the shape of a turd. And then there's poor Bob, tubby and bespectacled, who's the sort never to get a snog at the Christmas party, and Benoit, the so-called natty dresser of the group, whose fashion sense is limited to a cravat. The last time Kit Pedler set up an international operations centre, the intruders were held at gunpoint by a warmongering general. This time, they're welcomed by the space age equivalent of Ricky Gervais, a strangely benign boss who lets all his staff call him Hobby, and puts Ben to work in their equivalent of the stationery room. The change feels odd – we've never seen the TARDIS crew taken for granted so much before.

But I rather like it too. There's so much padding to be got through in a story where the regulars have to spend the first half hour of the drama overcoming everybody's suspicions towards them. (It's why Russell T Davies introduced the psychic paper in the new series, just so we could all jump over that initial hurdle and get on with the story.) There's a *normality* to this; the crew of the base are ordinary workers responding to a crisis not with panic, but the sort of weariness that comes of having to do overtime. And it's all against a backdrop that you feel really ought to have been used before: the moon. Looking back, I suppose an adventure on the moon didn't quite fit into the series' remit before – it was too humdrum a setting for bizarre tales about giant ants seen through Vaseline-smeared lens, and too outlandish for anything that was trying to be Earth-based. There's a lot of fun to be had here, especially after the strange insanity that was The Underwater Menace, seeing the Doctor and pals respond to *real* conditions on the surface of a *real* location off Earth. Spacesuits and low gravity and the like give a real contrast to *any* of the planets we've visited thus far, and as a result the moon looks all the more alien a setting.

T: If you're turning this into an analogy of The Office, let me go a step further and suggest that it's crying out for a second story where Controller Rinberg gets posted to the moon and proves to be more popular than Hobson, leading to the latter embarrassing himself with a terrible dance. (The moonwalk, perhaps?)

Otherwise, a lot of time in this story seems to be spent on Kirby wires, with added crazy comedy sound effects whenever anyone exploits the gravitational potential of their surroundings. I suppose we should be indulgent about this – Man hadn't conquered the moon when this was made in 1967, so all of this probably would have been far more fascinating than it is to our eyes. There is some padding, though – particularly the way the Doctor asks to be introduced twice, as if he's demanding some scene setting before the adventure can begin. Hobson's reaction to him is bonkers – a sort of glum resignation to the fact that his high security science establishment has been infiltrated by a group of misfits with no ID.

But, padding or no, there's much to enjoy here. The telesnaps suggest an impressive use of the Cyber-shadow to ratchet up the tension, and we have the return of the whirry-whirry music I so like. Also, I love the way the Doctor keeps his spacesuits in a chest – that's Doctor Who for you, the ancient and futuristic are so charmingly entwined! And the theme of the adventure as a whole couldn't be better encapsulated than by Polly's sweet response to the assertion that the medical machine can cater for all of Jamie's requirements, but "It can't be nice to him." No matter what technological advances are made, nothing can replicate human kindness – it's as fitting a riposte to the Cybermen as you could hope for.

The Moonbase episode two

R: Do you think Ben is really equipped to be a companion? In almost every single story, he has a moment where he's all for turning his back on the crisis altogether and leaving in the TARDIS. It's very sensible of him, and exactly what I would do in the same situation – but it's hardly his acknowledging the format of the series, is it? It does, in this instance, provoke Troughton's speech about how some corners of the universe breed evil that must be fought – which is pretty much a defining moment for his Doctor. (It's the bit they'll use on every clip show forever after.)

This episode does something very interesting – it's the first time Doctor Who has wanted

to mythologise a past adventure. We've had occasional references to old stories before, of course, but never to the extent that the events of The Tenth Planet are, as Hobson says, part of a history that every child on Earth knows about. It's a very clever technique, because it means that not only do the Cybermen seem suddenly elevated after only a couple of episodes' appearance to the status of Major Villain, but that the Doctor, Ben and Polly also feel like epic figures. It's something that the series will do many times, as it reintroduces monsters like the Yeti, or planets like Peladon – but it's never quite as striking as it is here.

And that impact is important, because although the Cybermen are back, and look silver and threatening, they don't really *do* very much this week. They seem limited mostly to carrying sick patients about (and, rather hilariously, never quite deciding which one to pick, as if they're stuck for choice in a supermarket). This is an episode which concentrates on Hobson and his team fussing over the Gravitron – one sequence in particular goes on forever. But the contrast between these rather dull scientists and the anarchy of the Doctor is brilliant – his collecting specimens and getting under their feet whilst they so seriously do by-the-book stuff sums him up exactly. He runs rings around Hobson, as desperate to find a cure for the mysterious illness as he is to *pretend* he may have already found one, just to buy himself more time.

There's another bit used on every clip show, and that's when Polly is asked to make some coffee whilst the Doctor does something clever. It's used to illustrate the sexism of the programme, of course – and it's unfair, because it's taken entirely out of context. Anneke Wills is rather terrific this week, busying herself around in the medical lab helping to find a cure, and finding time to cast aspersions on the Doctor's medical background. (And next week, she'll do something truly dynamic.) It's Ben who wants out of the adventure, remember, and Jamie who's lying about and moaning some guff about the Phantom Piper. Polly's doing fine. Leave Polly alone.

T: Let's handle the good stuff first... Troughton continues to be brilliant – he's mercurial, mischievous and likeable, but also capable of really hefty gravitas. He really sells the horror of what's happening here, and it's entirely down to his reaction that the episode gets away with the silly revelation that there's a Cyberman under a sheet in the sickbay. He's clearly taken ownership of the role, and in the 16 episodes since he took over, he's yet to have a duff moment. It's especially delightful when he cons Hobson, but with Patrick Barr playing the commanding officer like a slightly vexed but over-credulous uncle, this isn't quite the tense face-off it could have been.

But this story just isn't clicking for me, mainly because while it's as stupid and hokey as The Underwater Menace – while it has a similar reek of the B-Movie about it – it doesn't have the courtesy of providing us with performances either hilariously wooden or gleefully over indulgent. Try as I might to care about them, the moonbase staff are just *dull*, with their characterisation never really progressing beyond The French One, The Danish One and The Boss. Bloody hell, did you notice how in episode one, the black guy lived up to cliché by being the first to get zapped? As amusing as the regulars are, the supporting cast amounts to boring scientists wandering about doing boring things in boring T-Shirts.

The pity here is that I have such strong memories of Gerry Davis' novelisation. (It's for this reason that, deep down, I still think of this story as being called Doctor Who and the Cybermen rather than The Moonbase.) In the book, Hobson was a dour Northerner, and the Cybermen looked like the ones from The Invasion. When it was reissued with the correct Cybermen depicted on the cover, I mistakenly believed it was an aberration on the part of the illustrator; the proper Cybermen could *never* have looked like that, I thought, with their big letterbox mouths, golf ball joints and baggy suits. Cybernetics may be many things, but surely baggy ain't one of 'em!

I'm sorry that I'm getting a bit off-course in our efforts to stay positive, Rob, but it's a bit frustrating that I can so easily see how this story could have been a success – namely, if you're going to be bad, you should be *operatically* bad like The Underwater Menace. Because almost everyone involved is trying to play this straight, elements where they don't get it right – the moronic science especially – seem all the

more prominent. What, the Cybermen have entered the Moonbase after making a hole in the storeroom, and they've blocked that up with bags of sugar? Seriously? And if the Cybermen have been poisoning the sugar supply, wouldn't that mean that the latest scientist to fall prey to the illness somehow, someway, hasn't had a cup of coffee since the Cybermen started their dastardly plan? It's only when things get laughably naff – the Cyberboots sticking out of the bed sheets, and then the bed itself wobbling its way into the cliffhanger – that I start to like this at all.

I am amused, however, that Sam's surname is Becket. If Samuel Beckett had written the script, I'd have liked it a lot more.

March 18th

The Moonbase episode three

R: The Cybermen *sound* great. That electronic voice they have removes any sense of inflection or humanity. In The Tenth Planet, you almost felt they were amiable, creatures to be reasoned with – here they're just chilling. More obvious, perhaps, but chilling just the same. Sometimes the dialogue exploits this well; when they stress that they are without emotions, you believe them entirely – they refuse to accept that they are taking revenge by destroying the Earth, but are just being practical. And sometimes their lines sneer at stupid human brains, and they even indulge in a bit of sarcasm. It's inconsistent, and it ought not to work. But oddly enough, it almost works *better* than the pure emotionlessness. When you hear the words "clever clever clever" coming out in perfect unamused rhythm from the Cyberman, it takes you a moment even to realise what it could possibly mean. It only then dawns on you that it's a strange parody of gloating, it's mockery without any pleasure within it, and that these beings of metal and plastic used to be men as well.

Patrick Troughton hides in the background this episode, which only serves to emphasise him all the more. He leaves Hobson to do all the talking, and Benoit to do all the running; he's mostly silent, except for one very peculiar sequence when he literally discusses the situation with himself. I've talked before about the mad schizophrenia of Troughton's performance – and here it's played without any comic resonance at all, as a genius who cannot contain the debate within his head. It's earnest and actually very eerie – and in these few lines Troughton does more to sell the tension of the episode than anything else that's happening.

Polly gets to display a bit of genius too; she devises the Polly Cocktail – a concoction of solvents, including nail polish, that eats away at the Cybermen's chest units – and her ingenuity here may just be the character's peak. Ben and Jamie are left to fight over which of them like Polly best. It's typical boys in playground stuff – and a demonstration, perhaps, that the production team are trying hard to differentiate these two male companions by creating a false bit of conflict.

T: Mercifully, this is a much better episode. From the Cyberman killing Bob (aw, Bob was my favourite scientist – he was the Fat Keith of the Moonbase) and taking everyone hostage, to their climactic advance in *large* numbers, there's a palpable sense of tension. It's clever that Benoit is sent out onto the surface so you'll genuinely wonder whether he'll make it back or not, which you wouldn't do if Ben or Jamie had been shoe-horned into that task. Andre Maranne is probably giving the best guest performance here – he sounds genuinely terrified when he's confronted by the Cybermen, and he's rather likeable elsewhere.

The TARDIS regulars seem a bit off at points – Ben seems to have done a science degree and a dissertation on the Moonbase whilst they've been here, as he says some very uncharacteristic lines that he no doubt inherited from one of the crew in an earlier draft – but Jamie and Ben do have an unusual face-off that effectively diminishes the TARDIS crew's cosiness. Polly cocktail is good stuff too, as by its nature it creates goo. (Goo is good, I like a bit of goo.) And I note from the telesnaps that the Cyberman who gets offed on the moon's surface looks suitably gruesome. I was a bit rude about the Cybermen's costumes yesterday, but I've actually warmed to them and think the masks seen here are pretty effective.

Overall, I think this is an improvement because it's an exercise in action and adven-

ture, and it doesn't waste time trying to be clever, clever, clever. It's definitely not that, but it *is* becoming more entertaining.

The Moonbase episode four

R: I first saw this episode on a big screen at the National Film Theatre in London, as part of the twentieth anniversary celebrations in 1983. And I remember being rather offended by the audience's response – which was to laugh at rather a lot of it. (Hey, I was 13. I spent most of my time being offended by laughter.) The Cybermen's double take when they realise the laser gun doesn't work, or the way in which they start to pirouette up into the sky when the Gravitron is turned on them – they look a bit like idiots. And I recognise now that that laughter is utterly intentional: there's a real celebratory feel to this, as the monsters are beaten back by the Doctor's ingenuity and the humans working together. "Hurray, that's taken care of the Cybermen!", Hobson shouts after the villains are thwarted. We're meant to be jeering at the Cybermen as they fail, and cheering mankind on – and I don't think that up to this point any Doctor Who story has ended in such a jubilant fashion. This is an episode about humanity *winning*. Mankind has come up with a wonderful invention to benefit the world; the monsters want to turn it into a weapon; mankind uses it as a weapon, just the once, and turns it on the monsters. There's a poetic justice to that. It's not subtle, but it's nevertheless entirely *right*.

And it's also entirely right that the Cybermen's departure is so funny. They might have brute force and cold intelligence, but they lack a sense of humour. So it seems just that as they're defeated, they look comical. And how telling that it absolutely mirrors the opening to the first episode, in which the Doctor's friends also took advantage of the low gravity to jump about like children (accompanied by the same Clanger-ish sound effect). The difference was that Polly and Ben and Jamie were laughing and enjoying themselves – precisely what the Cybermen couldn't do. They're defeated by something that's supposed to be *fun*.

The Moonbase is a pretty simple story, with stock characters doing stock things. If it feels very formulaic, then that's because it's getting the formula right for the first time. It's the base under siege story done cleanly, without any of the structural oddities of The Tenth Planet. It's a template for something we're going to see done ad nauseam over the next couple of seasons – but that isn't The Moonbase's fault, and nor is it that we're going to see the template used with more skill and more depth elsewhere. It's a no-nonsense bit of children's sci-fi. It makes the kids scared at the right bits, and then laugh at the baddies when they lose. It does its job.

T: There is some good stuff here – the fate of the spaceship crew sent to help those trapped within the Moonbase is pretty grim, and we're left to ponder on their slow descent into the sun. Much of the action on the moon's surface looks jolly impressive – the forced perspective shot and the laser beam are no mean achievements. Troughton is again fantastic, especially in standing firm and facing up to the assault, then nearly fainting with relief when he turns out to be right. His performance is so chock full of clever little additions, it's especially tragic how many of his episodes are missing from the archives. I also think that postulating that the shooting star is the Cybermen is a sweet and exciting idea for the kids, who'll hopefully keep their eyes peeled on the night sky to see if they can spot them.

But, dear Rob, we've known each other long enough that I have to take issue with the way you've framed how the Cybermen flying off the moon's surface – in a moment that was rendered so brilliantly in the book (especially in the illustrations) – has a certain poignancy on screen because it looks like crap. Sorry, no… sometimes, stuff looks like crap because it *is* crap. It even *sounds* like crap (that's right chaps, the dramatic finale is crying out for a comedy whooshing noise). And this is really just the climax of an episode where, in entry No. 2 of my Hadoke's Hilariously Rubbish Sci-Fi Bits series, the triumph of humanity over cybernetics is shown in part as an attempt to plug a holed space dome with a tea tray.

I know I've been less than kind to this story, and perhaps it's because it rarely seems to cop any flack, and so I feel honour-bound to redress the balance. If I've been critical, though, it's out of love – The Moonbase hasn't

amounted to much more than some terribly generic sci-fi nonsense that any other series could do in its sleep, but *Doctor Who shouldn't because it's a more interesting programme than that*. Still, if The Moonbase is more fondly regarded than I can credit it, that's probably a good thing – different elements in Doctor Who are always going to appeal to different people, which is why the show works to well.

I think I've deduced, though, why the second Doctor's catchphrase was abandoned. Did you *see* the swimming caps that the scientists use to operate the Gravitron with? Not even Patrick Troughton could have said with a straight face that he'd like a hat like that.

March 19th

The Macra Terror episode one

R: We're back to the soundtracks again, since this one's missing from the archives. So the first thing that hits us is two opposing sound effects. There's an arhythmical heartbeat, and the laughter of a crowd enjoying a parade. I think it's a measure of what we now expect from Doctor Who, that people having fun and showing just that bit *too much* happiness is the more disturbing of the two. The colony is represented by high-pitched jingles and people being exhorted to work in cheery plummy voices, and everyone sounds duly contented. As is the custom for an Ian Stuart Black script, the TARDIS crew are welcomed immediately – but here that results in makeovers for the entire cast, and promises of beauty pageants.

And there's that voice of dissent: the Doctor. If I've gone on at length about defining moments for Troughton, then here's a whole defining episode. This is perfect for him. The sequence where he's put in a machine that smartens him up is lovely – his immediate response is to make himself thoroughly dishevelled once more. What could sum up his approach better? He arrives in a place that is happy, and the first thing he does is seek out the one man who believes in monsters. And it isn't with any fear, or out of a sense of concern, no – he listens to Medok's tale about swarms of insects with eager glee. This is the anarchist Doctor, never in his element more than when he can be the fly in the ointment, the one man in an idyllic society who'll find its weakness and bring it crashing down around everyone's heads.

The one real fault of the episode is that peculiar cliffhanger last week – where, for no very good reason but an old-fashioned urge to link one serial to another, the Doctor produced a bit of technology, a "time-scanner", that he'll never refer to again but which here enables him to show the future. It makes the eagerness with which the companions give in to their holiday camp treats look as if they're a bit stupid, as they forget the imminent danger the time-scanner displayed so quickly. And worse than that, it gives the Doctor a *motive* for hunting out Medok besides his innate curiosity and his devilish attraction for crisis. You can tell hearing the episode that Black didn't intend this, and Troughton isn't playing it that way either.

I had a girlfriend like Patrick Troughton once. Not that she dressed the same, I hasten to add. But put her in a hotel, somewhere perfectly nice on the surface, and she'd find the one thing in the bathroom that was broken, the one part of the carpet that wasn't clean, the one bowl of soup in the restaurant that had a hair in it. She could ruin nice holidays just as effectively as the second Doctor. If there had been one person on that trip we took to Lanzarote who had been running about the resort complaining about crabs, I just *know* she'd have picked the suite right next to his.

T: This marks director John Davies' sole contribution to the series, so we've no existing episodes to compare his work against, but the illustrious career he had in future suggests he's no mug. (By the way, he's *not* the John Howard Davies of BBC comedy fame that Wikipedia and others mistakenly list him as being.) The archived telesnaps and clips of this story suggest he's made some interesting choices – we open with a curious close-up of Medok's shifty, frightened eyes, as the soundtrack veers from sinister undulating heartbeats to the screechy bonhomie that permeates the colony. It's a very effective, beguiling opening that plays on all the senses.

And this is just the first volley in an episode that contains strangeness in abundance. Much

of this is wonderfully unsettling – particularly the weird, forced cheeriness and profligacy of hollow quotations, with scruffy old Troughton a perfect foil for this ersatz perfection. There's a telling moment where the band-leader Barney compliments Polly, saying that she's surely the most beautiful girl in the colony. When she coyly thanks him, he blithely tells her that, "It's all part of our service" – meaning his remark was superficiality personified, the sort of thing "nice" people are obliged to say. (Thanks for nothing, then!) It's a wonderful summation of the banality of this empty jollity. And the man playing Barney is Graham Armitage – he had quite an illustrious career too, so it's odd that his one foray into the Whoniverse is this slightly cursory one-episode cameo.

Events move along, and then the episode ends as strangely as it began, as a claw reaches out at the Doctor and Medok from the darkness. The soundtrack compliments this by replacing the ongoing throbbing noise with curious, warbling howls that punctuate the night-time hush. It's almost as if the programme-makers expected that this would only exist one day on audio, and decided to make an extra effort in that department.

Oh, and reading through what I've just typed, I'm further struck by my description of Troughton as "scruffy". As someone who doesn't own a hairbrush or an iron, I adore that the Doctor doesn't have time for superficial things like appearance. If it's true that we as fans tend to create Doctor Who in our own image, that might explain why Troughton is my favourite interpreter of the role.

The Macra Terror episode two

R: This is remarkable stuff. Ben is brainwashed and betrays the Doctor, whose unbridled delight in destruction and disorder is at its peak here. Now we've seen possession in Doctor Who before, of course – most recently back in The Moonbase, where those who were taken over grew helpful black lines all over their faces so we could tell. This is very different; what's so effective about Ben's treachery is that he hasn't been reduced to a servile automaton who no longer remembers or recognises his friends. Though the Doctor denies it –

quite often, as if he wants to convince himself – this is the same Ben, but one whose opinion has changed. There's a comparable moment in The Velvet Web episode of The Keys of Marinus, where another apparently utopian civilisation encourages the TARDIS crew to turn against each other, but in that far more simplistic episode the brainwash means that when Ian captures Barbara, it's as if he's another character entirely. When Ben cries with anger that the Doctor always claims to know what's best, there is an unpleasant truth being revealed. The Doctor may have, minutes before, told Polly to resist all orders from everyone, but the Doctor himself has always adopted a patriarchal tone not a million miles from the one the colony seems to speak in. Brainwashed he may be, but Ben's rebellion is the first genuine revolt against the Doctor since The Massacre, and is just as revealing. When moments later, Jamie declares, "I only take orders from the Doctor," it rings very oddly.

As I've suggested before, Ian Stuart Black is the real political rebel of the Doctor Who writers. This is his best and cleverest script. It's the first time he's able to put the Doctor right at the forefront of the action – in The War Machines he mostly *directs* the action, finding in new-found companions like Ben the willingness to take his orders and be the brawn in his battle against the mind-controlling antics of WOTAN. Here he's the iconoclast himself – but it's fascinating too that by putting his hero so much into the story's focus, the Doctor is as much a part of Ian Stuart Black's criticism as the happy happy colony he cheerfully rebels against. The Doctor is having a great time, amiably vandalising the Pilot's office as if he has a God-given right to spread chaos wherever he goes. And it's his companions who suffer – they're the ones who get slathered over by Buick-sized crabs, who have to question their loyalties. The Doctor is both utterly against the establishment, and the establishment itself. After all, the *old* Doctor never got his face in the opening credits, like this new upstart seems to have done suddenly! There's a lot of real feeling in Ben's rebellion.

T: It's so refreshing to once again have a story that – whatever its concerns with scary killer crabs – is *about* something. Medok is taken to

a hospital for correction, we're told, where he'll be made better by having his free will removed. The Pilot of the colony tells us that it's necessary to use force to create happiness – which is a wonderfully (and horrifyingly) paradoxical ideology. The spinning wheel onto which Medok is strapped whilst being interrogated looks giddyingly unpleasant, and suggests that this wonderful, liberty-loving colony will be putting him in an orange jumpsuit and torturing him next – all in the name of justice and happiness, of course.

From the scant evidence we have, the people in front of and behind the camera seem to be singing from the same hymn sheet as the script, and are trying to make this as creepy as possible. Peter Jeffrey, playing the Pilot, is being wonderfully wistful about the measures his character feels he must take with Medok. Gertan Klauber plays the chief of police (Ola) with relish, as if to suggest that his cheerful facade masks a cruel sadism; he could almost be a metaphor for the colony itself. Richard Beale, as the propaganda voices, has seductive tones that try to woo the regulars into submission. And there's something marvellously eerie about the way the Controller's strong, screeching voice (performed by Denis Goacher) is issued from a still picture – it seems weird to be shouted at by a photograph, as if everyone in the colony is only allowed to watch a telesnap reconstruction of the Controller (I know how they feel, actually). It's especially disquieting that, while it's a bit difficult to make out what's going on in the long pause between the Controller's revelatory appearance (he's played in the flesh by Graham Leaman) and his iconic dispatch as a claw pulls him off screen, it sounds as if he's weeping.

I should stop to mention how this marks the first of Leaman's appearances in the show (notably, he'll be along later as a Time Lord in the Pertwee era), but it here seems odd that the oft-used picture of him being menaced by the Macra claw ("Humans were the prey in the chilling The Macra Terror" is how The Radio Times 20th Anniversary Special captioned this photo), he looks *nothing* like he does on screen. Clearly, the publicity shots were taken before he'd had his baggy-eyed make up and scruffed-up white hair applied.

This is all going marvellously. After trying

my patience on the moon, Doctor Who has most effectively clawed its way back into my affections.

March 20th

The Macra Terror episode three

R: I think this may well be Michael Craze's finest hour. (Well... 25 minutes, at any rate.) I don't feel he's ever been given a fair crack of the whip as Ben. After a gutsy introduction in The War Machines, he's been allowed to take something of a back seat, always the character keenest to run back to the TARDIS and find somewhere else to visit – and it's hardly been helped by the introduction of Jamie. At this moment, Jamie is no better a character than Ben, *but*... he does wear a kilt, has a better accent, and being from The Past – and therefore in Innes Lloyd's Who, a bit thick – is amiably innocent rather than peevish and disgruntled. It's such a relief to see Craze being given something interesting to do. And the scenes where he wrestles with his guilt are terrific – all the better because, against the cliché, those qualms don't automatically lead to his salvation. His best moment is standing outside the Pilot's office, determined that if he's going to betray his friends, then he's at least not going to do it to an underling. Absolutely wonderful stuff. The sequence where he reveals that he let Jamie take the chief of operation's keys, and yet doesn't know why he didn't raise the alarm, is a carbon copy of the scene in The War Machines when the hypnotised Polly lets Ben escape. But it's much more interesting here, because Craze isn't playing Ben as a robot – it's a subtle thing, but even the way he calls the gassed Official "mate" while helping him shows it's the same person, not a mind-enslaved drone.

And the presence of John Harvey also reminds me of The War Machines – yes, it's Professor Brett back! Harvey seems contractually obliged to appear in Ian Stuart Black stories. Or maybe Black is obliged to write the stories featuring John Harvey. Either way, neither of them work on Doctor Who again after this. Harvey is rather wonderful here, though, as Officia – portraying a man who seems emi-

nently benign, but just happens to be in a job where he sends disgruntled colonists down in the mines to be gassed to death. He even tries to persuade his prisoners to make the best of it – "There are worse things than the Danger Gang!" We've had all the cheery muzak and holiday camp atmosphere in the previous two episodes, but it's in the part of Officia that we get a real sense of totalitarianism dressed up as a benevolent state. Even as he's considering punishment for Jamie's escape, he won't raise a finger to oppose it, wearily telling the Doctor that Control knows best. He's not a thug like Ola, but an ordinary likeable man who's been distorted by the state he lives in. And a big cheer too, therefore, for Peter Jeffrey, whose Pilot is the most dangerous fascist leader we've yet encountered, precisely because he genuinely believes he's a kindly man looking out for his people. He's thoroughly charming, and the way Jeffrey resists giving him even a *hint* of cynicism turns him into that most interesting of characters: a despot who's as enslaved by the system as much as anybody else. (We won't see anything of this nature again until Martin Jarvis' turn as the governor on Varos.)

This is a really great story, isn't it? One of the very best we've seen yet. It's a terribly clever study of autocracy, with bursts of bizarre heightened comedy, and moments with giant killer crabs. I love it.

T: It's almost as if they're having a War Machines reunion to mark Ben and Polly's last full story. In addition to Harvey, Sandra Bryant played the club-owner Kitty in that story, and she briefly appears here, in episode one, as a young woman named Chicki. (Although she's replaced in episode four by Karol Keyes, aka Luan Peters – quite why they didn't just change the character name, I'll never know, because it's not as if Chicki actually does anything noticeable.) I thought Harvey was rubbish in The War Machines, but his gentle, naturalistic performance in this is excellent – he elevates a potentially unmemorable character into something rather special.

It continues to be mysterious, this adventure – only being able to watch it as a reconstruction adds its mystique, and the Macra are probably more impressive in our imaginations than they would have been on screen. Even so,

Davies seems to keep everything quite shadowy; there's plenty of smoke and the music's spine tingling stuff, so I'm prepared to embrace this as a genuine classic. And I appreciate that the recovered censor clips give us some visualisation of the Macra themselves – sadly, the nice chap who took the off-air footage that exists seems keener to capture the oft-photographed Doctor and companions than, say, the rarely glimpsed giant crab monsters!

Troughton continues to shine. I love the bit where he scribbles his mathematical formula on the wall and marks himself out of ten. He then – to the audible frustration of the Pilot, which shows why the Doctor adopts such tactics – sounds childishly gleeful at the prospect of an almighty explosion. He has an air of jollity, but never lets you forget that underneath lurks a darker, graver complexity. And this week, he's got a script that behaves in exactly the same way! It's a thrilling combination.

And, it has to be said, Michael Craze is fantastic. He's always been very likeable and naturalistic, but here, given an opportunity to flex a different acting muscle, he's excellent at suggesting the layers of his possession – he shouts the work ethic and meaningless litanies like a man wrestling with inner conflict. It's tough to pull off being "possessed" or "hypnotised" acting without sounding silly, but Craze pitches his performance perfectly. It's also wonderful that when the real Ben seeps through, he urges Polly to run for it whilst he faces the killer crabs alone – in this regard, he's the perfect companion.

The Macra Terror episode four

R: So. This is an episode where a fascist state disposes of its dissidents and outsiders by gassing them to death in a room. And an episode in which Jamie tries to escape from his captors by performing a Highland fling to a bunch of overexcited cheerleaders. The Macra Terror's brilliance is the way that it contrasts its extraordinarily grim depiction of a totalitarian regime, with a happy bouncy style that delights in the silly extremes of its propaganda – and suggests, as a result, that they're all part and parcel of the same thing. Troughton's Doctor is just ideal in this setting, sending up the serious concerns of the story and tweaking the nose of

evil; the scene where he interrupts a coup d'etat by telling the Pilot and Ola to apologise to each other as if they were five-year-old children is very funny. But it's also very apt: Ian Stuart Black has written a tremendously angry piece of political satire, but dressed it up as a monster story for five year olds. The implication is that there's nothing quite as trivial and pathetic as the monstrous crabs, screaming at everyone to obey them – and that we're only in danger when, as killjoys like Ben, we take the anarchy that the Doctor represents too seriously, and prefer governed order. "Bad laws are meant to be broken," says the Doctor mischievously, and he's never before quite embodied the spirit of revolution as he does here.

And any story which has the regulars dancing their way to the TARDIS and to freedom gets a thumbs up in my book.

T: What makes this work so well is that Ian Stuart Black has taken the best elements of Doctor Who's very early years – the skewed oddness, the desire to terrify the kids – and melded them seamlessly with the more thrusting, gutsy, dynamic approach of Lloyd and Davis. At the same time, he has clearly nailed what Patrick Troughton is all about – the Doctor's line that "confusion is best left to the experts" is delightful, as is "I'm sure there's no need to be scared... well, I *think* there is." This Doctor never seems certain that what he's going to do will work (as opposed to the Hartnell Doctor's certainty that his intelligence would prevail), which makes him charming whilst concurrently upping the jeopardy. And how appropriate that the Doctor only decides to bugger off when he's told he's about to have an official position of authority bestowed upon him! He's becoming more anti-establishment with every passing story.

Meanwhile, Jamie's little bit of business with the all-singing, all-dancing colonists is great fun. Frazer Hines gamely throws himself into the comedy, and appears to stumble into a curious episode of Britain's Got Talent that's overseen by a mesmerisingly upbeat cheerleader. Despite the tits and teeth, it's quite disturbing to hear the words of mental enslavement sung to us; the mind-control at work here is nauseating and peculiar even by Doctor Who standards.

This instalment is a charming ending to a lively tale that could have easily been formulaic, but performs the estimable trick of being thought-provoking, delightful, weird, exciting and frightening. It could almost be the ultimate Doctor Who adventure.

I want to let everyone know how happy this story makes me. Ra-ra-ra!

March 21st

The Faceless Ones episode one

R: Having now established himself as an anarchic force, it's frankly wonderful to see Troughton for the first time in a contemporary setting – and having to deal with the suffocating inertia of British bureaucracy. The growing frustration he feels as he's asked to present his passport, and go through the proper channels to declare he's seen a dead body, finally spills over into complete denial. The scene where he's on the floor of the airport hangar looking for clues, utterly impervious to the thick sarcasm of the Commandant, is beautifully played.

And there's great use of Jamie too. The reality of aeroplanes ("yon flying beasties!", he calls them) is on the same level of his understanding as electrocution with ray guns. It'd be so easy to have written Jamie merely as someone who couldn't understand what was going on, a sort of kilted Katarina. But the brilliance of his character is, perversely, he blithely takes everything in his stride – and so can't differentiate between the technology of a contemporary Earth story and of a sci-fi adventure. The Doctor knows enough not to mention ray guns, but it's all the same to Jamie – and so accidentally makes the Doctor's story look ridiculous. It's a terrific reversal of that repeat gag that has bothered me so much this season, that people are thick just because they're from history – here Jamie assumes that if the Commandant can take flying beasties in his stride, he must be open to everything else too. But just because he's from The Future, it doesn't mean he's smart.

It's the first contemporary episode that feels deliberately *odd*. The War Machines went to such pains to establish some idea of normalcy, down to the Post Office Tower and famous newsreaders. The Faceless Ones pretends it's doing something similar, showcasing an ordinary working airport, and contrasting the Doctor and his police box against it for comic effect – and then presents us with images of uniformed air crew producing futuristic weapons, and helping horribly scarred men up escalators. And for the first time in ages, there's a genuine *mystery* as to what's going on. It's almost comical to see Donald Pickering (playing Blade – one of the Chameleons, a group of infiltrating aliens) fuss so much about postcards, and spend his time between kidnappings licking stamps. But in a series which usually makes its crises pretty obvious, episode one of The Faceless Ones provides lots of peculiar clues but no easy answers – and for once, you watch Doctor Who scratching your head and wondering what on Earth is happening. By the time it ends, you still can't get a handle on what the tone of this new story can be, and that's very refreshing.

T: The famed double-act of Patrick Troughton and Frazer Hines has clearly clicked by this point, and there's a telling – if unintended – subtext when Spencer (another of the Chameleons) snatches Polly while Troughton and Hines are seen walking away, looking so right together, unaware that she's even gone. Hines is now a fully-fledged foil to Troughton, the latter issuing comedy kicks as the former keeps putting his foot into it.

If the last story was about clinging onto free will, this seems to be concerned with having your identity removed entirely. Seeing familiar old Polly denying who she is – and refusing to acknowledge her friends – is disconcerting, and very off-putting. But I find that the credit for this episode's success lies more with the actors involved than writers David Ellis and Malcolm Hulke, because the script keeps giving people naff stuff to do. After Blade decides not to kill the Doctor because the authorities won't believe him (surely, it would be sensible to do so anyway, just to be sure?), he tells Spencer, "We'll gain nothing by questioning [Polly]." Sorry, what? If he means there's nothing to gain but answers to his questions, then yes, I suppose he's right.

Still, I won't let a couple of slips mar my

enjoyment of this. It's moody, it's interesting and it's funny. The setting really works, especially as the aeroplanes aren't just taken from stock footage. The villains are particularly good – Victor Winding is low-key and emotionless without being wooden as Spencer, and Donald Pickering's Blade positively ices up the screen; there's a really bold and eerie moment where he stares directly at us through the lens. And for ages, the only copy I had of this was an edited Australian print that lacked Gascoigne's death and most of the Chameleon stuff, so those lingering close-ups of the scabby hands – included in this uncut version I now possess – are rather novel and exciting to me. It's a simple but impressive make-up job, the gnarled mitts impressively contriving to be both scary and pathetic. (And it's just typical that with so much of this era gone entirely, we here have an episode that escaped the junkings twice. It's like when you haven't worked for a while, then get offered three jobs on the same day.)

Oh, and I should mention something that Victor Winding himself once pointed out to me – when Spencer goes into his office after murdering the copper, the door handle comes off in his hand, but he blithely carries on and places it on the table. Colin Gordon (playing the Commandant) was apparently shocked when this happened, because he hadn't really done TV in an electronic studio before, and couldn't believe how rarely it afforded the opportunity for retakes.

Anyway, I'm enjoying this – the final shot may be in a medical centre, but the series itself is in rude health.

The Faceless Ones episode two

R: The Doctor pretends that his rubber ball is a bomb, and throws it around an airport for comic effect. My God. You'd never get away with that nowadays on children's television. That's a sign of how times have changed...

Anneke Wills and Michael Craze here log their final week of work on the series. We last glimpse Polly unconscious in a packing case, and Ben frozen by a ray gun – neither what you'd call very auspicious departures. (We do glimpse them again in episode six, in a prerecorded bit that's intended to make their fare-

well "proper", but effectively both are being written off as abruptly as Jackie Lane's Dodo.) What's interesting is the way that just as the production team were determined to make Lane as unsympathetic as possible – all posh and stuck-up – in her final episode, they do the same here. And just as this was done in The War Machines to throw new girl Anneke Wills into a good light, here it's Wills being obnoxious to Pauline Collins. There's almost an aura around Collins' Samantha Briggs – a young woman looking for her lost brother, who is given spunk, a no-nonsense wit, determination, loyalty, the opportunity to flirt with Jamie and the honour of solving the postcard mystery. She's so clearly being groomed for a role as replacement companion. I like her a lot. I don't like her big hat, mind you. It'll have to go, or I don't think she'll last the course.

The postcard scam the Chameleons are perpetrating is one of those wonderful bits of plot which seem extremely clever at first, then rather contrived and unworkable the more you think about it – and then, ultimately, rather clever again, and for that very reason. It's perfect Doctor Who imagination, then. Basically, the scheme entails the Chameleons suggesting to all of their passengers that they write postcards to their family *before* they even arrive at the destination, and they'll take care of the bother of sending them out later themselves. It's utterly daft that people go along with it – and yet, and yet... because the flights are targeted at the Club Med-type age group, you can just about buy it as an especially smart comment on the indolence of modern youth. It asks the audience to accept an awful lot – and especially that this trick works time and time again on so many flights, and only ever one Liver Bird and one pipe-smoking detective ever think to investigate it – but it's not just a plot contrivance, it's also *funny*.

As is the terrific scene where the Doctor, Ben and Jamie have a council of war hiding from the authorities in a photo booth – only to pose with wide smiles if a customer thinks to pull the curtain. Cramped on top of each other like that, it's what travelling in a blue police box *ought* to be like.

T: I dunno... you're jumping the gun a bit with Ben and Polly, aren't you? You're mainly using benefit of hindsight; there's nothing in this story yet to convince us that it's pretty much the last we'll see of them. (For all we know at this point, they could wake up inside their packing crates next week and solve the mystery.) And it's quite a nice episode for Michael Craze, who looks as though he's going to make a breakthrough and rescue Polly, but then gets zapped. I will grant that it's pretty ignominious that his last line of dialogue is delivered via a small monitor in the corner of the screen, but it's quite horrifying having the Doctor watching Ben being overcome, impotently unable to do anything about it.

I really don't understand why Innes Lloyd was so bloody merciless when it came to dispensing with the regular cast members – sacking you is one thing, but shoving you out in episode two of a six-part adventure seems a bit rude. It also means that Anneke Wills spends her final minutes on the show either playing a character who's not the real Polly, or playing the genuine article as she's shoved in a box in a trance. It's hardly the ideal way to spend her last week at work on the series, and it must have left a nasty taste in the mouth.

But, I am heartened because Troughton uses the word "smithereens"! (I *love* the word "smithereens".) There's also a really clever bit where the Chameleon named Meadows knows a piece of information (that he's moved house) that isn't on his counterpart's records – it lets the audience know that the Chameleons don't learn stuff about their victims by rote, but that they've actually assimilated the information, somehow, from the minds of those they impersonate. And prior to this, there's another lovely moment where he gets used to speaking, and a dial is twiddled to sharpen his language skills. This is hardly a faultless script, but the writers are clearly thinking about the scientific elements of the fiction.

And I just remembered – didn't you comment, Rob, that you're not fond of Sam's hat? So (dare I say it?), are you saying you *wouldn't* like a hat like that, then?

March 22nd

The Faceless Ones episode three

R: Bernard Kay is rather fun in this as Inspector Crossland; he makes a spirited attempt at a Scottish accent, and sometimes gets away with it. Is this the first time that an actor has appeared in the series for three different guest star parts? (Dallas Cavell really doesn't count, does he?) I haven't really been keeping track – Toby, do you know? What I love about Kay is that every time he appears, he plays another character entirely – there's nothing to link his amiable Crossland, doing lots of lovely acting business with where to put his pipe, with the angry Tyler from The Dalek Invasion of Earth or the dangerously self-controlled Saladin from The Crusade. He's utterly out of his depth here, encouraging the Doctor to have free run of the airport with the sort of benign patience that can only mean he hasn't followed a word that the Doctor's been claiming, or warning a couple of aliens about the long arm of the law. ("I don't think it'll quite reach where you're going," deadpans Donald Pickering smoothly.)

T: To answer your question... Tutte Lemkow did, of course, have three roles in the Hartnell era, but they weren't exactly huge (he was relegated to playing shifty foreign nutters with various bits of their anatomy missing – still, it's a living). Bernard Kay is a far more versatile and brilliant actor – he's one of my absolute favourites. I especially love the Scottish accent he uses here – there's no scripted reason for him to do it (or the pipe, for that matter), it's just him putting some effort into thinking about character, as you expect actors to do. Kay's approach to the part also allows Troughton a lovely little moment of emphasis when he says "*Scotland* Yard".

In fact, have you seen the episode of Colditz with Michael Bryant's acclaimed performance as a prisoner faking insanity in order to be repatriated? Kay plays the guard charged with observing him to see if he's faking, and ends up being his only friend. Initially he's a big bullying bear of a man who becomes a touchingly gentle guardian angel. It's a heartbreaking performance, and beautifully underplayed. Bryant rightly gets loads of praise for that performance, but Kay is just as good; he's one of the unsung heroes of the small screen in my book.

Beyond Kay, though, *everyone* is good in this. Colin Gordon treats the whole situation with an affronted Britishness that is lovely – he goes a great double take when the Doctor blithely talks of alien beings. Pauline Collins, although having a shrillness that gives me horrible flashbacks because I've done loads of stand-up gigs in Liverpool in front of various gaggles of drunk harridans on a hen-do, is sparky and likeable. And look at Victor Winding – he's chatty, naturalistic and charming when dealing with Crossland's enquiries, but then gets all evil when talking to his own kind. It's a great contrast that prevents him from becoming the thicko underling that the script wants him to be.

If there's a disappointment here, it's only that the two episodes of The Faceless Ones that exist don't actually show the monsters' faces. (All right, they haven't *got* faces, but you get my drift.) It's something of a shame, as they look rather fab in the existing pictures. And as I'm on Day 22 and counting of my trying to kick the habit, I somewhat glumly noted Crossland smoking in the Commandant's office. Could you really get away with such a thing, back in the 60s? These days, it'd probably be tolerated about as much as the little bomb scare the Doctor performed last week. So I love how Kay implies towards the end of this episode that the principal reason he goes to the cockpit to find Blade is because he's slightly embarrassed – standing in the middle of the plane, unable to light up, with everyone looking at him.

The Faceless Ones episode four

R: I suppose you have a point, Toby... from our perspective as fans, we know that Ben and Polly are history, but the contemporary audience still doesn't have a clue. And yet, I think that Jamie has an inkling; he's now Top Companion, and he basks in it. There's a greater ease and humour to Frazer Hines' performance now that Jamie isn't playing second fiddle to everyone else, and it's the first sign of the Jamie that we'll accept over the next couple of years as the second Doctor's best friend – the

cheeky boy with a protective eye for the girls. This week he gives a kiss to Pauline Collins – and picks her pocket in the process! It's a far cry from the bemused kid who'd wonder if he'd meet the Man in the Moon, and who lay about in beds moaning for the Phantom Piper. I don't know how Jamie gets away with it, but it might have something to do with his Scottish accent. I wish I sounded Scottish; it's just so cool. Then I could have snogged and thieved like Jamie does. But I was born in Surrey, the blandest of the home counties. There's little opportunity for snoggin' and thievin' in a county that gets excited by weekend visits to Croydon.

This is the mid-point of the story, and frankly it's marking time. This is why the villains keep muttering darkly about how they should kill the Doctor, but always baulk at the chance, or decide to execute him in overelaborate ways involving moving lasers (without staying to watch, that typical failing of many a Bond villain). But the image at the end where the aeroplane just stops dead still in the air is wonderfully odd – as a mental image anyway, because from telesnaps alone it's frankly hard to tell whether it actually looked good. And I love the way that Patrick Troughton charms Wanda Ventham, who here plays the Commandant's secretary, into making a diversion so he can get into the medical bay. It's a rare time when I'm actually glad the episode is missing from the archives; that telesnap he took of Ventham winking at the Doctor to let her know she's faking may be the single sexiest thing John Cura did in his whole life... Oh, dear Jean Rock. What I wouldn't have given to be Scottish at a moment like that.

And deliberate or not, I love the way that the script so subtly reveals that the bureaucratic jobsworth at immigration control in episode one is just someone who lives at home with his parents. It's not necessarily meant to be pejorative – but it's a lovely reminder that these figures of arrogant authority can really just be mother's boys.

T: Steamy Wanda Ventham aside, it's all become a bit silly, hasn't it? Despite my admiration for the actor playing him, Spencer now ranks amongst the stupidest alien henchman we've yet seen in the series. There's a brilliant (for all the wrong reasons) moment where he says he'll give Jamie just five seconds to obey, and Jamie replies that Spencer will just have to shoot him because he won't leave the Doctor. Spencer then says, "I said five seconds...", as if acknowledging that it's Dim-Second-Fiddle-Alien etiquette to allow the heroes a window of opportunity to escape. And you've already mentioned the slow, unguarded death by laser, which saves me from frothing at the mouth and punching my monitor about it. It's as if Malcolm Hulke and David Ellis aren't able to pace the alien plot without making the Chameleons behave idiotically or slowly (or idiotically slowly, even). I do like, though, how it costs 28 quid to fly to Rome – does that include airport tax and luggage? You get the impression that Chameleon Tours are so evil, they don't just indulge in a spot of kidnapping, they have all sorts of hidden charges and tariffs.

It redeems things immensely, though – as you've said – that the aeroplane turns into a spaceship. It's pure, brilliant Doctor Who, isn't it? I love it too, when the Doctor is told how a high current RAF fighter can climb, that he dismisses its abilities; it's just like the Doctor to patronise modern-day technology, and it's a stark reminder that no matter how clever and advanced we think we are, we're in the company of someone who has seen the whole of space and time. The technological achievements of our brave new world – just like our petty squabbles over land or religious beliefs – can seem like trivial nothings in the context of the vast, boundless horizons that he's witnessed. All this, and it's the first acknowledgement of the existence of loos in Doctor Who! Ah, another milestone reached!

March 23rd

The Faceless Ones episode five

R: It's the third story in a row to deal with possession and identity loss, and I think that a lot of its impact is necessarily lost through overuse. But the simple idea of having the actors lose their regional accents when turned into Chameleon simulacra is very neat. It speaks volumes about Bernard Kay's attempts at

Scottish that Jamie doesn't even notice that Inspector Crossland is now speaking in RP – but when later on we see the same thing happen to Jamie, and after five months of accepting this Scottish companion we now hear Frazer Hines talk in cold English pronunciation, the effect is honestly chilling. It doesn't make much *narrative* sense, let's be honest; if the whole point is of taking people's identities, and playing every little detail of their lives, then you'd have thought it was a fairly basic failing of the plan that they couldn't preserve their *voices*. Be a bit of a clue something was up in Air Traffic Control, I'd have thought, when you sat at work one day next to a broad Mancunian, and the following to someone who sounds like they've been to Eton. But as a dramatic device, it works because it's just so *simply* achieved; in years to come, we'll have glowing eyes, or snakes on arms, or suchlike – just removing the vocal inflections we're used to makes Frazer Hines seem suddenly genuinely alien and unknowable.

And I think a lot of credit must go this week to George Selway too. The plot requires Meadows to give in to the Doctor's demands for help immediately, as soon as he reveals he's an impostor. In narrative terms, again, it's all a bit clumsy and convenient. But Selway plays very well the part of an alien aggressor who *won't* die for the cause, who's quite prepared to sell out his entire race for the sake of his own life. We'd accept it very easily if the storyline was reversed – the scared human who'll betray everyone else is a common stereotype – and that Meadows does the same thing suggests that the Chameleons aren't just another bunch of generic aliens all speaking with one voice and one agenda, but a race of people with different and individual characterisations. It's only inasmuch as they claim to have lost their identities in a big explosion that makes this so ironic. I suggest that when Chameleon Meadows finds out who *he* was, he'll be disappointed to realise he was the nasty weaselly one that, as a kid in the playground, none of the other Chameleon children wanted to play on their football team.

By the way, I love the tinkling sound effect of the space station, which has a little of the cheeriness of an ice-cream van. It feels so incongruous against the scene in which Jamie finds the human captives in miniaturised form – and makes that sequence one of the tensest we've had in the story for ages.

T: I have some misgivings about this, but I'm prepared to stick with it, as director Gerry Mill and his cast are working hard to keep things believable and menacing – to make what we're seeing concurrently realistic and unearthly. The accent thing is a bit daft yes, but a neat shorthand – and we see now why Bernard Kay went to such great lengths to make Crossland so affable and polite, in order to contrast with his harsher, more conceited doppelganger. It's nice when an acting choice yields a payoff, even if you can't immediately see the thought behind it at first.

But it's now episode five out of six, and I'm thinking that the motives and actions of the Chameleons should be making a little more sense at this stage. Captain Blade is in a glass house when he keeps banging on about how unintelligent humans are, as the Chameleons themselves haven't exactly displayed gargantuan levels of intellect. Then the leader of the Chameleons – "the Director" – has the arrogance to big himself up: he's so inappropriately self-aggrandising, you almost think it's a joke at the expense of a group of aliens who are increasingly looking so inept, they'd probably lose against the Moroks in an edition of University Challenge – The Aliens. And it's a tad jarring that the Chameleons refer to *each other* by the name of the person whose identity they have assumed – do they not have their own monikers, or did they lose those along with their identities? It's a pity this wasn't cleared up, although we might have then taken to referring to them as The Nameless Ones, which isn't such a cool title.

Blade himself, at least, correctly guesses that the Doctor and Nurse Pinto are imposters – so he's not all that stupid (even if he's suddenly decided that he needs to ask permission to kill them). Fortunately, Donald Pickering was born to play smooth, cold villains – he's been a consistently inscrutable menace throughout, wonderfully underplayed. It just goes to show that whilst big juicy performances can be fun, it can be just as effective if you play the part as an altogether calmer Chameleon.

The Faceless Ones episode six

R: When I was a kid, reading about this story in synopsis form, it all sounded a bit pat and twee. That at the end of the adventure, the Doctor just lets the Chameleons off – they promise never to be nasty again, and just disappear back into obscurity. Actually it's nothing like that at all, and it continues the interesting process started last week of making the aliens a lot less simplistic than we're used to. It's an unsatisfactory ending, but it's *deliberately* unsatisfactory. There's a stalemate – the Chameleons realise the humans can kill them, so reluctantly sue for peace. And it's telling that they *never* apologise for what they've done, for the people they've killed – that they still believe in their natural superiority. We hear a word that's rarely used on Doctor Who – "negotiation" – and it'll become a trademark of the writing of Malcolm Hulke, who'll later give the action hi-jinks of the Pertwee years real moral dilemmas. The difference with his stories about the Silurians and the Sea Devils is that, for all Jon Pertwee's attempts to broker peace, the compromise arrangements never work – aliens are either treacherous in the world of Doctor Who and have secret agendas for conquest (like the Axons), or the humans get cold feet and blow everybody up. The Faceless Ones is the single attempt in Doctor Who's history to come to a compromise between humans and the alien aggressors, and stick to it for real. The aliens don't get their conquest, the humans don't get their revenge – and, tellingly, the audience at home don't get their big climax and a big explosion.

And that means that the story doesn't quite pay off. However deliberate that might be, as a viewer, after six episodes, you still *expect* a climax. Intellectually, I love the scrappiness of this, that everything at the conclusion is a bit messy and open-ended. (And it ties in nicely with the otherwise perfunctory departure of Ben and Polly, and also with the way that the TARDIS is stolen in the last scene, so that you never really feel this particular adventure has quite resolved itself.) It's very real life, and I think it's very bold. And it's very *adult* in that, actually, in all the ways that fanboys like me want the show to be. But it does lay on rather thickly something that's been affecting the series ever since Troughton took over. And that is...

... that he never seems to *win* in the way we're used to. In The Power of the Daleks he plays off the idea that he's beaten the Daleks accidentally, in The Macra Terror he only wins the day in the nick of time by someone else saving his life, in The Underwater Menace most of the climax of the drama comes from his attempts to *survive his own plan*. Here in The Faceless Ones, he wins the day by sheer luck – his challenge to the Chameleons that the airport authorities can destroy them turns out, at the last minute, not to be a bluff after all. There's a wonderful tension on board the space station as Blade and Spencer are shaken by the Doctor's insistence that they can be dissolved at a moment's notice, and that comes of course from the contrasting scenes on Earth as everyone races around trying to make his threats a reality. But it becomes very clear, and more here than anywhere else in Season Four, that this new Doctor really *might* not win through. I love that, I love Troughton's performance of a genius in spite of himself, and I love the new danger to the stories that suggests the Doctor may lose. But six stories in, with a new actor playing the lead, I think it's time for a story which raises the stakes a bit, which really tests the Doctor so that he can be given a true victory. Troughton has been extraordinary since he took over, and there's an invention to the performance each week that has breathed new life into the show. But he needs to be given a chance to stamp his authority on the series once and for all, to establish that Doctor Who really *is* his.

I'm looking forward to The Evil of the Daleks.

T: Balancing out my constant niggles about the Chameleons being dim, some of the human characters in this story have been so well-written, they shoulder the weight of this final episode. I especially love the way Colin Gordon's Commandant has thawed out over the last few weeks, and become rather wily and heroic in a stuffy way (it's brilliant how he jauntily tells Heslington that the flap's over, and now they have to get back to work). Sam Briggs' character admittedly isn't as satisfying, and seems to fizzle out in this final episode –

she's involved in the action, but she doesn't actually say much, spending most of her time running around the car park. Fortunately, she gets a sweet and tender parting with Jamie, which beautifully complements her historical status as The Companion Who Almost Was. (Though I'd rather her and Jean Rock had got their own spin-off series – the story of two dolly birds having jet-setting, airport-bound adventures.)

But all in all, Rob, I think that we *are* given something of a climax here – it's just that it doesn't happen on the alien spaceship (where you might expect it), and instead occurs in the special environment that was the initial selling point of this adventure: Gatwick Airport. When the Commandant blasts through the Tannoy and exhorts his staff to join the search for the abductees, it opens the drama up beyond the confines of the few small rooms we've seen, and makes Gatwick seem like a more sprawling locale. The resolution you're seeking can be found in the way that the Doctor has spent the last six weeks trying to galvanise the human authorities into action, and here they finally pull together for the sake of mankind.

As for the Chameleons themselves... well, I'm more than happy for matters with them to be resolved thanks to an uneasy truce. It would be wrong if cold, calculating Blade suddenly saw the Doctor off with back-slapping bonhomie because it's the end of the story, just as it'd be off-putting if the Doctor had glibly come up with a solution to the Chameleons' plight. What we're shown instead is a bit more realistic and uncompromising, and the open-endedness is rather novel.

Which brings me to the exit of Ben and Polly from the series.... to my surprise, I'm less angry about it than I thought I would be, as it's not the brusque "See, you then..." that I had anticipated. Instead, it's genuinely affectionate and very moving, and it plucks at the heart-strings even if you're stuck (as I am) scrutinising fuzzy still-images and listening to a purloined soundtrack. I love that Ben offers to keep travelling in the TARDIS if the Doctor needs him to, and the way the seaman tenderly says, "I'm sure you will, mate," when Jamie vows to look after the Doctor. Anneke Wills sounds genuinely tearful and upset, and

Michael Craze is nobly quiet and sincere. It's terribly affecting, and there's even room for a little melancholy when the Doctor tells them that he never got back to his own world.

This is a true parting of friends, and I will miss them. Perhaps I'm being overly influenced by behind-the-scenes developments – I think Wills and Craze have been rather ill-treated by the production team, and it's hard to watch this without remembering that Craze deserved a much better subsequent career and died far too young.

I'm a genuinely a bit gutted typing this. For the first time since we began this quest, I actually cried. But it cheers me up to think that – as this story occurs on the same day as when Ben and Polly left in the TARDIS – anyone at Gatwick who had bothered to turn on the telly would probably have seen Kenneth Kendall warning everyone about the War Machines. If Ben and Polly hurry once they leave the Doctor and Jamie's company, they can probably watch themselves embarking on their first adventure!

March 24th

The Evil of the Daleks episode one

R: Dudley Simpson's composing the music... and for the first time, for someone so used to his work on seventies Who, it actually sounds like Dudley Simpson! It's a subtle point, and one that would obviously have been entirely lost on the contemporary viewer, but to fans of a certain age like myself – and you, right Toby? – Dudley Simpson's style defined what Doctor Who was. It was the glue that made The Horns of Nimon sound like it came from the same programme as Pyramids of Mars – his use of the orchestra, his use of tense themes. Up til this point, his music on Doctor Who has sounded rather inappropriately jazzy to my ears – but now, with his menacing Dalek theme, or the repeat of the woodwind to suggest "mystery", this links the programme with my understanding of where tonally it's going to end up in the Pertwee and Baker years.

On its own terms, though, this episode is rather an odd one, isn't it? It teases the audience right from the get-go with the title – it suggests that with its setting, this at last is going to be a contemporary Dalek story; we've seen them everywhere else in the universe, but not on modern-day Earth. And what we get instead is a curious game, in which the Doctor and Jamie are led to follow a trail of increasingly obscure clues – all of which seems to be very unDalek-like behaviour, and are instead the work of a peculiar antique dealer, Edward Waterfield, who seems to have a problem understanding twentieth century slang like "okay" or "dicey". Here's an episode that stubbornly refuses to give the audience anything it's expecting. At times it feels like a piece of Dennis Spooner-like whimsy (the suggestion being made that Waterfield is using time travel to sell genuine Victorian antiques is pure Meddling Monk stuff), at times it feels a bit like a thriller with heavies plotting against the Doctor and beating themselves up. And at other times, it's the best treatment yet of the modern day – Troughton and Hines sitting in a coffee bar listening to The Beatles feels so suddenly *natural*, a million miles away from the awkward overstatement of the sixties we got in The War Machines.

What makes it work so well is that the performances all seem – for once – to be deliberately at odds with the other. I love Griffith Davies' very natural performance as Kennedy (the baddies' all-purpose stooge), just as I love Geoffrey Colville's rather mannered comic turn as Waterfield's assistant Perry: they seem to be acting in different styles altogether, and that only adds to the strange unease that hangs over the episode. And that's all to the fore with the brilliant John Bailey, who is playing Waterfield as a mess of contradictions – he's a Victorian man in 1966, a man plotting against the Doctor but who seems less of a villain than a man threatened. It's a traditional game that we won't see a Dalek until the first cliffhanger, but in every story until this one, the opening episode has concentrated on establishing the world that they're going to dominate, and therefore what the tone of the story will be. At this point, when the Dalek materialises in front of Kennedy, we still haven't got the faintest clue what The Evil of the Daleks is trying to do, we simply haven't got a handle on this story yet. It's all rather disconcerting. And frankly, a bit thrilling.

Thank goodness that 70s stalwarts like me

can rely on Dudley Simpson's music to reassure us.

T: I'm not the biggest fan of set-up episodes from Doctor Who's early years – they often come across as prefaces, with the actual story only kicking in with the first cliffhanger. I'd expected the same routine here, as the Doctor and Jamie spend most of the time stalking/being followed by a couple of incidental characters. And yet, this episode really feels like we're gearing up to an end-of-season extravaganza – it's inherent even in the way the coffee-bar music fades out, to be replaced by the incidentals, as the Doctor grimly prepares us for a high-stakes encounter.

This is all the more remarkable when you consider how Doctor Who's seasons have been structured prior to this. With modern TV, we've come to expect that showpiece episodes, monumental occurrences and actor departures will generally happen at season's climax. The first four seasons of Doctor Who, by contrast, have been a much more organic affair – seasons have started and ended with unassuming fare such as Galaxy Four and The Reign of Terror, we've had cast changes (even that of the leading man!) occurring partway through the run (midway through a story, even!), and the longest story so far – a massive, 12-part Dalek epic – didn't initiate or cap off Season Three, it was bunged in the middle of it. None of the season-enders were designed to be any more spectacular, expensive or grabby than any other story – so here, for the first time, there's a sense that we're building up to something epic and extraordinary, and that the script and production absolutely intend this to be the case.

With the Dalek story postponed from starting until episode two (as we're obliged to have a Dalek appear in a "surprise cliffhanger", in a move so bizarrely repetitious, it now defies all attempts to understand it), writer David Whitaker relies on character, language and tension to carry things through. Bob Hall is a gruff gopher who won't resort to kidnapping, Kennedy is a jaunty little crook, Perry is wonderfully hoity-toity and Waterfield is haunted and eccentric – and it greatly helps matters that Whitaker has a discerning ear for the different idioms that highlight the contrasting

backgrounds of these men. And the tension I mentioned comes from a sequence of funny, daft little clues (Hall's overalls, the left-handed matches, etc.) that only happen in adventure series, but the beauty of this is that it's all a huge contrivance. All of the breadcrumbs that the Doctor finds have been deliberately placed to lure and ensnare him – wonderful!

Complementing all of this is a design style that works best on a time-travel series – notice how Waterfield goes from his contemporary shop into a futuristic room and picks up an old antique – it's a giddy melding of three time periods that plays with us on all sorts of levels. The antiques (and Waterfield's manner and costume) all give a classy period feel, while the hi-tech equipment promises sci-fi thrills and the modern-day setting ensures it's all believable. That's why Kennedy makes more of an impact than most Doctor Who characters who survive only for one episode – at this point in the show, we've rarely had modern-day baddies who haven't been hypnotised (The War Machines) or were really aliens behaving like cold space creatures (The Faceless Ones). Kennedy is a sprightly Cockney tough guy – a modern thug whose presence in the show is quite novel, even if he does sound like Harold Steptoe.

It's also the first time the alias "J. Smith" is used in the series – and not by the Doctor! (It's signed on a clipboard authorising the TARDIS' relocation by lorry.) And by the way... what was so special about 20th July, 1966? We have *three* alien/computer menaces now, all hanging around Earth on the same day! Flipping heck.

The Evil of the Daleks episode two

R: Consider just how good Patrick Troughton is here. In the early part of the episode he plays everything down – he's almost complacent as the Doctor, gently disregarding Jamie's (correct) theories about why the antiques look new, barely breaking a sweat as a corpse is found. When Perry goes to fetch a policeman, Jamie looks alarmed; the Doctor calmly says that Perry's doing the right thing, and carries on with his own investigation as if there's no urgency whatsoever. And then...! He's whisked back to 1866. And he's panicked and confused. He thought he understood what sort of story he was in, but he's now confronted by two Victorian gentlemen talking about mirrors and time travel, and he's angry and frustrated. Then static electricity is mentioned, and the look of fear that crosses the Doctor's face, as he begins to work out that his old enemies are involved, is wonderful. The Doctor's never been as out of his depth – and, conversely, Troughton has never seemed as in control of the material. The sly ease with which he responds to Jamie in 1966 contrasts with the awkward way he jumps on Marius Goring's lines in 1866.

And he's not the only one giving it his all. It's really great to have this episode in the archives, if only to demonstrate that new-found rapport between Troughton and Hines; I don't think a new companion has ever flourished away from the shadow of his predecessors as well as Jamie has. I love the way Jo Rowbottom, as the saucy young maid Mollie Dawson, flirts with Jamie (they're all at it), and even brazenly shuts the door with her bum on first entrance. And Marius Goring (as Theodore Maxtible, the scientist who accidentally summoned the Daleks to 1866, but is foolish enough to think he can exploit them) and John Bailey spark off each other beautifully – at first both seem cast in the same jeopardy, but just look at the ways their performances contrast, Bailey playing his fear of the Daleks with despondent horror, Goring with a cigar-lighting flourish that shows you he's really *enjoying* watching evil at work.

The Daleks are great too; as before, David Whitaker teases at them, trying to show them in unfamiliar ways. The scene in which one of them orders Edward's daughter Victoria not to give the "flying pests" her food is brilliant – partly for the sheer incongruity of it, but also for the callous way that it threatens to force-feed her. (Maybe at last, we'll find out at last what the sucker is for.) And it seems so typically Dalek that it'll devise a weighing machine that gives its subject such distress. The means by which Maxtible and Waterfield have summoned them, that they've broken their way into our world by the use of reflective mirrors, ought to be laughable – but it gives them a curious mythic quality we associate with our worst nightmares. And it's very telling that in his previous story, Whitaker kept the Daleks as polite for as long as possible before they went on the rampage – whereas the first thing he has them do here is exterminate the hapless Kennedy. They're an intimidating force, however bizarre they look in the Victorian setting.

T: I remember when this episode came back to the archives – I saw it at a convention, and it was the first episode I'd seen that was actually *better* than I'd imagined it would be. In fact, I think it's shown me what I like best from Doctor Who – good, scary monsters, a florid villain played by a big proper actor (Goring was a hell of a casting coup in those days) and a period setting drenched in atmosphere. David Whitaker's script helps the cause immensely, of course – just how much classier does the plot seem when it's explained by someone using 19th century parlance? The grandeur of Whitaker's dialogue, though, is matched by the BBC's consistent ability to mount impressive looking period pieces.

But much of the intensity of this story owes to Whitaker's ability in the Troughton years to keep finding new takes on the Daleks – he here treats them absolutely seriously, portraying them as alien and unknowable creatures who nonetheless have discernible traits like cunning and superiority. (I adore the fact that the Dalek doesn't realise that Victoria's weight loss might have something, just something, to do with the trauma of being held prisoner against her will.) And let me also sing some praises for Derek Martinus' directorial talent – he never lets an episode flag, and he's clearly paid a lot of attention to his casting. Even minor roles are filled by actors with impressive futures in the profession, such as Brigit Forsyth (playing Maxtible's daughter Ruth) and Windsor Davies (playing, unless you count Tobias Vaughn, the only classic series character called Toby – and no, that's not the reason I'm enjoying this story so much).

The scene with the Doctor, Maxtible, Waterfield and the Dalek in Maxible's lab (which is littered with paraphernalia, and has a pleasingly Jules Verne feel to it) is one of my absolute favourites in the series thus far. Troughton is just incredible, and really sells just how dangerous the situation is. "What have you done with your infernal meddling?!", he cries, before nervously checking to see whether the Dalek has gone. What's so disturbing about this is that the Doctor is *terrified* – he clearly doesn't have a plan, and nobody, not even he, knows what he's going to do next. You can see his mind racing, *racing*, trying to get up to speed. God, Troughton is so good – the desperation with which he scampers about, flapping and panicking, is childlike but never threatens to dilute the menace of the scene with unnecessary humour.

The only thing that's disappointing about this? The curious double mention of Victoria being the spitting image of her mother; it's a little hokey, especially as Frazer Hines hasn't actually bothered to look at the painting of Mrs Waterfield before asking who it's of. Oh, yes, and if I'm being honest, the whole "Human Factor" business is utterly nonsensical... and yet, I can buy it because everything else is being done so damned well.

So, hang on. What I'm saying is that this is brilliant even though the central conceit upon *everything* relies is ridiculous and unbelievable gibberish? Yes, I am. Few shows beyond Doctor Who could get away with that...

March 25th

The Evil of the Daleks
episode three

R: The depiction of Kemel is hard to justify by modern standards. To go into details – here is a black man who's mute and stupid (his brain, Maxtible says, is undeveloped), and only serves as a strong man. He's so strong, actually, that he's more animal than human – he can bend iron bars, and chop through planks. Now, within the very peculiar fairytale-like tone of this story, you can – just about – rationalise him as something from the Arabian Nights, not a character but an archetype. (And with Victorian maids and Arthur Terrall changing personality at least once every scene, and Windsor Davies – as Toby; a thug named Toby, that is, not *you,* Toby – playing every Dickensian lowlife rolled into one, it's clear that this is a story about stereotypes. Which is exactly why the Daleks are trying to tap into the Human Factor as if the traits of mankind were just like ingredients you could read off a baked bean tin.) It also says much about the increasingly

peculiar Maxtible that not only does he take pride in all the strange equipment he has in his lab, but he also has as a toy a foreign fella who can break things. Within the unnaturalistic style of this bizarre story, and set within the nineteenth century where you can imagine Kemel treated as a curio, you can *maybe* (if you're very, very forgiving) accept it. So long as the series doesn't do it again. Say in a futuristic story that should be more enlightened, with another strong dumb black man, in the very next adventure. Hmm.

It's all over the place, this episode. Arthur Terrall is an intriguing enough character, but after the third time he winces and grips the metal in his neck, even his unpredictability seems very predictable. The most notable part of the instalment is undoubtedly the argument between Jamie and the Doctor. It's brilliantly played by both Frazer Hines and Patrick Troughton, Jamie being genuinely upset to find out he's being used by his friend, and the Doctor trying to cajole him out of his mood by treating him like a tantrum-throwing infant. But I don't really buy it; it feels very contrived. This is a story right from the beginning in which everyone seems manipulated by the other – and although it's *thematically* on the money, it's emotionally very forced. Last week, the Doctor was adamant that Jamie must be informed about the test he's to undergo; this time round, he's being sly and cunning at the expense of a character I understand. This is only a few weeks after Ben's rebellion in The Macra Terror, and there I thought that the drama it created asked genuine questions about the Doctor and his relationship with his friends, and became a turning point in the plot. Here, though, it's just to make Jamie hot-headed enough that he'll be a hero and run off to rescue Victoria. As the Daleks list all the characteristics that define humanity, the first they should tick off is "gullible".

I must admit, though, I love Jamie's impatient reaction to the Doctor's mention of Daleks, as something he is always going on about. It's not dissimilar to Ben's reaction in The Power of the Daleks. I know I've said it before, but I do find it irresistible, this idea of a Dalek-obsessed Doctor, constantly mentioning them and pissing off his bored companions.

T: So, what you're saying is that the Doctor is like Uncle Albert from Only Fools and Horses. ("When I fought in the Dalek war... blah, blah, blah...") And while I certainly sympathise with your concerns about Kemel, perhaps our politically correct misgivings should centre around the casting of a West Indian as a Turk. Then again, this could all have been much worse... they could have hired John Maxim and got him to black up, or put Tutte Lemkow in a body suit.

Meanwhile, it's getting harder for me to gloss over this whole Human Factor business, and I'm trying to wrap my brain around it. The ingredients analogy you offer is nice, yes, but what *is* it? What, exactly, is going to manifest itself within Jamie that the Daleks can actually remove and inject into other Daleks? Is it a chemical? It *must* be – but if things like compassion, bravery, and improvisation all make up the Human Factor, how do you siphon them off as something tangible? And if it's not a chemical... what is it, then? *I can't stand the confusion in my mind!!!*

But if the scientific principles behind this story seem baffling, I can take some solace in the intriguing characters on display here. I think I love Molly Dawson – she's sweet and energetic and likeable and has a lovely dusky voice (she sounds like a ticklish Bonnie Tyler). She also sparks off Jamie wonderfully (he's later very gallant too, offering to escort her to her room) and brings out the Doctor's most charming behaviour. Arthur Terrall is also a stand-out character, shifting between being unsettling and yet sympathetic. And then there's Kemel.... okay, so Kemel's big, black, thick and mute, but at least he only resorts to hurting Jamie because Maxtible is lying to him. Kemel might be a stereotype, but he doesn't unquestioningly resort to violence because his master tells him to. By the way, did you know that Sonny Caldinez, who plays Kemel, wrestled under the same name after this? Does that mean that World of Sport is actually the first Doctor Who spin-off – boasting, as it does, a character from Who played by the same actor? The mind boggles to think about it.

The whole of this episode, though, is perhaps encapsulated in the confrontation between the Doctor and Jamie – a stand-off that's sparked by the Doctor's Machiavellian and shifty behaviour, plus Jamie's eavesdropping. Jamie is quite unlike the guileless Jacobite we're used to – Hines makes the most of this opportunity to show his dramatic chops, and Troughton is at turns patronisingly funny ("You're in a temper") and darkly manipulative in dealing with him. It's like watching an old friend being blackmailed by a clown. It's a surprisingly uncompromising exchange, and if it leaves a nasty taste in the mouth, it aptly demonstrates that there's nothing safe or cosy about any of this.

The Evil of the Daleks episode four

R: As ever – the test that Jamie undergoes *might* be very dramatic and exciting, and it's hard to tell by soundtrack and telesnap alone. (I'm betting it looked great; this is Derek Martinus directing, after all.) As it is, it all seems a bit strange, all these peculiar deathtraps of falling axes in a Victorian house. The Doctor spends the episode watching the events with great interest (so he's one up from me, then), and pointing out moments of bravery and compassion to a watching Dalek. Once you underline them the way the Doctor is doing, these moments feel a bit flat and obvious, really.

What works far better is that there's so much of humanity in all its forms on display in the rest of the episode. There's callousness in the scene where Arthur tyrannises Molly – but there's a surprising tenderness too, as Ruth Maxtible tries to find out why her fiancé is so altered, and Arthur himself clearly despairs at the inhuman brute he's turned into against his will. There's self-deception in Maxtible's efforts to persuade himself he's a partner to the Daleks; even as he's being physically forced to the ground, he's convincing himself that their insistence he's their servant, and not their ally, is just some cultural misunderstanding. And, best of all, there's the debate between Waterfield and Maxtible about their own morality being the "sleeping partners" of the Daleks. It's as unforced and as cogent a discussion on guilt and responsibility as we've ever seen in Doctor Who – and it's the turning point for this story about what makes a human and what makes a monster. Maxtible's insistence that he cannot be blamed for the deaths in the house is not unreasonable... but the moment he picks up a gun so he can murder his partner, he's resigned all moral standing. Whereas Waterfield is haunted by the chaos and tragedy he's unwittingly produced, and his eagerness to shoulder the blame is his redemption.

T: It's at this point that the cracks start to appear in fandom's received wisdom about this story – i.e. that it's an intelligent, action-packed and flawless epic – and we have to face the reality that we're now watching a plucky Scotsman and a Turkish wrestler evading lethal traps in a mansion. I don't know about *you*, Rob, but this isn't exactly what I watch Doctor Who for. And while we can give this some benefit of doubt because Martinus is too skilled of a director to have let the action get clumsy, there's a palpable sense of the story killing time when Jamie pulls Kemel to safety twice in the same episode. There are moments where I feel as though I've been put on hold so much, I half expect them to start playing Greensleeves.

That said, at least Whitaker has thought much of this through – this episode is a hymn to decent human behaviour, and shows admirable thematic rigour. The Human Factor may be scientific nonsense, but it has a moral core that isn't just reflected in the compassion shown between Jamie and Kemel, it's also in the interaction between Waterfield and Maxtible. The former embodies the Human Factor with his contrition and decency, whilst Maxtible has gone the Dalek route by selfishly wanting to ensure his own prosperity. To put it another way, this story's heart is in the right place, in more ways than one.

I said that Whitaker has thought *much* of this through, but I can't swear that he's given due consideration to all of it. To be entirely honest, it's getting a bit hard to reconcile Whitaker's classy characterisation and dialogue with the fantastical, almost childish, touches that he insists on throwing in; I'd accept Maxtible's belief in something as ridiculous and fairytale-inspired as alchemy as a sign of the character's avarice and stupidity, except I'm not entirely convinced that Whitaker doesn't believe in it too. How much of this stems from Whitaker's own views on science, and how much of it is just him writing to the sensitivity of a children's fable? That's one of the oddest

things about The Evil of the Daleks: it feels as if Whitaker has written The Forsyte Saga, but felt the strange need to occasionally include a scene with the Billy Goats Gruff.

But if nothing else, Whitaker resolutely and absolutely knows the Daleks. Their repeated inspection of Victoria – the way she's wheeled out and callously scrutinised – is pretty horrid, and it's a real shock when a Dalek pushes Maxtible to the floor. You might expect that they'd be a bit more manipulative and cunning with him, but they don't need to be – they know that dangling a financial carrot in front of this deluded, greedy man is enough to make him do the most wicked things. Perhaps they understand the Human Factor better than we think...

March 26th

The Evil of the Daleks episode five

R: Jamie tells the Doctor he's too callous, and that their friendship is over. Now, we know with hindsight that Jamie's not about to leave the TARDIS, and Frazer Hines will be debagging beskirted companions until they exit the show together. But in the context of how the series has been treating its main cast over the past year, dropping them suddenly and at a whim, there's a real force to this. Against the odds, there's a fine dramatic pay-off to the way that Innes Lloyd has treated Dodo or Ben or Polly – you can really believe that the producer may have tired of the little Scots boy.

It's so obvious that at the moment Doctor Who is looking about for a new companion, that it's all change in the TARDIS once more. The biggest surprise about spunky Sam Briggs is that when she and Jamie kissed goodbye at the end of The Faceless Ones, she didn't jump at the prospect of adventures in time and space with him – as a character she seems entirely *conceived* to be someone who can be brave and loyal, get captured a lot and help the Doctor with his plans. By the end of episode five of The Evil of the Daleks, it's also pretty clear who the new companion will be... Mollie Dawson, the cheeky maid. She gets to flirt with Jamie, she shows wit and courage, she gets knocked out and bullied by the villains. She's the one who actively helps Jamie in his plans, and she's the one who delicately suggests she has no present worth living for. What about Victoria Waterfield, the *real* new companion, you might ask? This is her *fourth* episode in the story, and it's only this week that she even meets another human being. So there's no chance for a rapport to be established – and from the moment Jamie meets her, he puts her on a pedestal. She's an idealised portrait of Victorian gentility (hence the name), and not someone you can imagine mucking in with Cybermen and Yeti. You just know that Mollie Dawson will give the monsters what for, and that Sam Briggs would have done the same. I'm not in any way criticising Deborah Watling, who gives the right sort of despairing anger to her scenes where she's interrogated by the Daleks, but at this stage of the adventure she's not the one you'd expect to be under contract for Season Five. That's all I'm saying.

It's a peculiar episode. David Whitaker is very clever – he wrenches the story into such a position that we have a scene where Edward Waterfield considers murdering the Doctor, just to prevent him from giving the Daleks what they demand. It's an utter reversal of where we'd expect the plot to be – just compare the steely resignation Troughton shows as he gives in to the Daleks' demands here, to his horror that Lesterson was prepared to give the Daleks any power at all. The debate that he set up so skilfully last week about morality continues here; the Doctor coldly telling Waterfield that it's too late to have a conscience is truly surprising. And it's why Jamie's outburst against the Doctor *here* feels justified. We're genuinely touching on aspects of his character we haven't seen before; the series is treading new ground. In the same way, the compassion the story shows Arthur Terrall is very welcome, not giving him the comeuppance we'd expect but a chance for redemption. The episode keeps on throwing us unexpected twists – until, in the final minutes, we see the Daleks as children playing games with the Doctor. It's all very fresh, and new, and not a little unnerving.

T: You swine! I wanted to use my word count suggesting Mollie as the next companion. She doesn't even reveal what she was doing up and

about when she heard Victoria's voice last episode. Was she being curious, using her initiative to investigate strange goings on, before getting captured and hypnotised? Oh, she's definitely through to the final of Companion Academy.

Otherwise, the Doctor's scenes in this story again demonstrate why he's such a fascinating character... "All forms of life interest me," he says, as if he's constantly observing what makes the universe tick – not just scientifically, but because he's empathic as well. He's gentle and understanding when Waterfield tries to attack him, in a fine scene where our sympathies fly about all over the place. And there's a moment of deep, deep foreboding, when Waterfield talks of the destruction of a race and Troughton mournfully states, "I don't think you quite realise what you're saying, but it may come to that – it may very well come to that." He's very mercurial, this Doctor – for all of his compassion, intellect and sense of justice, he's definitely prepared to contemplate the genocide of the Daleks.

There are some other good bits here. Maxtible insists that the Daleks are his colleagues, and thereby sets himself up for a mighty fall, the marvellously bewhiskered old loon. Gary Watson (as Terrall) and Brigit Forsyth (as Ruth) impress again in what are hardly the most rewarding roles. John Bailey (as Waterfield) has a timbre to his vocals that gives the impression he could break at any moment. And yet, he also manages to ooze conscience and goodness; Waterfield could so easily have been a dull, snivelling wretch, but Bailey gives him massive dignity. And I love the episode ending, in which the humanised Daleks are so playful and childlike, they take the Doctor for a ride; it's much more interesting than your run-of-the-mill piece of random jeopardy.

But I wish they would stop mentioning "the power of the Daleks" (they've done it three times now, I think!), as it only serves as a reminder of how good that adventure was. So far, I'd even rate it a bit better than this story – which is strange, because before we started this marathon of ours, I'd have ranked Evil higher. Nonetheless, I'm splitting hairs a bit – whichever of them is better, it's a crying shame that both aren't available for us to watch and appreciate.

The Evil of the Daleks episode six

R: The three Daleks endowed with the Human Factor are wonderful, their ordinary monotones replaced with excitable inflection. The joy they take from their new names is infectious – chanting them with utter delight. Then there's a moment, just a beat of silence – and they tell the Doctor in their childish sing-song voices that they've been recalled to Skaro. And a chill blows through the scene as the Doctor loses control of his new pepperpot friends, and you realise that for all their humour and curiosity these still *are* Daleks, and they're still receiving orders. The reminder of that is really chilling.

By taking the Daleks and tweaking what they stand for, both here and in his earlier story this season, David Whitaker is making them what Terry Nation couldn't – genuinely iconic. In The Chase, you'd get the odd thick Dalek who stuttered a bit, and that was simply because the production team hadn't cemented what truly represented a Dalek yet. But by writing stories which play directly upon what sounds entirely *wrong* coming from a Dalek voice – "I am your servant," "Alpha, Beta, Omega!" – David Whitaker is ironically able to define what a proper Dalek should be: callous, sly, pitiless and entirely inhuman. And it's therefore only right, after having the Daleks look so incongruous against the trappings of a Victorian house, that they're now transported right back to where they fit in entirely. We've barely seen Skaro since that very first season, and by now even its name is part of that iconography. (And it's great that Maxtible, still insistent that he's on an equal level to the Daleks, pompously refers to it as "Skarros" – brag about his importance all he wants, but the joke's on him, because even we as an audience know more about what's going on than he does. It's like Mavic Chen all over again; the more he claims superior knowledge of the Daleks, the more the viewer knows he's going to get a terrible comeuppance.)

As soon as you've made the Daleks icons, though, there's really nothing else you can do with them except play off that. It's why this is

entirely *right* that this was intended to be the final Dalek story – once you've played with the characters as freely as Whitaker does here, it's time to bring things to a close. (And it means that when the Daleks *do* return, in five years' time, it'll have to be done on first principles again, going back to telling very archetypal stories, reminding the audience of what the Daleks represented at grass-roots level. When the series starts to feel confident enough to play with their iconography again, it veers into another direction altogether, and introduces Davros.) It's why, with things coming to a head, that it's great we get the introduction of the Dalek Emperor; with the Doctor saying he'd always wondered whether they'd ever meet, this creature – who has before now only been mentioned within the spin-off merchandise, and *never* on screen – elevates this adventure to one of a new importance. Not only does The Evil of the Daleks riff off our expectations of what Daleks should be and subvert them, it also tells us at the same time that everything we've ever seen before was just a disposable preamble for this: the confrontation at last between the Doctor and his *true* nemesis. To take either stance is daring; to do both in the same episode is not a little breathtaking.

T: At times you're a master at seeing the subtext in a piece of work, Rob – and yet, I can't believe you're actually trying to pass off Marius Goring's fluff as a deliberate insight into the psyche of his character. If you're going to play that game, why did he call Waterfield "Whitefield" in episode two? Does he have a subconscious Aryan supremacist streak, which makes his eventual transformation into a Dalek an obvious thematic payoff?

Nonetheless, Maxtible is a terrific character – he's a real prat, mind you, but a very interesting one. What's most curious about him is his overriding obsession with turning metal into gold – has he not realised that he's invented time travel? With mirrors? In the nineteenth century? Has he not thought of the financial implications of *that*? He could earn a fortune... except that, hang on, he's rich already; he said he was in episode two. It's a ridiculous scenario, and it looks like those making this episode have begun to realise it – Goring goes a bit bonkers (repeatedly shouting "murder" when Waterfield attacks him, and bumbling about looking for the Doctor like he's a geriatric in a farce), whilst Simpson augments the man's escape with comic plinky-plonky music that is quite at odds with the deep, portentous score used so effectively elsewhere. There's an utterly superb moment, though, where he demands to know what right the Daleks had to destroy his house, and one sarcastically repeats the question "right?" over and over again as he blusters, then pushes him to the ground whilst they all start yelling at him. Like Mavic Chen before him, Maxtible just doesn't realise that he's not in control of the situation, but his presence allows us to see the Daleks as cruel and threatening.

But then events work towards a belting climax, as the Dalek Emperor orders the Doctor to take the TARDIS and spread the Dalek Factor throughout history. The design work on the Dalek Emperor is obviously stunning, and this scene is such a profound and terrifying moment, especially as it marks such a whacking great change in tone from where the episode started, with playground Daleks using childish speech patterns. The opening bits with the humanised Daleks could have been utterly ridiculous, but they serve as such a stark contrasts to the non-augmented ones, who even prior to the revelation of the Emperor's masterplan have underlined their callousness by sterilising the area surrounding Maxtible's house with a bomb.

This is a superb episode, one that's full of dramatic impact. It's powerful, and, yes, as iconic as its reputation suggests. And surely, this is the only Dalek story in which the title of its prequel and sequel are both mentioned, as Troughton talks here of "the day of the Daleks". It'll have to be very good to be better than this.

March 27th

The Evil of the Daleks
episode seven

R: In The Power of the Daleks, David Whitaker posed the question, why do human beings kill human beings? And in The Evil of the Daleks he asks, how would you get Daleks to kill Daleks? The answer's simple – turn them into

human beings. It's interesting that the first thing that the human-factored Daleks do is to rebel, to turn against authority. The great triumph of humanity is its ability to question – but as Whitaker shows, it leads immediately to dissent, and then to war, and then to annihilation. I'm not sure that this story is quite the celebration of mankind that people think; as in Power, there's something very impressive about the unanimity of the Daleks – the chaos that we see destroy Skaro is entirely alien to them. And I can't help but feel there's something unavoidably cruel about the Doctor's plan – no sooner does he give the Daleks consciousness, and make them vulnerable and likeable, than he allows them to be destroyed. It leaves a nasty taste in the mouth – deliberately or otherwise.

But what the episode does very cleverly is make it clear that the Doctor is fighting not only the Daleks as a race, but the Daleks as a concept. When Maxtible becomes imbued with the Dalek factor, and when a whole army of Daleks become humanised, the whole struggle becomes blurred; no longer is it simply that looking unhuman and having grating voices can be the focus of our revulsion. Now we can be horrified instead by the instinct to conform. It is that which makes these Daleks the strongest metaphor for Nazism in the programme – certainly more suggestive than in any Terry Nation story. And it's perhaps Whitaker's fascination with it, and that it is efficient, that it *does* look attractive, which gives the drama such power. Humanity is confused and eccentric, but there's something rather wonderful in that. If we look over the colourful cast of characters we've had over this story, it's their Dickensian individuality that has made them so memorable. On any logical level, someone who's had the ability to invent time travel obsessing over the secrets of alchemy seems preposterous – but that silliness is what makes Maxtible so appealing. And it's typically cruel of the Daleks that it gives him the formula he craves... just before turning him into a Dalek drone who wouldn't find it worth having. Maxtible may be capricious and selfish and corrupt, he's the very worst presentation of humanity on offer in this story – but he's also *bizarre,* and that wide-eyed larger-than-life performance he gives is so much more appealing than the efficient automaton he's turned into. There's no more disturbing moment in the entire story than hearing Maxtible chant "kill" over and over again, not as a Dalek but as a human who has no longer the imagination to think of anything else.

The subplot about the Doctor's own morality is nicely concluded too. When the Doctor apparently becomes Dalekised, it forces Jamie to decide finally whether he trusts him or not. And it is Jamie's decision to have faith in this Doctor – the Doctor who tells him to step through the Dalek factor archway – that redeems them both. It feels as if they make a pact together at the end, that they need to take Victoria with them and look after her – and it forges for them a new friendship.

So, that's the end of Season Four... Let's face it. It's not the same programme, is it?

I think I can't help but feel a bit guilty how quickly I've adjusted to a new Doctor. I thought it'd take longer to accept Patrick Troughton, but I'll be honest – I've been carried away by the sheer excitement he's brought to carving a new character altogether. Doctor Who is finding a formula for itself, and I miss the versatility it had in its earlier years; you'd never have had a situation before, say, when The Tenth Planet and The Moonbase repeated much of the same plot only a few weeks apart, and the last four stories of this season have so traded in the same themes of possession, it's becoming a cliché. But in a funny way, the repeated motifs do give the series an *identity*, something it seemed to be sorely missing last year. And yes, it's true, we'll never get a Marco Polo again – but we never got a Marco Polo back in 1965 or 1966 either. The science fiction stories of the Hartnell years always looked rather awkward and naïve besides their historical cousins. Whereas there's a far greater confidence and depth to them now than was ever even attempted before – and if we can have a series that can produce the thoughtful drama of The Macra Terror or The Power of the Daleks, then bring it on.

I miss the Doctor Who that was, the series that could offer *anything* in time and space. But I'm still enjoying this new sci-fi show about monsters nonetheless.

T: On a grand scale, what's changed since 1963 is that this bunged together, odd little show has become aware of itself. Just compare the ending here to the slapdash denouement of The Daleks – that was a so-so battle that wrapped up a jolly kid's SF adventure, but here the final showdown between the humanised Daleks and the, er, Dalek Daleks on Skaro has the deliberate air of an epic. We've been building up to this point, in a story that's been designed, specifically, to give the Daleks an appropriate send-off, their "final end" (at least, for now).

And it works – especially for me, as I so adore watching Victorian characters in a futuristic backdrop. It floats my boat much more than the B-movie shtick of The Moonbase; the Doctor Who of the Gerry Davis mould was more gutsy, but its emphasis on hard-nosed base personnel, clumping soldiers and high-tech establishments gave a sense, sometimes, that the magic of the series had been misplaced. In The Evil of the Daleks, it's the blend of the historical with the futuristic that provides a sense of the bizarre. And it's even *more* strange to witness the gruesome dehumanising of Maxtible – a nineteenth century man – as he stumbles about on an alien planet in the future, and mentally becomes a Dalek. And while it's unclear from the telesnaps and the soundtrack, it appears that Maxtible doesn't actually die on screen, and instead just wanders off shouting, completely demented – if anything, that's more horrifying than if he'd just been shot.

But for all that The Evil of the Daleks is chiefly remembered for the Dalek civil war at its climax, it stands out because it makes so many changes to the main characters. This is the most complex examination of the second Doctor that we've seen yet – although he's been the main source of whimsy in this story, he's been truly shady at times, and displayed moments of unstinting pragmatism. His trust is again called into question in the final episode, as he talks of sacrificing everyone's lives for the sake of a greater good. It's a very multifaceted characterisation that only the finest of actors could pull off; needless to say, Troughton does.

And what of Jamie? You rightfully mentioned, Rob, how this phase of the show has been patronising towards people from the past – but now Jamie isn't from the past. *That* Jamie – the Jamie who pointed, awestruck, at flying beasties in The Faceless Ones – seems to have left with Ben and Polly. He's become our eyes and ears, our moral yardstick, and to retain that empathy, he can no longer be surprised by the likes of toasters, or to start worshipping glitter balls. The new companion admittedly gets short shrift in all of this – Victoria's main character change is that she's now an orphan, although even this is more moving (with Bailey giving a terrific performance in Waterfield's final moments, as he says that the Doctor's life was "a good life to save") and realistically rendered than Dodo turning up and just *saying* that she was an orphan. Nonetheless, this adventure really *is* as seminal as everyone says, with the second Doctor and Jamie undergoing a sea-change, and looking miles away from their first appearance together in The Highlanders.

The Evil of the Daleks might be a couple of episodes too long in the middle, but that's already a distant memory, as the final two parts have been steeped in action, horror, high stakes and high drama. Despite all its flaws, and despite some moments of pure fancy and indulgence, those involved – from David Whitaker to Derek Martinus to Patrick Troughton to the guest cast and everyone around them – helped to make something truly special.

That's alchemy.

The Tomb of the Cybermen
episode one

R: This is all rather like one of those public information videos they used to show kids at school in the seventies, isn't it? Don't Play on the Railways, Don't Play Near Electricity Pylons, Don't Play in the Long-Buried Tombs of Alien Monsters. In the first episode alone, the hapless gang of archaeologists get themselves shot (don't muck about with weapons testing machines!), electrocuted (don't put your bare hands on high voltage doors!), and trapped within revitalising machines (erm... don't get trapped within... um, machines... yes). Never before in the history of Doctor

Who has such a group of people been assembled to look so much like cannon fodder.

And it's great fun, and beautifully tense, watching them get picked off. It has a similar feel to The Power of the Daleks – we as an audience know that the characters are treating these aliens in far too cavalier a fashion, and that their complacency will be an end to them. The beauty of Tomb is that a lot of the suspense comes from just waiting to see whether the Cybermen will *ever* emerge, or whether just the remnants of their technology alone will be enough to kill everyone. And it's helped enormously by Patrick Troughton's Doctor, never more irresponsible than here; at one moment he's frightened by the implications of the tomb and the dangers of the expedition, but he's nonetheless unable to resist displaying his own cleverness, showing everyone the right levers to pull and the right formulae to follow to get themselves into ever greater jeopardy. It'd be rather like, on one of those public information videos, seeing the policeman whose job it is to warn kids to stay off the train tracks trying to entice them onto the live rail to prove his point.

It's a Cyberman story, of course, so that means that Kit Pedler's got a bunch of scientists of all different nationalities and backgrounds for us. But this time, we don't get an opera singing Italian or a mad Dane – the acting is variable, and so are some of the accents, but there's no special attention drawn to the fact that the archeological crew are from all over Earth; it's simply a good, unforced representation of a multicultural team. (Barring the fact that there's only one black man, of course, whose job is to be strong, simple, and virtually mute. It's Kemel from The Evil of the Daleks all over again.)

And I love the TARDIS scene – which really feels like a prologue, with the titles withheld for *minutes* before the action proper starts on Telos. It's probably an accident that it's filmed somewhere with an echo, but it suddenly suggests the TARDIS as somewhere weird and cavernous. As a means of introducing the Doctor's time machine to Victoria, it's rather lovely. And bearing in mind it's the first time we've seen inside the Ship since The Moonbase of all things, it may well be an introduction to a lot of the kids at home.

T: I had hoped that K would be my companion on this part of the quest – so far, we've managed, somehow, to be apart for the stories that exist and together for the telesnap marathons. I couldn't justify encouraging her to watch lots of flat pictures and indistinct noise, so apart from some snatched moments of The Aztecs (and I think, a flash or two of Galaxy Four), she's not been about. Heck, I even tried to get the kids involved in watching The Tenth Planet – they were polite but hardly excited, and didn't want to see more the next day. So I've tended to watch my episodes on my laptop as I've travelled by train from gig to gig, or late at night when everyone's asleep.

But... The Tomb of the Cybermen is the earliest complete Pat Troughton story, and sadly it's the last complete story we'll get to experience for some time. And so, while fully acknowledging that I've wanted to show K a bit of Troughton, I'm also hoping that she'll give me a fresh perspective on a story that I think I may be unnecessarily prejudiced against. To be honest, even *before* The Tomb of the Cybermen was recovered in the early 90s, I thought it was terribly overrated. I do like Troughton, and I like base-under-siege stories as a whole, but I think Tomb is amongst the weakest of them. But, am I just trying to be cool by knocking a sacred cow? Will I actually be pleasantly surprised this time? Who knows, but the next couple of days might be difficult...

What strikes me initially is that approximately the first five minutes of this episode (barring the first, brief shot of the TARDIS exterior) are on film. It's a clever use of resources to begin the season on a glossy, expensive-looking note, even though it seems quite the luxury to squander some of this allocation on an exposition scene in the TARDIS. Still, director Morris Barry is clearly in his element – the scenes look absolutely first class, and the panning shots and high and low angles he uses on the "planet's surface" transform the (not yet standard) quarry pit into something altogether more alien. The bit where the expedition party blows apart the rock covering the tomb is rather less successful – after the initial explosion, there's a rumble that's probably meant to denote a subsequent rock fall that reveals the tomb doors, but it's confusing because everyone is looking disappointedly in one direction before Ted Rogers (one of Captain Hopper's crewmen) points in a completely different one. It's odd, and since K didn't quite get what was going on either, I don't think I'm just being thick.

Special mention must go to crewman Rogers. I know that's the character's name and not the actor's name – but it amuses me that he's called Ted Rogers! (Non-UK readers will probably need to be told that "Ted Rogers" was also the name of a fast-talking comedian who hosted the game show 3-2-1. It's for this reason that I hope the electrocuted crewman was called Lennie Bennett, after the host of Punchlines and Lucky Ladders.) Alas, in what's a fairly poor cast, *our* Ted Rogers manages to be the worst. Never has the line, "You'd better listen to him!", been issued with such a lack of menace.

Anyway, anyway – I must accentuate the positive. This *looks* magnificent. The design is very impressive (setting aside the nursery switches that populate control panels), and the scenes in the weapons-testing room are enlivened by having the lights turned down, making everything seem eerie in the extreme. I really, really like the soundscape as well – this kind of story works so well when augmented by offbeat, alien sounds rather than just music. Horror has always frightened me more than sci-fi, but this cleverly uses the best in both genres, and so has the potential to be thrilling as well as scary. And there are some gruesome little touches, such as the sparks that char patterns into the electrified tomb doors, and the black burn-mark make-up applied to Ray Grover's scorched crewman.

But it's (apologies to anyone who's getting tired of me talking about him) Patrick Troughton who makes the biggest impression on both of K and me. K is completely knocked sideways by his performance, and thinks he possesses a quick mind, which she regards as an essential element of the Doctor. She also spots how paternal he is, noting that the proactive nature of the new-series companions would undermine the authority that a Doctor like Troughton possesses. She also (for a Doctor we famously champion for his childlike vulnerability) feels completely safe with him – as if his innate power and wit is reassuring in spite of his shabby demeanour. She also laughed at the bit where the Doctor mistakenly takes Jamie's hand and they comically pull away, which made me very happy.

By the way, and I have a sneaking suspicion – just an impression, mind you – that the shifty, non-Caucasian members of the crew might be the bad guys. What do you think?

March 28th

The Tomb of the Cybermen
episode two

R: The sequence where the Cybermen are resurrected is justly famous; there's something grotesque about that moment when you can first see them inside their thawing tombs, beginning to stir, then breaking through their plastic coverings clumsily like sun-drunk bees. The whole episode, of course, is a build-up to this moment – it's a slow burn exercise in tension until the Cybermen make their inevitable appearance. And so it's a relief that director Morris Barry gives it a real sense of occasion. Never before in Doctor Who has something so beautiful and something so eerie been as well combined – as the familiar music of Space Adventure starts, and the Cybermen dwarf the frightened archaeologists... their Controller is awakened, and he dwarfs *them*. "You belong to us," he says. "You shall be like us." And you believe him.

Eric Klieg, frankly, isn't much of a villain. He can't even break into the tombs and set his masterplan into operation without the Doctor secretly giving him a helping hand, but I do love the pride that he takes in The Brotherhood of Logicians – it sounds like the sort of university club that all the nerd students belong to. And so it's so refreshing that when he starts on the predictable speech to the Cyber-Controller that he's their equal ally, he's interrupted in mid-sentence and forced to his knees. It takes the Daleks *episodes* of plot to get to this point in their stories, before their Mavic Chens and Theodore Maxtibles realised that you can't bargain with the devil. The Cyber-Controller might as well be saying, "We don't want to belong to your club. Come and join ours."

T: I have never quite bought the assertion that Troughton was a dark, manipulative Doctor. I'd always thought he had consummate skill in handling both drama and comedy, which – when combined with a clever, charming and original characterisation – made him the perfect Doctor. However, upon witnessing this directly after his behaviour in The Evil of the Daleks, I can see what people mean. There's the way he lurks about in the weapons room, and later manipulates the controls to aid the lead villain, Klieg – it's as if he can't stop himself from joining in the adventure, even if it means playing along with the baddies, and even if people will almost certainly get killed in the inevitable crossfire. It's as if he's *compelled* to be clever, even if it's not necessarily the *wisest* option. He is, to use his own words, an infernal meddler. All right, he tries to justify this by claiming he needed to see what Klieg was up to – well, if you hadn't *helped him* in the first place, Doctor, his intentions wouldn't have mattered, because he would've been stuck outside the Cybermen's lair!

It's much to this story's credit, though, that the Cybermen seem so imposing. As you say, Rob, they look impressive and powerful during their awakening scene (although I'm not sure that we really needed the squeaky cling-film sound effect), and they're greatly aided by Space Adventure, that brilliant piece of stock music that is now their theme. Once they're up and about, the director cleverly has them surround Professor Parry, which emphases their height and numbers. K was especially intrigued by the Cybermen's voices, and was visibly startled when the Cyber-Controller piped up. And yes, that's a point... isn't it interesting that a mere two episodes after we met the Dalek Emperor, we now get a bulbous-headed Cyber-Controller? It's as if the production team are trying to up the odds; whereas the return of the Daleks or the Cybermen used to be enough in itself, we now need the special/different-looking/Very Important Cyberman or Dalek. Perhaps it's part and parcel of an attempt to make the Cybermen as iconic as the Daleks, now that (we know with hindsight) the Cybermen are going to inherit the mantle of Top Doctor Who Monster for the next couple of years.

But I fear there's no escaping it – both K and

I feel that while this entire episode is fast-paced and action-packed, it's also fairly ordinary. It's as if writer Gerry Davis is trying to emulate Star Trek, po-faced clunkiness and all. And can anything other than a love for Americana explain the extraordinary Captain Hopper and his quite bizarre vocabulary? He says someone has "balled up" the ship – sorry, is that a swear word? I do, at least, like his line about wanting to leave Telos with his "skin still fitting tight all over" – it's lovely, as is Troughton's gentle, childlike interaction with this no-nonsense military guy.

I would be totally remiss without noting how Katherine likes Deborah Watling's pointy bra. See, I *knew* that having a female perspective would unearth some gems.

The Tomb of the Cybermen
episode three

R: The camera loves Deborah Watling. The scene in which she and the Doctor take stock of her family memories is beautifully played by both – and the way that Watling's face looks straight out of the screen, wide eyed and vulnerable and speaking of how she misses her father, is heartbreaking. If Troughton's Doctor has never seemed as irresponsible in earlier episodes of the story, here he is at his tenderest, gently chiding Victoria for letting him sleep because of his great age, and giving a surprising insight into the way that he copes with the absence of his never-discussed family. Amidst the scenes of tension and running about, it's a truly affecting piece of humanity.

Not that the running around bits don't work well; the first half of the episode in particular has a terrific claustrophobia to it, as the archaeological team are trapped within the tombs with the Cybermen. This is the first story to make explicit the threat that was only implied in The Tenth Planet – that these monsters won't give the easy luxury of death, but want instead to convert us all into plastic parodies of humanity. When they explain how the Doctor and friends will be a new generation of Cybermen, Jamie protests that they're not like them; the Controller's overemphatic response – "You... will... be..." – is so dispassionate and so certain, it's the most frightening the Cybermen have ever been. Klieg is utterly out

of his league here; he cheers up when the Cybermen agree to listen to his proposals as if he's got a schoolboy crush on them, and the way the Controller dips his voice whilst speaking to him is amusingly patronising. The Cybermats, it must be said, are rather less effective – you can see what the story's aiming for in one shot, when one of them appears from nowhere at such great speed that it looks like a jump cut – but they do look a bit cheap. They're still better designed than any Cybermats we see later in the series though, working best in close-up, when their eyes roll and bulge in a faintly disturbing way.

It's interesting to note that by now, Jamie is no longer an eighteenth century boy out of his depth, but has become the Doctor's comic foil. When Frazer Hines groans at Troughton's "metal breakdown" pun, it's very funny, but it's not a joke that the Highlander could possibly understand. When you bear in mind that, from Jamie's point of view, there's been no break in storyline since The Faceless Ones – his cry against the metal beasties at Gatwick Airport could only have been a day or two ago at most – it's an illustration that all the baggage of the character has been disposed of, and he's become a generic companion. (Indeed, from this point on, anything technological or contemporary will be explained to *Victoria*, even though he pre-dates her by more than a hundred years.) It ought to feel like a fault – but I much prefer it this way. It's so much better to play off the natural comic rapport of Hines and Troughton, than rely upon ever-contrived gags about Jamie's reaction to the modern day. Jamie McCrimmon may be watered down a bit, but Frazer Hines is allowed to flourish – and I know which one's the more entertaining.

And a word for Clive Merrison, who appears late in the story as crewman Jim Callum, and brings a refreshing bit of comedy to the proceedings. His amiable acceptance of the crisis, and Captain Hopper's shortcomings, are very natural – all the more impressive seeing as he's saddled with an American accent.

T: Like the Cybermen, my feelings towards this story have thawed somewhat. The opening minutes of this are great fun, with lots of impressive action as Hopper bravely hurls smoke bombs about whilst rescuing everyone.

At least one of the Cybermen has laser fingers, and there's that terrific moment as one of the creatures tries to force its way through the hatch, and then bashes away at it with its fist; classic Who, indeed. And the Controller continues to be riveting – he has a sleek design, and Michael Kilgarriff deserves some praise for bringing life (so to speak) to the role, especially if you compare the precise but graceful roboticism of his movements with the comedic lumbering of whichever Cyberman actor chases Jamie early on. And the Cybermats aren't quite as frightening as one might hope – K wasn't even sure what the Cybermats were for (when the Cybermen tested the Cybermats, she thought they were going to help Cyber-transform Toberman in some way), and when they attacked the Doctor's party, she wondered why everyone didn't just jump over or walk around them. (I told her that I'd explain later.)

And much like the effectiveness of the Cybermen and Cybermats, the guest cast continues to be a mixed bag. With the best of will, the villains are, on the whole, rubbish. Klieg is such a hopeless opponent that he starts in fear when Kaftan (his fellow collaborator) makes a noise in the weapons room, and goes strangely camp when calling the Cybermen "those vile things". Kaftan even has to do a comedy duck ("comedy duck" also being the sound effect used for when the Cybermen get lost in the smoke) when Klieg turns around while holding a lethal Cyber-gun.

But then, as you mentioned, Rob – Clive Merrison is rather fab, isn't he? It's a minor part, but rather than overstate his own importance, Merrison has clearly (and wonderfully) decided to make Callum vague and preoccupied – just witness the way he distractedly mumbles when Hopper asks him to hurry up with the smoke bombs. He endows the part with realism, and makes such an impression that it's surely no surprise that he, of all the guest cast here, went on to have the most illustrious career. And the two Americans help to bring out the best in Victoria – she's much more of a fun character when she's joshing gamely with the blokes rather than moaning in the company of a cardboard exotic villainess.

March 29th

The Tomb of the Cybermen episode four

R: Oh dear. They rather dropped the ball with this one.

Not to get too carried away – it isn't an outright failure, and we've sat through a lot worse. Patrick Troughton is still worth watching, of course – there's the way he pulls back from tapping the ailing Cyber-Controller on the shoulder, just thinking better of it at the last moment; and his amused dismissal of Klieg once he's tested the limits of his lunacy. And Deborah Watling makes the most of her sparring relationship with Captain Hopper, slyly putting him down when he baulks at the idea of going back down into the tombs.

And the emotional story is all in place, so you can see how this was *meant* to work. Toberman becomes part Cyberman, and yet turns against his new race when his beloved mistress is killed. There's a poetic justice to that. But it fails precisely because Toberman has been denied any real character anyway – he's just been simple and exotic. He has precisely one moment of dignity, and that's when the camera lingers on his determined face as he closes the doors – and that works only because it allows us to believe that Toberman knew he was sacrificing his life, and wasn't just electrocuting himself because he was mentally damaged. The Evil of the Daleks' storyline didn't hinge upon Kemel the way that Tomb's has on Toberman. But turning Toberman into Cyberman (and yes, the names are similar) isn't that dramatic, because aside from his metal arm there's precious little difference. Just imagine how much more interesting this might have been had Klieg been the one who was converted, or Parry, someone who had a character we might have seen robbed from them. Or imagine, even, how much more interesting had they bothered to give Toberman a character in the first place.

A lot of critics have complained that in the final reel, the Cybermen have no plan – all they can do is get frozen again. I've no problem with that in itself; Tomb is a deliberately *smaller* story than The Tenth Planet or The

Moonbase, and for all Klieg's rantings it isn't concerned with planetary threat but the intimate concerns of a small group of people. And after The Evil of the Daleks especially, there's nothing wrong with a story that sets its sights away from the epic. But it's nonetheless unfortunate that the plot has the Cyber-Controller running out of power and needing to be revitalised – it's only for the sake of padding, because the story's all but run out. And it means that moments of crisis which ought to have had greater impact by being small and focussed just look silly by being small and *trivial*. Kaftan's death is hilarious, because it comes out of nothing more than her stubbornly pulling levers back out of place, with the sort of petulant look on Shirley Cooklin's face that suggests she's fighting her Cyber-husband over the remote control for the telly.

T: My final assessment of Tomb would have to be that it's all right, but it's nothing special. We've seen better, we've seen much worse. I can, however, admit that my initial vehemence against this story was a pathetic reaction on my part to the fact that most people rate this very highly. But really, so what if they do? Good for them. I'm in a better mood today, so I can acknowledge that this has shortcomings but not get cross about them. I haven't got to work tonight, and I'm watching Doctor Who. Lovely. All is right with the world.

Well, *nearly* right with the world. The dummy Cyber-Controller that Toberman hurls into the control panels is famously deemed crap (especially in the way that its head falls off), but here it's made worse by the fact that K glanced over to me when Toberman hefted the dummy into shot. She said the look on my face said it all – it's that aghast expression that a classic Doctor Who fan affects when he knows that something on screen is rubbish, and he's painfully aware that all the non-fans watching with him are about to glance over, in unison, to see if he's noticed how terrible it is. (Come to think of it, it's an expression I pulled a lot during Season Twenty-Four.)

Which is a bit ironic, considering the sequence with the dummy is very short-lived, and if anything I continue to find the human villains more objectionable. Klieg is as daft a baddy as Professor Zaroff, but lacks the cour-

tesy of being funny as well (perhaps the Brotherhood of Logicians sent him away because they realised he was far too dim to be in their group). Even the Doctor, who is running intellectual rings around the ranting buffoon, has to stop and tell Klieg that he should kill them now – it's as if the Doctor himself is getting bored with all the self-aggrandising speeches, or maybe he's worried that Klieg is so inept that he won't *remember* to follow through on his evil-ness and gun them down. Anyway, how exactly *does* Klieg plan to subjugate Earth? It might not be enough to simply pitch up here and say, "I'm now in command because I've got all 12 remaining Cybermen with me. Could you all stand still, please, while they recharge? And then we'll get about our conquering." I'm also rather confused as to how he plans to keep the Cybermen in line with his little Cyber-pistol, once he lets them re-energize and re-arm to the point that they can overpower humanity, if that's even possible.

But, okay – the time has come for me to see the glass half full here. The regulars, undoubtedly, are in their element in this story. Victoria has been having so much fun laying into Captain Hopper, and Jamie now does all the brave stuff, with Frazer Hines playing the part as if he's doing so not out of fearlessness, but loyalty. Troughton's gag about giving Jamie a lesson in knot-tying (the better to trap Cybermen with) is splendid, and diverts us from the Doctor's highly illogical decision to assist the Cyber-Controller's revitalisation. Does he do so because he knows that the Controller will probably kill Klieg and Kaftan when revived? Is he really that Machiavellian? (Given that he subsequently rewires the tomb to become a deathtrap for any visitors, maybe he is!)

Also, there are some great visual moments – silly as Kaftan's death might be, I love that it's a *smoky* death, as is that of the Cyberman that Jamie shoots. And it's lovely that the Cyberman that Toberman kills oozes Cyber-goo out of its chest unit, then clutches vainly at it, as if it's trying to stop its innards from spurting out. K thought it was memorably grim, especially as the creature was still moving in agonising death throes. The Cyber-Controller's death is also a suitably jerky and twitchy demise – you've gotta love a bit of body horror.

And isn't the ending terribly effective (not to mention gruesome)? Poor Toberman's powerful body lies sprawled on the deck, and they evidently leave him there, not even bothering to bury him. (Thanks for nothing, chaps!) Professor Parry is suitably contrite (actor Aubrey Richards has looked decidedly wretched since the first death, bless him). But what's most telling is that the Cybermat that moves off as the Doctor and company struggle to shut the tomb doors, which hints that the Cybermen have a bit of residual power. Coupled with the Doctor's refusal to write the Cybermen off definitively, it seems that the production team want to leave us in no doubt that this isn't the second "final end" to a major Doctor Who monster that we've seen in the space of four episodes. Less than a year since their introduction, we've had *three* Cybermen stories – and it's only a matter of time before they surface again. They've already established themselves as Troughton's greatest adversaries.

The Abominable Snowmen
episode one

R: I like this very much. Even if I'm not entirely sure why. This is slow – even by 1967's standards. I don't think there's a Doctor Who episode out there that we've yet watched that's less concerned by pace as this one. After 25 minutes we still don't know that we're back in time or who the villains are (in fact, in spite of everyone's suspicions, we still haven't yet met a sentient enemy by the close of the episode). This instalment has but one function – that the Doctor deliver a holy ghanta back to a monastery – and by the episode's end he still hasn't managed a way of doing so. And to their credit, Jamie and Victoria have wandered off on a little exploration of their own, and still taken 24 minutes to find anything even remotely hostile.

Frankly, it all ought to be as dull as ditchwater. But it's the way that the episode doesn't even remotely try to disguise its pace that makes this so engaging in spite of itself. If there was even a sting of incidental music telling us to be excited or worried or amused it'd be crass – but there isn't, just the in-drama chanting of some monks to break up the silence. And for the first time in ages, there's a story which isn't telling us what we should think or feel. It allows us instead to explore the surrounding area of a new six-part Doctor Who adventure, and to *wait* for the inevitable jeopardy that we know our heroes must encounter. In the meantime, we can take pleasure watching Jamie's futile attempts to curb Victoria's curiosity, trying to keep her safe in spite of himself, and showing off to her that a hardy Scotsman like himself can withstand the weather of the Himalayas dressed only in a kilt. And we can enjoy the Doctor's enthusiasm finding within his cabinet an object that we can neither recognise nor work out its purpose, but which gives the Doctor a strange (if wholly bemused) nostalgia. As half an hour of hi-jinks, this fails. But as a depiction of the TARDIS crew in all their eccentricity, it amuses me greatly.

T: When I was a lad, we had a big, hardback book called The A-Z of Monsters – it had pictures of, and entries for, all sorts of creatures both real and fictional. Doctor Who was represented by some decent coverage of the Daleks, Cybermen and Ice Warriors, but the Yeti in this encyclopaedia weren't the Who variety, they were the "real" thing, complete with tantalising pictures of footprints and a skull fragment. And it's these little clues that help to provide this adventure with an atmosphere of mystique – we don't *see* the monster until the end, but its presence permeates the whole first episode. It opens with screams, darkness and a twisted rifle; then we see a furry beast on the TARDIS scanner (which Jamie quickly dismisses as the Doctor in his coat); then there's a murder in the murky night; and then there are large footprints.

It's all because this episode lives up to its name and is *about* the Abominable Snowman – a legendary rumour of a creature with only opaque indications of its reality. So while it's frustrating in most other stories (particularly those with the Daleks) that the reveal of the monsters you *know* are present is left until the very end of the episode, *here* it's a confirmation that the monster whose real-life existence is a mystery definitely exists within the Doctor Who universe. (Well, so we're meant to believe for now, at least. Actually, this story will trump and trump *again* the nature of the Yeti, which is why it's all so clever, but I don't wish to get ahead of myself...)

I can't quite make it out on the telesnaps I'm looking at, but I've read that the picture on the TARDIS scanner (and just look at that thing – it's round and in some sort of electronic contraption, and not at all like the scanner we're used to) shows snow. But when the travellers are outside, it's obviously beyond the production team's resources to represent Tibet by covering the Welsh hills with fake flakes. If the information I've read about the scanner is the case, though, it's the most blatant example we've had yet of the audience being asked to suspend their disbelief. It's as if the production team is saying that yes, there *should* be snow, but we obviously can't afford to show that, so we're just going to tell you that they're in Tibet and throw up some stock footage on the TARDIS monitor to denote what it should all look like. Just imagine that it's snowy and enjoy the rest of the story would you, please? This might sound a cheap strategy to some, but it's really just a means of the production-team putting the audience's imaginations to good use. You've got to admire them for that!

March 30th

The Abominable Snowmen
episode two

R: Harold Pinter's very good, isn't he?

T: Bloody Harold Pinter... I can't believe this chestnut still gets trotted out. When I did my Theatre Studies A-Level, I noticed Pinter had acted under the pseudonym David Baron, and got all excited that he might be the same bloke who plays the guard-monk Ralpachan in this story. Approximately 15 minutes of research (and this was pre-Internet, you understand) revealed that this wasn't the case. And *you*, Rob – I had always enjoyed your Big Finish work and your interviews and the like, but then you went and wrote to The Time Team at Doctor Who Magazine and perpetrated this myth! And they printed it! I have to admit that I went off you a bit – until of course, we met up and

I discovered that you probably knew the idea was rubbish, and were just joshing about with that twisted sense of humour of yours. Still, shame on you for spreading such lies! (Besides, if you insist upon going there, I have an alternative suggestion. Rinchen is actually played by David Grey – that's right, the singer whose album White Ladder hit the charts in 1999. Okay, so their names are spelt slightly differently, and even then, common sense suggests it might be a case of same name/different person, but what the heck – let's stick it on Wikipedia anyway. Or, better still, write in to DWM about it.)

Right, to punish you for this terrible, terrible affront to the truth that you've gone and done, I'm going to go *first* on the commentary with this episode, and mention all the really noticeable and interesting stuff while leaving you with only table-scraps. For a change, *you'll* the one forced to resort to bitterness and trite wordplay – hah!

I have to back up for a moment, though. Victor Pemberton was once asked at a convention what, as script editor, he'd contributed to The Tomb of the Cybermen – and he replied that he'd "added some atmosphere". It had become a byword for that serial – Tomb was "atmospheric", and I imagined that it entailed gloomy tunnels and Cybermen looming out of the shadows. So when that story was recovered, you can imagine my feeling cheated upon discovering that it contained cheesy characters in anoraks, and – apart from the weapons room – some brightly lit sets.

That's not the case here, though. The scenes with the Abbot talking to the monastery's master, Padmasambhava, entail gloomy, shadowy lighting, with flickering flames dancing about – *that's* atmosphere for you. It's especially pleasing that the cave sequences were filmed on location and weren't part of a studio set, and that the big stone sets and period feel of the monastery convey mood much better than a futuristic serial ever could. And it's also clever how – now that the Yeti has been revealed to us – we're given a new visual mystery, in that Padmasambhava is treated as an unseen, tantalising presence.

Meanwhile, the regulars have really bedded in, haven't they? Jamie gets to do the action stuff, Victoria guesses at things and is generally terrified, and the Doctor runs through the gamut of being scared, funny and grumpy – all within a second of each other. I especially love the way that Troughton has a serious discussion about capturing a Yeti, then nervously backs away because "Jamie's had an idea" on how to go about it.

Let me end by mentioning that the *real* David Baron is alive and well, still acting and very easy to track down. Even this, however, probably won't quash the rumour that an internationally renowned playwright took a five-week sabbatical to do a bit part in a children's TV series.

R: Hey, hold on! I didn't say Pinter was in the episode. It was just a greeting, apropos of nothing, really. Like, "Nice weather, isn't it?" or, "How are you this morning?" or, "Harold Pinter's very good, isn't he?" Now, *there* was a playwright who could get under the skin of late-twentieth-century paranoia. Nothing at all about him appearing as Ralpachan in an adventure about robotic Yeti.

... although I can't help wishing it were true. Because it'd just be perfect, wouldn't it? Our most lauded man of letters, the pillar of the theatrical community, putting on a fake moustache in a bit part consigned mostly to telesnaps. I'm still holding out for Tom Stoppard revealing on The South Bank Show that he was Sapan, or Alan Ayckbourn admitting that he's bumbling about in one of the Yeti costumes.

The Abominable Snowmen
episode three

R: This episode is solid and well directed, but the lack of incidental music means that we get a few too many sequences of brooding silences – Pinteresque pauses, if you will. And the point about Pinter's pauses is that they are heavy with menace and hidden meanings. I've no particular problem with the slow pace of this – but it's about time some of those menacing pauses paid off with a bit of action.

Nonetheless, in the monk Khrisong, writers Mervyn Haisman and Henry Lincoln have created a soldier who'll grimly devote himself to the protection of others, who'll put himself in danger more willingly than his own men, and who regards the undisciplined Doctor with

gruff suspicion before realising that it's his imagination and genius that will save the day. Remind you of anyone? Norman Jones is quite excellent as this prototype Brigadier. He's the most hostile figure within the story so far, and the clichés of a Doctor Who story would lead you to expect him to be an enemy, or a madman – early on in the episode Jamie considers him "daffy" – but it's quite clear that he is a man of integrity. And his frustration at the passivity of the monks he's sworn to defend gives an urgency to a drama which might perhaps be judged as a bit flaccid: his arguments for bold action rehearse once again a debate that's old to Doctor Who – that of the dangers of pacifism – and anticipates the entire plotline of The Dominators. But it's done far more subtly here, and to greater effect.

Indeed, it's a thoughtful script all round. I can't help but feel that Victoria's constant insistence on seeing a private sanctum is a bit crass. But when she mocks the young monk Thonmi for being in thrall to a master he has never seen, and cannot understand his own curiosity, it's surely a debate about faith itself: how can a monk devote himself to a lifetime of worship, when you can never look on the face of your god? At best, Doctor Who has taken a rather agnostic stance towards religious belief – you've either got your Aztecs who are gullible savages, and any number of cults worshipping Amdo or Demnos who'll sacrifice your average assistant as soon as look at her; or you've got your corrupt or hypocritical churchwardens and vicars, who'll either be ex-pirates or genocidal Time Lords in disguise. When Haisman and Lincoln set their story on a planet called Dulkis, and debate (endlessly) about a society's disinclination to defend itself, it's all rather too pat and twee. But when they depict a band of monks whose entire point is peaceful contemplation, something much more interesting is being asked when they're required to take up arms, or demand evidence of their faith. There are no easy answers here – as there shouldn't be – and whilst it's true within this story that Victoria has every reason to suspect Padmasambhava, the dignity with which David Spenser portrays Thonmi and his unwillingness to challenge his own religious doctrine is still very persuasive.

And Wolfe Morris' turn as Padmasambhava

reflects both sides of that debate. At one moment his voice is genial and warm, and then in a moment it'll become hissing and waspish. The schizophrenia of it is genuinely unnerving. But it also ensures that there's some respect given to these Tibetan monks; if we kept cutting to sequences where the man they regard as master kept on performing like a melodramatic villain, then they'd look no more than stupid stooges. The ambiguity of Morris' performance is the ambiguity of the way faith is handled in the story.

T: Norman Jones *is* magnificent as Khrisong, isn't he? Especially considering that he's undoubtedly the same Norman Jones who played football for Gillingham in the 1920s. Why, the man must be older than he looks – common sense might dictate that we're dealing with different Norman Joneses, but hey... the names match, so they *must* be one and the same. And it's not as if Norman and Jones are particularly common names is it? Off to Wikipedia again...

R: Dear God, Toby. Let it go.

T: All right, fair enough, I'll stop now. However, if the words "Bush" or "Kate" feature in your Kinda appraisal regarding who actually wrote that story, I'm going to write a bad review of one of your Big Finish audios – Scherzo, I think – and post it on Eye of Horus. I'll need to adopt their house style – something like "It sucked, were wuz the monstas?" – to get it past their rigorous editorial control, but I'm sure I can cope.

R: I'll bear that in mind. Even though that sounds to me less a threat than a challenge.

T: Back in Tibet, Professor Travers still has "bad guy" written all over him, hasn't he? He has a line where he seems to give himself away ("Now I must make a... find out for sure"); we're in a period of Doctor Who where this could be either a simple fluff or a character-almost-giving-himself-away-by-blurting-out-the-wrong-thing moment – and on this occasion it feels like the latter. We're never allowed to shake that feeling that Travers is hiding something, and it's part and parcel of the way

that Haisman and Lincoln have steeped the adventure in mystery, making it (oddly enough) much closer to the Universal horror movies than the tomb-of-the-mummy-flavoured story preceding it.

So many different elements, in fact, combine to make this story drip with a sense of unease. The scale of the location shooting is impressive, as is the fact that some of it is at night; it's very eerie, the bewitching blackness of the mountain's inky cloak. The board with the model Yeti effectively depicts – both in terms of visuals and storytelling – how a powerful, outside force is manipulating these events. And it's great that Wolfe Morris refuses to be hamstrung by his character's protracted invisibility, and gives a terrific vocal presence. In his "normal" state, he's both spiritual and chilling – but then he assumes the rasping, evil tones of the Great Intelligence, which is a smart way of suggesting that Padmasambhava is not necessarily a willing host to this baleful force.

And did you notice? Poor old Ralpachan gets hypnotised, which means he doesn't say much this week. He has to put up with plenty of pauses.

March 31st

The Abominable Snowmen episode four

R: There are definitely pay-offs to this deliberately slow pace. The last few minutes of the episode have a tremendous tension to them, as we realise at last that the claustrophobic menace is soon to break into violence, as the Yeti move to attack the monastery. And it's a great cliffhanger too – the grotesque smiling face of the ancient Padmasambhava urging Victoria deeper into the sanctum, and his lines genuinely scary because (guess what?) he makes them *even slower* than we're used to. And there are pay offs to the lack of music as well, the beeping of the Yeti spheres reminding us (and the Doctor and Jamie) that they're about to be set on by robots. Simple things, like fetching equipment from the TARDIS, the sort of stuff you wouldn't give more than a few scenes to in an ordinary story, become major endeavours; Travers is away from the monastery for an episode and a half, which lends his experiences in the cave far greater emphasis.

But I must admit, I wouldn't want all Doctor Who to be quite this minimalist. I think it's striking, and undoubtedly very good – but it requires an effort of patience I'm not used to giving the series. (And it's hardly the production team's fault, but struggling through it on soundtrack and telesnaps alone doesn't make it any easier.)

The highlight for me, though, is the scene in which Victoria tries to explain the workings of the TARDIS to the monk Thonmi. The way in which his Buddhism can accept a box travelling through time and space is actually quite touching – and even a little profound.

T: It's a bit slow, but it doesn't half build to a massive climax. The monastery's echoey, stony environs help to stoke the tension, the end of this episode sees the Doctor and Jamie imprisoned, the Yeti models moved into attack position and Victoria ordered to enter a creepy inner sanctum as Padmasambhava is finally revealed. Generally speaking, six-part Doctor Who stories tend to be marbled with padding, but this is a rollicking old adventure yarn, and it's coping well with the added time allotted to it.

I stumbled a bit concerning the dormant Yeti by the TARDIS – it makes the Great Intelligence look a bit foolish, as if it's gone to all the trouble of dressing up a robot to serve as a sentinel and lookout, but evidently hasn't bothered to keep it switched on. But conversely, I did like Thonmi's blithe acceptance that the Doctor can travel through time and space, as it's not such a huge leap from the notion that Padmasambhava can astral travel. I don't normally hold much truck with religion (I'm *areligious* rather than *anti-religious*, though – whatever one's opinions on the topic, they should be couched in good manners) and certainly don't want mysticism and magic in my Doctor Who. For that matter, I can much more easily accept a nonsensical attempt at rationalising something with science mumbo-jumbo (i.e. "refract the core of the plasma relay") than I can with mystical mumbo-jumbo (i.e. "summon the spirits of Isis to give us their spiritual power"). However, I can make an exception with this story, as the whole Buddhisty element

contextualises the Intelligence's malignancy. and so gives this adventure its own unique flavour.

Anyway... Buddhists are just, well, *nice*, aren't they?

The Abominable Snowmen
episode five

R: This is one of the most chilling episodes of Doctor Who we've seen yet, and it achieves those chills by dwelling upon human possession by alien intelligence with a directness rarely seen in the programme again. When Padmasambhava speaks through Victoria's mouth, it's truly disturbing – all the more so since the aftereffects reduce the girl to a puppet, only speaking when she hears the Doctor's voice, and only then with a frightened insistence that they should all leave. The Doctor breaks her hypnosis with such trepidation, and by stressing too that should her possession go unchecked it'll ultimately drive her out of her mind – it's a far cry, say, from the gentleness with which Hartnell helped the WOTAN-controlled Dodo, Troughton making the concept of Victoria's mind being so abused much more unsettling and real. When you bear in mind that a companion being taken over by aliens is already beginning to look like something of a cliché – since Innes Lloyd has become producer, they've all been at it – that Haisman and Lincoln are able to make it feel so *invasive* is truly impressive.

But the greatest example of alien possession in the episode is Padmasambhava, finally visible as a man rotting in his chair, who would have rather been left to die centuries ago. Wolfe Morris gives an extraordinary performance, inspiring both sympathy and revulsion. The scene in which the Doctor confronts his old friend, only to witness his apparent death, is very moving. That Padmas recovers as soon as the Doctor has left is genuinely unnerving, and makes us feel thrillingly that our sympathy has been abused.

And the imagery is great too. The lack of incidental music, again, makes the atmosphere truly oppressive, and lets the more disturbing moments speak for themselves. Travers moaning in fear at something that has been ripped from his memory, the Great Intelligence spewing out of a cave... and Rinchen, crushed to death by the statue to whom he is so desperately praying amidst all the chaos.

T: After all the build-up last week, this all kicks off as the Yeti break in and wreak havoc. Many of the Troughton stories are referred to by shorthand as being "base under siege", but this really *does* feel like a siege. Rinchen's death, which you've mentioned, is particularly gruesome, with him screeching as the statue is pushed on top of him, and he's horribly crushed. And it adheres to an odd dramatic device that's frequently used in a wide span of drama – from The Poseidon Adventure to Die Hard – which involves an annoying character who is just *begging* to get killed, even though their eventual death is in no way comic. In this case, Rinchen's intransigent insistence that Victoria is the baddie makes him slappably one-track minded, and you almost get the impression that the main motive behind Padmasambhava's orchestrated attack is nothing more than a petty desire to kill this moaning fruitloop.

Much of what else occurs, though, is entirely serious. Khrisong remains very honourable – he constantly berates himself whilst being brave and forthright, and Norman Jones oozes dignity and strength in the role. Wolfe Morris too gives a terribly multi-layered and impressive performance (even if the make-up he wears as Padmasambhava looks a bit stuck-on and latex), and adds an almost tearful shudder to his utterances. And Deborah Watling deserves a lot of credit for that really disturbing sequence where Victoria keeps speaking like a broken record. She pitches it in exactly the same way each time, and it's horrible – it's as if her personality has been scooped out, and she's now a brainless automaton.

So, we have here a great amount of action and discovery, and a despair-laden episode ending that 24 would be proud of – the monastery is evacuated while the Yeti are waiting outside, Khrisong unknowingly runs into danger as he charges out to save the Abbot, and the cave is so filled with the goo produced by the Great Intelligence that it starts to flow out onto the mountain.

April 1st

The Abominable Snowmen episode six

R: You remember that concern I had a little while aback, that Troughton never emerged with any clear authority at the climax of his adventures? Well, this more than makes up for it. In fact, it's probably the best stand-off with a villain Doctor Who has yet given us, the Doctor's battle with Padmasambhava coming off as a mental duel that uses all his reserves of power and concentration. The build-up to his entry into the sanctum, his trying to reassure his companions before going in to face battle, is exceptionally tense; that from Jamie and Victoria's point of view we only hear that battle commence with a scream of fearful agony from the Doctor hardly helps us. (And is this the first time the Doctor has been made to seem so vulnerable and pained? I think it might be.) That the production team raise the stakes so high that we really feel he *might* lose only makes the Doctor all the more impressive for winning through. On paper, it seems to be a similar conclusion to The Power of the Daleks, where the Doctor succeeds only by the skin of his teeth – but in realisation it's very different, Troughton in this story presenting a Doctor who's far less a bumbling clown than a man of enormous intelligence and mental strength.

And the very ending is lovely! So many Doctor Who stories will take urban legends or myths and demystify them. The Loch Ness Monster? That's a Zygon robot, you know. Vampires? Oh, they're deadly alien foes of the Time Lords. The joy of this is that the story puts its sci-fi spin on the abominable snowmen of Tibet, and shows they're the mechanical muscle of an extraterrestrial intelligence. And then, brilliantly, it reveals in the final minutes that there *are* real Yeti after all, that there is still magic and wonder in the world. Travers excitedly says goodbye to his new friends, and sets off after the creatures he's spent so many years searching for. His illusions haven't been shattered, and there's still innocence to be had. It's delightful.

T: It's that man Wolfe Morris again – he articulates Padmasambhava's turmoil extremely well, and later on emits a horrible, blood-curdling laugh. What's most interesting about this is that years ago, I was chatting to a fan who actually saw these episodes on broadcast, and who insisted that Padmasambhava's face melted when he died. Now, the memory *does* cheat, and there's no sign of that in the telesnaps. However, it came to light many years later that a face-melting scene had been filmed and then, apparently, cut. If that was the case, how would my friend have remembered it? It's an awfully large coincidence, and it can't be the case that he read about the supposedly abandoned melting and revised his memories, because that information hadn't come to light when he described it to me. Appropriately, it's a mystery about a story about a mystery.

Overall, I'd approached The Abominable Snowmen expecting a bit of a jolly – you know, that it'd be not bad, but slightly overlong and not all that special either. Well, I have to say it's surprised me – it's *very* well structured, *very* eerie, but most of all it's extremely weighty. Haisman and Lincoln impressively crank up the drama – that moment you mention, where the Doctor screams in abject agony, is doubly shocking as it happens almost as soon as he's disappeared inside a secret chamber for his ultimate confrontation. And that's *before* Jamie and Thonmi smash the Yeti-control sphere... and the heroes still haven't won. Then Travers shoots Padmasambhava... but to no avail. In the dramatic stakes category, this story with supposedly "cuddly" opponents is anything but resting on its laurels.

The Ice Warriors episode one

R: The first few minutes of the adventure are a bit disorientating. You've got all these scientists dressed in weird swirly designed costumes getting panicked about copious amounts of technobabble. It looks like sci-fi with a capital S and a capital F... and yet there's one little thing that grounds it. And it's that Peter Barkworth, as base-leader Clent, hobbles about with a stick. These may be people from the distant future, and they may be talking about ionisation and stuff, but they're *human*, and with human frailties.

And what's clever about the episode is that it contrasts the Very Very Futuristic – all the shiny computers and clinical sets – with the Very Very Old. It all takes place, rather bizarrely, in an old Georgian house for one thing, if only to make all this ionisation talk sound all the more incongruous. And, of course, it deals with a prehistoric figure buried in the ice. It's all the odder to have this caveman era giant resurrected somewhere another thousand years or so in the future – it only emphasises the yawning history between them. And right in the middle of this rather solemn scientific future and this unnerving distant past are our heroes, having fun and making jokes and refusing to take things quite so seriously. The scene where the TARDIS arrives on its side, and the crew have to climb out of the doors on top of each other, is just beautifully silly – and silliness is exactly the right sort of antidote to lots of engineers huddled around computer screens shouting numbers at each other.

Speaking of which, the Doctor takes against the base computers pretty swiftly, doesn't he? It's going to be a theme of the story, I know, pitting man's instincts against machine logic – but it's not as if the Doctor *knows* that's what writer Brian Hayles will be up to. And he hasn't been there long enough to realise that Clent and his assistant, Miss Garrett, are techie nerds yet. He reacts to the computers as if he's long had a horror of technology – and he *hasn't*, has he? This isn't the way he reacted to WOTAN or the Gravitron; it's all a bit too convenient. And although Troughton deadpans very amusingly, it does make him look a bit rude – like he's being shown someone's iPod and snootily saying he prefers vinyl records.

Another thing he doesn't know yet – and nor do the viewers at home – is that the defrosting caveman is going to be a new returning baddie like the Daleks and the Cybermen. It's hard for us, perhaps, to look at the Ice Warrior with ignorance, and not think of the Galactic Federation and Alan Bennion and Monster of Peladon – but in the closing seconds it looks like something utterly alien and unknowable, its strange face crumpling and pouting at us as this *ancient* creature returns to life. The Troughton stories have played a lot upon the complacency of its characters not realising that the Daleks on Vulcan are dangerous, or that the tombs of the Cybermen should be left buried – here it's Jamie, bantering about how he'd like Victoria's kit off (she should slap him, ye ken), and not bothering even to spare a glance at the reptile thing about to wreak havoc.

One final thing. Arden – the leader of the expedition that recovers the Ice Warrior Varga – is a pretty cool customer, isn't he? He reacts to the supposed death of one of his team members, Davis, with no more than the irritation that it'll get him into trouble with his boss. And by the time he brings his frozen warrior back to camp, he's all smiles and jokes and doesn't feel it's worth mentioning one of his party's dead. What a bastard. I hope he gets his just desserts soon. (Oh, and that was a pretty impressive avalanche, by the way.)

T: I'd go a step further and say that Mrs Davis could sue Ioniser International for the unnecessary loss of her son's life. It's pretty bizarre – perhaps Brian Hayles is showing us Arden's cavalier attitude to anything that isn't the advancement of his own legacy, and yet his other assistant, Walters, is equally jocular about the prospect of Davis being found dead. All right, people rarely react completely plausibly to death in Doctor Who – it's a staple occurrence in any adventure genre, and would soon become a chore if everyone responded to it by having a nervous breakdown. But it's *too* odd a beat here, with the writer making his characters deal with the loss of a human life as if they're aware that they're in a TV drama, and that fatalities are an unremarkable inevitability.

This seems like a funny (not to mention misguided) state of affairs, given that the other characters in this story have been thrown into the mix with such care and thematic validity. Clent, for instance, is clearly the personification of this highly defined and ordered future society, one where there's talk of a meeting that's scheduled to take place in *precisely* three minutes and fifteen seconds. So, are we meant to view Arden and Walters' callousness as a symptom of humanity being more cold, mechanical and computer-like in this era, or do they demonstrate that the world isn't nearly as ordered and regimented as Clent likes to pretend? It's a bit hard to tell what Hayles is getting at with Davis' death, but...

When you come down to it, this story is all about incongruity. There's a spaceman in pre-historic ice, futuristic machinery in a Victorian mansion, and a shabby Doctor amongst the slick conformity of the computer room. He looks brilliant scampering around trying to stop the base from exploding, doing comedy business whilst retaining enough believable authority to compel everyone to do as he says. And how right that he's a second out with his calculations – I don't like my Doctor invulnerable, I like him a bit imperfect. He's a hero for people like myself, who never get things exactly right.

So this is a wonderfully complex story with a lot going for it, and even though the schoolboy error in the science of how Earth came to experience a new ice age is completely, unforgivably bad (fewer plants meant less carbon dioxide, so the planet got cooler – sorry, did they ask Kit Pedler to consult on this?), I do like the one-line lament Clent uses when describing what's happened to the world: "One year, there was no Spring." So it's not global warming that got us in the end, it's global cooling. Jeremy Clarkson was right all along – so yes, this story is most definitely science *fiction*.

April 2nd

The Ice Warriors episode two

R: Peter Sallis, here appearing as the scientist-gone-rogue Penley, makes a fine surrogate Doctor – he's sensitive, intelligent, and iconoclastic. The scene in which they first encounter each other is the highlight of the episode, and feels like a true meeting of minds. Bernard Bresslaw is truly impressive as Varga the Ice Warrior. He plays a character who has to come to terms with the shock of being in a world several thousand years after the one he has known, and to think fiercely about how to protect himself and to ensure his own survival. He's big and brutish, of course, but in the way he so practically adjusts to the new circumstances he's very intelligent too, and oddly admirable.

All of Hayles' Ice Warrior scripts are based on the struggle between technological innovation and luddite conservatism, but this is by

231

far the best. Particularly memorable is when the Doctor bursts into the conference to announce the electronic connections in Varga's helmet, proving that he is an alien. In most Doctor Who stories, it would be the simple fact that there's a bulky alien walking around which would be the reason for Troughton's outburst. But when you realise his concern isn't for the Ice Warrior at all per se, but for the indication that he might own a nuclear-powered spaceship that endangers the ionisation programme, it is quite a surprise. And it is in the treatment of Varga as a conceptual threat, rather than merely as monster of the month, that makes this story so successful.

T: This continues to be very clever and well done (well, for the most part). Clent asks the computer to assess the Doctor's "work potential and community value", which sounds terribly sinister and is a fairly damning critique of the inhumanity of this ordered society. By contrast, we have Penley, who is amiable, witty, all-too human (he can't rush to Victoria's aid) and serves as a concrete riposte to the stark functionality of this world. And if it's remarkable that we have an actor of Peter Sallis' calibre pop up in this, it's *doubly* remarkable that he does so in a story that already has Peter Barkworth and Bernard Bresslaw in it. This is an astonishing line-up, and all credit should go to Derek Martinus for hiring three such respected and able performers.

I said this was clever and well done, though, "for the most part", and my reservation chiefly centres around Storr (an outsider who has renounced science) and Arden. In short, they're pillocks. It's to Sallis' credit that he reacts with such good humour to Storr's one-track-minded moaning – the two of them are so unalike, you expect that they'll next be performing in a production of The Odd Couple. Arden, though, has his own trademarked brand of selfish single mindedness when it comes to pursuit of his achievements. When the Ice Warrior comes to life and abducts Victoria, everyone panics and worries about her safety – everyone, that is, apart from Arden, for whom the fact that he's probably unleashed a homicidal lizard man seems secondary to what this will do for his career and reputation. He's an awful person – but good on

George Waring for adding some fear into his voice when he warns Clent how terrifying it is to be in the ice after dark. No wonder Arden is scared, though – night is probably when the ghosts of all the men he's casually lost out there over the years come out.

The Ice Warriors episode three

R: The speed-through reconstruction of these missing episodes on the VHS release does the job of filling in the gaps – but what it *does* indicate is that the best scenes are the ones you can safely excise and call padding. Take the confrontation scene between Penley and Garrett, for instance, in which she first tries to persuade him, then threatens him, to return to the base with her and work for Clent. She fails, so the scene achieves no useful progression within the plot, so it can be discarded. (If this were a new series adventure, there'd be no time for it at all.) But what's brilliant about it is that it actually allows two characters we've not seen together on screen before *talk* – and by doing that establish a relationship which gives them both a depth, and the situation a renewed urgency.

Season Five has adopted a story structure of six episodes; it's the first time Doctor Who has done this, until now largely settling on the four episode length as best. The added hour of storytelling does mean that there are longueurs to wade through; neither The Faceless Ones or The Abominable Snowmen have so much plot that they couldn't have been told with a couple of episodes lopped off. But the extra *space* that the six-episode format has gives so much greater an opportunity for character development. Khrisong in The Abominable Snowmen changes from obstructive military hothead to a figure of real dignity. And in The Ice Warriors, we can see the effect all the more. Penley describes Clent the way the nuts and bolts storyline sees him – as an emotionless man more interested in technology than people. Clent could so easily have been just another Hobson, a stubborn, bad-tempered base commander. He *is* all those things, but there's the time for Peter Barkworth to make him believably human and sympathetic, which makes his trust only in technology all the more shaming. At one moment he can interrupt Victoria's frightened grief for Jamie with demands for news about the spaceship power system, at others he can stammer out words of comfort to Arden. And when Arden (and Jamie!) are gunned down by the Ice Warriors, it is so much more powerful because we have already been party both to Arden's scientific enthusiasm and his guilt that that enthusiasm has been so disastrous.

What that means is that the scene between Penley and Garrett is all the better because Penley isn't even right; Clent is so much more than the soulless button pusher. And this has a knock-on effect of making Penley so much more than the Doctorish figure who is adopting Brian Hayles' own distrustful viewpoint about technology. It means that the scene doesn't work to advance the plot, and it doesn't even work as straight exposition – it's even *more* dispensable than we might have thought. And therefore it's so much more valuable too. Doctor Who at this stage isn't merely composed of moments which have a specific function, but scenes which give ambiguity and colour to the story. The way drama is meant to do. The Ice Warriors is slow by any modern standards – and it's telling that the events of the missing episodes two and three really can be summarised within 15 minutes perfectly coherently. But it's the steady pace that gives this atmosphere and depth, and that's what makes these stories still have such impact now.

T: Long ago in the murky mists of time, I once had a dream about this story being returned to the archives, only to wake up and become terribly disappointed when I realised it hadn't. (Yes, that's what young Toby used to dream about – not sexy ladies, but absent archive telly.) And then, at the very beginning of one of only two conventions I ever attended as a lad, it was announced that four of the six episodes of this story had been recovered! Two-thirds of my dream had come true! And eventually, I was able to see all sorts of funny little touches in this story that I never conjured from reading the Target novel or looking at the photographs – Clent's limp and walking stick, the sheer size of the typography in the opening credits (Brian Hayles' Mum must have been pleased – his name is massive), and the changing Ice Warrior helmet designs.

So now I'm watching a reconstruction of the still-absent episode three, and I'm obsessing about what we can't see here. The pictures suggest that the thawing Martians in the blocks of ice looked absolutely terrific, whilst the ambush of Jamie and Arden – and the unceremonious way they're cut down – is pretty brutal. Arden's death, surprisingly, comes only after he's shown pangs of conscience for no particular reason – he's not even reported the death he treated so glibly in episode one, and the last time we saw him, he was demonstrating vaulting ambition and anticipating personal glory. But if nothing else, Arden's sudden inclination to fret gives Peter Barkworth a chance to stumble as Clent tentatively attempts to show some humanity in response. It's a brilliant piece of characterisation – subtle, consistent and multi-layered, this is one of the series' finest guest performances up to this point.

And it's Clent who begins to really spell out this story's central conflict: that of science verses humanity. He insists on checking the Doctor's findings with the computer (a move that Troughton crossly resents), and talks of colleagues, not friends. The challenges they're facing are somewhat typical Doctor Who adventure and jeopardy – one of the companions has been taken hostage, another has been shot and there are deadly aliens thawing out – but the likes of Clent, Penley and Miss Garrett make the proceedings pop off the screen.

Oh, one more thing... Penley has been keeping notes on The Omega Factor, has he? It's good to know that an intimate knowledge of 1970s telefantasy featuring Louise Jameson will be vital when the world's under threat. (You and I, Rob, might end up becoming indispensable experts come the environmental apocalypse.)

April 3rd

The Ice Warriors episode four

R: I'm in a good mood. Because this – and another bumper two episodes after it! – actually exist in the archives, and I can watch them as moving pictures on my telly screen. You know, the way they were intended. It makes me much more forgiving of their faults. (God knows how I'm going to respond to the series after we reach The War Games; I'll be so overjoyed to be in a world free of blurry telesnaps that I'll probably love *everything*, just on principle. Watch this space.)

So, yes, intellectually, I think episode four has a few problems. It's that midway point in a long serial, so not very much really happens. Victoria escapes from the Ice Warriors, but is recaptured in time for the closing credits. The Doctor sets out for the Ice Warrior spaceship – but only gets there in time for the episode ending. And what an episode ending! Simply by refusing to be civil, and answering a perfectly innocuous question, the Doctor faces death and a contrived cliffhanger. If I were watching this by telesnap alone, I'm not sure I'd be getting much out of it. But with all the pictures in place, I can see how good Derek Martinus' direction is. On paper the sequence where the Ice Warrior Turoc lumbers after Victoria should do the Ice Warriors' credibility no good whatsoever, emphasising that they can't move very fast and have an alarming blind spot when people hide directly in front of them. But Martinus makes the slow heavy lurch of the Ice Warrior very intimidating – and coupled with Dudley Simpson's terrific music, there's a real tension to these scenes where a terrified Victoria runs for her life.

And there are some great moments. The social awkwardness of Clent, trying to express just how much he's come to value the Doctor – Peter Barkworth is quite brilliant in this scene. The casual cruelty of Storr's death, as the Ice Warriors assess his uselessness and dispose of him so peremptorily that their victim has only seconds to realise his life is in danger. The eagerness that Angus Lennie (as Storr) shows when finding in Frazer Hines a soulmate, someone who also cannot understand the science of the base, and the way that he throws away his life trying to help this new friend. And, as ever, best of all, the calm authority with which Patrick Troughton takes on the responsibility of talking to the alien aggressors – firmly telling his frightened friends that he refuses to take weapons with him. That he looks in his fur coat just as primitive as the hapless Storr, and that he too

is parroting the naïve belief that he can reason with the Martians, can hardly be lost on us.

T: This adventure continues to run the whole gamut of philosophical issues, using what could have been a bog-standard contest with some reptile men to focus on weighty issues such as science versus nature, technology versus humanity and man verses alien. Clent in particular is something of a marvel; lesser writers would have made him either an obstinate figure with whom the Doctor butts heads, or a helpful, sympathetic leader – yet in one scene here, he's both. He bullies Victoria in his efforts to find out what type of engines the Martian spacecraft uses – part of an effort to determine whether or not it's safe to use the Ioniser against the encroaching glaciers. But then, when the Doctor says he's going to personally investigate the matter, Clent gets all vulnerable and human – he can't quite bring himself to make a rousing speech that will keep the Doctor from going, looks to Miss Garrett for help at one point and finally snaps out his acquiescence. I hate to think that the nuances of Peter Barkworth's brilliant performance would have remained lost had these episodes not surfaced – Penley's description of his former boss is great ("He's got a printed circuit where his heart should be"), but Barkworth evolves the character into so much more than that.

The chief drawback to all of this wonderful character texturing, for me at least, continues to be the scruffy Storr (whose name, by the way, sounds like the monikers of Martians to come). He's a berk – someone who takes his anti-science views to such an extreme, he's blinded to all reality and pragmatism about the topic, and ends up looking like a stupid idealist. In short, he's an ill-educated loudmouth who gives the environmental lobby a bad name. Just look at how he chides Penley because the Martian weapons were "scientifically designed". Well, duh – so's your cooker, you numpty! I can't help but feel that Storr isn't in the story because he's a serious component of the unfolding discussion about man's relationship to technology – instead, I suspect he's just there as collateral damage, someone the Ice Warriors can bump off to remind us of their cold matter-of-factness. And it *does* work in that regard – Martinus famously cast shorter actors here as the humans, and seeing Bresslaw tower over little Angus Lennie is visually impressive. Matters get sickeningly terrifying when Storr is caught between Zondal and Varga as if he's a frightened rabbit, and they end up blasting him down after assessing his uselessness (or, rather, *non*-usefulness). In death, at least, Storr is a stark demonstration of the warriors' dispassionate soldiery.

Overall, I'm finding so much to like about this story. The sturdy, visually impressive sets look great on film, the chase scene is terrific, Bresslaw wonderfully looks like he's having a kip (as his head sinks into his body carapace like a turtle), and there's that superbly stylised music. It's an ethereal female voice contrasted with the sudden chomping, clunking solidity of a... er, is it a glockenspiel? Well, it's a voice and an instrument anyway, which work at odds to underline the themes of the story in a neatly distinct fashion.

The Ice Warriors episode five

R: Don't get me wrong here, I'm really enjoying my journey through Troughtondom. But it may well be a mark of the fact that the series has by now given itself over entirely to monster-led sci-fi japes, that there are fewer genuinely stand-out performances given by guest actors any longer. The stories are falling into certain types, and therefore the characters do too – in principle, there's little to distinguish General Cutler from Hobson to Leader Clent, they're all gruff leaders of bases under siege. Looking back at The Moonbase, I wouldn't necessarily fault Patrick Barr for his bland performance, because he merely played within the limits of the stereotype he was given.

So when Peter Barkworth gives his take upon a similar role, the fact that he mines so much from it is extraordinary. He's playing a man in an impossible situation, and goes from grim resolve to dreadful panic within moments. In one scene he's attacked by Penley for giving up hope, and then attacked by him minutes later because he's too hopeful. It'd be so easy for Clent by now to be nothing more than a series of tics – and we've seen so many characters recently descend quickly into insanity (Cutler, Lesterson, Maxtible, Klieg) that we're

quite prepared to add another loony to the list. But it's the way that Barkworth ferociously holds onto his character's dignity that is so impressive, sometimes in spite of the script. There's that very funny moment when he tries to rally his troops about him, only to be met by flat indifference from Walters – and Barkworth makes this attempt at optimistic cheerleading something that is genuinely touching. He makes the indecision of the character come to life quite brilliantly, understanding full well that any course of action he follows could be considered suicide. By this stage we can see perfectly clearly how the story must end, that the Ice Warriors can only be defeated if Clent pulls himself together and uses the Ioniser – and all these outbursts of angst are just delaying the inevitable. But Barkworth makes his agonies feel like a real character journey. And that's helped by the terrific encounter he has with Peter Sallis' Penley. Both Penley and Clent have spent so much time demonising the other, it's a jolt to realise this is the first scene they share on screen together.

I think Brian Hayles' script is so clever and thoughtful too – it's a story about the dangers of inaction (rather like the Yeti story was a month ago), but that it makes passivity so exciting is really rather an achievement. The Ice Warriors is a bit like The Moonbase, but with greater exploration of the themes it raises. Like the Cyberman story, it's all focussed around a weather-controlling device being threatened by a bunch of monsters – and how, in the end, turning the device upon those monsters will win the day. But whereas the only dilemma The Moonbase offers is in the practical difficulty of how to play the Gravitron upon the lunar surface (done in the end by pressing a button they'd forgotten – phew, that's okay then), with only lip service paid to the environmental dangers that might cause, The Ice Warriors is all about being given the solution to the problem and then not having the guts to implement it. In that way, the familiarity of the setting and the predictability of the plot are being acknowledged and discussed. This is The Moonbase rewritten with brains.

It's not all furrowed brows, though. Troughton at last gets to act off the big reptile monsters – and his first instinct upon seeing the giants, to run in the other direction, is very funny. And the scene he plays with Deborah Watling, plotting the use of a stink bomb as Victoria pretends to cry and he blows his nose, is a perfect bit of comedy.

T: Well, thanks for doing your job so well... you haven't left *me* with an awful lot to say, have you? So, all right, let's talk about the Ice Warrior costumes. They're imposingly bulky yet manoeuvrable, very sturdy looking and convincingly alien. It's a conundrum, though, as to where the armour stops and the warrior begins. Their outer shells look like genuine reptilian outer casings, but the helmets do seem to be just that – helmets. They're wired up for starters, and we can see the mouth below. So unless the *only* thing they wear is a hat, surely their main carapaces must be armour too? And yet, the armour seems hairy at the top – who wears hairy armour? And their hands must be gloves, as they have a laser gun attached. So is *everything* we see armour, apart from the space for their mouths? It *must* be, in which case, we've got to ask by what quirk of Martian culture they made their armour to look reptilian. (Human armour, after all, usually doesn't try to pretend to be skin.) Or (I'm getting an idea here), maybe they augmented themselves and are effectively cyber-reptiles, with technology grafted onto their heads and a gun onto their hands. Unless the new series revisits the warriors, we might never get a proper answer to these questions, but either way – it's a stunning and iconic design, isn't it?

Otherwise, the plot continues to give us an expertly crafted dilemma. It's a brilliant damned-if-you-do, damned-if-you-don't scenario where the central dilemma boils down to "Act against the aggressors and you might die; don't act and... well, you'll probably die." It allows all the characters involved to flourish, and the scene between Clent and Penley is especially marvellous – Barkworth aims certain barbs directly at Sallis, then opens out the argument and uses as a propaganda speech to underline his authority and undermine Penley's position. This man would be brilliant in the boardroom (playing some form of, I dunno, Power Game perhaps). Miss Garrett is interesting too – the admiration that she displays for

the central computer contains such reverence that it borders on the worshipful, and makes her seem automaton-like.

One character that's usually overlooked, though, is the cynical Walters, whose regional accent is quite rare at this point in the series. When Clent suggests that Walters didn't expect he'd be dealing with ice monsters when he volunteered for his job, Walters' response – that he didn't volunteer actually, but was drafted – echoes a similar exchange in the M.A.S.H. movie, so acclaimed for its satire. And yet, little old Doctor Who had already done it three years earlier.

April 4th

The Ice Warriors episode six

R: It's an episode of tough decisions. Penley operating the Ioniser, and risking a huge explosion, echoes the Doctor firing the sonic cannon and risking the death of Jamie and the other humans. And if inevitably the fact that we only get the best-case scenario is *something* of an anticlimax, there's enough honest angsting over the dilemmas to disguise that. We've had so many stories since Innes Lloyd has become producer about the superiority of man over machine, whether that's been facing down Cyberman or WOTAN. And it's nowhere better articulated than here, as Penley calmly takes responsibility for a decision that only Man can feel qualified to take. When asked to take a risk, Roy Skelton's computer voice goes a little doolally, and sounds a bit like a child crumbling under the pressure of pretending to be an adult. However abrupt the conclusion might be, it's satisfying and life-affirming.

It's interesting too that in the final act it's Penley who takes the lead – the Doctor surrogate rather than the Doctor. We've had to get used to that a lot in the latter Hartnell stories, where the production team sidelined the Doctor altogether; it was a sign of no confidence in their leading man. Here it's exactly the opposite. Troughton's Doctor is so assured now that the plot doesn't need to assert him unnecessarily – he can stand back for the good of the story without compromising himself. Indeed, it offers a conclusion in which we don't even get to see the Doctor making an exit round, either saying goodbye or sidling away. As Penley and Clent put their differences to one side, the regulars are already off set, their jobs done, ready to embark on another adventure – and we hear the sound of the TARDIS (impossibly) over the scene as if to suggest they're already impatient to move on. (I'd like to pretend that the end credits coming on too early, poised to start rolling, is another sign of that. But that'd be pushing it a bit.)

T: What's most interesting about this final instalment is the way the script allows Bernard Bresslaw to fully morph Varga from being an imposing alligator person into a fully formed character. He isn't just ruthless, he's snidely superior during his face-off with Clent, responding as he does to the man's brinkmanship with a blunt and dismissive: "I will tell you what I want, and you will give it to me." Then things *really* get engaged as Clent appeals to the Martian's better nature – saying the humans within the base will soon perish if the warriors leave it without power as planned – whereupon Varga starkly replies, "Whereas we would not." And there's even a bit of Martian black humour when Clent says Varga will regret what he's doing, and Varga says, "At least I will live to regret it..." It's marvellous how this intense confrontation boils down to a hobbling base-leader who has to deal with the intruders with finesse lest they decide he's expendable and shoot him, and a tall green reptile played by a whispering actor sweating under a mask.

All in all, Martinus' direction has been typically strong – the quick cross-fading as the Martians and humans writhe in agony from the Doctor's sonic-cannon attack is a typically impressive flourish, and it's also quite shocking and grim when Walters dies with his eyes open. (That's a change from the book, incidentally, in which he isn't first stunned by Miss Garrett. Instead, the Ice Warriors walk in as Walters is attacking the computer and gun him down, sparing him the indignity of being shot twice.)

What an excellent adventure – I wholeheartedly applaud its message about humanity winning through over technology, but did have a chuckle at the line "The computer says no." (Thanks to Little Britain, this sticks out a bit more that it once would have.) And it's not lost on me that I'm writing these words about Man triumphing over machine as I'm watching this story on a portable laptop that contains entire seasons of Doctor Who, during a train journey (London to Manchester in two hours and eight minutes) and then will send these words for editing and review to my friend Rob – who is in a different city – in a matter of seconds, thanks to an information superway of linked computers. Yeah, bloody machines. Who needs 'em?

The Enemy of the World
episode one

R: "Och," says Jamie, in irritation, "does he think we're children?" The Doctor emerges from the TARDIS, is delighted to find he's on a beach, and wants to go paddling and build sandcastles. And within minutes, he finds out he's not in a children's TV serial after all, but something much grittier, with helicopters exploding and men firing guns at them from hovercrafts. It's so nasty and so paranoid, and it feels like it's a world apart from the cheerful sci-fi show which tries to send kids hiding behind sofas from the big, bad monsters. It's telling that the Doctor has a very different attitude here than he would in most of his adventures, slyly refusing to trust Astrid Ferrier even after she's saved them from certain death, getting angry and demanding to know what she expects in return. It's quite clear that David Whitaker has plunged us into an adventure in which no-one acts just for the common good and there's no such thing as a good Samaritan; there's a world leader who's trying to save people from starvation, but that instantly suggests it can only be because he's a dictator in the making. There's such a contrast here between the happy-go-lucky Doctor who behaves like an infant wanting a swim in the sea, and the suspicious Doctor who instantly sniffs out the darker self-interest of everyone he meets. In a *normal* adventure he'd accept the fears of Giles Kent – a discredited security officer – on trust, or get the same sort of prickling sensation on his skin he feels around Daleks. Here evil is rather more nebulous – and, indeed, of all the characters we encounter, it's *Kent* who's immediately the most duplicitous, contacting his successor Donald Bruce to force the Doctor to adopt the identity of Salamander (a statesman and would-be saviour of the world, who might have aims of being a dictator) early on.

So this is all very different to what we've seen before. We get a helicopter, and we get a hovercraft – it is the directorial debut of Barry Letts, after all! – and in style it's closest to the first season of Pertwee, and in particular to Whitaker's own swan song, The Ambassadors of Death. And though Letts provides a hugely enjoyable action episode, with lots of shooting and running and falling over, you get the sense that all the energy he's putting in is partly to conceal the fact that this whole thing is really rather out of sync with where Doctor Who has been heading – the odd mention of ice and Ionisers are there not just as pieces of continuity, but as reminders to the audience that this is the same programme.

As a sort of James Bond pastiche, this is rather successful. The sequence in which Giles Kent shows the Doctor a series of slides of Salamander's victims is surprisingly chilling (one photograph shows a man backing away from an assailant in very real fear). There is an atmosphere of real world menace here; Donald Bruce's bullying of Giles Kent, as he asks him to refer to him by the security position he has taken away from him, is just one example of subtle writing. The cliffhanger is smashing, and indicative of the episode's tone as a whole – Bruce confronts the Doctor as he attempts a hasty impersonation of Salamander, and we're on the edge of our seats, waiting to see where the lies within lies will take us next. There's no real threat, but gripping suspense.

T: It's certainly *different*, I'll give you that. Really, it's an episode of two halves: the opening is an all-location extravaganza with loads of action but little plot, the second is a mass info-dump in a room. Whatever Letts might have done with the initial action sequences, however, it's a bit spoiled by the fact that Astrid and the thugs Rod, Curly and Anton are all working for Giles Kent, but they're *trying to kill her as well as the Doctor's party*. No explanation is given for this (are they so overzealous to assassinate Salamander that they don't stop to think that Astrid might be taking him into custody, or do they think she's switched sides

– what, exactly?), and I know that if I have a difference of opinion with a work colleague, we tend to stop short of shooting one another. Still, it's hard to argue with the action-packed kick-off, which entails some impressive hardware (there's a great telesnap of the hovercraft in action, with Rod lying on the side firing his gun), and some aerial shots which demonstrate a cunning use of the helicopter, both on and off screen.

And as you've touched upon, the Doctor is even more mercurial in this adventure than normal, isn't he? He seems to be in a bad mood in Kent's office, but he was previously sweet, mysterious and charming with Astrid, and prior to *that* he was hoping to happily scamper about on a beach with a bucket and spade. Just to make matters even murkier, when the Doctor is asked if he's a "doctor" of law or philosophy, he (delightfully) twinkles, "Which law, whose philosophy?" Mary Peach is slightly odd as Astrid, though, especially when she states matter-of-factly that the Doctor's helping her would probably involve his death, before opining that it'd be worth it, in a tone of voice that suggests that his not doing so would be about as disastrous as arriving five minutes late for the village fete.

And Troughton gets to indulge in a trait that will become much more frequent once he's left the show, when the Doctor claims that humanity's favourite pastime is "trying to destroy each other". You tell us, Doctor! Why, the political back-and-forth we're seeing here could only get shocking if we saw the Doctor himself turning nasty... oh.

April 5th

The Enemy of the World
episode two

R: 1967 ends with Doctor Who behaving very out of character. There's a joke about a disused Yeti, but besides that, you'd really hardly know it was the same programme. This is fascinating stuff, and after the claustrophobia of the last few stories, it's almost disconcerting to have a plotline that leaps back and forth between Australia and Hungary quite so freely. I don't honestly know how good Troughton's Mexican accent is while he's playing Salamander, and I suspect it's rather all over the place – but that doesn't matter a jot; he's clearly having tremendous fun being a tyrannical villain, and, not unlike within his "darker" Doctor moments, he is at his most dangerous when he downplays the role. The scene in which Salamander coolly blackmails his associate Fedorin into becoming a murderer is superbly handled. It is quite an accomplishment all told that, even saddled with the sort of outrageous accent he used in Season Four for comic relief, he comes over as someone who's in full authority. Indeed, in the one scene this episode where Salamander interacts with Jamie, Troughton's performance is so different you can honestly forget that he and Hines have ever met before.

And that's the nub of the matter, really; in The Massacre, the whole plotline of a Doctor's double seemed entirely out of place amidst the more sober machinations of the Catholic conspiracists, and a strange irrelevance to keep William Hartnell out of the action; in The Chase, the double was even played by another actor altogether! This is a story all *about* there being a doppelganger – partly to showcase Troughton's versatility, of course, but also to make the Doctor too seem a little more disturbing and unknowable. The sequence at the top of the episode in which the Doctor impersonates Salamander, then switches back to his familiar affability once Bruce leaves, is very telling – this Doctor suddenly looks a bit fake and threatening as well in his smart suit, someone who could become another man entirely within a trice. This all works because the Doctor has become so central to the series once again. By the end of Season Three, I'd become so used to Hartnell taking holidays or being written into minor parts so often, at times his presence on screen seemed rather out of place, a throwback to a style of story that Doctor Who had moved away from. But since he was introduced in The Power of the Daleks, there hasn't been a single episode in which Troughton hasn't been a major force. He's refined and reshaped his Doctor over the stories since then until we now have a performance in which we can have total confidence – he never looks out of place as Hartnell often could, he never seems to fluff his lines or seem unconvinced by the genre he's being asked to

play. So that's why now, halfway through his tenure, giving him a different costume and a different accent is so effective. When Hartnell appeared as the Abbot of Amboise, it always served to remind you that this figure *might* be the Doctor. When Troughton appears as Salamander, the shock is that he never could be.

It's not untypical over the Christmas season for children's TV stars to dress up in different costumes and play against what the kids at home would be expecting. It's what Blue Peter and Crackerjack would always get up to. This could so easily have been a variation on that theme – but Troughton here is resolutely *not* giving a pantomime performance, in a story so cynical and dirty that it feels about as unseasonal as it could get.

T: If you're acquainted with the Doctor Who novelisations as much as I am, the most notable absence from this episode is the word "bastard" – which Ian Marter shockingly added while writing the book version of this story, in the scene between Salamander's head-thug Benik (who is brilliantly given the first name of Theodore, I think) and Bruce. Oddly enough, I was someone who always wanted my Doctor Who to be grown-up (I was obsessed with telling people that it *wasn't* a children's programme, despite my being the ripe old age of ten at the time), but this left a bad taste in my mouth. There was something very un-Doctor Who about that swear word, and the televised scene certainly doesn't miss it, largely thanks to Milton Johns (as Benik) being so silkily threatening.

Bruce also gets a cracking character moment at the top of the episode, when he collars Jamie and tells him to watch his step – despite the fact that the poor lad hasn't said anything. It's a terrific example of impotent bullying that illustrates Bruce's anger magnificently. Indeed, *most* of this story is about the people involved rather than the action – both cliffhangers have entailed people putting themselves at risk (or, Fedorin's case, not having the courage to do so) to get involved. With only the telesnaps to guess from, I think it's safe to assume that the protracted silence at the end of the episode concentrated on Fedorin looking all guilty, and the disgraced Denes being inscrutably noble.

There are a few other things of note here... Salamander gets a splendidly horrible line about why Fariah became a food taster – "She was hungry" – and he calls the guards "boys", an interesting touch that brings him further away from the Doctor, who'd never be so matey with thugs. And it increasingly becomes obvious that the time travellers need to be extra cautious with regards altering the political balance of power at this point in Earth's history. Why, if they're not careful, this sort of incorrigible meddling is going to catch up with them...

The Enemy of the World
episode three

R: In his one scene as the Doctor, Troughton is a joy, lamenting the destructiveness of man as he holds up a broken piece of crockery. The problem is, he's still finding reasons not to take part in the main action – come on, we're halfway through the story! It's very strange, after a couple of stories which have been about the dangers of inaction, to have an adventure which is pretty much all a quest to give the Doctor enough reason to get involved. Jamie and Victoria going undercover as spies is strange as it is – like Patrick Troughton, Frazer Hines seems almost a different character out of his standard uniform – but when you consider that they're facing these dangers just to get information sufficiently lurid to prompt the Doctor into lifting a finger, it's all the stranger. And then you remember that this is by David Whitaker, script editor of the first season – and then this throwback to the style of those early Hartnell adventures which were more about running away than taking any responsibility makes more sense.

And that's one of the reasons why the tone here really does seem so downbeat. Jamie and Victoria have a plan to save the life of Denes – and it fails, completely and profoundly, and Denes is shot in the back. It's a shocking moment, all the more because Barry Letts rather throws it away – we don't even see Denes fall down as he's shot, he's not even given the dignity of a decent death scene. So all the initiative the companions have shown to get taken into Salamander's confidence was for nothing, and they're led away dismissively by

guards – not even to appear in the following episode. It almost feels as if they were operating by Doctor Who rules, and the story rather sharply has tripped them up to tell them they're appearing in the wrong show. It's impressive and startling, certainly, and unlike anything we've seen for ages – but it does leave something of a bad taste in the mouth.

Thank God, then, for Reg Lye as Griffin the cook. It's a terrific comic performance of such deliberate pessimism that it makes all the sour drama around him feel lifted as a consequence. It's Eeyore from Winnie the Pooh transplanted into a James Bond thriller. It's rare for a character in Doctor Who to come along where *every single line* is a gag – and even rarer for an actor to make every single one of them count. Griffin is never mentioned before this episode, and he's never to appear again, making this one of the oddest cameos ever in the series – and one of the best.

T: See, this is why I think that complaints about a story being "padded" are often overstated. Entertainment is about adventure, plot *and* character, as evidenced here. Griffin contributes absolutely nothing to the overall storyline of The Enemy of the World, but it doesn't matter, because he's thoroughly enjoyable. If he *hadn't* been so dourly amusing, his presence might have been an irritating diversion, but he's fab. It was once suggested that The Underwater Menace episode three escaped the archive purge because it was kept to preserve the majesty of the Atlantean Fish People Dance for future generations. If so, I'd like to imagine that they slapped a preservation order on this orphaned episode, purely so my children could savour the splendour of Reg Lye in this delightful role.

Otherwise, it's interesting how much people dismiss Troughton's performance as Salamander as a "comic turn" – is it because he's putting on a funny accent? – but I think he's rather more magnificent than that. He shapes his face to fit the part – his upper lip is drawn back, flat and terse; his lower jaw is stiffened; and even his cheeks contrive to be sleeker, less baggily humorous. Troughton also simultaneously endows Salamander with a coldness and a burning intelligence – just look at that superb final close-up, as his eyes dart about whilst his brain weighs up the implications of Bruce's confused claim that he met with "you... or, someone *like* you". Contrast this with the Doctor's lovely wistful mourning of some broken crockery, and his (ad-libbed, one suspects) line about there being enough air in the box in which he's hiding, and you can tell that this isn't just an actor showing off. There's a real sense that we're dealing with two different characters.

It's a very enjoyable episode, although it's very oddly cut (especially when compared to Letts' work in future). We chop in and out of scenes quite messily (Denes, denied a death scene here, at least has the honour of one in the book), and the decision to hold Denes prisoner in a corridor is so bonkers, it's more surreal than anything in The Celestial Toymaker. "It's easier to guard him there," we're told – easier than what, exactly? A room? With a door? Four walls? And a lock? And Letts went along with this? Was there not a room available, at all, in which to film these scenes? It's barking, absolutely barking.

One final remark: I can't help but notice that the actor playing the Janos the guard is EastEnders scribe Bill Lyons, who was nothing like as lovely when he was one of the judging panel on a horrible and exploitative reality show called Soapstars. (Well, perhaps I'm just mistaking him for his evil alter ego.) I almost wish I didn't know this – sometimes, too much high geekery can be a bad thing.

April 6th

The Enemy of the World
episode four

R: The cynicism of the episode's tone is a lot more consistent here, helped in part by the absence of Jamie and Victoria; they're not around to remind us what Doctor Who *should* be like. Giles Kent's attempts to blackmail the Doctor into killing Salamander are as amoral as Salamander's own blackmails we've already seen; it begins to feel that the Doctor isn't so much wanting the proof he's been asking for after all, but just playing for time as he struggles all the more feebly to avoid being part of this rather squalid little adventure. Certainly,

his insistence that he will never be an executioner, but only bring the dictator to justice via proper legal means, feels somewhat idealistic in a world as brutal as this one. And the emphasis upon brutality here is honestly startling – it's achieved in part by the use of the word "kill", a word used rather sparingly in Doctor Who, with "destroy" or "exterminate" being far more colourful synonyms. Benik's attack on Kent's base has a hysteria about it that is actually frightening, and there's a real sense of events spinning out of control into violence. Fariah's death is sick and nasty – Benik threatens to kill her for information even as she's dying from a gunshot wound, and her response is to spit in his face – and it's only tempered by the obvious horror his own soldiers feel towards the carnage. (I love the way the guard captain is so disgusted by the soldier who shot her, demanding to know whether he *always* follows orders; it's a subtle but heartening moment when you realise there's still a humanity to some of these thugs in uniform.) It's hard to believe that only last week, Benik's threat was confined to breaking plates.

And then, at the halfway point of the episode, it pulls off a real coup de theatre. When Salamander reveals futuristic technology hidden in his records room, and goes down deep into the Earth, it is as startling as when the First World War generals will start talking on television screens in The War Games. We've bought into the thriller format so completely (and it has become its most credible only minutes previously) that the shifting of styles is quite dynamic. The underground society who have been tricked into believing the world above has become a radioactive waste is a lovely idea; we get to see Salamander treated as another sort of saviour altogether. And we go from a world in which characters seem truly cosmopolitan, with names plucked from all over the world like Denes and Fedorin, to one that's jarringly *British*. We're now hearing from people called Colin and Mary – in contrast to the world above their heads, which is run by cynical politicians and gun-toting soldiers, they sound deliberately fey, a bit like tea-drinking Radio Four listeners. They're extremely gullible, of course; they've been in their underground bunker for five years! But Whitaker is making a satirical point. Having shown us a world stage which is so relentlessly cold, he now wrongfoots us by presenting the people who've so passively allowed that world to come into being – and they're not Eastern Europeans hiding behind exotic names, they're *us*.

T: Oooh, Benik *is* as horrible as you say – you really get the impression that his wardrobe is full of rubber, whips and gimp masks. Milton Johns has been a vaguely camp menace up till this point, but here he's a disgusting, slimy sadist of the highest order; he gives a performance that exquisitely veers between purred smugness to screeched psychopathy. Top marks too, to Elliott Cairnes as this week's guard captain – he's in no way important to the plot, but the genuine (albeit limp) way he apologises to Fariah for her fatal shooting is a fine piece of acting. And when Benik shoves the gun in her face, the captain snaps him out of his sickening fervour by pointing out that she's already dead... making the scene quite remarkably bleak and horrible. It's all capped off with Benik treating the news of her demise with a curt and frustrated "good", as if he's been denied his money shot.

Much of the rest of this episode is oddly sci-fi, as Salamander gets into a pod that goes deep into the Earth, and goes through seemingly endless procedures before unveiling himself to his mates sheltering underground. It's a neat plot twist that takes the story in another direction (something that is always worth doing, particularly in a six-parter). And it's also bizarre to hear chilling music that I normally associate with the following story – it's so effectively used in The Web of Fear that it almost cheapens it (to my ears, anyway) to use it in a scene that merely introduces some scruffy people living in a bunker. In my world, this should be reserved for the creeps and shadows of Web and the menace of The Shining – it shouldn't be wasted on this spangly speculative future. I'm quite relieved when it fades out.

This adventure is moving along nicely, but there remains a couple of odd lapses – both Fariah and Bruce asked a pretty reasonable question (how she was blackmailed, why he's visiting Salamander) and each brushes it off with a that's-not-important-right-now dismiss-

al, the ultimate "I'll tell you later" sort of writing. And by this point, the Doctor's insistence on waiting to take action against Salamander has become something of a joke – it's the end of episode four, and he's only just now decided to become proactive. In that regard, The Enemy of the World seems to be starting at the point when most Doctor Who stories have already finished.

The Enemy of the World episode five

R: That scene where Benik prepares to torture Jamie and Victoria is a bit near the knuckle, isn't it? We don't often get depictions of *real* sadism, where someone seems genuinely stimulated by cruelty to others – Milton Johns plays it very credibly, but the almost sexual thrill he gets from the anticipation of making the Doctor's friends suffer is very disturbing. As is what follows it – the Doctor interrogates Jamie and Victoria whilst posing as Salamander, in order to convince Bruce that their fears are genuine. After the way Whitaker had the Doctor manipulate Jamie in his last script, here he is again presenting our hero as a man quite prepared to use companions for the greater good if he has to. When he's finally driven Victoria to the point she needs to assault him physically, he says in his normal voice, "You wouldn't hurt your old friend, the Doctor!" It's as contrived a line as you can get, and deliberately so – referring to himself in the third person like that suddenly makes him more distanced, and we suddenly see Troughton *playing* the Doctor, just as he's been playing Salamander, and playing the Doctor playing Salamander. It's unnerving.

The problem with this demonstration of Jamie and Victoria's fear is that it still doesn't provide any proof that Salamander is a wrong 'un. And it's now become frustrating – we've seen he's a corrupt murderer right from episode two, so here we are, two hours into the drama, and we've known something for ages that makes the Doctor look at best overcautious, at worst rather stupid. He's been in the same room as Giles Kent now for five *weeks* – I genuinely cheered out loud when he behaves in character at last, giving Bruce his gun back to win his trust, and leaves to take part in the action. But it's perhaps indicative of this tale that when the cliffhanger is all about Salamander finally leaving evidence of his crimes, it's an assault on a man the Doctor has never met, from a part of the plotline no series regular has had a part in, and is discovered by a guest character. There's only so long you can sideline the Doctor before it begins to look a bit embarrassing.

Lots of good things about this, of course. Salamander's attempts to dissuade Swann – one of the underground dwellers – from reaching the surface are those of a man who doesn't want the extra blood on his hands; it's hard to tell from the telesnaps, but there seems to be almost a weary resignation as Troughton picks up the crowbar to brain him with. And Colin's despairing anguish when he realises that Salamander has taken someone else away from the bunker is very affecting.

T: I appreciate a cliffhanger that deviates from the "Kill them, kill them now!" mould, but throughout this story, David Whitaker seems almost hell-bent on daring us to find a single one that's even remotely exciting. It's as if this was shown in the UK as a feature-length adventure (which it wasn't, of course) that was then chopped into 25-minute chunks for the American market, and thus given extremely arbitrary cliffhangers imposed by timing necessities (as happened all the time when Season Twenty-Two hit the US market). And yet, I still quite like them – the one here entails the gravely wounded Swann identifying the man who betrayed him, and there's something arresting about hearing nothing but the baddie's name ("Salamander!!") from a dying man's lips as we go to the credits.

Troughton continues to play Salamander as an extremely plausible villain – a weaker actor would have been winking to us, aware that we know he's playing the bad guy, but I completely buy Troughton's commitment, and the forceful yet almost desperately pleading way he says, "Because I am right and you are wrong!", when Swann pushes Salamander about taking him to the surface, which threatens to undo Salamander's plans. It's great work too from Christopher Burgess, who as Swann hits the correct notes of a righteous anger tinged with an inner decency.

If anything, *the Doctor's* characterisation seems a bit harder to accept. He decides that Bruce is an honest and reasonable man – on very little evidence, and in spite of him being a total git to everyone in the caravan in episodes one and two. But then, this sort of reversal seems to be going around – by the end of episode, Bruce himself is convinced that Salamander is corrupt, even though he's been given no actual proof to that effect. Still, that means he was about four times quicker than the Doctor in working this out!!

But I would have to judge that this episode belongs to Milton Johns as Benik. I suspect we have a tendency to latch onto actors such as Norman Jones, Bernard Kay and Johns because of their recurring good service to Doctor Who over the years, but I honestly think that we've seen them all do acting of the highest order. And *what* a riposte Benik gives, upon confirming Jamie's suggestion that he was probably a very nasty little boy. Yes, Benik concedes, but he had a most *enjoyable* childhood. Creepy.

April 7th

The Enemy of the World
episode six

R: This doesn't end tidily. But then, that seems quite appropriate for a story that has so stubbornly refused to follow the familiar Doctor Who template, and has been keen to ensure there's an ugly ambiguity to everyone's motives. The underground prisoners are resolutely *not* saved at the episode's end; Astrid has determined that she'll keep her promise to the dying Swann, and she'll be helped by Bruce – and that the two of them combine forces after years of enmity is in itself quite positive. But it's made very clear that the operation will be dangerous and the outcome uncertain. And the Doctor isn't allowed to help; it's ironic, that in a story where for six episodes everyone's been asking for his aid, it ends with his resemblance to Salamander being an obstruction.

But I think that may be the fatal flaw in this adventure. I've admired it because it's been bold, and tonally so different. But it's rather reduced the Doctor; in the last story, he was needed because of his ingenuity and his diplomacy, and here it's because he accidentally looks like somebody else. At the end of the day, that's what feels wrong about that final TARDIS scene, where Salamander and the Doctor meet face to face. It ought to be a confrontation of nemeses – in fact, it's just one famous world celebrity encountering someone who could have done a turn at parties as a lookalike. The one really dramatic moment for the Doctor is the way he fools Giles Kent – and indeed us – into thinking he's Salamander in the research room. But once Kent has been exposed, he runs away to meet his *real* enemy in a pretty sadistic scene where Salamander delights in chasing him through tunnels and shooting him dead. It's horrible, but strangely uninvolving – it has nothing to do with the Doctor any more.

In the final moments, then, we have a telesnap of Troughton standing over Troughton, one telling the other that he'll make him leave the TARDIS and face the judgment of the people he's wronged. That seems right and fitting, after a story in which the Doctor has shown so much horror towards the casual violence and the needless death... and then Salamander dies anyway, because he gets sucked out into space. The whole sequence feels odd and strangely tacked on, as if the production team realised there ought to be one moment where the two Troughtons squared off. (Even though it makes no sense – why would Salamander know about the TARDIS?) And once you've got them together, with all that clever split screen stuff... they've really nothing to say to each other.

T: Strictly speaking, Astrid made that promise to the *dead* Swann, so that's *two* reasons why it'd be churlish of him to be disappointed if she doesn't succeed. It's also quite funny that Astrid decides that Colin and Mary must be the leaders of the bunker-people now that Swann has perished, when it was previously established that they're the youngest of those present. Perhaps by "leaders", Astrid meant, "the only ones alive who aren't extras".

Even so, good for Astrid – there's a real determination about her, and her resolute desire to do some good rubs off on Bruce. This whole story has offered a fairly grim vision of the future – complete with jack-booted guards, political machinations and kinky security

chiefs – so it's proper that the pair of them offer a glimmer of hope and humanity. This, despite Bruce displaying some of his earlier unpleasantness – but this time it's okay, apparently, because it's aimed at Benik. Fortunately, nothing is quite black and white in a Whitaker script, meaning that Benik gets all mimsy when asking for a fair trial, like the sulky little child he is. Good, it would have been too easy for his opponents to have just shot him, rather than going to the effort of properly bringing him to justice and watching him squirm in the witness box.

Everything is heading, though, towards an ending where Troughton has to flip between playing the Doctor, Salamander, the Doctor-as-Salamander and Salamander-as-the-Doctor. He seems deliberately off, just a bit, when the Doctor imitates Salamander (though as the real deal he's especially grave, serious and menacing in his face-off with Giles Kent in the caves). And I really like how the Doctor uses this to expose Kent's schemes, as well as his assertion that anyone who resorts to murder so easily is a suspect in his eyes. Yes, I do like it, even if the scripting for previous episodes doesn't exactly sell Kent's eventual treachery as a twist worthy of The Usual Suspects.

And it seems that, with this episode gone from the archives, we're cursed to wonder that the Doctor-Salamander showdown – requiring two Troughtons in the same scene – would have been like. The telesnaps aren't especially telling, but prove so tantalising that this is one of the top scenes I'd really like to turn up one day. It must have been great seeing the two characters in shot at the same time, and Salamander sucked into the void, even if it's all so abrupt that it doesn't really come across as a proper conclusion to the adventure at all. And isn't it typical that, after five weeks of rather low-key cliffhangers, we finally get one involving a bit of good old-fashioned action and jeopardy – and it comes at the end of the bloody story!

The Web of Fear episode one

R: There is, as you say, a certain frustration with the snapshot-information that the telesnaps convey. For instance, as this episode exists on video, we can see that Patrick

Troughton is wearing a plaster on his face! What happened in The Enemy of the World that I missed? Did Astrid claw him with her fingernails, did Giles Kent bite him, what? I know I could look it up. But I'd much rather, Toby, if you provided the answer. (Just watch, readers – Toby will know. He knows everything.)

It's hard to talk about this episode objectively. It's one of my favourites. It was my very first introduction to Patrick Troughton's Doctor, and I saw it at a small convention in 1982. I didn't know why it opened with everyone on the floor of the TARDIS (nor, of course, about that sticking plaster), and it didn't matter – I was mesmerised. And it made me fall utterly in love with the second Doctor (he's *my* Doctor, I might as well admit it, can you tell?). Over the years, I've seen it more times than I can tell you. And just as you think of Terence de Marney from The Smugglers whenever you stand on a London underground platform, Toby, I hear Troughton's warning to Frazer Hines about the live rails in my head. "Electrified! Braunched! Burned up!" ("Braunched"? What on earth does "braunched" mean? Like the sticking plaster, I never bothered to inquire. You can see that The Web of Fear did nothing for my curiosity.)

So I don't want to spoil this one by analysing it too closely. There are another five episodes to go that I'm barely familiar with; I'll put my attention onto those. I'll just say before going that I love it in part because it's so *funny*. We haven't had much comedy in Doctor Who for ages, and the regular cast delight in it here – it's not that there are many jokes in the script, but simply in the rapport between Troughton, Hines and Watling. No other Doctor can make eating a sandwich look as amusing as Patrick Troughton. It gives me pause to wonder, of course, whether they are *always* this funny, and the soundtrack alone doesn't reveal it. That may well be true, and if so, it makes me yearn for the episodes to be returned all the more. (Maybe *that's* how he got the sticking plaster, some hilarious bit of shtick whilst confronting Salamander.) But for the time being, I'll always have this orphaned episode to compensate me – the weary disdain with which Jamie drops the Doctor's gizmo when he's told it does nothing, the delight when the Doctor thinks that

he's being teased about the flashing light, Victoria's disappointment when Jamie doesn't bother to tell her that her clothes look sophisticated. Three of the very best of the Doctor Who regulars having fun.

T: I think we're in for a bit of a love-in here, Rob – The Web of Fear was your first Troughton, but it was my first exposure to "old Doctor Who" full stop, being the first Target novel I ever read. My copy still has a yellowed page from where it was left open on the back windowsill of a family friend's car, and wasn't returned to me for an agonising month and a half. I was later a bit disappointed when I first *saw* this episode, as it spent the initial few minutes rounding off the previous week's tale – "Come on!", I thought, "There are only 25 minutes remaining of The Web of Fear! I want to watch that, especially as I've just seen The Enemy of the World episode three!" (Remember my first bootleg tape?) With hindsight, I realise I was wrong – if nothing else, the opening provides some excellent "tilting spaceship" acting from Frazer Hines, even if the whole "TARDIS door not automatically shutting when the Ship is in flight" business strikes me as a bit of a design flaw.

But it's probably no exaggeration to say that this is the Doctor Who story by which I judge all Doctor Who stories, simply because the book made such an indelible impression on me, and got me started on the entire wonderful range of novelisations before I even conceived of being able to actually watch the old episodes themselves. I predominantly envisage this story as being about soldiers charging about and having pitched battles with Yeti, but this first episode is more spooky horror film than action/adventure. The scenes in Silverstein's museum – made on film and directed by Douglas Camfield – are terrifically gloomy and shadowy. That rumbling, ominous music is incredible, and the flickering light, which gradually dissipates thanks to the candles being blown out, is very moody and evocative. It's a bit odd that the programme-makers actually show the Yeti transform on screen – redesigns in this series are frequent and easily glossed over – and do you know, I think I actually preferred the previous Yeti; the big, glowy eyes of the new ones are a tad obvious, and the nose a wee bit beaky for my liking. Who cares, though? This is chilling, atmospheric stuff of the highest order.

And the scene where the regulars emerge from the TARDIS is very familiar to me, because not long after I got a video recorder, The South Bank Show did a film about depictions of the London Underground in popular culture. Lo and behold, the first clip featured was this sequence, and every time I'm on a Tube, I manage to banish Terence de Marney from my thoughts when we go past Covent Garden. Or, as the Doctor's words echo around my head: "Co-vent Gaaarden – oh yes of course, it's an Underground Station, we're standing on the platform." And I'm so familiar with this sequence that I take for granted David Myerscough-Jones' absolutely astonishing set design; it's not hyperbole to say that it looks like the real thing.

Talking of clips, I was very irritated when the Resistance is Useless documentary showed the bit of Captain Knight behaving like a prat to Professor Travers' daughter, Anne, as proof of the programme's sexist mores – did they not notice that the scene in full is actually a repudiation of boorish misogyny? You can prove anything if (pardon the phrasing) you doctor your evidence. And the scenes with the military, curiously enough, yield what I would judge as The Most Pointless Speaking Part in Doctor Who History – a title I bestow upon the soldier (played by Bernard G High) whose sole contribution to the illustrious history of Doctor Who is to be asked to help with some cable, and whinge "Oh, but Staff, I'm on this other job..." before being made to do it anyway. Couldn't the producers have saved themselves a few quid, and just got an extra to nod a bit? Or re-used High as the soldier who gets killed next week?

All in all, I just love how much of this feels like real, bare bones, 100% proof Doctor Who – it's got tooled-up soldiers, famous landmarks augmented by an alien presence, and (look!) a dead, cobweb-covered old man with a screaming, terrified newsstand headline by his corpse. And before I forget, Rob – you'll want to know that Troughton has the sticking plaster on at the end of The Enemy of the World, so it's probably as a result of the building collapsing after the explosion. Alas, I've no idea what

"braunched" means either – nor does Bill Gates, if the red squiggle currently nestling underneath it on my laptop screen is anything to go by.

April 8th

The Web of Fear episode two

R: This is ridiculous. But then it knows that. I'm not sure there's yet been an episode of Doctor Who which so glories in the ludicrousness of its premise. Yeti in Tibet who kill their victims with sheer brute strength makes a certain kind of sense. Yeti, in the *London Underground*, killing their victims with *cobweb guns* feels like it might just be a joke. (It's funny enough to imagine the Yeti holding any sort of gun, really – it'd be like taking a cheetah and giving it a fast car, or a wasp that doesn't sting its victims but instead drops masonry on them... oh, hang on, they'll do that last one, won't they?) The episode doesn't hide any of this, which is why there's that wonderful scene where the two soldiers sneer at the Tibet story, and speculate that the Yeti might be some bioweapon used by a foreign power. And it's emphasised all the further by the way that Anne Travers mocks the idea of the TARDIS flying through time and space, or by the fact that the Doctor turning up every single time there's trouble *must* logically make him suspicious. When you've got that terrific sequence where a character we only met a few months ago is back again, but this time 40 years older and made up to be an old man – and we're invited to see it from the young companions' perspective, that Professor Travers is the one to whom something bizarre has happened – then you know that the story is wittily turning Doctor Who conventions on its head. Yes, we had a monster called the Yeti, and they were in the Himalayas. And now for their sequel... modern-day London. Why not?

It's all the more uneasy because the one character that glues all the silliness together and makes it always look halfway acceptable is absent. This is the very first time Patrick Troughton has taken a holiday mid-story, and you can easily appreciate it's about time he was given a break. It has an interesting effect on the episode, though, making it seem much more uneasy and off-kilter. It's not hard to understand why everyone is so sceptical about the Doctor, and why everyone naturally assumes he must be a saboteur – in the atmosphere of paranoia, he does seem the most obvious culprit. Over the next few episodes, everybody is going to look guilty, of course, in fine Agatha Christie-like style – and so it's rather glorious they kick off the intrigue by having all the cast first suspect the missing Hercule Poirot. I've read many reviews of The Web of Fear which suggest that it's all just another formulaic base-under-siege story, but I think that's because it sets up a template which will become very familiar over the next few years. On its own terms, this does odd, brave things. For a start, setting a contemporary story against a recognisable London backdrop *after* the events of an invasion is something we've never seen before. There's no threat to be averted at the last minute, no distant future Earth wiped out to soften the blow. And then it offers itself as a direct sequel, so that we can return to characters aged by decades – the closest we've ever been to this sort of thing before was in The Ark, and everybody fell over themselves congratulating it upon the twist of making the second half a future comment upon the first. But that story didn't have the wit to use the younger Guardians now played as old men, and it didn't dare stick a couple of different adventures in the middle to give the return greater impact.

T: (Before people write in, I should mention that Troughton *has* taken a holiday before, in The Evil of the Daleks episode four, but that included some pre-filmed scenes with him and a Dalek, so the Doctor was still in the episode. It's more noticeable here, when he's totally absent. And before anyone can ask, no – source of trivia that I am, I still don't know what "braunched" means.)

It's interesting to hear you outline how ridiculous this seems in concept, Rob – you're absolutely right, but it never struck me as odd before, chiefly because Yeti skulking about the Underground with web guns seemed perfectly acceptable and normal when I was young, so I never really questioned it. And the *other* reason that this still doesn't seem all that bonkers is

because Douglas Camfield depicts events as unfailingly grim and down-to-earth. No funky technological hi-jinks from him, thank you very much, it's hard-nosed drama all the way. So, there are horrible death screams down the end of a phone line, which seem all the more terrifying because our own imagination pictures the slaughter and carnage. This adventure really has hit the ground running – I mean, we're only in episode two, and already the soldiers are undergoing a rearguard action while engaging in pitched battles riddled with casualties.

But I can't help but fixate on that clever moment when Sergeant Arnold says he doesn't think the Doctor has been slain by the Yeti; when asked why he thinks that, he says it's "a hunch". Now, this technically this isn't one of those daft moments where the traitor gives himself away, because the audience don't know there is a traitor to identify yet. It's just a little seed, probably one that'll be forgotten in four weeks' time when this character's duplicity is revealed. Sadly, I have always known the traitor's identity in advance – as I got near to end of the novelisation, I gave my brother (who had already read it) a rundown of where I was in the book, and he said, "Hmm, I won't give anything away, but you know how you said Sergeant Arnold was definitely a good guy..." The fool! He just gave everything away! I was scuttled by spoilers even before the term had been coined!

The Web of Fear episode two (interlude)

T: Stop me if I'm getting too personal here, but in-between watching these two episodes, I nipped upstairs to the loo, and – as is my wont – dug out a random old Doctor Who Magazine to have a read of whilst (ahem) I was engaged. Colin Baker and Nicola Bryant were on the cover, and inside there's an interview with... you, Rob! When I first read this piece, your Dalek episode hadn't aired, Moths had not been written, and we'd never met. Here I am reading it again, and I can now hear your voice as – in typically self-deprecating fashion – you confess to mishearing and subsequently misquoting a line from The King's Demons in a fanzine review. Aww, bless.

The Web of Fear episode three

R: It's the Brig!... except, of course, it's not the Brig at all, he's calling himself a Colonel, and wearing a funny hat.

When Terrance Dicks novelised The Web of Fear for Target in 1976, I'd imagine he faced something of a dilemma. By this stage, Lethbridge-Stewart had become an icon who had survived three Doctors, and was as recognisable a part of the series as a blue police box or a pepperpot with a sink plunger. And yet, episode three here *depends* upon the idea that we don't know who he is, and we can't trust him. He appears out of nowhere, and even soldiers in his own platoon don't seem to know who he is. (Logically, of course, he's just too obvious a suspect to be guilty – but the way in which he sweeps into the base, asserts his authority and expects everyone to respect him makes him deliberately suspicious.) Dicks' answer was not to pretend that this strange newcomer could be a traitor at all, and plays up the first meeting between him and the Doctor as being as meaningful as Stanley meeting Livingstone. And, of course, with the episode missing from the archives, it's the warmth of the novelisation that I best remember, and that reading it as a kid made me feel such affection towards UNIT.

But, of course, what's shocking here is that no-one making The Web of Fear has the remotest clue of the meeting's significance. This is not, as Jean-Marc Lofficier's Programme Guide taught me when I was 11, a "UNIT seed story"; there's no thought here of how to give the series a new direction for Jon Pertwee, and no thought of how to make the Colonel into a character that will still be appearing in TV episodes forty-ish years later. The tension between the anarchic Doctor and this suspicious authoritarian is, as you might expect, frosty – Lethbridge-Stewart's first act in the series appears to be to point a gun at the Doctor. And Nicholas Courtney plays the part, quite rightly, as a man cloaked in mystery, who seems blithely unbothered by the hostility he inspires – and as just another military man who at any moment might be murdered by a Yeti.

T: Think of the achievement here: Nick Courtney signed a four-week contract for a job that ended up being part of his career for *the next 40 years*. And it's not as if the estimable Mr Courtney just rested on his Who laurels either – he's had a decent and lengthy acting career, during which time, he's occasionally popped along to return as one of the most beloved characters in Doctor Who, one of the most famous television programmes ever made. The man is an institution, and it's amazing how certain inflections and mannerisms are uncannily present already, in week one of the televisual life of Brigadier (or Colonel, as we'll call him for now) Lethbridge-Stewart.

Yet again, this isn't the action/adventure I imagined in my head – there's a mounting sense of unease and paranoia, suspicion is bandied about in a very disquieting way, and the main suspects in this game of "Spot the Traitor" seem to be Chorley and the Brig (sorry, the Colonel). The model Yeti, so effective in The Abominable Snowmen, work equally well here, with the added bonus that their positioning enables the web of the Great Intelligence to infect the explosive store *inside the military base itself*, which is terrifying.

And, do you know – it's worth noting that for all we're meant to regard Professor Travers as an old, kindly and well-intentioned gentleman, all of this destruction is, in fact, his fault. After all, *he* reactivated the Yeti-control sphere, meaning that every single drop of blood that's subsequently been spilt is on his hands. They lock you up for that sort of thing you know, or even execute you. If he was from America, he might have got (this is the last time I'll mention it, promise) braunched in the electric chair.

April 9th

The Web of Fear episode four

R: Bloody hell, I bet this one terrified the young 'uns! I think that the scene with the trolley is one of the most honestly frightening in the show's history. Sergeant Arnold and Corporal Lane walk bravely into the fungus... We hear their agonised screams... and Driver Evans pulls on the rope to bring out the trolley they were pushing, and Lane's dead body is on it, covered in cobwebs. That's horrifying, even in telesnap form. And I'm 39 years old.

It's a brutal episode, in which a sizeable part of the guest cast are despatched swiftly and without sentiment. The image of Nicholas Courtney leading his troops into battle against an alien force, neither bullets nor grenades having any effect, is one so familiar to any Doctor Who fan it's almost burned onto the retina. But there's never carnage like this one; we know the names of the soldiers as they're all killed one by one (there are a couple of extras who get named just seconds before they're shot down, if only to make the point). And to hear Courtney crack under pressure, to bolt as the last survivor, to hear him give in to utter despair, is such a shock for that seasoned retina-scarred fan. There are three different groups within the episode, all on different missions – and all of them suffer terrible casualties. Within 25 minutes, the large speaking cast is effectively halved. As the Yeti close in on the few survivors at the cliffhanger, the series has never felt so claustrophobic. It must be gearing up for a climax – but no, we've still got two episodes to go.

I think this must be the first time that the guest characters start thinking of the TARDIS as a means of escape. It's the first impulse of the frightened child watching at home, of course – why don't they all just run away? – and up til now that's been the province only of the regular crew. But it's a measure of how desperate the struggle has become that the army are dying not in a battle to destroy the Yeti, but to rescue a blue police box that none of them truly believe can offer them salvation. That they're prepared to grasp at such slender straws of survival, and that the story is prepared to countenance them doing so, shows you just how grim this all is.

T: It's a shame that in the grand scope of Doctor Who, Mervyn Haisman and Henry Lincoln seem to get written off with, "they created the Yeti/fell out with the producers over The Dominators", and that's about it. They've also patently cracked how to structure a Doctor Who six-parter – pressure was built to the breaking point at the end of The Abominable Snowmen episode four, and we get a similar climax here. It all ends with a scant few

demoralised survivors assessing their losses, their drained authority figure despairing, and then their enemies bursting through the door. Ha! Get out of *that*! And there's a lot of tension in the set pieces that lead to this point too – early on, Arnold sounds genuinely but stoically distressed by the death of Craftsman Weams, whilst the Colonel is so distracted that he seems unable to recognise Evans.

But all of this is possible because there's a desperate fight with the Yeti that, as you say, butchers the cast down to size. It *sounds* like a cracking battle – we can't be sure of its actual effectiveness, of course, but we know Douglas Camfield and stuntman Derek Ware have form for this sort of thing, and the evidence we have at our disposal (the soundtrack, the telesnaps and the promising Australian censor clips) all indicate that it's absolute carnage (Corporal Blake's protracted bludgeoning especially) as loads of Yeti knock off a fair few soldiers. Evaluating the visual success of the web itself is admittedly harder – it looks impressive on the telesnaps, but we can't see it *move*, so it's entirely possible that the realisation of this amorphous glob is about on par with the giant rat from The Talons of Weng-Chiang, or the magma beast from The Caves of Androzani. I'm not sure it matters, though – as those two surviving stories prove, you can get away with just about any botched effect if it's reasonably brief, and the story otherwise is solid enough.

I'd like to stop and remark on two of the military men here. First, the huge fight allows Lethbridge-Stewart to be something of an action hero, whilst his pragmatic and ready acceptance of the TARDIS' abilities will probably come as a shock to viewers who are used to the befuddled, straight-laced stooge who in the Pertwee era refuses to believe that he's been transported off Earth, and instead must be in Cromer.

Second, it's ironic that whereas Douglas Camfield insisted that Nicholas Courtney had the bearing of an officer despite his only having been a private in real life, Ralph Watson – here playing Captain Knight – didn't even have those credentials, as he was a conscientious objector. I discovered this while talking with Watson – who is a chatty, amiable man – while we talked in-between sessions of doing the DVD commentary for The Monster of Peladon.

I came to admire how he stuck to his guns (or rather, his preference not to handle them) in the face of what must have been great hostility, and I was very affected when he said that his grandmother – who had four sons serve in World War I – felt incredible, intractable guilt that all of her boys survived, whereas everyone else she knew had lost someone. His description of her made him choke up a bit (not demonstratively or self-consciously), and I felt privileged to hear him talk about such things. Truth to tell, I also felt a bit remorseful that such important life stories are often overlooked while we as Doctor Who fans only seem to ask people of Watson's generation about amusing anecdotes and scary monsters. (Likewise, the publisher of this book assures me that Barry Letts' stories about serving aboard a submarine in World War II are even more riveting than hearing him talk about Doctor Who or his television career.)

Anyway, I continue to love this story. I love the action, the suspense, the monsters and the bits of humour. And I love how this exercise of ours has reminded me of all sorts of interesting people that I've been privileged to meet. It's nice to think about such things, especially whilst watching one of the very best Doctor Who adventures.

The Web of Fear episode five

R: Not a huge amount actually *happens* this week – and that's because for the first time Doctor Who has a go at telling an episode in real time (more or less). The Great Intelligence gives the Doctor 20 minutes before it'll suck out his brain, and we spend those 20 minutes until the cliffhanger in a state of tension. For once nothing actually happening is really the point; the Colonel and Jamie embark upon a scheme of rescue pretty much just to fill in the time, because as Lethbridge-Stewart says, making a show of useless action is better than doing nothing. We're back to this season's regular theme, that of pitting passive acceptance against positive resistance – except here there's little to be done but watch as the Doctor tinkers about with some technology.

And it's terrific. "Nothing" has ever been not done quite so brilliantly, and the atmosphere is so thick you could keep it in a jam jar. There

is no respite from the mystery of the traitor – scenes in which Evans pulls a rifle on the Colonel and Jamie, or in which Anne nervously asks the Intelligence for confirmation that her father hasn't always been under their control, reveal that the Intelligence's scheme is no more than a MacGuffin – what Douglas Camfield and the writers are really interested in is paranoia. Best of all, by the Intelligence revealing that its plan is to take the Doctor's intellect, the story suddenly focuses itself entirely upon our hero and exactly what he'll do to save mankind. Driver Evans, as always, is utterly pragmatic: if everyone's lives will be spared in exchange for the Doctor, why not just give them the Doctor? (In the novelisation, this remark is greeted by an outburst of anger from all the other characters – it's telling that in the televised episode, we quickly cut before we can hear what the reaction might be, and by the time we return to the fortress, no-one except Jamie seems too perturbed by it.)

I love the way too that the Intelligence doesn't want to kill the Doctor. That would be too easy and clean, and we're far too used to seeing him deal with threats of death. That he's going to have his brain altered, become someone with the mind of a child, is far more horrifying – it's the taking of something reliable and comforting and altering it beyond repair that disturbs more than its simple removal. (I'll talk about this more, I dare say, when we hit The War Games and that cruel ending in which Jamie and Zoe are made to forget all about their adventures with the Doctor, let alone what happens to Donna Noble in Journey's End.) To have the Doctor gently tell Jamie that should the worst come to the worst, he'll need his companions to look after him as an infant is somehow both quite funny and utterly sickening at the same time.

Favourite moment? It's just a little thing, and I might be misinterpreting it. But there's almost a callous satisfaction in the way that the Doctor notes that Driver Evans is frightened by the Yeti control sphere. This is the man who's cheerfully prepared to sacrifice the Doctor, and the Doctor hasn't betrayed the slightest nervousness about it (even giggling with delight when he's made the sphere work). But it only takes a little silver ball to roll across the floor, and Evans is jumping on a chair and aiming his rifle in terror. "Were you scared?" asks Troughton pointedly. Then walks out into the darkness to catch a Yeti.

T: As if to distract us from the fact that not an awful lot is happening right now, the script this week seems to beat us over the head about the quisling element of the storyline. Indeed, the Great Intelligence should really change its name after revealing that the mesmerised Professor Travers hasn't been co-operating with it prior to this, and boasting that it has another human agent. Camfield and his cast keep things gutsy and exciting regardless, and Jack Watling pulls off the difficult task of acting "possessed" with aplomb, but it does strike me as odd that nobody questions why the Intelligence has given the Doctor 20 minutes to co-operate. Why doesn't it just tell him that it'll kill Victoria if he doesn't do as ordered *now*? Even The Average Intelligence would have worked this out, and there's a part of me that's tempted to reevaluate my claim that Haisman and Lincoln had mastered Doctor Who's format. It's as if The Great Intelligence gives the Doctor its episode-long ultimatum because it's somehow aware that it's in a six-parter, and that it needs to stall for time.

With all of that in mind, this is still a fantastic episode in many ways. Jamie gets to act like a real grown up – he has to be physically restrained from going after Victoria, is curtly dismissive about the Doctor's tinkering and throws himself into the action whilst being scornful of Evans. Frazer Hines gives a more hardnosed performance than usual, and it suits him. And I think I've found evidence of how Camfield made the web seem effective in the tunnels – many of the telesnaps show that he's shooting from *inside* the web, meaning there's some cobwebby stuff in front of the camera and the audience has to glimpse the characters through it. It's a simple trick, but works very well.

April 10th

The Web of Fear episode six

R: There's an awful lot of effort made to disguise the fact that the ending is a bit anticlimactic. Right up until the last moment, we're still unsure who the "traitor" is – and the reappearance of Chorley, and that wonderful scene where Arnold gently voices all our suspicions about how he's managed to live so long, pull us in the wrong direction at a time when most stories working less hard would be content to tell us the truth. (That really is a wonderful scene, isn't it? And all the more once you understand that Arnold himself is the traitor. There's such a cruelty to it, taking Chorley's terror and using it against him, making him feel so paranoid that he'll even himself doubt why he has survived. And yet it asks the exact question that, directed against Arnold himself, would tell us all who the Yeti's inside man is. It's very clever stuff.)

Had the resolution really been a matter of the Doctor sitting under a helmet and draining the Intelligence, it would have been very simplistic. Had the resolution simply been that one of the Yeti turned on its fellows, it would have been simplistic *and* overfamiliar – it's been the ending for stories such as The War Machines and The Evil of the Daleks already. But because the story does them *both*, it somehow all works – and that's because the latter gets in the way of the former. The Doctor is so furious that his plan to defeat the Intelligence has been compromised by *another* plan to defeat the Intelligence, that for a moment we might even believe he's having a childish strop and that something adverse has happened to his brain after all. Either ending would have seemed a bit trite on their own; together, they give the illusion this has all been rather complex, and that a story which up until the final few minutes suggested that the Doctor had lost maintains its tension as long as possible.

That's in part thanks to Douglas Camfield, of course. The scene in which Evans is merely *captured* by a couple of Yeti is a bit disappointing on paper – killing the comic relief would have been more logical. But Camfield directs it so tensely, with Derek Pollitt making desperate jokes to the Yeti as they turn on them with their brute force, that it packs a punch all the same. The Web of Fear is the sort of story that's rather sneered at nowadays by some fans, the ones who complain that the shocks and thrills it offers are all fairly obvious. It's true; it's not an experimental work. But the military set adventures of the 1970s, and the monster in corridor romps of the 1980s, all look back to this and the genuine atmosphere it conveyed. And for moment to moment fear and suspense, not one of them did it better.

T: No, no, no, no, no! Hang on! I *hate* that Arnold is the traitor! Actually, I should restate that – I don't mind that Arnold is the traitor, but I hate that the Intelligence reveals that it was just animating his lifeless body, and that the Doctor postulates that he was probably one of the first to go missing. What a disappointment – Jack Woolgar has been so convincing and likeable as this no-nonsense (but not unpleasant) professional soldier. Even this late in episode, Arnold berates Evans and is suspicious of Chorley – is the Intelligence *that* convincing an actor? I'm pretty sure that in the book, it's revealed that Arnold was only occasionally under Intelligence's thrall, and that he was otherwise his normal brave and likeable self (as with Padmasambhava, whose most effective moments occurred when his humanity struggled against the evil invading his person). Furthermore, I'm certain that Terrance Dicks added in the book that if the Doctor had been allowed to see through his plan, Arnold would have survived. I'm aware that I'm criticising this story for not being something I thought it should be after reading the book, but I still find it a bit regrettable.

Other than that, I agree with you completely – I had no idea that some fans have sneered at this, and where I've offered disapproval about this story, it's mainly because I expect and desperately want it to be perfect. It's been such a terrific adventure, and whilst I won't embrace its rather basic ending (which entails the Doctor crossing some wires, whilst his companions don't listen and pull him out of a Perspex machine) as you do, I'll forgive it precisely because of everything that's brought us here. If so much of The Web of Fear has become over-familiar with time, watching the

series in order makes you realise *why* this was deemed a template for so much of what's to come. And as you say, from where I am at the moment, and even allowing that I may have tunnel vision, I don't recall any subsequent, similar tales being done quite so well as this.

Absolutely stunning.

Fury from the Deep episode one

R: If there's one thing doing this diary has taught me, it's that context is all. Stories from Hartnell's tenure that I may have dismissed before, like The Gunfighters or The Time Meddler, seem much more purposeful and surprising when seen as a contrast to what was going on beforehand. But it cuts both ways. And though Fury from the Deep has a reputation as a scary Troughton shocker – from this episode alone, it seems in context familiar and drab.

We've been here before. All of it. The regulars on a beach! (They did this two stories ago.) They get shot at, then taken prisoner, by suspicious guards. (That's par for the course.) They're within a scientific base (as ever), staffed by people of different nationalities (at least John Abineri's Dutch accent is a variation on the theme), and run by an angry authoritarian figure (whose name, Robson, is only one letter different from the chap who ran the moonbase).

I can see why it's so popular. It feels purpose-built Troughton. This ticks *all* the boxes. It even has the regular crew romping about in the foam, having a bit of a giggle, and showing us all the happy rapport between the cast. Watching it on its own, it probably comes across as definitive. But after months and months of this sort of thing, you look in vain for anything that's distinctive. Robson is played by Victor Maddern as a man who hates *everybody*. His bile isn't just directed at the TARDIS crew, but at his second in command, at his engineer, at some poor chap who only appears in the background on a monitor screen. Cutler, Hobson, Clent – at their respective introductions, they were all left with somewhere to build. Not here; it's the sort of character you usually see at the start of one of those Agatha Christie adaptations – a man who has to give, in only a few minutes, every single character different motives for stabbing him in the back. It might work if there was some other tension – but there's actually no jeopardy in the episode whatsoever. There's some foam, and some seaweed, and they make a heartbeat noise, but they do nothing to cause anybody any legitimate concern. Victoria's screams of terror at the episode's end are more than a little incongruous then; maybe if we had the visuals, we could see it's doing something suitably menacing. But since, so far this story, the most memorable thing about it is that foam fight on the beach, it's hard not to feel it's a cliffhanger that relies upon our understanding it's scary just because Doctor Who's formula tells us it must be so.

And that's the problem, really – lots of the Doctor Who formula on display, and none of its heart. (Heartbeats, yes.)

T: Believe it or not, for *years* this was my favourite Doctor Who story. Yes, yes, it's true that I've never actually seen it – how could I have done? Just like those young 'uns who wrote off the The Gunfighters without even watching it, I (as a Doctor Who fan) was also prone to assessing something sight unseen. After all, who needs facts when you've got an opinion? *Unlike* those lads, though, I didn't go along with received wisdom – anyone can champion the likes of Genesis of the Daleks and The Talons of Weng-Chiang, but I wanted to adore a story that made me look like an individual, a maverick... and yet, which no-one could take me to task about.

It was a bit arrogant and presumptive of me, frankly – I was basically saying that I knew Doctor Who *so well* that I was certain a story that hasn't been seen since first broadcast was the absolute best ever. (I realise I've just done something similar with The Web of Fear, but hopefully, despite all of my enthusiasm for it, I've added enough caveats to make clear that quite a bit of guesswork has gone into my evaluation of it.) I first got excited about Fury from the Deep when I read Gary Russell's review of the novelisation in Doctor Who Magazine. Later, I got a murky copy of the soundtrack – I held my ear close to the crackling speakers, managing to discern the odd sentence every now and again, and decided I was in the presence of greatness.

Then, when I checked a programme guide and discovered that van Lutyens (a technical expert at the refinery) was played by John Abineri – whom I'd appreciated in other works – it all seemed to come together. Even small parts were played by recognisable TV and Who stalwarts such as Hubert Rees (here appearing as the chief engineer) and Graham Leaman (Price, the communications officer), whilst the merely vocally present guard was played by Peter Ducrow (the Face from Adam Adamant Lives! – a series I knew was amazing despite never having seen an episode). Richard Mayes, an actor whose illustrious work in British theatre was getting excellent reviews at the time, was here relegated to appearing over a monitor, but no matter – this was the first Doctor Who story where I could confidently name the entire cast.

I realise now that I was acting like a bit of an idiot, but nonetheless some residue of that zealous advocacy remains for this story. But then, Rob, you send me an indifferent review about it! Oh. What's a boy to do?

All right, I would have to admit that this isn't shaping up to be an all-conquering classic just yet, but there's plenty to enjoy. The TARDIS' arrival is pretty impressive – it looks like it's descending from miles up in the air before landing with a plonk on the sea; so far, so different. And one story after the Brigadier's debut, we get the introduction of another icon: the sonic screwdriver. Furthermore, I'm not sure I buy the argument that this is overly familiar – yes, we have some weirdness happening at a scientific establishment, but we also have the refreshing invocation of domesticity. A family home with ordinary, everyday couple is quite unusual for Doctor Who in this period – for all that the Yeti just terrorised London, the military force they faced seemed less vulnerable than this plausibly domestic couple. And while "Robson" might be one letter different from moonbase-commander "Hobson", they're very much different characters. Hobson was the straightforward British officer type that Patrick Barr always played, whereas Victor Maddern's Robson is an obstinate bully whose single-mindedness could inadvertently help whatever is making noises in the pipes.

I have to say, though, that I once thought the

real-life gas board were a bit mean when they changed me to a card meter when I was a bit skint. Now I've reconsidered that opinion – in the Doctor Who universe, the buggers have sub-machine guns!

April 11th

Fury from the Deep episode two

R: I'll admit it – that sequence cut by the Australian censors is *brilliant*. Smiling like demented puppets, Quill and Oak gas a woman in her bedroom by no more than bulging their eyes and breathing on her – and to the clanky-clanky music of Dudley Simpson that suggests we should be finding this somehow *funny*. We've seen a lot of possessed humans on the series (and most of them over the last season and a half!), but none as chilling as these. John Gill's voice as Oak is smashing too, having some of the overstated melody to it of a children's TV presenter talking down to his victim.

But otherwise, I'm afraid this is still a strange bore of a story, with lots of earnest discussions about pumps and impellers and pipelines, and very little actual drama. And very little room for the Doctor and his friends either – Troughton sounds at best a little arch this episode, one remove from the action (which, frankly, he is). The only really human aspect to any of this is the relationship between the Harris family; the concern that Frank shows for his wife Maggie is touching and sincere, and the affection they have for each other gives the dialogue a lightness of touch. You suddenly realise how much Doctor Who shies away from this sort of thing; this is the first married couple shown on the series since The Celestial Toymaker, of all things – and that was a pair of playing cards! Just as the story feels it's drifting off into long arguments about scientific stuff, it's anchored by the refreshing domestic reality seen here.

T: It took me some time to fully discover Mr Oak and Mr Quill. The Gary Russell review of the novelisation eulogised them, and hearing John Gill's wonderfully fruity tones ("The bag, Mr Quill," he says with disdainful admonish-

ment) on the soundtrack did nothing to dispel my thoughts on how great they must have been. Then the telesnaps showed up, and I was shocked to see Quill standing there with his mouth wide open, his eyes bursting from his cadaverous face. And *then* the censor clips came back! Much of Doctor Who that I've experienced in book form has disappointed me on first viewing, as it wasn't as quite as good as my imagination (or in the case of the Nestene, what I had seen on the Target covers). But this marked the first time that something *exceeded* my expectations – Oak and Quill step forward in unison as Simpson's plonking, reedy music oozes in, and the camera moves onto Bill Burridge's terrifyingly contorting face. I was either 24 or 25 when I saw it first this, and even though I was watching it in the middle of the afternoon, it genuinely spooked me.

Other components of this seem very worthy... director Hugh David uses very inventive cuts, fades and close-ups in the 58 seconds of screen time that we can actually see; if the rest of the story was this good, something very special is indeed missing from the archives. Roy Spencer, as Frank Harris, exudes goodness and adoration for his wife – it makes a potentially wet character work as an extremely decent and devoted man. And Maggie Harris' possession is genuinely unsettling, her shuddering gasps suggesting that she's suffering acute pain (which, judging by her taste in kitchen cabinets, is something that she thoroughly deserves).

Really, my only disappointment here is that Oak and Quill aren't credited as *Mr* Oak and *Mr* Quill. But you can't have everything.

Fury from the Deep episode three

R: The cliffhanger is haunting and beautiful. All the more so because it's the quietest we've yet heard Victor Maddern – that's the power of this possession by seaweed, that it can turn such an angry man railing at the word into someone so calmly complicit. It's shocking too – having handed over the baton to Robson, Maggie silently turns and walks into the sea, until she's lost beneath the waves. Fury from the Deep is very good at this sort of thing – it's at its eeriest when it has the suggestion of menace. (You're right – the last cliffhanger was very effective too.)

Maybe, though, that's why I'm still having problems with the story. (Because I'm sorry, I still am.) Its threat may just be a bit too subtle for me – we're halfway through the adventure now, and I want more than *anticipation*, I want something to pay off. They're clearly seeding Deborah Watling's departure at last, as much to the Doctor's obvious bemusement she starts questioning why the TARDIS constantly takes them to danger. "It's the spice of life!" says the Doctor – and for me, I'm afraid, that falls a bit flat; I think the taste of this particular dish still seems too mild for me.

Perhaps I'll get into the swing of this story tomorrow. I can't help but feel that I'm missing out.

T: If there's a difficulty here (I know I'm highlighting problems when I shouldn't be; I think some of your negativity has rubbed off, Rob), it's that although Victor Maddern is thoroughly convincing as a man on the edge, the script asks him to be so *before he's been attacked by the weed*. The way he was going, parasite or no parasite, he'd probably just have cracked up and put Harris, van Lutyens, the Doctor – everyone, really – in the brig (I know they're in a refinery, but it's pretty tooled up in every other respect). And it's a stumbling block that the arguments in the complex aren't about life and limb (unlike, say, The Ice Warriors, where each course of action could have led to disaster), but rather about Robson's somewhat inexplicable stubbornness.

But the scenes here aren't *all* anticipatory – some pretty impressive terror occurs as foam and thrashing seaweed engulfs the Harrises' house. The gas that the weed emits increases the threat level, and the everyday sight of a ventilation shaft is terrifyingly transformed into the abode of the demonic. And the aerial shots on the beach and Simpson's subtle, moving music transform the episode ending into another classic, as Maggie inhumanely walks into the sea.

I'm a bit distracted while watching this episode, though, because I have a personal nerdy tie to it. My love for the intricacies of credits order – billing and other things that require making lists – is such that I once went to the

Birmingham library to look up entries for Doctor Who in old issues of the Radio Times. The first story I looked up was Fury from the Deep, and I was elated that the billings went: "Starring Patrick Troughton, with Victor Maddern and Frazer Hines, Deborah Watling." It seemed thrilling that guest stars could be deemed more important than companions (this may seem like a trivial detail, but when you grow up watching the likes of Matthew Waterhouse being credited above Emrys James, such things become important). Episode three was particularly exciting: the name of John Abineri – of whom I'm a huge fan – appeared in big letters just under that of Victor Maddern.

Call me overly pedantic if you like, but I think credits are very important – the quality of drama on the UK television is directly connected to the speed, size and readability of the credits, and that's a fact (or, all right, it might not be). Actually, I think *not* expecting that your audience is prepared to read words after watching a television programme is a sign that you think they're stupid. We need to do more to stop this trend towards crunching credits! Why, I refused to watch Spooks on broadcast because they'd done away with the credits – the irony being that when I later watched it on DVD, executive producers Jane Featherstone and Simon Crawford Collins justified that decision while their names were superimposed beneath them in big letters.

Credit lovers of the world, unite! (Yes, I know... this is all less about Fury from the Deep than it is about Fury from the Geek, but it happens.)

April 12th

Fury from the Deep episode four

R: I had a nightmare about Fury from the Deep last night. It wasn't foam, or gas pipes, or seaweed, or Victor Maddern getting angry with me. It was Dudley Simpson's music. Every time I closed my eyes, somewhere in my brain it'd come at me – that clanky-clanky theme he gives Oak and Quill. I got very tired of it, frankly. Say what you like about Arc of Infinity – and there's much that one can – but Roger

Limb's ooo-eeee-oo music never robbed me of sleep.

This episode has a desperation to it that's very recognisable and real. It's not the desperation we're used to from The Ice Warriors or The Web of Fear – by this stage in those stories, everyone involved had long realised that everything was going to hell in a handbasket. Not here, though; it takes until the end of episode four for there to be an accepted acknowledgement that an invasion has begun. I like that – I like the way that the most chilling scene is a subtle one between Robson and Harris on the beach, which is unsettling simply because it's so muted and inconclusive. I like the way that Victoria responds so badly to the atmosphere of *this* story, rather than ones of more obvious jeopardies, and more and more forcefully questions why she wants to travel with the Doctor. And I like the fact that Megan Jones (the chairwoman of the company who owns the refinery) can be so initially dismissive of the crisis – but does so (unlike in a lot of Pertwee stories to come) not by looking like a fool or a bully, but by being someone who's simply unable to recognise that there is that brooding tension we've had four episodes to get used to.

I think that's where I've gone wrong with Fury, and why I found it so hard to get to grips with it. It's taken the notion of a base in crisis, and played a game of nerves with its characters and with its audience. Something feels badly wrong, but it's not going to give us the relief of a dead body, or a villain issuing threats in a hissing voice. (I'm a bit of a coward watching horror movies; I jump at the slightest noise, I put my hands over my eyes. All up 'til the moment when I can see what level of gore the film is going to provide. Then the tension's gone, and I can relax and take it all for granted. It's the *waiting* for something nasty to happen that irks me. Fury from the Deep's effect on me is limited because – yet again – I'm squinting at it through telesnaps. If it actually existed, I think I might have more quickly realised what it was trying to do.)

Great to see, too, in Megan Jones a strong female character who commands respect – and by doing so, isn't either a defeminised automaton (as we'll see in Brian Hayles' stories), or a villain needing redemption. In its portrayal of a happy marriage, Victor Pemberton's script seems far in advance of its Troughton-era brothers in the way that it tries to characterise real people in real relationships in as unforced a manner as possible.

T: "Waiting" seems to be the keyword for these latest episodes – as van Lutyens said at the end of episode two, "It's down there, in the darkness, in the pipeline. Waiting." Here, the Doctor talks about the peacefulness outside, the calm, and tells Victoria that they need to wait until they know how to tackle the weed. But the tension causes her to panic; they're really putting Victoria through the wringer in this, which is great news for Deborah Watling, who gets some decent material for a change. And it's a fair point, because in real life, meeting disaster head-on is nothing like as bad as *anticipating* that it might happen, and things are rarely as bad as you expect. The expectation is the most uncomfortable bit – and that's what we have here in spades. Robson calmly waits on the beach, deadpanning his words to Harris before silently wandering off. When van Lutyens decides to have a peek in the Impeller, his justification is that "I can't sit about waiting." There's so much waiting going on, in fact, that Jamie falls asleep.

Because the viewers themselves have also spent ages waiting, it's really quite gripping when van Lutyens – having slowly investigated in the dark – gets sucked into the foam, his screams echoing up the shaft. Then the Doctor and Jamie go down to help, and we get that brilliant reveal that the technicians in charge of the lift are Oak and Quill (how fortunate for the story's fear factor that the weed chose the two most incongruously scary looking technicians to take over first). What began quite slowly starts to pay off – Robson goes bonkers to the extent that Maddern can suggest some alien manipulation of his mind, causing a mental struggle; it's a most convincing depiction of a man tipping over the edge. And Chief Baxter's on-screen demise is rather horrifying, as everyone watches aghast, unable to do anything.

So the tension finally *does* break in this episode, and very much works in its favour. It's a neat trick – it this hasn't been the most comfortable experience up till now, that's probably been the point. And it's an instalment that finishes with the weed-parasite inveigling its way through the entire control rig as a stepping stone to its moving onto the British Isles, and possibly the entire planet. Perhaps I was wrong. Sometimes, things *are* as bad as you expect them to be.

Fury from the Deep episode five

R: I'm in love with Megan Jones. Head over heels. She's so practical, so strong, and so decisive. Her very appearance in the story coincides with the seaweed monster actually pulling up its socks and *doing* something; even marine life wants to impress her. And the scene where she's alone with Robson in his room, trying to get information – and her voice drops, and she softly tries to reassure him she's an old friend – is one of the very best in the story. Her Welsh accent becomes more pronounced, and you can suddenly get this glimpse of a woman who's had to suppress even her own background just so she can justify her position in a man's world. It's a terrific performance, by a terrific actress. Toby, you're an actor, you know everybody. Could you fix me a date with Margaret John? Preferably as Megan, and not as the granny who got her face sucked off in The Idiot's Lantern – but, you know, I'm not proud, whichever's easiest.

Right, back to bed. I want to dream of forceful Welsh women tonight. And not Dudley Simpson. Thank you.

T: A friend of mine did a sitcom with Margaret John, and was perplexed by how excited I was when I found out. What's great about her scene with Robson (apart from the fact that the six-part structure here affords it to us) is that when she gives him the tough, stern, buck-your-ideas-up-chum speech, she's not doing it because she's losing her temper – she's trying to snap her old mate out of it by using the sort of approach he'd use on a wavering subordinate. Maddern builds upon last week's great work when he sounds like he's blindly flailing as he appeals for her help. It's as if he's trying to give the impression that the real Robson is in the dark, his mind being clouded over by this invasive creature.

You mentioned in episode one that context

is everything, and that Fury from the Deep suffers as a result, but I'm less convinced of this. It's become de rigueur of late to write off Season Five – the once much-lauded "Monster Season" – as a repetitive, formulaic bore-fest, but most of these adventures have used the "base under siege" template to fulfill different objectives. Tomb was a classic "get a small group together in a scary place to bump them off" tale, The Abominable Snowmen put an SF bent onto a mythical legend, The Ice Warriors addressed a "man vs. machine" ethical dilemma that worked within the plot and mirrored the subtext, whilst The Web of Fear was an action/adventure that sought to scare the beejesus out of you. But Fury from the Deep has been an exercise in mood – a steadily rising one started out at ominous, went to creepy and ramped up to anticipatory. And here at the end of episode five, as the Doctor and Jamie confront the nerve-centre of the weed and its minions, it looks like this thing from the deep is about to get *really* furious.

April 13th

Fury from the Deep episode six

R: I've got used to regular actors' departures feeling like afterthoughts, and so am still reeling a bit from this. The Doctor defeats the seaweed monster, of course – but that's not even remotely what this episode's about. He comes up with the solution a minute in, and it takes him about a quarter of an hour to implement it. The idea that it's destroyed by the amplified recording of Victoria's screams sounds rather twee and gimmicky in theory – but it's only as you listen to the episode that it hits you how cruel a comment upon what Victoria's been going through this really is: it's the expression of all her fear, and all her unhappiness, cheerfully stuck onto tape and made into an emotionless weapon. After weeks of trying to get the Doctor's attention, it's as if he only properly notices how upset she is in order to *use* it. I don't want to overstress this – but it's telling that the story ends as triumphantly as it can, with everyone safe and alive and friends with each other, almost to form a contrast with the way Victoria feels. The expected jubilation we'd usually get at the monster's defeat is tempered by the sound of Victoria dissolving into hysterics.

It's abrupt, this decision of hers to live with a family she barely knows – but not abrupt in an Andred/Invasion of Time way, the story isn't suddenly asking you to believe in a relationship which simply wasn't there. Maggie Harris sounds polite but surprised when Victoria wants to be with them – the "stay as long as you want" invitation is one I've made to friends in difficulties before, but it usually has the unspoken addition "but don't make it last for more than a fortnight" attached to it. That she goes off with strangers – not with a David Campbell, not with a Troilus – makes the stress Victoria's been feeling seem all the more acute. And the last ten minutes focus upon the different reactions of the Doctor and Jamie. The scene where Jamie talks to Victoria that one last time – and then promises he won't leave without saying a final goodbye – is full of pain and bravery and the confusion you associate with a break-up; the fact that, as far as the story is concerned, we never hear that goodbye almost makes a lie out of it. The Doctor instead is polite and practical; he's already accepted she's leaving before she knows it herself. That final scene in the TARDIS, with Jamie sulky and the Doctor defensive, and Victoria watching them silently from the beach, is heart-wrenching. We began the story with them fighting in foam, and all we'll get from now on are convention anecdotes about how the trio played naughty tricks involving knickers in rehearsal – but at this point it's a friendship fractured, and all the awkwardness of that comes clearly through. The protracted epilogue to this rather familiar monster tale is one of the most strikingly original things we've seen in Doctor Who for ages.

It's not all hard emotion. The sequence with the Doctor flying the helicopter is gorgeous. Without the pictures accompanying it, all the screams and shouts – and the Doctor's polite concern about how he can fly the thing – have a cartoon-like comedy to them. The fact we never find out *how* he lands, we just accept he does, means that this really is a great gag and not a bit of extra jeopardy. It's delightful, and feels like it's the programme giving one last burst of comic rapport for this terrific team.

T: At the end of the day, it doesn't matter to me how *good* this story is or isn't. How do we define "good", anyway? Something can have lyrical dialogue, splendid design, a well structured plot and fine acting, and inevitably someone will find it dull despite everything you can cite to the contrary. But you can't really argue with someone's opinion – I once saw a post on Outpost Gallifrey where someone listed their bottom, most-hated stories: Blink was on it, but Time-Flight was nowhere to be seen. And yet, how can I berate that person? I can't – not without being a patronising oaf. No matter how well I might argue my case, how dare I tell someone that the entertainment value they did or didn't derive from a piece of television is wrong? Sure, if you were to dissect the relative merits of Quatermass II and Gone With the Wind, the latter would win hands down, but that doesn't stop a lot of people on most days (myself included) from preferring to stick Brian Donlevy, miscast or not, into their DVD player.

I'm laying out this context because I can't deny that my experience of Fury this time around has felt a bit lacking. In particular, I think that having a silly helicopter chase in episode six, when the story is supposed to be reaching a climax, is unforgivable no matter how funny Troughton is, and how well shot the sequence might have been. It's the equivalent of having comedy escapades whilst King Kong is atop the Empire State Building; there's a time and a place for such shenanigans, and this is neither.

Don't get me wrong – there's great stuff here too. The final showdown with gallons of foam and the curious, thrashing creatures looks as though it could have been terrific, and it's wonderful how they use the echoey pipes to transport the sound out to the rigs and destroy the weed's nerve centre. Troughton puts in another gorgeous performance, Robson is restored to his old self (i.e. he's still a bit of a git), and – just this once, Victoria – everybody lives! And in a story with such a slow build-up, the relaxed, domestic coda feels just right and should be cherished; it's a rare moment of real-life in this fantastical series.

I could continue weighing the relative pros and cons of this story in some sort of cosmic scale of high geekery to determine its net value. I could. But actually, *none* of that is important, because I am so in love with what Fury from the Deep represents to me. It's permeated so much of my Doctor Who life. I vividly remember being a huge know-it-all kid, convinced I knew everything about Who – I had read all of the Target novels that were available, so I knew of companions such as Ben, Polly and Liz Shaw that my friends (the poor fools) were ignorant of. Occasionally I was caught out – I brought a copy of Planet of the Daleks with me for company on a camping trip, but I'd yet to read it. My tent-mate looked at the first chapter and read aloud, "Jo Alone...", whereupon I brashly informed him, "Oh, yes... Joe. He's a great companion...", and was then told, based on the evidence right there on the first page, that "Jo's a she."

After that, as you can imagine, I stuck to only talking about stories I actually knew. The problem being: there were a hell of a lot I *didn't* know about. I got The Doctor Who Crossword Book and thought it'd be a doddle, then got tripped up on answers such as "Rider From Shang-Tu". The Radio Times 20th Anniversary Special was very much an eye opener – look, it's Peter Purves from Blue Peter in a stripey top, was he a companion then? Who's this Dodo character? And there, tucked away in the synopses, was a small précis of Fury from the Deep. At the time it didn't make much of an impact on me, but there was a picture elsewhere of the weed creature and it looked enormous – a swishing mass of nautical anger towering over a cowering character. (Imagine my disappointment years later, when I discovered that the man was a special-effects bod, and the creature itself wasn't actually that big.)

But I still didn't give the story much thought until an issue of Doctor Who Magazine promised that in the next issue, they'd be covering the "special novelisation" of Fury from the Deep. I wondered: what could be so special about it? A month later, DWM revealed that it was a "bumper edition", which sounded terribly exciting. Unfortunately, Castle Bookshop in Ludlow – where I used to go sometimes go on a Saturday and rearrange the dozen or so Doctor Who novels they had into chronological order – had finally stopped stocking them. Fortunately, my friend Derek (a kindly handyman who'd do odd jobs for my Mum, and –

after he innocently mentioned that he'd watched William Hartnell as a boy – put up with a jabbering child asking if he remembered the intricacies of The Daleks' Master Plan) knew a man in Wolverhampton (Danny, a lovely bloke as it turned out) who was a Doctor Who fan. One day, I went with Derek to this man's house, where he lent me a number of old Doctor Who Magazines (to my shame, I still have them!), and, for reasons lost on the mists of time, *gave* me a surplus copy of the new novel of Fury from the Deep!! The excitement was electrifying!! I read it and read it and *read* it, and judged that everything Gary Russell had said in his DWM review was right.

Sometime later, I learned that you could get soundtracks on cassette from that shop I mentioned in Wolverhampton – the deal was that you took in take two C-90s and left with one full of crackly Doctor Who audio goodness (sans every other cliffhanger, sadly). I got a copy of Fury from the Deep – my first choice, of course – that made everyone's voices a pitch higher or lower. Abineri sounded like a baritone, Maddern like a chimney sweep, and it was so warbly it sounded like the weed's heartbeat punctuated almost the entire story. I huddled next to my cassette player, trying to discern what went on... and the pictures I conjured were multi-million dollar and as scary as hell. I was thrilled, I was elated, but I was also frustrated that I couldn't *see* it. I was intrigued by the mystique of the missing episodes, and prone to fantasise (as I still am, frankly) about their return. And as I've mentioned before, the recovered censor clips of this story eventually proved as terrifying as anything I had imagined.

In one fashion or another, Fury from the Deep continued following me. Anyone who has seen or heard Moths Ate My Doctor Who Scarf knows that I've always had a thing about John Abineri – I even taped highlights of an episode of Forever Green because he played the guest baddie and got top guest billing. I even had a brief dalliance with a girl at university who was his niece (which I *promise* was completely unrelated to his CV; I'm weird, but not *that* weird). Much later, when I was in Bath performing Moths, I was introduced to a man whose father had "been a Time Lord in Doctor Who with Patrick Troughton". I cockily reeled off the names Bernard Horsfall, Trevor Martin and Clyde Pollitt, but found that he was Graham Leaman's son! So actually, he was a Time Lord for *Jon Pertwee*, but guest-starred in Fury. I quizzed Giles Leaman about his Dad, and find out little nuggets about one of Doctor Who's most prolific odd-job actors. Months later, I was performing Moths in Westcliffe-On-Sea, and by sheer happenstance, the sound man saw the cue "John Abineri's niece" in the script and said that his mate Seb who lived down the road had that surname. Phone calls were made, and an absolutely delighted Sebastian Abineri (no slouch as an actor himself) bought me a drink and we had a wonderful chat. I subsequently got a lovely email saying how thrilled he was to have gone back to tell his family, and that his Dad would have been really proud and loved the show.

You can't write those moments. They happen, and you remain grateful for them, which I why I hope everyone will forgive me for being indulgent and mentioning them here.

So you can see why I really don't care that I haven't warmed to Fury as much as I'd hoped on this run-through. It's impacted me in all sorts of different areas more than watching a reconstruction of it over the past three days could ever compete with. Try as I might, I can't be objective about this story – but why should I be? Maybe that lad who hates Blink once lost a girlfriend to a DVD shop proprietor called Banto, or perhaps he enjoys Time-Flight because it cheered him up after he'd had a humiliation at school. For those of us who grew up with Doctor Who, it's so woven into the development of our lives that certain stories have a meaning above and beyond how we might view them as pieces of television. This show is a million different things to a million different people.

Rick and Ilsa may always have Paris, but I'll always have Fury from the Deep. And for that matter, it'll always have me.

The Wheel in Space episode one

R: Okay, now this is odd.

David Whitaker is an unpredictable writer, isn't he? Just as I'd got used to him as the man who'd scripted The Power of the Daleks or The Crusade, I remembered watching this that he's

also responsible for The Edge of Destruction. There's a crisis in the TARDIS! The Ship responds by doing funny things with the fault locator, and showing weird pictures on the scanner to tempt the Doctor away. (If its own particular way of warning the crew they were in danger seemed contrived in Season One, it just feels daft here in Season Five, now that the series is established. The day the Doctor fitted the Cloister Bell, and uninstalled the Bonkers Emergency software, was a very fine one indeed.) There's a lot of worry about the mercury in the fluid link, and then a few minutes' sequence in which the Doctor gets Jamie a meal out of the food machine, and you sort of want to ask – did the last few years of the show count for nothing? (And if so, did I sit through Galaxy Four in vain?) And when the Doctor takes out the time-vector generator, which means the TARDIS goes back to being just a police box (??), I smelled a rat. Has this David Whitaker even watched this programme before? It's a different David Whitaker, isn't it? It's someone they just called from the phone book by accident!

And yet, because we know that *can't* be the case – I mean, could it? – there has to be something deliberate about this. What we get here feels like an intentional deconstruction of what we expect Doctor Who to do in its opening episode. The danger comes not from any real active threat, but from the fact that there's no refuge for the Doctor and Jamie any more, that they're just stranded in space on some bit of floating jetsam. Victoria implied in Fury from the Deep that her life in the TARDIS was one of aimless wandering – and it seems that what was metaphor last week has been made explicit. So we get the Doctor prattling about with food machines because *there's nothing else to do*, a look at an unthreatening robot because *there's nothing else to do*; and Jamie eventually calls it a night and goes to sleep. And when the dialogue stops, the soundtrack becomes for long minutes nothing more than a series of bleeps and whirrs – it's Doctor Who not as drama, but as an ambient music album.

Why? Why be this dull on purpose? Well, the thing is, I'm not sure it was meant to be. I think it was intended to be disorientating. In what it attempts – the Doctor and his friend staying out of the action, being confronted with nothing but void, even being tempted by false pictures on the scanner – it's not unlike the opening episode to The Mind Robber later in the year. We all love The Mind Robber because it's original and it's eerie. In The Wheel in Space we're meant to be watching in a state of tension – the continuity announcer has told us that this is a Cyberman story, we know the way the series works, we know there'll be menace. Victoria knew it – that's why she scarpered. The TARDIS knew it – that's why it had a fit. We're denied all of that for 20 minutes. And then suddenly, shockingly, we're back with yet another bunch of Troughton-era scientists sporting a range of Troughton-era accents, and before we've the faintest clue who they are, they're turning their lasers on the spaceship that carries the Doctor and Jamie. Twenty minutes of ambience, crashing into three minutes of the achingly routine, crashing into the end credits. It almost leaves you blinking, dazed at the change of focus.

Or would do. If – and you can join in – It Existed In The Archives. It's honestly hard to tell. Either The Wheel in Space episode one is the most mind-numbingly tedious episode in the Doctor Who canon, or it's a rather brave experiment about audience expectations, trying to dislocate the way the viewers responded to space drama. (Not unlike the way Kubrick does in 2001.) The visuals might just have made this largely dialogue-free instalment weird enough to be intriguing. Not the visuals we see on telesnaps, of course – but scenes of empty corridors, of empty rooms, of emptiness waiting to be filled. And at that point I can feel Toby's credulity stretch to breaking point, and I'll go.

T: Don't worry, I won't take you to task *now*, I'll settle for giving you a Chinese burn next time I see you. But yes – it could be that Tristan de Vere Cole directs the hell out of this, and that it's a Kubrick-esque masterpiece. On the other hand, I've seen the extant episodes three and six, and unless he had a stroke in-between now and then, I suspect it's unlikely. Whereas the previous episode wrapped up the drama ten minutes early, this one doesn't even bother to begin it until the last five. Still, we should count ourselves lucky that it's not, as the opening few minutes suggest, a sequel to The Edge

of Destruction (especially as somebody somewhere would have insisted upon calling this Inside Somebody Else's Spaceship).

I can't help but feel a chill during the opening sequence – the TARDIS sound effect went on for ages during the closing music of Fury episode six, and here we have a reprise and a credit which means that this, and not Fury, is technically Deborah Watling's last story. And it's strange for me, as someone who grew up with even the companions as adult-identification figures, to suddenly realise that this young woman I'm watching fade away on the monitor is actually exactly 15 years younger than I am now. (Deborah Watling and I share a birthday, you see.) When did that happen? She used to be old enough to be my mother, but her Doctor Who-self is now young enough to be disgusted were I to make a pass at her. She's a cruel mistress, Time. And it's interesting that Jamie falls into the same bear trap as Ian and Barbara in The Rescue (is this a habit with Whitaker scripts?) when he says, "I wonder what Victoria's up to now." Strictly speaking mate, she's not up to an awful lot. By the time your current adventure takes place, she's dead, and has been for years.

You can tell, Rob, how interesting I find this episode – I've spent the last paragraph talking about someone who's in the first ten seconds, and no more. Yes, it's hard to judge because we don't have the video, so it's entirely possible that the Servo Robot moves in an exciting way, or that Jarvis Bennett's beard starts making Cyber-shaped shadow puppets on the back wall, but it doesn't seem very probable. However much we might pretend otherwise, this does seem to be killing time. I seem to recall Dennis Spooner saying he'd cut a load of nonsense about the TARDIS food machine out of The Power of the Daleks episode one – maybe Whitaker noticed the deletion, and kept it in a drawer in case of a crisis.

April 14th

The Wheel in Space episode two

R: Whitaker's dialogue – now that he's actually giving us some! – is actually rather stylish. There's a clever way in which he segues from the end of one scene into another to give the flow of them a bit more energy. Jamie asks for a report on the Doctor's health, and it's immediately answered by Dr Corwyn in another scene talking to station-controller Jarvis Bennett; that scene with Bennett ends with his suspicions that Jamie might be a saboteur, cutting into a scene which suggests a very good reason why our kilted friend might need to become one. And with Victoria gone, we're introduced to two new brilliant characters who might take her place. Wendy Padbury is really rather fab as Zoe, heartily amused by Jamie's insistence that he's not wearing ladies' clothes and his threats to take her over his knee and "larrap her". "I'm going to learn so much from you!", she says in delight. And Gemma Corwyn is an even better character – the way she can tell Jamie isn't a seasoned space traveller merely because he doesn't drink the water she brings him is the single cleverest deduction anyone bar the Doctor has yet made in this series *ever*. She's strong and compassionate and has authority – Megan Jones, I spurn you, I have eyes now only for Gemma. Zoe's bright and likeable, and the chatty way she lists facts so unselfconsciously is great fun – but is it too much to hope that the next companion might be an older brilliant woman scientist for once? (Well, it is *this* season. But Gemma's natural successor is on her way.)

Not all the dialogue works. We don't know these characters yet, so sometimes Whitaker's attempts to give them idiosyncrasies just looks a bit forced. "Did I ever tell you about my nose?" is Tanya's rather startling way of starting a spot of dialogue voicing her concerns about the rocket – Whitaker is trying hard to put a bit of colour into the clichés, but sometimes he's trying a mite *too* hard. Mostly these people talk normally and suggest they have an off-screen life – but it's so peculiar seeing the Kit Pedler stereotypes being given David Whitaker quirks that it disconcerts more than it convinces.

The details are fine – but ultimately there's not much of a bigger picture to look at yet. The cliffhanger boasts the eeriest image of the Cybermen we've yet seen, as they rock themselves awake and burst out of eggs as if they're warped parodies of babies – but it also reminds us it's the first time we've seen them in the

story, now two whole episodes in. And the Doctor spending this episode unconscious only emphasises that this week, the series is marking time. This ought to be very dull; everyone works hard enough to ensure it's merely *mildly* dull.

T: I'm surprised you didn't mention Jarvis Bennett's slow descent into paranoia – when Gemma tells him that they don't know enough about the approaching rocket, he rather bizarrely accuses her of subjecting him to psychoanalysis. He then starts mimicking the speech patterns of the child she thinks he's behaving like: "Bang, bang, blow up the balloon." Unlike Robson simply "cracking up" under pressure and Zaroff's rather sweeping "madness", Whitaker at least tries to characterise Bennett's psychosis. Unfortunately, despite being handed some of the most clear and realistic scripted depictions of a commander buckling under pressure, Michael Turner is easily the worst exponent of such a character this season; he growls and spits his lines in an accent that contrives to veer from Scottish to American, and is sometimes both at the same time. He's not the only one, regrettably – the crew babble includes Michael Goldie grappling with a wayward American drawl, whilst Peter Laird (a fine actor who has proved himself amply latterly) does an *unforgivable* Chinese accent, for which I hope he's velly solly. Still, who needs *glasnost* when you have Leo Ryan and Tanya Lernov, flirting their way through mortal danger?

Top marks too, to Jamie for addressing the issue of fashion. The 60s depiction of the future looks a bit daft to modern eyes, with snug two-pieces clinging to portly actors in an attempt to be space-age. So it's telling that when Gemma queries Jamie's dress sense, he points out that she'd look pretty silly to some people's eyes – as indeed, she does to ours. That's the thing about fashion: it always dates. Last decade's cool is this decade's naff, which is why I've never really bothered about hunting down the latest hot haberdashery. (Say it with me, everyone: "Wheel turns, fashions rise, wheel turns, fashions fall.") This random allocation of coolness means I'll probably be trendy by accident on a handful of occasions, and the beauty of that is, I won't have paid through the nose for privilege. In turn, this will leave me more money for Doctor Who DVDs.

And now, of course, Doctor Who is fashionable again – which makes me a winner!

The Wheel in Space episode three

R: Well, it's good to have Troughton back – but he doesn't get out of bed for the entire episode. This has a curious effect on the story; it means that halfway through a large cast adventure, he still hasn't met more than a couple of guest characters. And with none of the main characters having yet met a Cyberman either, this really can't be a good thing – I was ultimately prepared to forgive Fury from the Deep for the way it took its time before driving on with the action, but this is ridiculous. Troughton sitting up in bed makes him suddenly look very old, and really for the first time, this bundle of anarchic energy seems rather subdued and faded. The weary way in which he reacts to the news that he is Jamie's scapegoat for the sabotage, or that he is being confined to quarters, is really unlike anything he's ever done before, and Troughton appears to downplay his performance quite deliberately as a result. (He only really sparkles when he has the chance to flirt with Gemma Corwyn – the second Doctor and I have similar tastes, I think.) But what could easily have made the Doctor a bit dull actually gives him a certain freshness – I love his scenes with Jamie and Zoe, asking them both for theories to what's going on, as if he's a schoolteacher judging which is the most talented companion.

And the Cybermen have changed again! They just can't leave them alone. The new voices are – well, let's be charitable – a mixed blessing. At first they seem less inhuman, but at least more comprehensible. But then in the cliffhanger, when they give instructions to the hapless crewmembers in their control, they seem gabbled and garbled. I wanted someone to ask them to repeat what they'd just said, maybe a bit slower – but I suppose that might have destroyed the atmosphere they were trying to create.

Best bit of the week: the Doctor broods that there's some menace to be faced, and the close-up of his face cross fades with a Cyberman. It's

a lovely moment. Runner-up: technician Enrico Casali enjoying with a smile the romantic banter between Tanya and Leo, and then realising too late it was supposed to be private. Worst bit of the week: Kevork Malikyan's death by Cybermat. We've seen a lot of carnage on this series, but never has a man faced his maker quite so enthusiastically.

T: Vision on! Thank goodness for that. I've just done 13 episodes on the trot with barely a moving image, and now we have a whole 25 minutes of telesnap-free goodness. We should be thankful for the telesnaps – a decidedly odd creation that at least gives us some visual representation of those missing years. But The Wheel in Space episode three is a reminder that even when a Doctor Who instalment isn't overwhelmingly brilliant, we should be grateful that it was recovered. I remember when this was amongst the holy of holies – a missing Doctor Who episode! – but not any more. We can properly enjoy and evaluate it.

The Cybermen are undergoing a rebirth in more ways than one – the first shot is a nifty special effect of an embryo Cyberman bursting out of a Cyber-ovary, and I like their costume redesign too. The masks are excellent (especially the tear drops and the lack of gaffer tape around the eyes and mouths), and I applaud "sleekness" over "baggy" in the Cyber-designs. It's a pity, then, that the direction is a bit flat – we don't have any of the trademark visuals of a Camfield or Martinus here – and the decision not to use music gives everything a rather disjointed feel, as we have oddly silent establishing shots, or scenes augmented by Radiophonic sound. This occasionally works and comes across as expressionistically weird, but it's in spite of the visuals, not because of them. Basically, the "weirdness" here doesn't seem deliberate, and is more jarring than disorientating.

And while I take your point about the death of Rudkin, the only thing that's really wrong with it is what Kevork Malikyan does with his hands. Being zapped by Cybermats is bound to have an effect, but his clawed fingers look silly – I think he's trying to suggest that his hands are now paralysed, but it just doesn't come off. It's entirely possible that he thought this move was okay in the studio, then watched appalled at home when it didn't turn out quite the way he thought it would. (I can't name an actor who hasn't experienced that, myself included.) Given that the Cybermats were always going to seem pretty rubbish no matter what Malikyan did, the shot of the little creatures surrounding him and the close-up on his echoingly screaming mouth are actually pretty good. What follows Rudkin's demise is a bit odd – the script tries to give Duggan some reason not to report "Billy Bug" right away (everyone thinks he's daft for liking space fauna, so purportedly they'd all take the piss if he mentioned it), but in a high-security establishment that's been a victim of sabotage, it's very unlikely he'd keep schtum due to some potential social awkwardness. That's no disrespect meant, by the way, to Kenneth Watson – for my money, he gives the best guest performance of the lot. Duggan seems natural and unforced, and his self-flagellation at Rudkin's death, followed by an all too real "Oh what's the use of talking...", is terrifically empathic and believable.

Otherwise, as you say, there's a bit of playful banter here. I love that Troughton wakes up grumpy and automatically wants to cut cleverclogs Zoe down to size, and whilst your joy at the three-way banter between Leo, Tanya and Enrico is quite sweet, it's also a bit tasteless seeing as they're jollying about immediately after the brutal slaying of one of their colleagues. My favourite line of this episode, though? The Doctor saying, "Logic, my dear Zoe, merely enables one to be wrong with authority." One suspects that's what Whitaker himself said to many a poor script editor who had the audacity to question the nonsensical nature of his stories.

April 15th

The Wheel in Space episode four

R: Yesterday I took a pot shot at the new Cyberman voices. But now I'm back on soundtrack, what strikes me is how little they're used. Compare them to the Cybermen of The Moonbase or The Tenth Planet, who were so chatty that at times you felt they could be employed as speakers at a rotary club. These ones hide in the shadows, and kill without warning or explanation. The death of crewman Chang (more on him in a minute) is so abrupt I had to rewind the tape to check it had really happened – he's killed, then passionlessly dumped in the waste disposal, which is about as callous as you can get. Dear old Bill Duggan, played so amiably by Kenneth Watson, is in one moment cheerfully whistling as he sets about his work, and in the next losing his entire personality forever. I'll not make a secret of it – I've been a bit disappointed by the Cybermen so far in Doctor Who. They're a terrific concept, these emotionless men, wanting to convert the rest of us to their example – but in practice they've always been a bit too chatty and, therefore, *reasonable*. Here at last they seem as cold and merciless as they should be.

I'm not saying I couldn't wish they were in a faster-paced story, mind you. This week, we've got a sequence in which Zoe explains to an amazed Jamie the scientific magic that is the tape recorder. (It's a bit too late for this sort of thing, isn't it? And he didn't even blink last week when sabotaging a laser cannon!) And Jarvis Bennett is the latest in a line of Troughton base commanders to go round the bend. Michael Turner at least decides to stop shouting a la Victor Maddern at the moment his brain finally cracks, though – there's something at once very funny and rather unnerving about a man walking around his station grinning and cheerily telling everyone that there's nothing wrong.

And then there's Chang! As played by Peter Laird. Yes, you're right, the accent is shameful. But I worked with Peter Laird a few years ago in theatre; he's a terrific comic actor, and a thoroughly nice chap. When I first started working as a dramatist, I put my foot in things a few times on my first productions – some director would cast a Doctor Who actor in one of my plays, and I'd excitedly break the ice at the readthrough by reciting their credits at them. Not a good idea. They'd usually think I was a weirdo, and avoid me for the rest of the run. By the time I met Peter I'd learned my lesson, and so only revealed that I knew of his dubious Oriental background whilst we were both safely merry at the opening night party. "Oh yes," he said blithely, "I used to play a lot of Chinese back in the sixties. I got quite used to being made slanty-eyed with sticky tape." Peter was very good in my Ayckbourn directed comedy; he's rather less effective when required to get his "l"s and "r"s mixed up on a futuristic space station. It makes you wince to hear this Caucasian actor try to yellow his speech – but it's a sign of the times, and leaves me wondering just how awkward it would have been now had Innes Lloyd jumped at Patrick Troughton's initial suggestion to black up and wear a turban as the Doctor. Would we be able to watch *any* of his stories nowadays without shuddering? Would they be able to release them on DVD and put them in HMV shops? When Doctor Who Confidential announced the casting of Matt Smith back in January, and rattled through his ten predecessors in the role, would they have coughed with embarrassment over Doctor No. 2, and jumped straight to Pertwee?

T: You've pretty much covered it, so I'll just add that Laird isn't even doing a Chinese accent very well – at one point he sounds like Bronson Pinchot's character on Perfect Strangers.

I'm noticing a pattern, though... you asked after the previous episode for the Cybermen to slow down (and/or repeat themselves), and in the recap, their speech is noticeably more measured and not as fast. And then, in our next scene with them, they repeat their instructions! Someone out there is listening to you, Rob. (If only you'd asked for The Web of Fear episode four to come back to the archives.) Not only that, but you're getting all hot for Gemma Corwyn and – what luck! – she turns out to be a widow. You're a bit charmed today – have you been rubbing any magic lanterns recently?

And while I agree that Michael Turner is generally effective when he's being quiet and distracted, I think you're being a bit harsh on Victor Maddern by comparing them. The two parts are written rather differently, and Turner gets more interesting things to do, so it's easier to pull off. He's terribly unconvincing when pitching his performance up (not a criticism you can level at Maddern – he's shouty, but it's a *good* shouty), and he sounds like a pirate when he talks about morale never having been better. Add to this mix Elton's weird accent (which brings to mind Reece Shearsmith's

comically appalling attempts to read F Scott Fitzgerald in The League of Gentlemen) and this has made for one of the most bizarre audio experiences I've ever had. At least the programme-makers had the common sense to kill Chang – I don't think I could have faced a hypnotised mock-Chinaman.

Otherwise, this trots along amiably enough – I like Flannigan offering to take just a five-minute break before knuckling down to work again, and how the Doctor wants a coffee and is given it in pellet form, in a scene that looks geared to remind us that we're in space. Meanwhile, the newly pardoned Duggan looks all set to become the Doctor's main helper until he's unceremoniously brainwashed and rather callously zapped. I rather liked Duggan, he was nice – couldn't Leo have just knocked him out instead? Bye bye, Duggan.

And then there's poor old Zoe – she's not exactly likeable yet (but this is clearly deliberate), and she ends this episode being left out of the action, making us feel a bit sorry for her. She's desperate to help, to join in, but none of the other kids will let her because she's done well in school, is slightly annoying and awkward at social interaction...

Oh my God. I've just described myself.

That's it. That's the secret. Zoe is a Doctor Who fan.

The Wheel in Space episode five

R: So. Let's get this straight. The Cybermen's invasion plan is as follows. They contrive to make a star go nova, creating a meteorite storm that will threaten the Wheel. To destroy the meteorites the crew will be obliged to use the laser cannon, and use up essential supplies of the mineral bernalium. The Cybermen send Cybermats to the Wheel, which will eat the bernalium. Requiring further stock, the humans will fetch bernalium from the nearby spaceship, but the Cybermen will be ready, hiding in the bernalium crates, and gain access to the Wheel. From which they can launch the inevitable invasion of Earth (both of them). All as clear as mud, and begging only one question. Are we meant to take any of that seriously?

It's as contrived as can be, of course. And I'm not being fair to it, sticking it on the com-

265

puter screen like that, rudely staring up at me in all its aching daftness. Because the uncovering of the plot has a different effect on screen. You realise this is like one of those Rube Goldberg inventions – when a series of increasingly convoluted machine parts operate in order to achieve a very simple solution. The effect is usually comic – whether it be the bizarre means by which Wilf Lunn would crack an egg on BBC kids show Jigsaw, or Doc Brown would feed his dog in Back to the Future. But here, it suggests one of two things. Either that the Cybermen are so enslaved to logic that they're fiendishly clever at being able to harness so many variables – which is strikingly cold and alien. Or that they're rather stupid, and to quote a later comment about the Master, would get giddy if they tried to walk in a straight line. Take your pick. But suddenly realising in this episode that we're at the heart of such a staggeringly complex plot does cause the brain to flip – it's dizzying. And anything in Doctor Who that does peculiar things to the brain needs to be cherished.

Someone else enslaved to logic is Zoe Heriot. She's a much darker character than I'd ever realised. Whitaker's script rather brilliantly only *hints* that she comes from a pitiless totalitarian regime, where young children are taken and brainwashed so that they can come out the other end supergeniuses – capable of holding a huge amount of information, but not the wherewithal to respond to it emotionally. She's just another Cyberman. And it's telling that the crew of the Wheel are seen to recoil somewhat from her – just as, years later, those who work on the Sandminer are uncomfortable around the chiselled cool beauty of the Robots of Death. Zoe recognises this. She struggles against it. In a moving scene, she asks Jamie what possible use she can now be for, when all her logical training comes up short against a problem she couldn't have anticipated. She's a robot wanting to be a human being – and what makes Wendy Padbury's performance so powerful is that even in the recognition of this she *still* doesn't give in to emotion, she's still obliged to wrestle with the dilemma as if it's a particularly taxing game of sudoku.

parter. Oh well, there are some brilliantly tense scenes here. The first has the Doctor and Jamie relying on the help of people who aren't even in the same room to send a killer sound wave to destroy the Cybermats. It's quite nailbiting (possibly because we've no video, and so can't see the little metal critters). Their deaths take forever, no doubt because the production team wished to show off their cutting-edge radio controlled 'roaches. And whereas you complained before about the indistinct Cybervoices, what about the Cyber-lightbulb they report to? He's indecipherable.

The biggest disquiet I have about this episode, however, is the Doctor. He rather childishly forces a reluctant Jamie to go to the Silver Carrier to retrieve the time-vector generator, claiming Jamie was responsible for misplacing it (he wasn't). He responds with testy petulance when Leo berates him for putting Jamie, Zoe *and* Gemma into peril, and he's uncharacteristically callous – so much so that poor, brave Jamie must selflessly try to stop Zoe from risking herself. In The Evil of the Daleks, the Doctor's plan *obliged* him to be shady and manipulative; here, he's just a git. And then there's his reaction to Gemma's suggestion that they give Jarvis electro-convulsive therapy: "I wouldn't advise moving him." Yeah, because sending electric currents gushing through Jarvis' brain would be okay, but moving him is a no-no. I suppose we can be a little accommodating based upon the year in which this was written, but it's really disconcerting to hear such an awful technique talked about so blithely.

I do like, though, how we have another variation of a character being seen in mortal danger via telephone/on a TV monitor. This one's especially good, thanks to Troughton's guilty panic and the calm, detached professionalism of Anne Ridler as Gemma does her job before trying to make her doomed escape. It's a heroic death from a good character, and is as much the climax to the episode as Jamie and Zoe being under threat from the oncoming meteorites.

Both hazardous situations being the Doctor's fault, the swine.

T: So, *finally* everyone is coming together to fight the Cybermen – in episode five of a six-

April 16th

The Wheel in Space episode six

R: The best bit about the episode is – once again – Patrick Troughton. He's barely been in the adventure, and when he has he's seemed much more subdued than we're used to. But he rallies around, as if smelling the odour of season climax in the air. The way he insists that risking the lives of Jamie and Zoe was necessary for the greater good – but stands guilty and disconsolate when forced to admit that Gemma Corwyn is dead – is beautifully done. And even better is his confrontation with the Cybermen (the only one in the entire story!): his little moues of unhappiness when the villains keep bringing the subject back to his impending death are very funny, but also sell the jeopardy so well. As written, the scene is little more than exposition, but Troughton makes the whole thing seem as if this face-to-face with the Cybermen is actually *about* something pivotal. As it is, the story fizzles out as soon as the enemy stop skulking in the shadows and become plain for all to see – the skulking was really the whole point. But the skill of Troughton manages to elevate the episode into a discussion about the ends justifying the means, and give us a scene of extraordinary tension; we barely notice the plotline long ago ran out of steam.

And we're out of Season Five, and out of the cycle of telesnaps! Bar a few episodes here and there, Season Six exists entirely in the archives. It's a relief. I think my eyes were starting to go funny. Idly watching the last minute of the story, I note with interest that the Doctor prepares to show Zoe a mental video of The Evil of the Daleks. He seems to start with the beginning of episode two – and it speaks volumes about my obsession with watching these things, that this automatically makes sense to me. Of course, I think to myself, he's not going to give her episode one – she's not going to want to sit through a reconstruction.

T: He also gives away the ending to the next episode we're about to see, so he's clearly applying to be editor of the Radio Times...

The Cybermen are pretty easily defeated, especially as Flannigan somehow knows to spray them with space-plastic – are we ever told why this is lethal to them? – but at least he's rather winningly so miffed at the headache they've given him, he's decided to stomp about and give them a good seeing to. We *are* given an explanation for what he does to eject the ballet Cybermen into space, but it's a bit muffled under his helmet. I'm not sure it matters, however, because in essence the Cybermen are thwarted by that canny manoeuvre of pressing a button. Three times in fact! (The Doctor does it to electrocute his opponents, Leo does it to blow up the Silver Carrier and Flannigan does it in the airlock. What drama.)

Still, this has its moments. I've knocked some of Michael Turner's performance, but he's quite sweet in this, deciding – with the no-nonsense resolution of a child – that he's going to have a go at the Cybermen for Gemma's death. It's so pathetic that it's actually rather endearing, and Jarvis' death scene is very well (pardon my choice of words here) executed – the Cybermen pick him up and hold him aloft, but we only see this from afar on a scanner, so we're spared the embarrassment of a dummy or Kirby wires. And the Cybermen themselves are massive – they tower over Derrick Gilbert, James Mellor and Frazer Hines, really fulfilling their remit of being silver *giants*.

And at least Leo and Tanya have got all sexed up thanks to the death and drama. Jarvis and Gemma can rest safe in the knowledge that their demises resulted in a bit of space nookie – it's not just Tanya's nose that's tingling.

The Dominators episode one

R: Philip Voss is really good in this. He's cocky and arrogant – he fairly preens with self-confidence every time he checks the computer for radiation. And he's naturally charismatic. And, frankly, Nicolette Pendrell is very easy on the eye. The script isn't very sharp, but I could happily watch the continuing antics of their characters, the thrill-seekers Wahed and Tolata, for five episodes. I wonder what the Doctor will make of them?

... Oh no! They're dead! They've been zapped by some unseen robot called a Quark, and just before falling over, their faces have been blanked out and distorted. (Well, Tolata's has been, anyway. I don't think they could afford the special effect twice.) Another character called Etnin has just been zapped too, but he was neither charismatic nor pretty, so I wasn't as interested. Of the four Dulcians we've yet met, the only one left alive is the tubby chap in a toga. It's not that Arthur Cox is *bad* as Cully, per se – but Voss got all the charm, and Pendrell all the looks. Cully needs to be a bit of a wily rogue, an Arthur Daley sort. Instead, Cox just looks a bit *awkward*, running up and down a quarry with his toga flapping.

And we meet some other Dulcians. They wear togas too, except for the one who wears dungarees. Their performances are, at best, variable – but it seems rather cruel to name a character Kando when Felicity Gibson who's playing her so obviously kan't. And we meet some Dominators. They snarl a lot in contempt, usually at each other. Kenneth Ives, as the subordinate Toba, clearly likes blowing things up and killing people, and I like the little childish sadism he keeps on exhibiting – but it must be said, by the third time in one episode that his boss Rago (played by Ronald Allen) tells him off for doing the only mildly threatening thing yet in the story, it all gets very wearing.

And, of course, there are the Doctor, Jamie and Zoe. Troughton tries very hard in this, delighting in the idea they've landed in the perfect spot for a relaxing holiday. He shows delight in the atomic test dummies, and fascination in the spacecraft – but it all feels just a bit forced, because for once nobody else in the cast is even attempting to act with the same energy. When the Doctor finds out the TARDIS is threatened, it's all Zoe can do not to stifle a yawn – she decides to hang about with a bunch of strangers she's just met rather than see if they're in any jeopardy. And Jamie looks a trifle bored, and occasionally suggests they take off and go somewhere else.

It's a curious misstep for a season opener, this. Broadcast in August, when most of the audience are likely to be out enjoying the sunshine, this feels as lazy and as punch drunk as a warm summer's day. Doctor Who is back on our screens, straight after a repeat of an epic encounter with the Daleks, and the first thing

our heroes admit is that they feel tired and fancy a rest.

T: Hang on, why aren't we doing this properly, and watching The Evil of the Daleks again? They even went and sutured the repeat into the show's continuity, so surely, we should be including it in our marathon? We're going to get letters, I know it...

One of the more curious aspects of this project is that we're ruthlessly determined to get through it in one year, and so on a day-to-day basis, our takes on various episodes can't help but be influenced by what mood we're in. I'm feeling very good right now, as I have the day off, and I'm not working again 'till Tuesday. That might explain why, even though I've previously felt less than kind towards the episodes I'm watching today, I didn't massively object to Wheel episode six, and even The Dominators episode one seemed okay.

Mervyn Haisman and Henry Lincoln delivered two pretty damned good scripts prior to this, and for all that one could criticise the final result on this occasion, there are some interesting, well-conceived ideas going on here. The radiation on the island gives everyone a reason to be involved with it: the maverick Cully wants to get paid for shepherding the youths into the danger zone, teacher Balan and his students are monitoring the radiation levels, and the Dominators land on the island because there's radiation for their ship to suck up. Dynamically, there's a clever juxtaposition between Balan getting his student Kando to display her knowledge of the history of the island, and a later scene where the two Dominators postulate on the ramifications of a primitive weapon they find in a museum. Both teachers grill their pupils about war, but for diametrically opposed reasons. (Oh, and I must ask: why is there a *working* weapon in the museum? Health and Safety would go ballistic!)

Visually, this is better than you might expect. Tolata's death is pretty gruesome; it's quite the showpiece moment for a season opener, as is the whacking great explosion that destroys Cully's sea-paperweight. And director Morris Barry has an eye for framing his pictures on film, so we get another forced-perspective shot involving the bottom of someone's legs in the foreground and high up (like the Toberman shot at the beginning of The Tomb of the Cybermen), and a great moment at the end of the episode with the two little Quarks on top of a hill, joined by their towering master.

And I feel a bit sorry for some of the actors involved in this (but not for the reasons you might expect). Phillip Voss was previously the Mongol Acomat (hardly the best part in Marco Polo), and in this story, he's the first person to get bumped off! For pity's sake, this is a man who played Shylock for the Royal Shakespeare Company – he's one of our finest classical actors, use him more than this! Malcolm Terris (playing another thrill-seeker, and slain early on in the story) is no slouch either, another good actor who's not been well served by our favourite series. And while Arthur Cox always gets stick for his rendition of Cully, he actually plays the part with brio and a rebellious zeal. All right, he *looks* like a bank manager, but that's hardly his fault. Ronald Allen, at least, is remarkably right – he has a cadaverous, sunken-eyed face that seems chiselled from stone; he's impassive and cruel, with a hushed, gruesomely deadened delivery.

Why, though, do all the Dulcian men wear dresses or skirts? Some of them, at least, are students looking for experimental fun. And it happens that people dressed in such a fashion have turned up at the same location as some self-confessed Dominators; is this one of *those* sorts of parties? I hope the Doctor's brought his car keys...

April 17th

The Dominators episode two

R: As a comedy, this is absolutely marvellous. Much of the episode is taken up by the Dominators subjecting the Doctor and Jamie to intelligence tests – and Troughton and Hines are never funnier than here, trying to convince their captors that they're safely stupid. I so enjoy the look of delight that Troughton gives as he's told the answer to the simplest of puzzles ("Jump!"), his attempts to pronounce "electricity", and the sulky pout he gives when talking of the clever people who boss him about. And Hines is in his element

too, making the most of the comic rapport between the two of them that is by now second nature, playing a sort of bewildered fear that is very winning.

The problem is, though, that as a *drama* the laughs never go anywhere. After evaluating our heroes and dismissing them as idiots, the Dominators let them go with a warning to leave them alone. And that's it – the story really hasn't advanced any further, and before too long, the Doctor and Jamie are parading around gravel pits once more. Poor Wendy Padbury is stuck in a storyline which isn't half as interesting as theirs, trying to impress a bunch of bureaucrats with her alien origins. There's a comedy to all of this as well, of course – the council on Dulkis are *supposed* to be tedious old duffers, and on paper their dry academic response to what's going on is not without wit. But there's a limit to how long you can make jokes about people being boring without... well, being boring. The best gag comes from when Balan and his other student – Teel – draw a graph to show the radiation levels on the island of death, and take the inexplicable loss of that radiation as a natural phenomenon. ("It has happened, therefore it is a fact. We now know that the effect of an atomic explosion lasts for a hundred and seventy-two years.") If you're going to satirise pacifists as a bunch of gullible fools who'll take everything on face value without suspicion or intelligent inquiry, that's one thing. But it needs to be done consistently – why the story at the same time makes such heavy weather about the Dulcians not believing that the Doctor and company are aliens when they accept everything else so complacently is beyond me. So what we're left with on the one hand is a society who'll react without fear or great interest to the crises around them (which is a little dull), and on the other a society, conversely, who'll stubbornly deny the evidence in front of their eyes (which is, if anything, even duller).

As I say, Patrick Troughton is brilliant – and the sheer variety of faces he pulls for comic effect in this episode makes this an entertaining enough romp. But I think even Troughton will be hard pushed coming up with enough tics and mannerisms to keep this afloat for three more weeks.

T: I'm sure you can predict how I'm going to react to the rather patronising view of pacifism on display; it's as if the writers haven't quite worked out that an aversion to violence isn't the same thing as witless gullibility. It's also odd that they're knocking pacifism, and yet the movement that the writers are railing against predominantly, in 1968, stemmed from the young and rebellious cocking a snook at the pompous, patrician establishment. They can't quite inverse that for satirical effect without it seeming illogical, so it's still the young people – Cully (who doesn't seem to qualify as overly "young", but let's move on), Kando and Teel – using their intuition and energy to break the intransigence of the stuffy old guard (Balan and Senex), which doesn't really work to reinforce the script's reactionary stance.

Still, this isn't as awful as I feared. I like the nifty molecular bonding wall that flips back and becomes an examination slab, and I think the gossipy council members are rather funny. Arthur Cox has a great moment where he looks genuinely hurt that he's trapped in his father's shadow, and doesn't get treated as an individual. Troughton is excellent too – for all his keen intelligence, he assumes the role of clumsy schoolboy here with aplomb, and it's very plausible that the Dominators would see him as a nincompoop. I rarely laugh out loud while watching these stories, but I did when the Doctor asked Jamie if he could manage to pull off acting like an idiot. The friendship and rapport these two have is comedy gold.

Some of my perspective, to be fair, might be influenced by Ian Marter's novelisation of this story, which at times smoothes over what doesn't quite succeed on screen. Quarks in Marter's hands are giggling, chattering monstrosities – their childish jabbering is at odds with their murderous nature, which makes them unsettling and cruel. On screen, by contrast, their Orville voices and wibbly modulations make them seem inappropriately cute. The literary Dominators are closer to their on-screen counterparts – if I remember correctly, they have acrid breath, cracked lips and creaking skin, but these descriptions seem inspired entirely by Ronald Allen's performance. He's terse, direct and not unlike the walking undead. It's a looming, underplayed performance of considerable skill which helps

to disguise (sorry to say) the fact that many of Rago's decisions are stupid. It's rather ironic that although Toba is presented as a hot-headed, blithering idiot from his very first scene, his suggestion to scan the Doctor – and his desire to destroy the TARDIS and its crew – are the correct calls.

The Dominators episode three

R: To be fair, there's at least the attempt at something different with The Dominators. After a season of Earthbound stories focussed for the most part on scientific bases under siege, we're on an alien planet once more. It's the first time since The Tomb of the Cybermen that the production team have had a pop at that – and even if the planet looks exactly the same as the one we saw last time (presumably because Morris Barry has chosen the same quarry to represent Dulkis that he used for Telos), it does mean that we have an adventure which isn't just relying upon claustrophobic tension. But, that said, it still feels awkwardly familiar. It's that theme of do-nothingism again, as the Doctor once more tries to persuade people to take *action* rather than just wait for a crisis to resolve itself. We've seen it in The Abominable Snowmen, in The Ice Warriors – here it is again. This time though we're not merely dealing with passive resistance, but with passive aggression too: because, if anything, the Dominators are just as lethargic as the Dulcians. Every time Toba gets carried away and runs off with the idea of doing something nasty, he's restrained by his cautious commander. With the watchword of the baddy being one of patient investigation, and the goodies unprepared for more than patient debate, there's barely a plotline at all. When Senex laughs off the Doctor's pleas that the Dominators are callous and must be resisted, you can easily see where he's coming from. I see more dangerous people than Rago on London buses.

So to get the most out of The Dominators, you need to look for a series of moments, the chances taken by the cast to put a bit of life into the proceedings. The way that the Doctor can unravel a shuttle's navigation in mid-flight, so that when he lands on the planet the camera reveals him and Jamie charmingly buried within cables and wires. The little comic business worked out between Troughton and Hines over who gets to look through a telescope. And the beautifully funny scene where Zoe and Cully plan revolt from their slave labour, not lifting a finger to help as their other Dulcian captives stagger beneath boulders of stone. (Mind you, that last one may not have been designed to be funny. I take my chuckles where I can.)

T: It's all gone a bit pear-shaped, hasn't it? The scenes in the Dulcian council chamber are deathly tedious; I was mildly interested in the funny perspex thing on the table that Walter Fitzgerald (as Senex) decided to play with at one point, but it came to nothing. And it's difficult to get excited by a piece of a drama wherein a civilisation is based upon an unwillingness to do anything. The last unwilling warriors in the series were the Sensorites – perhaps the Doctor should poison the Dulcians' water supply, just to get them to do something interesting. And it becomes massively comical when Chairman Tensa proves his acclaimed intellect by telling the council they can either fight, submit, or flee – if your government needs to draft in Brian Cant to point out something that bleedin' obvious, it's time for an election. It is quite fun, at least, that well-known (at the time) Play School presenter Cant has been cast as this "revolutionary" thinker. Why, it'd be a bit like casting a CBBC presenter as a tooled-up freedom fighter in the new series...

The main appeal of this continues to be the Troughton/Hines combo (though their antics in the rocket seemed a little overzealous, as if even they realise how desperate the rest of this is), but I also appreciated Rago's order to work the slaves to the point of exhaustion, then observe when they collapse – it's marvellously callous, and Allen's stony faced, quietly grotesque performance has a dignity that dwarfs everything around him.

Oh, and I like the bit when the Quark's head wobbles about after Jamie blows it to bits.

April 18th

The Dominators episode four

R: I would also like to praise Ronald Allen. Poor old Rago isn't being given an awful lot of respect as Big Boss Dominator. Toba constantly defies his orders, and the Quarks don't seem to know which of the two they should be taking their instructions from. Allen isn't helped by a script that undermines him at every turn, making him seem a rather tepid villain – there's terrific potential in the scene where he dresses down Toba and threatens him with execution, but within minutes, he's off in a shuttle and leaving his subordinate to do what he wants all over again. But the performance itself is great – Allen downplays Rago to great effect, making every single one of his pronouncements much more threatening than the content of the lines could hope for. He shows cold amusement when he realises that he has reason to punish Toba, as if at last he's being given an opportunity to unleash the same sadistic cruelty that his underling so wantonly indulges in. It's not Allen's fault that the story itself then denies him the chance to wreak it. And he's terrific in the scene where he meets the Dulcian council, and cuts through all the bureaucratic blather by having Brian Cant shot dead. Allen keeps showing us the *potential* for a chilling and calculating villain – if only he'd been cast in a better story. As a Benik – as a Salamander, even – he would have been excellent.

And a word of praise for the Quarks too. The Troughton monsters have all powered their way round their stories by being big and thuggish. What makes the Quarks in theory much more interesting is that they're *cute* – but deadly. When you see one of them knocked down by a boulder, lying on its back with its feet wiggling, emitting high-pitched sounds of distress, your first impulse is to go and hug the thing. And I love the little Quark-shaped indicators on board the spaceship which flash on and off to show when one of them is being destroyed – it's rather sweet, and also suggests that these funny little robots get destroyed rather often, really. Haisman and Lincoln have tried before with the Yeti to create a deadly robot that played upon your protective impulse

– and it's easy to see why, in a story that took greater advantage of the dissonance that suggests, that they could have been eerie and memorable. (Certainly, the writers thought they were onto a good thing and wanted the merchandising rights, and TV Comic used the Quarks ad nauseam.) But, again, the plot doesn't do anything with them.

Ronald Allen. Quarks. An alien world. The elements for something fresh are in place. They only needed a *story* to use them to best advantage.

T: Arggg... I already used up loads of space praising Ronald Allen's blood-curdling performance in previous episodes, and now you've done it here, during an episode that has few (if any) redeeming features, leaving me high and dry. I played my Allen joker too soon – curses! Still, I should mention that it must have been easy for Allen to learn his lines; Rago and Toba have practically the same dialogue every week, mainly amounting to "Destroy!", "Conserve energy...", "But—", "Obey!", "Command [begrudgingly] accepted..." et cetera, et cetera, ad infinitum. It tends to undermine your villains if their main characteristic is squabbling – it's like being invaded by George and Mildred, or the sixth Doctor and Peri.

The best bit of the episode? When Rago storms in and begins making demands of the Dulcian council, and one of its members says, "If you'd care to make an appointment..." Allen's morbid amusement at their assumption that he's asking for their assistance rather than enslaving them, and his three-fingered point to Brian Cant's corpse, are winningly alien. Frazer Hines is on form too – he's rather gamely engaging in comic business at every opportunity, and the bits with a Quark shooting at him inject some much-needed excitement into this episode. Cully's big comedy boulder is great, smashing as it does a Quark to bits with unlikely accuracy.

But I fear that afraid the bad – actually, not even the bad, the *dull* – outweighs the good in this episode. While it's perhaps understandable that Rago doesn't think the Doctor is a threat, is that any excuse for giving him the run of the spaceship, with all its vital controls and equipment? I think Paris Hilton is a bit of a halfwit, but that doesn't mean I'd give her the

keys to my house when I go on holiday, let alone allow her access to my cooker. Oh and look, Toba is threatening to destroy everyone with a Quark at the end of the episode, again. What are the odds that Rago will wander in, just in the nick of time, and chastise him for wasting energy?

The Dominators episode five

R: For fun, I decided to count the number of times the word "bore" was used. I thought I'd be able to make a very witty play on words, there. I reached five in the first scene, and then somehow the joke no longer seemed quite so funny.

Once in a while you have to admit defeat, I suppose, in doing a book like this. I really can't find anything to say about this episode that is positive. No-one emerges from this one unscathed – not even Troughton, who's reduced to mugging in an attempt to get a bit of comic energy into the proceedings. He forgets he's holding a bomb that's about to go off, he forgets he's standing in the path of volcanic lava. Oh, my giddy aunt – it's the very first time I've seen my favourite Doctor reduced to something of a manic cliché, all gag and no heart.

But I do have one nostalgic memory about The Dominators. I first caught some of it at the big convention at Longleat House in 1983 to celebrate the twentieth anniversary. Famously, BBC Enterprises severely underestimated the attendance figures that Easter weekend, so that anyone lucky enough to get through the gates spent most of the time standing in queues. The tent that was screening old episodes was one of the smallest, and one of the most packed; there was one story selected from each of the five Doctors. I was able to get a seat somewhere in the middle and watched the Hartnell offering, The Dalek Invasion of Earth – I had to squint a bit, because it was playing on an inadequately small television set, and I had to strain to hear, because John Leeson kept on making announcements over the tannoy about face painting and car parks. I stuck out six episodes of Hartnell, however compromised, and was still in place for my slice of Troughton. Unaccountably, The Dominators was the second Doctor story chosen; it left, no doubt, lots of children with the impression that all black and white Doctor Who was about mining. And I remember craning my neck to make out what was going on the planet Dulkis – and realising, with some shock, that after a while I just didn't care. And I left to do something else. It was perhaps the first time I'd deliberately given up watching Doctor Who. It's from that moment that my obsession for Doctor Who was put into some perspective, that other things in life could slot into place. It's from that moment I stopped being a child, and became a *man*. Oh yes. Thank you, The Dominators.

T: Chris Jeffries *is* the Doctor! That much is pretty obvious even on the grotty picture that I'm watching, especially as there's an ill-advised (if slightly skewiff) close-up of him as Patrick Troughton's stand-in. To give Jeffries his due, he does a bit of comedy juggling with the Dominators' bomb, almost dropping it, in an attempt to convince us he's the real thing. It's not his fault that the director thinks we might neglect to look at his face. Once this is tidied up and made pristine for the DVD, I'm sure this will be even more obvious. Speaking of the DVD, once it's released, even a ropey piece of old tat like this will be fun to see – I'm currently watching the VHS print, which has numerous tiny little cuts (notably the various death scenes), so there will be a few snatched seconds of entirely-new-to-me Doctor Who to enjoy.

And there are bits – just bits, you understand – of entertainment in this last episode as well. Toba for once actually obeys Rago (he becomes a submissive Dominator!), and the tables are sweetly turned as the Quark alarms go off all around Rago in his spaceship, and he doesn't know where to look. To Morris Barry's credit, he's managed to suggest that there are far more Quarks than the three at his disposal. And while we know that Haisman and Lincoln fell out with the producers over exploitation rights on the Quarks – which, a bit optimistically, they hoped would become as big as the Daleks (does this mean the Dominators would have accompanied them on every subsequent appearance, which would have become tedious fast?) – they *did* get it right in one key area: "Quarks can't climb," says Jamie, thus allowing every lazy journalist, comedian and cartoonist

in the land plenty of ammunition if ever they became popular.

You can probably tell that I'm scraping for compliments here. The sad truth is that by this point, Hines and Troughton have been mucking about so much, they've occasionally veered too close to actorly hi-jinks in their efforts to keep the audience invested in what's happening on screen. You can't really blame them, though, as the script isn't sure at times of what it's trying to say. Cully becomes sad that Balan is dead, but he's thanked for rescuing Teel and Kando. But Balan would still be alive if Cully and Jamie hadn't attacked the Quarks, and yet any culpability on their part isn't so much forgiven as it's forgotten. Also, how does it continue to be the case that if Toba is such an over-eager young hothead, with Rago as his long-suffering commander, that all of Rago's decisions turn out to be wrong? These Dominators have snatched defeat from the jaws of victory – had they just paraded about shooting people as Toba has advocated for about two hours now, they'd probably have won. What's the message here, then? "Sadism works"?

And – oh hell – we even get another bloody space-food scene. Note to all Doctor Who writers: in the future, food will be nutrition blocks that look unappealing to our contemporary eyes. You can take that as read. It's not interesting, exciting or even funny. Please do not waste our time with it. It's perfunctory at best, irritating at worst. This is an ex-narrative device. The end.

[Toby's addendum, written 29th of May: Well, guess which lucky so-and-so was asked to moderate the spruced-up, uncut DVD of this story? That's right, me! The reinstated cuts *do* make a difference. I'm audibly shocked at how gruesome Balan's death is – it's a protracted, repeated onslaught of death-ray that adds real oomph to the episodes in question. As for the Doctor's double, I noticed Chris Jeffries because I was actively looking for him – the others present felt that they got away with it.]

[Toby's addendum #2, written August 2011 and included in this volume's second printing: Since writing this, I've discovered that James Copeland had actually passed away, unreported, in 2002, and that Maurice Selwyn is also deceased. Madeleine Mills died in 2010, and Roy Skelton in 2011.]

April 19th

The Mind Robber episode one

R: Of course, on any terms, this is odd. When in 1992 the BBC decided to root around the archives and show a repeat season showcasing one story per Doctor, this is the one that followed The Time Meddler. It was certainly different from watching a comical romp about a Monk in Saxon England, but not perhaps as jolting to the average viewer as when they settled down to watch The Sea Devils only a week later. Both the black and white adventures have Doctor Who doing strange things with a TARDIS – whereas the Pertwee story doesn't even feature a TARDIS at all! The Mind Robber boasts lots of surreal imagery, white robots in a void and strange sound effects – but cut adrift from the other Troughton stories surrounding it, it looks maybe like a bit of weird sixties absurdism done on the cheap.

But in context, it's the strangest episode Doctor Who has yet broadcast – and the greatest wrench the series has *ever* made from its established house style. And, as a result, the barrage of surrealism doesn't merely look imaginative and clever – the way it might have done to the patient viewer back in the nineties – but genuinely discordant. Even frightening.

As is generally known, of course, this first episode was an emergency script written to plug a gap when The Dominators was cut back. It had to be made with speaking roles for only the regular cast (save a quick voiceover for the next story's guest villain), the TARDIS set, an empty studio and a few robot costumes dug out of the storeroom. It's tempting to think that script editor Derrick Sherwin (who also wrote this episode, uncredited) looked to The Wheel in Space for inspiration, which had also opened with a Doctor and companion-heavy episode – hence the fluid links playing up again, mercury fumes all over the place, and the TARDIS showing tempting things upon the scanner. Indeed, to begin with, the episode seems deliberately to toy with us by offering only the familiar. It emphasises a direct link to the previous story by showing a reprise, and then plays around with the Doctor fretting about the TARDIS controls in just the same manner as he's done so often before.

The difference, though, becomes quickly obvious. Doctor Who has always revelled in the thrill of adventure. It's entirely what it's about. And the Doctor *loves* adventure – just think of the delight he takes in The Web of Fear when Victoria asks if what's outside the TARDIS will be safe ("Oh, I shouldn't think so for a moment!"), or his reaction to her fears in Fury from the Deep ("The spice of life!"). And Troughton is the most anarchic of all the Doctors, the one most likely to stride cheerfully into trouble without checking to see whether there's radiation on Dulkis or not. So when he insists that the TARDIS must not be left, it's very effective. And all the more because it isn't just Troughton acting frightened – we're used to that now as comic shtick. Instead he downplays his warnings again, and becomes as serious as we've ever seen him. All we can see through the doors is white blankness – and his refusal to look at it, his refusal even to *contemplate* it, makes it genuinely the most threatening location the TARDIS has ever taken us to. When Zoe first succumbs and steps outside, she just shimmers and vanishes into the void – and it looks as if she's just been erased.

And what makes that even more insidious is how the characters are tempted out. For Jamie and Zoe, it's the idea that they've returned home that is so appealing. Not so for the Doctor – the ghostly voice plays instead upon his heroism. What's shocking is that he fights so hard to resist it. He won't go to his friends – instead he sits down, shuts his eyes tightly, and refuses to listen to their cries for help. His weakness, inevitably, is his own predictable compassion. And one of the most chilling moments in the episode is the depiction (in his head? as he imagines it?) of a widely grinning Jamie and Zoe calling for him and beckoning him outside into danger.

It's extraordinary. I used to think that it was rather a shame that the limitations of the time meant that the viewer could easily see that this whiteness isn't a void at all, but has edges and corners in the distance. But now I find that strangely *odder* – that the "nothing" isn't as clean and as perfect as that. It's David Maloney's first time directing Who, and straight away, before he's had a chance to work out how the series should look, he does everything he can to dislocate it. He has Jamie and Zoe run directly to camera – as if they're actually looking out on us, the viewer, in horror. He has the camera pan upwards over their heads as they talk, only to reveal them again above, as if somehow in this mysterious place they're on two different planes at once. He has them dressed in white suddenly – all the better to blur them in and out of negative when he sees fit. (Negative, of course, by this stage the traditional death ray of both the Daleks and the Cybermen – it's as if he's killing them, and impassively, emotionlessly, set as statues, they don't even care.)

And then the story cheats. It cruelly suggests that the crisis is over. It allows us to believe the Doctor has rescued his friends. But the background sound effect we've adjusted to becomes a point of attack. The very sanctuary of the TARDIS is invaded. And the Ship *breaks apart*. The image of the central console spinning, with Jamie and Zoe riding it for dear life, is justly famous – but eerier still, I think, is that Zoe sees the Doctor, and screams: and he's in a different close-up, his head and shoulders filling the screen, turning around on the spot, unreactive. It's as if he's in another scene altogether, and there's no connection between the shots. We cut back to the console, getting smaller and smaller, then getting lost within the murk.

For the first time in Doctor Who, we really can have no idea what can happen next.

T: Technically, this episode is just padding – and yet, it's one of the most interesting, unnerving and well-realised episodes that we've ever seen, and ever will. It mainly consists of three actors and a blank set, but the set-up enables Troughton and Hines – who have been skirting perilously close to excess over the past few weeks – to get down and dirty with some proper acting again. And because of the limited nature of what we can see, Troughton really has to sell this hard – and he really does, throwing in a bag of suspense for free.

David Maloney is also very clever here – this is odd, yes, but it doesn't descend into confus-

ing nonsense; we're aware of the narrative rules within the surrealism. But while you're right about the slowly roving camera that displaces us, I would disagree with you on one point. My first copy of this was middling enough for the nothingness to be just that – a floorless, empty space. Now that the picture has been all spruced up on DVD, meaning you can see the joins and the studio wall (the visuals are now flawless, yes; floorless, no), I think it loses something. Sometimes, the murkiness of the past helps to give atmosphere to archival gems. I could get all metatextual and say that it's deliberately blurring the walls between reality and fiction because the nothingness now *looks* like a TV studio, and that the unreality of the production subconsciously reflects our complicity with the inherent fiction within the fiction of The Land of Fiction... but, well, I'm not you. That said, the words "Produced by Peter Bryant" appearing on the scanner at the start of the final TARDIS scene did tempt me to walk that route!

If there's a real shame here, though, it's that I've seen clip shows where that iconic bit of Zoe's bum, Zoe and the spinning TARDIS console has been used to illustrate the typical cliché of the "screaming companion". It's irritating, because they couldn't have chosen a more inappropriate example. Zoe's *first* scream in this episode is imposed over that shot of the all-white, Cheshire Cat-grinning Zoe and Jamie, who beckon and tempt the Doctor. Neither this, nor Zoe's scream at the cliffhanger, are "I'm-a-terrified-girly-who's-seen-a-spider" screams – they're peculiar cries of anguish that puncture the minimalist soundscape, keeping us on edge, and telling us that the normal rules of storytelling don't apply. Besides, if the TARDIS breaking up, followed by Zoe and Jamie clinging to the console while they and the adrift Doctor tumble into dark nothingness isn't cause for screaming, what is? Wouldn't *you* let out a bellow of terror? I would.

A final thought: it feels like familiar territory when the TARDIS scanner shows incorrect images to get the crew to react in a particular way. In that regard, this is a Land of Fiction as Written by David Whitaker Story. That makes me wonder, though – what happened to the food machine when the Ship exploded?

The Mind Robber episode two

R: And, I suppose, the maddest thing episode two could do would be to be so utterly unlike episode one. Whereas the tone for last week was fractured and chilling, here it's warm and whimsical. The weirdness this week is all about the mad characters the Doctor encounters, not in a madness that preys upon the Doctor – in that way this is *much* more traditional, showing our heroes wandering around a new planet and bumping into stuff. As fans we know the reason for this shift in tone, of course – we're now into the story as written by Peter Ling, not the filler episode written by Sherwin. It's an ugly fit – but, for once, that feels rather the point. When Jamie makes the one allusion to the events of last week, talking about how the TARDIS broke up, the Doctor reacts with panic as if it's something new to him – it feels like a dream, even compared to the dreamlike things that are happening here. It's so hard to imagine how this episode might have worked had The Dominators gone out in six episodes as planned, and the TARDIS had just plonked our regulars down into a world of giant jam jars and clockwork robots. It might have all looked rather twee. It certainly would have looked very disjointed. As it is, we've got used to the idea that *anything* can happen.

So maybe in a way, episode two is a little compromised by the brilliance of episode one. If you're told as an audience to expect the unexpected, then the twists can hardly have the same impact. (As anybody watching Roald Dahl introduce his Tales of the Unexpected on ITV in the eighties might have agreed, and as much as anyone going to see the latest movie from "strange twist-meister" M Night Shyamalan might think now.) But that's not a bad thing. Because the difference between Sherwin's weirdness and Ling's weirdness is that Ling wants us to see his story as a game to puzzle out. To go straight from the planet Dulkis to The Land of Fiction, we might have spent so much time reeling at the contrast that we wouldn't have taken part in Ling's little parlour games at all. There's a fierce logic to all of this, even if it's in a framework Doctor Who has never used before. That Jamie loses his face and becomes played by another actor is *bonkers* – but it's only as a result of the Doctor fudg-

ing the sort of puzzle the average child would have been used to from the filler pages of the Doctor Who Annual. The same thing's true for the picture-writing game, or the forest of words – what's striking about all this is that it's actually very familiar. That's the intention, of course. We don't yet know that Bernard Horsfall is Gulliver (and he's still credited as "The Stranger"), but sharp sixties kids might yet spot the references. The clockwork soldiers, once we see them in their full glory, should be utterly recognisable. (David Maloney realises this, of course, and reveals them very cleverly. We see first only their marching feet, looking a bit ungainly admittedly, but nothing compared to what we saw of the Quarks a couple of weeks ago. And then the first view we get of those painted toy faces is a throwaway shot on one of the Master's screens – so that as an audience we should be wondering, "Did I just see what I thought I saw"? Finally, as they surround the Doctor and his chums, we see the key in the back, and we understand at last.

So, brilliantly, if episode one just dropped us into chaos, episode two is more subtly subversive by parading on the screen things that seem endearingly commonplace but in entirely the wrong setting. It's not a million miles from giving Yeti guns and sticking them in the London Underground. And it might just be because Frazer Hines caught chicken pox, but to have a situation where Jamie is replaced by another actor altogether is part of that – even our trusted friends don't look right any more. Hamish Wilson is rather brilliant for two very good reasons – firstly, that he looks and sounds nothing like Hines, and secondly, that his performance nonetheless is eerily similar. He's got Hines' mannerisms down to a tee, the diffident head toss back at the Doctor. What's lovely is that Wilson plays Jamie as if we ought to like him and trust him just as always – he may look different, but he's our same Highlander friend, isn't he? – and we can't. He's sinister, simply because he assumes he isn't. It's very clever.

I love the children too, who are unsmiling and threatening. And the wistful way that Troughton wishes he believed in wishing wells: it's a note of gentle sadness in a story about imagination run insane, and his performance does so much to anchor the episode and give us something to relate to.

T: Once Zoe has fallen down the hole, and Jamie has been shot in the face by a Redcoat, it's Troughton who leads us through this crazy world – and he does so with the perfect mix of curiosity, fear and comic frustration. It's delightful and terribly funny how he's both guilty and haughty about Jamie's face-off, and is very slow to admit his own culpability in it. After the ordeal he experienced in the previous episode, the Doctor is back to his old self.

Jamie, on the other hand, is anything but. Wilson's main strength is the instant rapport he seems to have picked up with both Troughton and Padbury – he's laudably bold in being very familiar with them, and it helps sell the fact that this *is* our Jamie despite the deeper voice and different accent. (Perhaps there was, just out of shot, a still of the vocal chords the Doctor had to choose from.) What little we *do* see of Frazer Hines is odd, actually – whatever Jamie's confusion about a voice recording in The Wheel in Space, he's been a pretty modern sort of fellow for most of his tenure, and has seemed relatively unfazed by most technology and more literate than your average Jacobite. So it's shocking here, when the first thing he does upon seeing a Redcoat is to pull a knife and try to butcher him. It's a stark reminder that our loveable rogue of a companion is inured to the blood and guts of battle. And it's even *odder* that he throws a fair few words the Redcoat's way rather than just sneaking up on him – as Jamie should know, this isn't the most advisable way to engage in combat with someone with a big gun.

Outside of the regulars, we have a story that's trying to establish itself. The unrealistic nature of the sets is for once a bonus, especially as they depict such a wonderful idea as the Forest of Words. I applaud the design of the Toy Soldiers too – they have the visual flair and comforting solidity of a Dinky toy, augmented with a menacing expression and an inexorable and frighteningly stiff gait. And the human-looking characters that we meet in this strange land are slightly offbeat to the point that it's hard to read them. You can't help but raise an eyebrow when the children say that the Doctor might be "suitable" (for what we

don't know, but it's presumably a job for which the chief qualification is to solve a simple world puzzle after much prompting from a bunch of precocious kids). Emrys Jones (as the shadowy Master of the Land) seems to be channel the spirit of Wolfe Morris as he alternates between soft, benign sounding utterances and evil, whispered commands. And hooray for Bernard Horsfall, who besides being instantly trustworthy gives the impression at times that he's getting instructions or information inside his head. He's likeable enough, but we can't be sure yet whether he's an actual person, an android, or something altogether different.

Incidentally, you're wrong in that Horsfall is credited as "*A* Stranger" rather than "*The* Stranger". I like the "A" – it seems an altogether more literary denomination, and shows that a bit of thought has gone into the credits.

April 20th

The Mind Robber episode three

R: After the barrage of new ideas thrown at us over the last two weeks, it's a bit of a shock to find that in this episode there's really... only the one. And it's a clever idea, and potentially turns the entire series on its head. When Jamie finds a machine spewing out tickertape that is chronicling the Doctor's adventures, the suggestion is made that as our heroes walk around this Land of Fiction, they're just fictional themselves. In a way, why not? From the vantage point of 2009, when Doctor Who has now become a childhood hero that has inspired generations, that shares not only the time slot of Robin Hood and Merlin but much of its iconic appeal, this all makes perfect sense. I'm reminded of that moment (that so incensed fans without a sense of humour) in Steven Moffat's 1999 Comic Relief story, The Curse of Fatal Death. In that, when presented with the idea that the Doctor is finally dead, the companion Emma pleads for him to survive: "You're like Father Christmas! The Wizard of Oz! Scooby Doo!" And in The Mind Robber too, we've got the concept suddenly of the Doctor adventuring through time and space being of the same make-up as Sir Lancelot and

D'Artagnan. He's not just a character of children's fiction any more, he's one of children's fiction's giants. The unease that Troughton feels as he edges deeper into the labyrinth – why exactly does the Master want him so badly? – is surely that deep down, there's that sensation that the Doctor isn't actually real.

If you had to end the series – and let's face it, at this stage it's on the cards – how might it have played out? That instead of revealing that the Doctor is on the run from a race called the Time Lords (about whom we've never heard mention of before), there's the suggestion that he's a beloved and unforgettable character of family television. To quote the back cover of many an early Target novelisation, he's the children's own hero that adults adore. The series makes the decision in what may be its final gasp to push outwards into science fiction, and answer the mysteries of Doctor *Who* in a pretty prosaic way. (To be fair, it did ensure the programme's survival!) But at this stage, when everything's still up for grabs, before the Master becomes a psychopath with a beard from the Doctor's own race and is instead a strange magical storyteller directing the Doctor's adventures, there's something very persuasive about the weird turn into surrealism that's being presented here. It is, after all, the same sort of solution given to TV series as diverse as The Prisoner or Life on Mars – that all we've taken for granted is but a fictional construct. It's the story of a man who can change his face and personality travelling through time and space in a police box fighting monsters – it's no less fantastical than *any other character the Doctor is now meeting,* and there's so much sense to the idea that this is a fantasy too. The failure of The Mind Robber is that this *isn't* the end – that it's just another serial in an ongoing series – but I'd suggest that to contemporary viewers that sequence where Jamie finds out that the Doctor's adventures are coming from a writing machine is revolutionary. "It doesn't exist!" the Doctor will say to the unicorn, and then to the minotaur, and now to Medusa. What would happen to the Doctor, I wonder, if Medusa said it to *him*?

T: Tap-tap-tap-tap-tap... "Rob sent Toby a very clever treatise on Doctor Who's contemporary position as a classic children's fictional icon. As

Toby tried to think of something witty and clever to write back, Jeremy Kyle's voice blared through the thin walls of his terraced house, as Toby's hard-of-hearing neighbour regularly whiled away the lonely hours with such drivel. No matter. Toby was watching The Mind Robber episode three, an entirely different kind of fictional construct." Tap-tap-tap...

Tap-tap-tap... "Toby wondered, with a sigh, quite why Christine Pirie – here playing Rapunzel – never did anything after this, as she was sweet and pretty and was bang on in pitching her performance like someone reading a children's book. Toby was also very impressed by the stop-motion snakes on Medusa, the continued inventiveness of David Maloney's direction, and the convincingly evocative fairytale nature of the location filming." Tap-tap-tap...

Tap-tap-tap... "Toby could not, however, escape the troubling feeling that once an original premise such as The Land of Fiction had been established, there didn't seem an awful lot to do with it. The regulars had previously dismissed a menace by saying it didn't exist – so, surely, that's how they were going to escape from this latest one? Would every adversary the heroes encountered be overcome by the simple act of them marshalling their courage and pluck? Nonetheless, Toby revelled in this story's originality, and mused on the [deep breath] concepts of fiction presenting fiction as fiction within a fact which the viewer knew was fictional." Tap-tap-tap...

Tap-tap-tap... "As Toby typed the words – which would go on to form a bestselling book which would be garlanded with awards and tremendous sales – he sank back in his chair as the entire Jeremy Kyle audience stood up as one, and, with a screeching caterwaul, hoisted the posturing weasel aloft and impaled him on his own microphone. He wept for mercy and apologised to his guests, the nation and the whole of British television before expiring in front of a record-breaking audience..."

Tap-tap-tap... "Toby then sent this portion of the text to his friend Robert Shearman, who had just received postal notice from Buckingham Palace of their intentions to knight him for services to literature."

[Send]

The Mind Robber episode four

R: Emrys Jones gives a lovely performance as the Master, at one point fawning over the Doctor in a gentle elderly voice as if he's a long admiring fan – then becoming harsh and alien when issuing orders. It's rather clever, and does, as you've somewhat suggested, feel like a deliberate parody of Padmasambhava from The Abominable Snowmen, with a schizophrenic being controlled by an unnamed Intelligence. The Doctor may be concerned that his fate is to become fiction, but it seems that the production team are already taking familiar elements from his adventures and using them against him. (And there's more of that to come next week!) The wonderful cleaned-up version on the DVD also reveals that there's a strange white piece of thick spittle hanging at the corner of Emrys Jones' mouth; at first I thought it was accidental, but it's *always* there, and I think it's a subtle indication that there's something rather repellent about what's happened to the poor writer whose imagination is being siphoned off, as if for all his good manners he's something like a zombie.

But Toby has pointed out many, many times that I read things into these episodes that aren't intended. I can't wait to see whether somebody in the make-up department has taken a tissue to Emrys Jones by next week's instalment, and wiped away the hanging gobbet of phlegm. If it's gone, I'll concede I'm a pretentious git, and buy Toby a doughnut.

Wendy Padbury gets her best moment of the series yet, when she so cheerfully bests the Karkus with a lot of judo. Zoe is clearly having the time of her life tackling a cartoon character she's enjoyed from her childhood, and Padbury at last has the opportunity to make Zoe a little more human and likeable. The whole scene is a joy – especially when the Doctor tries to get in on the action, but, failing to recognise the Karkus as fictional, is simply flung to one side. She also gets her *worst* moment of the series yet, walking through an alarmed door she's only minutes before been warned about, and getting everybody captured. But you see, I *might* argue that by doing so she's merely being part of the parody of Doctor Who, and that it's really rather a clever comment on Peter Ling's

part upon the cliché of the clumsy companion. That's the problem with The Mind Robber – you can't be sure whether the sloppiness may not just be part of the point. (It all rests upon that spittle coming out of Emrys Jones' mouth. If it's there, the whole thing is intentional. If it's not, I'll shrug and admit defeat.)

The Master has been captured because, in 25 years, he produced half a million words. What a lightweight! The way things are going, Toby and I will turn out about three times that number with this diary alone – and we've only got the end of the year to finish it!

T: I'm on Weight Watchers again, so could I have a rice cake instead of a doughnut? The diet is my own choice entirely, in a "go on Weight Watchers or I won't marry you" kind of way (weigh?). Regardless, your ability to read things into episodes that weren't intended has gone loopy even by your standards – that isn't a deliberate glob on Jones, it's stray spittle without subtext. It's quite distracting, and makes me want to invent time travel just so I can go back and give him a hanky.

What *is* a deliberate policy of non-realism, however, is the excellent set design of Evan Hercules (and isn't that a *fantastic* name?). It conjures up pages of fiction and children's toyboxes with a deliberate, clunky hyper-unrealism – I particularly love the overly creaky door, which draws attention to itself as the ultimate cliché in creepy literature. Conversely, I'm afraid I found the fight with the Karkus less convincing than you did – it's very clumsily staged, and entails Wendy Padbury, in-between throws, shoehorning in references to which "move" she's using.

It doesn't really matter, though, because The Mind Robber continues to have such a dazzling premise, I can forgive so many of its shortcomings. It tells the story at quite a lick ("My, what short episodes you have..."), and there's a verve about the production from cast and camera alike. And *what* an incredible episode ending, as two beloved characters – Jamie and Zoe – are backed into an overgrown book that shuts on them. It's an image that's magnificent, exciting, terrifying and utterly bonkers all at once – in short, it's everything Doctor Who is supposed to be.

I hope Sydney Newman and Verity Lambert

were watching this. They'll have approved – and that's a fact.

April 21st

The Mind Robber episode five

R: Okay. I owe you a rice cake.

But, do you know, it doesn't matter to me whether it's accidental or not – there's still something disturbing about episode four's Master foaming at the mouth. Just as all the things that people often criticise this final instalment for (the way it reverts to being just another Earth invasion story, and that it's only got about 16 minutes' worth of action) also seem to me to be saying something rather clever, even if it wasn't the production team's intention.

Let's take that plot first. Last week, I thought there was a parody of The Abominable Snowmen going on. And this week, it's everything else! We've got a Jamie and a Zoe who are fictionalised – but behave (and are treated by the Doctor) as if they're merely possessed. We've seen so much possession in Troughton's run of stories that it seems apt to have it pop up again, but this time it's eerier because it's so skewed; the look of childish mischief on Hines and Padbury's faces as they rub their hands with glee and bend double like little kids is so much more sinister in this fairytale form. (And as a result, the pathos of Troughton realising that his best friends have become nothing more than two-dimensional stereotypes – who parrot nothing but the same lines over and over – is all the more moving too.) The Master Brain's cunning plan, to turn all mankind into a uniform race without individuality, is exactly the modus operandi of *the* generic Troughton monster, the Cybermen – and, of course, the villains waiting in the wings of the very next story. And the way that the Doctor is put inside a machine that'll feed off his brain, and the way he turns that against it, is a replay of The Web of Fear. We're being shown Doctor Who, sixties style, in cartoon format. And the brilliance of it all is that it doesn't come across as either funny or a bit cynical, but genuinely disconcerting. The story ends with a riff from The Evil of the Daleks, as the robots destroy their own world – and it's so utterly chaotic that it feels like a strange nightmare take on what the viewers have come to expect from Doctor Who. Even the abruptness of all this, and that the story finishes nearly ten minutes early, seems like a comment upon the way these Doctor Who adventures play out. At the end of the day, when the Doctor meets the villain, it'll always be about some sort of attempt to enslave the Earth, and how the Doctor wins through in the nick of time. We know the procedure, The Mind Robber tells us. Here it is, in sped-up form, without all the pretence this is anything you've not seen before. If this is all a dream that the Doctor and his friends are having, then what else would they be dreaming about?

I adore the way that Emrys Jones so gently pleads with the machine-intelligence speaking through his own voice not to destroy the Doctor – who is his only way out of writing's drudgery. (I worked on Crossroads too, you know, so I understand where Peter Ling's little fable about the way soap opera drains your imagination is coming from. And I was only on it for a couple of weeks!) I love that image of the Doctor lured into the TARDIS, only for the front side to fall away as a prop, revealing him (impossibly) already imprisoned – I love the cruelty of the children watching his misadventure laughing at the funny little man in peril and pressing their noses against the glass. It's all about the way that you keep on trying to feed the audience, and that there's never an end to it – Doctor Who going on, story after story, for years and years. For the first and only time, after the credits have ended, and the director's name has come up, we get a caption saying, "Next Week: The Invasion." That it's just "the invasion" without any more description than that – so blunt, so unadorned – seems almost part of this story's joke.

T: The final battle between the Doctor and the Master of the Land helps to fulfill, just a little, Sydney Newman's educational remit by having all sorts of fictional characters scrapping. (And it's a good swordfight too – fight-arranger John Greenwood was pretty highly thought of in his field, so well done to Maloney for securing his services.) It's all very charming and delightful, and if there's a shame about this closing episode, it's only that Peter Ling felt compelled to abandon surreal whimsy and resort to the old Earth invasion cliché. This might have worked if it had been a clever comment on the nature of fiction within the Doctor Who format, but the implication seems to be that a world of ideas isn't enough – a more tangible threat is required. It's not *all* that bad, though, because the threat to bring humanity into the Land means that we get to hear Troughton talk about how mankind would become "a string of sausages".

What a beguiling and strange adventure this has been. It's a testament to the skill of everyone involved that this story isn't a heap of childish twaddle, but actually has weight and requisite levels of jeopardy. If the *idea* behind this story is ridiculous, nobody is behaving ridiculously. Troughton is magnificent as usual, and Emrys Jones is convincing as both the sweet, rather charming old writer and the direct, powerful voice of the Master Brain. And it's an adorable touch that he's been carrying around a copy of the Ensign in his pocket for all these years, just in case he needs a visual representation of his achievements. (Go on, Rob, tell me you have a copy of The Chimes of Midnight secreted about your person, to flourish on social occasions!)

And it's all capped off by such a peculiar, abrupt ending. Was it a dream? Who knows? Lesser works of fiction have used a dream to over-ride an entire swath of stories, so why not this one? Let's hope they stop short of having someone wake up tomorrow, only to find a very much alive William Hartnell in the shower...

The Invasion episode one

R: We're out of The Land of Fiction – but suddenly everything's animated!

Obviously, I know the fact that The Invasion was released on DVD with its two missing episodes in cartoon form wasn't a deliberate follow-on from The Mind Robber. But rather like the Sherwin-written intro to the last story helps the audience adjust from the ho-hum clichés of The Dominators to the fairytale chaos of The Land of Fiction, so the cartoon helps us find a gradual way into a gritty urban thriller. To viewers in 1968, they'll have

jumped straight into an episode that's more brutal than they'd have been acclimatised to – the casual murder of the lorry driver, even as animation, is rather shocking. Cosgrove Hall have done a great job with their reconstruction – the way they've *stylised* the Doctor, for example, all sharp angles and eyebrows, doesn't try to hide the fact that this is only an interpretation of what's been missing from the archives, not an attempt to copy it.

And I realise it's probably heretical to say so – but I think I prefer it this way. On its own terms episode one of The Invasion is rather plodding. Our regulars hitch-hike their way into London, and the Doctor decides to check out his old friend Professor Travers to see if he's up to fixing the TARDIS circuits. Zoe isn't too bothered by this rather run-of-the-mill quest of his, so puts on a feather boa for the first airheaded photographer she meets – and the Doctor and Jamie run into some very *slight* bother with bureaucracy. But the animation makes all of this seem *odd*. What looked routine on the page now seems skewed. The long sequences with the Doctor, Jamie and Zoe in the back of a lorry are now very tense, their big eyes looking out at us in confusion. The Doctor's tirade against an answering phone service no longer feels like a bit of padding; in cartoon form, it feels broader and funnier, as it's become a pixie-like image of anarchy getting frustrated beyond measure with the inconveniences of everyday life. And Tobias Vaughn (the electronics tycoon working with unseen allies towards the conquest of Earth) and his henchman Packer are more sinister – the smile that Packer gives in anticipation of violence much more deliberate when it's been a choice made by the animators, the twinkle in Vaughn's eye as he reveals his alien ally hiding in his cupboard much more triumphant than anything recorded in a sixties studio could have given us.

I used to think it was rather a shame that when Cosgrove Hall were commissioned to fill in the gaps for The Invasion, they were stuck at first with an episode so unspectacular and low-key. (Check out the trailer they originally came up with, with the Cybermen advancing through the rain – it's *gorgeous*.) But as it is, they put a spin on what might otherwise have been forgettable and laborious. And for those of us following the series in order, it's a charming segue from the madness of The Mind Robber to Doctor Who at its most pointedly realistic.

T: I can't say that I've ever given much thought to The Invasion episode one. There's a certain kind of fan who prioritises episode recoveries for the somewhat-complete stories (such as The Crusade, The Reign of Terror and The Moonbase – don't get me started on that last one!) to finish out the set, but I'd rather *something* moving existed in the archives from the likes of Marco Polo, The Myth Makers or The Massacre, which are barely represented at all. I know only too well what happens even in the missing stories – I'm such a nerk that I've read and re-read, listened and re-listened to whatever material is available – to the point that they no longer hold any narrative surprises. Instead, I enjoy Doctor Who much like others enjoy music – I savour the mood, the tempo and the *feeling* a particular story provides, and I'm able to do that even with an orphaned episode. So I've never fussed much about the two missing eps from The Invasion being found, because the extant six instalments – like them or not – get the job done nicely.

All of that said, I thought the animated version of episode one was surprisingly good. I don't think that the animation can claim sole credit, though – Douglas Camfield has a knack for making everything edgy, and Don Harper's portentous, clanging music conveys an oppressive atmosphere; the first 15 minutes or so of this episode have a real moodiness to them. It also helps that Camfield casts intense, steely actors – the cameo by Murray Evans as the slain UNIT operative brings with it requisite grit (I imagine him stubbly, with beads of sweat on his forehead).

I do think you can start this story with the existing episode two and not have missed out on much, but I can't deny that this hits the ground running with a missile pitching towards the TARDIS, and Troughton in emergency mode from the word "go". And the Doctor's frustration with the automated machine is music to my ears – I spent much of this morning on the phone to a certain train company, and kept getting redirected to the wrong department by a robot, to such an

extent that I just screamed "For God's sake, can't I just talk to somebody real?!" with such anger that the cats all ran away.

But I digress. This was a potentially dull episode, but I found it reassuringly dramatic and well handled, animated or not. If you disagree with me, press four now. [Cue Greensleeves.]

April 22nd

The Invasion episode two

R: It's a subtle moment, but the bit that most struck me on watching this again is the fate of that poor lorry driver. The Brigadier shows the Doctor and Jamie a photograph of the hapless man who was shot dead last week, the Doctor breezily assures the Brigadier the man's probably all right – and we never hear of him again, never learn his name, and no-one ever seems to care that he was murdered. He's the first UNIT soldier we ever meet, and killed before we've even heard the acronym. Doctor Who has now entered the world of military organisations – and we'll get a lot of deaths like this, from characters who are introduced just to die bravely in the course of duty. The difference here, I think, is that for this one scene the viewer is supposed to know that the Doctor is wrong, and that the man's fate deserves more consideration than it's given.

And we get to see Kevin Stoney again! He's wonderful, isn't he? Tobias Vaughn makes such a likeable villain; it makes such a pleasant change to have a baddie who'll laugh with genuine amusement when he sees Zoe destroy his computer. He's the first enemy for a very long time – maybe as far back, even, as Mavic Chen – who's clearly shown he has a sense of humour. What Stoney brought to The Daleks' Master Plan was a depth of character to the blackhearted traitor, all the greater in contrast to the Daleks around him. You can see here that director Douglas Camfield wants him to give something of that character again: there's the same charm, the same wryness, and the same insistence to his alien allies that he should be given respect. The only time we hear him shout this episode is not at one of our heroes, but at the strange creature he's got hiding in his cupboard – he's *intrigued* by the Doctor and *entertained* by Zoe, but Vaughn need never even raise his voice against them. That's power.

I'm afraid I'll have to be honest, though – I *hate* Isobel Watkins. Not, I hasten to add, Sally Faulkner: she's a family member of a friend, and so I've bumped into her every now and then at weddings and things, and she seems very nice. But the only way I can read Isobel is as a talentless pseud. She wants to be a photographer, but is so friendless that the only person she can take pictures of is herself – that's until Zoe turns up, whereupon she dresses her in a feather boa, exhausts her with a photo session, and only *then* thinks to offer her a cup of coffee! The selfish cow. At which point she puts on some music – and it's the Teddy Bears' Picnic. The selfish, utterly insane cow. Tobias Vaughn may be a bit sinister with that non-blinking thing going on, but I'd rather spend an afternoon with him than with Isobel. She then accompanies Zoe to International Electromatics (IE), and laughs along as Zoe makes the computer there blow itself up with a logic problem, *as if she even understood a word of it*. So she's selfish, insane, and the sort of social misfit that will try to muscle her way into other people's jokes. You know the type. Don't trust her, Zoe. Get away from her now. She'll get her talons into somebody before the story's out, you mark my words. And the annoying part about her is that this lopsided-grinning airhead is a replacement for Anne Travers – who in The Web of Fear showed intelligence, bravery and an independence rare for this era of Doctor Who. For shame.

If Professor Watkins turns out to be some sort of trendy idiot wearing a medallion and calling everyone Daddio, then this series is on the slide.

T: Do you remember the furore when the Radio Times showed the Dalek/human hybrid on its cover, thus ruining the cliffhanger to Daleks in Manhattan? The Internet went bananas! Well, despite the circumspect nature of this story's title, the Radio Times had a picture of a Cyberman with its coverage of episode one. It's now a week later, and we still haven't seen or even heard mention of one – and we won't for another couple of instal-

ments. (Even then, it'll have the audacity of being an end-of-episode hook.) Talk about stringing us along!

These episodes really have to pull out all the stops, therefore, to be anything less than perfunctory scene-setting... and do you know, I think they're getting away with it? It opens with some fairly standard stuff that involves the Doctor and Jamie being followed, but it's transformed into something rather special thanks to Camfield's shifty camera work and Harper's excellent, oppressive music. And it's adorable how Troughton decides to give up and have a game of cards on the curb as the shady covert op guys surround him.

Camfield has always been rightly hailed as a fine director of action, but he's also very pretty canny in the casting department – he hasn't hired Kevin Stoney as his big villain again out of some kind of idle habit. Stoney delivers an equally skilful performance to the one he gave as Chen, but it's subtly different; he's so charming, and touches like his wonky eye and arched eyebrow only add to his brilliance. The *real* surprise though, is Peter Halliday as Packer. While reading the novelisation of this story, I pictured Packer as a Maurice Roëves type – you know, the tough, coarse, working class-sort of actor Camfield usually favoured to bring genuine grittiness to the "hard man" roles. And when I saw The Invasion as a youngster, I thought Halliday was woefully miscast – a character actor struggling to pull off thuggery. (My misgivings about this aren't entirely misplaced – Doctor Who is, after all, the series that asked Peter Laird to be Chinese, Rodney Bewes to be a mercenary and Beryl Reid to be Sigourney Weaver.) Watching it now, though, I realise I was wrong – Halliday's acting choices are obviously quite deliberate and effective. His nasal, reedy voice and the beginnings of a lank comb-over give him the aspect of a jumped up traffic warden wielding too much power, and his incompetence is so much better conveyed because he's a sadistic little weasel rather than a musclebound knucklehead. He's the worst kind of bully – someone who can only get away with it by virtue of his status, guards and big black helmet.

Overall, then, Camfield has worked his socks off to stop this from being sheer padding, especially as we're still waiting for the

Cybermen to be represented by more than just a talking chandelier. (Still, it's a step up from The Wheel in Space's light bulb...)

The Invasion episode three

R: I think this is terrific. It's a bit of a runa-round, certainly – but I also found it to be the most exciting episode of Doctor Who since The Web of Fear. And what can the link there be? This is a basic demonstration of Douglas Camfield's skills as director. The script is fine, but really nothing to write home about – you keep on waiting in vain for there to be some real spark between the Doctor and Tobias Vaughn, some wit to their confrontation. But there's a virtue made of this: Troughton's dialogue is so unusually functional, only speaking to Stoney in short answers or tones of measured politeness, that it only serves to make the Doctor look more disquieted than usual by the supremely confident businessman. By the third time that the Doctor is obliged to say "How kind" in response to yet another example of Vaughn's hospitality, it sounds like a guarded insult. It's in the spaces between the dialogue that Camfield lets the characters breathe. One of the funniest moments of the episode comes near the start, where Jamie is ushered into the back seat of a Rolls Royce... only to climb out the other side, and take Packer's passenger seat. It's that look of quiet triumph that Hines tips the bully, and the frustrated impotence that Peter Halliday gives him in return, which cleverly sets the tone for the entire episode – and suggests too a reason for Packer's vengeful sadism.

Halliday and Stoney make a wonderful double act – and, again, it's largely achieved through sideways glances and reaction shots. When Vaughn smoothly warns Professor Watkins of Packer's brutality, Halliday rolls his head sideways gratefully, in mock humility. Their relationship is one of the best things about this. Vaughn moves from condescending approval – treating Packer as his golden boy – through wearying sarcasm at his failures to outwit the Doctor, to blazing anger. What makes Packer work so well is that he's funny, but always dangerous – Halliday makes the thug look like a small and fussy little jobsworth, knocked to one side by his own

guards, but who quite clearly has survived in his job by being a cruel sadist. The anticipation on his face as he orders his lift to be taken to the top of the lift shaft, crossing his arms as if to brace himself for the sensation of squashing the Doctor on the way, is wonderful.

And there's a claustrophobia to it all as well. There is one inspired sequence where Vaughn takes the Doctor and Jamie to another of his factories – only to present them with exactly the same office set! Vaughn's dreams may be global, but he wants the world to be reduced to a small and tidy space he feels comfortable in. And his reliance on "uniformity and duplication" gives a clever hint to us as to just who his alien allies might be.

T: I would agree that the use of Vaughn's duplicated offices is clever – and it's budget conscious too! Perhaps this is when they earmarked Sherwin for the producer's job; after all, it's a clever conceit that's appropriate for the plot and nature of the menace, and also a canny use of resources. Everyone's a winner!

Plot-wise, however, this is a bit of a disgrace. What you call "the most exciting episode since The Web of Fear," I would call "lots of chasing up and down in a lift". I'm grateful that Camfield, Troughton and Stoney are all doing exciting things to distract us from the drying paint (why oh why wasn't Kevin Stoney better known – this is an extraordinary performance of suave menace and suppressed fury). But try as I might to see it otherwise, much of the episode seems an exercise in establishing that Vaughn's a baddy. And having previously lauded Halliday's unusual take on a stock character, I do think he overdoes it a little here, and gets very camp when he realises that the Doctor is responsible for the lift shenanigans.

There's so little else to say, let me use my remaining space here to tell you about a little detective work I've done. No-one seemed to be able to find Gordon St Clair, who played Grun in The Curse of Peladon. Now, I recalled seeing an advert in a fan magazine of some sort from years ago, for an event in Australia boasting appearances by Katy Manning and Gordon Stoppard (sic), with the latter cited as everyone's favourite King's Champion. I assumed that this was a spelling mistake for Gordon *Stothard*, who was a Cyberman in The Wheel in Space, and wondered if he and St Clair were one and the same. (It was difficult to tell, or course, because he was under a Cyber outfit in Wheel, and so we don't know what he looked like.) But sometime later, I noticed in the extras list for this story that Stothard was one of the tall men in overalls carrying caskets (the other is Miles Northover, for anyone who wants to know what a Kroton looks like). And look – there he is at the beginning of this instalment. Grun, in all his majesty! Yes, you read it here first, Gordon Stothard is Gordon St Clair. I've emailed this theory to my friend Peter, who has the ear of the Production Notes people on the DVDs, so I'll be interested to see if this info is used.

April 23rd

The Invasion episode four

R: I bet Douglas Camfield had a field day with all this! A helicopter rescue in mid-air, with guards machine gunning at it, and Jamie clinging to it by rope ladder as it flies away...! The action sequences have a scale to them utterly unlike anything we've seen on Doctor Who before; if I were writing a script for BBC Wales right now, with the budget and the kudos that the series now has, I'd hesitate before writing in something like this. Ambition is not necessarily something that looks good on screen in Who – but the fact that the majority of the episode is written to accommodate one glorious stunt suggests that they *must* have known they could pull it off. As it is, this looks epic enough even as a cartoon.

And after all this eye candy, at the end of the episode there's *still* time to show the Doctor and Jamie getting back into an IE warehouse... by canoe. The effort being shown by the production team to keep this story visually fresh is remarkable.

It's all sound and fury, and there's not much room for the little nuances I love to pick out. But I'm very fond of that pleasingly subtle moment when Vaughn uses the phone, only to find a *human* operator on the other end. He's so used to the system being fully automated, or to only talking to machine creatures from other worlds – and so when suddenly presented

with an attractive woman he audibly double takes, and turns on the charm.

T: The past two episodes have all been escape and capture – in fact, the past *four* episodes should really have been called Prelude to an Invasion – but it's become clear that everyone involved, rightfully, has faith that Camfield will keep things interesting even when there's very little substance. And while it's true that Sherwin hasn't given us much in the way of plot advancement, he's more than made up for this in stark realism and character development. Between the two of them, this has become quite a grown-up and uncompromising story – it's exactly the way my fevered childish brain imagined Doctor Who was when I read the novels. I'd have absolutely loved this had it been on telly when I was a teenager, and I have to acknowledge the great work of Cosgrove Hall in recreating these lost instalments. I stand by my previous comments that I'd rather have back an episode from a story that's entirely absent from the archives, but it is thrilling to have the gaps of this adventure animated for viewing on DVD.

And what a truly brilliant villain Tobias Vaughn is. I initially questioned the wisdom of his guards firing on UNIT, but it becomes a plot point – he can use force against UNIT because he has Major General Rutlidge under his control, and he can boast about double-crossing his allies because he's invented a machine that can harm them. Everyone is a pawn of Tobias Vaughn! Or I should say "prawn", as he's used marine metaphors twice in many episodes – he's all sprat and mackerel this, catching with bait that. I'm so glad you didn't notice this, Rob, because you'd probably have sensed a fish theme at work in the story, and written an essay on why Isobel is a mollusc and Sergeant Walters is a guppy. Or something.

Haddock out.

The Invasion episode five

R: The big mystery of the episode: whatever happened to Major General Rutlidge? In the novelisation there's no doubt. Rutlidge is murdered, and vomits a stream of blood as he does so (probably the nastiest example of overkill in any Target novelisation). On the television screen it's a lot more oblique than that. Vaughn senses that control over his puppet is weakening, so summons him to his office in London. There Rutlidge gives all the information he can. Packer asks what will be done with him, and Vaughn idly replies, "Leave him to me" – and then promptly turns his back on him, and goes to have a chat with Cyber-control instead. You'd be forgiven for thinking it was an error, that there's a missed scene – but Camfield focuses upon Rutlidge's face during this, picking out the beads of sweat, and a growing horror that he's in some way party to the invasion being discussed. We expect a moment of rebellion. Nothing. He's never seen again.

What's brilliant about it is Vaughn's very dismissiveness of Rutlidge. It only dawns on us as the episode continues that the Rutlidge story has ended. He was never meant to leave Vaughn's office alive – and it didn't need to be a big melodramatic gesture, Vaughn had the man killed so matter-of-factly, he did it after more pressing business *off screen*. It's subtly one of the most powerful deaths we've witnessed in Doctor Who for ages, and precisely because we *don't* witness it. Vaughn is that powerful. That he intends to kill Rutlidge is clear enough, and that he has him in his mercy is established. We don't need any more. The man is dead. It's chilling – and, of course, it succeeds so well because it can only be chilling in retrospect. This poor hypnotised man, made to be a traitor against his will, is nothing more than a loose end that doesn't need tying.

The power Vaughn shows this episode is so great that it almost overwhelms everything else. The scene where he attacks a Cyberman with emotions – reviving it "just enough to wean it out of its cocoon" to experiment on it – is so callously done that you actually feel sorry for the newborn monster. That's what's bizarre: the Cybermen have never looked so good or imposing, and you expect this to be the point in the story (as in Tomb) where they'll take over from their human ally. On the contrary – Vaughn is no idiot like Eric Klieg, and knows full well that his allies will dispose of him the moment they're able to. The Cybermen's voices are even odder here than in The Wheel in Space – but Derrick Sherwin has taken the best elements of that story, and cast

them here as the sinister mute giants skulking in the shadows.

Isobel Watkins, though. Dear oh dear. The scene in which she turns on the Brigadier for being anti-feminist simply because he's unwilling to let her encounter alien killers of superhuman strength in a sewer is so irritating that it makes my teeth smart. The programme can't have it both ways; Isobel can't be a freethinking woman with attitude one moment, and then be bemoaning the fact that the soldier she's chatting up isn't stinking rich the next. Here begins the long ugly take on feminism that characterises so much of Doctor Who in the seventies. A lot of bewildered male writers begin to recognise that women out there are starting to make a lot of noise about equal rights – and stick it into the show in such a caricatured fashion that any character caught banging on about Women's Lib looks like an idiot. When the Cybermen advance on those "crazy kids" in the sewer at the cliffhanger, you're left hoping that at least the annoying blonde one with the telephoto lens will cop it.

T: I have to say, these are my favourite variant of Cybermen. They're the first ones I saw, I think – they stared out at me from the cover of Doctor Who and the Cybermen (the novelisation of The Moonbase), and also featured heavily in that A-Z of Monsters book that I previously mentioned. Their face masks are simple; they're impassive, but also solid and unsilly. Their lace-up boots and zip don't detract from this more streamlined look, with stiff, solid looking support joints. Okay, they *sound* like Donald Duck, but that's not to fault the efforts of costume designer Bobi Bartlett. These Cybermen *look* fantastic, gleaming as they do in the sewers, and casting ominous shadows on the walls. It was such a great idea to have them skulking about in the underbelly of the capital, and it brings out the best in Camfield's direction.

There's much to like about this: the Doctor's distorted face in the magnifying glass, Ian Fairbairn's turn as the rather unkempt and downtrodden scientist Gregory, Jamie's cheeky grin when he tells the girls that man's superiority is a fact. In the end, though, Stoney once again is head and shoulders above everything else. His best line is when an underling worries that anyone meeting the rampaging Cyberman they've loosed in the sewers could be killed, and he responds, "Good, anyone fool enough to be down those sewers deserves to die..."

By the way, Happy Shakespeare Day. And RIP William Hartnell, who left us on this day back in 1975.

April 24th

The Invasion episode six

R: There's an energy to the direction we're simply not used to on Doctor Who, even from Douglas Camfield. Look at that quick sequence where a UNIT soldier beats a Cyberman down the manhole with the end of his rifle – he puts such passion into it that his cap flies off, and filmed from the Cyberman's point of view, it hits the screen with a real force. When there's the time or money for action scenes, Camfield frames them brilliantly – the scenes in the sewer, with Cybermen being bombed and scared soldiers being gunned down, is told with great economy that makes them very tense. And the sequence at the end of the episode, where we see Cybermen marching in front of St Paul's – their heads first appearing over the picture postcard image, then confidently taking full possession of it – is about as iconic and as epic as Doctor Who ever gets.

And the brilliance of Camfield is that when the time or money run out, he manages to make hastily scripted filler scenes just as effective. The rescue of Professor Watkins couldn't be shot as scripted – so instead we have a sequence in which a desperate Gregory tells Vaughn all about the action sequence, and is calmly sentenced to death as a consequence. It's shocking, and abrupt, and *cheap*, yes – but it's also so much more dramatic than another stunt set piece with the military. His extraordinary talent is being able to flip between scenes of large-scale action, with moments of dangerous intimacy. For my money, the best part of the whole episode is where Vaughn goads Professor Watkins to take his gun and shoot him. There's awful resignation on Watkins' face as he closes his eyes and waits for death, as Vaughn aims his revolver at his head – followed by bemused horror as he realises that

Vaughn is telling him to make something of his principles and take the opportunity to kill him. When Vaughn knocks him to the ground in impatience, it's done with real violence – and the way he laughs when the best Watkins can do is produce three smoking holes in his chest is the mark of a psychopath. The whole sequence is just beautifully staged for maximum tension, Camfield concentrating on extreme close-ups of Edward Burnham's face as we're asked to consider whether we too would have the courage to make a stand against evil.

T: Let me offer a fresh perspective on the Watkins-shooting-Vaughn scene. When I first watched this episode all those years ago, when the universe was less than half its present size, my sister stuck her head around the door. She was slightly confused by the scene, thinking that – thanks to the close-up on Watkins' face as he pulls the trigger, and lingers there as his head slowly falls back and he faints – that the gun had been rigged to fire backwards or something, killing him. So, I'm not sure if that particular moment is as 100% successful as we'd like to think. It's a *hell* of a sequence, though, with Vaughn goading Watkins and slapping him with enormous force. (I'm told that Edward Burnham wasn't too fond of Kevin Stoney – and perhaps that hefty whack in the chops had something to do with it!) Those smoking holes in Vaughn's chest are impressive too, and it's really quite an adult scene. The last story had a bunch of posh kids besting the Doctor with the old Adam, Eve and Pinch-Me chestnut; this adventure entails one man challenging his opponent's morality by demanding that he shoot him at point-blank range. Brr.

Otherwise, we're into Season Seven! All right, not really, but it's become very hard to watch this story separate from the knowledge that Derrick Sherwin will model the show in future on this template – loads of hardware, epic length and an overall feel of "contemporary grittiness" included. Fortunately, it's a hard-nosed approach that appeals, especially as the Cybermen are presented as being so powerful – grenade after grenade fails to entirely subjugate them. The effortless way that they bash manhole covers off is an economical demonstration of their strength, and that haunting image of their march down the steps of St. Paul's is one of Doctor Who's Great Moments. Brr again.

What we *don't* see of this display of military might is – as you say – the big battle between the UNIT forces and Vaughn's men, which happens off screen. However, the planned scene, which also appears in the novelisation, has Gregory (who in the book version, if I'm recalling this correctly, has dandruff – a deft character touch from Ian Marter) uncharacteristically drawing a gun. What we get instead is *so* much better: Gregory has already blotted his copy book by stepping in to stop Watkins being hurt during Vaughn's test of his emotion-generating gun, and after his subsequent failure to stop UNIT from rescuing the professor, Vaughn genially tells his minion that has no time left... before Gregory is subjected to a brutal, perfunctory dispatch in the sewers. Brr, brr and thrice brr.

On a more comical note, did you notice how Watkins' beard has grown? It was comparatively short and stubbly during his first appearance, but Burnham has now been on the job for a month, even though only a couple of days have passed for his character. Perhaps when the professor isn't working on the Cerebratron Mentor, he's been spending his hours inventing a hair-growth device, The Follicle Flourisher.

The Invasion episode seven

R: Now, as much as I've been enjoying The Invasion, there has for the last few weeks been an absence at the centre of it. And that's been the Doctor himself. If I were being harsh, I'd say that Derrick Sherwin and Douglas Camfield have got so excited at the template for this new direction of Doctor Who, they've rather forgotten to put Doctor Who into it. Troughton has spent the last few episodes poking about with microcircuits and neuristers, and looking pretty much like the able scientific boffin working for a military organisation – stick him in a smart uniform, and he'd look no different to anyone else buzzing around the Brigadier. And Troughton has looked none too happy about it, giving a rather subdued performance, left in the corner whilst the real action is between Kevin Stoney's delightful villain and a lot of

soldiers with guns. Wendy Padbury's barely had a look in either, popping down into the sewers briefly just to get herself into a spot of jeopardy. And Frazer Hines has been so redundant that in the last episode he went to sleep. On two separate occasions.

It hasn't entirely worked yet, this attempt to mesh Doctor Who as we know it with the sort of hardware tale that UNIT has to offer. It's peculiar to see this most anti-establishment of Doctors working so benignly with the military. And it's a lesson learned: when the Doctor returns to work for UNIT next season, it'll be within a much more adversarial relationship. It's the only way forward – as it is, the Doctor is in danger of disappearing into the background altogether.

And that's why this episode comes as such a relief. The Invasion has been so skilfully handled that it's only when that eccentric Doctor pops back into focus that I realise just how much I've missed him. There's room for some character comedy at last – he tosses a coin to determine which path he should take in the sewers, and with perfect timing sets off in the opposite direction. The way in which he floors Tobias Vaughn by so politely knocking at his door, so to speak, is absolutely priceless; it's apt that for the first time, Kevin Stoney actually looks *surprised*. And his discussion with Vaughn is perfectly handled, the Doctor looking relaxed and in control as if he's conducting a job interview with a sloppy applicant. Troughton looks happier than he has in ages, at last having the potential to show off the charisma we know he has at his best.

Wendy Padbury's better used too; the unflappable way in which she plots the destruction of the Cybermen warships is terrific. Frazer Hines is out of the story, though – Jamie is shot (with real bullets from a real gun!) to get him back into bed dozing where he belongs.

T: That's it for Professor Watkins and Sergeant Walters too – Edward Burnham must have been thrilled to collect an episode fee when he's essentially just bundled out of a back door. And while Walters' departure isn't really explained, the production text on the DVD says that John Levene replaced an actor who was sacked for persistent lateness – and said caption appears, by an almighty coincidence, over a shot of Walters-actor James Thornhill. Given that Benton takes over Walters' function, it's pretty obvious to whom they're referring. It's a shame, as Walters looks pretty nifty with his body armour and machine gun. Who knows? If he'd been more punctual, maybe he'd have become the series regular in Levene's stead (sliding doors and all that).

But you're right – it's odd how little we've mentioned Troughton in this story, considering he's generally the focal point of our raving. Still, he's not the only one who's been pushed to one side – having only come to this party at the end of the fourth instalment, the Cybermen are, after the cliffhanger reprise, not seen again for the rest of the episode. Meanwhile, having indulged in a spot of cuticle-chewing last week, Packer is now turning into an old woman, and moans to Vaughn who – brilliantly – refuses to be fazed. Vaughn is indeed surprised when the Doctor contacts him, but it's mildly piqued bemusement, rather than the shock of a man on the ropes. He's smooth and assured right up until his final confrontation with the Cyber-wedding-cake-thingy, when it's announced that the Cybermen are shifting into Plan B: the total destruction of Earth.

Tellingly, *who* gets the end-of-episode close-up? Vaughn, and it's thoroughly deserved. This hasn't been much of a second Doctor story, and in terms of screen time, it hasn't been much of a Cyberman story either. No, it's a *Tobias Vaughn* story, and he's magnificent.

April 25th

The Invasion episode eight

R: In a story of this length, it feels entirely right that the endgame should feel so drawn out. Other stories would have concluded much more blandly at the end of episode seven, with the Cyberships destroyed; it means that all of this week's episode plays as a desperate epilogue, with UNIT poised to stop a new and apocalyptic counterplot, and gives the viewer a sense unusual in Doctor Who that the climax isn't to be rushed at. In most adventures, the resolution of the crisis at best only concerns the last half of the final episode – which is why

Doctor Who stories often feel rather abrupt and unsatisfying.

There are two endings here: there's the Russian missile which takes out the Cybermen's mothership, and there's the death-defying attack on the Cyberman's lair by the Doctor and a bunch of soldiers throwing grenades at everything that moves. One involves standing around waiting, with lots of furrowed brows – and one involves guns and noise and the Doctor jumping about clutching his buttocks trying to avoid explosions. It's obvious which one should provide the final climax. And yet, bizarrely, that's not what the story does. It looks at first like a structural mistake. But in fact, after eight full episodes about an alien invasion which feels as detailed as the show will ever manage, it seems entirely right. Had The Invasion followed the usual Doctor Who formula and reached an easy resolution with guns ablazing, it'd have been trite. What's extraordinary is that the length gives the story a licence to play the ending more *realistically*, and show that wars end not tidily with a battle, but with people in conference rooms feeling anxious. There's a tension to those final scenes, as we wait for the missile to hit, that is utterly palpable. And although the story has nothing else up its sleeve now – there's no more jeopardy, the missile will strike home – it feels all the more realistic. Crises of this scale do not end with a big stand-off between one man being brave and a villain shown the error of his ways; as brilliant as the scenes between Troughton and Stoney are (Stoney so good at playing bitter disillusionment that you almost feel sorry for him), the story couldn't end with them. The scale of the adventure has been made so credibly huge that it can no longer be resolved by the actions of one hero.

And that's still why this doesn't feel entirely like Doctor Who – and why the series very rarely attempts anything of this size ever again. Doctor Who's great gift is its eccentric lead character, a little man fighting against the odds. There's only so much The Invasion can do with him – he's a bystander for the real climax at the end, and he doesn't even manage to destroy the radio transmitter; he needs soldiers to accomplish that for him. There's a very funny image of Troughton sitting amongst the dead Cybermen, trying to look his best for

Isobel's photograph, as UNIT rushes into action behind him – but the image is also saying, that's it, the Doctor's done his part of the story now, and it's time for the men in uniform to sort it all out. It's a brilliant bit of television. It's as spectacular as just about anything Doctor Who will accomplish again. But it rather overwhelms our heroes. In the final scene, as they're left to do their comedy shtick walking around a field looking for an invisible TARDIS, only Captain Turner and Isobel are curious enough to want to see them off.

T: Hmm, I buy your logic about the drawn-out ending, but in practice I'm not convinced. "It's going to be a long 12 minutes," says the Brig, and boy – he's right. The story climaxes with the Cyberman's mothership exploding before cutting immediately and abruptly to the coda in Isobel's flat. I'd have preferred a few more bells and whistles (not, mind you, the ones used in the inappropriately bouncy incidental music) during the final reel.

But then, this is a very curious ending all around. Jamie isn't present for the big finale not because of a story-development, but because of how the cast's holidays have been allotted. (His absence, at least, has enabled Zoe to have more input into the latter episodes, which is a pleasant change for Wendy Padbury.) Peter Halliday – a wonderful guest-star up to this point – gets a grand total of one line before Packer is slaughtered; so much investment was poured into the Packer-Vaughn relationship, it's lost a little quickly for my liking. Vaughn, at least, continues to be mesmerising up to the very end – his passing acknowledgement of UNIT's efficiency (although part of a throwaway moment) has a great truthfulness about it, and his deflated breakdown is mesmerising. His justly celebrated speech about why he wishes to control the world, and why he turns on the Cybermen – not out of altruism towards his own kind, but out of hatred for his former allies – ensures his character stays brilliantly consistent unto death. (It's an extremely odd juxtaposition, however, to see Vaughn's body ominously swinging on the ladder railing behind Troughton's lovely comedy jumping in the foreground.)

Much of the rest of this, truth to tell, seems very truncated. Once Troughton has amusing-

ly brushed himself down for the photo opportunity amongst the strewn Cyber-bodies, it's down to poor old Clifford Earl (as Major Branwell) and Norman Hartley (as Sergeant Peters) to provide the necessary urgency. This they do very well, but there's no escaping that the "exciting climax" occurs with those involved stuck behind desks and on a radio link. (For that matter, I was never entirely convinced that the UNIT control room set successfully represented the interior of an aircraft – it doesn't quite translate for me, I'm afraid.)

Fortunately, they've picked the best director possible to handle this material – save for Robert Sidaway's Captain Turner, who is rather impossibly cheery, Douglas Camfield has a gift for casting believable actors as military men. In particular, Clifford Earl is something of a wonder – before he was an actor, Earl was a soldier at Porton Down who was subjected to unlawful tests involving sarin nerve gas on unsuspecting human guinea pigs. (Those involved finally got an overdue, much-deserved apology and financial settlement last year, after decades of lobbying the government for them; it makes my long "12 minutes" seem like nothing.) In the previous episode, he got to say, "No hold-ups, please," with unflappable professionalism as the countdown reached its climax – and this week, he composes his hands after he's placed the firing keys in a way that suggests calm, standardised army procedure.

So, to review: The Invasion has been an impressively mounted production, helmed by a hugely talented director, with a stunning guest-cast and an excitingly adult tone. Has some of the Doctor's magic been lost in the process? Perhaps, but if the series can keep alternating between the likes of this and the inspired whimsy of The Mind Robber on a regular basis, we're in for a treat.

The Krotons episode one

R: This is such a contrast. We're back into cheap Doctor Who territory with a bump: the very first image is of a sliding door that wobbles and then won't shut properly. The Gonds are all dressed as simply as the budget will allow, and even the axes they carry have a distinctly hand-me-down whiff about them.

But it's a contrast to The Invasion in other

ways too. The regular cast are right at the forefront of the action again. The Doctor looks more relaxed here than he has for ages, taking in a gravel pit smelling of wet farts with a breeziness that suggests he's just materialised the TARDIS on a pleasure beach. And he influences events within the Gond society so swiftly that it beggars belief; a several thousand-year-old culture topples within minutes as soon as the Doctor points out that these Kroton benefactors are murdering people. It's as if Troughton is making up for lost time, after being shunted into the background by all those UNIT soldiers over the last few weeks. We're back on an alien planet, and the landscape looks suspiciously like Dulkis, and its inhabitants are as badly dressed as Dulcians too – and you grit your teeth expecting a story of a similarly arthritic pace. But the plot is dizzyingly fast; within 15 minutes, we've got rebels leading armed attacks upon the establishment – it normally takes us three episodes at least to get this far!

Jamie's been running on empty for quite a while as well, so it's heartening to see that the first thing he does upon meeting the first stranger who gets in his way is pick a fight with him. The duel is really well choreographed (let down only a fraction by the Doctor and Zoe ad-libbing squeaks of concern in the background).

I like this. It's back to basics Doctor Who, but none the worse for that. And it's great to see Robert Holmes' name on the credits at last. With Terrance Dicks for the first time being acknowledged on the previous story (as script editor), it's strange to think we've come this far through the series only now to see the work of two men we credit with being so hugely influential.

T: Well, I never had you down as the sort of chap that would use the phrase "wet fart". I have to say, it's not the most edifying of images to enjoy my breakfast with.

Anyway, poor old The Krotons... I've never really shaken off the disappointment I felt, ages ago, because it had the indecency to not be The Tomb of the Cybermen. When The Five Faces of Doctor Who season was announced back in 1981, I was extremely excited at the prospect of watching those Target novels I'd been reading come to life. When Troughton's turn came, and the BBC announced that they'd be showing the hitherto unheard-of (at least, in my world) The Krotons, it was my first inkling that perhaps not every story was available. Surely, after all, they'd have shown a well-known classic rather than this unknown entry into the canon? (That wasn't the only limit to my knowledge either; believe it or not, at this point I still laboured under the misapprehension that all Doctor Who stories were four-parters.) So, this cheap and cheerful little tale had a whiff of "if only" about it, for reasons that were never its fault.

The good news is that there are only *two* actual problems here – the bad news is that said problems are the production values and the guest cast. It's certainly not the first time that Doctor Who has been done on the cheap, but this *looks* cheap – the costumes are blander than a Hollyoaks cast list, the model shot of the Gond dwellings is dreadful and the computer banks don't spark when they're battered, possibly because they're as wooden as James Copeland's performance as Selris, the Gond leader. The rest of the one-off characters, though, aren't much better... Gilbert Wynne gives an over-wrought turn as the young man Thara, and dear old James Cairncross, as the scientist Beta, is a tad too plummy. (He was considered the main guest star of this, would you believe, despite his having less than a dozen lines in this episode.) Maurice Selwyn and Bronson Shaw are hilariously poor as, respectively, the learning-hall custodian and an unnamed student. Only Philip Madoc, as the demagogue Eelek, is giving a top-notch performance – when he thinks a hand on his shoulder contains poison, he glowers menacingly and removes it with clinical disgust. We're lucky to having him in such inauspicious surroundings, but it's like watching Olivier playing Rosencrantz at your local Village Hall whilst Prentis Hancock gives his Hamlet.

And yet, for all of those troubles... I like this. The script has a laudable economy; Robert Holmes is very good at setting up relationships, customs and backstory with very little fuss. The story bounces along nicely, and if nothing else, it's an intriguing premise (Holmes has only just left the starting gate, and already he's shaking a society to its foundations).

Troughton's mourning over the destruction of his favourite umbrella is sweet and funny, whilst the tubular probe that emerges to seek him out is impressive in length, girth and mobility (even if it does bring Doctor Freud a'calling).

Oh, and I'm glad you liked the fight. Jamie's opponent is Richard, my agent, so 15% of it probably used to belong to me.

April 26th

The Krotons episode two

R: I have to agree with you, Toby, that fandom has had something of a downer on The Krotons ever since it was repeated as part of the Five Faces season. As such, it was the first Troughton story of the video age – the only one for years that was readily accessible as a recording off the telly. My God, the fans I knew were sick of it. It opened our eyes to the state of the archives – that in a series of four-part stories, The Krotons was the only Troughton story then in existence of the right length. The Tomb of the Cybermen was still a good decade from discovery.

Of course, had Tomb existed, you could have been sure that John Nathan-Turner would have chosen it over The Krotons. And yet, I think that would have been a shame. I'm not arguing that The Krotons is a particularly sophisticated bit of Doctor Who. But as a showcase for the series regulars, I don't think there's anything better in existence. The rapport between Troughton and Padbury is extraordinary here – as they argue over their intelligence scores in the Learning Hall, and as they nervously enter the lair of the Krotons together, determined to "continue what they've started". I love Tomb, but we don't get as clear an interpretation of the second Doctor as he faces off to the Cybermen as we do here, when he bangs against the Kroton spaceship angrily because it's dared to call him "DoctorGond", or when he becomes alarmed once he realises he's begun to bask in their subliminal praise.

And Jamie is great fun too. His first instincts are to accompany the Doctor into danger, and he's only mollified when he's asked very particularly to look after a pretty girl. His frustra-

tion against Selris – who's so willingly sent the Doctor and Zoe into danger – and his furious attempts to get into the Kroton spaceship are really lovely; the episode makes it clear that of the three members of the TARDIS crew at the moment, Jamie is the only one who isn't a genius, but it's not a source of comedy at his expense. Instead, it demonstrates all that is great about Jamie – his courage, and his loyalty to his friends. Here's a boy who'll enter a death machine, confidently brandishing a crowbar, because he'll do anything in his power to rescue the Doctor.

T: It's interesting – we've both summoned up the ghost of The Five Faces of Doctor Who (my video copy of this still contains the promotional slide with said faces all together over a swirling, reddish starscape as the announcer tells us what's coming up), and we've both compared The Krotons to The Tomb of the Cybermen. But do you know, I like The Krotons more. I'm not sure it's any *better*, but where Tomb excelled was in moments of visual iconography, not the script. Here, there are plenty of decent, thoughtful ideas, all written with a certain witty flair, and all of them weighed down by a lack of money – something the makers of Tomb, fancy season-opener that it was, surely couldn't complain about. (Incidentally, all of my books are in boxes because I'm getting ready to move house, so do feel free to wipe the egg off my face if turns out they were similarly budgeted.)

I could be wrong, but it looks like David Maloney has been given such scant resources to realise this, he's opted to use some far-out flashing lights and distorting lenses on the Doctor and Zoe's faces, hoping to inject some kind of abstract visual flair to proceedings. And he's asked to pull off quite an ambitious sequence with the vats of slurry forming the crystalline Krotons (a nifty idea that pays lip service, in this case, to the science part of the fiction). It's all a bit confusing, though, as the montage doesn't really convey a sense of action or scale for the vats; are they big enough to create and house a Kroton?

The regulars are a mixed bag this time around... Zoe's ill-advised zeal to have a go on the learning machine is one in a long line of examples of TV producers thinking the general public might find smug, precocious geniuses who nonetheless do stupid things as somehow endearing (answer: they aren't). At least the Doctor tries to justify the scenario by saying that Zoe's genius "can be very irritating at times". He's no fool, this Doctor, but he's not one for exams or showing off – his intellect is served by instinct, not indoctrination.

And if nothing else, I quite like the Kroton voices – they're *not* Brummie, as everyone says. Roy Skelton once told me that he and Patrick Tull opted to give the Krotons a South African lilt, bringing a satirical edge to the Krotons' methodology of enslaving and exploiting the indigenous population. I tip my hat to their intent, and also appreciate the creature design. Designer Ray London always seems to get stories involving boxes (the box-like War Machines in their warehouse full of boxes, the Keller Machine), but rubber skirts aside, these fellas don't look half bad.

Isn't it odd, though, that two of the central protagonists that were established last week – Eelek and Beta – don't turn up in this episode? We've no idea what they're up to, but let's hope that next time, Madoc and the Englishman come out in the mid-day sun.

The Krotons episode three

R: There are some interesting ideas in this episode. But unfortunately, they're not being raised by the interesting characters. The Doctor and Zoe stroll out to the wasteland, and pick up a few sulphur rocks. Jamie spends the majority of the episode inside the Dynotrope. All three of them seem to have been elbowed out of the main action somewhat.

Which is rather a shame, because it means we spend the episode focused on all the wrong things. We give a greater importance to the Doctor and Zoe fussing about with the TARDIS than we do with the discussions about war going on between Eelek and Beta. And it's good stuff, too – just as the last story took the time to show us the real-world military consequence to an invasion, going on after the adventure would traditionally end, so The Krotons is all about the way that opportunists and radicals take power in the wake of a cultural revolution. In most stories, the Doctor flies off in the TARDIS at the point when the

enemy have been defeated, with the society left to pick up the pieces and rebuild itself anew. The Krotons haven't been beaten yet, of course – but most often the Doctor's battle is with convincing the populace that the status quo needs to be changed, and because that happened so quickly within episode one, there's now time in the script to deal with the political ramifications of that.

Now, I'm aware that when I use the phrase "political ramifications", I'm talking about the bloody Gonds. Get over yourself, Shearman. But the *intent* is there in Holmes' script, and I love that about it. Eelek was nothing more than a jobsworth bureaucrat in episode one, following the Krotons' wishes, and didn't even appear in episode two. Now he emerges as a man savvy enough to seize power, because by destabilising the Gonds' faith in the Krotons, the Doctor's also destabilised their faith in their leaders. Beta may advise Eelek to be patient and wait until they can devise a weapon to use against their alien aggressors, but Eelek is shrewd enough a politician to realise that to keep the people happy, you feed upon their impatience for immediate change, even if it gambles with their freedom. In most stories last year, the Doctor would be advocating *any* form of action, because most of the peoples he was fighting for had retreated into timid passivity. Here, though, the opposite is the case: the Doctor has set in motion the overthrow of a tyrant, but without having had a thought of a system to replace it with. Not to sound too crass, but it's not a million miles away from the war in Iraq nowadays. And to sound a bit *less* crass, it's not far from the darker Doctor of The Evil of the Daleks or The Tomb of the Cybermen, who is at least in part responsible for the crisis. (Note also that if the Doctor and Zoe hadn't been such showoffs with the learning machines, the Krotons would still be inactive in a pool of slurry. The thousand years of slavery might have continued, and the odd clever Gond might have been sacrificed, but the majority of the population would still have been happily cheering the society on in all its stability. Prior to the Doctor arriving and turning everything upside down, even the victims see their being taken away from their friends and family forever as an achievement to be celebrated.)

But all this is in a story with Krotons in it. I think you've pretty much got it right, Toby – their top halves aren't bad, and I love the spinning heads! The skirts and feet are dreadful, though. David Maloney does his best with a long sequence in which one of them sets off across the rocky terrain to find the Doctor. Other directors we could mention (well, Morris Barry, at any rate) would probably depict the thing shuffling along ungainly. Maloney gives us the point of view shot of the Kroton, its gun sticking out ahead of it, making it all look a bit like the computer game Doom from the nineties.

T: Oh God, you're getting nostalgic about the 90s. I remember when they were new. Heck, it's just sunk into me that The Five Faces of Doctor Who was more than 25 years ago – in other words, my off-air repeat of a piece of vintage TV is now older than the vintage TV itself was at the time.

I'm continuing to find this story rather charming, even if the novelty has worn off in parts. The Gonds are a pretty dreadful bunch – how many of them are there, anyway? In episode one, Selris addressed the assorted throng like they were the entire population, and despite mention of "the council", we don't get a representation of the wider community outside the squabblers we see on screen. Still, at least there are neat little sketches of character backstory – such as Beta chiding Eelek and telling him it must be novel being popular – that help to colour this world. Accent-wise, though, this has gone a bit off the boil – the South African ones are actually pretty ridiculous in practice, and it's awfully strange when Madoc's Welsh accent gets more pronounced (notably when he keep talking about a "little more time"), especially as he's appearing alongside the resolutely Scottish James Copeland. With Cairncross (also a Scot, actually) being absurdly RP English, you almost wish the hot-headed Axus had been Irish, because at least then you'd have the ingredients for a joke.

Nonetheless, I'm entertained by different components of this... there's a brilliant spinny thing that the Krotons hover above Jamie's head (I've no idea what it actually is, but I like it). The Krotons' spinning heads are fun too, and you have to enjoy a good-hearted laugh

when a line from a hitherto unseen, nameless Gond is reallocated to Beta, meaning that he's impossibly seen in the Learning Hall when the Doctor left him somewhere else entirely (that, or Beta discovered the principles of matter transportation instead of chemistry). Why, though, does the cast list at the end of this episode appear to have been cranked by someone suffering narcolepsy? I hope the Restoration Team recreates their slow, grinding progress when the credits are redone for the DVD release.

That's a point, actually – oddly enough, The Krotons is one of the few stories from this era in which most of the principal guest cast are still alive. Indeed, you have to get quite near the bottom of the list (i.e. voice actor Patrick Tull, who had a decent career in the USA after this) to find someone who is no longer with us. I have to plead ignorance regarding the Kroton operators and some of the cast (Madeleine Mills, Maurice Selwyn and Bronson Shaw), but the potential here for interviews and such is better than it is with some stories. I've been knocking wood lately regarding some of our more venerable actors – even since we started this quest, we've lost Laurence Payne and John Cater. At least Payne got an obituary in The Guardian; Cater hasn't, yet. A few years ago, I'd have done it myself, but – it shames me to say – I no longer have the time to do as good a job on such things as I'd like.

[Toby's addendum: Shortly after this entry was written, Cater got a very good obituary in The Guardian. Sadly, the cast of The Krotons was latterly depleted when James Cairncross died in December 2009. Please excuse that Rob didn't know this when he wrote the next entry about Beta living on borrowed time...]

April 27th

The Krotons episode four

R: There's one truly delightful scene in which Beta demonstrates a gorgeous disregard for life and limb as he throws himself into experimenting at chemistry with gusto. It's not just that James Cairncross reveals a gift for comic underplay that you'd never have guessed from The Reign of Terror – although it's really lovely

– but more that this is all actually *about* something. The joy of a scientist actually *allowed* at last to do scientific stuff, that this is what revolution means to people who've had their intellects quashed by the powers that be, is wholly infectious. (I mean, bless his heart, I don't think Beta's going to live much longer. Give him a week and he'll be exploded all over the wasteland. But at least he'll die smiling.)

This has all the hallmarks of a final episode from a writer who hasn't yet worked out how to do endings properly. Even the Doctor looks a bit embarrassed at the simple way in which he defeats the Krotons. But it'd be unfair to carp, when this is a story that feels quite deliberately as if it's playing about with awkward aftermaths and the messiness of loose ends. On paper Eelek is an out-and-out villain, the one who happily sells out the Doctor and leaves him to die in the Dynotrope. In any ordinary adventure, he'd get a lethal comeuppance – but Holmes leaves him alive, someone that Thara will have to fight against if he's going to gain any authority over the Gonds. I've not yet mentioned how good Philip Madoc is, but he takes a character that's fundamentally a bit of a caricature and turns him into a real politician. In the space of one scene, he shifts the aims of his campaign twice: at first he rails against Selris for taking action against the Krotons (and cleverly uncovers a dead body in disgust at the waste of human life), then within a minute is rallying his troops to take action against the Krotons! Then out come the Krotons and Eelek changes tack again, becoming their collaborator. The brilliance of Madoc is that what could merely look like inconsistent characterisation seems instead like cunning opportunism. The only false note about him is that in the previous episode it's said that nobody likes him – Madoc is so smooth and beguiling, I'd vote for him.

T: Everyone I know is moaning about the value of their homes right now, so it's appropriate that this gives us an indication of the value of Holmes. No, he's not the finished article yet, but he based this storyline on an inventive premise, and he's shown a flair for bending language and giving it an alien logic and consistency ("High Brains", "dispersed", "exhausted") without it seeming hammy or ludicrous.

The Krotons even refer to the Gonds' organic shells (meaning their bodies!) as "waste matter", a by-product to be disposed of once the energy has been sucked from their minds. That's horrible! And yet, the Krotons aren't being particularly mean, they're just dispassionate in their desire to survive – I'd be much the same, I suppose, if I was stranded and starving after a plane crash, and happened upon a passing rabbit. Holmes also enjoys writing the eccentric, and James Cairncross is positively liberated by the barmy boffin lines he's given here. He's very funny in these scenes, even if his profound staring at the melting Dynotrope in his final shot is a little desperate and unconvincing.

And like Holmes, David Maloney is in his salad days here – he hasn't quite got to grips with seamlessly fitting all the technical stuff into a logical narrative. Nor has he got his eye on the other departments (quite why they felt the need to give Vana's trousers an outer thong to accentuate her femininity is anyone's guess). But the main complaint here is the lack of connection between the model shots and the live action – we saw the tiniest glimpse of the honeycomb of the Dynotrope in relation to the Gond city in a rubbish model shot in episode one, but nothing really substantial until the confusing close-ups of it melting now.

So you could say that Holmes and Maloney are works in progress – much like this story, actually. But if The Krotons has been far from perfect, neither has it been a terrible calamity. It's not been without a sense of fun, it's had plenty of good ideas and it introduced us to Philip Madoc to boot! It's much, much more worthy than the "received wisdom" suggests, so all hail The Krotons! (Besides, it tickles me that all these years later, I have a professional, financial relationship with the actors from this story. One might say that I'm entwined in the claws of Axus.)

The Seeds of Death episode one

R: This is clever stuff. Broadcast just a few months before the moon landings, when the world is full of hopes about the wonders of space exploration, Doctor Who returns to the moon. But only to reveal a society in which the moon has become nothing more than a glorified post office depot, and where people's interest in travel to the stars dissipated years ago. In that way, it seems eerily to predict exactly what happened to NASA only a few years later. We've got futuristic people in futuristic clothes popping off in futuristic telemats – but they're doing *boring* jobs to crippling deadlines for humourless bosses. And carry briefcases! That's the image I most like – it's of Harry Towb (as the station overseer Osgood) arriving for work, materialising out of thin air, with his commuter briefcase in his hands.

Michael Ferguson smartly contrasts the sterility of the space age life with all the glorious artefacts found in Eldred's museum. The charm and magic of reaching out for the stars has been taken away, and we can see with pictures of Gagarin and models of rockets exactly how the future has taken all our dreams and rubbed the shine off them. Ferguson's camera work is rather tricksy: he'll give us close-ups on actors' faces whilst the ones who are speaking are lost out of focus, he'll film a sequence with technical expert Gia Kelly talking where she's entirely distorted behind a see-through panel. It so easily sounds like clumsiness, but it's clearly intentional – these people *are* all a bit vague and out of focus, and the camera gives them what they deserve. The story suggests from the get go that Osgood will be a hero; he's the only one who can make a joke, the only one who has any life to him. And the cruelty of that is that when he stands up to the aliens, he gets shot down instantly. The look on Towb's face is priceless – it's that of a man who thought he was going to be the hero too, and just lives long enough to be disillusioned.

T: Like The Krotons, it's very difficult for me to be objective about this one. The Seeds of Death was the first Doctor Who video I ever bought (from John Fitton Books and Magazines, as featured in Doctor Who Magazine, no less) – £48 it was, an absolute fortune. I devoured a preview in Doctor Who Magazine as I waited for the postman to deliver the tape – this was considerate enough to tell us pretty much how everyone died apart from crewman Phipps, I think. (Even this was helpfully spoiled, when someone later asked Matrix Data Bank for the episode endings, and so Phipps' fate at the climax to episode four

was revealed.) So, I knew a lot about this story even before it arrived. And while it *was* pricey, I just about got my money's worth because as I watched it over and over again. I can almost talk along to this (including Frazer Hines' line "Look at the size of this one..." and Troughton's murmured rejoinder, "Yes, it's very large..."), so familiar is the dialogue. I even have the old BBC Video music playing in my head.

But familiarity with this episode – as you can probably tell – hasn't bred contempt, and I *do* think that much of it is clever and wonderful. Harry Towb was a bit of a name at the time, so you'd be within your rights to think that he'd spend the story being the grumpy base commander who locks horns with the Doctor – so it's quite a shock when he gets wibbled to death! (It's less jolting when Harvey, an unspeaking extra, gets the same treatment – when you're played by Alan Chuntz, you should expect to get shot dead, and possibly to fall off something in the process.)

In terms of the story overall, this works very well. Brian Hayles starts off with a concept, then asks himself what his story is about and grafts an adventure serial into it. To put it another way, he uses the fact that Doctor Who can posit different futures and technological advances, and creates jeopardy within that framework. And what a brilliant idea to show the contemporary, brave new world of the late 60s as being quaint and obsolete by the time of this adventure.

Finally, I should mention that episode one as it stands on the DVD is far superior to the washed-out vagueness of the compilation video (you could tell when episode two arrived on the VHS, as the quality noticeably improved). I'm still not sure, however, if the images on the TARDIS scanner are meant to represent exhibits in Professor Eldred's museum, or if the obvious pictures are just that: pictures. (We don't see them, after all, when we eventually enter Eldred's gaff.) Either way, the Doctor seems very excited about being in a Space Museum – he's clearly forgotten what happened last time.

April 28th

The Seeds of Death episode two

R: Earth society may have lost its interest in space travel, but the production team haven't! This is mostly great, the first time that the Doctor becomes a hero just *because* he's prepared to become an astronaut and fly in a rocket. I love the way that it's very quickly established that the TARDIS just doesn't fit into this world view of space exploration – that at this stage of the series it's not a craft you can navigate, it's just the wardrobe that can fling you into any number of random Narnias. So for the very first time in a programme which is all about visiting alien planets, we subject the regular cast to the real-life rigours and risks of outer space. It all looks perhaps a bit quaint nowadays, and very long-winded; but again, this is an adventure broadcast in the very same decade of Gagarin, and before Neil Armstrong set his giant step for mankind – if the episode hadn't made the journey as painstaking as possible, they'd have been squandering it completely. We see the Doctor, Jamie and Zoe react to G-force, we see their lives threatened by homing beacon faults and communication problems – it's the very first time since the TARDIS took off in An Unearthly Child that we see space travel as something remarkable and hazardous. Last week it was a couple of hissing Martians that caused all the story's tension – this time there's nothing more dramatic than the slow countdown to the launch, the numbers from the computer playing in reverse over Gia Kelly's face, and the TARDIS crew inside the rocket looking cramped and scared.

The Ice Warrior storyline is, as a result, comparatively filler this week. Michael Ferguson films some scenes from the floor, giving the Martians extra height and menace. And it's quite a revelation that the slow lumbering Ice Warriors we met last year were clearly just the grunt soldiers – Slaar is much more elegant and mobile, and his skin wonderfully repulsive. The sequence where Christopher Coll (as Phipps) hides from one of the warriors by squeezing against a filing cabinet in full view is more than a little awkward – but I love it anyway, principally because after the warrior has

left the room, Coll nips out and closes the door tidily behind him! That can't help but make me chuckle, and turns a truly clumsy scene into something almost majestically silly.

For all this, though, my favourite moment of the episode is that single portrait of Terry Scully as Fewsham, sitting glumly by the T-Mat reception, arms hanging limply. He's a coward waiting miserably for the people he's allowed to walk into a trap. It just says so much about his desperate fear, and his self-loathing knowledge that he wants to survive whatever the cost.

T: I'd like to expand upon your point about the TARDIS, as I think it's vitally important that it *can't* help in these situations. For all the amazing properties it has, the Doctor's Ship is essentially ramshackle; Jamie even remarks, when the rocket starts going haywire, that it's as bad as the TARDIS. I like that about this series – it mocks its own icons and is wonderfully un-self important. I've lost count of the American shows where they set out in a spaceship that's the most remarkable/up-to-date/best in the fleet vessel that's available. The TARDIS needs to be a slightly temperamental, bodged, rather battered machine that never quite gets you where you need to go. (Unless, of course, plot expedience requires that it does – in which case it should, straight away, and with the minimum of fuss. Hey, I never said I was consistent.) So it's well and proper that the Doctor's party has to go to the moon via rocket. For that matter, I love Zoe's stern reprimand as Earth control nags them for an answer when they're trying to turn on the gravity, and Troughton's frantic wafting of the ominous black smoke emerging from the panels.

All of that said, the rocket plotline ran the risk of being desperately dull – so it's fortunate that Ferguson keeps coming up with nifty visual tricks to keep all the jargon lively. The man loves quick cut close-ups and superimposition, and places his actors carefully. There's a great shot of Slaar and an Ice Warrior in profile as Miss Kelly gets to work repairing T-Mat in the background, and the Warrior's death benefits from an expert synthesis of camera wrangling and vision mixing. An odd lapse occurs, though, when Phipps hides behind what looks like a cooker – he doesn't even bother to crouch or put the solar kettle thing on his head as a Warrior apparently stares right at him. It's the worst hiding-in-plain-sight moment we've had since The Keys of Marinus. (Mind you, perhaps the Warrior *did* see him, and just thought it was looking at a storeroom for wax-works of British character actors.)

And while I do appreciate that Eldred and Commander Radnor's ideological differences give Brian Hayles scope for scientific debate, the script does need something of a polish where logic is concerned. For a start, Earth's over-reliance on T-Mat – to the point that vast areas will starve if it breaks – is just painfully stupid. Worse, Radnor tells Kelly that she's *the only one* who understands T-Mat. How can this be? T-Mat, on which the planet depends, is only a heartbeat away from being completely unserviceable? Really, the only thing that makes sense about this is that Radnor is in charge of the whole project, but isn't actually certain how it works – he's akin to an ex-banker drafted in by the government to run the rail network on an enormous salary despite never having been on a train in his life, a situation I find all too plausible.

Oh, one last thing: how does Miss Kelly not realise that Fewsham's story doesn't hold water? He tells her, after all, that Osgood killed Locke – even though Locke informed them over the monitor that Osgood had died. And she doesn't even bother asking what happened to Harvey. (It's tough being an extra, no-one cares about you...)

The Seeds of Death episode three

R: There are these seeds. And they're of death! It's only in the final few minutes of this third episode that the title has any relevance at all, which is surely the longest the audience has ever had to wait to make sense of what the story's called. This isn't a criticism of that, by the way – I think it's actually very clever. One of my favourite movies is Miller's Crossing, directed by the Coen Brothers, and the importance of what Miller's Crossing is doesn't become clear until the second half of the movie – so that the first time it's referenced in dialogue, it has an effect that's electric. The same thing is true here. We've had threats of rockets and Ice Warriors and weird mirrored

corridors – and it's only as the Doctor is caught trying to find out what's inside the containers being sent to Earth that the story proper seems to begin. Slaar orders the Doctor to open up the box; inside we see the seeds; and for three weeks, what's been hidden in full view in its specially designed title sequence is shown on screen. Imagine not knowing the story as a seasoned fan – it's a sudden moment of connection, and we know something the Doctor can't, that he's in tremendous danger. The Doctor stoops to pick one of the seeds up, puzzled and complacent – and the tension is terrific, because we've suddenly understood that he should be frightened, that what he's touching is deadly enough that it's the title of this entire adventure. It swells up in his hand, explodes, and leaves him for dead – no warning, no explanation, just as abrupt as that. It's rather brilliant.

T: Setting aside for the moment that it would probably have been more accurate, but far less dramatic, if they'd called this story The Balloons of Death...

I'm continuing to have flashbacks to life in the 80s with my VHS of The Seeds of Death (it was the fourth-ever Doctor Who story released on video, right after three Tom Baker adventures). As I acquired more commercially released tapes and had more off-air recordings, I fell into the, er, curious (but, also, I hope some readers will find, endearing) habit of keeping various Doctor Who videos on stand-by, paused at an exciting moment, in the TV room at home. Then, if I heard someone coming, I'd press play so that they would walk in, see an *amazing* sequence, and – at last! – admit that they'd been foolish to mock Doctor Who. They'd then understand that it was, after all, the greatest thing ever. (It'd be a bonus if I could then show them other episodes and regale them with behind-the-scenes info and cast lists, but their simply validating the series' worth would have been a good place to start.) See, it wasn't enough for *me* to like Doctor Who – I needed everyone else to as well. I didn't relish being the lone lover of the programme, so it was vital I converted first family, then friends, then ultimately the entire world (bwa-hah-hah-haaaah!!) to the cause of celebrating the show's brilliance. And as you might expect, I failed more often than not, usually for reasons I found incomprehensible.

As part of this, I vividly remember my brothers and my sister howling with derision at a moment in this episode. Can you guess which bit plunged them into fits of hysteria? No? It was the shot of the three-pin plug adaptor. Oh, yes. My siblings had been brought up on Doctor Who and liked it – but they'd drifted away from it to such a degree, the sight of something so mundane yanked them out of the drama. I was baffled for the longest time as to why *that* of all things pushed them over the edge. You get so much more out of a programme if you just accept such things and get on with being entertained; could it be that we, as Doctor Who fans, interpret the language of television in a different way from the mainstream audience?

Anyway, back in the future, the Ice Warriors are vacillating between shots where they look fantastic and threatening, and others where they're just a bit silly. There's a *great* bit where, after they've shot the portly, waddling extra and the tall handsome extra (at point blank range!), they tower threateningly over Gia Kelly and seem really menacing. (I have to wonder, though – does anyone ask her what happened to the two extras when she gets back to Earth, or do they join Harvey in the Great Anonymous Supernumery Heaven in the sky?) But there are also more ridiculous moments where they wobble about in an ungainly fashion, complete with sound effects that make it seem like they have a grumbly tummy or a toilet cistern for a stomach. Alan Bennion, at least, is very good as the Ice Lord Slaar; he's very sleek and poised, and moves beautifully. You need someone with good body language if they're encased in latex, and he brings a grace and regality to his gait that's at terrifying odds with his guttural, hissed threats. It's easy to take someone like him for granted, but he's bloody good in the role.

Stylistically, though, this episode is probably most remembered for that sequence of pure padding where the Doctor gets chased, accompanied by such silent movie piano twinkling that it's no wonder Troughton capers his way through it, throwing his arms up in dialogue-free shock and comic horror. I don't really understand why a moonbase would be

equipped with a Hall of Mirrors, but at least everything climaxes with the Doctor's oft-quoted and (rightfully) much loved line, "You can't kill me, I am a genius..." Actually, what really sells it for me is the deflated way he delivers the end of this statement, and his look of genuine surprise when the gambit works!

April 29th

The Seeds of Death episode four

R: I remember when I first watched this, years ago, and what I thought. It all seemed very *contrived*. So the Ice Warriors have the Doctor, a man that at the moment they have no particular reason to see as any unusual threat, and against whom they wouldn't want to exact any special revenge. And they decide to kill him, as he lies on the ground unconscious. Not merely by shooting him with their sonic guns, as they've despatched everyone else so far, but by T-Matting him into deep space. Even though that requires the work of a technician to realign the setting of the T-Mat. Even though after this strange murder has been carried out, it'll delay their plans to send deadly seeds to Earth cities, and the T-Mat will have to be adjusted again. I remember thinking, *why*?

I was putting the cart before the horse, I think. This is sadism on the part of Slaar, certainly. But it's not sadism against the Doctor. He's not awake to experience what's going on, and his death will be instantaneous – of all the ways the Doctor *might* have been bumped off over the years, this is one of the nicest. No, this is sadism against Fewsham. Against the man who to save his own hide has been sending packages to Earth without question. He's a traitor, and the cruelty of the Ice Warriors is that after he's done what he's been instructed, they want him to *understand* the implications of that treachery. He pleads with them that he can't be a murderer, that he doesn't want to be directly responsible for the taking of another life. And this is the point – the Ice Warriors want him to appreciate that whether he kills the Doctor or not, he already has blood on his hands. Because of his cowardice, he's effectively destroyed the human race. By making him execute the Doctor too, they just want to rub that fact in. They're hard to please, these Martians. If you disobey them, they'll shoot you dead without a thought. If you follow their orders, they'll so despise you that they'll make you confront the guilt of what you've done in full force.

Doctor Who always hates the coward. Only a few weeks ago, in The Invasion, when the UNIT soldiers are down the sewers, you can tell which one of them is going to snuff it – it's the one that panics and doesn't show the proper British backbone that'll get blasted down by a Cyberman. (And as soon as Phipps begins to freak out in the ventilation tunnels, you know that he's a marked man too – sure enough, he's dead by the episode's end. Which is a bit unfair on him, really, because for the past few weeks he's been the sole human who's been courageous and resourceful – but one flair of nerves, and he's a marked man.) What's great about The Seeds of Death is that for the first time in the series it explores the cowardice of a character properly. Fewsham cooperates with the Ice Warriors because the alternative is death. Every single other man on the moon-base decides instead to take the admirable course, and to stand up against the aliens and their demands – and they all get killed for their courage. Doctor Who despises its Fewshams, but let's be honest – we'd mostly be Fewshams too. Ordinary people caught up in extraordinary crises, and out of fear doing anything in their power to stay alive. Other stories would have by now made Fewsham someone much more unsympathetic – a Klieg who's actively trying to betray his fellows, a Vaughn who thinks he can make the aliens his allies. Terry Scully gives a terrific performance as an everyman who puts the lives of everyone in Earth in jeopardy because when push comes to shove, he's just not a hero. And that's what I love about Seeds of Death: it's a story at first *about* heroism, about the remarkable men who'll travel into space – and then a study of a man who finds the resolve to become a hero in spite of himself.

The cruelty of the Ice Warriors – making Fewsham kill the Doctor, making Fewsham hate himself – is the same cruelty that we're habitually expected to feel to characters who aren't supercool and are just like us. The heart of The Seeds of Death is that it feels sorry for the weakling.

T: You're absolutely right, but I'd like to also mention the tragic "Oh no..." that escapes from Terry Scully as Slaar rubs in the enormity of what he has done. It's desperately sad, and Scully's wounded face and wiry frame really sell Fewsham as a broken man, battered by circumstance. I'm glad you mention poor old Phipps too – Christopher Coll has something very solid and likeable about him, and he gets to be all Bruce Willis in this episode, charging about in the ventilation tunnels and eavesdropping on the enemy. Give the man a white T-Shirt (as well as some advice about sticking your arm through any grille you're attempting to climb through – you'll never get anywhere going shoulder first).

Meanwhile, the Ice Warriors are slowly evolving in terms of their appearance and who enacts them. I notice their helmets are a uniform shape – for now, there are no big, outsized heads to be seen. And it's interesting to note how it takes some time for Sonny Caldinez to become the No. 1 go-to guy when you want someone to play an Ice Warrior; it's only here, in episode four, that he appears in this story, and he was the first Warrior they got rid off in the Martians' debut tale. Nonetheless, in future he will displace fellow Warrior enactors Steve Peters and Tony Harwood – they must have been irked, as Caldinez was only in the Conference League of Lizards, whereas they were in the Premiership. And yet, Caldinez will get all the Martian gigs from now on, leaving the two of them in the cold (where, as they're method actors, they should be quite comfortable).

I continue to have some logic-niggles, though. Having previously overlooked Phipps, an Ice Warrior here wanders into a storeroom and, astonishingly, fails to notice the unconscious Doctor. (Was my waxwork theory actually correct?) And in a continuing theme of the story, does the Ice Warrior who seems to perform the Arriving on Earth Dance only refrain from killing Eldred and Radnor because they're not extras? (Their guards, on the other hand, are toast as soon as walk into the room.) And why oh why is a big ship's wheel used to set the moonbase's temperature? If the Ice Warriors had been allergic to light, would all the dimmer switches have been the size of plates?

The Seeds of Death episode five

R: See, Fewsham came good in the end! I knew he would. His death scene is terrific. At the moment he meets his maker, Terry Scully refuses to overplay it – he grimly stares the inevitable down, gets shot, then just slumps over the Ice Warrior radar thing. Lovely.

I'm torn about the fact that this deadly fungus sucking the oxygen from the atmosphere can be foiled by water. I love the simplicity of it in theory – and I think the scene where a panicked Troughton refuses to run to safety, instead risking his life to find the right chemical that will destroy the seed, is really terrific. But I live in London. It always rains in London. It's raining right now. It'd be a miracle if it weren't raining. I can see what the production team are doing; we've already had weather control operations in The Moonbase and The Ice Warriors, so this story is rather cleverly feeding off the future history that the series has already established. (It's really rare for Doctor Who at this stage to build upon its long-term continuity like that.) But I think a story can be *too* clever – we're now required to keep in our heads not only a society that's based on instant transmission of matter, but also one where the weather is influenced by the flick of a switch – and it just dilutes the premise of both. So, yes, we've got scenes where an Ice Warrior goes over to a weather control station to destroy the controls so it can't rain. But that doesn't matter, we've already been shown exactly how this story is going to end. Someone's going to fix those controls, and by golly, rain it shall. We had this situation in The Ice Warriors too; but there, Brian Hayles was making the point that although we knew that the world would be saved by someone pushing a button, the drama was all about the characters finding the courage to push it. We don't have the same situation here. Hayles played upon the dilemma of Fewsham to brilliant effect, and in so doing made him the most interesting and developed character of the story. And he's dead. Without him, there's no dilemma left, and no mystery. Just lots of foam, and a few hissing reptiles.

T: Director Michael Ferguson doesn't get enough attention. Perhaps it's because he only worked on four stories, none of which are deemed classics, but you can tell that he's put a strong effort into this. He's even bothered to mount the obligatory opening titles in an interesting fashion, overlaying them on an establishing shot of the Earth and the moon. He also makes use of silhouetting people against that big glowing wall on the moonbase, and there's a wonderful shot of the foam and a seed pod gradually blotting out the camera's view of Weather Control.

It seems, however, that we've moved into a phase where it's not just the extras who are getting short shrift in death. Zoe rather dismissively announces Phipps' demise before banging on about how brilliant Fewsham is. "[Fewsham] saved my life," she says, sniffily... well, *so did poor old Phipps* – he even seemed to have magical hiding properties! – yet he may as well not have bothered, for all the ceremony he gets post-mortem. (We can only hope that poor old Harvey has a drink waiting for Phipps in the afterlife.) Fewsham, at least, gets as brilliant a send off as you've said – the only downside is that in his final shot, wherein he defiantly tells Slaar that Earth now knows about the Warriors' plans, he looks remarkably like David Jason. If only they'd shot him by the hatch of a bar, he could have earned a fortune from clip shows that continuously featured him falling through it...

Otherwise, little bits of this episode give me enjoyment. Sir James Gregson is the first, ahem, seed sown for the pompous bureaucrats who will lock horns with the Doctor's later incarnations. I adore the Doctor's response to Radnor's assertion that nothing will destroy the fungus – "Have you tried to understand it?", he says with the disarming patience of a grown-up trying to tell an infant not to attack its pet hamster with a cricket bat. And it's either amusing or irritating (take your pick) that the Weather Control prop has only got two settings, Wet and Dry. What about more subtle variations? Couldn't they have a switch for Light Showers with a Gentle Breeze and Moments of Sunshine Later? Or even Snow? And after the rewrites that plagued The Celestial Toymaker, and script editor Terrance Dicks having to do heavy surgery on this story, is it fair to say that we can expect a Hayles storm?

April 30th

The Seeds of Death episode six

R: Patrick Troughton's departure was announced by the press during the recording of The Seeds of Death. And so there's inevitably a valedictory air to the story. It feels like a celebration of all that made Troughton so great – and the images of him here are wonderful, whether that be of him running down corridors from big lumbering monsters covered from head to foot with foam bubbles, or of his taking on an entire base under siege armed with a couple of lamps and wires draped messily over his body. The general public weren't to know, of course, that this last stand he takes against the monsters was to be his last stand against *any* monsters. But we know – and it means there's a beauty to this, to the triumphant way he closes his eyes ready for death, having so calmly told Slaar that his plans have been foiled. Against the bulk of the Ice Warriors hissing and seething at him, this little impish Doctor has never looked so vulnerable – and has never been so wily either. This is a goodbye to all that made the Troughton stories such wonderful escapism, the little anarchist standing up to the monsters. For that it's gorgeous. And also terribly sad.

I love too the way that before dying, Slaar has to learn from his commander that he's a failure. That his operation has been such a cock-up that he's destroyed the entire invasion fleet, and sent it into the sun. There's not much room for expression on an Ice Warrior's face, but Alan Bennion nevertheless manages to manoeuvre it into appalled embarrassment. In his last scene, this vicious sadist is chewed out by his boss, is made to be just another loser. He becomes a Fewsham. Poor, picked upon, Fewsham. There's a wonderful poetic justice to that – that Slaar is killed accidentally by one of his lackey's guns, the clumsy death of a fool, is just the icing on the cake.

T: Gosh, the whole "Troughton has fought his last monster" thing hadn't occurred to me.

You're right, he'll spend his last 16 episodes bereft of any such opponents. Is that some sort of record? (I think it might be.) And it's also the first time a major con is used to resolve a cliffhanger, with loads of extra footage that places Zoe behind the door the Doctor is desperately trying to get through, even though she resolutely wasn't seen there last episode. (You could find the same sort of cliffhanger-cheat on a number of those hokey old serials that they sometimes showed on BBC 2 when I was a boy – Daredevils of the Red Circle was one, King of the Rocket Men another.)

But the Ice Warriors seen here would have drawn my attention regardless of their getting the privilege of having a last go at their hated enemy – I love the way one of them nonchalantly tilts his head as the famous ricochet sound effect indicates the uselessness of the guards' guns. Slaar dies like someone has punctured him, all the air escaping from his body in one big hiss, but he's been one of the most effective talking monsters we've ever had in the series. I can't think of a better Man In A Suit performance thus far, can you? I even liked his cracked skin and pointy teeth – a crusty and alien chin augmented by sharp and malevolent dentures. And it's a nice detail that Graham Leaman, as the Grand Marshall, can speak properly because he's in the Martians' natural environment; it gives his desperate, final lament an added level of grimness, as one realises that as a result of the Doctor's tinkering, the whole population of a space fleet is going to die a horrible, inexorable death. (And it just occurred to me: between this and The Macra Terror, Leaman is making a habit of getting bumped off on a monitor.)

Troughton himself is remarkably low-key in the finale... the Doctor seems almost resigned to death, which gives a fairly straightforward confrontation some unexpected depth and gravitas. I like to think that the actor himself is a little preoccupied, getting his head around the implications of leaving this career-defining part. (I know he's more likely just a bit tired, or bored, or thinking about the shopping, but I can dream can't I?) But if nothing else, the scene with him under a desk, pulling out a whole tangle of wires and cheerfully accepting that he's going to have to sort through them, is a wonderful, definitive second Doctor moment.

The Space Pirates episode one

R: Well, I'm sure it all looked lovely.

I've been spoiled. I've just got used to the idea that I can actually *watch* Doctor Who from now on, not listen to the thing and try to imagine. And up comes The Space Pirates, the very last story not neat and complete, and with a rather foggier soundtrack to boot. I can't help but feel a bit irritated by it.

The DVD extras on the Lost in Time package suggest that the model work for this was terrific. And I'm quite sure those shots of astronauts laying detonation charges whilst doing space walks were gorgeous. The problem is... there seems to be rather a lot of them. Just like The Seeds of Death before it, The Space Pirates takes its inspiration from awed fascination with space exploration. The difference between the two is that Seeds used that fascination ironically, presenting us with characters who were disillusioned by the whole process. Whereas it's rather hard to grasp any characters at all yet in The Space Pirates. A whole slew of conflicting accents do not personalities make. That it takes 15 full minutes before the TARDIS crew show up and start chatting on the soundtrack would be dangerous enough at the best of times – but here, where there's so little to distinguish the actors between pirates and police, it feels like a particularly bad idea. There's lots of talk about Beta Dart and Minnow spaceships, so that when we finally hear the traditional wheezing 'n' groaning, there's an almost comedic contrast. And it's lovely that the first thing the Doctor and his friends get to do is run around corridors dodging laser blasts. But for all the dazzling eye candy no doubt on display, this is painfully repetitious stuff. When at the cliffhanger one of the beacons blows up, this is the *third time* we'd have been expected to watch this in 25 minutes. That the Doctor, Jamie and Zoe are in jeopardy this time around isn't enough. Two times earlier, and this might have felt involving.

T: I remember looking in the Doctor Who Programme Guide and being shocked that this universally unadored adventure (even Doctor Who – A Celebration, which only had true ire for The Gunfighters, said this moved at a snail's pace) had such an impressive cast on paper. Jack May from The Archers as General Hermack? Donald Gee from The Doctor Who Monster Book (the only non regular actor to get a thank you in the back due to a picture of him as Eckersley) as Major Ian Warne? Even It Ain't 'Alf Hot Mum's George Layton as the lowly technician Penn? Impressive! *Especially* Jack May, as I was brought up having to endure The Archers (usually in omnibus form on a Sunday) as I helped Mum in the garden or kitchen, or we were on a long car journey somewhere. The only respite to the ooh-arrs and bumpkins droning on about butter and cows was the fruity and charming presence of the roguish Nelson Gabriel, played by May. He was easily the best character in the series, and something of a radio legend. And it was always good to see him occasionally crop up elsewhere, and to hear his reassuringly witty voice in Count Duckula. He even did the eulogy for Patrick Troughton on Radio 4, as a tribute to his recently deceased old mate.

But now, here Jack May is! In all his glory! On Doctor Who!... and, well, he's rubbish. I genuinely have no idea what he's trying to do. He seems to attempt an American accent for approximately his first two minutes on screen, then wisely gives up. His delivery is determinedly odd, it truly is. It doesn't help that most of this episode is spent with him and Major Warne, the two dullest spacemen yet seen in the series. They make Captain Maitland from The Sensorites seem positively wacky.

And the script isn't doing May any favours – to get the exposition out of the way, Robert Holmes resorts to giving Hermack a turgidly lengthy amount of info-dumping to his crew, and even Hermack admits that they already know much of what he's telling them. This Robert Holmes chap showed a bit of promise in The Krotons, the shortcomings of which I went out of my way to pin on the production team. But with this story, any culpability has to be laid firmly at Holmes' doorstep. And *maybe* at Patrick Troughton's too, if complaining about his workload resulted in this sort of non-event. Gosh, I can't believe I'm saying this – everything that is wrong with this is down to my two favourite Doctor Who people of all time! It's like having the worst night of your life with the girl of your dreams...

On the plus side, the sleekness of the models is very pleasing, and Dudley Simpson's music really catches the mood, effectively using the services of a (space) opera singer. And the space pirate leader, Caven (whom I had thought was "Kay-ven" rather than "Kavvan" until I first heard the soundtrack) is effectively unpleasant, telling his men matter-of-factly to bring the captured Lieutenant Sorba if he can walk – but that if he can't, to leave him to his inevitable death. Caven is quite a clinical murderer; he's not an evil sadist, he's just a brutal, cold, money-grabber.

Hermack tells us that he's going to find Caven even if it takes the next ten years. Good God! If the story carries on like this, it's certainly going to feel like that long.

May 1st

The Space Pirates episode two

R: The space drifter Milo Clancey may be the sort of Wild West parody who says "howdy" and "tarnation" a lot, but hey – he also moans about his solar-powered toaster, and is more concerned with his breakfast than he is all that dull space protocol stuff I had to listen to yesterday. So I think he's great. Yes, Gordon Gostelow gives a larger than life performance – but by God, it's what this story needs! And it's full of little subtleties. The mock amazement at realising that young Warne is a major, the deliberate way that in being *so* impressed by the quality of Hermack's spaceship he can show how much he despises it. If there's one fault to Gostelow, it's that he makes everyone else seem even more strait-laced and tedious in contrast. Even Donald Gee! I like Donald Gee. After Chesterton, I'm automatically sympathetic to any character called Ian. Before Milo turns up, Ian Warne is the likeable one of the story – and he becomes something of a miserable prig.

What's peculiar is that, with all this barnstorming comedy going on elsewhere, Troughton is offering in contrast an unusually serious performance. You can almost hear in your head how the production team expect Troughton to play the scene where his experiments with magnetism shoot him and his friends deeper into space away from safety –

that there'd be a little burst of comic wailing, as he calls himself an idiot. He refuses to do it. He plays all his scenes clean, and with solemn intent. The result is quite brilliant. All these sequences of the Doctor, Jamie and Zoe stranded on the beacon feel increasingly like padding, but by playing the crisis so straight – his telling Zoe off for being a pessimist not comic banter at all, but beautifully underplayed – Troughton brings a real tension to an episode that would otherwise have felt flaccid. It'll never be seen as one of his stand-out moments, lying on the floor with his friends, trying to suck out the last bit of oxygen from a canister, but it's the Doctor played with a grimness that we haven't seen for a long while. If only one episode of The Space Pirates had to be in the archives, then I'm glad it's this one, just so we can see Troughton in his penultimate story still approaching the part from a fresh angle. The pained defeatism he shows as he's forced to reveal to his friends that they've no longer any chance of survival, not even wanting to look at them, his voice drained of energy, is gobsmackingly good.

T: Call me old fashioned, but I think I'd prefer it if the episode of The Space Pirates that existed had some actual space pirates in it. And that the TARDIS crew did something of note. I mean, c'mon – it takes until the end of this episode for the TARDIS crew to even *meet* another character. For the majority of new Doctor Who, that's the length of an entire story!

Fortunately, it's so much easier to pick out the positives when one can actually see what's going on. You've mentioned most of them, as they generally come from Gordon Gostelow, who injects a bit of manic energy into this hitherto straight-laced little jaunt. Clancey not only hates his solar toaster, he bungs the burnt toast on the floor behind him. (You've never been to my messy house, have you? If you had, you'd probably know why I feel that Clancey's a bit of a kindred spirit.) Why, I was even going to call my firstborn Milo (*not*, I hasten to add, because of Doctor Who – I just like the name) until The Tweenies got there first. And Clancey mends his malfunctioning light by banging a panel with a hammer – which is about the extent of my technological know-how.

Meanwhile, it's clear to everyone apart from the characters themselves that the head of Issigri Mining Corporation, Madeleine Issigri (and her metal hair-hat), is a baddie. She comes equipped with some nifty tall silver wine vessels, and an equally sleek and metallic bottle – though the illusion is hampered somewhat when she pours Hermack a drink but no liquid comes out. (Perhaps she thinks he's had enough.) Hermack himself, much as I might wish otherwise, continues to succeed in the monumental feat of being both stultifyingly boring and astronomically thick. And my ears *must* be playing tricks on me – this week, I've decided that May might be attempting a Russian accent. But at least his really odd enunciation distracts us from the terrible exposition he is forced to do again, this time telling Madeleine stuff she already knows for our benefit.

I don't know what it is about this story, Rob... this close to the finish line for the Troughton era, am I running out of steam? Or is it because I empathically feel that since the TARDIS regulars haven't properly bothered to show up for this party, I needn't either? As you pointed out, last week's episode (barring Mission to the Unknown, of course) set a record for the longest time lapse between the episode starting and the arrival of the regulars. Well, recap aside (in which all they do is tumble about for two seconds), they look like they're having another go at it, not turning up for a full seven minutes.

Let me put it this way: there's talk of a mind probe. It's a damning indictment of this story that even mention of the infamous Gallifreyan Castellan Embarrasser isn't enough to distract me from the tedium on display here.

The Space Pirates episode three

R: I'm in a bit of a quandary. Here I am, halfway through No-one's Favourite Troughton Story. And unlike you, I'm rather enjoying it. Is it possible to enjoy something for the wrong reasons?

Because I think, left to my own devices, I'd probably concur that this really isn't very good. The plotting is very slow. The characters are

very broadly drawn. And, perhaps most telling of all, three episodes in, and all the Doctor cares about is getting his TARDIS back. He doesn't give a stuff about these space pirates, so why should I?

And the truth of the matter is, I don't *care*. The whole thing is rather washing over me. But I like it, strangely enough, for that very reason. This is Doctor Who so off-kilter that I find it strangely beguiling. You've got characters like General Hermack, who are so positively stupid that they don't recognise that Madeleine Issigri is the most suspicious femme fatale since Lauren Bacall told Bogart to whistle. You can use that as a stick to beat this story with – but isn't his dense detective work part of the fun? It's not as if the adventure is trying to disguise Madeleine's guilt – so isn't Hermack just a comic character (like Duggan, say, from City of Death) played so straight by Jack May that we're inclined to take him seriously? And then, on the other hand, you've got Gordon Gostelow, turning everything into humourous bluster – but all to disguise the fact that Clancey is the most intelligent and independent character of the lot, and that there's a darker side behind his comedic patina. (In that way, he very much anticipates a lot of Robert Holmes' most interesting characters still to come.) It seems to me that the actors are playing this all against type – the comic buffoon played straight, the wily maverick played like a fool. It doesn't necessarily work. But it's rather a clever intent, isn't it?

And the scale of the thing! After the way that Hartnell's Who tried to see the whole universe as its oyster, only a fraction of Troughton's stories have set foot off Earth. (Even Pertwee, who's exiled to the bloody planet, pops around different worlds more freely than Troughton does!) And yet, here we are with a story that genuinely takes pleasure in racing around different planets – there's Lobos, there's Ta; for the first time since The Daleks' Master Plan, of all things, there's a story which wants to use a huge canvas. Okay, we can't see these places, and they were probably just a bunch of corridors, but it's as if at its last gasp, Troughton's tenure has gone from its claustrophobic template into widescreen.

Yet this is as unlike The Daleks' Master Plan as you can get. Because for all that I've just described, this isn't remotely epic – Clancey delights in being mundane, and even the pirates themselves are coolly down to earth. This is a big adventure, and yet it's not at all, it's intimate. This is a space opera, and yet it's really a self-regarding comedy. This is Doctor Who, but Doctor Who's barely in it. It's a mistake, most probably. But there's nothing else like it. Is it possible to enjoy a story for that reason, the wrong reason, that it's getting it all back to front? Does that make me a bad person, Toby?

T: Nope, it doesn't. Doubly so, because I suspect that you're taking one for the team, and are letting me off the hook so I can just declare this is rubbish before nipping out to do my shopping. But if I did that, I'd owe you a favour, and who knows what story down the road you might insist that I say something nice about, just to balance the scales.

So... what do I like about this? Well, Wendy Padbury is continuing to shine. It's a common complaint from Doctor Who girls that whatever groundbreaking roles they were promised, their characters were gradually eroded away until they were reduced to asking stupid questions and screaming. That's not a complaint Padbury could legitimately make, I think. She had the learning machines business in The Krotons, her computer-trouncing and missile-plotting The Invasion, and her total recall of the base layout in The Seeds of Death. And here, she gets to be terribly clever regarding their course and location. It's a year into her tenure, and she's still the usefully precocious genius. It's admirable.

Even Hermack gets a good stroppy moment this week, when Major Warne asks to be rescued immediately and is met with a terse "Your request is noted..." before being left where he is! And thank God for Gostelow, who seems to ad-lib half his lines (he does one about Gruyere cheese which seems to genuinely throw Troughton and Hines). He has a refreshing unpredictability which is both believable and entertaining.

And this isn't a complaint per se, but isn't it strange that, just as I previously mentioned the threadbare contribution of the TARDIS crew up to this point, the space pirates seem to have taken a sabbatical also? Having been com-

pletely absent from episode two, it looks for a while like the titular bad guys aren't going to bother to turn up this week either. If this were a Hartnell episode with its own title, they'd have called it Waiting For Caven.

May 2nd

The Space Pirates episode four

R: There's some intelligence here – I love the way the Doctor surmises that there must be an exit from the pit, but because there's fragile crockery down there. And there's some decent comedy too – the Doctor's fondness for drawing pins is rather sweet. But what appealed to me yesterday about the way the TARDIS crew are almost unaware of the main plot happening around them is now beginning to grate. When the main villain starts getting concerned about Clancey, you think, fair enough, he's a guest star. When he starts giving attention to Sorba, who's not even been in the story since episode one, you grit your teeth a bit, but put up with it. But when he *still*, two-thirds of the way through the story, hasn't taken the slightest interest in the Doctor, it speaks volumes about the way this adventure has been structured.

And I can only imagine this must have been deliberate. We know from interviews and contemporary accounts that Troughton was unhappy with the series by this stage – hey, that's why he was leaving, after all. One of the reasons was the heavy workload, and that's why the episodes of The Mind Robber all ran so short: in a story that put so much emphasis upon the regulars, Troughton threatened to go on strike unless his lines were cut. You can well imagine by this stage that the production team asked Robert Holmes to sideline the TARDIS crew a bit, just to give Troughton something of a breathing space, and that he's simply done the job too well. So now that Troughton is leaving the show, we're in that frustrating position once again of seeing a Doctor bow out whilst barely being present within his own show any more. If what was done to Hartnell was insulting, though, here it's merely a way of trying to keep Troughton appeased. It's not as if we can lay the blame for the Doctor's ineffectual appearance within the adventure squarely on Robert Holmes' inexperience – as we've seen, whatever other problems it may have had, The Krotons highlighted Troughton perfectly.

So we're in one of those situations that we don't get again in Doctor Who until the days of David Tennant, where a story is constructed to give the lead actor a minor role. And so this week, the Doctor spends the episode trying to get out of a pit. Which rather says it all.

T: Whatever weaknesses Holmes has displayed here (and as you say, it's not *his* fault if he was asked to sideline the star), he does have a grasp for making space-age names seem unusual without being naff. He doesn't give us hoary old nonsense like Yartek, Zentos and Exorse or boring run-of-the-mill monikers like Hobson or Bennett. There's an almost retro Olde Worlde aspect to his nomenclature... so we have talk of Dom Issigri, Hermack's name is Nikolai (ahh, so maybe I *wasn't* imagining the Russian accent), and a reluctant, snivelling lackey called Dervish (that's positively Dickensian). I'm not sure about Caven being called "Maurice", though. That must be up there with "Keith" and "Tim" for the Most Unthreatening Villainous Name of the Year Award.

Otherwise, this story's attempts to underline the difficulties of space flight – complete with painstaking manoeuvres and lots of time spent in transit – would be laudable were it not for the fact that it's, well, so deathly dull. If really exciting things were happening to the Doctor, or if Caven was (I dunno) torturing a teddy bear, I could probably endure Penn's lengthy navigation processes. But they're not, so I can't. Especially as this episode compounds the sin of consigning the Doctor to a boring cave by having him escape by rigging up a fatal (!) trap. Tomb nearly got away with a similar scenario because the Doctor was sealing away a potent threat to the universe. Here, he's merely attempting to wriggle out of a comparatively minor jam. I know he only kills an extra – which at present is apparently no more heinous a crime than breaking a cup – but it does make me recall the brilliant bit in Clerks were they discuss the ramifications of the rebels kill-

ing all the freelance labourers working on the Death Star.

Let me close with a couple of positive notes. I'm pleased to see that Steve Peters gives a decent turn as the speaking pirate-guard – he clearly has more talent than his ability to fill a tall monster suit, so I'm glad he was given a slightly more rewarding role. And I do like the way Caven just starts blasting at the regulars – there's no grandstanding, questions or opportunities to escape while he gloats. Just bang, bang, bang.

The Space Pirates episode five

R: It began as a space opera, then became a cowboy western. Now the story becomes, of all things, a Victorian melodrama! The scenes with the Doctor are lit by candlelight, which I can only imagine change the atmosphere of the adventure quite considerably, and contrast with the steely brightness we'd have come to expect. And against this backdrop we've got something straight out of Bronte – the madman locked away for years in his own study, his daughter thinking he was dead. It's nonsense, naturally, but so long as the *style* was right, and the guttering lighting made the study look suitably old-fashioned, then this turn of the plot might have been just odd enough to have worked. Caven starts behaving like a Victorian cad, blackmailing the beautiful heiress; in one very good scene, Dervish explains that he fell in with Caven because of "one mistake" – if this really *were* Victorian, he'd probably have got pregnant with an illegitimate child or something. (That would have been rather fun.)

The change of style is welcome. That said – last week the Doctor spent the episode trying to escape from a pit, and this time he spends a good 20 minutes escaping from a locked room. It's getting a little beyond a joke.

T: Director Michael Hart (brother of Tony, don't you know) is a bit of a mystery where Doctor Who contributors are concerned. As far as I know, Hart is one of a very few directors – in a group that includes Henric Hirsch, Mervyn Pinfield, George Spenton-Foster and John Crockett – who have never been interviewed about their work on the series. It's hard to say if this is a great loss, however, because while I can credit Hart for trying to inject a bit of pace early on in this episode (by having Simpson's galloping music playing underneath the early scenes), it's a bit incredible that he's managed to assemble such a terrific cast (on paper, at least) and then, even allowing that the material is so uninspiring, got most of them to fail at lifting it in any capacity. It's like he's gone to the RSC with the script for Crossroads, and asked them to learn it the night before the first performance.

But the crux of this episode involves everyone getting chucked into a dusty library, and finding a bedraggled old man cowering under a desk. Yes, it's Madeleine Issigri's "late" father Dom, who has been mentioned too many times to *not* turn out to be alive after all. And as it happens, he's an even more enigmatic figure in Doctor Who history than Michael Hart – because there are no pictures or telesnaps of Dom, we've no idea what Esmond Knight looked like in the role, no clue as to the state of his hair, beard and wardrobe. Which is something of a shame, as he was a close collaborator of Olivier in his Shakespeare films, and so by extension was one of the most illustrious actors the series had nabbed to this point. I remember Donald Gee telling me how thrilled he was to work alongside Knight, who had been a childhood hero of his. And yet, nobody at BBC Pictures could be bothered to nip down and grab a shot of him.

I also know that Knight lost most of his eyesight during the war – not from any Who related research, but because my Mum told me. We were at the Grand Theatre Wolverhampton to watch Colin Baker and Jack Watling in Corpse, and Knight was included in some big pictures of stars from past performances. Mum told me about Knight's ocular deficiency – and it's funny that she knew that, because while she's no philistine, she's not a habitual theatregoer either. She's also the one who told me that Dudley Foster (who plays Caven) had tragically committed suicide; I think she's just from that generation who knew stuff, even if it wasn't necessarily in their field. And if it enriches my Doctor Who knowledge, so much the better!

May 3rd

The Space Pirates episode six

R: And sometimes a story just ends. In this instance, with the forced laughter of a Scooby Doo climax. That's its job. Fair enough.

No, the remarkable thing about this episode is that it's the final missing episode. Hurrah! From now on, every bit of Who I watch will come lovingly pristine from the archives, with moving pictures and stuff. The dialogue will actually issue from actors' mouths. I can't tell you what a relief that'll be. If not on my eyes, then on my *mind*. There were times during this project that I had to concentrate so hard on what was going on, I thought my brain would snap.

But the even more remarkable thing? Really? Is that this episode exists in any format at all. Because, let's face it, what are the odds?

When I became a fan in the early 1980s, weaned on Jean-Marc Lofficier's Programme Guides, and learning by rote not only all the story titles in order but even their bloody production codes, it took a while for it to dawn on me that a huge number of these episodes were no longer stored in the BBC archives. They all sounded so magical – my God, didn't The Underwater Menace sound like fun! – that it seemed almost criminal that they'd been wiped. It upset me hugely. And as my Who obsession grew, I remember lying in bed one night, with the pull-out posters from Doctor Who Monthly staring down at me, and praying to God. "Please restore all the missing episodes to the archives," I said to God. And, realising even at that age you don't get something for nothing, I added, "And in return, you can take years off my life."

That's honestly true. That's how much I cared.

It didn't work immediately, and that was okay, and I didn't blame God necessarily – he hadn't protected me from the bullies on the school coach either, or removed my acne. And it occurred to me some time later that God may not operate at quite the same speed as I might have wished. That just because, by the end of that week, all the Troughton stories weren't safely back in storage didn't mean that

God might not get round to honouring the deal later. After all, he's dealing with a lot of prayers – probably – and I can hardly expect him to answer them all at once. As the years went by, as we passed through the Colin Baker years, then the Sylvester McCoys, I began to regret the offer I'd made. At the age of 13, in the anticipatory mania for The Five Doctors, giving up a portion of my life in return for The Space Pirates seemed right and proper; at the age of 19, watching the final season of Doctor Who in the university common room and squirming with embarrassment as fellow students laughed at it, it didn't feel such a fair swap. In 1992, all the episodes of The Tomb of the Cybermen, at the time the most keenly desired story a fan could wish for, were found in immaculate condition in Hong Kong, and I genuinely began to fear that this might be the start of a trend. Maybe next week God would give us back The Web of Fear. By the end of the month, The Evil of the Daleks and episode four of The Tenth Planet. And by the end of the summer, as he finally plugged the last hole with The Feast of Steven, and William Hartnell wishing all us viewers a merry Christmas, he'd put me straight under a truck.

It didn't happen, of course. There are still 108 episodes missing from the BBC archives. My life is safe. (So far.)

As a fan I've spent an undue amount of my life mourning what's been lost. And not marvelling at what we have. Because it's extraordinary – we've well over *half* of the black and white episodes of Doctor Who, complete and in good condition. (And all the Pertwees too. Just because at that point we entered the colour age of television, it doesn't mean we necessarily moved out of some strange brutal philistine time where everything creative got deleted after broadcast – it's curious how lucky we are that it's only the monochrome portion of the programme that has gaps in.) But what's more remarkable still is that for most of these missing episodes, we have telesnaps. My God, we actually have visual evidence of most of the Troughton era, where some chap called John Cura was actually *paid* to keep photographing his TV set broadcasting Who every few seconds, as if somehow he twigged just how much an anal-retentive fandom, 40 years later, would need to know the exact facial expres-

sion that Jamaica would pull when killed by Captain Pike in The Smugglers. And, no, even more incredible: the fact that we have complete audio soundtracks for every single one of these missing episodes too. Not a single one is absent. *Not a single one.* (And my 13-year-old self would boggle at this – you can actually walk down to your local record emporium and *buy* each and every one of these lost stories on crystal clear compact disc. Fans these days don't know how lucky they are.)

So I've moaned a few times in this diary about having to find my way through episodes that don't exist as they were meant to be seen. Listening to soundtracks, following online transcripts, watching the reconstructions. But it must be said now, before we move on forever, that the reason that I'm able to enjoy them in any form whatsoever is down to the efforts of a few fans. As early as 1964, a mere 14 weeks into the run, there were already those as dedicated to preserving Doctor Who as I would be in my bedroom, 20 years later – and doing something rather more practical about it than praying to God.

It's worth repeating, and worth reminding ourselves about over again. Doctor Who fans are extraordinarily lucky. We have each and every episode of the series to enjoy again, even if in a compromised form. When sense would suggest that our tally of episodes should be riddled with holes well into Tom Baker's tenure, and that a substantial part of the 1960s offerings should be completely without shape or form. Here we are, Toby and I, and we're going through all the 700-plus instalments of Doctor Who in order. And we *can*. It's amazing.

... And, yeah, this essay is here in part because I can't be bothered to talk about Milo Clancey any more. So sue me.

T: Just a minute... does that mean that *I* have to talk about Milo Clancey? Dammit, you've played the Missing Episodes Joker when I had planned to! Suffice to say, if God knocks on my door with "the three Ms" (Marco Polo, Myth Makers and Massacre), and guiltily says he won't give them back because of some deal with you that he feels is a bit of a high price to pay for some archival ephemera... well, I'm afraid I'll have to snatch them off him, and just see you in the next life, matey.

But, all right, I'll write about the episode in question. History tells us that the regulars only appeared in pre-filmed sequences in episode six, as they were off fulfilling their massive obligations to the next story, so I'd expected their participation would be minimal. To my pleasant surprise, though, they feature heavily in this last instalment, and interact with many of the guest characters. And I can credit Dudley Foster for doing what he can with Caven, switching from no-nonsense, clinical villainy to snarling anger in a successfully brutal way. It's brilliant (and pretty hardcore) that he'd rather blow himself up and kill his opponents than be taken alive.

Two other characters, however, fail to live up to their potential. There's Dervish, who showed signs of breaking out and having some impact on the drama, but ends up as a Private Pike to Caven's Mainwaring – he snivels away, complains, and is told to shut up and do as he's told. Worse, poor old Esmond Knight, as Dom Issigri, spends the whole episode collapsing and being disorientated. Has an illustrious guest actor *ever* been so shabbily used by the series?

Oh, what's the use? I can't even pretend to muster any enthusiasm for this story. Do you know, it is my son's ninth birthday today – I thought *that* would make me feel old, and it might have done, had I not already been watching The Space Pirates. I feel like I've aged decades watching this... just look at how the V-Ship hurtles towards the climax by telling us it'll be there in 55 minutes, which makes The Invasion's 12 seem like the click of a finger. And *every* process that *everyone* engages in is complicated – the landing procedure for the V-Ship is slow, laborious and complicated; a lock is complicated; and there are complicated explosives which will be complicated to diffuse. Here in episode six, all these manoeuvres serve to slow everything down, as if Robert Holmes is wilfully refusing to be dramatic. He might as well have been more explicit about it, and just started the countdown at T-minus three and a half months.

But no, wait, I can be upbeat in one regard, even though you've somewhat paved this ground. The Space Pirates episode six is the final missing episode, which means that things will be very different from now on, because obviously I am – as with everyone reading this, I presume – more familiar with the stuff that exists on video. Sure, I've listened to the soundtracks of some absent stories many times, but usually while I've been pottering about doing other stuff, and not with the concentration that I've had this time around. That means that, whatever my reservations about a particular story, I've unearthed a few little nuggets that were surprising or mysterious or beguiling. The fact that so much is missing from this era, while deeply regrettable, does give it a magic that will be difficult to recapture with the more familiar and available. And let's face it: even if an episode as mundane as this one turned up, it would be *so* exciting! We'd discover what Dom Issigri looks like, how the other rooms and caves are designed, what sort of physical presence Dudley Foster brings to Caven, and so much more.

We can all lament at how much is missing from the archives, it's true. But there are times when the absence of video makes even the *potential* of something like The Space Pirates seem so much more alluring! You can bet that I'd be the first in line, cash in hand, if ever it was recovered and released on those shiny disc things – what a wonderfully joyful and giddy time that would be.

The War Games episode one

R: And to think – the Doctor and his companions begin the episode laughing. The very first spoken line is of disgust, the music is immediately doomy, the opening landscape of mud and puddles as immediately depressing as it sounds. And yet the regular cast, almost against the grain of the script, emerge from the TARDIS as happy as we've ever heard them. They've no idea what's in store for them. Nor has the viewer.

Because at first this feels very much like a return to the historical adventure. About eight minutes in, we're given our first anachronism – but it's subtly done, and we're left in doubt whether or not we're understanding what we're looking at. General Smythe opens a cabinet behind a picture and we see a little video screen. But we don't yet *know* it's a video screen; no-one's face appears on it; it all looks so decidedly lo-tech that it could just be the lens of an Edwardian camera. Smythe refers to the 1917 zone, and that of course sounds off-kilter – but we're given no further explanation of why he seems to be historicising the present, and it *could* at a pinch just be very awkward exposition. When Zoe asks the Doctor whether they're on Earth, the script (very cleverly) only says that they would *appear* to be – and the irony is that this very bogus World War I setting looks as credible a historical backdrop as we've seen Doctor Who do for years.

Film the Great War nowadays, and we'd be given sequences of soldiers being gunned down by machine gun fire in the trenches. (David Maloney will get his chance to do this, of course, and the imagery will be pure 1917 – but the action will be on Skaro, and by then Tom Baker will be the Doctor.) Instead, what we get to sum up the brutality is barbed wire and bureaucracy. The speed with which the Doctor and his friends are found, imprisoned, then sentenced, is almost surreal, and very dizzying – but that's precisely the idea. We're not seeing the ordinary Tommy killed without thought on the front line; he's being symbolised by what happens to our heroes, caught up in a piece of madness they can't reason their way out of, and then led off to execution. All of Troughton's wit and cleverness can't do a thing to stop it. The moment when he kisses Wendy Padbury goodbye has a despairing finality about it that is beautifully done – and very frightening, because we've never seen the Doctor so easily defeated. That final scene, in which he stands before the firing squad, and sighs with unhappy acceptance of his fate, is extraordinary. This is what the Great War did. It made death abrupt and commonplace.

What's horrifying is that the soldiers who sentence the Doctor do so very amiably. After Smythe appears, they all seem tragically human in comparison. The sergeant major who looks on sympathetically as he marches the trio to interrogation; the major who tries to comfort Zoe by chucking her under the chin as her best friend is led off to die. They aren't monsters. That's what's so terrifying. They're ordinary, even kindly people, who've got so used to institutionalised murder that in response to our regulars' cries for justice, they just exchange glances in bemusement. It's almost cruel, the way that the story gives the viewer hope this might be like an ordinary Doctor Who adventure – Zoe finds the key for the Doctor's cell, and goes to rescue him. (And after all the locking up and escaping we've just seen in The Space Pirates, this almost looks like a deliberate comment upon the series' clichés.) It's to no avail. He's taken outside and shot forthwith... or so it appears, in one of the most honestly shocking cliffhangers the series has ever done. It really doesn't matter that the way out of it will be a mite contrived. On its own terms, this episode appears to have taken children's hero Doctor Who out of his fantasy, stuck him in a very real and very grimy war, and, with undue haste and with awful credibility, killed him. If next week The War Games becomes a weird sci-fi adventure with ray guns and monsters, that's okay – this week, standing alone, it's played the Great War straight, and in the process has been one of the most remarkable episodes we've yet seen.

T: I'd like, if I may, to focus on the flipside of the casualness to murder that you've been writing about. There's an extraordinary (but quick) moment here when Major Barrington gets news over the phone that his men are to charge over the top of the trench in the morning – right into the waiting German guns, presumably – and notes the order with grim acceptance before he puts on a brave face to Carstairs, and cheerily informs him about tomorrow's big push. Then later on, after a kangaroo court has sentenced the Doctor to death, Barrington stoically gives Zoe some words of encouragement before returning to his command post...

... and we never see him again. Chances are, having told Zoe to keep her chin up, Barrington will have to be doing the same in a few hours. The Doctor's not the only one who's been sent to his death at dawn.

This isn't a production that shirks away from the horrors of the time – as is highlighted in the Doctor's lines, and the swift brutality of our heroes' condemnation – but what comes across even more strongly is everyone's ability to keep their basic decency in the midst of bloody madness. Yes, Rob, it's right and proper of you to point out the disconnect between the military personnel acting warm and personable while being callous where murder is concerned, which only goes to emphasise the sheer horror of war and what it makes people do. Apart from the gruesome, leering General Smythe (Noel Coleman has an air of superior military bearing, whilst being terrifyingly repugnant at the same time – he's terrific), everyone here is inherently a good egg. Lady Jennifer offers to look after Zoe rather than subject her to a night in the cells, and the barking sergeant-major offers the condemned Doctor some food. Even the northern sergeant who chastises the Doctor's party in the trenches issues a courteous, "You too M'am, if you don't mind..." to Zoe as needed. War will *always* be hell, and sometimes, the best that those involved can do is guarantee that chivalry and compassion have a place there also.

As this is Doctor Who's first venture into one of the two World Wars, it's perhaps not surprising that the morality on display here is trickier than on other occasions, when there are Daleks or Cybermen that need killing. In fact, so far, The War Games is notable because there isn't really much action either – the sequence of events that ultimately put the Doctor in front of a firing squad isn't an exercise in dodging bullets so much as it's about the TARDIS crew finding themselves (as was the case for a lot of real-life people in wartime, I'm sure) in a degenerating situation that they can't control. Moreover, it's a condemnation of the depressing reliance on military protocol – as if doing everything "properly" somehow excuses the destruction and butchery that abound – as is emphasised during the sham trial when the Doctor, Jamie and Zoe are made to march less than ten feet away, wait a couple of minutes, then turn around and march back. It illustrates a lunatic adherence to procedure, even when justice has just gone out the window.

I can't quite believe that I'm saying this, but after The Space Pirates, we've been thrust into an episode which is damn-near perfect. The script gives us jeopardy, character and mystery, and rollocks along from one interesting set-piece to another. The realisation of the period and ad-hoc dwelling places is effectively rendered in Roger Cheveley's excellent design

work, and even the grainy location photography is stark and terribly atmospheric. If this is Doctor Who's last black-and-white adventure, it should be celebrated as such – there's a certain breed of fan who thinks that the 60s stories would improve if they were colourised, but The War Games, and the grim period of history that it depicts, is manifestly at home in all its black and white majesty.

May 4th

The War Games episode two

R: A round of applause for Hubert Rees. His performance as the amiable Captain Ransom is an absolute joy – a pipe-smoking pencil pusher whose method of chatting up an attractive woman is to tell her all about his admin duties. The look of relieved delight whenever General Smythe hypnotises away any of his doubts is like a puppy dog being given a bone; here is a man who doesn't want to think for himself, and takes comfort in following orders. And that's what makes Ransom such a terrific comic character, but so sad and dangerous a figure as well – he's the exact epitome of conformity, of the plucky Tommy who'll die for his country without question. He's Hugh Laurie from Blackadder. The awful tragedy of it is that when he dies, it won't be for his country at all – it won't even be for his planet. This is a man who'll only moan about the cost of the Great War in terms of the number of shovels he has lost – he won't (or can't) bring himself to think about the loss of human life. Thoroughly likeable, and thoroughly dismaying, Rees gives the most interesting comic performance in the series since Barrie Ingham came over all Wodehouse back in The Myth Makers.

There's so much to enjoy here. The way that Jamie the Highlander is able to form a brief friendship with the Redcoat soldier is really rather touching – the two enemies coming together because they have more in common with each other than anyone else they could meet. That the Redcoat is so abruptly shot (albeit in the leg) takes the fantasy that two foes can find peace so easily and gives it a harsh twist – the reality of the war we see here is a lot grimmer than that. And I love the way that Troughton has the audacity to infiltrate the prison so bombastically and bully the staff. When he says that he is the examiner, his lie throws us right back to his very first story – and reminds us that this is what the second Doctor *used* to be like, the sly chameleon who'll take on any persona at will. In barking orders at the military and making them run around in small circles for him, it's as if, in his final adventure, Troughton is getting the chance to revisit the glory moments that established him. I'm just grateful he doesn't start admiring everybody's hats.

And for a truly magical moment – how about that sequence where the ambulance suddenly fades into thin air? At this stage we've no idea what that can mean. When it reappears before a set of Roman soldiers, it's as if Doctor Who has abandoned its police box, and replaced it with a time-travelling ambulance. It's as bizarre an image as – say – a London bus in a desert, and I think it's quite wonderful.

T: Troughton's turn as the barking prison-inspector while he and Zoe try to rescue Jamie is brilliant – just look at how he bristles with indignation and gets testy at the impertinence of someone having the audacity to query him. It's an act of desperation, of course – blustering chutzpah to cover the most fragile of disguises. Troughton emphasises this with a tremor in his voice that flits between quivering rage and desperate improvisation, and the way he storms about frustrating Richard Steele's delightfully stuffy Commandant is a joy. Steele first makes us laugh at him for being such a pompous twit, but ultimately engenders our grudging admiration as he snaps and refuses to be brow-beaten any further (even if this threatens to undo the Doctor's plan!). And then Zoe hits him over the head with a vase. You could argue that much of this is filler, but it's filler of the highest order. (Is it just me, though, or does Steele remind you of Richard Mathews' turn as Rassilon in The Five Doctors? Listen to his line about the inspector having to wait while he has his tea – the delivery is identical.)

So far, this has been a pretty sumptuous production, with plenty of location filming and impressive-looking sets. There's attention to visual detail – they've gone to the trouble of including broken glass in the windows of the

chateau. And let me add that Pat Gorman – one of the unsung stalwarts of Doctor Who, a perennial extra who was stuffed into all manner of monster outfits – finally gets a line, and a credit, and we actually see his face and everything! He sometimes gets one of those, but he's not yet had all three at once. It's all justly deserved, as he's logged so many hours with Doctor Who but so rarely gets any notice.

And let me not only echo your praise for Hubert Rees, but also use him to echo some of the points I made about episode one. Smythe orders the "creeping barrage" (two words that Coleman positively devours), and it's Ransom who reminds him that his target is, in fact, an ambulance with two women on board. Even in war, there are rules. In the mouth of madness, we still create a structure, a moral framework, which under actual scrutiny makes no real sense. That's the madness of human conflict – we allow ourselves to commit the foulest of crimes so long as we follow protocol, and obey the rules. War *games* indeed.

The War Games episode three

R: You could argue, I suppose, that the bit with the Doctor being interrogated by the German lieutenant as a spy is a bit repetitive. But of course it is. That's the nature of this war game – that for all their different accents, the soldiers on the front line are exactly the same stooges as each other, and will respond to the same events accordingly. The joke of it is made all the clearer when Smythe's counterpart, Captain von Weich, turns up and takes his lieutenant outside for a spot of hypnotism. Very rarely for the series, the whole sequence plays out in German, without subtitles – and we know *exactly* what's being said, the way that the naïve young soldier is being turned back into a simple automaton, because we've heard it so often already. The fact that David Garfield wears a monocle, rather than Noel Coleman's pebble glasses, feels like rather a witty difference – as if he's chosen another form of eyewear simply so he can show off his natty scar.

The best of this episode plays as a black comedy. We pass into three different time zones in 25 minutes, and all we get is the same pointless conflicts – it's hard not to get blasé about them. And just as we begin to relax a little too much, and watch Lieutenant Carstairs gun down nineteenth-century Americans with impunity, we're pulled up short by that *brilliant* scene where Smythe and Von Weich so callously discuss future battle plans as if they're playing chess. The more death and war we see, the more we behave like them – indeed, most of the episode plays upon the excitement of driving through a whole series of zones in which people massacre each other as if they were nothing more than pit stops. It's why the moment when Lady Jennifer realises that Carstairs has sacrificed himself (or so she thinks) to allow the ambulance to escape has such quiet power. There's no outcry, no grief – just a look down and a mumbled "Oh dear", the ultimate repression of emotion. That's what you do in times of war. That's how you get through – it's the "proper" way to behave.

T: The War Games is an infamously long story, it hasn't yet – for my money – shown signs of treading water. The script keeps feeding us tantalising clues with enough regularity to keep us interested, and it hasn't needed to reveal the answers quite yet. And it helps that we're benefitting from the presence of some great characters – Jennifer and Carstairs are delightful, wonderfully played allies, and there's an unflappable bravery to Carstairs as he stays put and tells her to drive on. It clearly demonstrates the duality of war; we get to simultaneously witness the best and worst of mankind.

David Maloney orchestrates the action like a maestro, using simple but very effective tricks to suggest that a vast number of troops are present. His film work is impressively staged (even if one of the Roman soldiers looks rather comical as he stares at where the lorry once was, his mouth wide open in shock), and his approach to that excellent scene between von Weich and Smythe is inspired, as he films them from underneath a table mapping out the battlefield.

Troughton is clearly giving his all to this – he obviously relishes the idea of blowing up the safe, and grabs one of the braids on Jamie's sporran – much to the surprise of his co-star! – when looking for a fuse. Let me also give a quick nod to Gregg Palmer, who gives a sweet little cameo as a German lieutenant, even if he's

a harbinger of doom for our leading men. (The only other occasion he popped up in Doctor Who was in The Tenth Planet, and you know what that meant for Hartnell!) And hooray for Lt Crane, the jolly toff – amidst all the fear and jeopardy, he's an opponent who impedes our heroes because of his polite, chummy desire to have a chat!

May 5th

The War Games episode four

R: Those funny little cardboard visors that all the alien students wear, with little black crosses for the eyeholes, ought to look rubbish. But actually when Troughton and Padbury put them on, it does somehow manage to dehumanise them. And I know Toby probably thinks I'm pretentious about such things, but I think it's honestly because they *are* a bit rubbish. It's like the strange swirly lined Batman sets, or the guards dressed in PVC – in any other story, if this were the alien world we were being presented, it'd be laughable. But it works here precisely because it provides such a contrast with the realism of the World War I set, or the striking normality of the barn in the American Civil War zone. It's as if from scene to scene we're jumping back and forth between period drama and cod sci-fi – and the effect is genuinely disconcerting. I love this strange alien world, of sudden hysterical alarms and background warbling mood sound, of overbright lighting and white walls. It feels artificial. And yet it's the reality of the story – whereas all that *looks* sturdy and designed to the nth degree, all the historical settings we visit are as fake as a three-pound note. It does clever things to our perception of the story, that, and what we regard as real and what we regard as fantasy – and over this long story it subtly destabilises what we're used to seeing around us, so that when co-writers Terrance Dicks and Malcolm Hulke drop their *big* surprises about the Doctor's background, we're in a mood receptive to accept it.

And talking of big surprises – we don't know yet what the importance of the War Chief could be, but the sequence where Edward Brayshaw and Patrick Troughton first see each other across a crowded room, and (my God!) *recognise* each other, makes me shiver. There's that one moment of horrified realisation (in which they're clearly *both* panicked by the encounter), there's that little pause – and then the alarms sound, the Doctor flees, the War Chief loses his composure for the first time, and all Hell breaks loose. You know that this is something big, and it's achieved in the subtlest of ways – purely through the right use of silence and noise, and through eye contact. It's brilliant.

So's the cliffhanger. David Savile has played a very likeable Carstairs. And so when he holds Zoe at gunpoint and begins talking so gently – dreamily as if he's stoned, even – that he's going to kill her, it's quite unnerving. (He doesn't do it half so well when they film the same moment as the reprise for next week – but that's because by that point, the script requires him to obsessed and vengeful, not as here the creepy man who has lost all his personality.)

T: I agree with you 100% on this – the alien set designs and costumes need to be outlandish (complete with groovy sets, bonkers specs and funky beards) to contrast the dirty, realistic and unflashy Earth conflicts. No other Doctor Who story looks like this – but then, no other story could get away with it.

Meanwhile, this adventure is one of the most consistently well-cast stories we've had yet. Edward Brayshaw has now come to the forefront as the War Chief, and he has such poise and elegance, coupled with an underlying glacial darkness. He looks *magnificent*, striding about as he does like a tall homosexual lion with his impressive mane, massive medallion and penchant for eye shadow. Such a performance would be too big for mundane hospital dramas, but it's pitched perfectly for slightly heightened sci-fi; it's impressive and Shakespearean, and not remotely silly. And the moment where he and the Doctor see each other really *is* a momentous occasion. We're used to seeing the Doctor arriving and *becoming* someone's nuisance or a nemesis, but here, he's faced with someone who is immediately afeared, shocked and desperate just from clapping eyes on him. With a jolt, we're reminded that the Doctor has a *past*.

Vernon Dobtcheff is also superb as the unnamed Scientist. Actually, Dobtcheff is something of a legend amongst the acting profession – he makes it his business to attend every single major opening night, and if he can't, he sends cards. He features marvellously in Rupert Everett's autobiography, and pops up all over the world to such an extent – seemingly conspiring to enter different actors' lives on different continents at the same time – that there's a jokey rumour that there are a vast number of Vernon Dobtcheffs. Sadly, I don't think he's on the forthcoming DVD of The War Games; it's a missed opportunity to talk with such a celebrated figure. (That said, he's never been out of work since his stint on Doctor Who, and might remember nothing about it.)

And beyond the casting concerns, the *scale* of this story continues to be impressive – no fewer than three factions encounter Jamie and Jennifer in the barn – and the developments keep us guessing. I'd like to tip my hat to the fact that it's the black character who is impossible to hypnotise, and displays bravery and defiance, and to say what a shock it is when von Weich turns up with a different accent but equal malevolence. And to cap it all off, we get that brilliant but disturbing shot of the frozen, upright soldiers awaiting deployment from inside the SIDRAT. They're erect cadavers, grotesque parodies of humanity waiting to be reactivated, then sent to kill or die. It's a gruesome image – intriguing, alien and unsettling – and it encapsulates this entire story in one shot.

The War Games episode five

R: What I love about The War Games is that it brings out so many really terrific performances. I'd argue that the Troughton stories as a whole have traded largely in stereotypes, and there have been fewer opportunities for guest stars to do as much with the parts as we saw in the days of Hartnell. But The War Games is making up for it. And what makes this story so wonderful is that the scope of the parts is large enough to encompass completely different styles of acting. You're right; Vernon Dobtcheff's Scientist is great – and hilarious, precisely because he's so downplayed. The scene where he allows Troughton to run rings around him as he experiments with his mind-wiping machine is brilliant, never quite sure whether to be irritated or impressed by this strangely-clothed student who's so much cleverer than him. Whereas James Bree's Security Chief is so very stylised, walking as if the movement of limbs is a concept he's not used to and takes no pleasure in, his every word clearly enunciated but just flat enough to feel inhuman. With Edward Brayshaw going the whole hog as a rather cavalier villain, displaying his golden medallion out to all and sundry, this collision of styles ought to be a complete mess. But for The War Games it works wonderfully, because the story is all *about* a collision of styles.

It's why there's such pleasure to be taken in those scenes where the rebels are together, this ragbag of different accents and different costumes. They all look as if they're from different adventures, all coming together incongruously in the BBC canteen. (I'm very sorry that Rudolph Walker bites the bullet so early, though – he gives one of the richest of the performances as Harper, one of the resistance members, and I'd have liked to have seen more of him.)

And that's it for Lady Jennifer, she's gone! As a companion in the making she's worked rather well, and Jane Sherwin has turned a woman who could so easily have been a prim and starchy aristocrat with a plum in her mouth into someone charming. (If you're going to cast the producer's wife in Doctor Who, better to go with Derrick's than Peter Bryant's, I think.) It's odd that she tells Jamie to pass on her best wishes to Carstairs, though, when she's every reason to believe he must be dead, and certainly no cause to expect him to be inside an alien base. It's one of those little instances where the writers presume the characters know the same thing they do, and clumsy as it is, it's an illustration of the enormous speed at which this epic story was composed.

T: I worried when we started this project that I'd bang on about the actors too much – because that's my field and one of my main interests – and although I'd like to think that I've restrained myself generally, here, on this final adventure, I haven't been able to stop. But can you blame me? There's so much to talk

about! You're right that it's a shame about Rudolph Walker and Jane Sherwin – they both did a terrific job, and made an impact even amongst this vast and flashy cast. But stepping up to bat is Graham Weston, who gets a great entrance as Russell – the man whose no-nonsense pragmatism is necessary to hold the ragtag resistance together. It's good that they don't shirk from the difficulties of bonding such disparate fellows together.

But I have to ask – what the bloody hell is James Bree doing? I remember reading an interview with Catherine Tate where she admitted that she thought the Daleks were the Doctor's *only* nemeses, and appeared in all the adventures. It's a reasonable enough supposition, but only if you've paid precious little attention to the programme. I bring this up because one suspects that Bree thought that too – did his agent tell him he'd be playing a lead villain on Doctor Who, and he presumed that he had to act like a Dalek? (His interrogator's headgear, at least, is a bit Dalek-like; otherwise, he's in entirely the wrong costume.) I wouldn't so much mind, except that he's acting in a manner completely at odds with everybody else around him. Oh, all right – I'm not convinced he's got the right approach, but I'll give him a bit of time and see if my opinion of it improves.

Watch. This. Spaaaaaaaace.

May 6th

The War Games episode six

R: It must be nice to have an influential Dad. Here's David Troughton in his TV debut playing Private Moor – in a little tale which allows him to be scared, angry, a bit heroic and to have a rather good fight scene. And it's a measure of how much *space* this ten-episode tale affords us; usually, if someone was to be given something for his first showreel, they'd be given a scene with a few lines in it, but the midway point of this long adventure allows Troughton's storyline to be stretched right across the episode. And perhaps it shouldn't work, perhaps it ought to look a bit tokenistic. But it's brilliant. Partly because it at last allows room for a small character, a young soldier of no great consequence, to have the focus placed upon him for a change – and by giving him his moment, the writers allow every him to represent every other frightened Tommy who's been exploited and become a victim of power politics he can't even begin to understand. The War Games is all the richer because for all its epic ambitions, it still has the room to remind us that it's a story about lots of ordinary people being treated callously. And it's brilliant too, because David Troughton is extremely good. There's an RSC star in the making here.

David Maloney gets his first chance to get actors into gas masks – a recurring trope in so many of the Doctor Who stories he'll direct over the next few years. And Wendy Padbury looks impossibly cute, flapping about in a great coat far too big for her, with a big hat perched upon her head!

But for contemporary fans, this episode has particular significance because it's the first time the phrase "Time Lord" is mentioned. It's without fanfare, without emphasis, and it just passes by the once in conversation. It will have meant nothing at the time to the 1969 audience, but it changes Doctor Who forever. Did it give you a shiver, Toby?

T: Yes, indeed... especially as it's the legendary Vernon Dobtcheff who gets to say such a legendary line! So, we now know that the Time Lords (the War Chief's people, and presumably the Doctor's also) have mastered dimensionary transcendentalism and time travel, and that – if the controls used by the baddies are anything to go by – they're able to manipulate such powerful accomplishments using fridge-magnet technology. But what's most interesting about this is how, in context, the term "Time Lords" *almost* sounds like it's nothing more than the peculiar vernacular to this particular tale. The aliens' ranks, after all, include a Security Chief, a War Chief and a War Lord, so the jump to "Time Lord" is actually pretty straightforward, and less impactful as a result. Well, less impactful at the time – for the likes of someone like me, it's hugely significant. I can't quite believe that we've entered the fifth month of this project, and it's the first time we've heard the term!

Whilst this adventure is still very good, the edges are fraying a bit. The Doctor tries to get

the mind-processing machine, is forced to leave it, sends Zoe away at the landing bay, and then goes all the way back for the device. This, in turn, facilitates a pretty grotty fight between Jamie, Carstairs and a couple of guards (whose method of attack is chucking themselves about in anticipation of as-yet unthrown punches that fail to make contact). And the Security Chief's assertion that the Doctor could only have escaped from a room with the help of a space/time machine is so ludicrous, it's comical. I know the War Chief points this out, but giving this staccato lunatic, who is prone to jumping to illogical conclusions, such an important position seriously undermines the aliens' credibility. (And they are running a deficit of it at present – after all, these are the same people who take Russell prisoner, but leave him with his gun and ammo.)

Still, these are minor quibbles for the most part. The writers have sensibly kept the adventure fresh and trotting along by adding new characters while taking others away. So we lose the creepy, weasally von Weich (it's a splendid turn from David Garfield), while Russell starts to become a heroic figure. The former's demise in the novelisation is rubbish, and he thankfully gets a better send-off on screen, as he impotently tries to raise his gun, in a final attempt to shoot his prey, before expiring. Talking of which, did you see how Carstairs rather gruesomely shot a guard, in the face, at point-blank range? And he's one of the good guys!

The best bit, however, is when Zoe asks the Doctor how he's so quickly acquired the knowledge required to use the War Chief's technology. He hurriedly brushes her off, with Troughton wonderfully conveying that this involves a terrible secret that he can't bear to tell even his loyal companion. It's very ominous. By the pricking of my thumbs...

The War Games episode seven

R: Two particular moments stand out for me. The one is the ingenious way that the Doctor uses his handkerchief as a white flag of truce – he comes out coughing on his knees from the SIDRAT groaning for all he's worth, and it feels like a typical bit of Troughton comedy shtick. And then he surprises us; he's going to use that flag as something to cover his nose when he gasses the entire room and makes his escape. It's very clever, and turns the scene entirely on its head. No wonder the War Chief is impressed.

And the other is such a simple facial reaction from Wendy Padbury, looking on in honest disgust as her own friends club down a couple of soldiers in the trenches. It's so easy in a story of this length, with so many hapless people being killed, to become desensitised to it – and that is, in part, exactly what this story is about, how decent ordinary people can grow so used to war that it's allowed to become something banal. Padbury's reaction pulls us up short at just the right moment in the story, as the music becomes ever jauntier, in an episode where a terrific number of ordinary men just doing their duty get gunned down by the Doctor's friends.

But it's Philip Madoc who stands out here as the War Lord. He's short and unassuming, and wears thick pebble glasses – he looks like an accountant, a grown up version of the kid who'd be ignored at school. And yet he commands instant respect. He quietly dresses down both the Security Chief and the War Chief, telling them to cooperate or be replaced, and you know immediately that this is a man of such power that he can conquer worlds without ever needing to raise his voice. When he comes up with a plan to defeat the rebels, having at last grown tired of the incompetence of his apprentices, it feels like Sir Alan Sugar has decided to step in and solve the week's task. You know he'll get his way. And within minutes, he's managed what no-one else has been able to do for weeks – he captures the Doctor. It's a rare cliffhanger, not of immediate jeopardy, but of despair; the look on Jamie and Zoe's faces says it all.

Only three episodes of Troughton to go. What do you say, we go hell for leather tomorrow, and finish off The War Games in one sitting? I think we owe it to the man.

T: Sure, I can happily do three episodes of Troughton. It's tidier for me too, as I fly to New Zealand the day after tomorrow. It'd feel wrong, somehow, saying goodbye to Troughton at an airport (I don't want to give him the same treatment that Ben and Polly got). So yes, I'm

sold – extra Doctor Who tomorrow! (Why not, as it's more pleasant than the 300 *other* things I need to sort out before I go!)

And hooray... there's brilliant, wonderful Philip Madoc. And such is his severe haircut and fabulously short, prickly beard, he doesn't even *look* like the same bloke from The Krotons, does he? Madoc has a great line in flickering, playful smiles that suggest a confident, quiet menace, and he provides a much-needed, fierce intelligence which thankfully gets between the increasingly interminable bickering of his two subordinates. Faced with the daunting task of writing a ten-part story, Dicks and Hulke have kept matters moving along by yet again escalating the level of villainy. And we're reminded of how far we've come when some unfinished business with the story's first evil protagonist, General Smythe, is addressed. The Doctor is pleasingly stroppy with him (and, to my delight, says "courts martial"), and eventually all the poise and authority Smythe displayed in previous episodes is stripped away, and he's revealed as the squalid little sadist that he is. And he gets a pretty miserable death as he's shot whilst scrabbling away on the floor, unmourned by his superiors.

And isn't it curious that the Doctor can't speak foreign languages, and that the one word everyone fails to communicate to a Frenchman during wartime is "resistance"? Even *I* know that it's the same word in both English and French!

Oh, and following on the heels of Patrick Troughton's son appearing last week, so Michael Craze's brother crops up in this episode. Before you know it, they'll be casting Jean Marsh's ex-husband or something...

May 7th

The War Games episode eight

R: I love that little scene where we see Russell and Carstairs manning the phones, cheerily taking down details of the latest rebel attack. They look like the minor celebrities they usually get to take pledges from callers at charity telethons! It works because (again) this is a story long enough to have the space to show a resistance movement stealing an advance upon the enemy; this sort of thing is usually confined to the second half of the final episode, and is led by the Doctor. But what's wonderful is that this is only *inspired* by the Doctor – Zoe says quite bluntly that the best way to help him in captivity is to carry out his plans. In that way, as an emblem of revolution rather than merely the man scampering around breaking things, Troughton's Doctor in his final story takes on a really epic status.

And it's a victory for mankind too, who can fight for freedom without his direct help. Mankind gets rather a rough ride this week otherwise, with the War Chief decrying them as the most warlike creatures in the cosmos. It's a fair point – and a rather witty one, too, to conclude an era of stories which feature monsters more than any other – but Dicks and Hulke very skilfully contrast it with scenes of humanity achieving much by working together. They're a strange ragbag, these resistance leaders – a whole slew of different accents and costumes, but they're all *characters* too. And that's why the broad comedy of Arturo Villar – the resistance leader from the Mexican Civil War Zone – works so well. The aliens are a humourless bunch who haven't even got the wit to have individual names, just pompous titles. We're better than that lot.

The cliffhanger has a hard job. It needs to persuade us that the Doctor may have betrayed his friends to the War Lord. And it just about gets away with it, because the scenes between Troughton and Brayshaw are so electric. We've never seen anything like this before in Doctor Who. When Hartnell played off Peter Butterworth, it was for comic effect, it was for the merry contrast of seeing Doctor Who scolding his irresponsible little brother. Here, though, there's a real sensation of new territory being explored, of the Doctor having a bond with a member of his own race. It's powerful enough that you can see it as the template for all those end-of-story climaxes between Pertwee and Delgado. And where it puts the viewer – we're learning secrets! At last! – is new and unsettling enough that the Doctor as traitor is far more credible than it should be.

T: What a contrast those two Time Lords make – Brayshaw is all poised, stalking about with

purpose and power, while Troughton is shabby and iconoclastic, grumpily rebuffing any notion of becoming a supreme being. The only thing that unites them is a shared, blazing intelligence, and a presence that only really good actors have. And it's a handy foreshadowing of what's to come when the War Chief mentions how the Doctor has changed his appearance – something that, after Troughton's first story, the series has gone out of its way not to talk about.

There are a couple of silly bits to this. The Security Chief hasn't improved with time, and to my eyes seems like the thickest villain since Spencer the Idiot Chameleon. And there's a very lame death from the resistance member who is manning the machine gun when the SIDRAT materialises – his method of expiration seems to entail straightening his cap, then having a snooze. Never mind that it's somewhat surprising to see him turn up alive and well in the barn at the end of the episode.

But as the *eighth* episode in, this has no business being as interesting and exciting as it is. Again, Dicks and Hulke have done a great job of gradually upping the stakes every week, and they're aided and abetted by what's a very cleverly mounted production in parts (to emulate the resistance's uprising, they just stuff a handful of extras into stock costumes, and – hey presto! – the sense of scale is yet again broadened). Speaking of which, it's pleasing that the resistance have a policy now of knocking out the conditioned soldiers rather than killing them; it's bad enough to die in a real war, let alone perish in an ersatz one.

The War Games episode nine

R: It takes us by surprise a little, even though as fans we know that this story is pivotal for the future of the series. It's that sudden shift in Troughton's performance, where what concerns him is no longer the good will of the rebels he's been helping, but his escape from his own people. The sequence in which he tells Arture Villar to shoot him if he wants to, but he's moving on to a new adventure anyway, is an acknowledgement that the last nine weeks have been small fry compared to the threat he's now facing. We've never seen Troughton so frustrated – note his sudden flare of anger when he tells Jamie to shut up and do as he's told. And it makes the fear he shows in summoning the Time Lords so very credible – and therefore his calling upon them a huge sacrifice. There's been an awful lot of explosions and gunshots in this story, but the climax of The War Games is the Doctor sitting on the ground and making a cube out of some white cards. It's such a small moment, but it feels absolutely *crucial*. It's the first time Doctor Who has saved the day by calling upon someone bigger than himself; this literal deus ex machina ought to feel like a complete swizz, but if anything it just raises the stakes as high as we've ever seen them. It's quite remarkable.

Edward Brayshaw helps sell this too – here's a man who would rather take his chances with the War Lord's cronies than wait around for his own race. The War Chief's last gamble, as he pleads that he's still an ally of the War Lord, is so desperate that you really feel for him; Brayshaw cleverly plays upon that same camaraderie with the Doctor that we're soon to see from the Master. You want to be on his side. The sequence where he settles an old score, and guns down the Security Chief, has you cheering him on, albeit a bit guiltily... well, it did me, at any rate. And Philip Madoc is never better in Doctor Who than he is in this episode. I know he gives a first-rate turn in The Brain of Morbius – but the amusement he shows in the scene where he evaluates whether or not he's going to accept the Doctor's treachery is so *very* dangerous. There's that little moment where the Doctor goes a little too far, and pronounces that the rebels are now his enemies not his friends – and you can see that Madoc doesn't believe a word of it, and is the more cunning manipulator. Indeed, when the Security Chief leaves the Doctor to be lynched by the resistance, there's a wonderful ambiguity to it – is this on the War Lord's instructions, and did he intend the Doctor to be killed after all? That there's room for such ambiguity in the first place is so refreshing – Doctor Who very rarely can resist the urge to spell out just how evil its villains are – but the way Madoc seizes upon it makes him by far the subtlest and most truly chilling adversary the Doctor has yet faced.

T: You've done it too! You called Villar "Arturo" in episode eight and "Arture" in episode nine – which is exactly what the credits do. There's nothing like a misspelt credit to get a pedantic little git like me all excited.

And Villar himself is great fun – likeable though Russell and Carstairs are (hats off to Graham Weston and David Savile for bringing such amiability to what could have been potentially dull, stock good guys), the rebel camp needed a bit of colour. Michael Napier-Brown is clearly having a ball in the role, making the most of his character's love for his guns and enjoyment of violence. It's an interesting nuance that we're meant to side with this man, even though he'd slit your throat for a bag of gold. Twice we're reminded of this pretty blatantly: when he insists on killing because "what else do you do with prisoners?", and his inability to discern the difference between shooting a man in the front or the back. This is the mankind the War Chief was telling us about last week.

(I should also mention that I owe Michael Napier-Brown my first professional engagement as an actor – he was latterly a noted theatre director, and he gave me three lines in The Merchant of Venice at the Ludlow Festival. So this mad, bloodthirsty Mexican will always have a special place in my heart.)

But really, I'm just digressing from the sheer amount of momentous stuff in this instalment. Troughton starts off low key and mischievous, clearly enjoying his game of cat-and-mouse with Brayshaw, and matching him for deviousness. For his part, Brayshaw really sells the terrifying consequences that will result if the Doctor calls the Time Lords. And even though the Security Chief discovers the War Chief's treachery (resulting in the Security Chief's prolonged line, "No, what a stupid fool *youuuuu areeeeeee*," which should be put in some sort of museum for cherished, hilariously-bonkers-and-brilliantly-bad Doctor Who moments), the War Chief later turns the table on his nemesis, and guns him down in a businesslike, unruffled manner. His final, desperate – and ultimately unconvincing – attempts to talk the War Lord round show how much the story is now pulling out all the stops. If the War Chief has become so surplus to requirements that he can be shot dead, then some even bigger guns are about to be fired – in the Doctor's direction.

Strangely enough, there's an inherent sense that The War Games as an adventure comes to an end here, with nearly everyone we've met in the last nine episodes sent back home. That Carstairs goes back to 1917 makes me concerned for his safety, but I like to imagine that he and Lady Jennifer hook up, get married, and have a daughter who marries someone called Crichton – enabling their grandson to later become the head of a shady outfit known as UNIT. Yes, I realise I'm walking this route only because David Savile plays both Carstairs and, 14 years later, Crichton, but why not? It's not the first time (nor the last, I'm sure) that lines have been drawn between two characters based upon an actor playing multiple roles.

One more thing: you know that something formidable is happening when even Philip Madoc looks coldly terrified, and weightily informs us that "[The Time Lords] are coming" in a way that sends shivers down your spine. It's interesting that this event is portrayed first with an ethereal howling, then with our heroes desperately struggling against some invisible force as they try to escape, and then some august and imposing organ music. Although this adventure hasn't been about them, the Time Lords here blast their way unforgettably into the climax of one of the most impressive and iconic episodes it's ever been my pleasure to watch.

The War Games episode ten

R: And he's gone! My favourite Doctor. Spinning into the distance, then into nothing, whilst complaining that he's feeling giddy. It's a little comical, it's rather surreal. I suppose it ought to be quite funny, really. But I found it rather upsetting, because it's the most *unjust* regeneration of all. (And, yes, I know it's not really called a regeneration yet.) The next few Doctors die at a moment of triumph – Baker saves the universe, Davison saves a friend, and Pertwee faces up to his fears and in a way saves *himself*. Troughton selflessly ensures that a bunch of ungrateful soldiers get to be returned to their own times and die upon their own planet's soil – and for that, he's stuck on trial. He's the only Doctor to bow out in a state of

defeat. And that's the part of the episode that makes it so very affecting. Look at the way, for example, that the Doctor responds when Jamie and Zoe try to persuade him to make one last ditch attempt at escape; Troughton plays it resignedly, hopping his way to the TARDIS, as if it's all for their sake, as if it's all so they can get one last little runaround together. When they're caught once more, the gravity with which he tells his friends that it's all over, and the emphasis with which he delivers his good-byes, is that of an adult telling the children it's time to put away their games and get ready for bed. The adventures are over. It's time to grow up.

Troughton gives such a clever performance here. Contrast the first half of the episode – which is all about manic flight, about the joy of being irresponsible and refusing to believe the party's over – with the sad acceptance of the end. Hines and Padbury look rather hurt as he decides to bow to his fate and give up on them. And all those awkward farewells, the mutual promises that they'll remember each other, are all the more poignant because you quickly learn that the Doctor has already realised their memories will be wiped. "They'll forget me, won't they?" is the first thing he utters after they've dematerialised out of his life forever – he knows that those well-meaning assurances of eternal friendship eventually add up to nothing. It's the saddest moment in Doctor Who ever since Hartnell reached the same conclusion at the end of The Massacre – that no matter how many companions the Doctor picks up along his travels, sooner or later they part company. Watching this as a kid I cried buckets, not so much that Jamie and Zoe were gone, but for the added cruelty that their many adventures were gone as well. And now it feels like a metaphor for moving on – that soon they'll see the Doctor as being such a very small part of their lives. And the same thing is about to be true for the audience at home; they'll move on too, into colour, with new adventures and new companions and a brand new Doctor – and the kids at home will soon have forgotten that this impish little Doctor ever existed at all. Troughton's on borrowed time now. All the energy of the Doctor we've come to know and love gets seen only one more time, as in his bad temper he demands that he decide what his next face can look like – it's all impotent bluster, the Doctor knowing full well that the game's up but refusing in his final moments to disappear gracefully.

It's a decidedly odd episode. The runaround bits of the first few minutes seem a bit pointless at first – until you realise that these clips from The Web of Fear and Fury from the Deep aren't exactly *disguised*; this is Doctor Who for the first time borrowing images from its past for a final hurrah. And it's a peculiar mix, really – the Quarks, the Ice Warriors, the Cybermen all make a final wave at the curtain call. (The Time Lords get introduced to a Dalek! There's a relationship that won't turn out well for either of them.) They go to all the trouble of filming a new scene on Zoe's Wheel, with Tanya Lernov turning up. There's a real sense, perhaps for the first time, of Doctor Who faithfully paying dues to its past, and reminding the audience just how far we've travelled these last three years Patrick Troughton has been the Doctor.

There are other things to mention, of course. I love the way that the Time Lords present images of the Earth wars by a series of pictures and photographs; rather like in The Massacre, it's as if the production team can most sincerely commemorate these real-life conflicts by suggestion, giving us glimpses of the art they inspired. I also think it's wonderful irony that these new Time Lord people have special laser eyes, and turn them upon the race that have used a variety of spectacles for the last ten weeks to emphasise their will. On its own terms, though, as a conclusion to an epic ten-parter, this all feels like a rather padded epilogue. But as a means of bringing the entirety of black and white Doctor Who to an end, it has an undeniable majesty to it.

I began this book believing Troughton was my favourite Doctor. Whenever anyone asked – and people do, don't they? They always do – he was the one I always plumped for. I thought it was because I loved all those monster stories. It turned out I was wrong. The monster stories as a whole lack the invention and care of so many of the Hartnell adventures, and although there's been a move towards experimentation in his final months, the series has been running dry for quite some

time. And yet it's been wonderful to watch and listen to – and that's almost entirely down to Troughton; the delicacy with which he's handled the comic and the serious, the sparkling way in which he's always made every least scene sing with energy, the fact that right up until the end he was clearly always trying to find new dimensions to the part... He's still my favourite Doctor. He was amazing.

T: Aw, Rob, you've just made me cry...

History teaches us that this story was ten parts long out of a production necessity, but if nothing else, it's helped to make the audience feel that they've really been through the mill. Here at the end of this, I feel exhausted, drained and rather emotional – especially because we won't see the likes of Troughton again. Sorry to echo you, my friend, but Troughton is definitely my favourite Doctor too. He was such an incredible, versatile, nuanced actor, the fact that he's really *only* remembered in association with Doctor Who – when like (say) Peter Davison, his talents ranged even wider than that – makes me rather irritated. He never gave a bad performance on Doctor Who, and only on rare occasions slipped into slightly over-zany antics – even then, he was usually dealing with material that probably deserved much worse treatment. He brilliantly sold the gravity of the drama whilst maintaining a joyful, shambolic lightness of touch that made him immensely watchable, unpredictable and fun. He might open this episode scampering around the TARDIS, flicking every switch he can, but the aura of defeat that hangs about him when they arrive on his home planet is immense. I think I shall miss this scarecrow most of all.

It's curious, though, how fandom is inclined to call this story "epic" when the Doctor's homeworld itself seems so very small scale (and comes complete with Time Lord Turkish Baths), and the second Doctor's swansong involves his head being manipulated on a monitor after some verbal jousting with three robed men. But really, it's the fact that this episode causes such a seismic shift in the series itself – that it unseats this most brilliant of interpreters of the role, as well as his faithful companions – that it seems so weighty. Anything less than this (the second Doctor being killed by a monster, or shot by a laser) would have almost seemed an insult. The way that Troughton takes a final bow – as he's basically sentenced for, well, daring to be an individual – accords his character so much respect.

What I *do* mind about this is that Jamie and Zoe are made to forget all but their first encounters with the Doctor. (It's as if the Time Lords have wiped almost all of Troughton's adventures – so, this wasn't just a bad habit on the BBC's part.) I really, *really* dislike this. Are there any moments in Doctor Who you pretend to yourself didn't happen, or write off as a mistake – you know, like everyone in The War Machines calling him "Doctor Who"? Well, I pretend to myself that the Time Lord conditioning is faulty and that Jamie and Zoe *do* remember, because I love them so much, and it's right and proper that they should have their memories of these fantastic experiences.

You say you cried watching it... oh hell, I'm comfortable enough in my masculinity to admit that I even cried when I *read the book*. This time around, it was Jamie being all playfully chiding, Zoe looking forlorn and, finally, Troughton's childish little wave that set me off – I really feel gutted that I won't be spending time in the company of this lot again. When Frazer and Wendy take that one last look around the TARDIS as they leave it early in the episode – as if the actors themselves are acknowledging that they are leaving it for the last time – I wanted to grab them and give them a big hug. And even now, I should give a special thank you to Frazer Hines, who appeared in more episodes of Doctor Who than many of the subsequent Doctors, and yet his enthusiasm and commitment were apparent every week. The man's a bloody legend.

And thanks to you also, mate, for letting me do this project with you – at this point, I really feel as though I've experienced something quite monumental. I know we will carry on tomorrow, but today feels like the end of an era in more ways than one. When we started this, we couldn't identify Matt Smith at 20 paces, I still smoked, had never been to America and had never attended a convention as an adult. But tomorrow, we not only start a new era of Doctor Who, I will fly to New Zealand for the first time, to do my one-man show about my love for this wonderful series. You and I have been extremely fortunate in that Doctor Who has taken us to new and exciting places in the real world as well as fiction. I wouldn't be making tomorrow's journey were it not for the good, the bad and the ugly of this brilliant show – and neither would I have had any of the fun times I've had so far this year.

I feel bigger on the inside.

ACKNOWLEDGEMENTS

Toby Wishes to Thank: Firstly, I'd like to thank Rob for asking me to do this with him – it was a flattering proposition from a bona fide *Doctor Who* writer which quite knocked me for six. He's been instrumental in easing me into a new chapter in my life and introduced me to all sorts of people, and I'm very grateful. A good friend.

2009 was a big year for me, and many friendships were forged and strengthened in the months that this volume was created (if I've failed to mention anyone here, fear not – I clearly didn't meet you till Volume 2 or 3). While undertaking this project, I'd suddenly find myself travelling around the country and headed towards, say, Inverness without a copy of The Krotons to re-watch – a quick text to John Williams, and he'd ensure it was there when I arrived. Steve Hatcher dropped everything on a couple of occasions to instantly furnish me with recons I'd not got or had packed away into storage (and a word here for those hardworking fans behind those brilliantly rendered labours of love – their skill and application are hugely appreciated and admired in Hadoke Towers). Neil Perryman, Martin Oakley and Simon Harries had a butchers at some of my early efforts and said nice and/or useful things. Mark Attwood will have a big grin on his face seeing his name in (another) Doctor Who book – he deserves far more, frankly. Lee Martin and Jason Cook occasionally remind me of a life outside of Doctor Who and have always been there when I've needed proper friendship, and Neil Smith, Ros Bell, Mike Thorpe and Leanne Burke are rays of sunshine who make my life easier with regularity, good grace and not enough credit.

I'm also indebted to Derek Fowler, Danny Jones, Paul Cornell, Simon Guerrier, Mark Wright, Steve Roberts, Sue Cowley, John Kelly, Michael McManus, Andy Murray, Jonathan Morris, Karen Baldwin, Ed Stradling, Steve O'Brien, James Seabright, Kat Portman, Steve Broster, Daren Thomas, Damon Querry and Matt Hayden, as well as everyone who made me welcome in the USA, New Zealand and Canada (which will feature in future volumes). From the comedy circuit, I am indebted to John Cooper, Dominic Woodward, Michael Legge, Andrew O'Neill, Mitch Benn, Dan McKee and especially Johnny Candon, who have all enabled me to discuss the Taran Wood Beast and Eric Pringle in green rooms up and down the country to the confusion of everyone else present. And especial thanks to Robin Ince, for suggesting that talking about such things on stage might be a funny thing to do.

Thanks to Lars and Christa for making it easy, and enabling this whole thing happen with good grace and skill. And really huge and heartfelt thanks to Peter Crocker, a close and valued friend, for going over the thing with a fine-tooth comb, making salient points and being there with good company and words of wisdom and support (not to mention curry and gin).

Louis, Ethan and Oscar represent the next generation, provide necessary perspective, and are duty bound to be the custodians of my Dapol collection when I am dead and gone. They also make me very proud (probably to the same extent that I make them very embarrassed).

Rob Wishes to Thank: As this is one of those very rare occasions when Toby has been allowed to write something first – ha! – I'd would like to acknowledge all the people that Toby is acknowledging, thank you. (Except for the bit about me, because that would be weird.) I would like to add, though: Owen Bywater – who got me into this Doctor Who thing when I was eleven years old, and is still a friend; my younger sister, Vicky, who was braver than I was, and dared to watch The Creature from the Pit when I was far too scared to do so (oh, that Erato blob was terrifying!); my parents, Joyce and Dennis, who despaired hugely of my Who obsession, but never tried to hide the remote control; my wife, Jane Goddard, for marrying me in spite of my love for Doctor Who; my agent, Suzanne Milligan, for *representing* me in spite of my love for Doctor Who; and Liz Myles, Nicholas Briggs, Ian Mond and Robyn Brough, for looking over the manuscript and egging me on.

OUT NOW... In Whedonistas, a host of award-winning female writers and fans come together to celebrate the works of Joss Whedon (Buffy the Vampire Slayer, Angel, Firefly, Dollhouse, Doctor Horrible's Sing-Along Blog).

Contributors include Sharon Shinn ("Samaria" series), Emma Bull (Territory), Jeanne Stein (the Anna Strong Chronicles), Nancy Holder (October Rain), Elizabeth Bear (Chill), Seanan McGuire (October Daye series), Catherynne M. Valente (Palimpsest), Maria Lima (Blood Lines), Jackie Kessler (Black and White), Sarah Monette (Corambis), Mariah Huehner (IDW Comics) and Lyda Morehouse (AngeLINK Series). Also featured is an exclusive interview with television writer and producer Jane Espenson, and Juliet Landau ("Drusilla").

ISBN: 978-1935234104
MSRP: 14.95

WHEDONISTAS!

WHEDON, J.
48 - 152342

A CELEBRATION OF THE WORLDS OF
JOSS WHEDON BY THE
WOMEN WHO LOVE THEM

mad
norwegian
press

Robert Shearman... is probably best known as a writer for Doctor Who, where he reintroduced the Daleks in the show's BAFTA winning first series, in an episode nominated for a Hugo Award. But he has long worked as a writer for radio, television and the stage. He has received several international awards for his theatre work, including the Sunday Times Playwriting Award, the World Drama Trust Award and the Guinness Award for Ingenuity in association with the Royal National Theatre. His plays have been regularly produced by Alan Ayckbourn, and on BBC Radio by Martin Jarvis; Big Finish recently published a selection of them under the title *Caustic Comedies*. His first collection of short stories, *Tiny Deaths*, won the World Fantasy Award. The follow-up, *Love Songs for the Shy and Cynical*, won the Shirley Jackson Award, the British Fantasy Award, and the Edge Hill Reader's Prize. A third collection, *Everyone's Just So So Special*, was published in 2011.

Toby Hadoke... is an actor, writer and comedian. His one man show *Moths Ate My Doctor Who Scarf* enjoyed a West End run, a major UK and international tour, a sell-out success at the Edinburgh Fringe and a Sony-nominated radio series. A follow up, *Now I Know My BBC*, premiered in 2010. He is resident compere at XS Malarkey Comedy Club, won The Les Dawson Award in 2003, and also a Chortle Award in 2007. His TV acting credits include *Casualty 1907*, *The Forsyte Saga*, *Phoenix Nights*, *The Royal Today* and *Coronation Street*. His writing includes *The Comedy Sketchbook* (BBC 1), *The Comedy Christmas* (BBC 2) and pieces in *The Guardian*, *The Independent*, *Doctor Who Magazine* and *SFX*. An experienced radio and theatre actor, voice-over artist, TV warm-up man and radio pundit, Toby has also moderated commentaries for the Doctor Who DVD range.

Publisher / Editor-in-Chief
Lars Pearson

**Senior Editor /
Design Manager**
Christa Dickson

**Associate Editor (Running
Through Corridors)**
Lance Parkin

**Associate Editor
(Mad Norwegian Press)**
Joshua Wilson

The publisher wishes to thank... Rob and Toby, for so enjoyably making this "great journey" through Doctor Who, and letting us play along; Peter Purves, for both the foreword and for being such a gentleman to work with; Lynne M. Thomas, for coming up with the title to this series; Katy Shuttleworth, for help with the "running men" graphics; Lance Parkin; Michael D. Thomas; Shawne Kleckner; Josh Wilson; and the incomparable Robert Smith?.

1150 46th Street
Des Moines, Iowa 50311
info@madnorwegian.com
www.madnorwegian.com